THE DIVINE ASSASSIN'S PLAYBOOK

ROBERT CHAZZ CHUTE

BIGGER THAN JESUS

HIGHER THAN JESUS

HOLLYWOOD JESUS

PRAISE FOR ROBERT'S WORK

Move over Elmore

Love the dialogue and the character studies...definitely a blend of Mickey Spillane and Elmore Leonard

~ Amazon reviewer, Alex Adamson

5.0 out of 5 stars Do Not Miss This Book!

Chazz is the master. Every story he writes immerses you so deeply in its world, you can barely crawl out when the pages are closed. "Brooklyn in the Mean Time" might just be his best yet. I don't know which parts of the story are reality and which are fiction. Chazz presents a version of himself where it might just be autobiographical. Then again, he may be messing with we readers to up the ante in our suspension of disbelief. Either way, it's an amazing book. I loved every syllable. Chazz ranks among the top tier of our generation's storytellers. Do Not Miss This Book!

~ Amazon review by Alex Kimmell, author of The Key to Everything

A unique and engaging novel with a compelling plot and well-drawn, idiosyncratic characters.

~ David Pandolfe, Amazon reviewer

Robert Chazz Chute is a versatile author, with books ranging from zombies, vampires, hit men, the end of the world, robots, dreams and time travel. Each book and series is well written, smart and leaves the reader wanting more.

~ Cavewoman reviews

Another good story from a master storyteller

Once again I got completely sucked in by Robert Chazz Chute. I could not put this book down once I started it. My only regret is that I got this book in November and waited until now to read it. The story is imaginative, engaging, and really not like anything else I've ever read.

~ Amazon reviewer Deborah630

DIG CHAZZ CHUTE

His writing style makes you part of his thoughts & conversations: you are part of his dimension Dear Reader and will "SWING" his every day. Only in Brooklyn can the 90's thrive and remain true. You can never truly return home after you ran from its hurts and pains, when naturally embedded during formative years are often hard to run from. Yet, the raw perspectives of your past with eyes wide open; does allow you truth and thus clarity. From there, knowing the negatives and going ballz to the walls with a cuppla hail Mary's; Chazz rocked it and lives the life he was meant to live and believed in.. HIGHLY RECOMMEND!

~ Amazon reviewer MIKALA RATED

Reviews of Bigger Than Jesus

Bigger than Jesus Captured My Imagination and Ran!

I have always liked the detective style books of the films from the 30-50's. This book captures all those best features. While reading the book I felt I was transported into a world that was inhabited by all the people and characters that made up the Humphrey Bogart movies, the Mike Hammer books, and the other gritty pulp fiction that I have always liked but somehow could not fully embrace. What helped me do that was the witty style that Robert Chazz Chute writes. It is funny, humorous, often serious and he speaks in a way that mixes the old style and current cultural references that make every one reading it feel included in the story.

~ Tidal Ashbrn, Amazon reviewer

The writing is just superb…. From beginning to end, this is one top notch crime novel. It is a smooth, easy read.

~ David Wilde, Amazon reviewer

Robert Chazz Chute proves that genre fiction can be inventive and unconventional in its use of language while delivering a suspenseful story.

~ Dream Beast, Amazon reviewer

An Excellent Read

I loved this book. It is well written, fast paced and unusual for a gangster book.

~ M Slott, Amazon reviewer

Bigger Indeed!

Oh wow. What can I say? Mr. Chute pulled me in with his POV and kept the twists coming through the whole book. I found the ending to be delightful and perfect. With comedy throughout and a wonderful cast of characters.

~ Jo Michaels, Amazon reviewer and author of The Fury

Excellent, fast paced romp

This book plays out like a Guy Ritchie film. The pacing is frenzied, the plot convoluted yet easy to parse, and the characters larger than life. Half the fun is trying to who's trying to betray who. I would whole-heartedly recommend this novel to action fans and can't wait to grab the author's next work in this series.

~Amazon reviewer Rev357

What a fun ride of a crime thriller!

In a short span of a couple of short stories collections and a few novelettes, Robert Chazz Chute has seriously become one of my favourite authors! You can count on him for well-written stories that pack punch, plot twists, clever dialogue and even some hidden wisdom in their pages.

~ Amazon reviewer johligo

Five Stars

Great treat, fun, unpredictable and gritty.

~ Kindle customer, Amazon reviewer

Love

Suspense, humor, love!

~ Shirleyjack, Amazon reviewer

Genuine characters, full of ups and downs. Intricate plot.

~ Julio Wickham, Amazon reviewer

Good Thriller

Kept my attention. Real page turner could not stop reading till I finished the entire book. Read it in one day.

~ Amazon reviewer A. Alpuche

Many people have donated their time and energy
to help make these books a reality. To

Kit Foster, Armand Rosamilia, Mark Victor Young, Janice Kurita, Brian
Wright, RCMP Cst. Leland Keane, Russ Sawatsky, Susan Toy, Claude
Bouchard, Johanna Goldenberg, Alex Kimmell, Tidal Ashburn, Mazie Lane
and Peter Hawkins: Thank you all so much for your support.

FOREWORD

I love Jesus Diaz. One of the reviews says, "He's the hit man you love to hate." I get it. He's a funny guy with bad luck. He's trapped and he makes a lot of bad choices. Given his life experience, it's easy to understand how JD got to be the anti-hero he becomes. He's not a good guy, but you will understand him. The author of Vigilante, Claude Bouchard, called Bigger Than Jesus, "Wickedly real and violently funny." That's the target and I think the Little Cuban hits it every time.

Special thanks go out to my friend and author Armand Rosamilia. Armand told me that if I didn't write another "Jesus book" we'd no longer be friends. I couldn't risk that so I came up with a fourth book in the series, Resurrection, A Hit Man Thriller. You'll find a sneak peek at the back of this omnibus. More books are in the editorial pipeline. Jesus Diaz is too much fun to be left alone for too long.

Thanks for picking up this omnibus. Grab a beer or pour a tall cool glass of something you like. Wiggle your butt to settle in, get comfy and enjoy the adventures of my quirky Cuban hit man.

And, not for nothing, thanks for being a reader! I hope you'll become a fan.

~ Robert Chazz Chute

July 1, 2019

THE HITMAN SERIES PART ONE

Bigger Than Jesus

ROBERT CHAZZ CHUTE

COME TO JESUS

Water drips from the soot-black gargoyle's tongue like thin saliva, as if the grotesque statue is mocking you and eager for blood. Panama Bob Lima clings to the gargoyle, using it as a shield. You are on a thin ledge on the side of a very high building and for once you wish you wore your Nikes instead of twelve-hundred dollar Tanino Crisci shoes. So far, this job is not going at all as planned.

"You know this doesn't end well for you, either," Panama Bob says. "Oswald gets Kennedy and Ruby gets Oswald. The first rule of a conspiracy is to kill the assassin."

"They didn't give Ruby a choice. I don't have choices, either."

It's a long way down, so far that Tribeca's streetlights and cars swirl together in one red and white and yellow blur. Is your vision going wacky as a defence mechanism? Is your mind letting go so you can let go, black out and be blissful as you plunge into the concrete's existential abyss? What is it about telling yourself not to look down that makes you look down?

You should have told Big Denny to chase Panama Bob, but Denny's too fat to do much chasing. Instead, Denny De Molina guards the parking garage exit forty-something floors down and you're out here listening to Bob plead his case. The wind picks up and you feel light, like a sudden gust might pull you out into space. Denny's first clue that Bob is not escaping in his white Caddy could be you, bursting like a sack of meat on the sidewalk. Tonight could be your private 9/11.

It's not like you could refuse this job, but you should have stayed home, eaten a pot cookie with *SpongeBob* for company and given the mission a little more thought. The rain has made every surface slick. Panama Bob is talking fast and all those lights are starting to spin faster and it's hard to concentrate on what he's saying. You watch his mouth, as if you can read his thick lips. The vertigo recedes, though the sick feeling in your stomach remains. It would be very bad form, not to mention dangerous, to puke out here. This will be a crime scene in a few minutes. You swallow hard, choke back your gorge and focus on Panama Bob.

"C'mon, man. You know me. I'm as honest as can be."

True. Panama Bob is as straight a shooter as a high-stakes gambler and drug lord can be.

"Jimmy sent me, Bob. It's business. This is not personal."

"Excuse me, but killing me? I take that personal. Besides, I didn't steal from the company. I skimmed a bit, sure. We all do that, but I didn't steal."

"I understand what you're saying, Bob, but Jimmy Lima doesn't make those fine distinctions."

"C'mon, Jesus! I *made* you. Jimmy didn't want to let a Cuban in and I said to give you a shot. Now you're coming after me?"

"It was Big Denny who brought me into The Machine. I do feel bad about this, Bob, but Jimmy gave me a job to do. You know how it is."

How it is. It sucks is how it is. You're dizzy and the ledge is slippery and you wonder how long it will take you to plunge to your death? You think of the World Trade Center jumpers again. Technically, if it weren't for the attacks on September 11, 2001, you wouldn't be here at all. If not for those crazy terrorists, you wouldn't have watched the smoke from the twin towers rise up into the Tuesday morning sunlight from your apartment roof in Queens. You wouldn't have joined up in a vengeful fury. The plan was to earn your US citizenship — not just have it given to you — through military service. You planned to kill Osama bin Laden personally and collect the $10 million reward. You fully expected to get shipped straight to Afghanistan to go hunting.

Instead, you guarded a checkpoint outside the Green Zone in Iraq. Then things went from bad to worse. You got your US citizenship, a broken ankle in boot camp, nearly blown up on several occasions and trained in a bunch of skills that did not translate well to civilian life. Then there was the incident with the Afghan civilians on your second tour, the sergeant who deserved his broken jaw and the dishonorable discharge you didn't deserve for breaking that jaw.

When you got back, you couldn't find a job. Then Big Denny got you a no-show job at a construction site and things got easier and worse at the same time. It's like you're on that wide, easy road to Hell your Army chaplain always talked about. And now you're on a high ledge trying to kill your boss's lying, stealing, murdering douchebag brother. Worse? You have to listen to him whine about it.

"Dude! Let's go back inside and talk about this. We'll go climb back in my office window, have a drink to settle our nerves and then we'll call Jimmy together. I promise we can get through this little tiff and solve this thing. Vincent is not going to like this one bit! It's Jimmy's idea, but it's you starting the power play. Vincent wanted us both as underbosses but Jimmy wants to be the only one. That's what this is really about. Divisions are not good for business."

You edge a little closer along the ledge. "This is me following orders. I don't know what Vincent will say about your high-dive suicide. I just know that if I don't follow orders, Jimmy shoots me in the head."

"See, that's the difference between Jimmy and me. I'd never do that to you."

"And you won't have my car blown up tomorrow morning if I let you go?

Yeah, right."

There's a thought. You should have blown up Bob's car. If you'd done that, you wouldn't be where you are now, rediscovering your fear of heights. At least when you rappelled from a helicopter in training it was over quickly and, when you threw up , all you had to do was endure the jeers of your platoon as your sergeant screamed at you for defiling his precious dirt.

Panama Bob is talking fast again, but you both know it doesn't matter. Jimmy sent you for Bob. That court takes no appeals, especially since Jimmy suspects Bob killed his personal bodyguard and best buddy, Cat Fornes. Martial arts fans remember Cat as a crazy, toothless cage fighter on TV. Big guy, big muscles, big yellow tiger tattoo that stretched from his neck to his feet and some mean jiu jitsu. His signature move was the spinning backfist. Cat might have been a champion except he got caught up in trying to use the backfist in every match so he'd have a brand. The other fighters caught on quick.

Jimmy loved Panama Bob like a brother, but he was a *fan* of Cat Fornes. You don't get to choose your family, but hooking up with a minor celebrity who had been on TV was more important to Jimmy Lima than any drug he ever sold. When Cat dropped out of the cage match game and came back to Queens, Jimmy made Cat a friend. Sometimes you wonder if he might have been more than that. The point is, Panama Bob may be a brother, but that's an accident of genetics and hormones and the back seat of a car. Jimmy loved Cat like the brother he *chose*.

When Cat went missing, Jimmy knew who to blame. Before Jimmy sent you for Panama Bob, he sent Cat to persuade the stolen money out of him. You stood in Jimmy's office when the underboss told Cat, "Bob's been skimming. Go have a talk with him. Show him that awesome spinning backfist and come back with the skim."

Bob might have weaselled out of this if their father was in the game. However, Vincent Daddy-O Junior, head of the family (father to Jimmy, step-father to Bob) doesn't know anything about all this. He's still laid out in a hospital bed recovering from getting his prostate cut out. This could blow up into a war and there's no good end in this for anyone.

Except maybe there is.

Bob holds up a key hanging from the fat gold chain on his neck. "Howzabout if I *bought* my way out of this? *You* could be out of this mess, Jesus. Don't you want to go back to Miami and be a wheel in warmer climes? Don't you want to be free of all this New York, New Jersey, rat race bullshit? "

You blink. "Tell me more."

"What I skimmed? It's in a storage locker."

"The money you said you didn't steal is in a storage locker."

"This is the key to that storage locker."

"Go on."

"Suppose I give you the location of this storage locker."

"And the key."

"Of course, *imbecil*. It don't work without the key."

"And you get to come in from the ledge."

"No. Big picture? *You* get to come in off the ledge, too. Everybody lives."

"Except Cat."

"I don't know what you're talking about."

"Sure. And how long before you think Jimmy finds us? A day? A week? What good is a sack full of money if I don't live long enough to spend it?"

Panama Bob is quiet for a minute. He looks down, gets a better grip on the gargoyle and when he looks at you again, he talks in a stage whisper, as if only you and God can hear. "There's enough, Jesus. There's enough there to run and hide for a long time. I was smart. I skimmed a long time and just took a little, but I was consistent. I wasn't greedy all at once. That's how they get you."

"Jimmy found you out."

"Not for years, Jesus. *Years!*"

"How much money are we talking about?"

"You'll never have to work again if you play it right."

"Yeah?"

"And you'll be living well. That sweet little señorita I seen you with in the club sometimes? Pete Vasquez's daughter?"

"Lily."

"You can play house forever and only stop for steak, lobster and oysters."

Hm. Lily *would* like that lifestyle very much. "And what are you going to do?" you ask.

"While you disappear, I'll be going to war. I was already making preparations when you showed up. I thought I had more time. I thought you'd come after me at home or something more discreet than hitting me at my own office. You kill Marv and Harvey? I didn't hear you throwing any shots, but when I heard your voice in the outer office I figured you'd come heavy and I climbed out here."

"I didn't have to throw shots," you say. "I just told your boys that Jimmy wanted to see them and that I'd do the babysitting. They went away."

"*Sonofabitch!* Fuckin' idiots!"

"Yeah."

Panama Bob looks up and blinks. The rain falls harder so you don't know if Bob is blinking away tears or water. The rain gurgles through the drains above you and the thin saliva from the big gargoyle's mouth builds to a little stream.

Readers Digest explained that the word *gargoyle* and *gurgle* come from the same language root. Somebody came up with the word gurgle from the sound the gargoyle made with the water going through it. That and movie trivia is the sort of crucial information that fills your head and kept you from learning anything useful so you could get an honest job. You're so stupid, you're wearing your shiny shoes with the too-smooth soles meant for office work and for show, edging along a tiny ledge, all the purchase in your toes. This is not what a smart ninja would do.

"Don't look down, Jesus," Panama Bob says. "Maybe you can walk on water, but you sure can't fly."

You think about Bob's skim for a full minute as the storm builds. The thunder rolls much louder out here, so close to the sky. You feel the boom in your chest and its force rivals your pounding heart. The first lightning flash strobes over Panama Bob and the gargoyle so, for a crazy second, they look like one grotesque, two-headed creature. Bob's got both hands wrapped around the gargoyle's neck, so his fancy nickel-plated .32 must be tucked into the waistband at the small of his back. He's no doubt still got a switchblade in his sock. You do, so why wouldn't he? Bob's got fast hands, too. That complicates things.

You inch back toward his office window. "Come inside before you get struck by lightning. You aren't any good to me if you're fried chicken."

Panama Bob's smile spreads ear to ear. "I knew you'd be a reasonable man. I know you!"

"I'm not reasonable, Bob. I just want out. With your skimmed milk, I can get away where Jimmy will never find me. At least for a while."

You almost slip. Almost. The smooth sole of your right shoe gives way and your heels dip. You throw yourself so hard at the wall you overcorrect and almost bounce off. You claw at the smooth wall and try to become part of it. You take another moment before you risk turning your head. Surprisingly, Bob is already around the gargoyle and coming up on you fast. When you glance down, you understand why he's so confident. His feet are bare. Bob moves along the ledge like he's climbing a shaky ladder: Cautious but in no real doubt he'll make it.

"I love these old buildings," Bob says. "Gargoyles! Can you believe it? Not only does it give the place character, so useful!"

"Yeah," you say as your left hand closes around the window frame to Bob's office. Bob's almost on top of you as you bend your knees and lean back, trusting the frame with your weight. Your right hand closes on Bob's calf, just below the knee. You miss the meat of the calf but you've got his pants leg and that's just enough. You drive with your legs so fast that you almost jump and Bob cries out as he twirls backward into the chasm.

If this were a Hollywood movie, he'd pull his piece from the small of his back and shoot in slow motion as he falls to his grisly death, the thick gold necklace and glittering locker key catching the city lights. In real life, he just has time for a short scream that cuts off with a bang as he careens into the concrete.

When you pull yourself through the office window, your legs and arms shake so badly you have to struggle to fish out your cell. "Denny! Get your fat ass up the ramp quick to the front of the building! Bob had a fall. Whatever's left of him is wearing a necklace with a key. Get that key off the body before the cops come!"

You don't wait for Denny's reply. Instead, you ransack Panama Bob's big desk. You don't have much time. Somewhere in this room there must be a receipt for a storage locker. When you find which storage facility is the right one, you and Lily are going to get away to fulfill some lovely dreams together.

That is, if the cops and Jimmy Lima and The Machine don't get you first.

THE KEY

You can't find the receipt for the storage locker in Panama Bob's desk. An ancient Underwood typewriter with black and white ivory keys sits on the desk. You lift it to see if a receipt is taped to the typewriter's bottom. Nope.

You thought you could be a cool and careful ninja about this and just roll the drawers out to find the receipt. Collect a zillion dollars. Do not go to jail. Instead, after a few minutes, all the drawers are dumped out on the floor and your hands are shaking.

Panama Bob wasn't such a bad guy, but he had no filing system you can discern. You wish Bob was less sloppy. If Bob had ordered you to hit his brother first, you'd be tossing Jimmy Lima's office now and you would have found the receipt already.

Jimmy's so anal, he changes three-thousand dollar suits to go from dinner to after-dinner drinks. Jimmy buys a new Beemer as soon as the new car smell fades on the old one. He uses a gold, jewel-encrusted lighter instead of a disposable one for $1.99. He's got a private courtyard under his bedroom window that's stuffed full of naked statues from Greece, all looking precisely east to greet the dawn with Jimmy as he drinks his morning espresso on his balcony. The coffee is the most expensive kind, the one with the beans that are eaten and then pooped out of a small animal before brewing.

The only items of interest in Panama Bob's desk are: one small baggie of green-brown weed, what appears to be the half-finished manuscript to the novel Bob was always tinkering with in his spare time and the nickel-plated .32 you thought he was going to use to shoot you out on the ledge. Sorry, Bob.

You call Denny on your cell. "You got the key?"

"Man, that was a mess."

"Yeah, yeah. That mess was almost me. You got the key?"

"Almost you?" The big bear sounds concerned. "You okay, buddy?"

"Better than Bob. Denny, if you don't tell me whether you got the key in the next two seconds, I'm going to throw myself out this fucking window."

"Got it. But he was—"

You don't need the details. You tell him to get out of the parking garage before the cops come. "Take your Dodge to the pizza joint around the corner and have a slice. I'll be there in a minute."

Big Denny's a mook. He's so big, he's fine for security gigs up front in a XXXL tee that's still too tight around the biceps. He's the bar bouncer who stops trouble just by showing up. However, in this situation, he's too hard to miss. He's not built for hanging around a crime scene.

Denny has been out of jail for more than two years — aggravated assault, but the other guy deserved it. Considering Denny's muscles and tattoos, he always looks like a guy on day parole. A sharp cop might think to ask him what he was doing there. Denny could get himself into trouble talking to a cop about the weather. You're the one who handles the nuance, art and public relations required if anyone in a uniform needs some lies thrown their way.

It's a big building. When the cops show up they'll set up a cordon and question anybody who leaves the building. Time is spiteful and speeding up and your hands are shaking more as you rifle a filing cabinet. Instead of the storage locker receipt, you find porn magazines. Bob really did hate modern technology.

You don't have time to go through every book on Bob's shelves. If Panama Bob had come to you first, it'd be Jimmy drowned in the big fountain in the center of his mansion's circular driveway and you would have found the goddamn receipt by now. All of Jimmy's books are fake: all-leather bindings and each of equal height, as if he's some scrub ambulance chaser in a late-night infomercial begging to be a legal beagle for clients with lung diseases caused by bad insulation.

If you had Jimmy's money, you'd know what to do with it. If. You can give yourself an ulcer thinking about If.

If you were Panama Bob, where would you keep the receipt for the storage locker that holds your fortune? Your eyes settle on a framed picture of Jimmy and Bob on a boat. Panama Bob's got a big, goofy grin on his face and he's holding up a small fish. Jimmy stands behind him, toasting the camera with a martini glass. Only Jimmy would think to stock a deep sea fishing boat with olives and toothpicks and only Bob would consider a baby sailfish a prize. You took that picture. You find the safe behind the frame. You hadn't known Bob had a safe. Maybe he wasn't so goofy.

You peek out the window. In the street, a crowd gathers to gawk at the body. There's no time to get a sledge and hammer that little safe out of the wall.

You scoop up the phone from the floor and speed dial Jenny, the woman who still thinks she's Bob's ex-wife, not his widow. She answers on the third ring. You thought you might just piss yourself waiting through rings one and two.

"Hallo, Bob. What do you want?"

"Jenny, it's Jesus."

"Hey, *Hay-soose!*" She drags out the syllables, just to bust your balls, like that's original. She does that even when she's not drunk, which she is now.

"Jenny, I've got some bad news. Bob had a fall."

"Yeah? How is he?"

"Dunno. I haven't seen him yet. Jimmy wants me to check something in Bob's office safe. Do you know the number or know where I could find the number?"

"Nope. I didn't know he had a safe. Tell him to open it up and pay my alimony. He's behind by two months. I got bills, too. Tell him that."

"Shit."

"Anything else, *Hay-soose?*"

"What's Bob's birthdate? The doctor will want to know for their records."

She hems and haws and you resist the urge to start swearing at her. That would make you feel better, but it won't help. Finally, she says, "April 20, 1970. Hey, is Bob going to be okay?"

"No. No, he won't Jenny. Sorry." And you really are.

You hang up and try spinning the dial on the combination lock. Past zero left to four, spin right to twenty, back left to 70.

When you try the handle on the safe door, it opens with a *chunk* sound. Bob was an idiot and you're a genius.

The safe is empty. You just joined Bob's idiot club.

Back to the window. There's a cruiser pulling to a stop with blue and white flashing lights and, even at night, you can tell there are upturned faces and pointing fingers. The police will "secure the scene" first, meaning they'll tell everybody to step back while they check on the body and dig out some yellow tape to rope off at least as far as the blood spatter. A shift supervisor will show up soon and they'll form a perimeter. That's what you would have done when you were an MP.

Once the perimeter is set up, you're trapped and trying to talk your way out. You've got to look like just another office worker on his way out after a hard day in a cubicle. You grab Bob's trench coat and umbrella on the way out the door and, after a moment's thought, you double back and grab his briefcase and sling the strap over your shoulder. In your suit and tie and briefcase, you look like another Joe Jobber. You take the stairs to the lobby.

You're almost out the back door when you realize you should have opened up the umbrella at the bottom of the stairs. High up in a corner, a security camera hangs from the lobby wall. Its red light blinks as it catches your movement and turns on, catching your mug perfectly. There's nothing you can do about that now so you hit the back door. The rain smacks the pavement so hard it bounces back up. Head down and hunching with cold water running down your neck, you open Panama Bob's umbrella and head for the pizza place.

Denny's got his face a couple inches from the table top, chewing the top of a loaded pizza. It's especially gross because he's not eating the bread. He takes your look and smiles wide, a dot of tomato sauce on his nose.

"New diet?"

"Low-carb. It's not so bad for you if you just order the works and eat the top but leave the bread."

Denny's last diet was all durian, all the time. Durian is an exotic fruit that smells like garbage. He stuck with that until he got the squirts and shit his pants running after a dealer for The Machine who was putting more up his nose than he was dealing. It's hard to be taken seriously as an enforcer if you lose bowel control while you're trying to have a serious conversation, even when you've got said deadbeat in a headlock.

"Is the low-carb thing working?"

"Down five pounds from three days ago," Denny says.

That five pounds must have come out of his feet because he looks just as fat as ever. "Yeah, I think I can see it in your face."

Big Denny smiles wider. It's safer to stay on the happy side of a felon who can crack walnuts with his hands. Denny saw Marlon Brando do that in that movie with Matthew Broderick and dedicated himself to the practice so much he's got early-onset arthritis.

When he hands you the key, you take a close look. Besides the number 408, there's no clue in which storage site Panama Bob's stolen fortune might be. This is New York. There must be a dozen such places close by. When the economy went south, lots of retail spaces emptied out and a bunch of them were turned into storage facilities. There's even a TV show about vultures bidding on storage lockers sight unseen so they can salvage the contents for cash. Before the recession, they wouldn't have all those lockers eligible for plunder.

"Too bad about Bob," Denny says. He's watching you carefully to see if you maybe need a hug.

"Anybody see you take the key from his neck?"

Denny nods. "Coupl'a homeless guys, sure."

"That's not so bad."

"And some tourists outside the coffee shop across the street from Bob's."

"Great." Your mouth goes dry so you look for the pizza waitress but she has disappeared. It's often difficult to get good service when you eat with Denny. He's too scary for most citizens. "How'd you know they were from out of town?"

"They stopped to watch after Bob went splat."

"Oh."

"And they didn't run away when I showed up. They just stood there with their mouths hanging open."

The red sauce is spread across his lantern jaw and his cheeks. It's like eating with a little kid, which, to you? Big Denny De Molina will always be a little kid.

"Congratulations," you say. "You just confirmed every stereotype the flyover states have about New York City."

Denny shrugs. "Gave 'em a story they'll repeat for generations." He tries to mimic a woman's voice and instead sounds like Miss Piggy. "This one time? My grandfather was in New York...like dat."

He offers you a slice he's torn off. He surely hasn't washed his hands since he took the key from Bob's broken neck. It doesn't matter if it's fresh dead guy. He should have washed his hands before digging into pizza. Your stomach turns upside down and you thank him but shake your head.

"So will the cops think old Bob committed suicide? Jimmy wanted it to look like a suicide."

The desk drawers are spread everywhere. The safe door is hanging open. "Maybe," you say. "Or maybe they'll think it was a robbery. Hard to say."

"You gonna tell me what the key's about?"

You thought about this on the walk over so your next lie is already in the chamber, ready to fire. "There's a storage locker somewhere. I don't know where, but Bob tried to get me to let him go with the stuff in the storage locker." You lean in close, whispering even though no one else is in the place. "Bob had pictures of Jimmy's wife!"

Denny's forehead furrows. This is a total fabrication this time, but there's precedent for it. "Babs? No way!"

"Solid."

Denny startles and jumps and does a double-take like he's mugging in a silent movie. You get a sick look at Denny's gold tooth and the red ball of mush and pineapple in his maw.

His eyes narrow. "I thought she was past her younger, wilder days, man. Jimmy and her went through couple's counselling and everything. Jimmy screws around. That's expected, a man in his position. Lotsa business trips and whatnot. But Babs? I don't see that in her anymore. Especially not after what happened to the last guy."

"You never told me about the last guy."

"Long story, long time ago, before you came on the crew. Some things you don't want to know and I can't tell you since I don't get that drunk and sad anymore. It was one of those *Pulp Fiction*-type foot massage situations. The guy...old flame. Long before Jimmy. One time only thing. But he's still a missing person's case, you know what I mean? Jimmy walks in on them, *in flagrante delicious pussy*. Next thing you know, the guy's begging to get to be a missing person. You get me? If Babs was screwing around, she'd be...you know...discreet now. Really. Jesus. Brother. Dawg! Really! Who'd be that stupid as to sleep with Jimmy Lima's wife?"

You didn't think you'd get this much resistance from Big Denny. You improvise. "Barbara is still a good-looking woman. Total MILF material. I'm guessing it's Jimmy's computer tech guy. Freejack Jack lives in the guest house so he's there all the time and Barbara is out by the pool sunning herself. Next thing you know? Porn movie."

"Nah. Freejack's got no balls."

"What about the personal trainer guy who comes around the house for those private hot yoga lessons?"

"Chad?" He shakes his head. "Gay."

"Yeah, but maybe he's the kind of gay that's flexible about it. Any port in a storm, you know. Jimmy's wife could turn on the Pope."

Denny's eyebrows furrow and he looks twice as scary. "This is…terrible news."

"We gotta find that storage place, man. And zip it until we know what's going on, for sure. Jimmy's not going to like this. We don't want him going off half-cocked and shooting Barbara in the face."

"No. We don't want that," Denny says. "What we going to do when we find those pictures?"

You shrug. "Once we know who we're dealing with, then we go to Jimmy with it. Maybe it's nothing. Maybe Bob was just blowing smoke so I wouldn't toss him off the building."

"Maybe." Denny brightens and returns to his pizza. "You really threw Jimmy's brother off the building, huh?"

"Well, it wasn't like Kevin Costner doing the bad Elliot Ness thing, throwing the guy off the rooftop in *The Untouchables*."

"How was it like?"

"Sort of like being Kevin Costner, only I almost crapped my pants and I had no hate for Panama Bob. It was just a thing I had to do, you know?"

"I know." Denny stretches out a paw and pats your hand. "Sorry, Jesus. I shoulda gone up myself. You know how you are with heights."

You went on the ferris wheel at Coney Island once and almost threw up while waiting in line, but since you were on a   date with Lily, you held it down and she thought you loved the ferris wheel.

You reach inside the trench coat and your fingers close around a thick leather wallet. "I think I've had enough excitement for one night. Your dinner is on Panama Bob tonight, may he rest in peace."

"Pieces. Jimmy is okay with killing his own brother while the big boss is in the hospital? What you think he'll do to whoever's screwing Barbara?"

"Slow death. Vice grips and fire might be involved. Bad karma all around." You open the wallet and there's a bunch of the usual cards. You slip out the bills, a fifty and twenties and tens and count it out under the table. There's just over three-hundred dollars in your hands. You tell Denny it's about two-hundred bucks and give him half that before slipping the rest in your pants pocket.

While Denny trudges off to the bathroom to wash his face, you take inventory of Bob's wallet. There's a slip of paper with Chinese characters on it that's obviously from a fortune cookie. The English side reads: "You will be a great and persuasive writer."

You pull out a bent business card for a hair salon The Machine owns and a business card for Chad, Barbara's personal trainer. It's got a telephone number on it written in ink and "Chad" is written out in childlike, block letters. You hope Denny can keep his mouth shut so nothing bad comes Chad's way. He's not much more than a kid and, with that lisp and those lycra shorts, it's obvious that any violence that went his way would be unfair, collateral damage. You just need time to figure out which storage business is the right one so you and Lily can get away from this life and start a new one that doesn't require you to chase anybody out on high ledges in the rain.

Another business card catches your eye and this one's a surprise. The card advertises a jazz spot called Thackeray's Horn Club. On the back, in loopy, girly letters, someone had written "Melba." A telephone number with a prefix for cell phones sat cramped beneath the name. Whoever Melba was, she'd left a thick greasy lipstick kiss, now smeared, but no less visible in bright, do-me-quick red. Poor Panama Bob. He had hidden depths and lived fast until the pavement stopped him short. You plan to feel really bad for him later. *Push that thought away and save the grief for later.*

Denny punches you in the shoulder gently. "Jimmy called me while I was in the can. He says he wants a meet, right away, do not pass go."

You tell Denny you want to swing by your apartment first.

Denny shakes his huge head. "No time. When the Underboss calls, gotta go."

You want to ditch the key so it's not on you when you see Jimmy. You can talk in circles, but Denny's a straight line kind of guy and could blurt out something to make Jimmy suspicious. You trust Denny with your life, but not with a secret or to tell a solid lie.

Denny's like a brother. You almost want to tell him, "Sorry, man. No one's doing Jimmy's wife. I just told you that so I could keep all of Panama Bob's skim to myself." Almost. But half of a fortune might not be enough to get far away for a long time before The Machine finds you. Sure, Denny's like a brother, but Lily is *the one*, plus she sleeps with you. No contest.

You tell Denny you're still sick from the vertigo as you run to the bathroom. You pretend to throw up. Making lots of noise, you stand on the john and hide the key above a ceiling tile. You give it a few more minutes of theatrics before you come out wiping your mouth with your handkerchief.

The pizza girl is back behind the counter, looking worried about what she might have to clean up in the men's room. You ask for an extra-large decaf to go, "just to get the taste out of my mouth."

Then Big Denny's driving you to Jimmy's house and you're thinking that this is going to get deeper and darker before you see the light.

But if it all works out, you can get out of The Machine. Belonging to Lily would be different than being owned by Jimmy. Lily is the most gorgeous

Latina in all of New York. Her love is the kind of slavery any man would choose gladly.

LOVE & NOOKIE

You know you're in trouble when Denny doesn't want to talk baseball. He's a Yankees fan and the easiest way to wind him up is to talk about the Mets. "Santana's going to be healthy in time for spring training. D'jou hear that?"

Big Denny shrugs.

Uh-oh.

The java is bitter and burns your tongue. You put the steaming coffee in the cup holder to let it cool. The meeting with Jimmy could go south in all kinds of ways. What does Jimmy want with you tonight? Bob's dead. Jimmy shouldn't want to be within 100 miles of you. He should be sending you to Atlantic City to let the heat ease. Your stomach feels like you swallowed an ice cube. What if the big boss, Vincent, is awake? He just had the prostate surgery today, but that old son of a bitch is tough. Maybe he's up and making decisions again from his hospital bed. Could Vincent suspect that Jimmy gave you the contract to take out Bob?

Jimmy is a hothead who made mistakes from the get-go. He told you to hit Bob at his office. "Send a message, but keep it away from his house on the Upper East Side. I paid off Bob's gambling debts and I paid the fucking mortgage on his overpriced house. I don't want any trouble turning around and selling it, what with blood smeared on the walls. That shit *stains!*"

Jimmy's second mistake was to send Denny with you. Denny's not ninja muscle. The third mistake? Jimmy said Bob would be alone. As soon as you walked into the outer office, there were Bob's guys, Harv and Marv. You had to improvise so you told them Jimmy wanted them to take the night off and you'd take over babysitting Bob.

That could be bad for you. Maybe Jimmy was wrong about those guys. Maybe they were more old school than new school and, when the reorganization happens, they'll stick with Vincent instead of Jimmy. You just killed the contender to the throne. The old man won't take kindly to you if he finds out you're the hit man. Not that Bob was much of a contender. As criminal masterminds go, poor Panama Bob would have made an okay fisherman.

What if, like Bob said, Jimmy's plan is to blame everything on you? Bob would be out of the way and Jimmy could go crying crocodile tears to Vincent about the Cuban outsider. Vincent is a smart guy, but a father suffering cold grief might order Harv and Marv to do some creative origami with your scrotum before he began to suspect his other, conniving son.

"Denny," you say, "I'm starting to think this might be a trap."

Big Denny's head jerks and he swerves right to pull into a construction lot by a black pit. You follow Denny's lead and open your door. You can't see the bottom of the hole and it looks like no one's around. Is Jimmy late or are Harv and Marv going to show up, shoot you in the back of the head and throw you in the hole?

The rain makes the car roof a snare drum and drowns out Big Denny. You lean closer to make sure you hear him right.

"Whaddayamean, Jesus?"

"I said, a *trap*. Like *Star Wars*…Death Star…General Akbar. It's a trap!"

"Explain."

You tell him Jimmy might be setting you up. Jimmy might be setting *him* up. "There's lots of hit men. Maybe not with my flair for fashion, but still, expendable. And you? No offense, dude, but to get more of you, all Jimmy has to do is snatch up the guys with bad knees who drop outta pro football tryouts who were supposed to play Special Team."

"Yeah. I gotcha. Where's the trap?"

"We're scapegoats, man. Jimmy blames us and gets the empire when the old man steps down. Vincent will retire in Boca to play golf and go to oncologist appointments and Jimmy will be king."

"I get it," Denny says. "You hand Jimmy the locker key and tell him who's screwing his wife and Jimmy will put it all on him. Whoever's screwing Jimmy's wife will take the fall for Panama Bob's hit and you're in the clear, Jesus." Big Denny smiles and you can see his gold tooth glint in the light cast up from the dashboard. "You're a smart guy, dude. You'll figure out which storage place that key belongs to and then Babs and her *lovuh*? They are *so* screwed."

"I hadn't thought of that."

"Christ, Jesus, if I thought about it, you must've. You got that key. The key is the key to the whole thing." Then Big Denny De Molina, your brother from another beaver, balls up his fist and pops you hard in the face. Before you can say anything pithy about that, he pops you again.

You fumble for the open car door to get your balance in the soft mud. The pain is explosive when Denny hauls back and nails you square in the face again. You're propelled to your back. Bright raindrops flash through the glow cast by the streetlight and fall cold on your face. You're slow and your gears are disengaged. Denny hit you hard enough to push the clutch in your brain. *The raindrops fall from far above. If you were a raindrop, you'd stay high up where it's safe.*

You're still fumbling for your SIG Sauer when he lifts you off the ground and slams you down, knocking the wind out of you. "I'm the guy sleeping with Barbara, dawg! You playin' me? You think Big dumb Denny dudn't know what *time* the motherfucker *is*? Who would be stupid enough to mess with Babs? *I* would. Me! I fuckin' *love* her, dawg!"

How did you not see that? He looked you dead in the eye and asked who would be stupid enough to screw Jimmy's wife. Of course, there are lots of guys dumb enough. You might have caught on, but you thought you were just making it up. You had no clue he was doing Barbara.

He picks you up again. If he gave you time, you'd tell him it was all a ruse so he wouldn't want in on the skim. He won't believe you now, anyway. Besides, you can't move any air. Your nose is broken and spewing blood. Maybe those are raindrops or maybe they're stars.

He takes your pistol from your belt and tosses it through the open car door onto the driver's seat. You're still rolling around and grabbing your face, trying to get your lungs to work as he rips the switchblade from your sock. He checks your pockets. If you had the key on you, you'd be dead.

You're up in the air again and Denny's holding you in a bear hug from behind, his fists crushing into your solar plexus. You look down into nothingness. You're over the edge of the construction pit with nothing between you and the darkness but a flimsy yellow boundary tape flapping in the wind. It's a hole for a high-rise. It's a long way down. You try to focus on one good feeling. You tilt your head back to feel the cold wash down your forehead and open your mouth to drink a few drops of water. The rain tastes sweet. It's the last thing you will taste besides blood.

"Where's the *key*, dawg? Down in that pit, tomorrow morning, they're going to find you impaled on a bunch of rebar, maybe still dying but begging for the fire department to pull you off so you can die proper. You know what I'm sayin'? Stigmata ain't the half of it, *Hay-soose*! Where's the key? I hate to do this to you, brother, but for me and Barb's sake, I gotta get those photos!"

The blood from your smashed nose is running into your crumpled and soaked thousand-dollar suit. Your feet don't even touch the ground. You finally move enough air to laugh.

Until Big Denny squeezes tighter.

"It's back at the pizza place!"

"Bullshit!"

"Would I lie to my big bear?"

He throws you into the dirt like a broken doll. Your wrist scrapes raw and the elbows and knees on your suit are wrecked. *Armani!* Why couldn't Denny have had this tantrum when you were wearing the Hugo Boss with the stupid striped lining?

"If you're shitting me, dawg, it's you with rebar sliding through your guts. You get me that key and it's just a double tap behind the ear and sweet dreams."

You're up on your knees, scrabbling toward the yawning passenger door.

The mud's turning softer and slides under you like you're trying to crawl up the down escalator. You hear a grunt as Denny bends to grab you by your belt, no doubt to slam your head into the side of the car. You feel that big paw making a grab for that fine python skin belt you bought at a flea market in Florida, but he fumbles the ball and you slip away.

You get one foot underneath you and you launch yourself at the car. You get some weight on the other foot and you're doing a Superman. You are flying, parallel to the ground. You crash land into the passenger seat.

Your SIG is close, waiting for you on the driver's seat. You almost have it when a vice circles around your left ankle and yanks you back. You struggle to dive for it again, but there's no traction in the mud giving way beneath you. You're half in and half out of the car on your knees when Denny wraps a big paw around your left elbow and flips you on your back, still half in and half out.

"Jesus, I'm sorry to do this to you, but you ain't gettin' in the way of love and nookie. You gotta ride in the trunk till you simmer down so we can go make sure that key gets safe in my pocket."

Denny grabs your legs and starts hauling you out.

You are not getting your gun. The hot coffee will have to do. You grab it from the cup holder and scald your hand as you squeeze to pop the top.

Big Denny sees it coming and stumbles back, but not before you splash it in his eyes. He's grabbing at his face and screaming, stumbling back and reaching for the pistol in the back of his waistband. You scramble up, push off from the side of the car and throw your shoulder into his big belly.

You almost slip in the mud again. You almost fall short of pushing him by a foot. Almost.

Big Denny has his gun out and would shoot you in the face, but the edge of the pit gives way under his heels and for one almost comical moment both the big man's arms pinwheel in the air, trying to grab traction from raindrops.

He falls back, out of the light, straight as a tree, down into darkness.

You collapse in the mud, gasping.

For the second time in an hour, you've thrown a man you liked from a great height. You could do this professionally.

RUN

You park Denny's ride around the corner from your apartment and go up using the service elevator. Maybe those tourists saw a well-dressed Cuban man fitting your description throw Panama Bob from his office tower and maybe they didn't, but the cops will have your picture from the security camera soon. Denny's either dead or bleeding out at the bottom of the construction pit. Worse, does Jimmy really want you to report to him, or was that just Denny's ruse to get you to the construction site? Is there already a contract out on you? Are you the goat in Jimmy's nasty power play to take over the Lima empire? These are the sort of nebulous complications that get a dude dead.

If you just barrel into your apartment, you're going to make a mess of the carpet and blood never comes out of shag. You put Panama Bob's briefcase on the tile floor along with the knife from your sock, your SIG Sauer, belt holster and the spare mags. You take your clothes off just inside the front door and leave the ruined black Armani jacket and pants on the tile. Everything aches and it seems to take a long time to accomplish what should be an easy task. It would help if you could breathe through your nose.

You stuff the suit, muddy and torn, into a green garbage bag. You'll miss that suit. Two gay salesmen at a clothing store fawned over you while Lily sat back with a cappuccino and giggled. She kept the salesmen busy running back and forth, fetching you more linen shirts and silk ties to try out. The ruined jacket didn't make you feel good because the fine cloth fit you perfectly. It made you feel charged because it reminded you of Lily in that store's leather chair. Her little black dress and high heels showed off her long legs. She pointed at each shirt and tie with long manicured nails, a large gold ring for every finger except the ring finger on her left hand. She sat, sipping cappuccino and laughing, directing the festivities like a queen. You so want to be her king, her jester and her slave.

In the six minutes it takes the hot water to kick in, you keep the cold shower spray on your nose, trying to numb it to the terrible throbbing. When the hot water winds its way up to your shower nozzle, you turn around and let the water pulse over your back and have a good cry. You can't remember the last time you cried, but this seems like the right time.

You learned English from Tia Marta, a German immigrant in Miami. It was Tia Marta who insisted you break the stereotype and assimilate like she did. "Don't say 'Chit!', little boy! Say 'Shit!' like a goddamn American." She started you out with the same books she learned English from: Mickey Spillane novels. None of Spillane's heroes would be very proud of you tonight. Mike Hammer never cried in the shower. But Hammer never got hammered by Big Denny De Molina.

The hot water runs out and you shake through your core. You climb from the tub carefully and wipe the steam from the mirror to inspect your face. Your nose is swelling badly. Worse? It's not at the lovely angle you're used to. Your eyes point straight ahead, but your nose is looking off to the side in dismay.

"Dennis De Molina, the monster who was the closest thing I had to a best friend in all of New York City was such a slob, he never left things the way he found them," you tell your reflection. The pain is bad, but you're crying a little for him, too. With your nose broken, your voice sounds squeezed. You sound like a constipated duck.

Not long after 9/11, you found yourself at Fort Drum. At the end of your third week of Basic, you were on night maneuvers. The idea was to find another squad, camouflaged and hidden. The Drill Instructor didn't trust anybody with night-vision equipment yet, so the task was an exercise in working together, being thorough and not panicking. A little wrestling to get captured men back to your squad's flag was supposed to be the fun bonus. To amp up the tension of competition, if the other team eluded capture until dawn, it meant shit duty for your squad. You can't remember why that seemed to matter at the time because further experience proved that everything in the army was shit duty.

The DI didn't allow flashlights, either, so aside from the aforementioned "work together, be thorough, don't panic," finding the opposing team was really luck and moonlight. The guy in front of you was lucky, at least at first. He "found" one of the other squad by stepping on him. Your squadmate either panicked or was hyper-competitive because, when the guy popped up to run, he smashed the dude's face with the butt of his M4 carbine. Good thing no one was trusted with live rounds yet or the moron might have shot him.

"You fucking idiot!" The guy with the busted nose stepped close and kicked panicky guy right in the balls.

You could only make out the silhouettes' interplay, but it was your team member's sickened moan that turned your stomach. The guy with the broken nose sounded like a constipated duck. He continued to yell at the fallen man and kick him in the ribs to punctuate his cursing.

A DI appeared with a flashlight and asked you why you weren't helping your fallen teammate.

"Sir! Because my teammate is a fucking idiot, sir, and the guy with the broken nose is not kicking the shit out of my squadmate, sir!"

"He's not? Then what the hell is that man doing?"

"Sir! He is training my squadmate, sir!"

That got a laugh and the DI turned to the guy with the broken nose. "What is your damage, boy?"

The guy's nose was smushed to the side, just like yours is now. In the yellow circle thrown by the DI's flashlight, the recruit put one hand on either side of his nose and with one savage move, made it straight again. You heard his nose click into place, even over the sound of your teammate at your feet, vomiting.

The DI didn't blink because DIs don't blink. "Can you continue with this night exercise, son, or do you need a medic like this pussy rolling around on the ground is going to need?"

"Sir! This recruit can continue with the exercise, sir!" He still sounded like a constipated duck, but less so.

"Well, then carry on, boy!" the DI bawled.

Before running off into the night, he turned to you, gave a cruel smile and kicked you in the balls, too. You doubled over in agony. The DI doubled over laughing. The guy with the broken nose had been a paramedic before the army. Later, he became an officer. You did not.

Back at the mirror: You try to set your own nose with one savage twist. It takes quite a few savage twists and more crying. You have to commit to the move, but every time you put your hands on either side of your nose to straighten it, the throbbing pain rises to a silent scream from prescient nerves. The anticipation of pain is so bad, you might start to believe in auras because even raising your hands in the vicinity of your face is enough to make your eyes water more. Was a watery eye okay with Mike Hammer? You can't remember, but surely even Mickey Spillane would allow his hero to get a bit teary with a badly broken nose. That's wrong. This nose is actually very well-broken.

You're stalling.

"In three…two…one…*nnnnnope!*" You pound your chest with one fist but when that makes your whole head throb, you think better of trying any macho bullshit to pump yourself up.

"In three…come on! In two…don't wimp out now! One, so I can be pretty again!"

Clunk!

Agony.

And you got a *clunk*. Why a *clunk*? Captain America-Kick-You-in-the-Balls got a *click*. Why did you get a *clunk*?

You breathe hard (through your mouth, of course, since a wad of bloody toilet paper is stuffed up each nostril.) When you dare to look in the mirror again you see that, yes, your nose is straight. The nose will be okay, though both eyes are going black fast. No problem, you tell yourself. Jack Nicholson got his nose sliced open in *Chinatown* and he solved the mystery or got the bad guys or whatever the hell he did in that movie. He probably didn't cry about it as much as you do now, but you've got a whole broken nose and his wound was just one cut.

You ruin a bathroom towel, the bathmat, a t-shirt and a tea towel in the kitchen waiting for the bleeding to stop.

You hear your apartment door slam and you figure Jimmy has sent Harv and Marv to kill you. That would be fine with you just now. When you look up, the lovely Lily Vasquez is upside down. You must have passed out a little because you're lying on kitchen tile, caught in the soft light from behind the open refrigerator door, ice cubes clutched to your face. You're on your back and Lily only *looks* upside down. You glance up her dress as far as you can see, and then begin the laborious task of righting yourself and making it to your knees.

She stands at the edge of your tiny galley kitchen, hands on hips and pissed. She surveys the geography of your face, one eyebrow quirked high. "Are you in trouble?" she asks.

"I don't know why you'd think that." Your voice sounds too high and nasal, but thankfully less duck-like.

"Jimmy Lima's looking for you and being rude to me."

"Oh." You take a few centuries to form the next thought. Civilizations rise and fall while you cogitate and formulate. Oddly, she's still here when you finally manage, "I'm not sure about Jimmy. I think the Irish Mob might be after me."

"The Irish Mob?"

"Yeah," you say, slightly more swift now, gathering steam. Only one eon passes before you answer. "The Irish Mob. You know. As in…the cops."

"Get up."

"I'm not feeling altogether sexy right now, sweetie."

"Dead or alive, you're coming with me."

"A *Robocop* line? Now? Baby, you're my dream girl."

"Come with me if you want to live."

"That's definitely *Terminator*. And *Terminator 2*. And *Termin* —"

"Jesus, either get up and get going right now *before* the Spanish mob or the Irish mob busts in here or I'm leaving."

"You wouldn't leave me like this, would you?"

"With the mob or worse on the way? I'll get the hell out of here and I'll take your left nut in my clutch purse as a memory of all the wonderful times we had."

"Don't talk like that. Please."

"I thought you liked the dirty talk." Lily leans on the doorframe. No matter how she stands, Lily looks like she's in a glamour pose, like she should be stepping onto a movie screen or off a magazine cover.

"It's not the dirty talk that breaks my heart, sweetie. It's you talking about us in the past tense. Can't have that."

She's one of those women who is beautiful when she's angry, though she's stunning when you make her smile. Smiling's better.

"Move faster, Jesus." She sweeps her bejeweled hands up and down her torso, "Or you'll never have this again."

You get your feet under you.

Move! Feel the pain but walk anyway and, no matter what, don't lose Lily.

MORE LIES FOR LILY

Lily gets you dressed and out of the apartment. You're all the way to the service elevator before you have to run back to the apartment to pull two more black Armani suits (still in their dry cleaning bags) from your closet and fish your go bag out from under the bed. Lily gives you the look when she sees the suits but she asks about the big backpack.

"My sergeant taught us a few phrases in Latin. *Non semper erit aestas*. It means be prepared for hard times and zombie attack. We've always gotta be zombie-ready."

"Jesus, you're delirious. How's your nose?" She reaches out to touch it and you flinch away. "If you're going to be a tough guy, keep in mind for next time that a bag of frozen peas or hash browns conforms to your face and works much better than holding ice cubes on your skin. I think you've got freezer burn on top of everything else."

"Sweetie, I'm such a tough guy, I got no frozen peas and no hash browns."

She pinches your nose and you shriek like a little girl. Well, not if the little girl was Lily. She tells you to squeeze the bridge of your nose to stop the bleeding. When you tilt your head back, you taste blood. Before you can bring your chin down, Lily slaps the back of your head. "Just pinch your nose. Don't let your head fall back or the blood will run down your throat! I swear, you throw up in my car, I don't care how bad you feel, you're cleaning it up!"

You step on the service elevator and ride down. Staring at the wooden planks, both of you are silent. By the time the service elevator's door opens, she lets you in on what happens next. "We'll go to my father."

"Pete works for Jimmy."

"He's my father more than he's a bookie. You get in trouble, you go to Dad."

"My dad was eaten by a shark, so I never got that." Still pinching your nose, you sound like a chipmunk's squeak muffled by heavy snow. "What's this about Jimmy insulting you?"

She shrugs. "I'm a big girl. I told you because it pissed me off, not because it's a problem for you to solve."

The rain has let up a little by the time you are out in the street and you think how great a night in the city smells after a hard rain. It's like all the sweat and stink and dirt gets flushed down the sewers and the air is cleansed. You have to think about it because you sure can't smell it. "I wonder if my smeller is broken forever. I'll miss your perfume most."

"That would be a shame," Lily says, but you detect no worry or warmth in her voice.

"I know what's up with me, babe. What's up with you?"

"S'up? Huh. Well, let's see. I get a call from my father's employer asking me for my boyfriend. He says you have been calling Panama Bob's ex and asking about a safe. He asks me where you are and, of course, I say I don't know. I tell him it's not like we're an item or anything. We just go dancing sometimes."

"You're saying we aren't an item?" Your head is beginning to throb again.

"I told him we're no item."

"Are you saying to me we aren't?"

"Baby." She reaches out to caress your cheek. "The way you're looking right now and the trouble you're putting me through? It's not a good time to ask that question."

"Ah."

Lily hits her key fob button, the Toyota beeps and the door locks click open. As she climbs behind the wheel, she reminds you not to bleed in her car.

"So Jimmy asks me straight out what's this about a safe and I say I have no idea and he says some rude things. No name-calling, you understand. Just hinting that maybe I know more than I'm saying and if that's true, he'd get hot about that. Then he says he was at my christening and my confirmation and tells me that good Catholic girls should listen to their parents and godparents and 'fess up before things get complicated."

"That doesn't sound rude."

"Oh, that wasn't the worst of it. Then he told me to give the phone to my father. Daddy listens and nods so hard, you'd think Uncle Jimmy can hear his brain rattling around in his head over the phone. Then Daddy tells Jimmy he'll have a talk with me as if I'm, like, six years old. As soon as he hangs up, he starts in on me."

"Did Pete hurt you?"

She throws you the first smile of the night and it is a sight to behold as the streetlights flash by. Her full lips pull back over pearl white, even teeth and she's all dimples. "Daddy talks big but he'd never lay a hand on me. I'm my mother's daughter. Any man lays a mad hand on me, he'll pull back a quivering stump."

You believe her and when you nod, the throbbing in your nose reminds you how hard Big Denny could hit. You wonder if your best friend is even now being slowly impaled on a grid of steel rods and praying for death. You'd feel bad and cry some more if that hadn't been what Big Denny had planned for you.

"I told Daddy that I'd find you and he wasn't so keen on that, you being you. But what Jimmy wants, Jimmy gets. That's his problem. He gets it all and still wants more."

"Did he say anything about Panama Bob?"

"Uncle Bob had a fall."

Yeah, he had a great fall. And all the king's horses and all the king's men…

"Is Uncle Bob going to be okay?"

Uncle Bob. Not a real uncle. Panama Bob is an uncle to Lily like Tia Marta was your aunt. Children adopt neighbors and family friends and strangers and sometimes even mafia bosses and call them uncle and aunt. Bob and Lily weren't close, but close enough that Bob came around with Christmas and birthday presents. Lily might not understand that you had to kill the guy who set her up with her Barbie collection, Malibu dream house and whatever that toy RV for Barbie was called. Lily might not understand that when Jimmy Lima tells you to kill somebody, you do it or somebody else gets the job but they have to kill you first.

"Jesus! I asked you a question."

"Uncle Bob is not going to be okay."

"I figured that much since you were asking about his safe." She lights a cigarette off the car's lighter and rolls down the window a couple of inches to let the smoke trail from her lips to the wind. Her father, Pete Vasquez, is the most successful bookie on the East Side. He's so sharp at his job, he gave her this car for her twentieth birthday. He's not so sharp that he knows she smokes yet. Or maybe she's just that much smarter.

"Where's your portly friend with the bad breath?"

"Denny's missing in action. Prolly killed in action."

She waits until the next red light for the next question so she can look in your face when she asks. "Did Denny De Molina murder my Uncle Bob?"

"Yup." It's close to the truth. Jimmy told you to kill Panama Bob and Denny drove. He knew the mission.

"Did you get Denny or did Bob?"

"I got Denny." You're squirmy over that truth, but rush to it so you can get back to being the hero.

"Shit." She pauses a moment after the light turns green and drives on, a little faster and weaving her way through traffic.

"Yeah," you say, thinking of how you had owed Big Denny for rent from when you first moved to the city. You never got around to paying him, but that debt is erased now, along with all the good things about Denny. Funny how he could be a badass and there were lots of things to not like about him, but it's the good stuff that makes you hate him more now. Each good thing about Big Denny De Molina demands that you feel bad. And you do, worse than about Bob. Bob was a job. Denny's dead because you lied to keep his big paws off Bob's skim.

"You said the cops are after you. Did they do this to you?"

"Nah. Denny gave me my facial redesign."

"Then he deserved to die," Lily says.

You get a warm feeling in the pit of your stomach.

"Twice over," she adds. "Once for self-defense and once for Uncle Bob."

Back to ice.

"The cops know you killed Denny?"

"Uh…no, too early, but they might have a witness I got to worry about." Another lie to Lily, though you guess you could call the camera eye a witness. You can't tell her which crime scene you were fleeing at the time. You can't be honest and still keep her. Without Lily, there wouldn't be much point in getting hold of all that storage locker money.

Heh. 'Storage locker money." It isn't Panama Bob's skim or even Jimmy Lima's money anymore. It's storage locker money — money with no owner until you can get to it. You'll have enough money to get away with Lily and never look back on this shitty night. Or all the other shitty nights since Big Denny pulled you in and got you a job working for the Limas. You turn your head away from the lovely Lily, even managing to tear your eyes away from her long legs exposed through the slits in her dress. Instead, you look at the last spatter of rain caught in the city lights. Rivulets of water find each other and streak back, sliding down the glass like tears down cheeks.

You tell Lily to pull over by an all-night drugstore you know has a bank machine. You pull some cash out of your account. You don't need much for now, just enough to operate until you can get out of town. The machine's jaws open and two hundred dollars in crisp, new twenties slide out. You break a twenty and buy a bottle of painkillers and a couple of bottles of water. Back in the car, you knock back twice the recommended dose of pills and finish one of the water bottles in one go. You close your eyes and wait for the medicine to do its work, but before the throbbing eases, Lily swings the wheel and you're in the parking lot behind Pete's after-hours club. You first met Lily on the dance floor here on salsa night.

"Daddy wants to see you," she says.

If you had time to think this through, you never would have gone in to face Pete Vasquez. Lily's already out of the car. You follow her like a puppy dog.

You'd follow Lily across heaven and earth. And hell, too, as it turns out.

THE CIRCLE OF LIGHT

The line of Tuesday late-night party-goers stretches down the alley that leads to the side entrance to the club. They're mostly kids of the ungrateful living generation, ironically trying to keep Goth alive. Their clothes match their black eyeliner: *tons* of black eyeliner, drugstores and mothers' bathroom drawers full of black eyeliner. It's a parade of sad raccoons who don't have that much to complain about and they're pissed off about that, too.

The posers are interspersed with a few hardcore, outlandishly dressed party kids. They look like they all escaped from the same circus. The theme tonight appears to be Irish Vampire Clowns. They're beyond pale, dressed in bright green. They wear curly antennae on their heads that end with big cherry lollipops. It's like they're part of some kind of twisted sports team, if cutting were a sport. You're not much older than these kids. Not in chronological age, anyway.

The club, called *Como Si*, is in the basement. Officially, Pete owns the bodega on the main floor and the top floor houses his accounting business. Pete's crew of two old guys and one old lady — Lily's grandmother — work the phones for his bookie operation upstairs. Pete doesn't get along so well with his mother, so he hangs out in the back of the bodega smoking and talking on his cell phone and admiring his black Caddy in the rear parking lot.

Pete only drives the Cadillac to make the rounds of a few laundromats he says he "has an interest in." Pete started out as an enforcer for The Machine and still picks up weekly payments, leaning on mom and pop businesses. "I came up when the Korean laundromat biz was exploding. Koreans don't call the cops. Protection's a beautiful thing. I swing in, maybe pick up or drop off some laundry and there's always a white envelope. It's like being a bill collector for the government. It doesn't even occur to them to give any flack."

Maybe that's because Pete's rep as a guy not to mess with lives on from the old days.

Lily's halfway to the back door and you're stumbling after her. Sitting in the passenger seat for the ride to *Como Si*, you've stiffened up and your body feels old. *Thank you, Denny.* Likely Denny's body is slowly sliding down some bloody rebar, so you really can't hold a grudge over a few aches and pains. You're only halfway across the back lot and you can already hear the thump of electronica from the building's basement.

Como Si is the perfect New York after-hours club if you know the schedule. The regulars are a cult that somehow know the drill without taking notes. Wednesdays, local kids with electric guitars squeeze on the tiny stage to try to bring back the hair band, though everything sounds like REO Speedwagon on bad acid. Thursday the club is closed for cleaning, but it's really poker night on the underground circuit. Friday is always gutless '80s music. Saturday nights at *Como Si* are supposed to be like a Saturday Night Fever disco — AKA gay guys' night. That always devolves into an ABBA marathon. Sunday, Dyke Night, features a lot of Justin Bieber early in the evening and Melissa Etheridge lyrics rapped over synth later on. Monday is Lady's Night: Cool jazz and hot blues for the first half of the evening followed by salsa till dawn.

If Lily had taken you to *Como Si* on any of those other nights, you could handle this meeting with Pete better. But Tuesday nights like this? A DJ spins house music until 3 a.m. and *Como Si*'s walls thump until dawn with industrial clash mixed with that ambient shit that's only tolerable to sweaty kids on MDMA.

The beat, even in the parking lot, matches your headache's pace. This ear beating makes you wish you were back in Havana by the Hudson. Salsa till dawn (every night) is your preference. Tia Marta taught you salsa and English to make you a more acceptable boy. Sometimes, when you're on the dance floor with Lily in your arms and lost in the music, you could almost forgive Tia Marta everything.

Instead of heading to the side door, Lily steams straight at a steel door by the bodega's loading dock. She rings a doorbell that's hidden above the door frame. She has to lift up on the tip toes of her high heels to do it and you watch her bare legs working, the long calf muscles contracting under taut skin. Lily teaches Zumba part-time at a nearby gym and it shows. Her exercise class was your in with Lily and how you found the courage to talk to her. Since she did Zumba, she thought she knew salsa. You showed her the difference between what she was doing and true salsa from Miami. Salsa is the only thing you and Lily both do that you execute better. You've got the looks and the clothes — at least you did until Denny's fist pounded your face sideways and flat — but, no salsa? No Lily.

The peephole darkens for a moment and you hear three heavy deadlocks ratchet and clunk. Jake Cibrian swings the door open and drinks your girl up and down slowly. "Hello, gorgeous." Jake has one of those too-wide, shark smiles that shows two rows of sharp teeth. "You looking to skip the line and do some thumpin'?" He's hard-muscle packed into a suit that doesn't fit him in the shoulders. The jacket hangs straight down like he bought a big polyester shopping bag off the rack.

Jake sees you step into the light behind Lily and his mouth forms a big zero through which a trilling, girlish giggle escapes. "If it ain't the little Cuban! Hey, Cube! Jesus Diaz, the Cuban sensation! The Cuban *burning* sensation. You get hit by a truck?"

"Cut myself shaving."

"Was you shaving with a machete?"

You would have come up with something cutting, but just then your nose starts to bleed again, defying the sheer force of your will. You cover it with your handkerchief and step in front of Lily.

"Never mind busting his balls, Jake. Busting his nut is my job."

Despite the pain in your jaw, you give Jake a smile. It hurts, but for the look on his mug, it feels better somehow, too.

"He's here to talk to my dad," Lily says.

"Pete's in back with his noise-cancelling headphones. You musta messed up real bad to get Pete out of bed, Cube. He's hardly ever here once *Como Si* opens. C'mon in."

He steps aside and you look back to make room for the lady, but Lily's already retreating to her car. She blows you a kiss. "Keep pressure on it, up near the bridge of your nose. Come see me after, if it's not too late." She's already floating away like a rose petal on the wind.

Your stuff is in the car and you're about to say she should wait, this won't take long. Then Jake yanks you inside by the collar. He shoves you back a few feet while he turns the deadlocks.

"You shouldn't put hands on me, Jake. I don't like it."

"Easy, Cube. Pete wants to see you now, not later. The longer he stays, the more pissed he gets. I like it, but he's too old for this music."

The wooden floor vibrates with the pumping bass line while something wafts up, muffling a chorus that sounds vaguely familiar. Madonna or Gaga? As you follow Jake down the hallway, you're almost sure the beat is banging over a song from *Annie*, trying to obliterate it with equal measures of decibels and irony. Jake pounds his fist twice on another metal door and opens it, pointing you in. When the door clangs behind you, the music is muffled. You're in the loading dock at the back of the bodega. The concrete floor cuts some of the thump from the banging beat from *Como Si*'s pit. Sound tiles do the rest.

Pete, wearing the big cans of noise-cancelling headphones on his ears, sits in a circle of white light, smoke in one hand, a Kindle in the other. He looks up, holds one finger up and you stand at ease. A trickle of blood is thinking about trailing down your face again but you snort it back and tough out the ugly iron taste in the back of your throat. Damn Denny. He sure gave you something to remember him by.

Pete stands and tucks the e-reader into an inside pocket of his brown leather jacket before removing the headphones. "Jake bought me these headphones last Christmas. Says I can wear them on the plane. I tell him, where am I gonna fly? I come here, a drive once in a while, I go back home, I come back here the next day. When am I going to use these big headphones? Wear them on a plane, they're gonna think I should be flying the plane, am I right?"

He seems to really wait for an answer so you shrug and nod.

"No! I'm not right. Sometimes I work late and these headphones? It's a beautiful thing. All those freaks downstairs can go deaf, I'm up here counting their parents' money. I don't go deaf, I win twice, am I right? Sure, I'm right."

You nod, but you're thinking of Panama Bob disappearing into the dark air, then visible again, sprawled in the lit street. You couldn't see it from your high perch, but you can see the spreading pool of bright red blood all too well in your mind's eye. Did some woman across the street scream, or is that your imagination, filling in holes? Maybe you were the screamer. You're never going out on a ledge again unless the building's on fire.

"Siddown, kid. You look like you been through the wringer."

"Yeah."

Pete vacates the folding chair and waves you to sit. "Jimmy's looking for you. Wants to talk."

"He coming?"

"Don't worry about that. You talk to me. I'll fill him in."

How much has Jimmy told Pete about the demise of Panama Bob? Does Pete already know? You don't want to insult him by spooning it out on a need-to-know basis, but you don't want to be stupid, either.

"You want a drink or something? Some wine? Or maybe something cold from downstairs? You let me know and Jake'll be right back with a seven and seven, rum and Coke, whatever you like."

"No thanks, Pete. I'm okay. When I have a drink, I like it without Jake's spit in it."

Pete smiles for the first time. He gestures for you to wait and disappears into the gloom. When he returns to the circle of light, he's got two more folding chairs. He opens each one and sits opposite you.

You eye the empty chair. "Jimmy's not coming, right?"

"Nah, nah. I got a special guest coming. Actually, that's something you can help me with. He'll be here any minute. Jake spotted the guy in the line outside and we were just waiting for you. When Lily called and said how beat up you were, I had an idea."

"Lily called you?"

"Yeah, while you were getting your stuff and clearing out of your apartment and whatnot. Looking at you, Jesus, I have to say — and I don't mean this unkindly — my Lily, she did not underestimate. Did *Bob* do this to you?"

"Big Denny."

"Really?"

"Big Denny."

"How many times you shoot him before he went down?"

"Didn't. Humpty Dumpty had a great fall."

"Holy shit, people are falling all over the place tonight. Maybe I should sit on the floor, huh? Could get dangerous in here."

"I think that's it for falls from high places for tonight, Pete."

He laughs. "You killed Big Denny without an iron? Respect. And all this time I been thinking you were a pussy. No offence, but I guess Lily's right about you."

"Oh?"

"Yeah. She said you weren't that big a pussy."

You watch him laugh and you think how much more you love Lily than she loves you. You can salsa your way into her heart. She'll love you because you'll always treat her the way a goddess deserves to be treated. The skim will help with that project immensely.

Pete's laughter winds down as he picks up your silence. "Good. Good. Hey, now. You know what I miss? The angles used to be shallower and easier. Used to be, you bet on a dog race, you had a decent chance you could win. Used to be, you want to *fix* a dog race, that was even easier. This one time, I'm at the track and I pay this guy, just another ham-and-egger. Pay this guy a hundred bucks and he clips all the dogs' nails, you know? On their paws? He clips 'em all short but the one dog I bet on. You clip a dog's nails, he doesn't run quite as fast as the dog with nails. I look back, I think that was the easiest money I ever made. Made thousands on that one dog race and was home in time to watch the soaps with the wife. The soaps, I don't miss, but that afternoon with my wife, first and only time I banged her three times in one afternoon. No disrespect to Lily's mother, but you and me are talking here. Money is more than just money. It's juice. Not even on our wedding night did I have it like that afternoon."

"I understand." You don't. He's talking like he already knows about Panama Bob's skim.

"You know what else I miss, Jesus? Phone booths. Where did all New York's phone booths go? The other day I saw a homeless guy and he's talking into his Bluetooth." Pete laughs. "A fucking Bluetooth! On a homeless guy!"

You laugh politely. It hurts your ribs.

"All these civilians are walking around and it's the Jetsons. Everybody's talking to somebody who isn't there. People come into the store up front and no matter what time of day it is, there's always some woman in there talking to her friend while she shops. The friend's prolly got a job, but with the Facebook and the thing...they're not really doing their job. It's crazy. We all got jobs we gotta do, am I right?"

"Of course," you venture.

"Of *course*, of course! So I know you did a tough job tonight. You were doing your job. You got beat up, but there's no shame in that. The opposite, right?"

"Yeah."

"Yeah? Yeah."

Something about his delivery feels rehearsed.

"You know what else was good about phone booths back in the day? You want to shoot a guy, you just follow him around. At some point, the guy's going to go into a phone booth. You come up close, pop him in the ear while he's calling his mistress or saying goodnight to his Mom and *bang*! He's down between the 'good' and the 'night.' Phone booths! No place to run. No extra drama when you do your job."

"A phone booth would have been helpful tonight. Couple of 'em." The headache's hammering harder. How does anyone know if they have a concussion? Maybe you've got one of those hairline fractures that kills skiers when they run into a tree or something without a helmet, like what happened to Liam Neeson's wife and Sonny Bono. Maybe blood is slowly filling up your brain pan right now and you should have just gone to the hospital instead of coming here. And wouldn't it be great if Pete could just shut up or maybe just shoot you so you could go to sleep and be done?

He looks you up and down. "Listen. Seeing as you're here and all messed up already, I got another job for you, but don't worry, all you gotta do is sit there. This is going to be strange, but I got an idea to shake up the deadbeat I got waiting outside. You in?"

"What have I got to do?"

"Nothin'. Just sit there and look beat up. You can do that easy."

"For the next few weeks, probably."

"Ha. Yeah. But listen, as the guy who is dating Lily, you're going to have to trust me like I'm trusting you with my daughter. When the guy comes in, I'm going to put on a show. I love the theater. You understand?"

"Sure."

"Put your hands behind your back, behind the chair so it looks like you're tied up." You hesitate a moment, but you put your hands behind your back while Pete opens up a cell from his pocket and says, "Jake, bring the guy to the dock." He mumbles into the phone, circling you and you're feeling sleepy. You're still thinking about your brain bleed when the hard plastic loops of the zip tie cinch up and cut into your wrists.

You sit straight up like an electric shock has shot up your spine. You're wide awake and about to protest but the flat look in Pete's eyes tells you it'll be better if you shut up.

"This is even easier than a phone booth, huh?" he says. He gives you a grin and all you can do now is wonder how such an ugly animal could produce the beautiful woman you love.

THE DOCK

A knuckly fist pounds on the heavy door twice. The music from the pit below blares a moment as the door swings in. Jake Cibrian shoves a squirrelly guy dressed in black toward the circle of light. He wears a silver chain that hangs from the hoop in his ear to the piercing on his lip. When dealing with a guy like Pete, this is a mistake so obvious, it's visible from orbit.

"Edward! So glad you could join us," Pete says. By his tone, he could be calling a puppy to come get a treat.

Edward looks back at Jake. "There's no need to be rough about this. I called you guys. I called you and you said we could work this out!"

Oh, boy. This isn't looking good for you or Edward. You pull at the zip ties. Useless. The sharp plastic edges cut into your wrists. Pete left you your gun in the small of your back, but what good does that do? Throwing yourself to the floor and shooting the bad guys from behind your back only works in movies. In real life, the effort might annoy Pete. Then he might have Jake drag you over to the loading dock door and crush your head.

Edward rushes to Pete, the reasonable, older guy. He doesn't know Pete. He only thinks he does. The kid pulls crumpled bills out of his pants. "Just like I said! There's $400 there!"

"And that would leave the remaining bill for your bets at…?" Pete still looks reasonable.

"About thirty-nine thousand dollars."

For an older guy, Pete's fast. Edward didn't see the bitch slap coming. It knocks him sideways. "Never say the word 'about' when you're talking about money, Edward. Money's serious. Now *siddown*. I want you to meet my friend, Jesus."

Edward touches his cheek and sits at the edge of the chair, as if he might try something stupid like popping up and running. Jake stands with his back to the door, arms crossed with one hand inside his jacket. You know Jake's already got his snub-nosed .38 in his fist. Standing like that is an old bodyguard trick. He looks like a guy standing with his arms crossed and looking surly, but his hand is already wrapped around the gun so if Edward runs, he'll whip it out, looking like some kind of fast draw cowboy in a bad suit. That's what you'd do if you were standing there. Wouldn't it be great if Jimmy had sent Jake to kill Panama Bob? If he had, it'd be Jake tied up in this chair and you'd be standing there with a smug look on your face instead of a spreading bruise.

Pete sits in the last folding chair and watches Edward closely. "I'm going to ask you some questions, Ed. I know you will answer me honestly. While we talk, I want you to look at my friend's face here. Note the obvious pain that he is in. The busted nose and the puffiness. He's working on blowing up into major shiners on each eye, don't you think? Most guys, they get worked over, it's mostly one eye 'cuz a lot of guys just think with one fist. Wild haymakers, same fist every time, pounding away. Most guys fight like they masturbate, one hand pounding away, am I right?"

Jake's girlish giggle makes you want to gut him even more than usual.

"But Jesus, here, got worked over pretty professionally, don't you think? You got to respect the work. His wounds look…symmetrical."

"Who *is* this guy?" Edward says.

"This here is Jesus Diaz. He's dating my daughter."

"Is that why you beat him up?"

Pete guffaws. "You don't know my daughter, Edward. Lily, she does what she likes and I just nod and say, 'What can I do for you, sweetheart?' And she still gives me a hard time. Nah, if Jesus is man enough for Lily, I got no complaints."

"So — ?"

"I wasn't done talking, Edward," Pete warns. "This is listening time for you. I'll let you know when it's your turn. Just keep looking at his face."

Edward shuts his mouth and looks at you.

"I *like* Jesus. He's a nice kid. But he's here in this sad state because you and Jesus have something in common. You're dealing with big problems, big people. You're over your head and I don't think you understand that. Jesus doesn't know the forces that are coming together. We're talking continents sliding around. Molten magma erupting in your face. Constellations turning upside down. And here you sit, a small person. You know what you guys are? You're Job, like from the Bible. You're both sitting on top of a shit pile and you're thinking of complaining about it, but you complain to God, you know what happens? You piss Him off. Trust me. I was an altar boy. I know. Job said, God, you take everything away from me. You beat the living shit out of me and kill everything I love and leave me just on the edge of fuckin death! What are you doing to me?"

Edward looks at you and says nothing. He's looking very pale, like the blood's draining from him. You're probably looking pale, too, and not just from blood loss. Pete's speech is as much to you as it is for Edward's benefit.

"So Job's a whiner and you know what God says to him? He looks down at Job with his ass on a shit pile and he says, 'Who do you think you are, Job? Where were you when I made the stars and named them and fuck knows what else? I am God and you are nothing to me. I can make you or I can break you and what I require of you is faithfulness. Never mind anything else, God says. Be faithful. Do as you are fuckin told or I'll pull you apart, put you back together and pull you apart again just for shits and giggles because I am God and you are not.'"

Pete pulls out a fresh cigarette from his pack and lights up. Edward glances his way and Pete points the lit cigarette toward your face. Another warning for both of you: for him to look at you while Pete is talking and a reminder to you that you are helpless.

"My old priest grew up Baptist in Indiana before he converted to be a Roman Catholic. He tells it better," Pete says. "He says, 'Don't box with God! Your arms are too short! Don't play head games with God! He made your head!' That's somethin', isn't it?"

Pete pauses for a thoughtful puff before continuing. "I usually say *Roman* Catholic. Romans ruled a long time. I like the idea that I'm part of something huge. Me? And Jake over there? We're Roman soldiers. We got an empire and if you think you're Spartacus or some shit? We'll crucify you and burn your body and you'll be a goddamn streetlight."

Edward does not sob aloud, but he's crying now. Pussy. A real man curls up and cries on his kitchen floor when no one is around to hear him. A real man cries in the shower.

"That's what the Romans used to do. They'd barbecue a couple thousand slaves alive on a stick and the fire would eat at their fat and they'd be human candles, lighting the roads. Which were also bad ass by the way. I read that the space shuttle was the size it was because the Roman roads were just so wide for a couple of carts to pass each other. I guess it had something to do with the width of the axles. All roads lead to Rome and all roads are based on Roman measurements. Somebody decided the railways should only be so wide and the space shuttle couldn't be bigger than what railway cars could carry, so they based their specs on some Roman guy who built a road a couple of thousand years ago on a goat path. Amazing, isn't it?"

Pause.

"Edward!"

He jumps.

"I asked you a question —"

"Yes! Yes, it's amazing!"

"Good. Now you know what that's all about?"

Edward shakes his head.

"College boy." Pete takes a long drag and when he speaks, the smoke puffs out with each syllable. Pete transforms into a dragon spewing white smoke. "God. The Romans. Their roads. The shuttle. The railway. It's all about *faithfulness*. Faithfulness is the root of how things work. We got a *system*."

Tears roll down Edwards cheeks.

"I take the time to tell you this because I don't know what they are teaching at that school you go to, but it seems you don't understand the system and your place in it. You bet on a basketball game and you win, I pay you. You lose that bet and you pay me. You string me along and give me some bullshit, I start boxing, Edward. You're just like my friend Jesus, here. You're a babe in the woods. You don't know your arms are too short."

Pause.

Pete arches his eyebrows, inviting Edward to speak.

"I understand."

"Good. So my question to you, Edward, is how did you get here this evening?"

"I drove."

"Uh-huh. What do you drive?"

"Toyota."

"Toyota. Toyota, what?"

"Echo."

"Ah, the little one. Makes sense. You're a kid. You got a gambling problem. You own it?"

"Yeah."

"Is it in good shape?"

"No. I'm the fourth owner, I think."

"Okay, but you can get some bucks for it. The thing I'm trying to instil in you, Edward, is that you roll in here with four hundred bucks on this big a debt, I think you've got the wrong idea about our relationship. One time a guy came to me and he had his kids' piggy banks. That guy understood the system. He understood our relationship, see? The guy with the piggy banks? Bad guy. Bad father. Bad husband. But a good risk. He squeezed everything he had to come up with more dough before he came to me. When I look at you, I see a kid who's never been hit. Never got a real education. Edward, you are a guy who owes me a lot of fuckin money and you act like you can work this out without inconveniencing yourself. That inconveniences me, Ed. I got a daughter with expensive tastes. Am I right, Jesus?"

It hurts your face, but you give him a smile.

"Huh. That's good. You didn't lose no teeth. A miracle is what that is, Jesus."

You brace for the punch you're sure is coming.

"Give me until morning and I'm sure I can come up with more money. I just need more time. I can get $2,500 maybe even $3,000 if you give me until morning. Mom cut me off, but I'll make sure she knows…about God and Job and stuff."

Pete laughs. "Good! And I can help you help your mom understand, too." Pete flicks the lit cigarette into Edward's face as he rises and kicks him hard in the chest. The kid gets knocked over backward in his chair and goes sprawling.

You saw a guy get kicked like that in Basic once. The sergeant's boot heel drove so hard into the guy's chest that it messed up his heart's electrical system and stopped it. That recruit had to be shocked with a defibrillator. Unfortunately for Edward, he's still moving.

"He looks as pale as the vampire Edward from those movies," Pete says. "And dressed all in black, you look even more white. Is that the look you were going for? I ask because I'm a people person. Some guys, it's only about the money, but I got into this business for the people. Does that look work with the little chickie-poos in the club? Do you use lines on them like you used on me? 'Next week. I promise, I'll love you tomorrow —' "

The kid drools and sobs, which as answers go, doesn't accomplish much. Pete stands over him. You're relieved he's not thinking about you for the moment.

"You said we'd work it out!" Edward screams.

"We are working it out. This is me working out." Pete picks up the folding chair, collapses it and raised it above his head before bringing it down on Edward's ass again and again. "You're a little boy in need of a spanking!"

Edward doesn't so much cry as bleats. You've never heard a person in pain do that before, but he really does sound like a lamb getting the shit beat out of it.

"Your mom is going to believe you, Ed! She's going to help you pay down a lot of cash!"

You'd think the sight of Pete beating on the boy with a folding chair would remind you of old-time wrestling. It doesn't. In fact, the horror of his helplessness freezes you. All you can think about is the pain in Edward's ass and the look on his face because Edward knows somewhere deep down that Pete isn't even half done. Pete's just getting started.

Edward's cries grow louder. Pete stops and you think maybe God does have mercy. Then God pulls the noise-cancelling headphones over his ears and steps on the fingers of Edward's left hand, one by one, with his heel.

Jake ambles over, reaches down and rips the chain from Edward's face. The lip and ear hoops come away with the flesh and blood. Edward's cry of anguish is unforgettable. You want Edward's torture and the terrible bleating to stop, sure, but when they're done with him, they'll start on you. The scared and scarred part of you hoping they'll keep wailing on him? That's bigger than the human being praying they'll soon finish. Even in terrible moments like this, you discover there's still room for self-loathing. If you survive, you really should think about finding a shrink.

Pete's kicks are slowing.

Edward stops bleating and, somehow, his silence is worse.

Pausing to stare your way, Jake licks Edward's blood from his knuckles and grins. "You're next, Cube!"

You know monsters. You grew up under the rule of sadists so you know that, for Jake, a beating isn't a means to an end. Pain and power is an end in itself.

You are next. Think of something. Quick.

THE PUNISHMENT

Jake drags the kid away. Pete lights his next cigarette as he turns back to you. Pete's smiling. He's more scary when he smiles.

"As the guy who's possibly going to be your son-in-law, Pete," you say, "I'd really appreciate you untying my hands."

Pete smiles wider. "Let's talk first. Tie a guy's hands behind his back and sit him in a chair and…well, it keeps you sharp, thinking about how I've got a burning cigarette and you're sitting with no way to cover your crotch."

You cross your legs.

Jake burbles his little girl laugh, his back against the door again, arms crossed, his fist wrapped around the butt of the .38 in his fancy cross-draw shoulder holster rig. Some guys even have holsters with springs in them for a faster draw, like this is Tombstone and every day they face another desperado.

It's time to take control before Pete's burning and beating you and Jake is dragging you out, rolled up in a rug from one of the offices upstairs.

"In the old days, they called enforcers like you 'leg breakers.' It was a bad strategy. You break a guy's leg, he'll respect, but how's he gonna run and get you your money? Later on, we called the guys who were most persuasive 'dentists.' You break a guy's leg, he's only got two and he's fucked up. Knock a tooth or two out and the guy's motivated to keep the rest of his smile."

You smile, showing your pearly whites. "Whose side you on, Pete?" You don't feel it, but you have to inject calm into this situation, feel him out. He knows something you don't, but you've got to introduce a little doubt and make Pete think it's him on the dumb end.

"Panama Bob's dead, so not much use being on his side," Pete says. "So I'm on Vincent's side. Always side with the big guy with the big guns. Respect. Faithfulness. Crucifixion. These are the things that build empires."

"There's more sides to this than just Vincent's."

The folding chair scrapes across the cement as Pete pulls it close and sits to stare in your eyes. On the one hand, he looks intrigued, but he's also close enough to reach out and burn your eye with that cigarette. He waggles his eyebrows and you start talking, unsure what the end of the sentence is going to be until you get there. You lay it out, going slow:

"Jimmy sent me to do a job with Denny." True, sort of. He gave you the job and you asked Denny to drive.

"Denny killed Panama Bob." A lie.

"I just drove the car and didn't know what the job was until Denny already did it." A lie.

"Jimmy said the hit was Vincent's order, just before he went under for his surgery." This is what Jimmy told you, but you didn't believe it for a second.

Pete's right. Sitting here helpless does make you sharp. At least you thought so until Pete's first bitch slap rocks you sideways and your nose is gushing blood again. Pain is such a tiny word for the huge wave that crashes over you.

"I already talked to Jimmy, kid. *Jimmy* says Bob planned to take over The Machine. He had something big going on that he wasn't letting Vincent in on. Bob was making moves on his own and cutting the organization out. Jimmy didn't know what. Vincent didn't know what and Jimmy didn't want to let his father know what was going on until he'd confronted Bob. *You* were just supposed to bring Bob to Jimmy's house."

And there it is. Jimmy's got what the military calls plausible deniability and he's making *you* the goat. Edward may have bleated like a lamb when they beat him, but they'll have you making whatever sounds a goat makes in a moment.

"Jimmy Lima says there's a lot of money involved. Then you call up Bob's ex-wife to ask about the combination to the safe in his office. We don't know what happened with Big Denny. You and Denny are friends, Jesus. It's hard to imagine you killing him. Actually, it's hard to imagine you trying to kill him and being successful. Is he really dead, Jesus? Was it Bob who beat the piss out of you? If you come clean, I won't have to beat the shit out of you. Where's Denny and where's whatever was in the wall safe?"

When you catch your breath and the tide of pain in the bridge of your nose ebbs a bit, Pete's still waiting. You decide to tell some truth and see if that works. "Jimmy sent me to kill Panama Bob. Jimmy wants to take over The Machine." Then you get an inspiration for an idea that could be the truth. "I called the ex-wife to try to get into the safe because I thought there might be evidence in there." That sounds plausible.

Pete stares. Maybe he's considering what you're saying. Who can tell what's going on behind Pete's eyes?

"You and Denny went about this all wrong. If it's supposed to look like a suicide, you don't hang around and rifle Bob's office. If it's a clean hit, you don't leave a body around. Murders? The police take murder seriously. Missing persons? Not so much. If Bob were a missing person instead of a murder victim, there'd be a lot less heat on us, stupid." He slaps you again, between the *stu* and the *-pid.*

When you open your eyes, he's still staring at you, waiting.

"Jimmy wouldn't have sent you to kill Panama Bob unless he'd already considered whether Bob was careless, a thief or a rat. You think the boss is an idiot?"

"*Ow*," you say. You want to say much more about the pain you're in, but that might encourage him to do it again. "Jimmy had already sent Cat to talk to Bob and Cat never came back. We don't know what happened to him. Jimmy and Cat are tight, you know that. Jimmy was through the talking phase. He wanted his half-brother dead. It was supposed to look like a suicide but it didn't go down that neatly…though Bob did fall down pretty neatly in the end."

"You're asking me to take the word of a tiny Cuban whose pretty new to The Machine. The one guy who could stick up for you, you say is dead. Are you sure you don't want to rethink your story and give Big Denny a call? How about I get out my cell phone and we get Denny back from the dead and he confirms your story."

"Denny wasn't so trustworthy. He was banging Jimmy's wife."

That gets Pete's attention. He looks like you slapped him. From the door, Jake bursts out with "Bullshit!" but Pete isn't so sure.

"*Sh!*" you tell Jake. "The adults are talking." You might have seen that in a movie once. As bad as things are, it still feels good to watch Jake turn red and go from simmer to boil.

"Jimmy's wife…" Pete is thinking. "They say the best predictor of future behavior is past behavior. Fuck! If there is anything I can't stand, it is faithlessness and ingratitude."

"Denny was trying to kill me when I pushed him down into a construction pit."

Jake leaves his post by the door, anxious to get in on the slapping action, though if Jake gets involved, it'll be punching and kicking. "You're saying Denny threw Panama Bob off a building and then Denny fell to his death, too? That's a lot of falling in one night, man."

You look Jake dead in the eye. "Shit happens. Life really is like a Coen brothers movie sometimes."

Pete slaps you a third time. If he slaps you again, it feels like no one will ever have to again. Your ears ring with bells that peel *pain, pain, pain*.

"What were you doing calling up Bob's ex? What was in the safe?"

When you bring your head up, you want to shake it, but that seems unwise. Something might come loose. You need ice over your eyes and you need to stop the cut that's opened up over your left eyebrow. Pete really does just think with his right hand. He's not working you over as professionally as old Denny did. "Careful, Pete, you're going to make me asymmetrical."

Jake laughs that stupid, trilling giggle. With the headache you have, that sound drills into your skull and feels almost as bad as the slaps.

Mixing the truth and lies together isn't working so well. If Pete slaps you again, your head will spin around on your neck. You think about the pistol in the small of your back. It's still just as useless. Pete knows it's there, but he's not worried. That makes the pain worse. He knows about the switchblade in your sock, too, and he doesn't think enough of you to bother to take your weapons away. He respects you not at all. If you try to go for it, the best case scenario is you shoot yourself in the ass. Worse case, in the spine. Worst case, you shoot yourself in the spine and then Jake and Pete kick you until you bleed out. Yeah, that would get the goat sounds going really good.

Once you're out of the picture, there's no one to warn Vincent that it's Jimmy who's taking over The Machine. Jimmy who ordered the hit on his stepbrother because he thinks Bob killed Cat. The fact that you happened to kill Jimmy's wife's lover, too? Happy circumstances all around for Jimmy. Not so good for you in any way. Bob was Vincent's stepson too, of course, so there's no mercy in your future and enemies at ever turn. That's why Jimmy picked you, the relative newcomer and outsider for the job.

The fact that Bob was skimming from The Machine might even be a minor thing to Vincent. When Jimmy ordered the hit, you should have jumped the chain of command and gone to Vincent. The truth is, the moment Jimmy ordered you to kill Bob, you were screwed and from where you sit now, it's hard to imagine how you ever thought this would work out any other way. For Jimmy, this is about getting even for Cat's death, getting the power, getting the skim and blaming the whole mess on you.

Jimmy sold you out. Pete just wants the truth about the wall safe before he kills you. The truth will *not* set you free.

The arc of your life will go from Castro escapee to slave to soldier slave, to bag man to enforcer to a crime lord's goat. There'd been girls, but there'd only been one woman. Lily was your only port in this shit storm and she'll never know what happened to you. You're going to be a missing person. Soon she'll be doing the salsa with someone else. You'll just be another guy she knew for a time.

"What was in the safe, moron?" Jake Cibrian yells.

You ignore him and focus on Pete. "Future father-in-law. Remember when I asked whose side you're on?"

"Yeah. What are you telling me? That I should be on *your* side?"

"Nope. You should be on your side. When Vincent finds out Jimmy had Denny kill his own stepson, you don't want to be standing so close to Jimmy. Jimmy's poison. I just drove the car. I'm the innocent bystander in the struggle for power that started tonight."

Jake raises a hand to his forehead. "I'm going to need a roadmap. This trip is all twisty."

Pete ignores him and keeps his gaze on your eyes, looking for a flicker. "Vincent isn't going to kill his only surviving son, kid—"

"Which is one reason you should be listening to me, Pete. Vincent isn't going to kill his only surviving son, but he will erase the people under him. Jimmy's only as powerful as long as he's got lieutenants, like *you*. You should start thinking that I'm looking out for my future father-in-law. That maybe I came to warn you how things are going bad."

"Because you love me so much?"

You see it now. Pete has a tell. Just before he bitch slaps, he takes a slightly deeper breath and his jaw gets tight. His jaw is getting tight now.

"Because I love Lily so much. Something happens to you, she's not happy with me. Something happens to me, you're in the doghouse and Lily isn't the forgiving type, is she?"

That stops him. His jaw softens. "I think you're the only one getting erased, Jesus."

"Yeah," You roll your eyes. "Like Vincent rose to run The Machine because he's such a patient, understanding-type guy."

"Watch your mouth, kid."

"What if I am lying? What if you're right and Denny is still alive? Maybe he's out hiding the money we found in Bob's safe. Like you said, Denny is my best friend, but we both know he's not the sharpest. Maybe he runs with the money Bob skimmed or maybe he goes to Vincent to make himself a hero."

"If you believed either of those things, you wouldn't be here now. You'd be on the run with Denny. You guys would be taking the skim and running back to Miami."

"Lily doesn't want to go to Miami, so you know I gotta stay. You know I love her. She's your daughter, Pete. You tell me how anybody could not love her."

"You're trying to make me go soft on you, Jesus, but I still got a raging hard-on here. Just tell me about the skim. Tell me why you really aren't on the run already. Did Denny want half? More than half?"

That's when you get a new idea. It's really an old idea. You heard about it from Denny. You drove around with Denny for hours dropping off drugs and picking up money. You and Denny spent so much time together, most of it with Denny doing the talking. He talked baseball and who was an asshole and who wasn't and he talked about what he read. All Denny ever read was weight loss cookbooks and books about the mob. Denny told you about the grift. It's how a Boston gangster set up a guy for a hit once.

"Where's the skim, Jesus?" Pete asks. Pete's jaw tightens again and he takes a deep breath before he slaps you. You try to roll with it, but you've been hit too many times tonight to be that fancy.

Pete hits you, not so much with the savage whip of the back of his hand this time. There's more meat in it as he drives the heel of his hand across your jaw. Pete really puts his shoulder into his work.

You've got one shot at the grift before Jake comes over and joins in. Then, whether you've told them anything true or not, it's all over and you will never hold Lily on the dance floor again.

THE GRIFT

A good grift depends on the greed of the mark. The believable lie is one that doesn't make you look too good. The best lie is in line with the worst people expect from you. If you say you did the worst thing the mark would do themselves, they want to believe.

"Look in my wallet, Pete."

Jake comes forward and opens your jacket slow, as if he expects you to be booby trapped with a rattlesnake.

"Not you, moron. This information is not for apes. It's for my future father-in-law."

Jake draws his fist back to punch you square in the face. It would have been agonizing beyond belief on a night when you'd set new records for pain, but Pete catches Jake's elbow.

"Take it easy, Jake. I can't have a civil conversation if he's unconscious from concussions. Haven't you noticed? He's had enough punishment and we're getting somewhere."

"You heard him, wage ape. Go over and guard the door. When Pete and I are done talking, maybe even an idiot like you will figure that you aren't guarding that door to keep me in. You're on that door to keep the devil out."

Jake looks at Pete, pleading with his eyes to scratch up his knuckles on your chin. Pete's eyes flick to the door and Jake steams off.

Pete reaches inside your jacket and pulls out your wallet. When he opens it, his face softens. There's a picture of you and Lily on Coney Island. Big Denny took that picture. Pink cotton candy made beards for your smiling faces. Denny took the pictures and went on the rides while you and Lily walked the boardwalk holding hands.

"I want to believe you, Jesus, but this is serious. This is not about you and my daughter. This is about Jimmy and Bob and the big boss and money."

"It's not about the picture, Pete. It is about the money. Look at the money."

He pulls out the fold of fresh, new twenties. They are so new, they look like they've been ironed. Real ballers in the mob do what gangsters in the movies do. In *Pulp Fiction* and *Goodfellas*, bills are always rolled up with an elastic around the wad. You're too neat to do that and you'd like to think you're too smart to act the way Hollywood movies say you should. You use a Calvin Klein wallet made of glove leather.

You might never have heard a chortle before now, but you're pretty sure that's it. Pete's gone from violent to amused. That is, until Pete says, "What is this shit? This is — " he counts it out, "$180. Are you seriously — ?"

"Pete," you begin to pitch the grift. "Look at me and look at you. Do you think I'm a dumb guy?"

"You're pretty jammed up to be called a smart guy, don't you think?"

A swing and a miss...

"I'm sitting here and I'm out of lies. All I want to do is be with Lily and be safe."

"Where's the skim, Jesus? Are you trying to play me? Jake can't wait to take you apart and see what makes you work, you know."

Strike two...

"I'm out of options so all that's left is to tell you everything because you are so right. Anybody hits me again tonight, I'll swallow my fucking tongue and call on God to kill me."

Pete looks you over, still holding the bills, forgotten in his hand.

Ball.

"Take a real good look at those bills, Pete. If those aren't just about the best counterfeits you've ever seen in your life, stub your cigarette out on my balls right now and I won't even complain."

He guffaws. You went from a chortle to an actual, certified, fully legit guffaw. You definitely got a piece of that one, but it's still a foul ball. You aren't out of this yet.

Pete stares at the bills, one by one. His forehead makes three deep lines as he squints at each bill, holding them up to the light.

"You asked me why I'm not running already. Doesn't make sense that I'm not running already, does it? You're right. I'm not running because I'm going to have to take care of Lily soon. She's not going to live in a walk up in Queens over a deli, forever, *Dad*. Lily is meant to live on the Upper East Side and travel the world and go to those art museums she dreams of. Maybe our kids will grow up in a brownstone and we'll have a view of the Park. For that to work, I gotta stay and make big money. No trucks or heists or highjacking or shakedowns or running around like errand boys for Jimmy Lima. Bob wanted to make big money. *Literally*, *Dad*. Bob wasn't so smart that he could skim from The Machine and not slip up long before now. But he knew a guy from the joint who was an artist who gave him an idea."

"What guy?"

Uh, shovel faster boy!

"I dunno. Some tourist guy named Kit from Scotland, traveling through the US, got pinched on a bogus marijuana conviction. He and Bob talked in the yard and Kit gave him the idea."

Pete looks from the bills, to you, back to the bills. "You're saying these are *fake?*" He leans forward, studying your face. You hope the blood covers up any trace of a lie that's leaking out.

"It's amazing what they can do with scanners and printers, huh?"

You need a name. Who knows anything about computers? You spit out the first name that comes to mind.

"Freejack Jack figured out how to make it work."

"Freejack?" Jake says, incredulous. "The guy who lives in Jimmy's guest house?"

"He used to be a straight citizen college boy before Jimmy picked him out of the unemployment line."

Your feet are braced, your shoulders hunched. You're on a roll and talking fast, but if you don't hit this one out of the park, it's going to be a long night of cigarette burns and body blows and your pulped face will go through a sieve by the time Jake is done.

"Panama Bob talked to Freejack. Told him to work on the idea of scanning currency."

Pete looks at the bills again. The corners of his lips turn down. "These?" He rubs a twenty between his thumb and forefinger, testing the texture. "You're telling me *this* bill is a fake?"

"It really is amazing what they can do with graphics programs. They're even coming out with 3D printers now. You load up the back with plastic chips and out comes a Nike running shoe out the front. Currency is on the way out, anyway. By the time we're done, nobody will believe in money at all, anymore."

"Bullshit."

"Think about it a minute longer. You *already* can't pass a hundred-dollar bill anywhere. There isn't a grocery store from here to the West Coast that would let you give them a hundred-dollar bill, US cash money, no matter how real it looks. Try any store and they won't give you any change."

Pete leans back and you watch his face as he works it out.

Home run.

Now for the tricky part. How do you walk out of here?

"What was in the safe?"

"A few of these bills. Freejack's samples for Bob." Swallow some blood and stall.

Pete leans toward you, more interested than threatening now. "And the kid, Freejack. He's not working for Jimmy because…?"

"Jimmy wanted too much of a cut. I'm not saying it's wrong, but you know how Jimmy is."

You catch Pete's slight, involuntary nod at the truth of that. Jimmy Lima is notoriously cheap in doling out cuts to employees. "Holy," Pete says. "Jimmy went to war with his own brother for a counterfeit scam."

You blink. Uh…why not? "It's a lot of money, Pete. Enough for all of us to have a view of the park. For generations."

"I don't buy it." Jake pipes up from his place at the door and ruins everything. Almost. "Hell, I don't even *get* it."

If you had to lay it out again, you'd screw it up and they'd change your name in the obit from Jesus Diaz to Cigarette Burned Balls. Fortunately, you do not screw it up because Pete comes to your rescue.

"You don't get it? What's not to get, dummy? Bob has Freejack Jack make fake bills, right under Jimmy's nose. Jimmy can't kill Freejack because he's the fuckin golden goose. Or the goose that laid the golden eggs or whatever. Bob tried to keep it all for himself and now Jimmy wants it all for himself."

Pete's turns in his chair, holding the bills up to the light to admire them. "Bobby...poor Panama Bobby should never have kept this from Vincent. That was a sin and ungrateful."

"Unfaithful," you say.

"Fuckin right!" Pete says. "Vincent takes in Bobby. Stepson, son, doesn't matter. Treats Jimmy and Bob the same. Then Bob sees this opportunity and wants to keep it for himself. Selfish. Selfish and unfaithful are the only words. I don't know how I'll be able to show my face at the funeral knowing this about him now. And Jimmy? Jimmy lies to me about Bobby skimming. Lies to me about the counterfeit money. I've known that kid since diapers. Knew Vincent since Sing Sing. And lies and betrayal is all we get."

"Where's the skim?" Jake asks.

"There *is* no skim!" Pete says. "The skim is counterfeit bills! Bobby was going to keep it all for himself! Jimmy was going to keep it all to himself! It's a disgrace!"

"All that was in the safe was these bills," you say. "Samples." You've switched from bleeding to sweating.

"This will kill Vincent," Pete says, his shoulders slumping.

"Only if he finds out what this is really all about," you say.

Pete's eyes come up and you can't tell what that look means. His jaw tightens but his breathing is shallow.

"Of course, the best thing for all concerned would be for Jimmy to get hit. Vincent would never have to know his own sons tried to screw us all over. Panama Bob's dead. If Jimmy goes away...it all looks like gangland stuff. Say it was the Italians or some other gang. It usually is."

"You're talking mutiny. You're talking about starting a war to save your skin," Jake says.

"I'm talking about ending a betrayal and stepping up and finally getting what we deserve. We do all the work. We should be rich, too. When Vincent passes — and how much longer can that be? —- *you're* the man running The Machine, Pete. Vincent's true legacy will be secure, despite his lousy sons."

Pete smiles and, for the first time, he doesn't look scary.

Home run.

THE SKIM

The official story Pete will tell Jimmy Lima is that he couldn't find you. Unofficially, he told you to go get cleaned up until he figures what the next move should be and when to make it. Pete tells Jake to drive you where you need to go and you accept on the condition that Jake doesn't say one word to you on the way. Where else can you go? You arrive at Lily's place.

When she buzzes you up, she's waiting for you in the hallway, her hair pulled back in a ponytail and wearing tight jeans and a peasant top. Lily looks great in Vera Wang and heels, of course, but you prefer her like this, barefoot and casually gorgeous. She runs to you as soon as she sees you at the top of the stairs. "Oh, my god! Jesus! You looked better before! Did *Jake* do this to you?"

"Yeah. Jake's an asshole." You smile to yourself. She thinks you're being brave, but really, you're relishing the thought that Jake will never have Lily now. Every guy in The Machine wants Lily, of course. You tell the guys she's your girl, though she won't call what you have with her exclusive.

"I have an idea," you said one day not long ago. "How about you roll up those posters of yours, marry me and we run away together?"

"They aren't posters. They're *prints*. *Starry Night* and the Dalis. And, no, not yet," she said. "I'm only twenty-three. Rush in like my parents' whole generation did? No thanks. That's stupid. Let's enjoy being young and see where it goes, okay?"

It was either agree or lose her. You agreed, but soon, with Panama Bob's skim and Jake and Pete chasing wild geese made of fake bills that aren't fake? Maybe Lily will teach Zumba in Miami all the way into her eighth month.

By the time a baby comes along, you and she will have set up and can play house on the same beach you washed up on so many years ago. Lily, pregnant with your child and playing in the sun and sand forever in back of a big house. That's a good dream.

She puts your left arm across her shoulders and tells you to lean on her on the walk down the hall. It's awkward and mostly unnecessary, but you lean on her anyway and put your face in her hair. Lavender. She bathes in it. Her shampoo is lavender. Her perfume is lavender. Every lavender candle and waft on a breeze outside a soap store will always carry a sense memory of Lily.

"I'm not here," you tell her.

"I'll make you some eggs," she says.

"You're going to cook something for me? Really?" Maybe you needed to get beaten up to ignite her maternal instincts. Nice to know she has some. Lily with maternal instincts is part of that misty dream of a life making sandcastles with your kids.

"I'm not hungry," you say.

"You need to eat."

"If Jimmy calls, you haven't heard from me."

"Eggs and toast make everybody feel better."

"Fine. Anyway, I'll have a nap and figure out what to do next but I'm not here, okay?"

"I got it, nowhere man."

She breaks off to let you enter her apartment door first. Your clothes are strewn across the floor and your go bag is dumped out on the coffee table. Given a second longer, you might have reacted, but someone pushes you hard from behind. You land softly on the couch. You look up to see one of Bob's lanky bodyguards with the tattoo of a letter *H* on his neck above the collar. His twin brother, Marv, has a tattoo very much like it on his neck. Same size and style, Marv's tattoo reads *M*.

"Hi, Harv."

"Hey, Jesus."

Lily shrugs. "Sorry Jesus. Harvey was insistent you get in the apartment right away. In case you were followed, he said."

Your eyes shift to Harv. "Jimmy want a report?"

"The boss is feeling hinky about the feds tapping his phones and his cell and his club and his car. Panama Bob's death has him way too edgy."

"So he doesn't want to meet."

"You tell me what goes, I go back and tell him in person tonight. Hey, Lily, can you make us some coffee, baby? Decaf for me, please, if you got it."

"Ain't your baby," Lily says, but she walks to the small kitchen just the same. Harv comes around the back of the sofa and kneels down. With his back to the kitchen and kneeling, Harv is a puppet show and all you see is his head and shoulders. He doesn't slap you, which is nice, but when he asks you where the key is, it's just as bad.

"What key?"

He sighs. "The key Bob always had around his neck."

"I imagine it's still around his neck or in an evidence bag down at the morgue."

"Don't shit a shitter, man."

"Easy, Harv. Sounds like you've got as much to tell me as I have to tell you."

Harv studies your eyes for a full minute before he speaks again. "You were in the army. I was in the army. Both a couple of grunts in this mess. Jimmy told

Marv and me you'd be showing up at Bob's office and if we wanted to be on the right side when all this shakes out, we'd go see him as soon as you showed up."

"That's reassuring," you say. "Bob was convinced you guys were stupid, leaving your post just on my say-so."

He shrugs. "Marv and me, we're pretty worried. Jimmy's talking about telling Vincent another gang hit Bob. Last thing we need is a war with somebody just to throw blame off on them. Why can't everybody get along and make their money for Christ sakes?" Harv surveys your clothes strewn across the little living room. "Sorry about your clothes and stuff, man. I didn't take nothing. I just need that key fast. Nice suits."

"Thanks. What's the key all about, Harv?"

"Oh, man! You know it's about the skim. Enough money to get away from here. Enough for me and Marv and you, too, if you're smart about it. How about we pull the pin and get out before Jimmy's plan for world domination gets us jammed up? Marv talked Jimmy out of blaming the Italians, but he's still only thinking about covering himself. He decided to blame the Romanians! He'll tell Vincent the *Romanians* hit Bob."

"Why the Romanians?"

"The Italians are too big to wrestle."

"The Romanians are crazier. Smaller the mob, the more psycho they are."

Harv wipes sweat from his forehead and nods. "Valid. The Liberians have a block in Queens. One block, but they'd gut your whole family for squinting their way on a sunny day. Some Samoan kids? Midgets and punks really, but they got half a block in Washington Heights. They'd kill anybody over a rainy day."

"Seems these smaller gangs' moods are very weather-oriented."

"My point, smart ass, is, whoever Jimmy blames his brother's death on, it's war. Jimmy is only thinking of his own hide. What does he think Vincent's going to do about me and Marv? We were supposed to be watching over Bob when Bob got himself killed! Before this is done, me and Marv are done. The doctors are keeping the big boss in the hospital another couple of days. We gotta get out before the sky starts raining shit."

"I feel for you. And it sounds like your true calling is to be a weatherman."

Harv looks at you as if he just clued in that he's not talking to himself. "Hey, what happened to you, man? You look like a prize fighter."

"A prize fighter after his final fight. Denny rearranged my furniture."

"He try to stop you from doing Bob or something?"

"Nah. We had a disagreement. Keep it to yourself, but uh…Denny was doing Jimmy's wife."

"Christ! Him, too?"

"*What?*"

"Never mind. Jimmy's on enough of a rampage. He was pissed at Bob and wants the skim, sure. Jimmy wants Cat Fornes back, too. I told him, I don't think Cat's coming back and Jimmy got pretty hot at me. All he can talk about is Cat. You'd think a big, tough son of a bitch like Cat, jiu jitsu fighter, tattoos and all, could handle himself."

"Yeah, that is a mystery," you say, "but nobody's too big for bullets."

Harv looks away. "You got any cream, Lily? Marv doesn't let me have any cream. He's on a health kick. He wants me to be thinner. Every day, I look at him and think I could look like Marv and be more muscular, if lifting weights didn't bore the living shit out of me. Excuse my language, Lily. I got an allergy to the gym is all. Thin is okay without all the veins popping out. Marv's my funhouse mirror."

"Where is Marv?"

"Waiting for Denny. He hasn't shown up at his place yet. You weren't at your apartment, so I figured you'd be here." Harv looks over his shoulder, studying Lily's ass like he's cramming for an exam. "I sure would be here all the time if I were you."

"So the cops have the key," you say. "What was the key for? Safety deposit box?"

Harv shakes his head. "Storage locker."

Lily starts up the loud buzz saw in the stainless steel box she calls an espresso machine to grind beans and Harv looks back to study Lily's ass again while you bend a knee and reach for the switchblade in your sock.

"Where's the storage locker?"

"Dunno. Bob ditched us like once or twice a week. Said he didn't like all the babysitting all the time, but we figured he was sneaking off to make deposits."

"Then how do you know it's a storage locker?"

"We saw the key. You sure you don't have it?"

You're weary, but your switchblade opens at Harv's throat in such a casual move of your arm, he doesn't see it coming. "Where's the storage locker, Harv? Let's not let this get weird."

As the espresso machine's blades wind down, you hear the hammer of Harv's pistol click back. He's scared but he manages a smile.

You take the blade from his throat. You took a knife to a gun fight. Rookie mistake. You're going to have to talk your way out of this. You talked Pete out of killing you, but Harv was Bob's bodyguard. He knows too much. The counterfeit grift won't work on him. Or you could just give up the location of the key and Harv could kill you. That might be a mercy after all that's gone on tonight. But then he might hurt Lily. He'll kill Lily for witnessing your murder if he really plans to make a run for it.

You don't just retire from The Machine. You ask permission to retire and usually that's refused unless you're too old for the life. Harv's desperate and just wants to get the key, hit the storage locker and get out of town. He probably dreams of a beach in his future, too. A care-free beach is the American dream, as far away and unlikely as a lottery win.

"Harv, we need to talk about this. You have to think about what side you're on."

"What? You think I should be on your side? I be Batman and you be Superman and we team up? I never liked those comic books."

"No. It's not about that. Everybody's on his own side, but if you give me a minute, I can show you how pulling that trigger is not in your interest."

"I got a bead on you right through the back of this couch, man, so tell me where the fuckin key really is." His tone is scary because it's flat. You see fear in his eyes, but his voice is steady. He won't hesitate to pull the trigger. "Are we going to stay friendly or am — "

Kang!

Kang!

Harv's gun goes off, a crack that echoes off the walls. There's a new hole in the leather couch that's even with your heart. You *feel* the bullet whiz by, missing you by maybe an inch.

BONG!

Whiff!

BONG!

BONG!

Pete gave Lily fancy cookware when she moved out of the house. One of those gifts was a heavy iron skillet.

Lily's eyes are wide and she's breathing hard. Her pulse races in her neck. She drops the skillet with a clang into the pool of blood flooding from Harv's skull. She comes around the couch, listless as a zombie, and falls into your arms. Her tears are hot on your cheek.

"You did a good thing," you say, "especially since I had no idea what shit I was going to tell that fool."

Lily's breath is fast and shallow on your neck. Her voice is muffled. "I *told* you you needed eggs. God! When do I ever cook for you? Take a hint next time! What happens now?"

"Which would you prefer? A life of riches on sunny beaches or to disappear into the country?"

"Do I get to be wealthy in the country, too? I can't be a hick."

"Yes, of course, you can be wealthy in the country, too."

"I want to go to Paris and I want to go to Spain. I want to see the Salvador Dali museum. I want to be anywhere but here now."

"Agreed. But first, I suggest you pack a bag quick and we have to do something about the corpse behind the couch."

"Solid thinking, Ace." But she doesn't move. She's still crying.

*   *   *   *   *   *

Lily dials her father and hands her cell to you. "Clean up, Aisle 3. The key's under the mat."

Pete says Jake is on his way back to take care of the spilled ketchup and the broken bottle, but you and Lily are already in her car driving away. You hang up on Pete without going into any more detail and turn it off. You tell Lily to slow down and drive the speed limit. After a couple of blocks and several urgent warnings — okay, pleading — that she's going to get you both pinched, she listens and eases up on the accelerator. After another few blocks, Lily speaks for the first time since she closed the door to her apartment. "Has everybody gone crazy? Harv… He was at Dad's barbecue last summer."

"The Machine's broken. It's already a civil war. Jimmy's going to make it bigger. Jimmy has his way? There's gonna be no crew left."

"Harv said it was all about Uncle Bob skimming."

"He did, huh? What else did he say?"

"He said he wasn't going to hurt you. He just needed to go through your stuff and ask you a few questions."

"You didn't believe him."

"Maybe I did. I wanted to believe. He was rude about it, though. I told Harv he shouldn't go through your stuff and he got very impolite about it. The way he talked to me…he talked to me like I didn't matter." Lily's upper lip curls. "When I got pissed about that, he softened up and apologized and asked me not to tell Dad. As if I'm a little girl who runs off to tattle to daddy. What a punk." She looks like an angry goddess. "Harv knows better now, doesn't he?" she says.

Lily really is like a goddess if it's true you're supposed to worship and love and fear deities in equal parts. You watch the streetlights flash by.

"So where's the money?" she says.

"I don't know exactly," you say.

"You better find out. I don't know anything much about civil war, but Dad made me watch *Gone With the Wind.* If that's civil war, I got an idea we should get out of town for a while."

"Absolutely!" But you don't know whether to feed her the same bullshit story about counterfeit bills you told Pete or to tell her you really are after Panama Bob's pirate treasure.

You decide to shut up and pray to God for help while she picks an out of the way hotel. You don't know which deity to fear more. God or the goddess? Looking at Lily, it feels like you are underwater, drowning again. You haven't felt trapped like this since…since when? Since the tire.

This is somehow worse than getting tied up and sitting in the chair at Pete's mercy. Lily's beside you, but you are so close to losing her. You close your eyes. You can't tell Lily the truth, so you pray silently, your head against the cool glass as the indifferent city flashes by. What can you tell her?

THE TIRE

The men who smuggled people weren't called coyotes back then, not in Cuba or Florida, anyway. It's only 90 miles of open water. America used to worry about nuclear missiles just off their coast, with Castro's finger on the button. Castro worried about Marines landing on his beaches. Your parents weren't political. They just wanted a better life for their sons. That, and there was the incident over the Montreal Expos baseball cap.

Marco Diaz worked as a bartender at the pool of a major hotel. Maritza was a maid at the same hotel. They met in May and married by the end of June. The ceremony was held in your father's childhood home in Pinar del Rio and Maritza gave birth to you eight months later. A couple of years later, you had a little brother. Rodolfo looked like you but thinner and more frail.

Your family was poor, but still better off than most. Your mother got the best tips. The tourists, especially the ones who returned year after year, were often generous. The newcomers left money behind at the end of their stay and wondered why the hotel help was surly. The seasoned travellers brought an extra bag filled with toothpaste, small toys and spare clothes and dealt out their goods for services on a daily basis. Those people, your father said, always left thinking how happy and cheerful all the people of Cuba were.

One day, an old French Canadian tourist arrived with a charter group. The man sat by the pool for most of his stay, slowly burning himself lobster red and ordering a steady supply of daiquiris. He wore a Montreal Expos baseball cap your father admired very much. Marco served the man well and spent much time engaging him in discussion about the Expos.

"I told the man how much you would love to own a cap like that," your father said. "I told him how our favorite pitcher was Nelson Santovenia. He was born just down the street from me in Pinar del Rio!"

For all his attentiveness and blatant hints, Marco went unrewarded. The day the man left for the airport, his Expos cap still on his head, your father came home, determined to go to America. "I *crawled*," Marco said. "What more could I have done? I wanted to get you that hat, Jesus!"

"It's okay, Papá. I don't need the hat. Don't be angry."

"I'm not angry at you, *mijo*. It's not even really about the hat. I'm angry at callousness. That man took advantage of me. I have a job, but still no respect. I fetch drinks for drunks. I've got no power or pride."

"We are servants," your mother said. "If we go to America, we can still be servants. This is our home. Different countries, same problems. Where's the pride in that?"

"It's only ninety miles away!" Marco thundered. "A better life where at least we have a chance. We'll have lots of friends there. So what if we're servants there? At least I could buy my sons baseball caps."

"The Expos don't play in Florida," you said. "They're in Canada."

Marco's laugh was a bark. He rubbed your short hair. "Montreal is too far to swim, even for men like us."

"Florida is too far to swim," Maritza said.

Your father found a man with a boat willing to ferry his family safely.

It wasn't safe. It was a dirty, old fishing trawler manned by the Captain, a strong-looking fellow with a stubbled chin, and his mate, an older fat man with a long gray beard. You shivered, surprised at how cold you could be on the water at night. You huddled with Rodolfo and your mother, trying to comfort your brother and warm him.

The boat's engine droned on through the night and, as the waves grew in height, the bow rose and fell. You and your brother vomited over the rail until there was nothing left in your stomachs. Next came the dry heaves. With each tortuous spasm, it felt like your scrotum might come up through your mouth. You can't remember how long you were on the boat. All you know is that you promised yourself that, after this trip, you would never set foot on a boat again.

You woke around dawn to a loud argument. You rose from the deck and saw land ahead. It didn't look far, but the Captain of the boat refused to take your family any closer.

"The weather slowed us too much. We spent more fuel. The Coast Guard will spot us any moment. Give us more money if you want me to risk my boat!"

Your father refused.

"Fine," the Captain said.

You thought it was over. The man shrugged, his palms out, with a "What more can I do?" look, but a minute later he returned from the cabin with a rifle. Your father's back was turned. He was still staring at the Florida coastline, smiling, as the Captain swung the rifle's butt into his temple. He was knocked cold, a red gash gushed crimson blood down his neck and across his white shirt.

Maritza screamed but she did not run to her husband. Instead, she pulled you and Rodolpho to her and cried, burying her face in your shoulder. She begged for her family's lives. She had hidden a wad of American bills wrapped in a white handkerchief in her underwear. She reached under her skirt and threw it to the deck at the Captain's feet. The Captain laughed and handed the rifle to his mate.

Marco Diaz, helpless, moaned and grabbed at his head. The Captain and his mate swung your father overboard. Then the Captain held up the rifle and pointed over the side, toward land. "Jump!"

"The children can't swim to shore! It's too far! You're killing us!"

The Captain considered for a moment and his gaze flickered. He ordered the mate to cut the rope that held a truck tire to the side of the boat. As soon as the black tire hit the water, the Captain pointed again to the water.

Maritza shook her head.

He and the mate picked up your mother and threw her overboard. You grabbed Rodolpho's hand and pulled him over the side with you.

Rodolpho panicked and flailed. You had underestimated the strength terror can bring. He wrapped himself around you and you had to fight him off, kicking and pushing, trying to stop him from pulling you down, drowning you both. You had tried to save him, but then you wanted to kill him to save yourself.

When you began to choke, you tried to swallow the saltwater rather than drown. You thought you could but it was too much and you choked more. Your brother was killing you. Your father's pride was drowning you and your mother was helpless. The light in the water dimmed. Dark depths called up to you.

A strong hand thrust down and grabbed you under the chin and hauled you up to the air. Your father, his head still leaking blood with every heartbeat, had one hand on the truck tire. He pulled you and Rodolpho to it. Rodolpho sputtered and choked and held to the tire as tightly as he'd held to you. Maritza cried. Marco smiled at you, but one eyeball was rolled up so all you could see was the white of his right eye.

The fishing boat roared away. Your mother was still pleading for the boat to come back long after you couldn't hear the engine's drone.

"We have to kick," your father said. "We are going to make it to land. When we make it to land, everything...everything will be fine."

You kicked. Your little brother complained until your father slapped him. It was the first time he had ever raised a hand to Rodolpho. "*Mijo*, you kick so we swim this tire to shore, or we all die."

Your little brother shut up and kicked.

You remember the burn in your calves and thighs. The salt stung your eyes. The brine splashing down your throat made you vomit again. All you had was more salt water to throw up. Your arms and shoulders ached and your hands cramped in their death grip on the tire. Waves slapped your face and splashed water into your gasping mouth. You choked and sputtered and puked more brine in a torturous cycle. The land didn't seem to get closer or farther away. It hung in sight, mocking and full of bright potential you were sure you'd never see.

But you kicked. Little Rodolpho kicked. Your mother stopped crying and she kicked. Soon, your father could not. He slipped in and out of consciousness, at first for less than a moment. Draped over the tire, he dropped out of the waking world. He slept more and longer each time, losing the battle for light. Each moment he did not kick was another moment you were all losing to the ocean's waves.

The last time he awoke, he asked his wife how long he had been asleep. She didn't know.

She blamed him for getting all of you onto, and then into, the ocean. In the end, she blamed your father for being dead weight. You're sure of that. She didn't look at him. The care drained from her voice. Her eyes were fixed on the far away land. She did not turn her head to look at Marco. She only kicked.

"Boys," he said. "Take care of each other. Take care of your mother. And keep kicking. Always, keep kicking." He shrugged. His last words were, "*Se mire como se mire, te quiero.*" *However you look at it, I love you.*

Marco Diaz let go of the tire and slipped down and away.

Maritza Diaz said, "Don't look back. I told him we should have tried for Isla Mujeres."

You could hear your father struggle weakly, trying to swim or float, but he had too little strength left. You heard a few weak splashes and then only the welcoming ocean and the crash of the next wave over you as it tried to tear you away from the tire and swallow you as well. You imagined him dropping away, deep and below you, from light into darkness. Looking up with two eyes — one ruined, one keen and sharp — Marco Diaz would be looking up at you and your brother and Maritza through a thin cloud of the last of his blood.

In your memory, Marco Diaz has faded like an old photograph — there, yet not all there. You can still see him on the deck of the rusty fishing trawler, smiling at the beckoning coast, an oblivious, dreaming fool. The day he came home angry over his wounded pride is vivid. Your father held a beer but was too upset to drink it. He could only complain about the Canadian tourist. You see your father in that vignette as a broken man, bitter that he could not give you a baseball cap you didn't want.

In your clearest memory, you see Marco Diaz for the best of the man he was: You see his smile as he lets go of the tire.

And you see him in your nightmares: a one-eyed, white-eyed zombie, still searching for you on the sea floor, clawing and scuttling through the dark in warrens and labyrinths of cutting coral.

You gripped the tire, gritted your teeth and held your breath through relentless, crashing waves. You, your brother and your silent mother came shoulder to shoulder to push the tire to the beach. You did not swim toward America and the dream of a better life. You kicked harder and swam in terror, swimming away from that vision of your drowned, grasping father, somewhere below and behind you, watching in a solitary death…and *waiting*.

To die with those you love and to be responsible for their deaths is a horror beyond measure. A lonely death is bitter solace.

THE FUTURE

You wake up in a cheap little motel in Jersey and no one wants that. You don't remember falling asleep last night and this morning, Lily doesn't want to get out of bed. She's not hungry. She just wants to sleep. She's never killed anyone before, so she's feeling a tad sensitive about the whole episode with Harv. The fact that Lily saved your life by crushing his skull with an iron skillet doesn't appease her and when you make a zombie joke, it does not go over well.

You won't pine over Harv's untimely demise. The shower spray bothers you much more. Each water droplet feels like a stick pounding on a drum. Your nose is straight, thanks to your painful efforts in first aid, but it feels thick and both your eyes are black. You taste blood as you run your tongue over your teeth but none are loose.

Big Denny was a bulldozer in his day. "In his day." Like he wasn't alive as recently as yesterday. Your sense of time is screwed up. So much has happened since last night, it feels like everything is slowed down and you're noticing everything more.

One of your combat instructors was a hard rock named Sgt. Devin, but of course, everyone called him The Devil. The Devil said something about focus and time once, how when the adrenaline is pumping, your eyes will dilate and you'll think you can actually see the bullets whizzing by. You go into bullet-time like in a video game and you focus on details.

"Don't focus on the wrong details," The Devil said. "The wrong details will get you killed." Is that what you are doing now? Jimmy Lima's on the warpath and he doesn't care who gets hurt as long as it's not him. Instead of sitting at the bottom of a motel shower in Jersey crying over Denny, you should be getting the money and grabbing Lily for a run back to Miami or even someplace boring as long as it's far away from here.

Focus on the storage locker, dumbass.

Reassess: You have to find Panama Bob's storage locker before anyone else opens it. Jimmy wants the skim. Pete thinks the skim is a load of counterfeit money and a ticket to becoming the Boss. Now is not the time to hit the pause button.

The shower and fresh clothes make you feel a little more human. You may never feel like your old self again, but Armani salves a lot of wounds. You tell Lily you'll be a while but you'll bring back coffee. You slip out the door and take a walk. Within five blocks you find an Internet cafe. You order a bagel with some lox and a medium roast Tanzanian Peaberry coffee. Even in an armpit off the Jersey turnpike, you can still order a fancy coffee.

Your Internet search reveals a couple of storage companies by the Brooklyn Bridge and another cluster north of the meatpacking district. The heat is soothing and the caffeine helps you focus, but your jaw is so sore, the bagel takes a lot of time to get down. Halfway through the bagel, you think you've found the most likely target.

Most of the storage facilities are the indoor type with lots of security. Bob would want a place close to his building, but easy to get in and out of without a lot of fuss. Bob never walked anywhere unless he had to, so it's hardly a surprise when you discover a storage business on Greene Street. It's less than two blocks from Panama Bob's office. It's not a converted office building like most storage places. Instead, from Google Maps, it looks like several rows of little garages across from a big Post Office. Bob's key looked like it would fit a padlock rather than a regular door.

Next all you have to do is grab the key from the bathroom at the pizza place, get to the storage locker and get out of the line of fire. "Easy-peasy, lemon squeezy," as Tia Marta used to say as she gave your balls a rough squeeze.

"I love American idioms," she'd say in her thick German accent. "They are so nonsensical. A fat chance and a thin chance is the same to them. They say across the street and *right* across the street and that means the same. Americans say a healthy helping of food but that looks very different from a healthy helping of food."

Tia Marta looked down on Americans, but she'd chosen to come here. She called you a dirty boy when she found you in the basement, but then she'd held you all night and let you cry into her shoulder when you told her about how your father died. She helped you, but hurt you, too. Americans weren't the only people full of contradictions. She made you love her…at first.

You're almost back to the motel with a BLT and a coffee for Lily when your phone rings. The caller ID says it's Pete. You let it ring through to voicemail as you search out a public telephone. Pete's right. Finding a phone is harder than it used to be and there are no phone booths.

At a strip plaza, you find a bank of three phones with the telephone books ripped to pieces and only one of the phones works. You wipe it off with your handkerchief before you put the receiver anywhere near your mouth. You remember Tia Marta saying that a gentleman always carries a handkerchief, which was ironic because she did not allow you any clothes. She was right, though. With a handkerchief you can blow your nose, bandage a wound, conceal your identity, gag or even strangle a guy if you have to.

You call Pete on his private phone, the one he's sure isn't bugged. He answers after one ring.

"Lily safe?"

"Yeah." After last night, it's nice to hear worry in Pete's voice. "She's freaked out and won't get out of bed, but that's natural."

"Oh God… Listen, don't go back to her apartment."

"Does Jimmy have somebody watching it?"

"Ah. Geez. I wasn't thinking about that possibility. No, Jake, the idiot, used way too much bleach. We'll have to air it out before it's safe. The moron put bleach on top of ammonia! By the time I showed up to see what he was up to, he was almost passing out on top of the…uh, ketchup."

"Tragic."

"Bleach and ammonia don't go together! Am I the only one around here who knows anything? Christ!"

There are so many ways to die. Denny's dead yet Jake lives. There are so many ways for things to go ugly, so many ways to end up dead and disappointed.

"Too bad you found him. Jake could have been on one of those *Most Moronic Criminals* shows or *1,000 Ways to Die* or something."

"What did Harv tell you before he got his bottle broke?"

Pete assumes it was you who killed Harv. That's fine. "If he was telling the truth, we got a civil war within The Machine up one nostril and war with the Romanians up the other. Jimmy will do whatever he can to make Vincent think it wasn't him who ordered Bob's hit. But no matter what Jimmy says, the Romanians have nothing to do with it. This is an in-house matter and Jimmy's making things worse."

"If Jimmy blames the Romanians, then you're in the clear."

"I thought about that. It would be nice to be in the clear, but as soon as the police let Vincent know how the investigation is progressing, I'll be the slaughtered goat. Camera caught my face on the way out and witnesses in the street saw Denny. Maybe me, too, if somebody was looking out the window at the lightning storm. Either you move up in the ranks and save me from Jimmy and Vincent, or I'm dead."

You listen to Pete breathe and when he says nothing, you add, "Jimmy sent Harv over to Lily's apartment. With him dead, Jimmy might decide to clean house, including you and Lily. It's not mutiny when the officers are trying to kill their own soldiers, Pete. Your loyalty is to Vincent, not his asshole son who is too ambitious for anybody's good."

"Yeah," Pete says. "I get it. It's me or him. I should have known. Jimmy was an asshole even when he was a cute little kid."

"Is the old man awake? How'd his surgery go?"

"Of course. He'll be fine. Vincent can't be killed. He's bulletproof. He's fuckin' immortal. Vincent Lima took three bullets in the '80s on three separate occasions before he got to the top. You watch. They whipped out the guy's prostate" — he pronounces it *prostrate* — "through a smokin' hole. Give 'em a few weeks and a Viagra and he'll be down at the strip club talkin' a stripper out to his car with nothing but a smile and a bindle of coke."

You ask Pete if he's talked to Vincent yet.

"How am I supposed to tell him one son's dead by the other's hand and his heir apparent is going to get us all killed?"

You consider this and think about the seeds you planted last night when he had you tied up and was threatening to burn your balls with cigarettes. "There's the other way," you say.

"What are you saying, Jesus?"

"I'm saying Vincent needs a new heir apparent. A guy with a steady hand on The Machine's wheel. Somebody who goes back a long way with Vincent. You could do the right thing and kill Jimmy and never tell Vincent you did him a solid."

"You're talking mutiny and treachery and some evil Shakespearian shit there, Jesus."

"I'm talking about being faithful to Vincent's legacy. Jimmy's already stirring up trouble with the *Banda*. If Jimmy were to end up shot, it would follow that the Romanians got Bob and then they went after Jimmy."

The wrinkle for Pete is that there'd still be a bloody gang war. Not your problem. The heat would be off you long enough to disappear with Lily. The security cam won't be a problem with you a thousand miles away.

"The old man thinks his dumb ass *sons* are his legacy," Pete says.

"Man plans, God pulls down Man's pants and mocks. Vincent's legacy should be preserving The Machine, not grinding the gears and ripping out the works."

"What I've said before sarcastically, I now say in earnest. You're smart, Jesus. Look after my little girl while I sort this out. When I'm Vincent's Number Two, you're coming up in the world and we'll have a sweet project what with all that sweet fake dough and all."

Good. Let the wise guys chase each other around while you slip out of the way and down the I-95. You could go Down Under (mob-speak for Florida and your old stomping grounds.) They do have some useful gun laws down in Florida and you do miss the beach.

Orlando is a nice, relatively war-free zone. Mob clashes too close to Disney would alarm the tourists and bring down the Feds' wrath so organized crime steers clear. The Families, Companies, Corporations, Machines, Bands, Clubs, Tribes and Offices all leave Orlando alone so the profits go to the Mouse. Besides, even gangsters want to take their kids to Disney and not have to worry.

Maybe Florida is too obvious and Jimmy would come looking. There's that little town up in Maine along the coast you've heard about. Poeticule Bay. All they've got up there is a lighthouse, a tiny police department that hands out speeding tickets and a view of the seagulls to one side and a view of the woods on the other. It was in the papers when the town's sheriff went missing. The body was never found. If they can lose a cop, you can certainly go invisible ninja and disappear there. Poeticule Bay would still be close enough, you might even duck into the Big Apple to visit your tailor down in the Village.

But what are you going to tell Lily and will she come with you? When Pete rises to the top, he'll leave you alone as long as you're married to his daughter. Once things settle down, maybe you could come back to New York. You'll need a couple kids by then, just for extra insurance. Pete's tough, but he won't mess with the father of his grandchildren. At least, you don't think he will. A lot of this will depend on Lily. You'll give her whatever she wants if she'll just stay with you, anything at all for her smile.

You've already been away too long and it's not like your body has recovered from Denny's beating and getting slapped around by Pete. In fact, if anything, you're more sore now than you were this morning. You need to get the coffee into Lily, cheer her up and make her eat. Then you'll curl up next to her, sleep, recover and wait until dark to get back to the pizza place in Tribeca. You'll get the key.

Then it's on to the Greene Street storage locker to see what treasures Bob buried. It seems like the perfect plan, but there *are* so many ways to die. Even as you snuggle up, spooning Lily, feeling her warmth and the softness of the pillow at your cheek, you have an inkling. Things have not gone well for you in the last twenty-four hours. The worst should be behind you. It should be easy from here on out.

Then you think of what you told Pete last night. It was the one thing you said that was unadulterated truth: Sometimes life really is like a Coen brothers' movie. Coen brothers movies are your favorites: *The Big Lebowski, Fargo, O Brother Where Art Thou?, No Country for Old Men, The Man Who Wasn't There, Blood Simple* and *A Serious Man.* Their movies ring ludicrous and true because things keep going wrong on the wide and easy road out of town.

"What are you thinking about?" Lily asks.

Your face is in her hair and your nose must not be too bad because you can get a whiff of lavender. You can't tell her any of this. "I was just thinking about *Fargo.* Remember how it was raining and we bought it from the guy with the box of DVDs on the sidewalk down by the Chambers subway, after we went into that Jamba Juice that time?"

"Yes."

"Remember how neither of us had seen the movie and we didn't have any expectations? We didn't know a thing about that movie. It had slipped below our radar somehow so when we watched it, it was this big surprise because we expected so little and got so much. Wouldn't it be great if everything worked like that?"

"Are you saying I expect too much out of life?" Lily asks.

"No, no…. I'm just saying how great it is when things work out, like you go for normal and you get great."

"Do you think we'll ever get to normal after this?"

You're still talking into the back of her head. "Wouldn't regular, old *normal* be great? We could live like regular people. Be one of those citizens you see all the time, running off to a job somewhere, paying taxes and having kids."

She rolls over and stares at your broken face, studying your black eyes. "You want to have a regular job and pay taxes?"

It still hurts to smile. "Well, maybe not that part. But something close to normal would be great. Great is great, but for people like us? After this? Just normal would be great, too, wouldn't it?"

"I guess so. When can we start with normal, Jesus? I mean, we're falling asleep in a cheap little motel in Jersey. No one wants that."

You laugh and tell her that's what you thought, too.

"I can't stop thinking about Harv. He was going to shoot you."

"He *did* shoot at me. He missed. Not by much."

Lily is quiet. When she finally speaks again, you can tell by her eyes that she's still back in the apartment murdering Harv. "I read once that they did this study about free will."

"Who's they?"

"They. Them. You know. People who study the brain and stuff. They did this study where they asked people to choose something. I don't know what, but they could see on some kind of brain scanner that the choice is made before people think it's made."

"What do you mean?"

"I mean the choices we make…maybe they aren't our choices. Maybe we're just puppets and there is no free will, like this is a play and God's just watching it for His amusement."

"So you didn't choose to hit Harv in the head to save me?"

"It's not that I didn't choose exactly. It's that I didn't really have a choice. Free will might just be an illusion. If it is, we're all innocent. I want to feel innocent. I'm asking, what's it all about? Do we really have free will or is everything predestined? Tonight, for the first time, I don't want independence. I want God to take the blame and leave me alone."

"Despite my name, this is too deep for me. You need to talk to a priest. I don't know about free will. All I got is…making choices? That's for other people. People with money get to make choices."

Lily lays her head on your chest. Her warm tears soak through your shirt. And you think of Panama Bob's skim. How much could it be? Enough to have choices, anyway.

"The worst is behind us," you assure her.

The worst *should* be behind you. Pete kills Jimmy. You pass go and do not go to jail, either. You get the skim and evaporate into the wind with the girl of your dreams. But the more you think, *the worst is behind me*, the more sure you are that you will trip headfirst into some deep Shakespearian shit.

Easy-peasy, lemon squeezy.

LIES & PIE

You find a place to park Lily's car near NYU and take your time, strolling and doubling back, winding through the city. You try to look casual, checking in reflections in store windows and scanning for any sign of a tail. It pays to be paranoid. You only have to screw up once and your head will end up on a pike.

There's a murder house in Jersey. Denny told you, though he was fuzzy on the details. He would only say that he'd been there once when he was inducted and it took two days for the tortured rat to die.

"I didn't have a hand in it," Denny was quick to point out. "I had to watch. Made me dirty. They got a couple of guys from out of town to do the work. They enjoyed it too much. One guy had a blowtorch. The other guy used vice grips."

That's the problem with The Machine. If Vincent has a place set aside just for the purpose of murdering rivals and traitors, he's wasting a lot of energy and operating on a bad business model. When you came back from Iraq and Afghanistan, you should have looked harder for work instead of letting Denny get you into Vincent's business. It looked like easy money at the time and the military had left you with a limited skill set.

You pass the Silver Center for Arts and Science. When you first got to New York City, dark from the sun, you did what every newcomer does and what no native New Yorker would ever do. You took bus tours with people from all over the world and stared up. Awful histories aren't just for poor people in the desert. Before the Silver Center was an arts and science building, it was the Brown Building. Before that, it was the Asch Building.

You remember because the name was ironic. Up there, 146 garment workers died in the infamous Triangle Shirtwaist Factory Fire, just over 100 years ago. Ninety years before 9/11, New York saw sixty-two people, most of them young seamstresses, leap to their death from a high building, some of them on fire as they fell. Just the thought of it makes you dizzy and you're out on the ledge with Bob again. You close your eyes and wait for the feeling to pass.

It was March in 1911 when all those people died screaming. Rusty fire escapes collapsed. Locked exits trapped young women in an inferno. That fire was a testament to the greed and unsafe labor conditions of the garment workers' workplace. The squares have their murder houses, too. You don't have to be a bad guy to get screwed over permanently by the boss.

It takes almost half an hour to get to the mom and pop pizza joint. You look around one more time and, sure no one's watching, you enter. The girl who was here last night (could it really be that it was only *last* night?) is nowhere in sight. Instead, a late middle-aged man with wispy white hair parted in the middle stands behind the cash register. You're halfway to the bathroom to retrieve the key when he stops you.

"Bathroom's for customers only."

"Sure. I could eat."

"What?"

Taking in the yellowed walls and the orange grease stains running down the proprietor's apron, you're not in the mood for pizza. The big pizza chains dress their kitchen workers in aprons that are the same color as orange pizza grease. Maybe this place is just as clean as anywhere else, or equally dirty, anyway. In a glass case behind the line of pizza slices — lukewarm for the flies under heat lamps — you spot pastries.

"You make that pie here?"

He shakes his head. The bakery next door supplies them. "It's why the small place is always better than the chains. We got the extras. You want apple or cherry?"

You order a slice of cherry pie and he tosses you a key to the bathroom. If you go south tomorrow, you'll be eating key lime pie in the Keys. If you head north…what kind of pie do they eat in Maine?

You unlock the bathroom door. You lean your weight against it to open it without touching the doorknob just as Jimmy Lima steams in.

You aren't obvious about it, but your hand is already in the front pocket of your trench coat wrapped around the SIG. You don't pull it out. You're pretty fussy about your clothes, but if you have to shoot through the pocket to wipe out Jimmy, you will. The skim will buy a lot more trench coats.

Jimmy puts up both hands, empty, and smiles. He nods slightly left and right. Two heavies stare in through the front windows. Juan and Twist each give slow nods and narrow their eyes, like they're daring you to draw in an old Western. Their hands are stuffed in their pockets, just like you, so maybe this is *High Noon.* Unlike that scenario, if Juan doesn't get you, Twist will. God writes a mean script.

In the movies, even the guys who are wounded pretty bad end up getting bullets pulled out by a mob doc or a veterinarian. In real life, if you're lucky, you get dumped outside an ER. In the unlikely event that you survive, you're handcuffed to a gurney and have to answer a lot of uncomfortable questions from steely-eyed detectives.

Not that you have any hope of getting dumped out of a car at the entrance to Bellevue tonight. Not with Jimmy coming at you. If you live, he'll call in a guy with a blowtorch and a guy with vice grips. Jimmy's the kind of guy who holds a grudge so hard he won't let you die for days.

Time to switch tactics quick: You show him your empty hands and surprise him by stepping forward and hugging him.

"What the fuck, Jesus?" he says. "Why haven't you called?"

And, now, ladies and gentlemen, the Academy Award for Best Performance Under Threat of Horrible Death goes to...

"What the fuck? What the fuck! What's going on? Did Pete find you Bob's stash or not?" You've watched Pacino do this in so many movies, you're sure you can carry this off as long as you sound angry instead of shit balls scared.

Jimmy's eyes narrow. "What are you talking about? Talk fast, Jesus."

"Did Pete find the fuckin' money?"

Jimmy glances at the guy dressed in the dirty white apron behind the counter. The guy's listening but he looks bored like he's practiced looking bored all day from an early age. He puts your slice of pie on the counter in a casual move. With just a little more oomph, he'd be tossing it at you. In Miami, the old Spanish waitresses smile and hold out the key lime pie on a saucer with two hands, like you're still a kid and they're playing *mamacita*, giving you a special after school treat. In New York City, the move is, "Take it or not. I don't give a fuck. Just eat if you're gonna and get the fuck outta here!"

New York. That's the attitude you have to make Jimmy believe. As in: *Take my word or not. I don't give a fuck. Just swallow my story if you're gonna and get the fuck out!*

"Gimme a slice of cherry," Jimmy says.

The guy behind the counter nods and cuts another slice. You take yours and head for the booth along the wall, but before you can cut the shooters' angles outside, Jimmy takes your elbow and guides you to a table in front of the window.

Shit. You might not just *say* shit, either. You really wanted to get the key, but you have to go to the bathroom, too. Like The Devil used to say in boot, "You will be challenged not only when you are at your best, but when you have a fever, when you are unready, unsteady, sleepy and when you have to take a gargantuan shit. Persevere, anyway, and no whining!"

Okay, but the heroes in the movies never got the piss beaten out of them, two big black eyes and a broken nose. Bruce Willis or Clint Eastwood or Al Pacino never had to con the bad guy, escape danger, save the girl, make an awesome getaway and at the same time desperately yearn to hit the can. The worst Harrison Ford ever got was frozen in carbonite or a scratch on his forehead as Indiana Jones. Boo-fucking-hoo. The guy from *24* never went to the bathroom though the show tracked every second of the day.

You glance at Juan on the other side of the window. Both his hands are in his pockets and his scruffy beard makes him look hard. Twist leans over and gives you a smile, but not a friendly one. Could these be the two guys who enjoy hobbies with blow torches and vice grips? Denny was always fuzzy on the details of the murder house incident.

"Can I get a large coffee, too, buddy?" you call to the proprietor.

He shrugs and tells you a fresh pot is brewing. When he asks you how you take it, you tell him black and hot.

Your gun hand is away from the guy at the window, but as you sit, Jimmy makes a great show of putting his hands on the table and spreading them out, lifting his chin in a jab that tells you to do the same. You put both hands on the sides of your plate and smile at Juan and Twist. "Won't the guys be cold, boss? We should invite them in."

"I don't think so, Jesus. They stay cold out there so things don't get too hot in here."

"What are you talking about? Hasn't Pete talked to you? I filled him in on everything last night." You lower your voice and lean in, "Obviously, you didn't want me calling you."

"Pete said he couldn't find you. Even had Lily out looking but no luck. I've been worried about you, Jesus. I thought maybe you flew the coop with Bobby's skim."

You drop your jaw and then concentrate on looking more angry. "What? Fuck Pete! I went straight to him to report."

"Usually it's Denny who comes to the house to report."

"Usually Denny doesn't think on his own. Denny follows your orders, not Bob's. *Usually.*"

"Wait. Are you saying Denny tried to stop you from killing Bob?"

"How do you think I got this?" You wave at your face and dig into a big forkful of pie to slow down the conversation. You've got a lot of lies to keep straight.

"What happened? Break it down, step by step."

"I got Bob. I imagine you already know the details about that."

"Took the big dive, yeah."

You scan his face for any trace of regret at having his brother killed. There's still a difference between hard rocks like Jimmy and guys like you. His eyes hold no regret.

"I told the cops he was depressed," Jimmy says, "which might have worked except somebody in the street saw a well-dressed guy who looked remarkably like you out on the ledge with him before he went over. The detective tells me Bob's office was ransacked. When I gave you the job, did I not say to be discreet?"

"That was me on the ledge, yes. I chased him out there because Denny warned Bob I was coming. While I was in the outer office telling Harv and Marv to beat it, Denny betrayed us."

"You're claiming Denny warned Bob you were coming?"

"I'm not claiming it. I'm saying he did it. Must've called him on the cell while I was getting rid of Marv and Harv. Then Denny showed up behind me as I snuck up to Bob's office door. He was supposed to stay with the car and make sure Bob didn't get past me and make a run for it in his Caddy."

Jimmy seems satisfied and tells you to go on.

"Denny almost stopped me, but when Bob went out the window, I followed right after him to the ledge. Denny's not that fast on his feet."

Jimmy takes a small piece of cherry pie and dribbles some red juice down his chin. His eyes never leave yours. "You got the key?"

"I'm your hero. Bob handed it to me."

"He just handed it to you?"

"He was bargaining."

"And he lost that bargain. Uh-huh. I get it. What happened with Denny?"

"Screwed up. He was tearing the place apart looking for the safe, looking for money. I thought if he had anything incriminating, it's probably in a safe deposit box. It would have been easier to find that information out if Bob hadn't run out on the ledge first. I had been hoping to ask him some questions before we were one inch away from the drop of doom."

"So you're telling me Denny was searching Bob's office and he let you back in the window with the key?"

"Naturally. If he wanted the key, he had to let me back in safely. We had to get out of there before the cops showed up. We couldn't very well have it out there and then. If I remember my *Star Trek* properly, the Klingon proverb is, 'Only a fool fights in a burning house.' There wasn't a lot of time to dance, Jimmy."

"And later Denny blacked your eyes and made your face a balloon?"

Better to stick as close to the truth as possible. "No. The cops were already on the way, so he didn't have time to try to kill me for the key until he pulled into a construction site. He did all the hitting, but I got the last lick in."

"Uh-huh…. That's a good story, Jesus. So where's the key?"

"If Pete hasn't got it already, it's in that bathroom, sitting on top of a ceiling tile over the john closest to the door. I brought Denny here to try to hash it out. I needed to know why he warned Bob when I went after your brother…on your orders."

Jimmy's face darkens. A storm's coming.

"You gotta understand, Denny and I were good friends for a long time. I wanted to work it out between us. I was hoping he'd get his head on straight, maybe make that lapse go away."

Jimmy takes another bite of pie and chews angrily, giving you both time to think. You wonder, how much did the cops tell Jimmy about Bob's death? People saw Denny in the street retrieving the key from Bob's broken neck. He said they were tourists. Tourists talk to police. If it had been New Yorkers, you'd have a decent shot of them moving on before the heat arrived. You begin to sweat. You shouldn't have told Jimmy that Denny was upstairs with you. You tripped up.

The manager comes around the counter and sets the steaming coffee on the table. He drops the handwritten bill beside Jimmy.

"Pete didn't tell me any of this. He said he couldn't find you. You saying Pete isn't on my page?"

"That's not for me to say, boss," you reply. "All I know is that I told him everything last night at the bodega's loading dock over *Como Si* so he could tell you what happened. Sounds like Pete is trying to hang me out to dry."

Jimmy leaves the crust and finishes the cherry filling, chewing with his shark mouth open, grinding and mashing. When he swallows, Jimmy says, "That's not a bad story, Jesus, trying to put it all on Pete and Big Denny like that. Except, I happen to know it's not true. You're a good liar, though. You must be a good liar to have such a big supply. You must be Bullshit's East Coast distributor. I already got the key. We searched for it and found it twenty minutes ago. It was *you* who called Bob's ex about the safe, not Denny."

Shit. Forgot that. Maybe you're *aren't* the best bullshit artist ever.

And then it occurs to you. How did Jimmy know to find you here? The only person who knew you were coming here tonight was Lily.

SMART OR GOOD?

"Jesus. Now that you know that I know that you're fulla shit, you want to start again?"

"Who told you you'd find me here, Jimmy?"

"A little bird told me."

"I see."

"Did the bird tell you that Harv is dead? Or how he died?"

Jimmy's shark mouth drops open another fraction of an inch. You've hit him with news. "Harv's brother's been asking about him," he says.

"He came after me. Harv died...horribly, but relatively quick."

"When it's locked on you, Death never comes quick enough."

"You'll be happy to know Harv wanted to get Bob's skim and get the hell out of town, so I guess that's another traitor you won't have to worry about, though there will be plenty more. Remember *The Godfather*, Jimmy? You're Sonny Corleone all over again. The hotheaded son of the boss everyone loves. I love movies so much, I'm amazed I didn't spot the parallel before. Only you killed Michael. Well...Panama Bob was no Michael. Pacino played Michael as a real smart guy. Still, Bob's dead and he's still got us running in circles for the skim, so maybe we all underestimated him."

"Don't talk to me about my brother, Jesus."

"You remember what happens to Sonny, right? A lot of machine gun bullets."

Jimmy's turning red. Good. It sure looks like Lily's betrayed you. What's to live for? Maybe if you get Jimmy mad enough, he'll do you a favor and nod to one of his mooks and they'll open up right through the window and kill you relatively quick, too, in the stereotypical hail of bullets. With the civil war coming, it's bound to happen, anyway, right?

"You know what other movies I like?" you ask. "*Star Wars*."

"What?"

"Especially the first one where we first meet Han Solo in the crazy space bar."

"Chalmun's Cantina, also known as the Mos Eisley Cantina," Jimmy corrects you. You blink. He smiles for the first time. "I'm older than you, kid. I saw it in the theatre first and own every incarnation up to Blu-ray. I've seen the first trilogy over and over."

"So you know the controversy about whether Han shot first?"

Jimmy Lima takes a deep breath. "Heh. You think I'm Sonny Corleone. I think you're Greedo. You're the alien guy with the weird face that Jabba the Hutt sends to get Han Solo — "

"But Greedo just wants the money Han owes Jabba," you add. "I always thought calling the bad guy alien Greedo was a little too on the nose, didn't you? Greedo? Greedy?"

"In Mr. Lucas's defence, asshole, it's a kid's movie."

You shrug and nod. "So who shot first?"

"Han Solo shot first in the original." Jimmy's leaning in, looking at your hot coffee. "That's what I saw in the movie theater. Later, Lucas changed it so it looked like Greedo fired first."

You nod. "In the 1997 incarnation, yeah. Lucas wanted to make it clear to the kids that Han was the good guy. But in real life, if you don't make the first move and shoot your enemies before they shoot you, you end up a dead sucker. Better to teach kids to be smart. Good is easy. Smart is hard."

Jimmy clenches and unclenches his hands, getting ready for action. "But they shot at each other under a table meant for cocktails. How could Greedo miss? It's dumb. Han shot first. Had to, if he didn't want his balls shot off. Shooting first is always the smart thing to do."

Jimmy Lima's eyes are fixed on the coffee cup. He braces, telegraphing his move a second before he goes for the large paper cup, grabs it and tries to toss the steaming coffee in your face, just like you did to Denny.

Jimmy would have burned you badly, too, except you've already ducked and deked right to step beside Jimmy, putting his body between you and the guns outside. You jab the business end of your fork into Jimmy's exposed neck and run. It doesn't go in far. In the movies, you'd snag the jugular or the carotid and Jimmy would be a jigging, pumping fountain of blood. Instead, you get a band of muscle and open his skin up pretty well. Either way, he's screaming and you're running.

You jump the counter and you're already running past an open pizza oven, past the manager and out the rear fire door as Juan and Twist focus on Jimmy. You hope. You don't dare glance back in case one of Jimmy's boys is lining up his shot.

As you hit the door, a high-pitched alarm goes off that pierces your eardrums and shakes your nerves. It spurs you to try to sprint harder. You can run hard or long, but no one can do both. You run until you're out of breath and leaning on a wall in an alley. It would be easier to breathe and you could run much farther if your nose wasn't a solid hunk of pain. Running makes your face throb.

Jimmy's got the key, but there's good news, too. Maybe Lily didn't betray you. Jimmy went for that coffee cup so quick and easy, like he knew that's how you got a fighting chance over Big Denny De Molina.

Denny is still alive and talking. Big Denny, you're almost sure, is Jimmy's "little bird" instead of the lovely Lily. Lily loves you, or at least she didn't rat you out. That's a start!

That moment's pause almost finishes you. You hear a boom and cement from the wall you're leaning on chunks out to fall at your feet. Another boom and this time you hear the bullet whine by, smack and ricochet. You look back, expecting one of Jimmy's hired guns. Instead, it's the manager with the bad haircut.

He's got a huge silver revolver in his mitt. He might have got you, but his hand is shaking so badly, you can almost see the electric current of fear jangling through him. He steadies the hand cannon — a Dirty Harry .44 — and spreads his feet wide and drops into a two-handed shooting stance. He'd definitely have blown you away with his next shot, but he's breathing hard and trying to hold his breath and thinking too long about sending you to hell.

You pull your gun and point it at his head. You feel the energetic connection between your muzzle and the middle of the man's forehead. Pull the trigger now and he'll have a small red hole in front and a sick, yawning maw of brains squirting out the back. The pink mist will be followed by gray and white and red: All the colors of a head shot.

The shakes take over the pizza man's body. Hunters call it buck fever when they have a stag lined up in their scope but can't stop the tremors. He sees your steady eyes.

As gently as you can, you say, "You ain't Batman."

The pizza man understands now that he's not a killer. He's a worker ant who manages a little place that sells bad food. You are the hit man. He lowers the revolver and, still trembling, drops it to the sidewalk. He raises his empty hands, shaking so bad it looks like he's waving goodbye. A tear rolls down a cheek. He closes his eyes and begins a Hail Mary as he waits for you to throw him into whirling red blades.

You should shoot, but he's just a civilian. You've done a lot of things, but you don't shoot civilians. There's enough war without bringing civvies into it.

You're off down the alley, running again. You run with your chest thrown out, your head tilted back, opening your throat to your lungs to suck in as much air as you can gasp, driving your legs hard, long gone and far away before the pizza man is done his prayer.

THE BUGMAN OF SURFSIDE BEACH

'*B*alseros! Balseros!"

You don't remember the last 200 feet to the shore. You remember the waves pushing you away from America's promises and back toward Cuba. Your mother gasps and curses your father. Your brother whimpers and kicks as hard as he can, which isn't hard at all.

Sometimes, maybe once or twice a year, you wake from this same nightmare. Sometimes the nightmare keeps going and you can't wake up. You relive the moment the Captain threw your family overboard and Rodolpho panics again. This time he succeeds in drowning you.

Usually, the part that wakes you with a start and in a sweat is you, close to shore but still no sand under your feet. Your thighs burn. Your calves cramp. The ocean floor rises under you, but not fast enough. Somewhere behind you, your one-eyed, white-eyed zombie father is still reaching up, grabbing, pulling you back, pulling you under.

The safety of the beach is close, but as you and your brother and mother kick and kick and kick, pushing the old truck tire, you're sure it's just a tease and a cruel trick. As soon as your foot touches sand, your dead, drowned ghoul of a father — a moray eel where his tongue should be — will rip you away from the air and yank you down into the dark with him.

"Balseros! Balseros!" someone yells from the shore. A cluster of people gather and point your way. Are they pointing at you or are they pointing at a shark fin rising out of the water behind you? Maybe a shark will get you before your dead father can. Either way, at least you will rest. You've got no energy left to kick. Instead of pointing, they should be swimming out to you and helping.

Then you remember something your father said about feet. What was it? It was important. Wet foot. Dry foot. You have to get to the shore and then you'll be safe. No one will punish you and send you back to Cuba if you can get to the shore on your own. Your father told a terrible story of the US Coast Guard drowning Cubans who were trying to get to safety.

"White men, privileged to be Americans by accident of birth, might use water cannons on us. *Us!* People who just want to have a better life! They would kill us for having the temerity to grasp for what they were given for free and take for granted!"

Your mother said attacks by the Coast Guard rarely happened, or might even be Castro's propaganda, but Marco was firm. Until you step on dry land in Florida with your legs under you, you're a slave. Stand up, and you won't be any man's slave ever again.

"Wet foot? We get sent back to Cuba," he said. "Dry foot? We go see spring training."

The baseball, you admit, could be fun, but you're not quite twelve and all you can think about is men with water cannons shooting you far out into the ocean to die.

A man in a boat is coming. It is a fancy, fast boat like you've never seen. It is loud and painted white. A small American flag flutters behind the driver from a red and white stick that looks like a candy cane. You have heard of go-fast boats, but this is a rich man's boat made for racing. It is mostly made of throaty engines. Go-fast boats from Cuba could hold ten or more people, but this long, low-slung cigarette boat swings in front of you, between your family and the shore, and the engines seem to roar even as they idle. The man is tan, but his low-riding Bermuda shorts reveal bright white skin. Big mirrored sunglasses make him look like a bug.

You thought you'd drown. Or your father's hand would wrap around your ankle or that you'd die of exhaustion or that sharks would rip you in two and eat you and your mother and brother. Then you were sure the Bug Man was going to kill you with his monster boat. The wake rolls over you and you spit saltwater. Rodolpho cries out weakly and the wash nearly pulls him from the tire. Somehow, you and your mother hold on to your brother.

"Help!" your mother cries.

The Bug Man smiles and twirls his wheel. Far off voices shout from the safety of the sand, but you can't see land anymore. There are no buildings rising up to give you hope of rest and shelter as soon as your feet are dry. The Bug Man stretches out his hand and hauls you up first. Spent, you collapse to the deck gasping.

"Landed a fish," the tanned man says.

You thank him and beg him to save Rodolpho and your mother. He hesitates and pulls down his glasses to look you up and down. He smiles and turns to haul up Rodolpho. He's not ten yet. "Scrawny fish."

Your mother is spent, but she swims over with the last of her energy in an awkward, one-handed stroke since she doesn't dare let go of the tire. She reaches up, smiling at the Bug Man, one hand still on her makeshift life preserver. The Bug Man is still smiling as he reaches down to touch Maritza's fingertips. He then straightens and waggles his fingers goodbye. He turns back to the wheel. Your mother's screams are swallowed as he guns the engine.

You try to stop the Bug Man from taking you away from your mother, pulling at his elbow. You plead. You bite the meat of his upper arm.

The Bug Man elbows you in the forehead and you are dazed but somehow grab a rail and keep your feet. You go back to bite him. You were in an after-school fight once. A bigger, older boy got you in a headlock and hit your head with his knuckles. He laughed until you wriggled out a little and bit him on the back of his arm. He screamed in pain. Then he screamed you were a girl for fighting that way, but that ended the fight. You go for the same spot and the Bug Man yelps, too, but he shakes you off and backhands you to the deck. As your head hits the rail, you turn to see your beautiful, terrified mother, her mouth making a huge "O".

As the Bug Man drives you away from your mother, you do the only thing that's left to do. You pull Rodolpho to his feet. His legs are wobbly, but for what you need to do, he doesn't have to walk. He only needs to fly past the sharp and savage propellers whirling and cutting the water behind the boat.

The engines roar louder. The bow rises high as the props dig in and churn. The boat jets forward, throwing you and Rodolpho back against the rail. The shift in inertia helps you throw your little brother away from the clutches of the Bug Man, but not quite enough.

You're about to jump, too. You hesitate only a second or two, preparing yourself to follow Rodolpho into the darkness. That's just enough time for the Bug Man to bring a fist down on the top of your head, all his weight behind the blow. It's much worse than knuckles. It makes your knees bend and you can't straighten them. You are the nail to the Bug Man's hammer.

Dazed, you see the sun come out from behind gray clouds. It's going to be a beautiful day somewhere else not far away.

"You let my scrawny fish get away!" the Bug Man says. He hammers you again and bright day drains to night.

*   *   *   *   *   *

You stand by Lily's car parked next to the NYU campus, bent over and gasping for breath, waiting for your heart to slow. A civilian just tried to kill you. Bob's dead. The cops have your picture from Panama Bob's murder scene by now. Big Denny is alive — you're almost sure. If you're right, Denny's talking to Jimmy Lima and the boss has the key to the skim. If Jimmy's listening to Denny, Pete's going to jam himself up, too. Harv is dead by Lily's hand.

Lily. The woman of your dreams, the one who balances out all the nightmares, is waiting for you in New Jersey. She's waiting for you to save her from a murder rap and this life of blood.

You are Maritza abandoned in the water, screaming and unheard. You're watching the life you could have had slip away.

You are a helpless boy, denied victory and trying to do the next best thing.

Worse: All this? You're doing it again. Loss is the loop of your life. You've fallen into the propeller blades.

TOOLS OF THE TRADE

Big Denny De Molina's flop is Apartment C in a building in Washington Heights. The C is a real problem because, as Brad Pitt mentions in *Fight Club,* lettered doors are for sad basement apartments. You can't look in a window or check to see if the lights are on. You're going into the situation blind, but you've got to get into Denny's apartment. He's got hardware you'll need stashed in there. It's even possible that Denny survived his fall into the construction pit and he's in there, covered in bandages and waiting for you to show up so he can kneecap you and demand a sincere apology before he puts a hole in your head. Or Marv is in there, waiting to take you to Jimmy Lima and a very uncomfortable death.

There's no doorman or security. There used to be two secure doors to the street, but even the residents stopped blaming the slum lord after the locks were destroyed every time they were replaced. Poor people robbing poor people isn't just illogical, it's downright stupid. If you're well off and a junkie wants to run off with your TV to fund a fix, you'll have the fun of picking out a new TV at Best Buy that afternoon. When all you've got is a dirty mattress on the floor and a coffeemaker, you'll blast whoever comes through the door with .00 buckshot to keep your coffeemaker.

You've been to Denny's plenty of times, but never with such trepidation. You're operating off a hunch based on Jimmy trying the same scalding coffee move that saved you from Denny. However, you have to trust your instincts and the alarm bells in your head are going off.

Years ago, every door in this building had a gold-plated door knocker. When those were stolen, silver knockers replaced them. Now there are no door knockers. Now it's all colorful spray painted tagger designs and wary eyes peering from peepholes.

You slip down the stairs and a couple of black kids, a boy and a girl of about seventeen, walk past you. They barely notice you. The cliche is true: They only have eyes for each other. You take a moment to watch them go.

Lily is just the right height so, when you walk side by side, your arm across her shoulders, you both move as one person. She's your perfect fit. You don't believe in soul mates, but Lily is so powerful you *want* to believe. You're ashamed you ever suspected for a moment that Lily would rat you out to Jimmy. You look at her the same way that young kid looked at his girl. One day soon, once you have Bob's skim and you can get away from all this, you could be your true self. When Lily sees the real you — not the enforcer — she'll see you the same way you see her. You're almost sure.

You don't know who your real self will be, but you're excited to find out. Getting away with no money worries or responsibilities? That's why everyone plays the lottery. That kind of freedom makes you a kid and you can finally have that childhood you missed out on. The way you grew up, the real Jesus Diaz never had a chance. You and Lily can find out who you really are together and you're almost sure that's going to be great.

Bare bulbs hang like dead men above dim yellow pools of light down the basement hallway. You wait at the bottom of the stairs for five...ten...fifteen minutes. Somewhere above you, maybe on a landing far up the old iron staircase, a woman is screeching. You only hear one side of the fight, so it's like you're listening to a hysterical woman screaming into a phone. "It's mine! That's all mine! No, no, you are *not* taking that with you! *That's* mine, too!"

Christ, man, just go. Don't stay to haggle over an iPod full of James Brown, pirated ironic Manilow albums and LMFAO. If all the sinners in hell screamed out their torment in one voice, this woman would be their spokesperson.

Tia Marta is in your head again: Ugly threats, jibes and bullying. You push those thoughts away, but she's never far. If you could fix it so thoughts of Tia Marta would never return, if you could erase her with a well-aimed, sharp stick in the brain without anaesthetic, you would.

You wait and listen for any sounds of life down the hallway. Harv said Jimmy sent Marv to stake out Denny's place. A new thought: Maybe Marv is in the apartment, standing over Denny's corpse and he's the assassin waiting for you to come through the door. If Denny told Jimmy Lima everything, Jimmy might thank him and then whack him so his plans for The Machine would be safe from Vincent. Fathers and sons, bosses and underbosses: All had secrets from each other and would go to great lengths to keep them secret.

Or maybe it's simpler than all that and Denny and Marv are just playing a quiet game of poker, their weapons ready for you to poke your stupid face in so they can shoot off your big, puffy nose.

You move up and unscrew the lightbulbs as you go. Only the dim light cast down the hall from the stairwell reaches after you with thin yellow fingers. You stop at the door before Denny's apartment. The door reads: *Mechanical.* Old pipes gulp and gurgle and some kind of equipment hums unevenly, like something needs a tune up. Denny often complained that he had the worst apartment in the building because of that hum. The sporadic hammer and bang of water in the pipes kept him awake nights. Sometimes it was so bad, Denny left the TV on with the volume way up just to mask the noise from the mechanical room.

If you had the job of knocking somebody off in this situation, you'd be a smart ninja. You'd pick the lock to the mechanical room and wait in there. As soon as you heard anybody messing with Denny's door, you'd pop out and blast him. That would be a smart ninja way to solve this equation, given the variables.

You don't want somebody popping out of that door behind you. You listen before you make your move. You can't hear anybody breathing behind the door. If it were Big Denny, you could hear his heavy breathing for sure, but Marv is in shape. He could be waiting to send you to hell, easy. You stand to the side and try the knob. Locked, but it's nothing but a lock made for bathrooms. A child could defeat that with a straight piece of hanger wire.

You thought hard about how to get into Denny's without getting bushwhacked. One tool you'll need tonight, you already had in your go bag. You thought you might need it to get into the storage locker facility. The other? Super glue. You picked that up at a corner store on the way here.

You take the little cylinder of super glue out of your pocket. You've already cut the tip off the long nose of the plastic cap in the car so you wouldn't have to fuss with it here. Quiet as a smart ninja can be, you run the tip of the cap down the side of the mechanical room door as you squeeze the tube. The glue solidifies almost instantly. You smile. This is one level up from smart ninja and into James Bond territory. Makes you wish life had a movie soundtrack.

Maybe you're acting paranoid and Marv isn't in there, but you would be if you were Marv. Marv is smarter than Harv. Twins aren't really identical. Marv was in better shape and attributed his smarts to being twenty-one minutes older than his brother. "I'm more experienced in the world," Marv joked. Well. The first few times it was a joke. Then he kept saying it.

The super glue might not hold for long, but it would slow Marv down long enough for you to whirl and unload your SIG into him. Satisfied with stage one, you creep down the hallway to Denny's door.

There's no sign of forced entry, as the cops say. You had hoped Marv had come earlier and ransacked the place to find the key and left. From your conversation with Jimmy, it's clear Denny figured out where the key must be. You'd told him as he was beating your ass by the pit, so there's more evidence Denny must still be alive.

Despite everything, you really do hope Denny isn't dead or even hurt badly. You guys have a lot of history behind you. He saved you a few times. He was a good partner. No. More than that, Denny was like a brother right up until he tried to kill you. If you end up having to kill him twice, you will be genuinely upset.

You stop again and listen. The woman upstairs still screams in spasms of anger. It sounds like she's following someone out. Whoever she yells at remains quiet. You can't even hear a murmur under the hysterical woman's cries as she comes down the stairs. "This is it, this time! Don't come back! You come back, the locks will be changed! I'm better off! Don't you look at me! You don't *deserve* to look at me!"

Again, Tia Marta rises, a thought zombie that won't stay dead. The last time you saw her, she kind of sounded like the woman upstairs, though Marta's thick German accent made everything seem more ominous. Of course, with Tia Marta, everything really *was* more ominous.

More screaming as they bang down the stairs.

Just go! I'm trying to hear if there's someone in my ex-best friend's apartment waiting to kill me!

Eventually, you hear the front doors on the ground floor bang shut as the woman follows her ex out. Other guys would have rushed in by now, but you're a smart ninja. You wait next to Denny's door, holding your breath and straining your ears.

You once saw on TV that doctors pitch their hearing when they listen to a patient's heart through a stethoscope so they sense the finer workings, listening for murmurs and catches that spell doom. It sounded like bullshit, but right now, your head cocked and straining, you believe it. Getting through this door might be the key to getting back in control of your destiny. If you get hold of Denny's stash, and if you live through tonight, you could spend the rest of a rich, long life with Lily. Most straight-edge citizens wait for extraordinary things to happen to them. But you? You could make this happen.

There's no sound of a TV or whispered conversation or the clink of a glass. That's good, because the stealth phase of this mission is about to end. You take the second tool out of your trench coat. You've had this stick since you traveled north to Havana on the Hudson.

At first, you were worse off in some ways. You saw snow for the first time in Hudson County, New Jersey. It was colder than you imagined, but you escaped the Bug Man. You were still a scrounging kid on the streets, but you were back among Cubans and Havana on the Hudson felt comforting and familiar. You thought you'd find your mother there. That fantasy sustained you for a long time. If you had stayed in Jersey, you might have grown up to drive a *guagua*, but standing here in your last good suit and a thousand-dollar trench coat, it's hard to imagine living the life of a humble bus driver. Bus drivers can't be Batman, ninjas or James Bond and they don't feel the comforting weight of a SIG Sauer P220 in their pocket. Well, most of them, anyway.

You're not big enough to run at Denny's steel door and just burst through to toss the place, so you're going to have to make some noise. The tool is a couple of feet of hockey stick. That's the handle. The business end is a bicycle chain. Wrap the chain around any doorknob, use some leverage, wrench it and you're through. The trouble is, you're about to make all the noise you've been avoiding up until this moment.

You have your gun out and ready in case Marv really is about to burst out of the mechanical room. A breach like this is really a two or three-man job to do it right. If you had your druthers, you'd have one guy watching your back and another working the chain around the knob. As long as you're making wishes, it would be best if three guys were taking care of this while you drank mojitos in another state.

No one tries to open the glued door to the equipment room. No one was waiting for you after all. For a moment, you're hot with embarrassment about what a bitch you're being about this. Then you remember your training. The paranoid soldier is the one who survives.

You try to be quiet, but the bicycle chain clinks and clicks and scrapes on Denny's steel door like a slow snare drum. Fuck it. If you can't be ninja stealthy, you'll have to opt for speed. You wrap the chain around the lock and try to open it with one hand. Nope. This is a two-handed job. You stuff the gun in your pocket (guns in belts are for stupid tough guys who shoot their testicles off in the middle of a job.) With two hands, you brace one foot against the frame of the door and haul on the hockey stick handle. The door knob comes away clean and you lean on the door.

Shit. You push with all your weight and the door gaps at the bottom, but there's another lock above where the knob was. You hadn't remembered that one. So much for genius ninja. You look to the apartment across the hall: Apartment D. You step up to that door — it's been quiet over there, too — and you run at Denny's door. Bang! Wow, does your shoulder hurt.

What you wouldn't give for a SWAT team on your side: One of those battering rams for the quick entry, a sledge hammer, a couple of flashbangs and a few canisters of tear gas to plow the way would do nicely. Then you go for old faithful, the ninja stamp. You plant your feet and kick hard, your heel delivering the blow as close to the lock as you can manage. The door swings open with a bang.

An idiot would do a textbook tuck and roll as soon as the door burst in. That's the sort of Hollywood *Beverly Hills Cop* bullshit that will get you shot while you're still trying to roll up into a crouch, still searching for a target in a dark room while your assassin sits in an easy chair with a sawn off in his hands. Tarantino got it right in *Kill Bill*. Uma was the most dangerous assassin in the world but bad old Bud easily bushwhacked her with a shotgun full of rock salt from the comfort of a rocking chair.

As you were messing too long with the door, Marv or Denny could be sitting in the easy chair or on the couch or just on the floor beside the door, the sawn off in his hands already lined up with your chest. You'd hear a boom and the shotgun pellets would tear through you. The hydrostatic shockwave of the punch through your torso would blow a lot of viscera and fluid out through the hole he made. You might have a short flight through the air while you were still figuring out what happened. Then the searing pain would hit you repeatedly, pushing you into the dark.

They say no death is ever instantaneous and the best anyone can hope for is to die in their sleep. The odds of a guy like you dying in your sleep are just about nil, unless you get the ordnance in Denny's stash so you can get the key back from Jimmy Lima. Panama Bob's skim might be the ticket to you dying peacefully in your sleep some day far off, surrounded by children and grandchildren and Lily, old but still somehow beautiful, holding your hand as a nurse pumps up the drugs.

Maybe it will be Propofol, the same shit that let Michael Jackson go in his sleep. You'll go out high and dreaming sweetly instead of gut shot and dying in the doorway of a shitty basement apartment in Washington Heights. The pain and loss will be pushed away by the best drug cocktails that American pharmaceutical companies can supply. Marco was wrong. Baseball isn't the pinnacle of the American Dream. Escaping life painlessly on clean, white sheets is the ultimate goal.

There's no sound from Denny's apartment. Even the mechanical room's hum has gone away. The air feels alive and electric. You aren't just listening with your ears. You reach out with sensors in your skin. You tingle and crackle with life as your heart slams against your ribs.

A smart ninja would take a walk now and come back later. Maybe you could wait by the stairs and see if you can make the other assassin the idiot. Let him pop *his* empty head out around the corner of the door frame to get it shot off. A smart ninja would make whoever's in there chase you out into the hall where the odds are even and you're the guy lying on the floor in wait, presenting a small target in the darkened hallway.

But the sad truth is, you don't consider any of those smarter choices in the moment. Your adrenal glands are kicking out adrenaline and testosterone is seething through your bloodstream.

You slip to the floor on your left shoulder and peek in from the bottom of the open door, your SIG out in front of you. You can't see a thing in there.

Denny's little apartment is as dark as the inside of an ass and smells almost as good. You've been here but you never stayed long. Denny complained the building's water was always too cold so he rarely took showers. You told Denny as sweetly as possible that he gave big sweaty guys a bad name. As you drove around with him and made your rounds for Jimmy and Bob, you rolled down the windows, even in January.

Marv or Denny could still be in there, waiting for you to do something manly and stupid. Then, smart ninja inspiration strikes and you pick up the fallen doorknob. You had an evil DI who pranked a tank crew with a dummy grenade once. The tank driver pissed his pants and another guy came out a hatch so fast he banged his head and knocked himself cold.

You toss the doorknob into Denny's dark apartment. It clanks satisfactorily. "Grenade!"

Nothing. No one is waiting to kill you. Marv must have gone home. You laugh. You even giggle. You reach in the open door and find the light switch.

No one is sitting on the couch with a shotgun levelled at your chest. The La-Z-Boy chair is pointed at the television, but neither Denny nor Marv is in it, cradling a machine gun. Getting shot at and almost getting killed has you jumpy and more paranoid than ever, but everything's fine.

Then you stiffen as the cold muzzle comes to rest behind your ear. You aren't a smart ninja. You weren't nearly paranoid enough.

You drop your gun and it hits the floor with a disheartening clunk. It would be embarrassing if it had gone off and shot you through the head, but only briefly. Such a clumsy death would be quite a relief compared to the alternatives that await you. You turn slowly to face the reaper and there's Marv with his precious Tech 9 pointed at your head.

Behind him, the door to Apartment D is open. Behind that, you see the body of a woman on the floor. Marv's been waiting for you so long and so patiently, the blood's drying on the dead woman's floor. A housefly lands on the dead woman's face and drinks deep. Her head sits in the pool of blood. Her eyes are open. Her look is accusing. Her face, drenched red from her vicious head wound, is a chilling combination of *I'm not really surprised* and *You're next, you prideful idiot, you useless tool. You're no better than your father.*

THE GAMBLER

"The little Cuban," Marv says. "You're ten feet of trouble in a 5'9" sack of shit."

Your eyes are still fixed on the dead woman's face. "You didn't have to do that, Marv. What did she ever do to you? She was a civilian."

"Collateral damage," he says.

"I never liked that term. It's jargon. It's a term made up by bureaucrats and press secretaries to cover up killing innocent people. You and me, we're not innocent, but that lady was. When Denny was sick last Christmas, she brought him baked beans and gave him an ice pack for the fever. He told me. Her name was…was Mrs. D. Denny could never remember her name but it began with a D and she was from apartment D so that's how Denny remembered that much."

Marv digs the Tech 9's muzzle into your sternum and you step back. In the movies, the hero grabs for the gun or kicks it out of the gunner's fist. That's stupid. Try anything fancy and Marv will tighten up. He might not even mean to shoot you — yet — but that won't be much comfort as you bleed out on Denny's dirty rug. Hand-to-hand combat is for when both guys' guns are empty. Even then, it's much better to fight just long enough to go find more ammo and reload.

Time to go into lying and negotiation mode. "Can we talk, or," you nod at his gun, "is this going to be a short conversation?"

Marv gestures with the gun and you sit in the La-Z-boy.

"I can't wait to tell the guys about you throwing that doorknob and pretending it was a grenade. Hilarious, man."

"You saw that, huh?"

"All through the peephole."

"It'll be a good story. You want to hear another?"

Marv doesn't miss a beat. "Are you going to tell me about where the key to Panama Bob's skim is or are you going to give me that same bullshit story about how Bob was into some crazy counterfeiting scheme with Freejack Jack?"

You blink. "I was going to try the bullshit story about counterfeiting, actually."

Marv smiles wider, like the corners of his mouth might get caught up in his ears. "Yeah, see that worked great on Pete. One, because you can sell a story, and two, because Pete's greed is bigger than his brains. That's saying something because Pete's pretty smart. But I worked for Bob. I knew about the skim, but he slipped us enough, Harv and me, that we could keep our traps shut."

You settle into the chair. It's best not to look too freaked out with Marv waving the gun your way. If he is going to shoot, you may as well go out acting cool. You're genuinely afraid the doorknob as hand grenade story might be your legacy. You've got a lot to live down. Sure, you looked like an idiot, but you'd have been a genius if the ploy had flushed out a bushwhacker.

Keeping the Tech 9 on you, Marv walks backwards and closes Mrs. D's door. When he comes back in, he closes Denny's door and paces back and forth. "How about I tell you a story for a change?"

You shrug. It might give you some time to say a few Hail Marys. "Sure."

"Once upon a time there was a traveling poker game. Different place every week. High rollers. Sometimes in the back of a restaurant, all night long. Sometimes at somebody's house in the suburbs, out among the civilians with their barbecues and 2.5 kids and picket fences. Could be anywhere, but this one night, it's in the back of Con Carnies. You know this story? It's an oldie but a goodie."

You shake your head, hoping it's a good long story because you've just discovered you can't remember a single phrase beyond "Hail Mary, full of grace."

"One of the guys who works in the back of Carnies? He was a dishwasher. He overheard the boss talk about how these underworld types were coming in after midnight for a high stakes poker night. There's going to be thousands of dollars on the table. Maybe a hundred thousand. Maybe even more. And this little dishwasher starts getting ideas. He starts to think about how his life sucks and if he had that kind of money…if he made one bold move? Well, he wouldn't be a dishwasher anymore, would he? Maybe he could take his girl and escape to Miami, huh?"

Sweat trickles down your neck while jagged ice turns in your stomach.

"This dishwasher gets big ideas about himself. He gets a plan together. He figured if he could crash that poker game, he could steal all that money and he'd get away free. They're a bunch of bad dudes around that table, but there's one good thing about robbing bad dudes. They can't very well call the cops, can they? He figures, with that kind of money, he can disappear far enough down a hole, he won't get tracked down. It sounds like a good plan, doesn't it? Does it remind you of anyone, Jesus, you stupid fuck?"

"No, but keep talking. You're exciting me. Sexually."

"Heh. Smart mouth on a dumb guy. *Grenade!*" Marv laughs and then settles in, his eyes never leaving yours. "The little dishwasher realizes he should probably have some muscle. Bad dudes carrying big cash will be armed, for sure. They might even have bodyguards in the room to complicate things. He knows he's got to go in hard, but he can't bring himself to get anybody else in on the scheme because more guys means more mouths to talk and more mouths to feed afterward. He doesn't want to split the cash up. That would screw up the point of his gamble."

"Right."

"Which reminds me, did you even check on Denny after you threw him into that hole? Or did you just leave him to die? Pretty cold way to treat a partner."

"Did Denny tell you why he ended up in the hole?"

Marv pauses. "That's kind of the point of my story, Jesus. You screwed yourself by betraying Denny, by being so greedy you didn't want to share the skim with anybody."

You shrug. "The way I see it, he betrayed me. He did try to kill me and he gave me this mug." You gesture to your face.

"Denny says different."

You now have confirmation: Denny is alive. Not surprisingly, in Denny's version of the story, he wasn't giving up that he was sleeping with Jimmy's wife. Interesting. You think you can use that, but then Marv tells you the rest and that little burning hope is extinguished.

"The little dishwasher gets an idea that he should go in hard with a machine gun. That's a good instinct, but his trouble is, he's still a dishwasher. He doesn't know anything. Where's he going to find a machine gun on a few hours' notice? But, he figures, this is the Bronx. If you can't scare up some serious hardware in the Bronx, it's not the Bronx, right? So he asks his buddies and phone calls are made but the best anybody can do is to give him a double-barrelled twelve gauge. You want an M-16? Come back tomorrow. You want an Uzi? Sure, but not till next week. Plus, all that didn't matter because, like I said, he's a dishwasher. He can't afford to pay for major ordnance. He's only got enough scratch for the shotgun and he's lucky it's not a little squirrel gun."

Denny said you knocked him into the pit so he couldn't be in on the skim. Does *Pete* know this isn't about fake bills, yet? He must, if Marv knows. In which case, you're screwed twice. Again.

"Hey! Am I boring you? Can I shoot you now?"

"Nah, I'm riveted. Shoot me at the end."

"Agreed. Where was I?"

"Dishwasher with a twelve gauge. Big dreams. Gets the money. Escapes. Lives happily ever after because that's how all mob stories end."

"Heh. I'm going to almost miss you."

But Marv won't miss with that Tech 9.

"Dishwasher with a twelve gauge comes into the room hard. He's all hyped up. The underworld types are appropriately surprised anyone could be so galactically dumb that he thinks he can rob them and not end up with his nuts getting roasted for breakfast. Still, for a whole minute there, the little guy is large and in charge, as we used to say back in the day. He rushes in and bodyguards are there, but he owns them and this little guy gets that first charge of power. Probably the first charge he had since he discovered his own dick. He jumps up on the poker table and screams, 'All you motherfuckers put your dough on the table!' And just to emphasize his point, he lets go with the scattergun and puts a hole in the ceiling. Clearly, the little dishwasher is bone crazy."

"Clearly."

"So these wise guys mutter and scowl, but they pony up and start putting wads of cash on the table. Wads of it, man. More money than the dishwasher has seen in his tiny life. He gets all excited. About then, the guy realizes he doesn't have anything to put all the money in. A pillowcase or a big garbage bag would have done the job easy, but he didn't think it through. There's all this money for the taking, if only he can get out the door."

"What's he do? Talk slow. I'm getting horny."

Marv gives a genuine smile. "You may not like how I punctuate the period when I say 'The End'. Anyway, the little guy is screaming for somebody to give him something to put all the money in. And the gangsters around the table? They really can't help it. This guy is screaming and jumping around and one of them laughs a little. It's just obvious it's amateur hour. The guy doesn't know what he's doing. Nobody's brought a bag to the back of the restaurant. There's no briefcase full of cash. What did the guy expect? Amateurs always think they're going to bulldog their way in and figure it out once they're in there. It's crazy time. The theft doesn't begin and end with getting a gun. You gotta have a brain behind the trigger."

You think what a happy coincidence it would be if Marv had a brain aneurysm just then. That would be ironic and helpful. Maybe if you could remember all the words to the Hail Mary, whatever psycho is in charge of the universe would give you a break. You close your eyes, make an earnest wish, and snap them open in a hard blink. Nope, Marv still looks remarkably healthy. Harv did say Marv worked out a lot.

"So this little dishwasher gets pissed off because what started as a chuckle spreads around the room. 'Gimme something to put this money in! Gimme something to put all your money in!' And the wise guys just start to laugh harder. That only pisses off the little guy more. They ain't taking him seriously. That's the one thing on earth nobody can stand for long. So the dishwasher? He screams louder! And then, just to make sure they see his point of view, you know, for emphasis? He fires off another cartridge into the ceiling! Just to make his point! You see the problem?"

"It was a double-barrelled shotgun. He's out of ammo."

Marv touches his index finger to his nose.

"The wise guys all stop laughing at once and everybody round the table, the bodyguards, even a couple of the hookers, according to legend…they all pull out their gats and take a bead on the idiot. He doesn't show up for work again, you know what I mean?"

"I like that story. Would you like to tell me a few more, say until the sun explodes? I can wait."

"Heh-heh. You just get one, but do you know the point of the story, Mr. Diaz?"

"Observe the golden rule? Temper your ambition? It's always darkest right before everything gets really fucked up?"

Marv gives you another genuine smile. How he does it, it's creepy. "My point is, you're that guy and you've shot your wad. You gave Pete some story about counterfeit cash that got him to hold off on killing you. That's one shot in the ceiling."

"In my defence, I was also avoiding torture at the time and I was improvising."

"And you had the key to the skim and you lost it."

"If I'd had it on me, I'm pretty sure Denny would have beaten it out of me. Like, even if I'd swallowed it. Like I said, I was improvising at the time."

"Uh-huh. The upshot is, you're out of stories. Jimmy wanted you to know that he knows you're fulla shit. Pete knows there's no counterfeit scheme that will make him the new boss and he's not going to clear Jimmy Lima out of the way. You've got nothing left to bargain with."

He raises the Tech 9 and you sense the straight line of the energetic connection between the muzzle and the spot in the middle of your forehead where the bullet will drill in. "And we've come to the period after The End."

"I might have one thing."

"No, thanks, Jesus. I enjoyed our chat, though. You were a funny guy."

"Do you know who killed your brother?" you ask.

His hand tightens around the gun. If the Tech 9 had a hair trigger, it would have bucked in his hand by now and you'd already be dead. You close your eyes and count to three. You're going to live, maybe another moment longer. You heard on some morning radio trivia show once that the technical definition of a *moment* is just 90 seconds long.

"Harv is…dead?" Marv asks. "Who did it? Was it you?" He raises his gun again.

You shake your head vigorously. You can't tell him it was Lily, but there are plenty of people you hate on whom you can throw blame like flaming napalm. "Jake did it. On Jimmy's orders."

"You're lying. That's all you do."

"Have you heard from Harv?"

Marv's eyes flicker and, for the first time, three deep worry lines appear on his forehead.

"I killed Panama Bob on Jimmy's orders because Bob was skimming and Jimmy wants to own The Machine. Jimmy obviously wants me dead because I know about the skim and Jimmy wants it all. I was supposed to get it, or the key to it, anyway, before I whacked Bob. I didn't expect him to go crazy ass and run out the window onto a ledge and hide behind a gargoyle. Jimmy assumed the skim would be on the premises. Now that Jimmy's got the key to the skim, he wants everybody who knows about it dead. That's me, Denny, Harv and you."

Marv lowers the gun and pulls out his cell phone. It rings and rings. At least it does on Marv's end of the line. On Harv's end, maybe it's burbling underwater somewhere deep and dark. When his twin fails to answer, Marv grows another worry line. He gives you snake eyes. "You have a history of bullshit."

"Let me dial Jake. If I'm lying, you can shoot me in the balls."

Marv's eyebrows shoot up. After a short pause he says, "Respect." He presses the key on his cell for speaker phone and hands it to you.

You dial Jake and he answers on the first ring. "Jake! They already found Harv's body! You moron! What did you do? You don't know your job, man!"

"Bullshit!" Jake says. "He's never going to pop up. Where'd you hear different? And why are you talking this shit on a c—?"

You close the cell and hand it back to Marv.

"Bastard!" Marv cries.

You look away and study the carpet to give him a few minutes to grieve.

When he quietens, you clear your throat. "Harv and I were talking about a truce so we could combine forces and go after Jimmy. He won't stop until anyone who knows anything about his power grab or the skim is dead. You know that."

Marv tosses his handgun onto the couch cushion beside him and buries his face in his hands, holding nothing back. You'd cry, too. Harv had that *H* tattoo on his neck and Marv has his matching *M*. As muscle, a team of identical twins, they did look pretty cool, like a couple of heavies out of a Bond movie. Without Harv, Marv's just another douche nozzle with a neck tattoo.

"Jake's gonna die for killing my brother and Jimmy's gotta die for giving the order," Marv says.

"Then you better let me live so I can help you. You're going to need me if you're going to storm the castle. You don't want to run in there without enough firepower like some amateur dishwasher."

"Valid," he says. His face still in his hands, he asks in a small voice, "What do we do for firepower?"

"Denny keeps his arsenal behind you in the kitchen. That big freezer doesn't work as a freezer. It's all in there."

When Marv composes himself, he looks up at you with puffy red eyes, looking like the little boy he must have been at some point. We're all little boys. Sometimes, in moments like these, it leaks out.

"Jimmy's got some guys on high alert," Marv says. "How are we going to get to him?"

You consider that a moment and an idea forms. It's not a good one, but it's all you've got. "Your job is to find me and maybe get the locker location for the key, right?"

"The main thing was to kill you, though." He shrugs. "Up until a few minutes ago, anyway, but the idiot little Cuban enemy of my enemy is my friend."

"Did you call them to let them know I was here?"

"Of course not. I wasn't going to give away my position and give up my front row seat to the grenade thing."

"Yeah, yeah. Stop bustin' balls. My point is, as far as Jimmy's concerned, you're still on Team Lima, right?"

Marv gives you a reaper's smile. "Yeah, Machine-ready."

"Then I got a way into the castle. No idea how we'll get out, but there's a safe way in."

"Safe?"

"Safe-ish."

"Rock it, Rocket. Lay it out for me."

THE ULTIMATE LIAR

"Paper or plastic?" Bug Man asks. In his mirrored sunglasses, you hardly recognize yourself. You have never seen yourself in terror. Terror makes your face longer. Your hands are tied to the rail of his boat. He can do anything he wants. When the Captain struck your father with the butt of his rifle, there was no time for hatred. When the Captain threw your father overboard, there was only room for fear. Later, you hated the sea, but even then, you knew that it was nature. Nature is not personal. But there is time to hate the Bug Man. There will be much time to discover new depths of loathing.

"Are you going to be a good boy? Good boys get paper."

You piss yourself and the yellow puddle wets the Bug Man's leather deck shoes.

"Bad boy." He slips a clear plastic bag over your head. "I own you. You belong to me."

Your face is hot and the bag tightens, wrapping your face in a transparent shroud. You didn't have time to hold your breath. You want to scream but that's a waste of breath. Your vision fills with black spots. At first you're afraid, but soon you welcome the nonexistence the spots bring. The black spots grow large to meet each other to build infinite darkness. You are dead and the Bug Man can only kill you once.

No, you aren't that lucky.

*　　*　　*　　*　　*　　*

When you wake in the dark, you feel small. Your body aches. The Bug Man pushed you down the stairs. You sort of remember that: flight, like when your father threw you into the air to land in the water of the shallow end of the hotel pool he was supposed to be cleaning. Then you realize you were not flying but falling and the pain came. You crashed, banging and scraping against the jagged edges of rough wooden stairs to the cold, concrete floor. You are in the basement of what must be a large house and there is someone here with you.

You pray to Jesus. You ask the Virgin Mother for help. You ask God if it's an angel breathing in the dark. (Do angels breathe, or are they more like fish?

Are they more like divine birds with gills? You hope so.)

The angel listens to you until you tire of asking God for the same thing over and over: Deliver you from evil and give you your family back. As the silence stretches out, the angel moves, shuffling. The only light is a line under the door at the top of the stairs. Moving to the stairs, the silhouette reveals himself. He is a boy, older than you, or at least bigger. As soon as he speaks, you are crushed again. God, Jesus and the Virgin Mary would understand you. They would speak kind and comforting words, but this boy speaks in English. You don't, not yet.

God has turned his back on you, even though you are named for his only begotten son. "For God so loved the world, he sent his only begotten son…" God the Father didn't send help when Christ was on the cross. You never understood that, but you think of your mother's Bible lessons and the fear is fresh. If God didn't send help for Jesus Christ suffering on the cross, he probably won't send an army of angels to rescue Jesus Salvador Umberto Luis Diaz.

The boy chatters on. It's gibberish. He repeats something and you pick it out of the torrent of English words. You ask him to speak slower, not to understand, but to commit the words to memory in case you live to understand more later. Maybe he understands you a little, or maybe he just repeats the same thing, like he's praying, too. He says the words into the night because God's not listening. The boy says the same words until you're sure you will never forget. That night, you dream your first English words: "My name is Darren Hill and I'm from Sarasota. If you try to run away, they'll kill me. I'm next. I'm next! I'm next! I'm next!"

*   *   *   *   *   *

Bright, white lights behind cages of thin wire mesh blaze on, dazzling you. A tall woman with her hair pinned high on the back of her head clacks down the wooden stairs carrying a silver tray. Before she is two steps down, the heavy metal door swings fast on tight springs and slams shut behind her with a click. She puts the tray on a portable table against one wall. The basement isn't as large as you imagined. The walls are cushioned with a padding you soon learn is soundproofed. In the dark, you had been too afraid to explore the dimensions of your prison.

"I am Tia Marta." The woman speaks in Spanish, but with a German accent you had heard from some guests around the hotel in Cuba. "If you behave, there will be rewards. Wonderful rewards. If not? Not."

Your mother read fairy tales at bedtime. Evil kings held princes in dark chambers. Evil witches trapped princesses in high towers. The Bug man imprisoned you in his dungeon. Tia Marta cast a spell. You never knew if she drugged you with the chicken sandwich or the milk.

Before you finish eating, your body slows until it feels like a single blink could be measured with a watch. You slip to the floor and stare as Tia Marta turns the white boy around to show you the danger. Across his buttocks and back are lines. Some are old and healed. Many are fresh slashes of angry red welts.

The first English words you learned were: *sir, mistress, yes, please and thank you.* Tia Marta told you in Spanish that was all you'd need to know for the first few weeks. She didn't add "…until you are broken." You learned that later, too.

The word *no* is not a word you are permitted to utter. They beat you until you understand. They take away your name, too. You are not a person. You are just a boy, which is the same as being a thing like a lamp or a dishrag. Tia Marta and the Bug Man make clear in English, Spanish and with their fists and whips: Things can be thrown away easily.

*   *   *   *   *   *

You run your finger down the list of vocabulary words. Each time your Spanish accent creeps in, Tia Marta corrects you with a sharp rap of her ruler across your knuckles.

"After the age of nineteen, it's all over," she says. You aren't sure what Tia Marta is talking about but you nod earnestly. "There's a switch in the brain. After a certain age you don't get any taller and you can't talk like a native speaker anymore. Arnold Schwarzenegger came here from Austria to become the American dream, but he still got here just a little too late to lose the accent. Once it's bred in the bone, it doesn't come out. He still says '*Cully-fornia*' and 'red vine and vite vine' not 'red wine and white wine.' You're lucky, boy. The Sir brought me to this country too late. I was twenty. A little earlier and I could be speaking English like a Southern belle. Wouldn't that be charming?"

"Yes, mistress." You speak up clearly or she'll slap you.

"But my accent is pretty as it is, isn't it?"

"Yes, mistress." But not too loud or she'll slap you so hard, her fingers will leave a red outline on your cheek. Or she'll use her long fingernails and leave a mark, like she does more and more with the other boy.

"I'm very pleased with the progress in your attitude, boy."

"Yes, mistress. Thank you, mistress." Like the story Tia Marta told you of the Medusa, you must never look her in the eye. And you must never, ever, look too long at the key on the heavy gold chain that hangs from Tia Marta's neck.

"Good boy. So good, in fact, I think you're ready for some training. I've waited long enough. How about we watch a movie you'll like? You are going to love this. It's an old one called *Fast Times at Ridgemount High*. To improve your English, listen to the actors' diction and pay particular attention to the girl in the red bikini."

"Yes, mistress."

You don't understand the jokes and you're afraid to laugh at the wrong times, so you smile for Tia Marta. Then the pretty girl in the red bikini opened the front of her bikini top to show her breasts. Tia Marta reaches for you, her long fingers pushing into your lap, grasping and clawing as you squeal. You are so shocked you stand as if you could leave. Tia Marta is so upset, she calls the Sir.

The Bug Man strides in wearing a three-piece powder blue suit. He is especially angry because you interrupted a business call. He has to take off his jacket and vest to give you what he calls "a proper punishment." He leaves big splotches of purple bruises that take weeks to finally yellow. Tia Marta slashes her long nails across your chest.

Under terrible circumstances, time passes so very slowly.

Finally…"Paper or plastic?"

Paper is just for scaring you and keeping you off-balance and clueless as to where you are and when the next blow will come. Plastic is near-death, or at least it has been so far. You've learned to gauge his moods and there isn't a chance he'll put a paper bag over your head tonight.

For the first time, you answer bravely, "Plastic, Sir! And please don't stop. Use the plastic bag and don't stop!"

But you aren't that lucky. The countless days and awful nights melt into each other and for the rest of your time with Tia Marta and the Bug Man, you are no longer allowed the dignity of clothing, just like Darren Hill from Sarasota.

*   *   *   *   *   *

"You are my smartest and best student, boy."

"Thank you, mistress."

"You've earned your new place."

You don't know what she means until Darren Hill from Sarasota, your companion in the dark for three years, disappears. You didn't try to run away, but the Bug Man took him anyway. Darren was growing into a man and so Tia Marta is done with him.

One night, soon after Darren's exit, a little boy crashes down the wooden stairs to the floor. The light from under the door catches the boy's terrified face for just a moment. He cries out and babbles in Spanish how he is afraid and he begs you to take him home. You hold him and rock him. This is…familiar. In the dark, the boy is as small as Rodolpho. You beg him not to cry. "If you cry, Tia Marta and the Bug Man might come down here."

You haven't been allowed to speak Spanish for a long time but, to calm the boy, you risk it and, once spoken, you find you can't stop. "My name is Jesus Salvador Umberto Luis Diaz and I am from Cuba. Don't try to run away or they'll kill me. I'm next. I'm next!"

Footsteps.

"Sh! Sh! Please, shut up. Please!"

The footsteps are sharp and fast. That's not the Bug Man. His step is heavy and slower. Tia Marta almost always wears high heels and sometimes she uses them in terrible, painful ways.

"Please be quiet! *Sh! Rodolpho!*"

And there it is. Rodolpho. You have cried for your brother many nights after the lights were out, but you have not spoken his name since the day you tried to save him and, instead, the water turned a frothy pink.

Tia Marta moves around in the kitchen, close enough to hear your words, but you can't stop crying and the boy won't stop crying and you can't stop saying, "Rodolpho! His name was *Rodolpho*! My father's name was Marco and my mother's was Maritza and I am Jesus Salvador Umberto Luis Diaz! I am here, Rodolpho! I am Jesus Salvador Umberto Luis Diaz! I am Jesus Salvador Umberto Luis Diaz!"

The lights blaze on. Tia Marta clacks down the stairs carrying the silver tray. The door swings, slams and clicks behind her. The boy is a slight kid with a bowl haircut. He looks surprised at your naked body, or maybe it's the criss-crossed scars that shock him more.

"Boys, boys, boys! There has been a fracture of decorum in the Sir's house."

Tia Marta puts the tray of food on the little table and, with an expansive gesture and a cunning smile, she invites the little boy to eat the food. Then she turns to you and her smile fades to a thin, hard line. "A fracture deserves a fracture, don't you agree, boy?"

"I am Jesus Salvador Umberto Luiz Diaz."

"I heard those words. I thought we'd beaten them out of you. I thought you were grateful."

You test the forbidden word: "No."

"What did you say to me? Aren't you still my little boy?"

"No."

She comes at you, nails slashing for your eyes, clawing for your throat.

You leap back in fear and try to run. The first strike isn't the cut of her nails or a blazing slap but a hard thrust to your jaw with the heel of her hand that sends you reeling.

"Don't worry, Jesus! I'm going to beat that name out of you and you *will* be grateful again. I'll squeeze you like a pimple. I put you down so hard you won't even *remember* your name." She swings at you again and you feel the wind of her dangerous arc past your eyes. "And I'm doing it all for love. Of all the playthings the Sir has given me, you have survived the longest and I'm not done with you yet! You aren't a man yet. You've got a few miles left in you. I want more! Only when I decide you've earned it, do you get plastic for the last time."

You duck under her next swing, infuriating her.

"Remember, this isn't a beating, little boy! I'm *training* you!"

The little kid cowers in a corner, covering his face with his hands. His cheeks are wet. He's praying, but you've already tried that so many times, any hope and power your prayers might have had is drained.

You need a weapon. The plastic cups and the paper plate Tia Marta brought down here are useless, but the silver tray has weight. She follows your gaze and lunges to stop you. You avoid her, but not for long. Her arms come around your neck from behind and you know what comes next. Black spots. Later you'll wake up, naked and staked down. The torture will begin.

She's choking you out, but your left hand fumbles for the tray. You fumble. You reach. You miss. She's taller and stronger and outweighs you by at least forty pounds. Your hands reach for her arms but she's wrapped around your throat, tightening and squeezing like a python. Her hands are fists so you can't grab at her fingers to try to pry her off. You've imagined gouging out her eyes a thousand times, but now you're flailing and failing.

You're out of air.

You kick at the tray table, hoping to pop the silver tray up into your hands. Instead, you only succeed in kicking the tray away from you farther. You've risked everything and lost.

Tia Marta is laughing in your ear. It's a cruel sound, like there's metal in her throat. Despite all the anatomical similarities with which you're familiar from the vast amount of sadistic pornography she's shown you, you suspect Tia Marta is not human.

"I'm going to make it last, boy!"

You're losing the world. The black curtain is coming down and when the curtain comes again and you reluctantly surface into the light, the physics of the world will end. The earth will rotate slower, almost to a stop, as Tia Marta explores the nerves of your skin in exquisite detail. "Nociceptors," she calls them. "The pain nerves. Even more fun than the nerves we use for pleasure."

Time will slow as the torture begins. She might take so long, all the clocks on the planet will stop.

"*Tómelo!*" *Take it!*

The little boy slides the cool silver tray into your sweating palms. You're so weak without air you almost drop it, but something more is still left. Your hands are rigid claws. You slam the tray behind your head in blind desperation.

The edge of the heavy tray slams into Tia Marta's face. She won't let go, not yet. And surprise! That is a *good* thing. You twist your chin to try to pry under the blade of her forearm. You slam the heavy tray into her face again and you suck in air through your nose even as you sink your teeth into the meat of her arm.

She shrieks, lets go, stumbles back, but not without a ripping sound. Her eyes go huge as she stares at the gash pumping blood from her wounded arm. You spit the meat to the ground in front of her and she looks at you with…is that…*glee*? She is not human. Shaking, bleeding, smiling, Tia Marta reaches up with the arm that is whole and draws out one of the long, sharp pins that holds her hair up and points it at your eyes. "This will be a fine demonstration for my new playmate!"

She lunges at your eyes and you use the tray as a shield, deflecting her thrust up while you kick out as hard as you can, nailing her in the belly and doubling her over. The hairpin spins away as you knock her arm to to the side. You bring the edge of the heavy, silver tray down on her neck. It's as if God has wished away all her bones. She is a heap on the floor. But you keep hammering at her head with the tray, punctuating each savage blow with your newfound words: "I! Am! Jesus! Salvador! Umberto! Luis! Diaz!"

You're crying as you grab the chain around her exposed neck and strangle her to make sure she has nothing left. You can't be sure. Tia Marta only *looks* human. You open your eyes when you feel the little boy's cool, shaking hands on yours, gently pulling you away from the thing on the cold concrete.

The Bug Man was out of the house, away on business. His clothes are too big for you, but you'll grow into them some day and when you do, fine suits by Armani will conceal your scars.

You and the boy head north and you don't stop running until you get to Havana on the Hudson. The boy thought he'd find his parents there but he never did. Instead, the little boy becomes your new brother, Little Denny De Molina. When he gets to be Big Denny De Molina, he'll save you. He'll get you into The Machine after you come back from Iraq with a dishonourable discharge.

You've been telling yourself the man you pushed to his death in a construction pit was just a friend. You are such a good liar, you lied to yourself the most and the best. Big Denny was always more than a friend. But he's alive and you're afraid you're going to have to kill him again, if he doesn't murder you first, of course.

THE WAY OUT IS THROUGH

When you walk in, Lily's in bed but still in her dress, the bed covers pulled up to her breasts. Lily's drinking rum and Coke, sort of. She tips back the rum, gulping straight from the bottle and, once she's made room, adds some soda and gives it a gentle swirl. She'll be plastered long before it's all Coca-Cola.

You close the door, peer out through a gap in the curtains and watch to make sure you haven't been followed.

"You pick up a tail? You got a shadow? You worried you're going to get whacked?"

"Don't talk like that."

"Why? Does it sound dumb when I say it?"

You turn from the window. "I just don't want you to jinx us."

"Why not? I'm a moll now, aren't I? I killed one of Jimmy Lima's soldiers. That's something. Lily in the library with a candlestick! Lily in the conservatory with the lead pipe! Lily in the living room with a big ol' frying pan! Lily swings for the fences! I thought I'd never get sucked into Dad's world. I had plans. I was going to go to Paris and study art. I was going to be one of those girls. Berets and books and Euro passes for the trains and backpacking."

You sag. "I guess you shouldn't have gone slumming with the help then, huh?"

"Don't be petulant, Jesus. It's not sexy."

You reach for the bottle but she frowns and holds it to her chest. "Mine."

You retrieve a little plastic cup from the bathroom and unwrap it from its paper sheath. You hold out the glass and Lily pours you a couple of fingers. Your drink tastes stiff. You sit on the bed and watch her throat as she tilts her head back and swallows.

"How did you find out Pete does what he does?"

Lily shrugs. "Lots of little girls and boys don't know or care what their parents do for a living. For a long time, all anybody in the family said was that Dad was a businessman. You get that early enough, you don't question it. The mob's like religion. You get in early enough, the weird doesn't feel weird."

"And later?"

"I wasn't a dumb kid. I had an inkling. One time, over Christmas dinner — maybe I was twelve — Dad toasted 'the suckers'. I asked in front of everybody who the suckers were and the men laughed and the women got quiet. Mom told me Dad's business was trading stocks. Mom wanted to keep me in the dark forever. She kept up the pretence of Santa Claus and the Easter Bunny long after I found out where Christmas presents and Easter eggs come from. Friends from school told me the truth about the Easter Bunny and Santa. I didn't tell her I knew the truth because I *liked* the presents. If I said I didn't believe, the presents would have stopped."

"When did you know Pete was connected for sure?"

"I began to get it over time. I knew Dad was important, how other guys talked to him. When he met a client in the street, they were extra nice to him, like he was their boss or a kind of celebrity or something. I started to get it watching guys like Jake. The way those young guys defer to him, like they respect him, but they fear him, too. Fear is easy to spot. It's everywhere."

"What did Pete say when you figured it out?"

"I'd known for a while but I had the mob talk with him when I turned sixteen. I asked him to tell me about his business."

"He said his business wasn't any of my business because he put food on the table. Almost ruined that sweet sixteen party." She takes another long swallow.

Lily's hair is mussed and hangs over half her face. Her red lipstick is smeared and uneven. She looks sexier than ever.

"Mom took me aside and told me Dad was in the gambling business, that it was technically illegal, but it wasn't bad. It was only illegal because the government doesn't want competition for all its own gambling and lotto schemes."

"So you didn't make a scene at your sweet sixteen?"

"No, I did with Daddy what I did with Santa Claus and the Easter Bunny. I chose the presents."

"You chose your family. That's not so bad. I wish I had that option."

"Is this finally the moment where we open up to each other, bare our souls and you tell me why you never want to take your clothes off to have sex?"

"I like my clothes."

"You do take them off, right? Like to shower, I mean."

"Of course — !"

"Chillax, Jesus. I'm only picking at you. You're an exotic scab, you are."

You drink. You don't like the taste, but it's better than talking. Why does anyone have to talk at all?

"So why don't you want to get naked with me? Are you covering up embarrassing tattoos? From what you've let me see, you don't seem to have any tattoos. I was thinking you had an ex-girlfriend's tattoo on you somewhere and you're worried it will piss me off."

"Would it piss you off?"

"No. Of course not."

Not the answer you were hoping for. "What if I have dozens of tattoos all over from my exes?"

She laughs and takes a long drink. "You? I don't think so, Jesus. The way you are, I don't think there are a lot of girls in your history. You're the kind of guy who thinks he has to be in love to have sex."

It hurts you, how true this is. Your first sexual experience wasn't just loveless. It was hate-filled. Love and Armani are insulation from those memories. "Staying in the suit hasn't stopped us from doing anything," you say.

"A girl gets skin hunger, Jesus. It's not just about getting off. It's about the closeness, too…at least when it's good."

You shrug and have another drink, waiting for a new conversation thread to pull. You can feel her eyes on your neck.

"Fear is easy to spot," she says, slurring her words. "I said that before, right?"

"Yeah. How are *you* doing with fear, Lily? You killed Harv. You doing okay with that?"

She jiggles the bottle at you. "I'm dealing with it. What about you? Who was the first person you killed?"

"I'm not going to talk about that." But the mere question raises the spectre of a scream cut short and pink water in whirling blades. You push that thought away with another. "I'm more worried about the last person I killed. I thought I got Denny, but he's still around, and probably very angry with me."

"Okay. You thought you killed Denny but he lived. Who was before that?"

You can't tell her you threw Panama Bob off a ledge. He's still Uncle Bobby to her. You hold out your cup and wait for her to pour. She does and you knock this one back.

"You're afraid," she says. "Why can't you tell me anything? I took a frying pan to Harv's head. I've earned my bones. Did a good job of it, too. The Machine should have an equal opportunity employment policy. I could be an enforcer."

"Yeah," you say. "You've got an air about you that's definitely *Kill Bill*."

"What is it with you and movies? Start with that. I just saved your life and we're on the run and I don't really know what the fuck is going on, so how about you tell me? We could have a real conversation. We've had fun. Then I killed a guy for you. We should really move on to the next step in our relationship and have a serious discussion, don't you think?"

You tell her you'll solve all the problems. You tell her you'll take care of her and she doesn't have to worry anymore and she'll never get any blame for Harv's death. You tell her it's better if she doesn't know. You say anything you can to placate her, to shut her up and to make her stop asking you questions. And her answer is to cry, dig under the covers and hand you a newspaper.

It's on the front page of the City section. A bomb killed Derek "Cob"

Cobzaru, a Romanian mobster from Washington Heights yesterday afternoon. His two children, a boy and girl aged six and eight, were also in the car when it blew up. "I caught some of what Harv said. He said Uncle Jimmy was making up that the Romanians killed Uncle Bob. He said something about how he was trying to throw blame. Did Jimmy really make the order for Bob to die?"

"I guess so."

"You guess so? What does that mean, you guess so?"

"It means I want to tell you as much or as little as it takes to keep you calm." She sneers.

"And to keep you out of this as much as I can. The less you know, the better for you."

"The Romanian guy. His kids were little, Jesus. Suffer the little children. You know what this means? It's war. The Machine is supposed to be about making money. How is a gang war going to help that? And how am I supposed to keep calm? I've known where Dad's money came from since that not-so-sweet sixteen, but I never thought about anybody getting killed."

"Things get complicated." You're beginning to lose the thread. How much has Lily really heard? What does she suspect? How long was Harv in her apartment before you showed up? Did they have long to talk? Did Harv say anything that points Bob's death straight at you instead of Big Denny? Could Lily forgive you if she knew? How much longer can you keep all the lies straight? And why did you drink so much before you got lost in the lies? Is it because the truth is too heavy to carry and you just need to lay it down?

She looks in your eyes. "What's your part? What exactly do you do? Tell me."

"Mostly? I threaten people to make sure they pay up."

"That doesn't sound so bad, but I don't really know, do I? You ever kill a little kid? You won't fuck me without one of your precious suits on. What else goes on behind your eyes? How deep does the sickness go?"

You close your eyes. "I don't kill civilians. If I show up on somebody's doorstep coming heavy, they're already dirty and brought it on themselves. I don't do car bombs. I am not an indiscriminate monster who kidnaps kids. I've killed people. You know that. But I'm not killing anybody who's in danger of curing cancer. They're all lowlifes. If I show up, they're probably already rotten."

"So you've got a code. Good for you. It's better than none. What about Dad? Has he got a code?"

"Everybody's got a code. Pete's got a code of silence and loyalty. He'd die for Vincent, but he knows Jimmy isn't worth that sacrifice. And Pete would rather stick a knife in his eye than be a rat. That's pretty standard."

"What's his policy on hurting people?"

"The other night when you drove me over to your Dad's place? Pete threatened to burn my balls with cigarettes and he would have if I didn't tell him something he wanted to hear. That's the kind of business your father's in. That's where your car and your apartment and everything else comes from. That's where studying art in Paris and Spain was going to come from."

Lily goes gray. She sits back and drinks some more. There's not much left to drink. It's quiet for a long time. When she speaks again, she sounds different. She sounds like a woman who has grown older. "Thank you for telling me the truth. All this time, I thought I was so smart. I thought it was just about taking bets, like Dad just really loved sports and that was as far as it went."

You drain your cup and hold it out again but she's shaking too much to pour and you take the bottle from her before she can drop it and drink the last. It's all Coca-Cola now.

You get into bed with her. Lily turns her head away, but she lets you take her in your arms and hold her.

"You asked me about the movies," you say. "Let me tell you about movies. When I got here from Cuba, I learned a lot of English from the movies. I learned to talk like the actors and lose my accent and be an American. That's all it was at first. Later, it was different. Movies became about escape. I imagined that I could step into the screen and become part of the movie and everything would turn out okay. For a long time, it was like being really sick and staying indoors in bed, all the while knowing that other kids were playing outside in the sunshine. Escape was so close. I could almost touch the life I wanted. Freedom was in front of me, if I could just step through that window."

"Why couldn't you be like the other kids?"

You ignore her question. "Movies are what set Americans' dreams so high. Every guy wants to be the best of the guys they see on screen and we all want a woman like you to tell us we've made it. We all want a woman like you, Lily. I want you to say...to be able to say that I pass. I met the movie standard and I'm one of the good ones."

Lily turns to look at you and puts her head on your shoulder. "As long as we're part of this mess, this war, the Machine...as long as Jimmy Lima's alive and as long as my father can find me...you're never going to be that guy, Jesus."

You're quiet for a long time before you tell her you have a plan. "The way out is through."

"Are we free on the other side, Jesus? Is it like we're in a movie and everything works out in the end and we can look each other in the eye when we're done and be sure we're the righteous ones?"

"Somebody once said that life is all about sex, death and mind control. If you can get the first, accept the second and use the third, you can be happy. We could be happy if we exercise a little mind control."

Cars start up and rumble off from the parking lot. You hear a maid vacuuming the room next door. Finally, Lily tells you the thing you have feared most.

"If you want me with you on the other side of that plan," she says, "you're going to have to tell me the truth. All of it. Harv said something about the skim. What's the skim? How did Uncle Bob die?"

"You can be a hard woman, Lily."

"Tell me everything or I walk out that door. I'll go to the cops. I'll get protection from the FBI and you'll never see me again. I'll tell them I killed Harv to protect you and you're mixed up in a gang war that killed two little kids. If you hold anything back, I'll never forgive you and you will never, ever have your movie ending. You'll never have me and I'll never love you and I'll spit on your grave. And, yes, 'spit' is a euphemism. Believe it."

You don't consider your options. You don't even hesitate. You tell Lily everything.

MISSION POSSIBLE

A couple of Vincent's soldiers are watching the emergency entrance and another guy you recognize hangs out by the elevator on Vincent's floor. Hospital security is the easiest security to bypass if you are wearing scrubs and stick to the stairwells. You wear a lab coat over a scrub top with tiny ponies running across it. The only thing that doesn't fit are your black eyes. You still look like a raccoon so you wear big sunglasses. To top off the disguise, you carry a clipboard and wear a stethoscope around your neck. You blend in with some nurses coming in a side door from a smoke break. You're in.

Denny told you stories of mobsters who dressed up as women to whack somebody, but it's hard to imagine most hit men would do it because if things go wrong, you don't want to die wearing pantyhose. You wonder how Denny is now and if they've found the storage locker yet. How much money is the skim, anyway?

The hospital's cleaners try to cover up the smell of fear with industrial bleach. It's an insult to your intelligence, trying to make you forget that this is the place people come to die. In Vincent Lima's case, it's the place to put off dying a little longer. He had to argue to get the prostate surgery. His doctors refused him at first, declaring that at his advanced age, the anaesthesia might kill him before the cancer got the chance. He's a tough old guy, a bullet eater and much loved, if for no other reason than that he has survived this long and he's still in the game.

Behind schedule, you get lost in the rabbit's warren between Radiology and hallways of empty offices that all look alike. You have to wander around, but you finally spot Marv by the entrance to the cafeteria. As soon as he spots you he taps his temple as if he has forgotten something — all systems go — and heads out the far door with you trailing behind. He gets on the elevator. You take the stairs.

Vincent is on the fifth floor. He's supposed to be discharged today around five. It's 4:30. As long as the guys downstairs don't come up to ask if the big boss is ready, you might pull this off without a hitch. It looked good on paper, but everything looks good on paper on the first pass. In the military, they taught you all battle plans are solid until you actually confront the enemy.

As you come to the top step, you see down the hall and spot Paulie Munoz at Vincent's door. Marv stands behind him, looking sharp in a blue pinstriped suit. If not for the *M* on his neck, he could pass for a tall, buff accountant. According to plan, Marv tells Paulie that he's to help out by providing a little extra security for the boss on Jimmy's orders. Given that the Romanians will be out for vengeance as soon as they get over the shock of their loss, that makes a lot of sense.

Paulie's eyes are on Marv, but as soon as Marv sees you coming through the stairwell door at the end of the hall, he gives Paulie the nod. Paulie spins and sees you coming with the clipboard out front.

"Jesus Diaz!" Paulie smiles and waves, a huge toothy grin spreading across his face, but he's reaching for his gun as Marv smacks him behind the ear with the butt of the Smith & Wesson taken from Denny's arsenal. Paulie's legs wobble but he's not out. It's easy to give anyone a concussion, but that doesn't mean they crumple and go to sleep. For that, Marv wraps his arms around Paulie's neck while you pry the gun from his hand.

Paulie's eyes roll back and he's out. Cat taught Marv that chokehold well: under the chin, scoop up, squeeze in and lock down the carotid arteries and it's beddy-bye time. Paulie didn't have a chance with you and Marv coming at him from both sides. In the military, you learned that if you find yourself in a fair fight, you've failed to plan properly.

Marv holds Paulie under the armpits while you grab his legs and carry him to a gurney. A patient, an elderly woman with frizzy hair, pokes her head out of her room. She looks worried. "Should I call a nurse?"

"No worries, ma'am," you say in your best Australian accent. "He doesn't care for the bleach smell. Fainted. You know how it is. Some people have a hard time with hospitals."

She comes out of her room a few more steps tied to an IV pole by the needle and hose in her arm. "Yeah…my dad had that problem. Fainted at the sight of blood."

You turn your back to the old woman and block her view of Paulie. "We should get the patient into a room, don't you think, doctor?" you tell Marv in your most official voice. You're already pushing a door open with your back and wheeling the gurney into a large room.

A man lying in a bed by the window looks up from reading a book. "Excuse me. This is a private room."

Paulie's coming around so Marv pulls the curtain closed, screening him in so the guy by the window can't see him. Paulie's undoubtedly going to have a huge headache. You zip tie him to the gurney while Marv takes off his tie and stuffs it in Paulie's mouth. Paulie's eyes lock on yours and you hesitate, just for a second, before pulling the pillowcase over his head.

You lean close to Paulie and whisper, "We're here for Vincent. There's a Romanian guy outside the door with a straight razor. He's under orders to cut your throat if you call for help. I'd be really quiet if I were you. That was his little niece and nephew you guys killed. The Romanian won't need much provoking, you know what I mean? "

Paulie nods.

"This is going to be over in a few minutes. Just relax." Paulie nods again.

You've done some jobs with Paulie. He's not a bad guy. He is just doing his job just like you were when Jimmy told you to whack Panama Bob. You do Paulie a favor. "Stay away from Jimmy Lima's house. When you get out of here, go home and have a long nap and put some ice on your head. Lay low. A storm's coming."

You slip out from behind the curtain and the man in the bed still looks pissed. "Excuse me! I told you this is a private room! I paid for a *private* room!"

You pick up his chart from the end of his bed and pretend to study it. You take the pen from the breast pocket of your lab coat, circle something at random and sign your name: Dr. James Bond. "Cutbacks, sir. I'm sorry, sir. You shoulda voted Democrat."

"Wh-whuh?" He looks white, fat and puffy, like just about anybody who can afford a private room.

"The charge for the private room will be deducted from your bill. Please be quiet. If you disturb the other patient with excess noise, his throat might collapse permanently. A nurse and someone from hospital administration will look in on you shortly to sort out your room assignment. We're moving you to a room with a jacuzzi." You return the chart to the end of his bed and turn away. You leave the lab coat and scrubs in the bathroom before you're out the door.

Marv stands at attention outside Vincent's door when you pop into the hall. He doesn't conceal his admiration. "Respect, bro! It's amazing how easy the lying comes to you. You don't hesitate. If I were Lily, as fine as she is — don't get me wrong — I sure wouldn't trust you with all the maids around your mansion you're going to have when we're done with this."

"As a kid, I was trained by experts to think one thing while saying the opposite," you whisper. You're thinking of the words *yes,* and *I love you* and *thank you.* "Plus, I've seen all the *Mission Impossible* movies and watched a lot of improv."

A moment later, you're standing in the old man's hospital room. He sits in a wheelchair, dressed and ready to go with an orange paperback in his lap, facing the door.

Vincent Lima's lined face betrays no emotion, but he says, "Marv! And young Diaz! I didn't expect to see you."

"We gotta go, Boss," Marv says. "The *Banda* is out for revenge for car bombing the Cob."

"After what happened to his children, I don't blame the Romanians. Cob was a good target but getting the kids…that's too bad. Jimmy really screwed the pooch all the way around on this one. Killing kids gets everybody in an uproar. After the funeral of the little boy and girl, they'll come for us."

"We got a tip that they're going to assassinate you here!" Marv says. "We've got to get you back home where we can protect you."

"I was going home today, anyway. I was supposed to talk with the doctors before I left, but I guess they can call me."

"Are you in pain, Boss?" you ask.

"At my age, pain is all I've got and all I can do is to try to give it away and not piss my pants too much. Where's Paulie?"

"Driving the decoy car."

"That's what he's good for. I'll be glad to let you boys give me a ride."

Marv takes point and you push the wheelchair. You're halfway down the hall before Vincent peers back at you and says, "You look pretty good for a dead guy. Jimmy told me you were dead, or as good as."

"Aside from a couple of black eyes and a bad beating, I'm feeling pretty good, sir."

"Sir. Heh. What's the plan? You gonna whack me for the *Banda*? How much are the Romanians paying you? I can top it."

"This isn't about you, sir. But I need to have a talk with Jimmy."

"So you're telling me on your word of honor, on your mother's name, that I'm not going to end up in your trunk today?" He smiles. The old guy has old school style.

"My mother's name was Maritza and I'm not here to kill you, sir."

"Respect."

Marv plows ahead, scanning for Machine security, but there's no resistance along the escape route. You're already out a side door beside Radiology and headed across the back parking lot to the street.

Vincent looks up at the late afternoon sun, closes his eyes and his shoulders loosen. "What do you want to talk to my son about, young Diaz?"

"He ordered me to murder your other son, sir. Bob was skimming, sir. I'm sorry to say it, but it's true. The car bombing wasn't necessary. He killed that Romanian guy and his two kids for nothing. He knocked off Bob so he'd be your only heir to the throne. He wants me dead so no one's around to say otherwise when he takes the whole Machine to war against the *Banda*. Jimmy's gone nuts."

The old man's chin sinks to his chest and you almost miss his mumble. "Some throne. I'm a king of idiots."

Just for a moment, from the side, you think you catch a hint of a grim smile. You should know what's coming next. You aren't driving Vincent Lima to Jimmy's house as a hostage. Vincent's taking you for a ride.

WHAT WILL STOP HIM

Marv sits behind the wheel and revs the engine while you help Vincent Lima into his car. You sit in the back seat of the 1966 four-door, hardtop Cutlass Supreme with the old man. The make and model, also known as the Holiday Sedan, is the same as Vincent's first car when he was coming up. Everything is original except the custom paint job: "It's bright red, for the flag of Navarre, where I was born," Vincent explains. "After the Italian Families blew up my first car in '73 — a misunderstanding — I bought another one just like the original. It's a lucky car and we all need luck."

"So the bomb went off early or something?"

"An old friend of mine, name of Jimenez, was borrowing the original for a date. Good guy. He first brought me into The Machine before I spoke any English at all. Fresh off the boat, as they say. He never made it to the date. That car was lucky for me. Not so lucky for Jimenez. The girl he was going to meet later on became my first wife. Funny, huh?"

"How long before the Italians stopped trying to blow you up?"

"Give up enough money and territory and they can be very reasonable and forgiving. I love the Italians. Good food. There's a shake up every ten years or so, but they understand the Code and they get that we all make more money when we're peaceful. We are kingdoms. We respect the borders of those kingdoms and there's room for everybody. Usually. Sometimes...sometimes it's worth it to shake things up so you get more territory. It's not about the lives it costs in the short-term." Vincent looks at you pointedly. "Good soldiers die for larger causes. Just like with the whole country, it's about the money and the respect."

The old man's smile is full and unforced. He's supposed to be your bargaining chip, but instead, you're the one with fear skittering up your spine like cold spiders. What was it Lily said? *Fear is easy to spot. It's everywhere.*

"You know, Jesus... What old guys like Pete and me understand, 'cause we've been through the worst of things, is *loyalty*. We need guys who know how to follow orders and keep their traps shut. You were in the army. You know. The Machine's a private army that serves a business, just like any other army. In the regular army, no matter who a guy is, he doesn't do what he's supposed to do? Treason. Dead. Simple."

You sit back and nod and cross your arms, your right hand slipping around the grips of your SIG Sauer. You could shoot him right through your jacket and surely Vincent knows it, but he speaks with the confidence of a man who Death has missed on so many occasions, he's sure he can't be killed.

"When I was coming up, younger than you, Diaz, I found that I had a talent for working things out with people. My old boss? Anbessa. Long before you came along, Anbessa called me The Ambassador. I could make things right. Maybe a few eggs would get broken and there'd be some ketchup in the omelette, but I could do what it took to make things right and make The Machine safe. We respect the Blue so the local cops stay out of our business mostly and we respect the Code…mostly. The threats to The Machine's business are often not from the outside. It's ungrateful people you take in and feed, people who sit across from you at your table in your own home where you cooked the food. The ones closest to you are the ones to watch, Jesus."

"Yes, sir."

"You won't remember this, but some guys got remote car starters when the remotes first came out."

"Denny told me about it. He said he's done some wiring for you over the years."

"Yeah. Well…car starters are a great way for fat, lazy people to get fatter and lazier. Hard to believe the citizens we got now come from the same people who travelled across the world's oceans in sailboats. Most people won't get off the couch now unless it's for candy. But for guys like us? Those remotes sure beat getting your wife to start your car. Trouble was, it caught on too much and the big bosses started looking harder at the guys who bought those car remotes."

Your palm feels wet on the SIG's grip. All this talk of remote starters and car bombs makes you sweat.

"Guys thought they were pretty clever. They said it was to warm up the car, of course, but it doesn't get *that* cold in New York. New York can get chilly, but we're soldiers. We make the city tough and the city makes us tough, am I right? If they thought there was a chance they'd get blown up some morning, they got a car starter installed. Those guys were scared and it started to make us think somebody was definitely up to something. Least that was the word. Then Anbessa — great guy, smart guy even for a wise guy — got suspicious of these three guys with remote car starters. One morning, they got blown up. It was in all the newspapers. The Machine got a little smaller that year, but I moved up faster."

"So you didn't get a remote because it might make your old boss suspicious of you? I thought you wouldn't do it because you didn't want to mess up your classic car with wiring for a remote starter."

"It wasn't quite so classic then. Then it was just old. No, I moved up because *I* was the guy wiring three cars to explode one morning. Three jobs in one night! I never had a remote starter, but I did keep my car locked up in a garage every night, which is what those guys shoulda done, the rats."

"That's why those guys got blown up? They were all rats?"

"Well, I speak too harshly. One of 'em was, for sure, yeah. We heard later that the feds' investigation stalled out after that morning. It's a shame."

You hear his words, but you can't detect any tone that sounds like true regret.

"We never figured out which of the three was the one who wasn't righteous. It's a terrible thing, Jesus, to kill a friend, a fellow soldier, a *brother*." The way Vincent looks at you, you know he knows about Rodolpho and the red churning water beyond the propeller blades. The only person you ever told about Rodolpho was the kid you adopted as your new brother. Vincent has had long talks about you with Denny, you're sure.

"Yes," you say finally. "Yes, it *is* a terrible thing to lose a brother."

"But you gotta do what you gotta do to save The Machine. In Viet Nam, they said we bombed the village to save the village. Sacrifices are made so we get to keep what we fought for. Sometimes terrible sacrifices. Sometimes, you even have to kill a son to save a family."

Marv pushes the button on the visor to activate the first gate to Jimmy Lima's place. He turns the wheel and you're through and on your way up the long drive to The Castle. Denny will be there with the key. Or maybe they figured out where to find the storage locker and already picked up Panama Bob's skim. All that doesn't matter anymore. Vincent sees your game and he is ice.

We all need luck, he said. Your luck drains away, flushing your life with it.

"You sleep okay, Jesus? I sleep okay. My own prostate swoll up and tried to kill me, but I still sleep okay. You know the secret?"

"Sir?"

"The secret to success and dealing with all of life's troubles and sleeping fine and letting go of worry and stress…. Everything civilians don't get but we have to learn if we're going to be soldiers and make ourselves useful cogs in The Machine? You know that secret to overcoming all of life's difficulties?"

"What's the secret to all that, sir?"

"Not minding. Not minding, doing what you gotta do. But you, my young friend? I think you've learned this lesson too late."

He knows you've got your hand on your SIG, yet he doesn't look the least bit worried. Now you know what Vincent won't do and what will stop him: Nothing.

You *do* mind. You should worry, so you do, all the way up the long driveway to Jimmy Lima's castle in Great Neck. The end is coming fast.

DESCENT

Bald Van is on the inner gate, strutting back and forth with his heavy combat shotgun, a SPAS-12. Van has told you on many occasions it's the same model used in the video games he loves. The SPAS-12 in Van's hands is a very dangerous thing. Unlike most of Vincent's guys, Van spends time practicing with his weapons at a range. All mob guys carry, but few can be bothered to put in enough time to know how to put bullets in the right places.

Back in Denny's apartment, Marv tried to convince you a night attack on Jimmy's castle would be the smart way to go. You told him going ninja was the quick way to breaking an ankle jumping down from the high wall that surrounds Jimmy's place. The grounds are patrolled by dogs at night and getting your throat ripped out is a hard way to go. The closer you get to the big house, despite your muscle and your surprises and an old man for a hostage, now you wish you'd taken your chances with the guard dogs' teeth.

Marv slows the Cutlass for a moment so Van can see Vincent sitting beside you in the back. As soon as he sees him, Van signals Chico to open the gate. Chico carries a bolt-action Remington Model 700 sniper rifle with a long can — a noise suppressor screwed into the end of the long gun's muzzle — and he quickly steps up to slide the heavy iron gate back on its wheels. Chico's weapon has a bipod folded under the barrel for stability and accuracy on the long shots. It's a standard issue police rifle used for containment, but it's a slow, stupid choice for a sentry on a gate. Assuming you get to live long enough to fight your way out past this dunce, it's not a good time to tell him he should be making smarter hardware choices.

As the Cutlass slides up the driveway, you spot Freejack Jack. He's out on the front lawn in cutoffs tossing a disc back and forth with a pretty girl in a barely-there-in-the-right-spots tankini.

Twist and Juan, each carrying Uzis, run out and herd Jack and his squeeze toward the guesthouse by the pool in back of the mansion. You look through the back window and catch a glimpse of Chico talking into a walkie-talkie. Jimmy already knows you're here with his father. There doesn't seem to be any other muscle around, though, so Jimmy's not worried about you and he must not expect trouble from the Romanians until after the funeral for Boss Cob and his kids.

Twist and Juan stick too close together as they follow Freejack Jack and the tankini girl. That might come in handy. Twist and Juan are best friends, but they joke around too much while on duty and stand too close together to be smart. A single spray of bullets, or a nearby explosion, could take them both out at once.

Freejack disappears out of sight around the corner of the mansion, safely out of the line of fire. When Jimmy brought Freejack Jack in, he was way outside the world of The Machine. He went to college and made no bones. He's a computer guy and the accountant. Every gang has some guys who are good at math, but he just wasn't street enough for the job. Before he moved into the guesthouse and girls started showing up, Denny told you he was sure the guy was a twink.

"No man wears cutoff jeans that short, dawg," Denny said. "I'm telling you, Jimmy wants a little strange nearby, but it's not pussy he's looking for. It's some guy's mouth-pussy."

You shrugged and had nothing to say. "Jimmy's business."

"Jimmy's done time, man," Denny persisted. "You know how that goes. Some guys go to jail and they're gay for the stay. Sometimes when they get out, they still can't pray the gay away."

When Cat Fornes got hired, Denny started speculating about Jimmy's love life again. The cage fighter's muscles were huge, but his masculine image was softened by his high voice and his lisp. Big Denny was sure Jimmy Lima was banging his bodyguard instead of Barbara. Looking back, maybe it was then that Big Denny decided to risk his life and move in on Barbara.

You didn't care then, but now you wonder if Cat Fornes got Bob's skim and took off and that's why no one's seen him. Maybe you're risking everything for nothing and you should just be running with what little cash you have on hand. If you had the courage to leave Lily drunk and asleep in that Jersey motel, you could be a bus driver in California in a month.

Maybe the skim is what Hitchcock called a MacGuffin: The one thing everybody in the movie is after but either nobody gets it or it doesn't really matter, anyway. In *Pulp Fiction*, the MacGuffin was just something shiny and valuable in a case, but Tarantino let you squirm and speculate what it might be as the body count climbed higher.

Then you think about Lily crying into your chest, looking for an out, God's blessing, forgiveness or at least escape. You think about all her talk about free will versus fate. To you, the skim is no MacGuffin. The skim matters plenty because you've got to get out of The Machine, stop being a cog and get away. You want a chance at having choices. The farther you roll up the driveway and the closer you get to the key, the less likely it seems you'll make it back down this driveway.

You've visited Jimmy's house many times, but your palms have never sweated like this. Marv wheels the big Cutlass around the fountain in the circular driveway and parks at the front door. Jimmy Lima trots down the stairs with a bandage on his neck. When Marv steps out from the driver's seat, Jimmy gives him a nod and you can't see any change in his expression. Has Marv turned on you? Jimmy only slows half a step when he spots you beside his father.

He freezes when he sees your arms are crossed with your hand under your suit jacket, but before you can speak up, Vincent takes charge for you. "Young Diaz would like to have a talk, so I think we should call a meeting, Jimmy. We can clear the air. How's the neck?"

Of course Jimmy already told the boss that you stabbed him in the neck with a fork.

"It's fine, Pop." He rubs his neck, nonetheless. If he could set you on fire by sheer force of will, you'd already be screaming.

You had hoped Jimmy would keep his father out of the loop as long as he was in the hospital, but that was too much to hope for. It's not just that Vincent wasn't flustered when you showed up. He must have *expected* you.

He's right. The trick is not minding and Vincent has that knack. You've got Marv on your side and a couple of surprises to come, but despite the SIG in your hand, Vincent is still the man driving this bus.

You get out on your side, closer to the house, your hand still under your jacket, as Marv helps Vincent out of the car on the other side.

"Where's Paulie?" Jimmy asks.

Vincent leans on the Cutlass's trunk for support and barks out a laugh. "These guys took him out easy. I didn't hear a thing. My hearing's not so good anymore, but still, very pro. I didn't know for sure he had me until he walked in my hospital room. Very smooth. Jesus, you'll be a real loss to the organization."

You ignore the compliment and the threat. "Paulie's alive and tied to a gurney. He probably still thinks there's a Romanian on the door waiting for an excuse to cut him up."

Jimmy points at Marv. "You turning your back on us, too, Marvin? You throw in with the little Cuban? What? Did he tell you a story and you believed him? You should never believe a word from this guy."

"This isn't about you or Jesus, Jimmy. This is about *family*. Jake killed my brother. I know he's here. You know what I've got to do." To everyone's surprise, Marv is crying. He pulls out the Smith & Wesson ahead of schedule. He doesn't point the pistol at anyone — it's down by his side in a listless hand. "Give me Jake Cibrian so I can avenge my brother and I'm done."

You don't have time to shout a warning or get the situation back under control. Jimmy's still pointing at Marv, two fingers out and thumb up like he's a kid pretending he's holding a pistol.

"You're already done," Jimmy says. He raises his other hand to his ear and tugs the lobe. Marv's head explodes with a very precise one-shot kill from a .308 round.

You underestimated Chico. He must be putting time in at the range with Van. You throw yourself to the ground behind the Cutlass before Chico can chamber the next round. Your gun is out but Jimmy stomps on your arm. You might have kicked out and taken Jimmy down with you, but there's Bald Van with the SPAS-12's muzzle digging into your back. You never saw Bald Van coming. You were focused on the wrong details, watching faces instead of watching your back. You drop the SIG.

You walked in with an old man for a hostage and Marv for muscle — a guy you conned into being an ally. Now you have nothing.

Almost nothing.

You still have hope until Van tells you to get up. At the top of the stairs stands a big man with cold eyes. Big Denny De Molina, the friend and adopted brother you killed. It's hard to imagine you ever worried about having to kill him again. He's on crutches with one leg in a plaster cast that reaches from his right ankle to his crotch. His lower lip trembles and you take in at a glance that when you nearly killed him, you hurt him in ways no cast can heal. But that's not the crazy part.

Big Denny is flanked by two beautiful women. One is Jimmy's wife, Barbara. She is the woman Big Denny loves so much, he tried to kill you to protect their secret. But that's not the craziest part.

The other woman is the only woman on earth you'd kill for. Lily is dressed entirely in red, down to her three-inch, come-hump-me pumps. But you're the one who's really fucked, aren't you? In the next few minutes, before you're murdered, it might be nice to figure out if Lily is the one woman on the planet worth dying for. That's pretty far out there, but still not the craziest part.

"Take it easy, Jesus," Lily says. "I talked to Daddy and Papa Vincent. They have a plan. We're all going to get out of this alive as long as you don't do anything stupid." Lily says that like she believes it. That's the craziest part.

YOU'VE COME UNDONE

Pete and Jake are waiting in the great room. In most houses, this would be called the living room, but not in a castle like Jimmy's. From the front window, beyond Vincent's Cutlass and the fountain, the vast front lawn — the "grounds" when they're this big — stretch out to the inner gate. It's a long way to run and, assuming you can get out of here, Chico will have a few shots at you before you cross the lawn. You probably won't even make it as far as the fountain.

Bald Van is thorough. He takes your trench coat and removes your chain and hockey stick tool. He takes the knife from your sock and, careful not to scratch the white wood, places it delicately on the Baby Grand piano beside your SIG Sauer P220 and the extra mags . You've eaten with these guys, played pool and poker with them and worked beside them. They know your usual weapons and where you keep them.

Van leans on the wall by the window but keeps his gaze fixed on you. He flicks the shotgun muzzle an inch and waggles his eyebrows and you take a seat. Big Denny lowers his bulk to the loveseat awkwardly, his broken leg straight out. Pete and Jake sit on a sectional couch and glare at you. Jimmy and Lily sit behind you along the back wall. Vincent sits across from you so he can look into your eyes.

"You've forced my hand, Jesus," Vincent begins. "I'm going to have to air the family's dirty laundry, though maybe that's for the best anyway. Baldy, you sweep this room? No bugs?"

Van nods.

"For sure?"

"Swept for insects twice, sir. The Feds don't have a prayer."

"Fine."

Pete trembles as he stares at you. His fists are clenched. "What were you thinking bringing my daughter into this?"

If they're going to kill you anyway, you may as well go out with style. "She likes black eyes."

"What?"

"Denny gave me black eyes and Lily found me irresistible. I understand your confusion. At first, I thought she meant that she liked black guys."

Jake guffaws but Pete silences him with a hard look. Vincent at least has the grace to smile. From behind you, Lily whispers for you to shut up.

"Yeah, better you shut up, Jesus," Vincent says good-naturedly. "This is the point in your story where all the interested parties gather and things get explained, just like in an old Nero Wolfe detective story. Only you're no detective. You think you're smart, but you're not so smart. You're the guy things happen to. I'm the guy who makes things happen. Understand?"

"So far I do. Speak slow."

"You punk!" Pete rises and steps close, drawing back his hand. He hasn't taken his ring off. You imagine that ring will hurt when it connects and you wince and turn your head, hoping to roll with the expected blow. The strike never comes. When you open your eyes, Lily stands between you and her father. She says nothing. She just shakes her head and Pete lowers his hand.

"Everybody have a seat," Vincent says. "I'm going to break this down for you. There are complications coming our way because of a lack of discipline and loyalty in the ranks. This, I will not tolerate. You don't get a house like this, Jimmy, by being sloppy. You especially don't continue to keep it if you're going to be sloppy. We've gotten weak and lazy. If we're going to grow, we need to toughen up and clear out the dead wood. With discipline, we could be so much bigger than we are. For the rest of The Machine to work better, we've got to make examples of those who would fail us. Harsh discipline builds a legacy. Remember this: I am not the bad guy here. I'm the fucking king. I make the tough decisions today to make sure there's a castle here tomorrow."

Vincent turns to Pete. "Speaking of things that make me sad, the kid played you with an old scam and that's one thing that's got you pissed. The second thing that's got you pissed is that your only daughter is still hanging out with this loser."

Vincent turns to you. "Pete came to me months ago and asked me for permission to whack you, Jesus. I said no. I told him the little guy could be useful and if there's a shit job that comes up that could get him killed, then maybe I'd use you. I also told him that Lily is a beautiful young woman and she should make her own choices…up to a point. Let them date and be young and feel their wild oats and later, Lily will settle down with someone of substance."

Lily crosses her arms and looks sour.

"Don't even," Pete says. "This is not the place or the time for you to be the rebellious kid. I'm sorry, Vincent. I spoiled her."

Vincent turns to Pete and shakes his head. "That's not what you should be apologizing for, Pete. Jake tells me that as soon as you fell for Jesus's grift — magically making counterfeit money out of real bills — you were plotting against Jimmy and telling yourself it was for me and The Machine's own good. Think about it a minute longer and it's clear you were thinking of promoting yourself."

Pete glares at Jake, but before he can move, Jake stands up, pulls his pistol and levels it at Pete's midsection. Pete sits back on the couch, his mouth a thin line, while Jake reaches into Pete's jacket and removes his pistol and sticks it in his own belt.

"You thought you saw an opening," Vincent says. "You thought I was weak. I'm old. You, of all people, should know the difference between old and weak, Pete."

"Dad, can't we deal with this somewhere else?" Jimmy says. "I don't want this to happen in my own home. Marv's corpse is bleeding on my front step, for Christ's sake!"

"Shut up, Jimmy. I'll get to you in a minute. Ordinarily, I'd agree. But we're all here and I just had prostate surgery, so you'll excuse me if I'm not up for any more travel and shenanigans today. Where were we?"

"You just made Pete aware that I'm going to be buried with him," you say in a cheerful, helpful tone.

"Pete's an old friend. I'm not going to let Jake shoot him in front of Lily. Lily's like a granddaughter to me. It's not that kind of day. But Pete? You disappoint me. Deep. Jimmy's the heir apparent, but you would have still been his chief adviser when I give up the ghost. That's not going to happen now. You're demoted. You get to keep your book, but I'm going to need to take ten percent more starting now. Also, the after-hours club is all mine. Any questions?"

Pete looks at the carpet and shakes his head.

"I didn't fucking think so," the old man says genially. "Jake, put the heater away. You look a little too eager to use it. You were loyal, so you'll be working with me from now on. Paulie's a good guy, but obviously too stupid since instead of being here he's tied to a hospital bed. You're my new driver, Jake. Congrats."

"I just want to pipe up here, sir," you point out, "Lily doesn't want to see *me* killed in front of her, either. And you should know I'm a bleeder, Jimmy. I'm really going to mess up this fine carpet."

"We'll use a plastic bag, then," Big Denny says.

A plastic bag. That cold bastard. You wish you'd never told Denny the truth about your history in that terrible basement in Florida. You wish you'd never saved him. You wish lots of things. Except for getting Lily, your wishes have never come true. Now that's slipping away, too.

Vincent ignores Denny. He's back to watching your eyes so you stare back. All the lies are out. All you can do is own them and wait for your moment. Your moment better come quickly, before Denny steps behind you and slips a plastic bag over your head and seals it off with a zip tie around your throat.

Vincent shifts uncomfortably in his seat and takes a pill bottle from his jacket, opens it, and knocks back a couple oblong tablets, swallowing the painkillers dry. "You think just because I went under the knife that *now's* your opening? I'll give up The Machine when I choose. I didn't work my way up for so long to have one of you apes just step in the moment I hit a speed bump. I'm bigger than cancer, boys. I've dodged bullets for years. I sure as shit can deal with you humps. Get it?"

The men nod. You allow a shrug. You consider telling Vincent that you just wanted the skim so you could get out and far away. You didn't have any designs on a quick promotion. The old man doesn't look so genial anymore, so you shut up.

"Next, just so you all understand once and forever that I am not weak, *I* gave the order for Bob to get whacked. "

The blood drains from your face. You can feel it.

"I told Jimmy to order Jesus to whack Bobby. It tore my heart out to do it. My own step son. I never thought of him like that. I always, always just called Bobby my son. But he got greedy. I could even stand that. I understand that. There's too thin a line between ambition and greed. Under the right circumstances, Bob might even have been a good boss someday. But he had his gambling problem. I can't abide weakness. Stupid, I'm used to. Weakness, I can't stand. But worse, Bob was talking to the feds."

Mouths drop open around the room. Even Bald Van, who you thought wasn't listening, looks more pale. He leans back against the window pane, cooling the back of his head.

"So…" you venture, "this was never about the skim."

"Nope. I could tolerate a little of that. I gave him rope. I knew about his gambling debts in Atlantic City. I wanted him to grow up and deal with it himself. If I had stepped in earlier, maybe the feds wouldn't have gotten their hooks into him so deep. They picked him up with a limo outside a casino in Atlantic City and gave him a dream of escape from us, after we gave him so much."

"How did you know for sure?" you ask, thinking of how Vincent car bombed three guys, knowing only one of them was the rat.

Vincent shrugs. "There's lots more going on behind the scenes than you imagine, kid. Like all little guys, you think the game is all about you. You're the worst kind of dummy. You're the kind of dummy who thinks he's smart. You think all I do is sit back and drink wine while you run your little errands and it's your world. Meanwhile? I'm a business man. I cultivate people. I have meetings. One day I get a phone call from an FBI agent. He tells me I've got a rat and for an exorbitant amount of money, he'll show me proof who it is. I met with this bastard, heard a tape and saw some photos and I was still crying when I paid that FBI bastard his money for the information. I would have excommunicated Bob and left it at that if it weren't for the feds. Bob threatened the entire Machine. Bob wanted out, but he wanted us to fund his retirement and then live high off the hog in some WitSec program. A fat guy like Bob, he wasn't going to testify and let the feds ship him off to be a shoe salesman in Arizona with a new name. He wanted to get out, to send us all to jail where we wouldn't chase after him and keep the skim, too."

"My brother was a rat?" Jimmy looks ashen.

"Easy, Jimmy. When I told you to have the little Cuban whack Bob, you didn't fight me so hard. You thought this was just about the skim. You couldn't have loved Bob that much. You're not so different from Pete, here. You saw your ascent in Bob's fall."

"You told me to give Jesus the job. I don't question your orders, Dad."

"Sh. *Sh!* Don't pretend it was loyalty. Sure, there's that, but it was self-interest more. That's the problem. We aren't a machine until you get that we are bigger than you. The Machine is bigger than any one of your little dreams. Which brings us to you, little man."

"I'd like to point out that I'm almost 5'9"," you say.

"Good for you. Your legs reach all the way to the ground. Your problem is you got your head in the clouds. Diaz, Lily tells me you want out of The Machine, too. You saw the skim as a way out. You wanted to take Bob's skim and whirl our little Lily far away from all that we've given her."

"Would you have let me go if I'd come to you?"

Vincent laughs. "You were in the army. Did they just let you go when you asked to go home?"

You shrug. "I got out. At first I thought all I had to do was kiss a sergeant. Turns out that doesn't work with all sergeants. Some, you have to break their jaws."

"You're a funny guy, Jesus."

"You say that like pretty girls say they like a guy with a sense of humor. Then they end up dating some prick with money whose jokes are lame."

"Why am I here for this?" Lily says. "You said it was going to be all right. You said I could be in the room. I thought if I was in the room, that meant you were serious that everything was going to be okay. You'd give us the key to the storage locker and your blessing and we'd walk out of here. You promised me everything would be all right, *Abuelo!*"

"Shut up, kiddo. I'm not your *abuelo*. Since Pete has proved himself disloyal, sadly, I'm now simply your father's pissed off employer. I said everything would be all right. I didn't say *how*. I got a machine to oil if we're all going to stay out of federal prison, so you just shut up. You aren't hearing me. You're too pretty for your own good, Lily. Always were. We have always spoiled you and this is our reward. You think everything is just about you, too. You think the money for your car, your apartment, your education…that it all falls from the sky and you stay clean? Nobody's clean. Everybody has a dirty hand in."

Lily steps back and leans her hip against your shoulder. It's a silent apology that's way too late. Moving slowly so Bald Van won't blow your head off, you offer her your hand and she takes it.

Vincent sighs. "Young love. The most stupid love of all. Lily, you got the curves but you don't have the brains. You don't understand what it takes to do what we have to do. I had my own son killed. What makes you think you're so special?"

Lily looks up and with a defiant sneer you know too well says, "I killed Harv with a frying pan."

Vincent didn't know that. You can see it in his face. Jake must have told him *you* killed Marv's twin.

Pete leans forward, his head in his hands. "What am I going to tell your mother? Oh, God…."

"Shut up!" Vincent yells for the first time.

Jimmy smacks you in the back of the head as he steps in from behind your chair. "What the hell is wrong with you? How could you let Lily get in this deep? I thought you said you loved her?"

"She killed Harv with a frying pan because she loved me," you reply. "The rot in The Machine is deeper than you think, Jimmy. Lots of us want out. As soon as Marv and Harv heard about the skim, they were both ready to kill for it to get out and away. Harv was going to kill me to get the key and Lily loves me so much, she killed for me."

Lily squeezes your hand and you feel her warmth flow back into you. The ice in your stomach goes away and you feel more strength. "Marv was going to kill me, but then he thought Jake killed his brother and all he wanted was to get revenge and get out with the skim, too."

"Who told him *I* killed Harv?" Jake asks, bewildered.

"Oh, who do you think, fuckface?" Jimmy says. He fishes out the locker key from his pocket. "Take a good look, Jesus. This is the closest you'll ever get to Panama Bob's skim and the cozy little life you've been plotting with Lily. Millions of women in New York City and you gotta… It's just not done! If Lily weren't the headstrong little princess we all allowed her to be, if anybody in this goddamn room asked permission —"

"Marv was really gonna kill me?" Jake looks at you with new hate in his eyes, but that's okay. He was pretty much full up with hate for you, anyway.

You manage to smile back at him. "It's human nature, Jake. Nobody likes you. And everybody dreams of escaping their regular job, winning the lottery and getting away where there's no boss and we can all live the lives we see in movies. The end part. The happily ever after. We've all got that in us. We've all been sold happily ever after but that's just for movies, I guess."

Vincent's eyes narrow. "And Denny? He rearranged your face pretty good, so can I trust him, or is he a happily ever after guy, too? Was Denny going to kill you for the key, grab the skim and get away from us? Who can I trust, Jesus? If you speak the truth, I'll know. I need to know."

You nod toward Jake. "You can trust him, but he's a moron." You tilt your head toward Bald Van at the window. "You can trust him and he's no idiot, but in a few minutes, he won't be part of the equation."

Vincent's forehead furrows, but before he can interject, your gaze falls on your old friend on the couch, the brother you chose. "Of all of us, Denny's motives were the most pure. Denny didn't care about the skim. He was just trying to get me out of the way to make sure I wouldn't tell anybody his secret. I wish he could have trusted me with the secret. If he had, none of us would be in this mess now and maybe me and Lily would already be living our happily ever after."

Harv and Marv and Panama Bob won't stir up any great sadness in you. You'd planned to kill Marv before this was done, anyway. But the innocent civilian? Denny's neighbor? She didn't have to die. You don't know her name, but you'll never be able to forget her bloody head and her dead eyes staring back at you with accusation.

"What's Big Denny's big secret, Jesus?" Vincent asks. "Convince me. It's time I cleaned The Machine and got it working right. No machine can work right if it's got too many complex parts. Help me clean The Machine and I promise you this: You'll die easy."

"Denny's a loyal cog in The Machine," you say evenly. "He didn't try to kill me for the skim. He tried to kill me so I wouldn't tell anybody that he's in love with Jimmy's wife."

You should expect the punch, but it comes quicker than you can think. Jimmy drives his fist into the side of your face. Maybe you hear a crunch, you're not sure. Certainly, your left eye is going to stay blackened for a long time with all this ongoing abuse. It would if you lived that long, anyway.

Jimmy starts screaming for Barbara but it's Denny he wheels on next. He runs at Denny, who doesn't move from his place on the loveseat. Jimmy's almost on him when Denny lifts one of his crutches and drives the point into Jimmy's solar plexus. Jimmy goes down, clutching his stomach and gasping for air.

Barbara heard Jimmy scream her name and comes running. She stands over him, watching her husband writhe on the floor. He can't talk yet, but he reaches out, his palm up, pleading with his eyes as he struggles for breath.

Barbara doesn't rush to her husband's side. Instead she watches him flop around like a fish on a dock. Her little smile proves that sometimes you do tell the truth.

Jimmy's open palm closes and he points at Barbara. His fingers make a gun. Jimmy's getting his breath back and he uses it to scream. "Kill her! Kill Denny! Kill them both! Do Jesus, too! Do them all! Clean house! Clean house!"

Jake pulls his pistol out again, pointing it first at Denny, then at Barbara. Vincent struggles to stand. It pains him, but he's shouting at Jake, "Don't shoot! Don't shoot! Not here! Not *here*! Not *yet*! No!"

You want to get up in front of Lily, for the little good that will do, but Bald Van trains the SPAS-12 on you and shakes his head.

Pete leaps up from the couch to lunge at Jake. Jimmy shoots him in the shoulder before the bookie can take another step. Pete cries out and spins to the floor, holding his shoulder.

"*Papi!*" Lily screams.

The wound doesn't look bad from where you sit, but everybody knows that once you commit to shooting somebody, you empty that mag so they can never get up and come after you.

Jake's committed to the craziness of the moment now. He draws a bead on Barbara. He's only listening to Jimmy's screams, blocking out everyone else. Jake must have never imagined he'd be ordered to whack the boss's wife. He hesitates and in that moment, Barbara looks her would-be killer in the eyes and crosses the floor to sit on the loveseat beside Denny. She wraps her arms around him and the big lug kisses her. It's the most romantic fucking thing you've ever seen. You could never have dreamed the most romantic gesture you've witnessed in your life would involve Big Denny De Molina.

Lily has slipped behind you by the bookcase full of fake books, her eyes on Jake, screaming to be spared and pleading for her father who writhes on the floor.

"Kill them both, goddammit! Do it!" Jimmy bawls, struggling to his feet.

Jake takes another breath to brace himself for what he's about to do. Barbara and Denny are about to die. The SPAS-12 booms. Jake leaves a bloody smear on the wall as he slides to the floor out of sight behind the big couch.

Your eyes are on the key. *Happily ever after.* It's there, embodied in the little key on the floor at your feet where Jimmy dropped it. Sure, they'll find you wherever you go — earth's not that big — but you could at least escape with Lily for a little while. Ever after isn't in your cards, but escaping for a little while is better than a lot of people ever experience.

However, your prospects to survive the minute are poor. "*Not here, not yet,*" Vincent had said, but soon, obviously. Vincent has the key and now he knows how deep the rot goes. You've got nothing left to give him besides the location of the locker, but since you figured it out, surely Vincent has figured it out, too. Vincent doesn't need you. He'll kill you. He'll clean house just to make sure no one questions that he's still the alpha dog and he's smarter than everybody.

No doubt Vincent is smarter than you on the fly, but you did have some time to prepare. You glance at your watch. The Romanians are late.

TAKE IT

*C*rash! The Romanians hit the outer gate.

The great room's floor-to-ceiling windows provide an excellent view of the battlefield. The crash is eighty yards away, but the commotion inside the house ends as everyone swivels to look out to see Doom hauling ass up the driveway. A big armoured cube truck — a United States Post Office vehicle — hits the gate and the sheet of iron bars bursts almost all the way inward.

Figures. An armoured truck used by banks is a tough get, but the armoured postal trucks sit in rows beside the regular delivery vehicles, waiting to be stolen. The outer gate is heavier than the driver expected and the truck has to back up and take another run at it before he crashes through. Had the driver committed to hitting the gate at full speed, the element of surprise wouldn't already be slipping away. Two cars following the truck too closely have to wheel out of the way, their tires screeching and smoking to make room for the second run at the iron obstacle.

"It's a bunch of white guys!" Bald Van yells.

"It's the *Banda*," Vincent says.

An alarm starts up that sounds like a submarine klaxon. From the first floor, running feet pound through the house and, below, Juan and Twist come into view as they run down the front steps. They deke around the Cutlass's back bumper and kneel behind the fountain in the center of the circular driveway. That should be decent cover for them to pick off the Romanians as they pour out of their cars.

Jimmy forgets his adulterous wife and stares out the window in shock. "We got defenses that will make these bitches shit kittens." Even as he says it, five more guards carrying heavy ordnance — four AKs and one guy with a Rocket Propelled Grenade — run out the front of the house to join Juan and Twist. Three kneel in defensive positions behind the fountain. Another squats behind the Cutlass's trunk and the guy with the RPG takes cover behind the car's engine block and shoulders his weapon.

The truck's engine roars, using power rather than speed to slowly push through the steel of the first gate's moorings. It plows a path on to the estate with two cars tight behind, bumper to bumper to bumper. Cracks of gunfire begin. The guys in the back of the second car lean out of their windows to fire at the house. Vincent steps back from the windows.

"Never mind, Dad. The windows are bulletproof," Jimmy says.

"No such thing as bulletproof," Vincent says. "You don't know what they've got in the back of that mail truck."

"We can handle this. Get to the panic room till this blows over. I built this house like a fortress. We don't call it the castle for nothing."

The Boss looks at you. "Is this supposed to be the cavalry coming over the hill for you?"

"We had a talk," you admit. "The Romanians are very angry and vengeance drives a postal truck."

The old man is still ice. He smirks and shrugs. "So you don't just want out, after all. You're a fucking traitor to The Machine, out to destroy us."

"I'm the slipped gear."

Vincent ignores you. "C'mon, Pete. We got a safe spot while the boys take care of business. Barbara? Lily? This isn't your world. Let's go. You've got to be a young idiot with too much testosterone and too many bullets to stay out here and deal with this shit."

The boss has a right to look untroubled. That RPG will tear the vehicles into metal shards, charred flesh and bits of bone. The guys with the Kalashnikovs will clean up the *Banda* before they get anywhere near the front door.

The guys behind the fountain wisely hold their fire, waiting for closer, more realistic targets. However, from behind the inner gate, Chico does a very macho, idiotic thing he probably learned from movies. He stands behind the gate's bars and levels the big Remington at the truck. You can't hear the rifle with that big can on it, suppressing the report, but you see Chico rock from the rifle's kick. He looks like a kid with an air rifle plinking at a tin can with a bb gun.

There's enough space between the outer and inner gates that, this time, the van gets some speed up before it hits the second gate. You're sure Chico will get chewed up under the big truck's wheels in an ugly death, but you're wrong. Nervous and fooling with the rifle bolt too long, he has just enough time to take one step toward safety when the mail truck hits the second gate. When it busts in, the wall of metal sweeps him away like it's a giant's open hand. Everyone stands still, transfixed, as Chico is thrown aside, his body and brains shattered against the wall of the gatehouse. Marv is avenged in a grisly fashion.

"*Ooh!* I thought they'd wait until after the kids' funerals, at least," Jimmy says absently.

"I was sure they weren't going to hit us till at least tonight, after dark." Vincent sounds like a general, surveying a battle, safe behind the front lines. Or so he thinks.

Time to pipe up. "The *Banda* had some inside information, Mr. Lima."

"Shut up!" Jimmy can't look away from the battle. One of his guys opens up. The AK fire is close, but the gunfire is outgoing, not incoming. "This is already over. We can hold off a hundred guys with half a dozen."

You rise from your chair and Bald Van wheels from the window's distractions, the SPAS-12 up and ready to send you bleeding and flying, just like Jake Cibrian. You can't take your eyes off the shotgun's muzzle. Its darkness looks like the future.

"Run Lily! Get out of here! The Romanians are coming. They want vengeance for their boss and his little kids and they're going to get it. Vincent, in a moment, you're going to wonder if murdering a rat son and oiling your machine was worth it. I know you don't care about the money because you've already got plenty. You care if *we* care about the money. You wanted to know who would stay and who would go if they had a chance at a blank slate. Surprise! Anybody with imagination wants out. The Italians have it right. At least they call their mobs 'families.' You call us your Machine. We ain't cogs and gears. We want to make choices, too. We want to be free."

Vincent looks at Bald Van. "Christ, Van. He's making speeches like fucking Castro over there. Why haven't you blown that little motherfucker's head off, yet?"

The Boss is on the move. It's time.

Bald Van shrugs and raises the shotgun.

"Uh-uh-uh!" You raise one fist high above your head and, perplexed, Van lowers the muzzle a few inches, trying to decipher your play.

"Vincent, you should know that not all the parts on your precious Cutlass Supreme are original anymore."

You open your hand to reveal your keys. On the key ring is a bright red car remote that has big googly eyes and a cartoony smile glued to it. Denny bought the novelty car remote from the same street vendor who sold him the disposable camera on that sunny summer day you took Lily to Coney Island. Denny recognizes it from his own arsenal. With his good leg he kicks, throwing all his weight backward and tipping the loveseat over backward, taking Barbara over with him.

Vincent processes what you said about his car and has just enough time to let his jaw drop slack. Jimmy, oblivious to the real danger, turns only half a step from the window. Bald Van raises the SPAS-12 and tightens up, ready to blow you apart as you throw yourself backward and cover your head with your arms as the shotgun booms. The buckshot cuts the air over your head.

You press the remote's button. The receiver in the Cutlass's trunk detonates the Semtex.

A bright, white flash. BOOM!

You feel the thud of the bomb's concussion through your body as the floor shakes under you. The roar deafens. Your eardrums whine in shock at the concussion.

The remote in Denny's freezer gave you the idea for this frontal assault in daylight. Denny had a brick of C-4 stashed in there, but it was the Romanians who helped you and Marv pack the trunk and wheel wells with Semtex.

The Romanians knew Vincent's car, of course. If you and Marv hadn't driven straight to the *Banda* with the Cutlass, they surely would have shot you in the head when you showed up at their headquarters. When you offered them vengeance for their boss and his two dead children, they didn't smile. They nodded grimly and got to work. You weren't really sure the Romanian electrician who wired the car bomb had done a satisfactory job until the bomb's blast rocked the mansion.

Time warps and you don't know how fast or slow it's passing as the Earth's turning gears of time pause and hitch. Eventually, after who knows how long, you shake your head and roll on to your back. You spot the Baby Grand tipped on one side and roll toward it. You're screaming for Lily, but your voice sounds muffled and far away. You can't find your SIG.

When you chance a peek over the piano, you find that the outdoors is now indoors. Something's on fire and white smoke rolls over you, getting thicker by the minute. The mansion's stone facade has melted away and much of the second floor is gone.

A huge shape with four legs looms haltingly out of the smoke. It's Big Denny De Molina, covered in ash except where his bleeding wounds trickle down the side of his head. His left shoulder sports a deep gash, too. He looks like an angry ghost on crutches. He's got your pistol in his fist. That's it. You're dead. Goodbye Jesus Salvador Umberto Luis Diaz.

You wonder what happens next. When you open your eyes, will you be in Hell? Is it like the priests say? Everlasting pain and flame that burns but never consumes? Will Denny's dead neighbor look down on you from heaven and piss on you from fluffy white clouds, laughing at your pain? Or will Hell mean you're trapped again in the Bug Man's basement, this time forever? Will Tia Marta be a devil holding a plastic bag in one claw and a burning whip in the other? Will all the scars on your back open and never close?

Or will nothing come next? Is Death just darkness and nothingness, a return to the blissful unconsciousness of whatever you were before you were born? That wouldn't be so bad, except there will be no Lily. Lily makes you want to live.

When you open your eyes, Big Denny is leaning on his crutches and Barbara stands by her man. The way Barbara looks at Denny, they're like teenagers who have just shared their last first kiss. You wish Lily looked at you that way, but maybe you've still got a chance at becoming the man who is worthy of that look. Denny grips the SIG by the barrel and holds your weapon out to you. "The pussy's out of the bag now, man. No point killing you now."

You take your pistol and, when helps you up, you discover your switchblade at your feet. Denny tips his head toward the rear of the great room. Barbara leads the way to the bookcases. She steps over Vincent's legs to do it.

The Boss is slumped against a wall. His shirt is so bloody, it's sucked to him. The old guy is still alive, but the way he looks up at you, you wonder how many of you he sees. He gives you a brave half-smile and closes his eyes.

You don't look back. "Lily? *Lily!*"

Barbara slides the bookcase back to reveal the panic room's steel door. Barbara knocks three times. "Open up! It's me!"

Two locks click open. Lily peers out, her eyes wet. Tears stream down her cheeks as she points behind her. She dragged Pete in there in the confusion of the Romanians' attack, but Pete's just a heap on the floor now. His eyes are open. Even in death, his eyes are shark's eyes.

Lily's cool hands clasp your face and you pull her to you. Your hearing is recovering. That distant screaming is Jimmy Lima. He must have fallen through the floor as his castle walls collapsed. He's screaming that his legs are broken.

Barbara covers her ears and leans into Denny. You knew Jimmy was mean, but in her face you see yourself the night you killed Tia Marta. Barbara has no pity or regret left for her husband. All that's left for Jimmy's demise is...relief?

"That screaming will make it easier for the Romanians to find him through the smoke. Don't worry, Barbara. They won't let the fire take him. They'll want the satisfaction."

There's more gunfire. It sounds like it's coming from behind the house.

You grab Lily's shoulder and pull, but Denny's big paw holds you back. He holds out the locker key. "Tómelo." *Take it.*

"You're sure?"

Denny grins. "The cops will be here soon. Barb was talking about redecorating, anyway. We'll stay. It was always the plan that she'd get the house in the divorce. Now we're going to get everything. And besides," he looks down at his leg and his shoulder wound, "I'm not up to running. Running is your thing."

You take the key. "Gracias. Sorry about the leg, bro."

"I should have trusted you about Barb, but you always cheated me on splitting the restaurant bills."

"You...The restaurant tabs? Really?"

"I can do math better than you think. If a dude will take me on the little things, I can't trust him with something as big as messing with the under-boss's wife."

You want to say something. There isn't time. Lily pulls you away and Barbara pulls Denny into the panic room. The door slides closed and the locks click.

You've thrown a brother away again.

THE GARAGE

A couple of the *Banda,* Ion and Mihai, are waiting for you in Jimmy Lima's underground garage. Before you can say anything, Mihai, the tall black-bearded Romanian who wired the Semtex, claps you on the shoulder. "Jesus!"

"I told you, it's pronounced, *Hay-soose.*"

"Sure. Big bang boom, huh?"

"You have no idea."

Ion, looking amped up, steps from behind Mihai. He carries an Uzi and you wonder if he got it from one of Jimmy's fallen guards. He gives you the fish eye. You're glad you have the SIG tucked into the back of your waistband so your hands are empty and he can't take anything you do as a sign of aggression.

Mihai gives you a broad smile. "The *Banda* thanks you for your help. You did the right thing. Boss Cob and his children will rest in peace."

"You're welcome," you say. "The ride I came in on is a jigsaw of thousands of tiny pieces. I need one of Jimmy's cars. It won't be long before the cops are on the way. We made too big a bang boom."

Mihai laughs and points you toward a sporty Toyota. "Yeah, we gotta finish our business and get everybody out. The keys are in it, Jesus." Behind the Toyota is an older model Ford sedan.

You tear open the Toyota's driver's side door and yell at Lily to jump in. You climb behind the wheel. In your rearview mirror, you catch Ion and Mihai running for the far side of the garage. Lily's cool hand covers yours as you're about to turn the ignition.

You duck your head. A green and blue wire snakes out under the steering column and disappears under the dash. "Sons of bitches! The Romanians had a little bit of Semtex left over. Just enough to blow us back to a basement in Florida."

"What?"

"Never mind. We're about to conduct a science experiment to see how stable Semtex is." You reach under the dash and rip the wires free. "Put your seatbelt on." You pause and hand Lily the blue and green wires. "Better keep your head down and hold these wires apart, okay?"

Ion yells out to you from the darkness. "Go! Go! The police will be here soon! We're clearing out in a few minutes!"

You roll down your window. "What?"

Ion steps out into view. "I said — "

You gun the engine and, to Ion's disappointment, you're still here. Ion's face snaps shut into a grimace of hate and frustration and he's pulling the Uzi up as you slip into reverse and press the accelerator into the floorboard. The Toyota jumps backward. Ion raises his weapon to take you out but hesitates when he realizes that even if he shoots you in the head, the momentum of the car will still run him down. That moment is all you need. He leaps to the side, you twist the wheel and slam his body into a pillar. The thug is pinned upright at the waist. The shock doesn't take him. Instead, he screams.

You roll out of the Toyota and come up into a crouch and raise the SIG. You put Ion out of his misery with one shot through his forehead.

Mihai rises up behind the Ford. He doesn't have time to reach for the Beretta in his shoulder holster. Your aim is already locked on the center of his chest. You take the Beretta from him and hand it to Lily. She holds it as if you just handed her a full ashtray.

"Mihai," you say, "I'm having a pretty bad day, man."

"Mine's worse," he says. He puts his hands high over his head.

"Why? We had a deal."

He shrugs, staring at your pistol as if, through sheer concentration, he can transform it into a wad of cotton candy. "A guy like you? An enforcer who can turn his back on his own people? You did the right thing helping us avenge the children, but...it was decided."

"That makes no sense. You knew I was getting out, anyway."

Mihai shrugs. "Clean slate. A guy like you — "

"Yeah, a guy like me.... The best friend I ever had just told me in not so many words that I'm a piece of shit a few minutes ago. Turn around and get on your knees."

Mihai does as he's told, but he asks, trying to get in one last dig, "Was Denny wrong?"

"There were...circumstances, but no, he's not totally wrong." Then you see the double-cross. "I didn't say it was Denny."

"Um..."

"You called me *Jee-zuzz*. You don't think I know a Judas by now?" You stick the SIG's barrel along his cheek so he can hear its cold mouth whisper promises of a dark future. "What was Denny going to give you?"

"Expansion into New Jersey and no more competition from The Machine there."

"What else?"

"Nothing else."

"You ever see *Cop Land* with Sly Stallone? Serious movie. He's a half deaf sheriff."

"I've got nothing to tell you!"

"A gunshot next to Sly's ear — *this* close, Mihai — almost deafens him. Bursting an eardrum? I'm told it hurts so much you just wish someone would do you the favor of shooting you in the head so it's over. *What else?*"

Mihai spits on the concrete and shrugs. He's an old soldier, but even the code of silence can't matter that much to a guy who's about to be executed. "Denny called us right after you left with Vincent's car. Denny's going to be The Machine's new boss. He made a better deal. He said as soon as you are dead, he'd tell us where to find a storage locker stuffed with money as a bonus."

"I'm very disappointed, Mihai."

He chances a look back at you and says, "Denny could have let you walk away. We didn't care as long as we got Jimmy and Vincent Lima. New territory and less competition from The Machine, respecting boundaries…that was more than we expected. You think Big Denny's your best friend? You really *must* be a piece of shit, huh, Jesus?"

You glance Lily's way. Her wide, wet eyes tell you this is too much for her. You've got to get her out of here.

"Mihai, I'm going to prove to you that I'm not as bad a guy as you've been told." You turn the SIG over in your hand and bring the butt down on the spot behind his ear as hard as you can. It takes a few swings, but after some flopping around, he's finally out.

"Christ, Jesus!"

"Relax. He's not dead. He's got a concussion. He might not be able to do long division any time soon. Explaining to the cops why he's here will give him a wicked headache. By the time he gets out of jail, that beard's going to be long and white. Let's go."

But Lily doesn't move. "He tried to kill us. You killed his buddy. He'll come after us. Or he'll send somebody after us from jail. Why didn't you kill him?"

Mihai is already coming around, moaning. His fingers touch his skull and come away bloody, but he's feeble, dazed and no threat now.

"I don't want to be the guy Denny knew, Lily. I want to be the guy you want to know. I'm going to be the guy who studies art with you in Spain and Paris. I'm going to be the good guy, babe."

"You're not." Lily raises Mihai's Beretta and shoots him in the head. His body shudders and is still. She keeps firing until the pistol clicks empty. The Romanian's head is a bowl full of salsa.

THE MAN YOU ARE NOT

L ily tosses Ion's Uzi into the Ford's back seat and puts the Beretta to your head. Sirens wail in the distance. "Get us out of here!"

It will probably be firefighters who arrive first, but a properly executed getaway would be a great idea, preferably at least several minutes ago. There's a little business to be taken care of first.

"You don't need that," you say, but Lily can only hear the sirens. "Put the gun down, Lily."

"What if I — "

You grab the barrel and push the slide back while twisting the Beretta upward. Trapped against the trigger guard, her index finger is pulled back painfully. Lily's shoulder drops until the muzzle points at her face.

"What if I say no? What if you shoot me in the head? I'd still love you. Don't you get it? I fucking *worship* you, Lily! You don't need a gun with me." As soon as she lets go of the Beretta, you twirl it around and give it back to her. Then you give her the storage locker key. "Got it?"

"I got it solid. Please, let's go." Lily sits back against the door and you gun the engine. She leaves the Beretta in her lap and pushes back in the passenger seat, bracing herself. No big bang boom through your temple. It would sap energy from your chivalry to point out that the Beretta is empty, so you keep that to yourself.

The Ford shoots out of the back gate and the tires squeal in protest as you twist the wheel and head toward the city. The gate's hanging open and Freejack Jack's car is gone. How many of The Machine's guys got away and how many will come back? The Machine is made of a couple of hundred associates: punks, wannabes, overseers, loan sharks, bookies, regular muscle, fronts, lawyers, enforcers and the thirty-five higher-up, made soldiers. Denny's got about the same number as the DeCavalcante crime family used to have in Jersey: about a hundred guys. The DeCavalcantes thought *The Sopranos* was based on them and a lot of guys thought they might be right. Denny will be a real threat once he reorganizes. Unlike the DeCavalcantes, The Machine will carry on. Now is the time to disappear.

"Why didn't Denny kill you himself?" Lily asks.

"Old time's sake."

"No, really."

"I'm on his to-do list, sure, but he's safe up in the panic room with no gunpowder residue on his hands. When the cops show, they'll take everybody left alive to jail, but he won't stay there long. Jimmy's lawyer is also Barbara's lawyer so he'll have high-powered legal muscle on his side. He'll just be the big guy on crutches comforting the widow as far as the cops can prove."

"So Denny will be after us, too? Really? Why won't he go to jail?"

"The lawyer will just say he was in the wrong place at the wrong time, that he was Mrs. Lima's bodyguard or something. That's what I'd do if I were him. Play dumb. All this time...I think Big Denny was pretty good at playing dumb. Nobody knows what goes on in anybody else's head, I guess. All this time, I thought I was the ninja."

"So Denny's really going to walk? That's bad for us, Jesus."

"He'll limp, but yeah. The cops will know the score but they'll call today a victory over organized crime, anyway. We kill each other and the cops pat themselves on the back for a job well done. They'll be very happy Vincent and Jimmy Lima are dead. With Pete and Bob gone, it leaves a power vacuum, but not for long. Five minutes, maybe. The Fed's anti-drug task force will throw a party with strippers and blow this weekend. It's quite a week for them, but before they're over their hangovers, The Machine will be back in business and allied with the *Banda* now."

You check the rearview mirror and realize you're making a rookie mistake. You're speeding away from a crime scene. You ease up on the gas pedal and drive a few miles over the speed limit like a normal citizen.

"What happens next?"

"When The Machine comes back, Denny will step in and be an important guy. When he double-crossed me, he bought a truce and standing with the *Banda,* though maybe not as much if we have Panama Bob's skim."

Lily opens the glove box and finds a pack of cigarettes. She puts the Beretta in there, too, and your shoulders relax as a ladder truck and a water truck scream past, heading to Jimmy's castle. It's Barbara's home now, be it ever so bombed, aflame, water-damaged and humbled.

Vincent made a classic military error: He underestimated his enemies. He didn't pull in all his available numbers from the streets to defend his perimeter. He thought he'd get another afternoon of earning out of The Machine before the war began. It's a common flaw: The arrogance of a smart guy who gets too comfortable. That attitude killed Vincent and it almost killed you. In *The Godfather*, Michael never got comfortable so he got to live, though he wiped everyone out until he ran out of friends.

In *Apocalypse Now*, Martin Sheen's soldier knew that every minute he stayed in his hotel room, Charlie was getting stronger out in the jungle. You let yourself be weak. You didn't see what was happening beyond the day-to-day bullshit. You had no idea Denny was banging Jimmy's wife. You didn't find a way to get out from under the shit assignment of whacking Panama Bob. Bob was right all along. Out on the ledge, hiding behind a gargoyle, Bob told you that the first thing they do in a conspiracy is kill the assassin. You let Denny get stronger while you dreamed on about the skim like a stupid lottery player. You are not a smart ninja.

"What are you thinking about?" Lily asks.

"Movies."

"I'm thinking about my father."

"Right. Sorry about Pete."

"Yeah." Lily's quiet for a long time. "You know those prints on my wall? The Dalis?"

"The melting clocks guy and the other one?"

"Salvador Dali. The artist's name is *Salvador Dali!*"

No idea why she's so pissed, you shut up and wait, keep your gaze on the road, and keep glancing in the rearview mirror, alert for bad news.

And Lily tells you about Salvador Dali's life. "He thought he was the reincaration of his dead brother. He was as old as I am now when he illustrated his first book. He dressed weird and acted weird, but he could paint. People know all about the melting clocks, but before that he messed around with Cubism. He could paint anything. It didn't have to be strange, but he had to be different. Some of his paintings are floating around with forged signatures. Dali sometimes got his chauffeur to sign his paintings for him. It made him laugh to think of rich people paying big bucks for his paintings, putting it on their walls and saying 'There's the master's signature!'"

"That's kind of a cool 'fuck you.'"

"You'll like this part, Jesus. Dali experimented with Bulletism."

"He shot at a painting or something?"

"He'd shoot paint at paper and develop an image out of the ink blot."

"Okay."

"He even lived in his own museum! He was crazy, but genius crazy, not the regular kind of crazy like the guys in The Machine. Not like guys like you."

You turn that over in your mind. You don't like where this is going. "We can get away and live a different life. We can reinvent ourselves. I've already done it a couple of times. I started out as a swimmer, shit happened, I got in the Army, I got out — "

"And you got into another army. You didn't change, Jesus. Wherever you go, you'll always drag a heavy bag of bad behind you."

You stop at a red light and dare to look over at her for the first time. Black mascara slides down her cheeks.

"You're a great salsa dancer, Jesus, but that's not enough," Lily says. "I want to be crazy like Salvador Dali. I want to live a big life, live long, and when I die, I want to inspire a bunch of bitches I never met to say they want to live like I did. If I go with you, all we'll do is hide. I don't want to live my life in hiding, Jesus. I want to live a big, Salvador Dali-sized life."

You swallow hard.

She talks some more, but you aren't really listening for the meaning of her words anymore. Instead, you listen to her soft accent, memorize the musical rise and fall of her voice and breathe in the faint hint of lavender. No matter where you go, you will always have a bottle of lavender with you as a reminder. Part of Lily will never get away.

You say, "I'll drop you off at the locker." You mean, *"Please don't leave."*

When she steps out of the car, Lily doesn't look back.

THE MAN YOU ARE

You slip around the "Restroom Closed for Maintenance" sign and climb the steps two at a time. The Post Office's second floor is the perfect observation post to surveil the storage locker business. You didn't know for sure the federal agent would be there, drinking coffee and peering through a camera with a huge zoom lens, but it's the obvious spot for a lookout. The fed wears a sweater vest over a blue buttoned-up Oxford shirt and Mom jeans. If that weren't enough of a clue, the baseball cap that reads FBI in bright yellow stitching confirms all you need to know.

"Agent! There's a *gorgeous* Latina moving in on the objective! Have you spotted her yet?"

"Wha — ?" The guy looks up and that moment of indecision between reaching for his weapon and reaching for the walkie-talkie is plenty of time to whip the Uzi out from under your trench and smack him across the face with it. He's knocked against the wall and face down on the floor before he can get to the *t* in "What?"

You grab the walkie-talkie. "All units, stand by. Do not move in. Keep this channel clear. Over."

When you handcuff his wrists, they make a satisfying ratcheting sound. You should have been a cop. In retrospect, that would have been a better career choice. Who knows? You could have been the guy on the floor with the swelling jaw.

"Nice sweater vest. What's your name?" you ask.

He says two words. The second word is "you." The first word is not "thank."

You fish his ID out of the FBI jacket hanging from the camera tripod. "Agent *Smith*?"

"You are in for a world of trouble, mister."

You have to chuckle. The guy sounds like a high school principal, not a supercop.

You read his home address to him off his driver's license. That settles him down immensely. That, and saying, "Sh!" while putting your SIG to his head.

You key the walkie-talkie's mic. "This is Smith. The Latina going for the storage locker. Do not move on her. Do not move on her. Maintain radio silence. Over."

"That won't work," Smith says.

"Your name is Agent *John* Smith? Really? Agent *Smith*? I suppose it's a common name for a white guy, but your buddies must have made a lot of *Matrix* jokes about you when the movie came out, huh?"

"Yeah, they did, but I haven't heard a *Matrix* reference in months. Listen — "

"Is this the part where you tell me we're going to be besties? Let me guess: If I put the gun down, give you back your driver's license and forget your address, we'll go around the corner to Saluggi's. We'll share a pizza pie and a few laughs, right? Bad things happen to my friends, man."

The radio crackles. "Smith? Come in?"

You key the radio and just say, "Stand by." Thanks to Tia Marta and her insistent elocution lessons, you sound like a white guy to the FBI.

"They are going to be all over you in a minute."

"How'd you find the locker? How long you been on this stakeout?" He doesn't say anything until you ask, "You got a wife and kids up there in Elizabeth, New Jersey?"

"There was a body in the locker. Shot in the head." Smith says. "It was wrapped up, but the smell still got out and the owner of the lot called the police. I've been on this stakeout for about a week.

So that's what happened to Cat Fornes. Panama Bob Lima shot him. Cat was a tough guy, but nobody's tougher than a bullet that's worth about two bits and no amount of sit-ups makes anyone immortal. Old Bob was tougher than anyone thought.

"You the shooter?" Smith asks.

"Nah, but you can close the case with this: Big Denny De Molina did it. Take it from me. In fact, I'm here on Big Denny's behalf, so when you start with your chasing and beating, start and end with Big Denny De Molina."

"You still talking? Sounds like a lot of hot air," Smith says.

You can't help but smirk. "Yeah, I get that a lot. You need evidence. You know who Denny is because you know who Jimmy Lima is. Jimmy's dead. Get a warrant for his records. Somewhere in the paperwork for one of his legit businesses, a property management company, is the money trail for pay that goes to Denny De Molina. He's listed as the Assistant Super and his rent is free. Denny could break a toilet by sitting on it, but he sure wouldn't know how to fix one. Then get a warrant for the Assistant Super's residence, Apartment C, in the basement. There's a big freezer that doesn't work. You'll find a lot of explosive residue there and some very illegal firearms. That should give ATF something to get excited about."

"Interesting. Anything else?"

"That'll be a good start."

"If you're here for him, what have you got against the guy?"

"Family feud. And I don't want to have another family reunion any time soon." That ought to keep everybody busy for a little while, at least.

You look through the camera. The old guy up front at the storage facility's office is peering toward you holding a walkie-talkie. Lily thinks she's talking her way to the storage locker and getting by on her looks and charm. The agent would let in anyone with a key to locker 408. In is easy. The trick will be getting her out.

You angle the camera and zoom in. There's the lovely Lily. She unlocks the padlock, bends to pull the metal door and it slides up. It probably still smells bad in there. Otherwise, the Feds would have a guy in there waiting to arrest her. If you don't do something drastic soon, the rest of Smith's stakeout team will ignore your walkie-talkie antics and put her in cuffs. Handcuffs aren't the sort of bracelets she's destined to enjoy. She's going to study art in France and Spain.

Lucky for Lily Vasquez, lover of Salvador Dali, ex-lover of the loser you have been, it's new leaf time. You take Smith's pistol and his FBI cap and sling the trench over the Uzi to hide it.

Lily comes out of the locker with two suitcases, one in each hand. The old agent from the booth moves toward her. You smash out the bathroom window with your elbow, stick the SIG out and fire two shots into the air. The old guy wheels and dives for cover.

Good luck, Lily.

The walkie-talkie crackles. "Johnny? What's going on up there?"

"This is Mr. Anderson," you say. "I have an automatic weapon pointed at Agent Smith's head. Pull back and let the girl go or I will blow his stupid head off."

"Anderson? Who are you?"

"Don't you remember Mr. Anderson? Code name Neo? Keanu Reeves played me in the *Matrix* movies. I'm Agent Smith's nemesis. Pull back and let the girl go with her suitcases or I will kill your man. Guaranteed. No kung fu. Just *bang!*"

There's some cross chatter on the channel as the FBI crew regroups to figure out what they're going to do. You're hoping embarrassment will slow their response, but you've learned your lesson: Never underestimate the enemy. SWAT's surely already on its way. On the other hand, SWAT will be way too late. You have no idea how many guys the FBI would spare for a stakeout like this, but not enough to set up a perimeter quickly enough.

"I should kill Agent John Smith just for his fashion sense. If you're going to carry a gun, you can't wear a sweater vest. Make a choice. The shirt's okay, but I don't know if I can forgive the pussy sweater vest."

"Hold on!" It's got to be the old agent pretending to be the storage locker guard. He'd have to be the senior agent on the stake out. "Don't do anything crazy! Let's talk about this before you do anything you can't take back."

"I'm already ten past crazy o'clock." You mute the walkie-talkie and slide it under your trench just as three guys with FBI emblazoned in yellow across their backs race across the street and up the Post Office steps. They pass you without giving you a glance. In their rush to be heroes, they're focusing on the wrong details. You empathize. You've done that.

Once they're out of sight, you raise the walkie-talkie and key the mic, "Back off or I'll kneecap your boy!"

Sirens wail, coming fast, but you're already a block away by the time they figure out you aren't in the observation post with Agent Smith.

You cross Canal street and slide up beside Lily. "The FBI will be after you. The money will be real so they have evidence but there have to be tracers in there. Grab a cab uptown and as soon as you can, get those suitcases underwater. A fountain, a bathtub, a hotel swimming pool. Whatever it takes. I'll draw them off and stall them."

"How'd you know that would work? I saw the guy coming toward me with his gun out as soon as I came out with the suitcases."

"Han Solo tried to bluff the Stormtroopers when he and Luke Skywalker rescued Princess Leia from the Death Star's jail. He tried to bluff, but Han didn't have my gift of gab."

"I guess not." Her eyes are wide and shining. Before she can turn away and hail a cab, you kiss her for the last time.

As you steam away, you turn up the volume on the walkie-talkie and tell the feds if they leave the Post Office, three cars on the block will explode.

Smith answers immediately, "You son of a bitch! When I find you, you are going down so hard. We don't believe a word you say, you fucking piece of shit liar! You can't sucker us twice!"

"Three cars, pigs! Just like the Cutlass Supreme that exploded outside of Jimmy Lima's house this morning in Great Neck! Three cars wired with Semtex just like that one. I'll detonate them one at a time, killing civilians up and down this busy block. Try me, Sweater Vest! One explosion for every FBI jacket I see."

The key to a great bluff is specifics, conviction and evidence you've already taken the full tour of Crazy Town. You drop the walkie-talkie into a garbage can and keep going.

When you glance back, Lily's already in a cab, going away and getting away. Soon she'll be just a dot on the horizon. Then less than a dot. Then just a memory.

To her, you were always and forever going to be nothing more than the salsa dancer she had fun with for a while on her way to Dali. As you head down Greene Street, you promise yourself that, as good a liar as you are, you'll never lie to yourself again.

But how can anyone know when they lie to themselves and when they do not? Maybe you're lying again right now. Every day you talk to yourself. There is no "I". There is only "you." You have to be your own friend. Talking to yourself, separating the pained, tortured "I" from the cool, smart ninja "you"? That's what got you through the hell that was Tia Marta and The Bug Man's basement prison and every bad thing that's happened since.

You spot a cab and make a run for it. You don't see any FBI agents chasing you. "They better not," you tell yourself, "With a gun in your hand, nobody's bigger than Jesus."

THE HITMAN SERIES PART TWO

HIGHER THAN JESUS

ROBERT CHAZZ CHUTE

UNFORGIVEN

Thirteen years ago, Tia Marta taught you how to please a woman who was hard to please. She took away your name and beat the Cuban accent out of you. She also taught you the word "sidle", which, she explained, was acting sneaky and casual at the same time. "It pays to improve your word power," she said, waving a *Reader's Digest*.

"Get on your knees, boy. You may look me in the eyes if I see love and devotion in them. If I do not see love and devotion, I'll take out one of your lovely brown eyes."

Tia Marta taught you English. She taught you how to lie well, when to hate and how to kill.

Early on in your confinement in a Miami basement, you once dared to complain to your other captor, the Bug Man, how terribly mean Tia Marta was.

"Actually," the Bug Man replied, "Marta's little bits of fun sound pretty close to my British boarding school experience." Then he slipped a plastic bag over your head until you almost passed out.

He did that several times until you lost consciousness, but somehow, lots of brain cells survived. For instance, you remember the word "sidle" and tonight you used that knowledge in the commission of a murder.

*　　*　　*　　*　　*　　*

A few hours ago, as soon as *It's a Wonderful Life* ended, you sidled up beside the target at the bar and asked him if you could buy him a drink. You want to get out of the business of sidling up to strangers and thinking of people only in terms of predators, prey and potential witnesses. However, this is a special case. You were doing this job for a damsel in distress. Whether she thinks she fits that quaint description, the guy who ordered the hit sure thinks so.

Suspicious, the target asked you why you wanted to buy him a drink.

You checked your watch. "It's officially Christmas."

"I'm more of a Hanukkah kind of guy."

"We're in a shitty bar."

The Bartender of Undetermined Asian Descent cutting limes into wedges looked up from his knife.

"Sorry," you told the bartender, "but it's no secret."

He shrugged and returned to his work. To the target, you offered, "All over

Chicago, people are either asleep, having Christmas sex or swearing up a storm trying to put a toy together for their greedy, ungrateful kids. We should be much more hammered than we appear to be, don't you think?"

"Test: name your two favorite TV shows."

"*Dexter* is uneven but delivers great moments. *Breaking Bad* is best overall."

The target smiled. "I would have also accepted *The Walking Dead.*" He turned to the bartender, "Gimme a Singapore sling. He's buying."

"Make it two," you said. "What is a Singapore sling?"

"It's a sweet drink that was popular when I was in college."

"Sad holiday nights are for nostalgia."

"Yeah, or, through the magic of association and sense memory, I'm getting back in touch with the slutty college girls I remember." He swept his hand in an arc. "When I was a journalism major, *this* place used to be quite the hot spot. A meat market! Sense memories like taste and smell are strong. For me, a Singapore sling is a time machine. Fires up the brain full of Jon Bon Jovi, feathered hair and girls falling out of their tank tops."

The bar looked dusty and the only sense you got was the feel of old beer on the sticky floor and, over toward the bathroom, a bottle of bleach did battle with the sharp stench of fresh Christmas Eve vomit. Somebody toasted Christmas with something red and green, so at least the puke was festive.

The Bartender of Undetermined Asian Descent had to check his iPhone to look up how to mix a Singapore sling. When the slings were finally mixed, they arrived sweet and went down easy. You'd already tipped the bartender not to add alcohol to anything he gave you. For the job ahead, the target had to get obliterated mentally before you could finish him physically. You had to be able to find the door and drive.

"Grenadine," the target said. "I don't know if that's just sugar, or flavored syrup or something else."

You nodded to the little TV mounted high on the wall behind the bar. *It's a Wonderful Life* was over, so whoever was in charge of irony at the TV station had switched to news reports that featured the year in review. The riots, both foreign and domestic, looked disturbingly similar. Plumes of smoke and fire rose behind grim-faced correspondents speaking into microphones in news stories that looked interchangeable with all news reports since 9/11.

"We're just consumers and destroyers now," you said. "We buy everything made from anywhere but here and we don't make anything besides guns and ammo. How would we know about anything nice, especially sweet stuff like grenadine?"

The target turned and looked you over, apparently considering you seriously for the first time. "Nice suit. I like the red tie. Christmasy."

"Thanks. Silk. The last gift my ex-girlfriend gave me."

"*Ex*, huh? So that's what brings you to this hole on Christmas? I'm guessing the 'ex' part is recent?"

You gave him a cagey shrug and, perhaps reassured you weren't coming on to him, he offered his hand. "I'm Thomas."

"Sully," you lie. "Sully Martinez."

He shook your hand. "You look like a Martinez, but I never met a Sully who looks like you."

"It was Sal, as in Salvador, but when you get called *Sally* in elementary school enough days in a row, you switch to Sully as soon as you can."

"Heh. *Sally*. Can't blame you there, son. Bad bounce."

"What brings you out in the snow tonight, besides memories of college girls?"

Thomas finished his drink and ordered another, switching to Scotch. "I read a novel a while back. It was called *Still Life with June*. Good stuff. I'm here a lot, sure, but I remembered something in the book about how people in a bar on Christmas have the best stories. How about it? Got a story?"

You could have told him you'd been following him off and on for a week and he'd gotten wasted in this bar five days out of the last seven. Instead, you told him, "I'm only here because my girl broke up with me. Not much interesting in that. Happens all the time. Sorry."

"Shit. I'm a bit worried, Sully. There's only you and me in here and Chinese Rick doesn't talk. Not much English, anyway. It's a bit concerning when I come here for the sad stories and I might be the saddest ass in the place."

"Rick's Chinese? I couldn't tell."

Thomas burst out laughing. "I don't know his *name*, *Sally*, but he's running the bar and the original title of *Casablanca* was — "

"*Everybody Comes to Rick's*. I get it. And it's Sully," you added, curiously defensive over your fake name.

He toasted you, tossed back his Scotch in one go and winced. "A cinemaphile, huh? Or is it cineaste? I used to know lots of shit like that. I should have gotten a job in journalism, but I got into it too late, born too late. Freelanced for a while here and there, but it wasn't paying the bills. Now so-called journalism is all about working for free and linking to some shit-for-brains blogs. No money in that and I'm *still* paying off my student loan."

The line of work he ended up in, he can easily pay off those loans.

"Why'd your girl dump you on Christmas, Sally — uh, Sully?"

"She wanted freedom and travel and I wanted to settle down."

"You're too young to settle down."

"I'm one of those guys who needs stability, I guess. This time next year, I'll either be sleeping in my own bed or having Christmas sex with my new wife or maybe even swearing up a storm, trying to put a crib together."

"Christ, you're young and in a hurry."

"I've always been in a hurry to get married. Feels…safer, and love — especially *new* love — is a drug, right? Besides, it's always later than you think."

You made a show of trying to catch up and knocked back your Cuba Libre. Only you and Chinese Rick know that it's only Coke.

You bought the target all his drinks and watched him get steadily plastered. He did most of the talking and he did have some interesting stories. "Kennedy said we had to beat the Russians to the moon, but that was really about developing rocket technology. He had to justify those huge budgets so he told America it was about the Space Race instead of developing better ICBMs to nuke the Russians."

He switched to Seven and Sevens — two ounces of straight grain whiskey, five ounces of 7-up and a wedge of lemon. Chinese Rick just gave you the lemon and 7-up.

"Now NASA is all about *unmanned* space missions," the target said, gesturing with his glass. "We don't even have *shuttles* anymore. Unmanned missions, just when we need the best flying killer robot drones possible. You think that's a coincidence? It's the Space Race all over again, but this time, with the tech they're developing, they'll use it on us, on American soil. Just wait until those DEA and Homeland Security douchebags get hold of surveillance drones that are the size of houseflies!"

Thomas ordered again without even pretending he might reach for his wallet. You kind of liked him. You might have liked him more if he wasn't so cheap, but you'd had that problem, too, lately. You reminded yourself that your annoyance was really a case of the reformed sinner getting more annoyed at an unrepentant offender.

"I'll tell you another thing. Nixon said, go after marijuana users and keep the whole *Reefer Madness* propaganda going. Our government is *still* doing that shit. We got a recession and they're spending billions on policing weed instead of making billions taxing it. Organized crime — this should tell you all we need to know — *wants* to keep weed illegal so their business model isn't interrupted."

You nodded, knowing from personal experience that this was true. You're not surprised that he sounds informed. He bloviates — thanks Tia Marta and *Reader's Digest* for more word power — but he's informed. Given the main reason you're killing him — besides the money — his views on drugs surprise you.

"You know why Nixon and all the other douche nozzles in authority wanted to go after marijuana? Because weed is the drug of all those protesters and the jobless and the kids with student loans they'll never pay back. Cocaine users aren't protesting shit, but you want to have another handle on Occupiers so you can lump more charges on them when you arrest them for getting the snot beaten out of them? That's how you do it, son, and the scared middle class just nod and say, 'Thank you, sir, may I have another? Hope you don't come after me with a cannon that shoots sound and melts my eyeballs.'"

"Somebody once said, 'Question Authority before Authority questions you.'"

"Hell, yeah!" He toasted you again.

His politics bored you, but the more toasts, the better.

"Have you noticed that there are no major drug busts anymore? The feds have all this new technology and weaponry that Homeland Security gave them so they're all militaried up, but you hardly ever hear of huge cash and drug seizures like in the old days. I think it's because the cops are doing the seizing *before* they get the drugs and cash back to headquarters. Safer to send SWAT through a door to squeeze a bunch of stoners. Try that shit with a bunch of meth heads and they'll shoot your balls off and fry 'em for breakfast."

You gently pushed that subject, seeing where Thomas would take it. "I've done some weed, but I never thought about it like this. I mean, I know the underground economy is tied up in the regular economy. Gangsters mix with banksters."

"Heh. That's not the half of it! In the late '80s, the locals…big Chicago gangs like the Black Kings and the Latin Kings? Crack was the drug of choice then. It's a cheap, quick high. Now we got meth, which is some crazy shit. But it's the prescription drug companies that are the huge pushers. International conglomerates, and they're the ones killing off all our celebrities. Prescription drugs have their uses, but a bunch of these kids have no idea what the wrong dose of Vicodin will do to their livers. I've seen some crazy shit. You see that earlier this year? Sly Stallone's kid? Sage? Gone. Too many prescription pain meds. And Heath Ledger? Shit. He's gone, too."

"Heath Ledger played the Joker the best it has ever or will ever be played," you said. That was the first earnest statement you'd allowed yourself tonight.

Thomas slammed his glass down so hard, you thought it might shatter. His words had grown more slurred. "Right! To Heath Ledger! Best Joker ever! Hot damn! Made you totally forget Nicholson's Joker and the totally unrealistic anal sex in…in…!"

"I hope you're talking about Heath Ledger having 'totally unrealistic anal sex' in *Broke Back Mountain.*"

"Right." After a few minutes he leaned closer. You resisted curling your lip and turning your head from his boozy breath. "You say you've done a little reefer, Sally?"

"Sully, and yup."

"Do you realize the resources that go into stopping people from sacrificing a harmless plant to the fire gods? The government is so stupid, they even outlaw hemp. Hemp can't even get you high. Makes the best clothes, paper, fuel and rope and, just because William Randolph Hearst wanted to keep his lumber companies profitable in the last century, we *still* can't have hemp in *this* century. This country is crazy. Henry Ford's first car was made out of hemp and you could hit the fenders with a hammer and not leave a dent!"

Thomas fell forward. You caught him before he could fall into your lap.

"It's about time," you said. "I thought you were going to bore me to death."

You slipped one of Thomas's arms across your shoulders and helped him to his car. You already knew which car was his just as you knew where he lived and that his garage door opener was clipped to the sun visor over his driver's seat.

You slipped your gloves on before touching his car door. As soon as he was inside, Thomas lay slumped in the passenger seat. You fished his keys out of his pants pocket, but he didn't stir. "No more political lectures," you ordered, sure now that the murder would be righteous, if only to shut him up. Thomas began to snore.

*   *   *   *   *   *

Twenty minutes ago, you parked the car in the target's garage, pushed the button to close the door and left the engine running.

Every assessment of a crime scene is based on the easiest theory of the case. It's Christmas day, so when detectives are eventually called, Occam's Razor will go in your favor. The easiest narrative is that Thomas drove home, drunk and depressed. The cops will think he decided to end his life as a Christmas gift to himself, though you happen to know his death will be a gift for a stunning blonde.

Christmas, you reasoned, is for suicides, domestic and child abuse and family fights. Even though holiday suicides are really a myth — you Googled— it's a persistent lie and who could say the victim himself didn't believe the myth so much he acted upon it? More people commit suicide than murder and someone offs themselves once every seventeen minutes — Google again — so why wouldn't the police jump to the easy conclusion?

Besides, hit men usually take Christmas Day off. Not you, but most.

When you were a Military Policeman, you saw far too many suicides. The target's crime scene would look open-and-shut clean and DIY. Checking out via carbon monoxide is one of the easier ways to leave this world and find out if hell has room. Bullets and blood get complicated and you've had all the complications you can stomach.

You left him in the car, engine chugging and tailpipe spewing. You planned to go out and check on him once you completed your search. If he had receipts or any clue he was in Chinese Rick's bar, the evidence leaves with you. The hardest part of this hit would be to muscle Thomas into the driver's seat.

*   *   *   *   *   *

Five minutes ago you checked the refrigerator and freezer. You looked in, under and behind the stove. The cupboards stood nearly empty except for bags of chips. The client promised the money and drugs would be hidden in the house. However, Paulie, your only remaining contact with The Machine back in New York, didn't know where the target stashed the drug money. Paulie owed you his life, but more important, you're pretty sure he's too afraid of you to screw you over. You continued the search.

The tough part of the job was not to make a mess. Tossing the small house wouldn't take so much time if you didn't have to worry about keeping the suicide narrative intact. You moved from room to room, confident you were alone, but losing faith in Paulie as you searched. The house seemed too bare for this to be the target's only flop. The cupboard held one dish and one water glass. Where were all the empties and the cleaning supplies or even a bottle of ketchup in the fridge? The living room held just one chair, a large square glass coffee table and a plasma TV with a PS3 game system beneath it. He only had one game: *Lego Batman 2.*

Only one small picture hung in the entire house and it was in the bedroom. You paused to note that it was a photo in a cheap frame: a stacked blonde in a red tankini whose face was turned away from the camera toward the setting sun. Since it was the only picture in the house, you were sure you'd found the treasure. You checked behind the frame for a hidden wall safe but again, came up zeroes and snake eyes. You looked under the mattress and found nothing but dust bunnies. There were no sheets, just a sleeping bag and a stained pillow. Despite your surveillance from the street, from where you stood, the target's house looked more like a front by the minute.

Finally, you discovered Thomas's stash of Vicodin — a bundle of pill bottles wrapped in plastic held tight with thick blue elastics. He'd hidden the stash behind the toilet tank in the upstairs bathroom.

* * * * * *

A few seconds ago, you heard the crash and tinkle downstairs. You pulled your SIG from your waistband and raced downstairs, pausing at the landing to peer around the corner.

"H-help!"

Of course, it was Thomas.

* * * * * *

And now, having stumbled in from the garage, Thomas smashed through the glass coffee table, ass first. He's trapped on his back, helpless as a turtle. He looks up at you through red, bleary eyes, coughing and bewildered. "Dude…Sally…my car's out of g-gas, man."

You thought you were cool, but you forgot to check the gas gauge.

A trickle of blood drips beneath him, but he doesn't seem to notice. It takes him a while to work through the equation that you're standing in his living room, a pistol in your fist, the business end pointed at him.

"Where's the money, Thomas?"

"Wh-what? What are you doing here, Sally?"

"Jesus. My name is Jesus Diaz."

"R-really? *Hay-soose?*"

"Where's the money, Thomas?"

"H-hey, man…are you…are you the bad guy?"

"No, man. I'm not the bad guy. I'm just *a* bad guy. You're *the* bad guy."

He tries to get up. You push him back down.

Thomas straightens his legs, which makes him sink deeper into the well of the broken table. It's like he's trying for a sit up with his ass in shattered glass.

"This is not Cirque de Soleil, Thomas."

Still, as he reaches up awkwardly, his pant leg slides back and — surprise! — he's packing a little .22 in an ankle holster. Ankle holsters suck to wear and are slow to use, so you have just enough time to shoot Thomas in the upper chest once. His body jolts, his arms fall back and he makes a sound that starts with a growl and ends on a high note of despair followed by a long wheeze.

He looks up at you, glassy-eyed, draining and fading fast. Breathing in tiny birdlike gulps, he manages to say, "I'm not... *Thomas*."

*   *   *   *   *   *

Tomorrow you will skim the news websites and find a reference to an unidentified man found dead in a nearly empty house on Chicago's east side. Police will say they found $20,000 behind the kick plate under the kitchen cupboards.

Paulie told you the target could have at least $80,000, maybe more, and Paulie expected a heavy finder's fee for being your agent in addition to your cut of whatever cash you found. The rest would go back to the guy who ordered the hit. Maybe the guy who called himself Thomas was right. Maybe the DEA doesn't have major drug and money busts anymore because cash and drug seizures are the only reliable retirement fund left. They've got kids with student loans to pay, too. You pop some pills because the only thing you know for sure is that you will never know.

It will bother you that you missed out on at least $20,000, but you'll be so high on Vicodin, it will lessen the pain. You will stay in your room, play *Lego Batman 2* on Thomas's PS3, and dream of finally meeting the woman in the red tankini face to face.

The Vic-induced euphoria will kick hard and sweet, but you will wish the Vicodin could do more, like make the woman in the photo speak to you. You will hold up her picture close to your face and whisper, "I'm not really the bad guy. I'm just a guy. I can dance and we'll play pool and have fun and I'll never leave you. It'll be good. I'll be good. I've been trained to make people happy who were very hard to please."

But who is the real you? Which is the higher self who will graduate from this life and deserve the girl in the red tankini? What happened to the innocent kid from Cuba, pushed into this life?

"Jesus," you coach, "you're losing the thread. You're losing yourself. You can't think in terms of what you've done. You have to cut the past off and burn it. You have to forgive and forget. Everybody says that so it must be true."

When you start to hyperventilate, you resolve to stop taking any more Vikes for a while.

You tell yourself aloud, your voice bouncing off the hotel room's walls, "It's always later than you think! You've got to live in the *now*, not think about what might have been."

The counsellors at Veterans Affairs call what you're doing "dissociation". You call it the only way to be you and live.

You will fall asleep holding the photo of the girl in the red tankini to your bare chest, so only she will see your scars. You hope she's as nice as she seems from a distance. You want her to be pure. You want to be pure for her.

TICKING CLOCK

Ordinarily, you would never sit with your back to the entrance but, halfway down the middle of the diner, you get the best continuous view of the girl from Thomas-not-Thomas's photo. You'd have chosen differently if you knew that ten minutes from now, two thugs are going to burst in the front door of this greasy spoon and point their Tech 9s in unsafe directions. You don't know that yet. You're just trying to enjoy the Blue Plate Special: tough steak and runny eggs. The food is bad, but the waitress who took your order and brought it out to you is the girl from the photo. That red tankini did not lie, but now that you can see her face — those cheekbones! Those eyes! If you could order a pot cookie with your decaf coffee, you'd stay here all night.

Still, you're never off the clock. People are after you. Before you could even look for the girl of your dreams, you scoped out the diner's clientele. An old couple left as you arrived and you held the door open for them. They looked at you with suspicion and hurried into the street.

The only other person in the diner when you arrived was the big, black bald guy in the rear booth by the bathroom. It was Ving Rhames, the actor. Then you decided it wasn't him, couldn't be, not here in a greasy spoon on the edge of Logan Square late at night. Then you wondered if Ving Rhames has a twin brother. You felt the same startling jolt everybody gets when they spot a celebrity. You'd felt it before. You saw Kevin Smith, the director, in Times Square once and you'd even said hello to Christopher Walken twice in the street in New York.

The guy in the rear booth looks up and scans you, too. Celebrity or not, you try to do a threat assessment in a glance. You should have given the guy more serious consideration when you first spotted him. His size is intimidating, but he passes the can-I-take-him test for two reasons: he seems more interested in reading his Kindle than looking at you and the vest under his suit jacket is bright purple. The vest was a bold choice for the otherwise conservative, dark pinstripe suit. The dude has style. On a lot of big guys, a suit either fits them like a paper bag or they look like they're stuffed into a sausage casing. His suit is tailored and fits well. With that purple vest, there's no way he's a cop, so he seems safe. You take him for a musician having a bite after a gig at a local jazz club, but when you get up to go to the bathroom, you spot the big Bible on the table in front of him and decide he has to be an evangelical preacher. He has the look of a former football player who has found Jesus — not you, the other one.

Settling into the booth and watchful for the goddess from the photo, you try to live in the now because that's what the counsellors at the VA say to do. They tell you to look for details and notice things, like where the exits are and how many windows are in a room. They call it "mindfulness." You call it being on high alert every day of your life, as if memorizing wallpaper patterns is the answer to your problems.

Your life coach says you should live for today, too. Sgt. Billy doesn't work at the VA. He lives on the street but he still has lots of advice, telling everybody who comes within a few feet of him how to live their lives. Mostly you just politely nod to him as he babbles at you and pretend you don't speak English.

But Sgt. Billy said something Christmas Eve Day that caught your attention as you passed him. "The three most powerful words are 'I love you.' Say it more and you live better! Now gimme a dollar!"

With the money from the Christmas Day hit lost to the cops, you're off to a slow start on beginning again. Either way, you will try to start fresh. You may as well since you're starting at zero. You ran from New York. Yes, "ran" is the right word. There wasn't a lot of dignity in the way you left. That wasn't a retreat. That was a run-away-before-the-FBI-arrests-you situation. That was a disappear-before-the-Machine-shoots-you-for-treason sort of deal. You may as well have run away holding your hands over your head and screaming like a little kid. Even the Romanian mob wants you dead and they barely know you.

Ah, but when you're in the greatest city on earth, where do you run? East was the ocean. North was boring. They'd know where to come looking for you if you'd bolted south to Miami. That left running west, so you ran away to Chicago to lose yourself in another big city. The cops and the mob probably won't find you as long as you start being the smart ninja you only thought you were when you got in that mess in New York.

The key to staying alive and living in the now is to keep your profile low, avoid playing with guns and, above all, don't fall for the first pretty girl you see. Not again. Of course, you're already screwing that up as soon as you look up and see your waitress walking toward you smiling. Even though the photo didn't show her face, you know who she is. You've seen her before at a distance. You memorized her rack then, but it's her blue eyes that hold you now. You've never gone out with a blue-eyed girl.

She's already plenty tall so she sure doesn't need the two-inch heels in a place like this. Most diner waitresses wear white orthopedic shoes with lots of cushion for all the miles back and forth from the kitchen. Occasionally a hand reaches up and dings the bell on the counter, but the short order cook must be awfully short because you haven't spotted him yet. Maybe the waitress is trying to give the diner some class. She's fighting a losing battle with the neon sign out front that says "Good Eats". The second *o* has flickered so it looks like "God Eats". Still, the high heels do wonders for her calf muscles and it's impossible not to imagine how her long legs would feel wrapped around you, urging you on.

"More coffee?" she asks.

The name tag on her left breast says Willow. The old joke is "What do you call the other one?" You resist the urge. Instead you give her the nod. As tough as the steak is, there's nothing wrong with the view and you want to make the good times last. You dip your head slightly and give her your slow smile. Tia Marta instructed you in how to throw down your most seductive look and this is it.

"Undress me with your eyes," Tia Marta said. "Look hungry. Make me feel desired, like you want to tear my clothes off with your teeth. Even women who prefer shy men don't want men who are shy about their desire. Make me believe you are the answer to all my questions and all my needs, boy."

Of course, the context of Tia Marta's instruction was kidnapping, statutory rape and murder, but your seductive look still has juice. Willow doesn't call the 14th District cops. Instead, she smiles back as she refills your cup. A flame leaps up where your heart has been cold.

As she turns away, you savour the way she moves. There's something different about the way Willow carries herself, like she spends a lot of time at the gym when she's not slinging hash on the edge of Logan's Square. If you can get your shit together, Willow is the perfect girl for getting over the last girl, She Who Must Not be Named.

You pour in the sugar and cream. You need the calories. Your suit is stylish, but it's hanging off you lately.

*   *   *   *   *   *

You applied for a job at a gym just before Christmas, but it wasn't the sort of place for a woman like Willow. Stale sweat and anger hung in the air and every few minutes some juice monkey would grunt and yell with effort and drop his weights to the floor with a clang. All the guys at the gym looked the same: big biceps and spindly legs. They're making bar bodies so they can pose with their beer and wait for somebody to ogle. Men who can't dance do weights until their muscles fail. The place had looked promising from the outside, but the moment you climbed the stairs you knew this wasn't the sort of place that would need a Salsa instructor.

"You box?" the bored-looking guy behind the counter asked. His name tag read: Dravon MNGR. You didn't ask him what he'd named the other tit, either, though his chest was a muscled shelf that a flat-chested girl in junior high would envy.

"Yeah, I box."

"Any good?"

"Golden Gloves."

"I knew right away. Your face says you've been in the ring a lot."

Your face had been pounded harder outside the ring than inside it, but you didn't correct Dravon's assumptions.

"We could use a boxing instructor on Friday nights in the New Year. Just Friday nights. The regular guy always wants to start his weekend early. Start at five, teach a few members one on one. Maybe a class with a few more people if I can get them to sign up. People keep asking for it. You know, the weight loss people, not the regulars, so it's an easy gig. I pay you by the hour at the end of the night. We good?"

"Part-time's better than no time. Sure, I'll be your boxing instructor."

"Got a name?"

"Jesus Diaz."

"You Cuban, *Hay-soose?*"

"Yeah."

"I knew that, too. All Cubans make great boxers."

"Yeah. My Mom was Cuban. She had a surprise hook. My grandmother's uppercut was mean."

Dravon looked at you a moment too long, trying to decide if you were messing with him and how much smartassery was okay for a guy he'd just met. "You got the look is what I'm saying."

"If I were prettier, like Ali, you'd know I was great. You know that scene in *The Magnificent Seven?* Yul Brynner is in a bar looking for hired guns to protect a Mexican village from marauders. One of the farmers he's working for says, 'What about him? Did you see his face? Lots of scars. He must be tough.' And one of the other farmers says, 'No, we're looking for the man who gave him that face.' "

Dravon looked at you like he was going to change his mind about giving you the job. "Don't know that movie. Is that just out? I haven't heard of that one yet. I don't see many movies stuck behind this counter."

That's what passed for the first regular conversation you'd had in a while. You couldn't remember the last long conversation you had that didn't end with you having to kill somebody. Dravon seemed nice enough, but sadly, Thomas-not-Thomas was a better conversationalist.

You do talk to the people at the VA, but they're too hippie earnest and never want to just talk about movies and things that don't mean something else. They make a big deal about staring you in the eyes to make sure you're listening or to let you know they're sincere when they tell you they care. If they really cared, they wouldn't have to try so hard.

Even Sgt. Billy, your life coach from the street, stares in your eyes as you pass. He street preaches about how he was a stand up citizen before he got behind on his credit cards, started drinking and got in trouble kiting checks. Your first day in Chicago, he sat on a stoop a few doors down from your fleabag boarding house and offered you a drink from his bottle. You shook your head wary of what might crawl from his mouth to your lips if you drank from it.

"Good, man!" he said. "Stay off the wrong drugs! The wrong drugs release the bad mojo of our true natures. I can tell by looking at you, that's a valve you want to stay stuck. Stay out of trouble! Now gimme a dollar!"

*   *   *   *   *   *

You watch Willow wipe tabletops and straighten chairs. She wanders to the last booth by the bathroom to offer the huge, well-dressed bald, black man ensconced there more coffee. Maybe the salad is as bad as the steak because the Ving Rhames lookalike ignores the salad bowl at his elbow. Instead, he focuses on reading a book. Maybe he's just camping here to stay out of Chicago's winter chill. He waves the waitress away with a smile.

Willow lingers and straightens menus and salt and pepper shakers. She's doing busy work, going slow and enjoying your unwavering attention. You would love to have a conversation with Willow. She's the sort of woman who makes you think you should plan things out and think about what you're going to say so you sound as smart and funny as you imagine you are. You want to dance slow and close with no music at all and she could talk into your neck about movies or TV shows or nothing much, her hot breath measuring out each soft syllable. You could have a conversation and not be anyone's burden or case. With a woman like Willow, you could feel so good, you could skip over all the stuff you have to fix about yourself and just be who you only imagine you are. You could claim your best self and not be a bad guy.

The people at Group, the people who say they've heard it all before, are do-gooders who can't understand people like you. They think they've heard it all, but they don't know the horrors you've seen. And the worst things? That's when you're standing outside yourself, seeing yourself do bad things and seeing bad things done to you as if you were another person while light and shadow battle for who gets to drive your brain around in this body. There are a few people at the VA, the do-badders. They might understand, but they might understand far too well and turn you in for the reward.

Your coffee cup isn't half-empty when Willow's back at your table, smiling sweetly. She doesn't show her teeth when she smiles, but her lips are full and her eyes light up when you give her your I-am-the-answer-to-all-your-prayers look. "You okay?" she asks.

"Um." What had you planned to say that sounded so smart and funny in your head?

"For coffee, I mean? You okay?"

"Um." Beat. "Yes."

"You took too long between the 'um' and the 'yes' and maybe I'm reading too much into it, but there was a hint of a question mark in there. Like you said 'yes' but I heard 'yes?' "

"Uh." Two beats. "Okay."

Willow's giggle makes you want to laugh, too. It's a Betty Rubble giggle, lips closed and her head nodding ever so slightly. It's the most charming thing you've seen a woman do since She Who Must Not Be Named woke up in the morning wrapped only in bedsheets with her hair mussed (but sexier for not even trying to be sexy). You shouldn't be flirting, using your head dip and slow smile on her. You should keep this to business, but you've also heard the best cure for an ex is sex with the next.

"Sure you don't want me to brew a fresh pot?" Willow says, but she's already pouring and leaning closer.

What is that perfume? It's subtle. You didn't catch it over the smell of fried food before, but at this range, you can't miss.

"You know you've been talking to yourself, right?" she asks, not unkindly.

You stare at your spoon like it contains all the secrets to the universe. "It's an old habit. Sometimes I do that. Sorry."

"Don't be sorry."

"Did I say anything…" — *incriminating* — "interesting?"

"No, no. It was all an under your breath sort of thing. Don't worry. I didn't hear anything. You know, they say if you talk to yourself, you must have money in the bank." Before you can bark out a laugh, she rushes to tell you she has another theory. "But whoever 'they' is, they're idiots. It's pretty obvious. I think the people who come in here and talk to themselves are lonely."

"Ah."

Willow surprises you in a way that delights: "Like Tom Hanks and his volleyball on that island in *Cast Away*."

Then Willow surprises you even more by setting the coffee pot in front of you and sliding into the seat beside you. Her perfume, you decide, is made of roses. You imagine her in bed, wrapped in a thin sheet and the smell of roses in the air. You gaze at her, stunned and wordless.

After a moment, she says, "Dude, you do speak English, right?"

"Yes," you say. "I had a very mean teacher who made sure."

"Good, because I just gave you your opening. I can't make it much more plain without one of us getting embarrassed. I caught the way you looked at me, but don't stick with the shy thing. The cute and shy thing will only take you so far."

"It's so funny you say that. That's exactly what the mean teacher said."

"Well, mean teacher or not, it's true. A girl likes to be chased by a go-getter, you know? When a girl flirts with a guy, the polite thing to do is to flirt back harder and ask me out, for Christ's sake!"

"It's the twenty-first century," you say. "A guy likes to be chased sometimes. If you make me feel pretty and keep the free refills coming, this might be the start of a beautiful friendship."

There's the Betty Rubble giggle again. "Since you've already got the cool trench coat, you be Bogart and I'll be Louis."

"Willow, you picked up on my *Casablanca* reference."

"Netflix," she says.

"Still weird. My life seems to have more *Casablanca* references than usual lately."

"Sure, though who wouldn't catch that?" she says and you almost fall in love with her right then. "Happens all the time. You think of a word or a person you haven't thought of in ages and suddenly it seems like it's everywhere. It's called synchronicity. It's also why we have to watch what we're thinking so the bad things don't creep in too much."

"I agree completely," you say, though you have reservations about the whole synchronicity thing. "I try to watch my thoughts all the time. Where'd you pick that up?" already guessing the answer.

Willow shrugs, looks away and says she reads a lot of self-help books. You already know the problem she's struggling with. Maybe you're the answer to that, too. Some people would say she's way too tall for you. Fuck those people. You're her answer and she is yours, no matter what the question is.

"I'll be your Bogart," you say. "You know the coolest thing about Casablanca?"

"That it's the film that launched a hundred movie cliches? That it has the most romantic end in movies? The 'Maybe not today, maybe not tomorrow,' speech where you know Rick Blaine loves Ilsa but he sacrifices himself and tells her to get on the plane and he loses her forever for the greater good?"

"Um. I was going to say that the plane at the end was just a cardboard prop and they used little people for the ground crew to make the plane look big…. Your answer's better."

Willow's lips part to break out a killer smile. She shows her teeth. One tooth on the top is doubled up a little, like she has two canines that decided to live side by side rather than insist the adult kick out the baby. Willow is a beautiful woman made more beautiful by one precise flaw. A flaw like that can stop a gorgeous woman from knowing she's gorgeous. A flaw like that can perfect her so she never becomes a bitch. That's the moment the scales tip over hard and you go from almost falling for her to deep in love. You told yourself not to fall in love with the first pretty girl you see. However, when you look at Willow and smell roses, the pain of She Who Must Not Be Named recedes, the same way you can't remember an old tune when you hear a new song playing.

That's also the moment the two thugs burst through the front door of the diner, guns out and looking for trouble. They find it.

RAGE IN HEAVEN

Two black guys, a big handsome, tattooed thug and a thin, rat-faced banger, rush in. They carry Tech 9s, so scarily inaccurate that your weapons instructor referred to them, and all machine pistols, as spray and pray guns. You assume they're on a mission from Big Denny De Molina, once a brother in The Machine and now the guy who wants you dead — well, *one* of the guys who wants you dead, anyway. Though the diner is long, it's also narrow, so missing you is a long odds bet.

Your hand is on your SIG, but if you get into a firefight with Willow beside you, she's dead. You hold off, take a breath, and wait to die. You close your eyes and your last thought is, "Gee, I hope they're good shots and don't screw it up." Your heart ramps up to pound at the inside of your ribs as if it's trying to get out of its cage. You are definitely living in the now.

"Samuel Clemont!" the thin one at the door screams.

You open your eyes. Neither of them spares you more than a glance. New York's Machine is not going to kill you tonight, but there's a better than even chance one of these guys will. The big guy steams your way and grabs Willow by the hair, yanking her up from her seat in the booth. You wish they were here for you. Not only have they taken Willow hostage, but Samuel Clemont is the client who hired you for the Thomas-not-Thomas hit. Paulie was pissed when you told him the cops confiscated the dough, but you argued that services were rendered and the client still had to pay up.

"Jesus, you were supposed to find the money *and* the drugs."

"There weren't any drugs, either," you lied and swallowed a pill. "Guess the cops took them, too. I'm told, they do that sometimes, but I'm not interested in making the client's problems mine. I gotta get paid."

Paulie wasn't even going to tell you who the client was until you reminded the idiot that if you didn't get paid, neither did he. Only when he understood how the problem affected him did Paulie give up Clemont's name.

"Paulie, you're what's wrong with this country," you said and hung up.

Back to living in the now: "Samuel Clemont! We need a meeting!" The big thug turns to his partner and with a tilt of his head, indicates the rat-faced guy should come closer and cover you. The slim guy is light-skinned, which does nothing to conceal the red and purple birthmark plastered across his throat. Even though he's wearing a mock turtleneck — that's probably all he wears — the raw mess crawls up to his chin. Mr. Bad Birthmark should think about wearing scarves until he can grow a thick beard. The birthmark is such an obvious identifying feature, he is not meant for this type of work. When God gives you a birthmark like that, He's saying, "Get in a police line up and go to jail, sucker!" The dude really should have studied harder in school. He could have been something more useful, like a tax collector dying of a heart attack in an empty office after hours. You would have preferred that happening to him in the now. That would be most excellent compared to what he's doing, which is pointing the mouth of his Tech 9 your way.

"Anybody moves, shoot them in the face," the beefy one says. He has the air of entitlement most leaders have. He reminds you of a young army officer you once knew who got the rank for the wrong reasons. This guy is as jumpy as that guy. Busting in here without scoping the place out was a stupid move. After all, you're in here. Only an idiot assumes he's the only one with a gun.

The slim guy is the smarter one. He at least thinks to go back to the front and turn the sign on the door around to read: CLOSED, and lock it.

"Samuel Clemont!" the beefy guy yells again. "I've got your girl here. You come out and we'll have a chat. You make me come back there and it'll be bad. Don't make me come looking for you or I'll make it real bad. You got cleavers and a deep fryer and all sorts of things to play with back there so do *not* fuck with the Lone Wolf!"

The way he announces it would make you giggle under different circumstances. It's not just that he's not busting in alone. No one sane gives even a street name in the commission of a crime any more than a bank robber would give a bank teller his account number, though some idiots have actually done that. What it tells you about the Lone Wolf is that he's stupid and reckless. You might have to jump to taking a chance with Willow's safety and shoot him in the head. The Lone Wolf will have to be put down first, in any case. The guy who is the most aggressive is the one who wins most fights, true. However, this guy is too jittery. He's liable to shoot Willow. Considering you've just decided she is the love of your life, that would prove untimely.

"All right! All right!" a gravelly voice comes from the back.

You slide one hand off the table and reach under your trench coat again. Right about then is when you glance straight ahead and catch the eye of Ving Rhames's twin brother at the back of the diner. The shake of his head is so subtle, you almost miss it. Watching the big man watch the bad guys now, you see how you read him wrong earlier. He's not the kind of guy to save sinners. He looks back at you and, with the slightest narrowing of his eyes, a hint of a smile in one dimple and another subtle head shake, tells you: *I've got this. Do not to go for your weapon.*

You smile back and quirk an eyebrow. *Your move.* You're trying to look cool, but you feel like an idiot. Appropriate. Only a moment ago you were telling yourself that only an idiot assumes he's the only one packing.

You're still sure he's not a cop, not with all the expensive fashion and style he wears. Ving Rhames's twin is so cool he's not even staring at the Tech 9 in the Lone Wolf's hand. Under stress, most people focus on the wrong details and stare at the gun. Talk to any witnesses after a crime with a gun involved and they can probably describe the weapon, but descriptions of the assailant will range from a clubfooted Asian pygmy to an albino basketball player.

The lookalike slips a massive hand up to his mouth, takes out his two front teeth, and drops the plate into his water glass. He picks up his Bible, touches it to his forehead and slides out of the booth.

The beefy guy holding Willow by the hair swings his machine pistol around and screams for Ving's twin to sit. Your hand tightens on the grip on your SIG as you glance back at the slim guy with the unfortunate birthmark. He's looking out the front window nervously and trying to cover you, too. They should have brought three guys for this job.

The Lone Wolf gets even more jittery. "Get down you big, dumb sonofabitch! I will shoot you in your goddamn face if you don't get back in your seat!"

Instead, Ving's twin goes down on one knee, holds his big Bible up in front of his face and begins to pray with a lisp in a surprisingly high voice: "Oh, Lord, deliver us from evil!" The us comes out "*uth.*" "Though we may walk through the Valley of the Thadow of Death, deliver uth from theeth two men who have lotht their way! Pleathe, Lord! Deliver uth by releathing the Devil'th hold on their thoulth!"

The word *thoulth* strikes you as particularly ridiculous. If you could watch this as a *Saturday Night Live* sketch, it would be *hilariouth.* You knew another big, scary guy with a high voice and a lisp. Everybody you've ever known who suffered a lisp either came out of the closet early or they became very motivated to lift weights and get huge. Nurture or nature? Bullies or genes?

The Lone Wolf shakes and screams louder for Samuel to come out of the kitchen. He doesn't know what to do with the man praying for his "thoul", whose entreaties to God wail louder. "Oh, Lord, spare us from death, despair and dismemberment. Spare these sinners, these thieves in the night, from Hell's tortures."

'Thpare theeth thinners'? This guy should have been an actor considering how thick he's laying it on. You're 100% sure it's a con and that man is a killer. Fortunately, the big jittery guy still has no idea there's a train coming down the tracks. The thug doesn't even know he's tied down yet.

Your job will be to take out the rat-faced banger with the birthmark. In your mind, it's already done. Some civvies think guys like you have faster reaction times than normal humans. Not true. It's just that people like you plan how to take people out, even if you're just at the store, shopping for almond milk and egg whites. Planning ahead and preparation only makes it *look* like you're faster than average. You measure the distance between you and Rat Face.

Meanwhile, the preacher who is not a preacher is speeding up his train: "Don't, please, don't Lord, make them gargle each other's genitals in a lake of fire! Don't send them to hell and make them give each other blowjobs with an unholy gnashing of teeth, each forever consuming the other, and the fire consuming them to ash and yet devouring them anew, never letting them expire, that they may be pierced by flaming swords wielded by their dead mothers in a gleeful dance of ecstasy at their bastard sons' infinite punishment!"

It's such a fine performance — you might have laughed if the asshole with the Tech 9 wasn't holding your future wife hostage by the hair. Maybe that really is Ving Rhames. It's not just the lisp. It's the tears in his eyes and the high sing-song pitch, like a Mike Tyson lullaby, that sells the con. It's like he's high on helium.

"Don't shoot!" another voice calls from the kitchen. "I'm coming out!"

Samuel Clemont, you judge by his greasy white smock, is apparently the short order cook who undercooked your eggs, overcooked your steak, and sent you to kill Thomas-not-Thomas. Since you couldn't see him back there earlier, you'd assumed he was what people used to call a dwarf. Since Peter Dinklage rocked his role on *Game of Thrones*, pretty much everybody's got the memo by now that the label is not "dwarf" or "midget". They're now called *little people*.

However, though technically Samuel Clemont *is* short, he is not, in fact, a little person. Both his legs are missing below the knee. He rolls his wheelchair out, just into view. Judging by the high and tight haircut, the tatts snaking out from his three-quarter length sleeves and the M-4 Carbine across his lap, Samuel is a former Marine. No one, no matter how short they become, is ever an *ex*-Marine. It's an easy guess that he probably became a double amputee in a desert war started by a lying Texas oil man and wannabe cowboy. You were sent on that errand by the same Texas oil man and still have a locker somewhere that holds a neatly folded uniform with a few grains of sand in it.

Willow's crying. Just thinking about that really makes you want to shoot somebody. The angle's wrong to take out the big guy. You could shoot him, but there's an excellent chance you'd shoot your wife in the head before the bullet drilled into the Lone Wolf. And what about the rat-faced baddie with the Tech 9 at the front door? The Lone Wolf's death depends on the man who is not Ving Rhames, or a preacher, either.

*   *   *   *   *   *

When you were an MP, you got called to a PMQ one night. Private Married Quarters are like regular homes, but everything is smaller. The doorways are narrower. There's less room to move around so, though a happily married young officer might enjoy the privacy and married bliss of a little house away from the pure animal raunchiness of the barracks, it didn't work out that way all the time.

The night you're thinking of in particular, at the base in Germany, you got a call over the radio to respond to a domestic disturbance. Some lieutenant was drunk and beating on his wife again. She wanted him to get out. He threatened to kill her. It wasn't the first time you'd been to this lieutenant's house. In the civilian world back home, the drunk asshole would have been dealt with differently. Instead of breaking his nose, you had to call him sir and pretend that his wife's beatings wouldn't end tragically some night.

When you arrived, another MP — a guy named Leland — was already on the stairs, backing up from the young lieutenant and screaming, "Stay back! Stay back, sir! Please!"

The drunk asshole kept coming down the stairs with a combat knife in his hand, held high and heading toward the MP. You drew your weapon and shouted warnings, too. Leland stumbled backward a couple of steps, grabbed for the banister and shot the lieutenant in the wrist.

Stunned, the asshole officer dropped the knife. The lieutenant slowly raised his arm to stare at the blood pumping in spurts into his face and blinding his unbelieving eyes.

Astonished, you congratulated Leland on his amazing marksmanship. "Good shot!" Even if it was an accident, it was an amazing accident. The rule is: pull your weapon, mean it and aim for the center of mass. In stumbling backward, for a few seconds there, you were sure Leland had managed to save the asshole lieutenant's life with a fortunate wound. Your relief didn't last long.

Dead, the asshole wife beater dropped and slid down the stairs to the landing face first. Leland's bullet hit the bones in the wrist and a fragment zipped up and ripped into the bad husband's heart.

*   *   *   *   *   *

Hostage situations can go so wrong even when you have the advantage, which, in this case, you certainly don't. If the preacher's train is going to obliterate the guy with the gun to Willow's head, it better pull into the station soon.

The scene in front of you slows: Ving's twin brother says, "Let us read from Galatians!" He pulls a blued .357 Magnum out of that big Bible and puts the muzzle to the Lone Wolf's forehead as Willow yanks herself away and drops to the floor. The beefy guy goes wide-eyed and freezes, one arm still in the air, a hank of Willow's long blonde hair still clutched in his fist.

In his soft, high, Mike Tyson voice, the preacher who is definitely not a preacher lisps, "I think ith time you guyth thtarted prayin' ." A big smile cracks his egg head wide open to reveal the empty space where his top front teeth should be.

The Lone Wolf — the big beefy bad ass with whom no one was supposed to fuck — lets go of his Tech 9 and control of his bladder. The gun clatters to the yellow linoleum as he pisses his pants. Samuel Clemont raises his M-4 Carbine to lock on to the skinny guy at the front of the diner. By the way he stares into the mouth of death, his birthmark bobbling up and down as he swallows hard, the Lone Wolf's accomplice knows he's outgunned. Mr. Bad Birthmark lowers his weapon and turns his back to the short order cook's mercy, scrabbling at the front door's lock.

You could leave it at that, but that's your future wife crying on the floor and you don't want to be the guy who did nothing to defend your future wife. She'd always remember this night as the time you watched her be taken hostage. You've got too much pride to be the guy who sat back, helpless and humiliated by your helplessness. What kind of future could you have with Willow if she always wondered what you would have done, how far you would have let it go before even saying a word when Evil grabbed a Tech 9 and a hank of her beautiful hair?

You are caught up in the moment. You want to be a hero. You are not being a smart ninja. You'll understand all this in the future. You don't know it yet. You're living in the now.

You make your move.

THE UNDERCOVER MAN

There are stereotypes about Cubans. When people think about Cuba, they often think baseball players. There's often some truth in stereotypes. That's how stereotypes begin. However, you never played little league. Your parents were always too busy working at the hotel to take you. Instead, you stayed home, cared for your baby brother, Rodolpho, and kicked a soccer ball back and forth.

But you do have a good throwing arm. To take out Mr. Birthmark, you have several choices of weapons available to you: the SIG in your waistband and the steak knife are the obvious choices. Instead, you go for the weapon Willow left in front of you. You grab the handle of the coffee pot and stand in one smooth motion, twist and throw it at the bad guy as hard as you can.

The scene slows down as the coffee pot turns in the air. He has the door unlocked and yanks it open. Glimpsing some movement in his peripheral vision, he swivels slightly. His head turns to the right as the glass shatters and the coffee scalds his face and neck. His scream is high and loud. He stumbles into the street in misery.

"And stay out!" you roar.

The scene speeds up again as the big bald black man strikes the Lone Wolf with the butt of his pistol in the temple. The Lone Wolf's limbs go loose and he collapses the way a building implodes. When his head hits the floor, there is nothing left in him to resist the fall or to cushion the sickening smack of his shaved head against the linoleum.

Mr. Bad Birthmark is still screaming down the street as you look down and offer Willow your hand to pull her to her feet. She cries and rubs her scalp where the hank of hair was ripped out, but, honor defended, she smiles at you. She closes the gap and throws her arms around you in a desperate embrace. Willow is warm and soft and strong.

The last time you saw your mother, she clung to a tire in rough water off the coast of Florida as you were kidnapped. You have dim memories of being hugged by your mother. Willow is so tall, her embrace is kind of like getting a hug from your mom. Strangely, you feel like a very young boy again. You like it. A lot. It feels like...beginning again.

She pulls back, still holding you, and says, "I-I only saw you sitting down! I had no idea you were…uh."

"Short?" You manage a laugh. "How tall are you?"

"6'2"."

In her two-inch heels, she's seven inches taller than you. "I'm 5'9". No wonder your name is Willow. You're a tree."

"You think that's the first time I've heard that, don't you?" she says.

"Sadly, I thought it was original. And 5'9" isn't so short."

You look up at her and pull her close again, holding tight. "I'm so glad you're okay."

"Me, too."

"No, you don't get it," you whisper in her ear. "I'm glad you're okay because I don't know you, but I'm going to know you. I don't know if the height thing is an issue for you. If it is, that's too bad, because when we lie down, I'm going to make you forget about it completely."

Samuel Clemont rolls out and nudges you in the knee with the butt of his rifle. "Hey! Will, who the hell is this?"

When you and Willow part, she does so reluctantly. She turns to the man in the wheelchair and says, "Dad, say hello to my little friend!"

Ouch. And a nice *Scarface* reference! You love her even more so you are going to forgive her. Still, *ouch!* And *"Dad"?* Oh, sweet Christ.

You stick out a hand. "Nice to meet you, sir. I'm Jesus Diaz."

He looks at your hand as if you just pulled it out of your ass. "Christ."

"Common mistake, but it's pronounced *Hay-soose.*"

He gazes back at you sourly.

The Ving lookalike stands over the Lone Wolf, who was thinking about getting up until the big man pushed him back down with his foot. He does not need to use any martial arts finesse or leverage to trap the beefy man beneath him. He pushes the bad guy down like he's stepping on an ant. He scoops up Lone Wolf's Tech 9 from the floor. "Easy, son. You are messed up!" The Lone Wolf doesn't look near as scary as he did a moment ago.

The big black man looks at you, nods and kicks his prisoner hard in the ribs with the toe of one of his pointy shoes, which you suspect, despite their style, are steel-toed.

Samuel Clemont zips forward and rolls over the Lone Wolf's right hand.

The Wolf shudders. "Mother— !"

"Don't talk. Don't come back." Clemont sticks the muzzle of the carbine behind the Wolf's ear. "If I have business with you, I'll call you. Tell your boss, he's not the only one with muscle. If you understand, moan softly." He raises the butt of the rifle and brings it down on the Lone Wolf's collarbone with a thunk and a crack. It only takes twenty pounds of pressure to snap a collarbone, so that's done. The bad guy moans, but not softly, gets up and stumbles his way to the door holding his right arm with his left hand, his mashed fingers to his chest.

"Lock that door after him," Willow's father says. "We're done business for the night. At least, we're done with regular business."

You recognize the tone. Before he was in that chair, he was an officer. He's used to giving orders. Officers have that sure tone of entitlement. They don't say please and they have no doubt whatever they command will be acted upon immediately.

The big man locks the door, and turns to look at you.

"Oscar-worthy performance, Mr. Rhames."

"Thanks, but that's not original, either. I hear the Ving Rhames thing all the time. People used to say I looked like Michael Clarke Duncan, but they really meant Ving Rhames when they said it. Since Michael Clarke Duncan's death, they don't make that mistake anymore."

Michael Clarke Duncan would have been easier on him. There's no lisp when he says, "Michael Clarke Duncan." Now he has to deny he's "Ving Rhameth."

"The resemblance has probably got you laid plenty, though, huh?" you ask.

He finally breaks into a tight smile, but crosses his arms. Mixed signals. He's still trying to figure out your place in his universe.

"Good job taking that guy down," you say. "It was a smooth con. I didn't see the .357 coming out of that Bible. That's something out of a western. I saw you reading an ebook, but for pulling a cannon out of a book, you can't beat an old Bible."

"You a pro, Jesus? Or are you just a good Samaritan? You have the look of a pro. You talk and move like a pro."

Sharks recognize each other as sharks. Still, you shrug. "A pro? I dunno. Right now I'm not getting paid. It preserves my Olympic status as an amateur."

That makes the big man smile more, but Samuel Clemont eyes you up and down like you're a rusty car at the back of the used lot. "You from around here, smartass?"

"I've only been in Chicago a couple of months."

"You plan on staying?"

You look at Willow like she's a new and shiny Ferrari. "Oh, hells yeah."

"Then, for your own safety, I guess you're on my team. Maybe our safety, too, if you're useful."

"He's useful," the big man says, although with his speech impediment, it sounds like he's calling you youthful. Your hand disappears into his as he shakes it gently. It's like putting your hand into a warm loaf of bread. Most guys squeeze your hand hard to prove how strong they are. He doesn't have to prove a thing.

"I'm Chilli Gillie," he says. "My friends call me Chill. The way you nailed that guy with a coffee pot from half-way across the room? You call me Chill."

"Cool."

"How'd you do that, anyway, man? Just overhand a coffeepot like a baseball and nail him like that?"

"Dunno. It's only my second time scalding somebody with hot coffee. A few more times and I could reach expert level, but I'm afraid the act might get stale."

He looks at you like he's still trying to figure you, fails, shakes his head and smiles. Smiling seems to remind him he doesn't have all his teeth so he goes to the back booth and retrieves his top plate from the water glass. When he turns away and dips his head to pop his false teeth into his mouth, his back looks like a wall. He reminds you of Big Denny De Molina. It's nice to have a new friend who is well armed and just as big as the one who wants you dead.

You don't know how much to say in front of Willow, but you can't very well talk to Samuel Clemont about the money he owes you for killing Thomas-not-Thomas.

"Jesus, you escort Willow home," Samuel says.

When he catches your grin he tells you to come right back. "I'm guessing we got a lot to chat about. No dawdling."

He gestures to Willow and she bends to bring her ear close to his mouth. It's a long way down. He whispers and she shakes her head. Then she nods.

You were hoping Willow would take you home and pump you. Instead, she'll be pumping you for information.

NIGHT AND THE CITY

Willow has questions, but not the ones you expect.

"Do you drink?" she asks.

You take a deep breath. You already had your lies all lined up and here she is, getting the truth out of you. "There was this girl I really liked once. I was at a bar and she asked me if I wanted to buy her a drink. Of course, I did, and then she asked me what I was drinking and I made the mistake of telling her I was drinking a Coke with a lime in it. She called me a pussy and walked off with the drink I bought her."

"So you don't drink. Does that mean you drank too much before or — ?"

"Sometimes I'll drink alcohol, but not often." You could tell her that the last time you were in a bar you only faked drinking to set up a target so he looked like a carbon monoxide suicide. You hold back. "I just never liked the taste. Those uh, fruity drinks with umbrellas, are sweet. The kind that disguises the sharp taste of alcohol, like a Singapore sling. Is that the right answer?"

"Fruity drinks with umbrellas? Really?" She lets go with her Betty Rubble giggle. "That girl who called you a pussy might have been right, but not drinking is the right answer. "

"Great. Just what I was hoping to hear."

When Willow laughs next, she snorts a little and covers her nose. Embarrassed, she laughs and snorts again. You're charmed. This *must* be love.

As you both walk up the street toward the apartment she shares with her father, people bustle back and forth, heedless of the fact that you and Willow had guns pointed at your heads just a few minutes ago. "Nobody knows what we just went through," you say. "Weird, isn't it?"

"You think I'll get PTSD, like all those soldiers?"

You shrug. "When I was a little boy in Cuba, my father, my brother and I built a treehouse. It was just scraps of wood and it didn't hold together very well. We weren't exactly a handy bunch of guys."

"More evidence of being a pussy. It's not looking good for you."

"Anyway," you continue, "I was trying to drive a nail and I hit my thumb instead. I dropped the hammer and started dancing around in pain and my father looked at me and said, 'That hammer probably hurt a bit, but at least it wasn't on long.' "

"Helpful."

"Made me laugh. And you just laughed...*at* me, but you laughed. All things considered, I think you're getting over your life being threatened remarkably quickly."

"I'm sure it looks that way to the casual observer."

"I'm looking at you, but not casually, Willow." You look away when you realize your look veered off into a leer. "There are military folks who go through a lot and they don't fall into the stereotypes about Post Traumatic Stress Disorder. There's people who go through several tours, look fine, then kill themselves. I hear that even those guys in Nevada who pilot drones to kill people halfway around the world? They're eating dinner at home every night with their families and their work looks like they're playing a video game. Some of those guys get PTSD even though they're safe. Maybe I'm wrong, but you weren't held hostage very long before Chill and your Dad and me did our thing. Don't worry about PTSD."

That doesn't seem to comfort her. "Makes me think of Dad. Even when he was safe, he was pretty messed up," she says. "After he got hit with the IED and his wars were over — at least until now I thought they were over — there was a while there when I thought he was going to kill himself. Maybe it was the drugs he was on then, but once, when he looked up at me after one of his surgeries…. He was coming out of the anaesthesia and he told me, 'Will, we should never have gone over there. Not just because it was what the enemy wanted. By going after them, we bring ourselves down. ' "

"Wow."

"It didn't last. As soon as the drugs wore off, he was back to wanting to kill them all. 'Nuke 'em and turn the desert into a glass parking lot,' is Dad's annual Christmas toast."

"Mental note: I do the Christmas toast from now on."

She laughs, squeezes your shoulders and leans down to lay her head on yours for a moment as you walk together.

The air is crisp and a light snow begins to fall. You and Willow pause to watch the flurry fall out of the darkness and into the city lights. *You and Willow.* What great words they are when put together. "Look," you whisper. "We're having a moment and God approves."

"Thanks. I guess I am feeling pretty safe with you. Seeing you get that guy…" She gives a full-throated laugh that exposes her fang. "If you'd asked me an hour ago if I thought that was a good thing, I would have said no, but as soon as that guy hauled me up by the hair, I didn't just want them dead. I wanted them to suffer. I wanted to watch them burn in hell and I wouldn't even piss on them to put out the fire." She does something with her jaw. She looks a little harder. You suppose you look that way all the time.

"Priorities rearrange themselves, Will. Somebody once said that a liberal is a conservative who hasn't been mugged yet."

"Oh, I've been mugged before, but this was more personal. That guy was calling Dad out by name."

"Yeah, you gonna tell me what tonight was all about and why I'm on the team for my safety and possibly yours?"

"What?"

"What Samuel said. Not exactly a ringing endorsement, thanking me for swelling the ranks."

She shrugs with one shoulder. "It's about protection money. Those guys have come around before. Dad says they want too much. It's not like the diner is doing that well."

That one-shoulder shrug bothers you. Is she telling the truth? Her face tells you she knows more than she's saying. You want to press her, but the snow is falling. "I can't imagine why the diner isn't doing better. *You're* there. Why doesn't everybody come there? At least all the hetero guys and a platoon of lesbians."

"It's a diner, not a strip bar, pal."

Pal. A girl has never called you that before. The way she says it reminds you of a moll from an old Jimmy Cagney movie. That makes you feel warm. You love those old movies, and like you, Jimmy could fight *and* dance. When done right, fighting is dancing.

"Besides," she adds, "they still have to eat the food. I told Dad we should class the place up with some fancy coffees. In fact, coffee is *all* we should sell. I don't think he's a very good cook."

"You say that like it's a matter of opinion. It's a fact. I don't usually do this, but since we're pals with an option for more, I agree with you. The steak and eggs were awful."

Willow punches you in the shoulder. "You don't usually agree with people?"

"I don't usually tell the truth. Not on a first date."

Willow pulls you around a corner to head south on North California Avenue. "Nobody tells the truth on the first date. The first couple of months of a relationship, at least, it's like a job interview that just goes on and on. No farting!" She laughs and snorts again.

"No farting, I promise. Not for a while. For you? Not for *years*."

"Maybe we should try something different," she says. "I'll tell you the truth. I'm laughing and having a good time with you but I'm also on the edge of throwing up. Those guys... I don't know what Dad and Chill are going to do about them, but I'm glad I'm not them. And with what they did? Just grabbing me like that, like I was nothing? I don't really care what they do to them. I know I should care, but it's like looking for something on a shelf. You think it should be there, but it just isn't. Wishing doesn't make it so. If it makes me evil to want them dead, then I'll be evil. You know what I mean?"

"I know exactly what you mean. You're not evil. You're a brave woman."

"No. I'm all exposed nerves. Feels like I'm a toothache. It's worst over my heart. I'm like my mom. While my Dad was in Iraq for his first tour, she was diagnosed with breast cancer. She was all nerves, too, but the deeper she got into her treatment — the chemo, the radiation — the funnier she got. The sicker she was, the more jokes she made. You remind me of her, actually."

"Oh, no. I remind you of your Mom."

She pulls you by your lapels and kisses you hard.

"If you kissed your mother like that, it's not PTSD you gotta worry about."

"Shut up. We're still having a moment, smartass."

"Kiss me again."

She does.

"Okay, go on."

"At the beginning? When Mom went into surgery, this orderly wheeled her down to the OR and while they were waiting, she made him laugh and laugh until he was just about to pass out. Later, one of the nurses asked how my mother knew that guy. The nurse had never seen him laugh like that. Mom didn't know him, but getting scared, just opened something up in her."

"I've seen that. I've even done it and felt it. I used to be an MP in the army. Cops, medics, paramedics, funeral home directors…they all have a weird sense of humor. When you're that scared all the time, it's a reflex. When you see the world the way it really is, you can cry, but it's mostly so hopeless, you might as well laugh."

"Mom was funny right up until the end. I guess you're right. You can be hysterical or in hysteria. Better to make jokes on the way out."

"It's why I always liked the *Spider-Man* comics," you say. "Spider-Man is one of the few superheroes who makes jokes while he's beating up the bad guys."

"I've never gone out with a short guy before. I don't know if I can handle it if you turn out to be an ubergeek, too." She lessons the sting by leaning down and kissing your cheek.

"One more," you say. "Jesus said, turn the other cheek." You tap your other cheek and when she leans in, you turn your head at the last minute and your lips touch again. This turns into a softer, sweeter, lingering kiss. It's a *real* kiss. This is the one. This is the kiss you will count as your last first kiss. Her lips taste like cherries.

She looks you in the eyes for a full minute and you think, just for a moment, that she recognizes you. She's seen you before, maybe in a glimpse, but she's seen you. But she didn't *consider* you then. Not like this. The moment passes and you're relieved when she puts her arm over your shoulder and you walk on. You slip your arm around her waist. Her hip is against your side, but the mismatch doesn't bother you a bit. Sure, this is the sort of abrupt start to a relationship that addiction counsellors warn about, but since this must also be what lottery winners feel like, fuck that noise.

"I'm supposed to find out more about you."

"What does Samuel want to know?"

"The way I'm feeling, he can ask you himself. I have my own questions."

"Can I ask you one?"

She shakes her head. "It didn't actually occur to me that the whole question and answer thing would go two ways."

"Too bad. When your mom got breast cancer, did your dad come home from overseas?"

She takes a deep breath. Blinks. Her jaw is moving but no words come.

"Never mind," you say. "I know all I need to know about that. Ask me something."

"I asked about drinking," she says.

"And we established I'm a pussy."

"Yeah." The smile is back. "What about drugs?"

"Weed makes the inside of the top of my skull feel like it's packed with peppermint gum if I smoke it. I prefer edibles."

"Weed doesn't count."

"Not unless I'm a pussy and —"

"You can throw a full pot of steaming coffee with deadly accuracy and take out a guy who's threatening me and my father. I'm going to take a risk and declare, you aren't a pussy."

"I worked on my ninja skills since the hammer and thumb, treehouse debacle. It's a good skill, but it's difficult to monetize."

"Ah, have you got a job?"

"I teach boxing over on North Fairfield on Friday nights." You haven't actually done that yet, but Dravon gave you the job for the new year, so you're managing to stick remarkably, unusually and excruciatingly close to the truth so far. You hurry on, "I could teach Salsa, but I haven't found a place to teach it yet. I play guitar, too, but I'm not good enough to teach that and the pay's for shit, anyway. The economy — well, you know how it is. Everybody knows how it is."

"You said you were an MP. You ever think about being a cop? They need lots of guys. The mayor keeps talking about cracking down on gang violence. It's gotten crazy, like those assholes tonight. Last Memorial Day, there were a bunch of people killed not far from here, including a kid in the crossfire. They also need a lot of police for crowd control. I swear with the economy and the protests…it's all just getting bigger. Things are getting worse."

"I thought about being a cop. Lots of times, actually. But I don't have the temperament for it. I don't take orders well. I've been given a lot of orders from a young age. I decided I don't like it. I don't like wearing a leash."

"That must have been a tough way to go in the military."

"It was."

"Huh. Well, Jesus, so far you're enough like my father to like a lot and so different from him I might…" She doesn't finish.

"I'd like to hear the end of that sentence."

"This is my building." She gestures up at an old apartment building indistinct from all the others. "And you should get back to the diner. Dad will be waiting."

"Let him quiver in anticipation a few minutes longer. Suspense is good for the adrenals. You were about to say something interesting."

"We giants don't reveal everything to our dwarves." Willow wraps her arms around you and kisses hard. Heaven must be like this and chocolate croissants all day long. She's shaking when she finally pulls back.

"You are Queen of the Giants. Queens need knights. I'll be yours."

"So are you going to tell me about the gun in your waistband?"

"Yes. On our next date."

"My dad will want to know about the gun when you get back to the restaurant."

"Then let him ask me."

"You won't tell me?"

"Only if you agree to a date tomorrow night."

"What will we do?"

"I don't care as long as I make you laugh and snort."

"That's not something you tell a girl on the first date."

"I'm feeling unusually confident and truthful tonight."

"The way you say that, I'm not sure if you're messing with me or telling the truth."

"Truth. It's a new thing, but I'm trying it out. When you meet the Queen of the Giants, it's a rule: either tell the truth or leave out the tough stuff. It's the custom of my people, the noble dwarves."

She laughs and snorts again. "This is going to be strange, isn't it? It's the custom of my people to slouch a lot and deal with a lifetime of back and neck pain. It's that or only date basketball players."

"Don't slouch for me, Willow. You don't have to be anything less than you are for me. And obviously, since a gorgeous queen like you is available, the basketball players aren't working out. It's time to try a dwarf. We all Salsa and, if your back hurts, I'll just stand on the front steps and you stay on the sidewalk. The goodnight kiss will work out fine."

"I'm not into basketball, anyway."

"Whatever you're into, I'll be that, though getting taller might require ropes, pain and some persistence."

"I've never met anyone quite like you. You're funny."

"The secret is the same one your mother figured out. I'm terrified all the time."

"Is that why you carry a gun?"

"That's second date talk and I like mystery and suspense, don't you?"

"Okay. Tomorrow night, meet me at the diner."

"As long as we don't have to eat there, fine."

"Huh. Okay. I'll play, as long as you can answer one question correctly. If you don't like that rule and don't want to wear my leash? I'll have to say goodnight and we'll just have to part ways and chalk all the smooching up to facing death without pissing ourselves."

"I did piss myself a little, but I wouldn't mind wearing a leash if you're on the other end of it."

She laughs and snorts again and struggles to give you her serious face. "For reals, though. One correct answer and we go on from here. Wrong answer and we do not proceed. Got it?"

Reluctantly, you give her the nod. "Respect."

"Do you do any drugs besides weed? I can't be around anybody who does hard drugs. For serious."

"I don't." It's your first real lie to Willow, but you were almost honest for at least eight blocks.

MEAN STREETS

There's great power in pointing a pistol at someone who deserves it. When you aim, you feel a connection to the point of impact, like a line of energy ties the path of the bullet to the spot between the target's eyes. When someone points a gun at you, you sense that same energetic connection. You've felt it several times: a spot between your shoulder blades; a crawling feeling on your forehead where the slug was to drill through; a laser's dot over your heart. New love is like that.

After you check Willow's apartment — no monsters under the bed or hiding in the closet — you kiss her goodnight. You take it slow, your hands in her hair. Her lips are soft. After, even though you're on the other side of her thick, reinforced steel door secured with three deadbolts, you still feel her presence.

As you walk down the street, you feel light. You want to keep this feeling. When you wake in the dark on sweaty sheets and the walls lean closer, crawling with shadows, this is the feeling to hold onto until the sunlight finally marches to Chicago's dawn and outlines the city's horizon like uneven, broken teeth against the sky. To sleep at all, you always need a room with a window, so when Tia Marta's basement nightmares return, you can wait and watch for the softness to disperse Miami's memories.

Big Denny De Molina used to laugh at you for falling in love too quickly. He never understood your need to share the night with someone. While he was out trying to get laid, you had few girlfriends, you were often too serious too quickly. You drove a lot of young women away and went into a funk for months at a time over each one. "Jesus, the answer to an old love is a new one, or at least a booty call," Denny said. "Why you gotta fall so hard?"

Big Denny never understood because, back when he was still Little Denny, you saved him from Tia Marta's chamber of horrors. But don't think of Tia Marta tonight. Tonight is for love and cherishing first kisses. Kissing Tia Marta doesn't count as a first kiss. That wasn't your choice.

But it's already slipping away. Happiness reminds you to be sad. Telling yourself not to think of the past ensures you will.

*   *   *   *   *   *

In Union City, you learned the power of choices. For the first time, you had them. Bankrolled from what you stole from the Bug Man's mansion, you and Little Denny ran away from the crime scene in Miami, got on a bus and wound up in Havana on the Hudson. Tia Marta's master, The Bug Man, took Denny from his parents like he took you away from your mother. Denny was sure he'd find his parents in Union City. They were on their way there when he was kidnapped.

Union City, New Jersey is small but dense. From its streets, New York beckoned. The twin towers still commanded the city's skyline and commuters streamed through Havana on the Hudson, always on their way somewhere else. If anyone asked, you told them Denny was your brother. Little Denny couldn't replace Rodolpho, your real brother, but he was fun and didn't hesitate to dumpster dive with you. Denny was small, but he wasn't a whiner.

Back then, when the homeless did it, everyone called it dumpster diving. Now, with the economy all messed up, a new movement of poor people and nouveau hippies call it living Freegan. Most people who live on discarded food aren't part of some anti-consumerist movement. They're hungry. Maybe some wackos think that's "progressive" or maybe they're trying to make people without choice think poverty is cool and noble. When soccer moms and Wall street banksters take up the freegan lifestyle — not just white stoner hippies in dreads — you'll reconsider.

The dumpsters behind grocery stores were best. Denny would sniff the thrown food and declare most everything "Vamos a comer!" *Let's eat!* You stopped him to look at the best before date. If the food was only a day or two past that date, it was dinner.

The Bug Man owned a mansion, fine clothes and slaves. All you had was what you could steal and stuff in a hockey bag. During the day, you and Denny scouted places to stay and each night you counted the Bug Man's money, trying to make it last. Your first job was washing windows up and down the Miracle Mile. While you worked the squeegee, Denny carried the water bucket and soap, pitched pennies and searched the crowds for his parents' faces.

As that first summer in Union City ended, you had to find a warm place for you and Denny. A lanky blonde hustler named Jinx often wandered the Miracle Mile. You weren't sure how old he was. He couldn't seem to grow a beard and his skin was cracked from too much time in the sun. His thin hair looked like mange on a lost dog. You often saw him getting shooed away by the local store owners. Jinx said one of his tricks owned a rug warehouse where you and Denny could squat.

"I'll tell you where it is, if you and the boy want to party."

"We're not into that," you said. "Leave us alone."

"Everybody's up for a party when it gets cold, boy."

He shouldn't have called you "boy."

"Jersey's so cold at night in the winter, you little brown boys have no clue. But hey, it's a free country. You let me know when you're ready not to freeze to death some night."

A couple of weeks later, bleary from a night spent shivering in a big metal Salvation Army donation bin, you could see the steam of your breath even at noon. That night, you told Jinx you were down for a party. Little Denny looked worried, but you soothed him. You would take care of everything.

The rug warehouse was a large old gray building that stood by railway tracks. Jinx surprised you by producing a key to the big padlock on a side door.

"How'd you get a key?"

"It's *my* key, dummy. I broke the old padlock and put on my own. I take all my tricks here when there's no place else to go. Lots of guys' wives wouldn't appreciate me in their living rooms, but their husbands don't mind me in their mouths."

The darkness beyond the doorframe freaked Denny out and he pulled on your arm. In a torrent of Spanish, he pleaded with you to run with him back to the Salvation Army clothing bin for another night of shivering. When you tore your arm away, he cried and tried to pull the hockey bag off your shoulders. You slapped him across the face and pulled him inside.

"Easy! Easy! This can all be easy, boys. All that carpet makes for a good flop. Just cover yourselves with the rugs and you can be cozy. We can all be cozy. Just be out at six. Nobody shows up to work here until nine. Leave the place as you found it and it's fine. There's a scuzzy bathroom past the freight elevator, but the water works."

There were no light switches, but Jinx showed you where to find the circuit breakers. When the lights snapped on, the rolls of carpet looked like hills, big and small.

"You boys can sleep here whenever you want. All you gotta do is pay the tax."

Without ceremony, Jinx pulled his pants down to his knees, his hard penis bouncing up. "I suggest you work together!"

You'd never pointed the Bug Man's SIG Sauer P220 at anyone. Your hand shook. The bullet was to go through his belly button. Where life had first come to him as a baby, death would enter and it would be deliciously agonizing. You could see Jinx's guts explode in your mind's eye. You relished the power because it was the first time you had ever felt any power.

You took a deep breath before pulling the trigger. That was just enough time for Jinx to slap the pistol from your hand. It spun off into the darkness and Jinx laughed so hard, it sounded like a howl. His next slap burned across your face and Jinx howled louder and longer in delight.

Plan B kicked in: Little Denny leapt from a rug roll to Jinx's back. Jinx kept to his feet but, with his pants at his knees, staggered. Denny used the Bug Man's switchblade, cutting him off mid-howl. Jinx burbled and fell, his neck spraying blood. He grabbed at his wound, trying to stop from bleeding out, but once the carotid is cut, it takes about four minutes to die.

Technically, Jinx would have been your third kill. Denny didn't seem so bright, but he had a head for this. You cut the rug on which Jinx bled to death and rolled up his body. Together, you carried and dragged him outside to the railroad tracks. It was Denny who suggested you take off Jinx's clothes, fold them neatly and put them beside his shoes. "People who commit suicide do that," he said.

You took his suggestion and, despite the cold, you and Little Denny De Molina huddled together and waited for the train to decapitate Jinx the hustler. You never knew his last name. All he had in his pockets were a few dollars, three condoms and the key to the padlock. That rug warehouse kept you and Denny alive that first winter in Union City. The killing itself was distasteful. You were afraid and sick as you carried Jinx to the tracks, but you clung to that rush of power, the feeling of holding the SIG and pointing it at a target who needed killing.

*   *   *   *   *   *

Now, as you look up into Chicago's city shine, you pick a snowflake and follow it to the ground. The sound of a distant train shuttling into the night reaches out. It's probably just the El, Chicago's elevated train system, but the sound of a train always gives you a familiar warm feeling. After Jinx, you were less afraid. You learned that to survive, you didn't have the luxury of indecision and hesitation. You learned you had to grab life by the balls and squeeze.

A wino, listless and palm up, sits on a stoop. He looks at you from under a black hood with white lettering that reads: Ezekiel 25:17. The Bible reference looks like it's scrawled on with white paint or seagull shit. You've seen him on the street before, another of Chicago's permanently disenfranchised. His eyes look scared. The street is a time machine that makes people age faster.

"Hey, guy," you say. "The shelters are closed to new guests this late at night. Better go crash somewhere safe or at least find a heating vent."

"Yup. Already colder than a witch's tit, praise God," he says. "You been saved? Do you know Jesus loves you? Do you know the truth? Do you know someone's watching over you, sir?"

"That's too many questions, buddy, and I only have one answer. The truth I know is that life is too long if it's bad and way too short if you live it right," you reply.

He nods. "Amen."

You give him five bucks. "Stay warm, brother."

Chilli Gillie and Samuel Clemont are waiting. You trudge off through the deepening snow toward the diner with hope that your new life is about to start. This is the happiest you've been in a long time, but you try not to think about how happy you are for fear you'll jinx it.

THE UNKNOWN MAN

When you get back to the diner, Chill is waiting outside the front door holding his hollowed-out Bible. "Before you go meet with Mr. Clemont, I wanted to talk a second, man."

"Shoot."

"Funny you say that, because I was wondering if Mr. Clemont hired you as a troubleshooter. I told him all I do is provide security. No black bag and wet work nonsense for me. The man wanted to turn downtown Chicago into downtown Baghdad. When I told him that's not my thing, Clemont was pissed. Now you show up. Are you a hired gun, Jesus?"

"I didn't come in on the noon stage."

"Huh?"

"Look, I didn't have to shoot tonight, so I didn't."

"Technically, you didn't have to burn that man, either. You appear to be afflicted with a temper."

You note that there was not a single s in that sentence and it's vaguely disappointing. You didn't realize how much stupid, juvenile enjoyment you were getting out of hearing Ving Rhames with a lisp.

"If Sam had hired me to shoot somebody," you say, "I didn't do that job tonight. And I wouldn't have gone through some kind of play just to convince you. I'm mostly here for the girl."

"It's pretty clear Mr. Clemont hates that idea."

"I'm charming. He'll come around."

"Jus' helluva coinkidink, you showing up, packing heat and ready to rock." The way one eyebrow shoots up, you know for sure he's not buying your con at all. He's too good at cons himself to be fooled.

"Everybody's gotta be somewhere," you say. To change the subject, you ask how he knew you were packing heat.

"You had the look when you strutted in."

"Really? That makes me sound like a douchebag. Maybe I'm not quite as charming as I thought."

"Well, mostly it was that your belt buckle's pulled over a few inches and riding low on your concealed carry."

"I should have gone with the shoulder rig, but I wanted to be casual."

Chill looks your suit up and down. "You dress pretty fancy for a guy trying to look casual. Usually it's fat guys trying to conceal a gut who dress up this nice to go to a greasy spoon so they won't be too embarrassed to order a milkshake."

"Like I said, I'm here for the girl."

Chill checks the street. "No girl here now. Why you back? You could just date her. You don't have to get pulled into her father's business."

The way he says the word business — *bidnith* — reminds you of Eddie Murphy in *Beverley Hills Cop II*. You have to suppress a smile. That's one hell of a speech impediment he's rocking. If you laughed, you'd feel bad though. Chill is one of those guys you want to like, and not just because he's so big you pray he's always on your side.

"Jesus. Be real with me. I'm a good listener. I don't believe in coincidences. You try to sell me on coincidences and I'll start to think that you believe I'm dumb. I got a list and that's high up on Things That Piss Me Off."

You nod and choose your words carefully. "I don't have much going for me in the employment department and Clemont brought me in to protect the girl, too." That much is sort of true. Eliminating her drug dealer, Thomas-not-Thomas, is supposed to help with that. "I thought I could get a few free meals."

"Make sure Clemont pays you more than a few meals, Jesus."

"What's he paying you? You called him Mr. Clemont. Sounds pretty formal. He's not a friend?"

"Friend of a friend. The friend of a friend called me in to help. I grew up in Chicago and my name came up as someone who could help deal with a gang problem. I live in Los Angeles, doing security gigs for celebrities." He catches the surprise on your face. "Yeah, I know. We're a long way from Hollyweird, but no matter where you go, the problems are all the same. Mr. Clemont's got lots of problems. He brought you in to solve the problems I refused to solve for him."

The snow falls heavier now and the city seems to settle, muted under the fresh white blanket. The streetlights light up the snowflakes and in a few hours, this dirty stretch of town could look pretty, at least until morning. The silence stretches out until you have to snap it. "What do you want to know, Chill?"

He shrugs. "You don't show up in a Google search, or maybe you do on page eighty-six or something. There's a lot of Jesuses in the world."

"I imagine you got a lot of hits on the well-known, formerly Jewish magician."

The big man looks grim. "Beware the blasphemer."

"Looking up Jesus is like looking up John Smith. I actually met a John Smith a few months back. The dude looked exactly like I imagined all John Smiths should look like. White guy with an alligator on his shirt and a stick up his ass."

Chill laughs a little, lets that settle down and then looks at you as serious as a knife in the eye. "You asked me what I want to know. I can probably guess quite a bit, but the main thing I need to know is, who am I teaming up with? Are you a good guy?"

"I think I just had this conversation with Willow. I gotta tell you, man, you aren't my type."

"You, either, man. I'm gay, but don't believe the hype. I'm picky. You're cute, but too petite for my taste. "

"I'm both insulted and relieved."

Chill laughs again. "So? How about it? Good guy or bad guy?"

"I told Willow I'm a good guy. You seem like a good guy. But here's the thing: those two pieces of shit that walked in Sam's diner an hour ago and grabbed Willow by the hair and threatened to kill her? Those guys think they're good guys, too. I'm not sure there are good guys, except in bad movies for simple people, maybe. I've seen things. I've seen guys who were supposed to be good do stuff that turned my stomach. Guys with stars and bars."

"I just hang out with stars in bars and babysit them," Chill says, "but I think I got your flavor. Go on."

"What do you want me to say, Chill? Clemont called me in and I just happened to be here when the shit went down and I burned one of the sinners with holy water. What else is there? I'm righteous. I haven't done anything else for him yet." (Except the little matter of putting a bullet in Thomas-not-Thomas, the turtle with an ankle holster.)

Chill nods and looks at his shoes.

"But you aren't up for any illegal shit." It's a statement, not a question, but Chill takes his time answering.

"I'm 37 years old, Jesus. The illegal shit is supposed to be behind me."

"I'm not 30 yet. I got a few more years of stupid left in me."

"It's the testosterone overload, you know."

"I know. What do you want done?"

"Just like that?"

"Can't be worse than what I just got out of."

"What did you just get out of?"

"It's a long story. It'd take up a whole book and it's cold out here."

"How about I do my thing and watch the girl? I provide security and when I need back up, I'll just call the police. You say you're not the bad guy, but when shit goes down, you're not the type to call the police, am I right?"

"Yeah. I'm Batman."

Chill's chuckle sounds like it could come from a little Macy's Christmas elf. "The guys that came in heavy tonight went down easy, but the Lone Wolf and his sidekick will be back, and maybe not alone."

"I read you. I was hoping I'd get the job of watching Willow."

"I have a feeling you might get distracted and she'd get you out of that nice suit."

You nod. "Willow is distracting, but I never take off this suit. I'm too pretty in it."

"You are." He smiles again. This banter between a couple of guys just bullshitting? You've missed this. Everyone in Group is so bare-their-soul earnest, they think the earth turns on the axis of their every conversation.

Then it comes to you. "Chill, I don't want to mow your lawn, but, you're solid gay, right? Not iffy, even when you see a girl as hot as Willow?"

"Solid. No offence, but pussy gives me the heebie-jeebies."

"Excellent. Okay, then you can babysit my future wife and the mother of all my many, many children while I work for her dad and take care of business."

Chill nods. "Is Willow in for the night?"

"All locked in. I even checked behind the shower curtain and under the beds before I left."

"That must have been quite a challenge, getting away from her bed."

"Please. A girl like that, you don't go near the bed until the third date. Respect!"

"Righteous."

Chill turns and opens the door to the diner for you. You step in out of the cold and stomp your feet to get the slush off your shoes. Chill waves goodbye.

"You aren't coming in?"

"You're on your own with Mr. Clemont. What he asks you to do, I don't know and I don't want to know. From here on out, my favors begin and end with protecting the man's daughter and your future wife. Favors weigh heavy, man. The guy who brought me in? I owe him a *ton* in favors, so I couldn't say no. You taking care of this for me so I don't have to do some sketchy shit for Clemont, though? Now I owe *you* a favor."

"Cool."

"Probably not."

Chill lets the door swing closed. He pauses for a moment on the sidewalk, raises one hand and makes the sign of the cross, blessing you through the glass. The big man tucks his Bible under his arm, turns and the night swallows him.

It's warm in the diner, but you feel dead cold and alone.

ROPE

After locking the door, you find Samuel Clemont making a fish patty for himself in the kitchen. The counters and stoves are built shorter so he can reach everything. You feel taller. Then your shoulders sag when you consider that Willow sees you the way you see this Oompa Loompa kitchen.

Clemont scrapes the burnt fish patty off the grill with a blackened spatula and dumps it on a stiff bun beside a pile of french fries on a chipped plate. "Shoulda set up shop in New Orleans. You burn your food in the Big Easy, you just call it Cajun and nobody complains. Just add hot sauce." He bites into his sandwich and grimaces. "I grew up in Maine, so I hate fish. Ate too much of it when I was a kid. Sick of it. This halibut is about to turn. Might as well eat the profits. Still better than most food I ever had as a grunt."

"Is the Marines where you learned to cook?"

His laugh has a cutting edge. "Hell, no!" He drops the fish sandwich back on the plate. "Though, that would explain a lot."

While Clemont focuses on the fries, you look around. The M4 Carbine is propped against the wall in a corner beside a table with a box of rounds. Clemont snaps his ketchup-stained fingers and waves you over to a stool by the counter. "I talked to Paulie again. He said you'd come."

"It sounds like you've got much bigger problems than Willow's drug dealer."

"I thought Gillie could take care of these guys. Apparently, I was misinformed, so I guess people *can* change. Should have seen what he did back in the day. Gillie's still bad ass, but inflexible about what else I need done. Since you've already shot Willow's supplier, I guess you're up. You pass the test. You can help me with the Lone Wolf and his sidekick."

"Maybe Gillie's got the right idea — "

"You like Gillie? Kinda faggy, huh? I wouldn't tell him that if I were you, Gee-Zuzz. He'd pop you like a little boil on his ass."

"Is that a short joke? I suspect you used to be taller but you're probably shorter than me now. It's hard to tell with you sitting all the time."

His laugh is a seal bark, but you can tell you scored a point by hitting back.

You've run into crusty old guys like this. Clemont comes off tough and gristled, but he's really testing your skin for thickness. He wants to see how long it will take before you tell him to go to hell.

It would have already happened, but he is your future father-in-law. You can be polite and appear to have all the social graces. Tia Marta taught you how to look like you were in love while waiting to strangle the life out of her. You can keep your temper on the chain and never let it show. You'll wait. When the time comes, he's not living with you and Willow and the kids. You'll remind him of what an asshole he is as you drive him to the cheapest old age home you can find.

"You owe me one coffeepot. Gillie cleaned up your mess."

On the other hand, why wait to frost his nuts since he's trying to bust your balls? "From what I gather, you want me to clean up a much bigger mess. And you already owe me a chunk of change. The man at the address you specified is dead."

Clemont digs out a cigarette and lights it. He must have had the habit a long time because he cups his hands around the lighter's flame, as if he's still out in the field, bracing against a stiff wind. "You were supposed to get the money and the drugs from the premises. Paulie told me you were good."

"Paulie's right, but I don't have X-ray vision."

"You botched the job."

"If you had dealt with me directly instead of going through Paulie, I'd have had more details, like knowing where to look for the cash. After I shot him, there wasn't a lot of time to hang around and tear the place apart brick by brick."

"Excuses. From where I sit, you screwed up."

"You're always sitting. It's different when you're standing up and walking around, taking care of business. The place was a front. Maybe the guy did business there, but he was cagey. He even gave me a false name."

"What name did he give you?"

"Thomas LeClerc."

"And he didn't even live there anymore?" Clemont looks genuinely surprised.

"A lot of drug dealers don't want anyone to know where they really live. I knew a guy in New York who had a dozen apartments and houses, weed growing in every one. You take a walk and see windows with black out curtains, five will get you ten."

"Uh-huh. So I'm out my money and you want yours. You're going to be disappointed when you find out how the world works."

"I've seen how the world works and I'm beyond disappointment, Samuel. The only light I see is in your daughter. How did an angel like that come out of a guy like you?"

He smiles. "Her mother was a peach."

"Must have been."

"How's this? You double down on the job and keep the Lone Wolf out of here and I'll get you your money. Gillie and I disagree about possible solutions to the problems I've acquired, but a Cuban dwarf might do."

"You've been talking to Willow."

"She called."

"What'd she say about me?"

"Says you don't do drugs and I should ask about your gun."

"It's a SIG Sauer P220 and you already know why I carry it. What did you tell Willow?"

"That you're the shortest bodyguard I could find through my old military connections and she shouldn't count on you being around for long."

"That's hurtful." You flip him the bird and he smiles wider.

"The local gang is giving me trouble. You're a troubleshooter, Jesus. Troubleshoot."

"If those guys are in a gang — "

"They aren't exactly. They're a faction out of the exurbs and they think they're on their way up. They want to be part of the core business and be in the big time downtown. The gang calls themselves The Victorious."

"Sounds like a boy band."

"The Lone Wolf and his burnt buddy had a meeting with me last week, when they started the hustle. If they can do well by the gang, they're not simple foot soldiers anymore. They want to move up the chain all at once on my back."

"So they're trying to make their bones. Guys trying to make bones are dangerous."

"I got my M4 and you got your SIG. Why didn't you go for the P226? You'd have fifteen rounds instead of just nine."

"I hit what I aim at and I like my rounds to have more punch. Chill wanted to bring in the cops to deal with those guys, right?"

"Yeah."

"What did you tell Willow? How much does she know?"

"About the drug dealer you killed, she knows nothing. She's been a good girl lately."

You wait for him to spill more and he stares at you through the smoke. He's the first to break the pregnant pause, so you win. "All Willow knows is those guys tonight came for protection money."

"Keep her in the dark. Here's what you say if she starts looking at you funny: if you call the police, they ask a lot of questions, make arrests and then the bad guys get out on bail. Then they come looking for you. Restraining orders aren't bulletproof. You can have 911 on speed dial, but cops are for after the fireworks are done and blood and brains are smeared all over the walls. No matter how many times you paint, blood and brains always show through. Cops show up late. They're for after-the-fact problems. They're less useful before the fact."

"Sounds about right."

"In my experience, it's exactly right."

"In your experience," he says and lets that hang out there a little longer than you like.

"Let's focus on the real problem," you say.

"I need to discourage these guys so they don't come back. Ever."

"We discouraged them pretty well tonight. They might even get hang dog depressed for a while, what with the burning, scarring and pain."

"Guys like this?" Clemont says. "The Victorious is a *gang*. If it spreads to them beyond the Lone Wolf and his sidekick, the rest of the gang will get involved. That's when things get tricky. You beat 'em senseless and if you let them wake up after the beating, they come back for more, but harder next time. They're used to intimidating people and when they run into somebody who can't bend, they have to come down even nastier just to be sure everybody on the block gets it. We've got to get the Wolf and his pal dead — not connected to me — and nip this thing in the bud. They're seriously bad."

"What do you know about the Victorious?"

"They've been around a while. A few years ago, there used to be a barber down the street. He didn't want to pay protection. They made him drink that blue stuff used to clean scissors."

"Barbicide."

"Yeah. How'd you know?"

"Getting my hair cut is one of the few things that relaxes me. I like the scalp massage. The barber got very sick I assume?"

"Killed him. Took some time, though."

"So you want a cost-benefit hit?"

His head comes up. "A what?"

"You got that M4 and Chill, but you've also got a business and a daughter. You're vulnerable. The gang no doubt have a place they hang out. What you want is to make them feel vulnerable and off balance so they get distracted with bigger problems — AKA me — instead of coming after you for protection money. Maybe they come after me or maybe we can blame a rival gang. That's a cost-benefit hit."

"Right! That's exactly what I need! Blaming a rival gang. Could that work?"

"Only in theory, for a short time. I've seen it tip upside down. It's a lot of death and destruction. I'd have to hunt Wolf and Mr. Birthmark fast before they got to you. They might have already swallowed their pride and called in reinforcements from The Victorious, though if they can't handle a simple protection scam, they might not want to share that information. After what happened tonight, if I were them, I'd just come right back and firebomb the place."

"So hit them fast, before they get reinforcements."

"Downside: they might get me first."

"What's your price?"

"Money's no object?"

"Within reason. Look around. I'm trying to build a legacy here for Willow. I've got too much invested in this place. Do you know how much it costs to custom fit a kitchen for wheelchair height?"

"Uh-huh."

"I was thinking you could take care of this for me for a few thousand dollars."

"My suit is worth a few thousand dollars and you still owe me for the first hit."

"Then a few thousand dollars more," he says.

You sigh and wait for him to come out with it but he's still under the impression you're an idiot. It's time to let the old guy know you are not going to let him drive this bus. "Sam. As the man who will be your future son-in-law, let's not throw feces, okay? We are not monkeys at the zoo."

His eyes narrow but he's still not going to give.

"Let's spray some air freshener," you say. "You get me to hit a drug dealer to keep him away from Willow. You figure you'll take care of a protection racket problem, and pay my fee, by having me steal all of said drug dealer's cash on hand. That hangs together in theory. Almost."

"That was the plan. What's the loose string?"

"I mean, sir, that I don't believe a word of that story. That story — pardon me for honesty in the face of death and disaster and family discord — sucks a big fat clit."

PLAY IT AGAIN, SAM

"What gave me away?" Clemont asks.

"Those guys came in way too heavy for a protection job. You can't give up a hundred or two a week for protection? The math is bad. My expenses alone would cover the cost of paying these gangster wannabes. You could easily slide the gang a little money, or move, or even call the police if principle really is more important to you than your own neck. The hanging string is that you aren't going to risk your daughter no matter how much of a hard ass you want to make me think you are. You're not an idiot — at least I don't think you are. *Yet.* I'm reserving judgment depending on what you say in the next couple minutes."

"Shit," Clemont says, admitting defeat with a chagrinned look.

"So try again."

"All I care is to find someone to take care of the problem. I'd do it myself but…" Clemont gestures at the spot where his legs are not.

"If I was supposed to feel sorry for you now, you shouldn't have acted like such an asshole before. This isn't a favor. You're asking me to clear out a wasp nest. You ask me to kill again, you gotta tell me why I'm doing it. I'm not in the army anymore and I recently made it my policy not to kill people for no good reason. Getting rid of that Vicodin dealer to protect Willow was a good cause. Killing the dealer so you could pay the gang protection wasn't so righteous. I need another righteous reason."

"Keeping the Victorious out of my business is a good cause."

"There might be other solutions than going at The Victorious all *Call of Duty*, so don't give me the good soldier bit, Samuel. After 9/11, I signed up to kill OBL in Afghanistan and got stuck in Iraq instead. I don't follow orders blindly, especially since we haven't fallen in love with each other's undeniable charms yet."

Clemont smokes and thinks and takes his time capitulating. You wait for him to catch up with you at the finish line.

"I guess…"

"Start at the beginning."

"I knew a guy who knew a guy."

"Good start. Go on."

"You know the Scorpion?"

"The car or Mac Gargan, sworn enemy of Spider-Man?"

"Oh, sweet Christ. The *pistol.*"

"I'd be more intrigued if the Victorious were actually led by the Marvel Comics character dressed up as a big scorpion, but go on."

He takes a long drag on his cigarette and, as he speaks, the smoke piles toward the ceiling. "The Scorpion is a nasty little machine designed by the KGB. The guy who knew a guy got a shipment of Scorpions. He had Russian connections. All these handguns had been sitting in a warehouse along with lots of ammunition."

"The ammo is still good after all this time?"

"Cold war issue. Keep it dry and it's good forever."

"How'd it get into the country?"

"Container ship. The container was marked 'Machine parts for dishwashers.' The ports are hit and miss. It wasn't much of a risk. After 9/11, they upped security everywhere except where it counts. One of these days a freighter sent by Pakistan or Saudi Arabia is going to blow up in a harbor and destroy all of New York or Boston. Everyone will wonder, how'd that happen?"

"You're scaring me. Talk to me about the guns to calm my nerves."

"There was this guy I knew named Harry. Harry needed a safe place to keep the shipment until he could find a buyer. He started talking to a few people to feel them out to see if they had the scratch for the buy."

"Who did Harry contact?"

"I don't know who all he talked to exactly. Somebody in a militia in the midwest, a religious bunch in Georgia who are getting ready for the race war, some Minute Men in Texas and Michigan."

"Hold up," you say. "The Texans are trying to keep Mexicans out, but there are Minute Men patrolling the northern border in *Michigan?*"

"Yep. Trying to keep out the one Canadian who wants to live in the U.S."

"*Heh.* Okay. And Harry talked to the Lone Wolf and his scabby little friend?"

"Yeah." He looks gray.

"So if the Wolf gets the Scorpions for his gang, he's a hero and he moves up to the big time."

"That's my complication. There's a group up from Florida that wants the shipment, too."

"Who?"

"They call themselves the Recipients."

"Recipients of what?"

Clemont shrugs. "Christ, I think generally. In this case, guns. Harry said they're a mix. Most of them would consider themselves religious folks, but they're determined to get the Scorpions. Getting ready for The Fall."

"As in next autumn or the fall of God, Satan, the Empire? What?"

"Satan or Obama, maybe. I'm not sure they make those fine distinctions. The Recipients are pretty hardcore churchy and they're willing to pay. These guys repping for the Victorious? They don't want to pay anywhere near a fair price."

"Hm. Well, I'm against that on principle, even if they hadn't grabbed Willow by the hair. It's that exact thieving attitude that makes a few drug deals go wrong and gives all the everyday, peaceful drug deals a bad name."

"I need to deal with The Recipients. They talk the end of the world now, but they're still making vacation plans for next year on Disney Cruises," he assures you. "Convictions are slippery things. You ever see the TV show *Hoarders*? That's mostly what stockpiling guns really is. They aren't dangerous. They're hobbyists who want to play with my Scorpions on their compound's gun range. No big deal."

"Sure. That worked out so well for Koresh at Waco."

"Take my word for it. The Recipients aren't any more of a threat to anyone than the Amish. In fact, they're just like the Amish. They just want to be left alone."

Bats beat leathery wings against the walls of your stomach, trying to escape. If your future wife weren't in danger, you'd already be out the door, after you lit the place on fire.

Clemont seems to read your thoughts. "The way you talk, I thought you were more flexible. A tough guy. You're sounding like Gillie."

"It's not a question of being flexible. It's a question of dealing with crazy people who act off their politics instead of their principles, especially when both are nuts. You deal with the right people, they won't come knocking later. This is America. The only color anyone should care about is green. Business is America's religion. People who make money their god, I understand. Money means freedom. Religious nuts aren't about making choices. They're about cutting everybody else's choices down."

"You and I care about the green and we can make some," Clemont says. "Focus on that."

"But the people you're dealing with *don't* focus on the green. Doing things for love, I understand. Doing shit jobs for money, I understand. Doing things because you have to? I've been there plenty. Cults and compounds? That leads down a road that ends with hateful bullshit and little girls burned in churches. The most successful gangs and mob organizations stay low profile and keep the peace in their neighborhoods so they can do a profitable business."

Clemont shrugs and you can see the responsibility fall from his shoulders. "The Recipients are who I'm doing business with. The choices customers make isn't my end, anyway." He looks at his cigarette as if it holds all the answers. "This is all Harry's fault. I was just a storage guy. Harry wanted a safe place to put washing machine parts. I had a place. Harry had opening talks with too many people."

"What could go wrong there?" If you roll your eyes at him any harder, you might sprain something.

"He imagined a bidding war, as if the shipment was real estate and the Recipients and the street punks would sit there all civilized. I told Harry this isn't some fancy auction house, bidding back and forth with ping pong paddles with numbers on them. Harry thought he could up the price by setting up a little friendly competition."

"What happened to Harry?"

Clemont stares at the ceiling for some time. Finally he admits, "The Lone Wolf killed Harry to let me know that there would be no goddamn auction. These people don't play that way. They want an ass load of Scorpions. You said you understand doing things because you have to. You gotta do this. Before he died, Harry told the Lone Wolf who to go to for the guns. Me. Me and Willow are in the crosshairs."

"I see. Valid."

"Fix it so I can sell the Scorpions to the Recipients unharrassed and Willow's safe. The Recipients might shoot a few gators out in the swamps, but what kind of damage do you suppose a street gang like The Victorious might do with that kind of firepower? I say no to the Wolf and he — or maybe the whole gang now — will kill me and Willow. You, too. Actually, you first."

"I get it."

"Gillie didn't get it. He thinks the way out is to move to Alaska."

"Can't be much colder than Chicago."

"I'm guessing the wheelchair access in Alaska sucks and I don't want a polar bear to eat me on my way to the mailbox."

"So just tell both groups where to find the shipment and you're done. Walk away…say sorry. Roll away and let the Wolf and the Recipients fight it out."

"That leaves too much money on the table. I'll make five times my money back with this deal. No way. Life is too expensive." He glances again at where his legs should be.

You give Clemont a slow nod.

"When can you get the deal done so the Scorpions are off the table?"

"The Recipient guy is coy," Clemont says. "Didn't even give me a phone number. He said he'd call me. The bigshot wannabes gave me a phone number, though. I'm damned if I do and dead if I don't make the call. Neither party thinks I have the guns yet. I've been putting them off, saying the container is still in transit. I've been sitting on the shipment for over a week. You want to ship something scary, do it during the Christmas rush and there's even less chance of getting caught."

"The Wolf's impatient. He must have guessed you're stalling."

"Yeah, telling him I'm out of stock isn't going to get it done any longer. The

Minute Men I could blow off. They're a bunch of paranoid patriots with binoculars. But the Wolf? He killed Harry. We should have killed The Lone Wolf here tonight, but Gillie is too pure for that job. I'd have murdered those two idiots myself tonight. I had those assholes in my sights, but I couldn't do that in front of Willow. With what she's been through…"

"Making Willow an accessory to murder would be bad form?"

"I'd be more concerned about her sobriety. Staying calm and clean…it's a fragile thing." He looks away and studies the ceiling. "I get this deal done, I'll be able to send Willow to a nice rehab out in Colorado."

"I got the picture. I'll help you solve this problem for fifty percent."

"You're dreaming. Me and Harry set this whole thing up. You're late to the party. Ten percent."

"You just lost Harry and now you've got a partner back. You pay Chill out of your half. Fifty-fifty and Willow never finds out you're an arms dealer."

Clemont barks out a big belly laugh. "Willow doesn't know about you killing her drug dealer, but she *already* knows her daddy's an arms dealer." His eyes are steady. You believe him. The Queen of the Giants has a darker side than you had guessed. You try, too slow, to rearrange your face so he doesn't see how much that pains you. You wanted Willow to be pure and you wanted to be pure for her. You should have known she couldn't dress as well as she does and still manage to live off tips.

Sgt. Devin, AKA the Devil, was one of your combat instructors. He warned you that true warriors see the world the way it is. You saw Willow through a gauzy lens. You took her uptown-labelled clothes as a sign that she had fine taste, a perfect match for your preferences for double-breasted Armani suits. You focused on her Jimmy Choos and your Tanini Crisci shoes. The Devil was right: you are an idiot. But you're also a knight. It's your duty to save the Queen of the Giants.

Clemont lights a fresh cigarette off the dying nub of the old one. "Look, kid…I got screwed over. Willow understands because she was by my hospital bed and watched while it happened. The wheelchair is a bad deal, but I could have accepted that. It was the low payout that got me into this. It's a free, capitalist country and an ass load of guns is part of being free and capitalist. Nobody's holding back on buying oranges, iPhones and sneakers just because they get 'em from slave labor. Willow's no different. She doesn't want to know where the money comes from, but she doesn't turn it down, either."

You've been down this road before. Family is family and daughters accept whatever their fathers do. "The deal is *sixty* percent or I walk and you can deal with the crazies on your own," you say.

"Sixt— ?"

"I don't see any other job applicants here and I've got the experience you're looking for. You're going to give me a thousand up front just for expenses and the phone number you've got for The Victorious wannabes."

He soaks that up and smiles. "You sound like you got a plan."

"Not yet, but I will. I always come up with something."

"'Cuz you're *experienced*, huh? New York, mob-type stuff? Does Willow know you're a hit man, not just killing her drug dealer but — hey, how many people have you killed?"

Just like that, he's got you. You sigh. "Forty percent and you keep your mouth shut. I'll tell her my history, but just let me tell her in my own time. Till then, I'm just another bodyguard for hire. And whatever deal you got going on with Chill, pay out of your sixty percent."

Samuel Clemont smiles so wide you see the gaps where his bicuspids used to be. He flicks the butt of his cigarette into the sink. "You and Willow won't last a week, anyway. She'll cut you off quick. Or the Wolf will cut you into little bits. Slow."

He may be right. You need to go recruiting. If you're going to war, you need to get help from the Army. You head out, wondering exactly what your cut on an "ass load" will amount to.

HOLLOW MAN

The next day you find Sgt. Billy at his regular hangout down the street from the Salvation Army's men's shelter. His sloped shoulders look thin even though he's bundled in several layers of clothes. It's easier to wear everything you own rather than to carry it. The nights he doesn't make it to a shelter must be brutal this time of year, even with the sweaters he wears under his big coat. Sgt. Billy is one soldier in Chicago's army of invisible men who wander the streets. When you ask him for his help, he's pissed.

"All this time, I *knew* you could speak English! I knew it and you just kept walking by, throwing a few dollars in my hat."

"Easy, man. I'm talking to you now."

"Yeah? And why's that?"

"Got a job for you."

"A job? I haven't had a job in a long time."

"It'll be easy. It will hardly be different than what you do now."

"That doesn't sound like a paying job. If it was, I'd have heard of it already. You want me to put up posters or something?"

"Even easier than that. C'mon, let's go get a sandwich. I'm buying."

He doesn't move. "They won't let me eat inside."

"Then I'll go in and get it and I'll come out and have breakfast with you."

A few minutes later you're sitting next to him on his usual stoop in front of an abandoned building. Despite his invisibility, there's something left in him from when he was a citizen. He's grateful and polite. Sgt. Billy wants to know more about you before he'll talk business. When he demands to know where you're from, you tell him New York City.

"You know about the Molemen?" he asks.

"Spider-Man went up against the Mole Man. Or do you mean the Molemen, like the enemies of Superman? I'm not a big Man of Steel fan."

"Don't be an idiot."

"Are they Chicago hip-hop guys?" you venture.

"You are an idiot. I mean the Mole People under New York! People said it wasn't true, but it's sort of true. There were a lot of us under the city. Fewer now. There were books about it. Actually there are more underneath Vegas. I'd live there, but I can't take the heat. Chicago gets cold, but you can get to a shelter or sleep on a vent or whatever to get warm. You get too hot, what are you going to do? Homeless, the cops leave you alone. Homeless and naked? They ain't gonna leave you alone."

"Where'd you serve, Billy?" you ask.

"Korea."

"Wow."

"Not so much. You?"

"Sandy places."

He finishes half his sandwich and folds the plastic over the rest to save for later. He stuffs it in one of his pockets. The coat is tattered and filthy. Sgt. Billy smells like onions so you tell him you aren't hungry and give him the rest of your sandwich. That disappears into another filthy pocket.

"Sgt. Billy, can I trust you?"

"I wouldn't, but I suspect I'm smarter than you." His smile splits the space between his gray beard and his broom of a moustache. His eyes are not unkind.

"You know The Victorious?"

"I know who they are. Assholes."

"Do you know where they hang out?"

"Everybody knows. Nobody says. They hang out at a garage up a few blocks and around the corner, less than a few minutes walk from here."

"How would you like to hang out across the street from them? I need eyes on the street."

Sgt. Billy looks to the sky. He might be counting to ten. "Henry David Thoreau said that it's not what you look at that matters. It's what you see."

"I need you to be a proctologist, Billy. Watch the assholes. Recon-only mission from a discreet observation post. If they move in force or if you see something that looks weird, you call me. You tell me. I'll give you a description of two guys to look out for in particular."

"Proctologist. You're a funny guy, but what you really want is a spider crab." He explains when you quirk an eyebrow: "Spider crabs are covered with algae and detritus. Even sea anemones attach to its shell and a spider crab sits in the sand and the silt of the seabed. Living camouflage. A guy like you in that suit can't hang out for more than five minutes without drawing attention. You go over there dressed like you're going to church and you'll get rolled. I'm your spider crab."

Your eyes narrow. You have to know now. "What did you do after Korea?"

"Married a sweet girl from Texas. Got a degree and taught high school English and sometimes biology."

You nod and clear your throat. "Anyway, you gotta hang out somewhere. Why not for pay?"

"Depends. I can see why you wouldn't like The Victorious. The only people they like is their own people. But I have to know why you want me to do this,

Jesus."

"A couple of guys who want to move up fast in The Victorious threatened my future wife last night. I'm trying to figure out how to get rid of them."

"Sounds righteous."

"It is." You hand him one of the disposable cell phones you picked up this morning and show him how to call you.

"What's the wage?"

You hand him a hundred-dollar bill. Sgt. Billy looks at it like he could eat it, but he hesitates. He tears the bill in two and hands half back to you. "Hold on to that and pay me when you're satisfied I'm done, Chief. Give me all that at once and I'm liable to do something I shouldn't with it. Once you pay me, I won't be so useful to the mission."

"Okay, Sergeant."

"This young lady…the future Mrs. Diaz? Let me tell you what you need to know."

He's back in life coach mode. You hold back on a heavy sigh. "Don't tell me anything you don't want me to know."

"If I don't pass it on, what use was the pain? The key to keeping my sweet Texas girl was to keep the drinking to only the weekends or at least really late in the day. If I could have even managed that bare minimum, she would have stuck. A woman in love will put up with a lot. That's why they're better than us. If you find a good one who will put up with you, stick with her 'cuz she's rare."

"How come you couldn't keep the drinking to the weekends?"

"Because, like the poster at the VA says, no soldier comes back unwounded."

"Roger that."

"She deserved better. Drinking's no good when you got kids to watch out for. Parenting and husbanding is tough enough when you're sober. Texas is better off without me. She was *good*, man. If I hadn't been so drunk, I would at least have more memories to cherish." When he stands, you offer your hand and instead, Sgt. Billy salutes you.

Talk of kids and sobriety: Willow called stuff like this synchronicity. Maybe it's just your body reacting to stress that makes your monkey brain whisper, "It would feel so good to get high. You still have a lot of Vikes and ooh, the euphoria!" Maybe it was Sgt. Billy's salute, crisp and unexpected, that triggered your hunger for more Vicodin.

You had planned to go visit Willow and discuss how many kids she wants. Instead, you feel the familiar ache of the hunger that isn't hunger. The counsellors say it's a craving for the kick and the rush of dopamine. Throwing coffee pots and pointing guns at people, wielding the divine power of life and death delivers the same dopamine trick. Maybe adrenaline unlocks the same brain chemicals as dopamine to sate the same needs. To be pure for Willow and lift yourself up above the bare minimum, you're going to have to get past running after these furious rushes and dangerous highs. Batman never gets the girl.

Is your career a solution you fell into because your body got addicted to fear under Tia Marta's fierce tutelage? Does the SIG fill a biological craving to even out that terrifying high? Is the switchblade in your sock the answer to a psychological twist in the branches of your cosmic tree? Is this how God made you, or did He fashion this shit life for you as a challenge to grow out of and overcome?

In *The African Queen*, Katherine Hepburn says to Humphrey Bogart's character, "Nature, Mr. Allnut, is what we are put in this world to rise above." Maybe God wants you to be Charlie Allnut.

When you look at your life, the God and the Devil look like twins on a bender. You may as well ask these questions of a magic eight ball. What you really want to do now is escape questions and doubt and suck down an eight ball.

You push off, heading east. If you don't get to a meeting soon, you might slip, and you are determined not to slip. You're doing this for Willow and all those beautiful little kids you'll have with her.

The counsellors in Group say you should stay clean and sober for yourself first. Alone? You aren't worth that much effort, but maybe your hopes and dreams for you and Willow will pound that mountain road flat.

You go to Group.

FIGHT CLUB

Twelve vets in a mustard-coloured room sit in a circle. You don't care for circles. They demand too much eye contact.

Kyle is the Jamaican nurse who has access to drugs. He says he knows he should switch specialties, but he thinks he can control his addiction. That much, you're almost sure, is true. At the last coffee break he told you he was clean and sober and he deserved his chip. Then he leaned in closer. "But I'm still *selling*, if you're interested. No pressure, mon, but just let me know. On a nurse's salary I got more month left over at the end of my money than I can stand, yeah? If you feel the need, I can hook you up."

The familiar craving gnaws at you, but you turn away and guzzle more acidic coffee to try to drown the Vicodin urge. It's like trying to fight a house fire by peeing on the potted plants.

If this were AA or something, Kyle might have worried that you'd rat him out, but in the VA programs, the code is still in force. Close ranks and be the badass robot. Help each other, cover your buddy and no matter what you do, don't trust the brass. You covered each other when there was sand under your boots. Why should scuffed tile be any different? Vets suffer double the unemployment of civilians and veteran suicides outpace combat deaths. Everybody needs a break.

Official policy is that anybody who sells isn't allowed to stay in group therapy. If you care enough, the group leaders say, you rat out threats to the common sobriety. If you were solid in your commitment to staying clean, you'd rat out Kyle for your protection. Instead, you let Kyle slide. You don't do it just to ignore The Man and official policy or even the desert code. You hold back on dropping the dime because Kyle is a high interest credit card. You should cut him up, but what if you need him someday? What if the drug-hungry tingle comes on too strong and you need a hook up? You keep him around, just in case, even if he could jam you up.

The group leader, Tim, is a swell guy. Everybody says so. He's friendly and smiles at your jokes, but you don't like the former lieutenant. You suspect that to Tim — Smug Tim, in your mind — you've got a life sentence. You're filed under a case label that will never change: Vet with Substance Problems. There's

212 | *The Divine Assassin's Playbook*

something so mortal and terminal about that. Sure, things are screwed up now, but doesn't anybody ever get *over* the bad shit? To heal, do you have to accept a higher power? The only divinity you know is that feeling you get holding a SIG and pointing it at someone. Will you ever just be Jesus Diaz, and not that cloying thing: "A survivor"?

Talk therapy feels like masking tape on a broken car window. Cover it up all you want, but what's broken is never really fixed and it looks like shit. Slather on the same true confessions, add tears, muted applause and "Thank you for sharing!" Rinse and repeat, as if speeches about weakness and victimhood are a magic spell that, once spoken, fire up a time machine that change history and your DNA.

If you live long enough (which seems unlikely) you don't want to be stuck in a mustard-colored room like this as an old man. You don't want to end your days the same way you now spend them, avoiding eye contact with the survivors and addicts. When you look around the room, you see people who can't get over the past because they are too busy talking about what got them here. They're reliving it, wallowing in it. Everybody says Group helps, but talk therapy never made you feel as good as holding the SIG in your hand.

There are a few others here who have PTSD, too, though, unlike you, they picked up their Post Traumatic Stress Disorder in the desert while wearing a uniform. Your PTSD comes from a basement in Florida. Your captors didn't allow you the dignity of clothes, let alone a uniform.

You feel a headache coming from the horizon and zeroing in on your forehead, so you push those old thoughts away and focus on why you hate Tim. Oh, yeah. Group leader Tim has his shit together. He has a house and he says his wife is a hottie, all sideways smiles and aw shucks. He has a couple of kids and a regular job and he knows where he's going to be next year and the next and the next. He's going to be here, in this room with mustard-colored walls, listening to vets like you and pretending not to judge.

Smug Tim says he "had a little Percocet problem" — coyly — the same way a brainless reality show star might say, "I have the sweetest little dog. Fits in my purse. What breed? It's a Percocet!"

Tim picked up his little Percocet problem after an IED took his right leg. You envy Tim his little problems. The mental scars and emotional stumps no one can see? Those don't fix with a metal leg.

"Good to see you again, Jesus. I was worried about you," Tim says. "Haven't seen you for a few meetings."

His crooked, smug smile has too many teeth. You could fix that. "Been looking for a job," you say.

"Excellent! Did one of our counsellors hook you up with a fresh resume?"

Heh. That's funny. What's your resume going to say besides: Hit man; recently let go from The Machine for trying to steal skim; dropped one boss off a high building. Most recent achievement: shot a drug dealer. Current position:

Fugitive from the FBI for questioning in a car bomb case. "Been looking on my own," you say.

"Good for you!"

Excellent! Good for you! Does he mean that or does he go back home to his hottie wife and cute children and laugh about how everybody's so dumb they never catch his irony? Aside from only being three-quarters present and accounted for, what's this guy really all about? If you lose your leg, do you get to be this positive and chipper all the time, too? Maybe you're overestimating Tim. Maybe he's just stupid. You read somewhere that some psychologists believe happy people are delusional and depressed people see the world as it really is. If getting your shit together means being stupid and happy, maybe it would be worth it to get a few more concussions.

Smug Tim rambles on. You look attentive, but you're looking at the poster on the wall behind him. In blood red it reads: Casualties of 9/11, the War on Terror and the Invasion of Iraq: 0.28% were 9/11 victims; 0.55% US casualties in both Afghanistan and Iraq; 4.39% civilian casualties in Afghanistan; 94.78% civilian casualties in Iraq. While he talks, you try to figure out the math in real numbers. If the 0.28% was about 3,000 people, then...damn. Tia Marta was your only teacher. The bitch never taught you math.

You knew some of those casualties: Iraqi, Afghani and American military. Listening to Smug Tim is part of the penance. When the little Muslim kids come to you in the day, they are just daydreams you can unhitch. They aren't scary then. When they come at night looking like skinless, burnt zombies? Different story.

You come out of doing the bloody math in your head. Shattered Crystal is talking. Skulls are tattooed on her knuckles. Shattered Crystal always wears long sleeves and covers herself up, but the edges of more tatts appear now and then at her ankles and collar. As she mows the same psychological lawn again, Tim puts on his listening face — or maybe he really is listening, who can tell?

You watch the sharp end of a yellow eagle's beak dance along the line of the sternocleidomastoid muscle in Crystal's neck. When she turns her head to address Tim, it stands out and ripples.

You know it's the sternocleidomastoid muscle because a buddy in your platoon had his shot out by an enemy sniper one bright sunny day while he was burning shit in a barrel with jet fuel at the edge of the base.

"Sternocleidomastoid. Somehow missed the arteries. It's a lottery wound!" the medic had said. The guy lived, but he was never going to look left to check his blind spot again.

Shattered Crystal was raped by two superior officers in Iraq. Some people put on weight to try to make themselves less attractive to their abusers. Living mostly on table scraps, you weren't given that option in that basement in Miami.

As a tank commander, Crystal couldn't put on weight and get sloppy, either.

Making herself tougher, pretending to be another person: that's how all those tattoos started. Then she kept going and the tattoos grew and spread and came together. Trapped, Shattered Crystal figured she would never come back from Iraq. She never thought she'd have to apply for a job at a Denny's with all those scary tattoos.

You didn't turn to tattoos. There wouldn't be much point since you never take your clothes off in the presence of another human being. You didn't get fat, though that sounds like a more pleasant way to defend unwanted advances. Instead, you became another person. There are two of you in one body. To protect yourself, you usually let the smartass with the flexible morality do the talking. He's kept you alive so far.

The question is, who is the real Jesus? You can never trust your brain to answer your questions honestly. You'd have better luck figuring out whether Tim's really happy when you lie to him about your progress.

"Forgiveness." A new voice cuts in on Shattered Crystal's practiced monologue of undeserved shame.

You look up. It's the guy with the salt and pepper hair — you can't remember his name — and he's eyeballing you with a familiar, hyped-up look. The nice guy half tells you to smile back at him and look away. The tough guy in you says stare him down and if he doesn't look away, take him out in the alley after the meeting for "a lesson in deportment." That's what Tia Marta called your beatings.

"Deportment and comportment," Tia Marta teased as she ran the flogger up and down your bare leg. "I'll go a little easier on you if you know the difference, Jesus. It pays to increase your word power. See how your balls jump as I bring my cat-o'-nine up your thigh? That's called the cremasteric reflex. Your testicles are trying to hide from me. Funny, isn't it?"

"What are you doing, Jesus?" Salt and Pepper Guy says. "You got any forgiveness going on in your life? I don't think you do."

"Excuse me, Hans," Tim says. "Crystal was speaking."

Hans! That's Salt and Pepper Guy's name. Hans as in Hans Gruber, the bad guy from *Die Hard*. How could you forget?

"Now I'm speaking, Tim! Now I'm speaking! Crystal's always talking and you listen and you nod but nobody has any answers for us and meanwhile, this guy here," — Hans points at you — "is planning some evil shit. I see the signs! He's got a shadow soul, man! Don't you see that dark cloud? Don't you see the metal teeth in the gears working behind his eyes?"

"Calm down, Hans. We do not talk to each other like that in Group!"

"Talk like what? Tell the truth? Save a soul and maybe the freak's life?" Hans has that shiny-eyed earnest look unique to spiritual gurus, true believers and the terminally crazy. "Jesus! Listen to me, man. To err is human, to forgive is divine."

"I'd like to find it in myself to forgive," Crystal says, "but I'm not good enough. I don't have it in me."

Everyone goes quiet. Hans somehow manages to look even more smug than Tim.

You feel a rant and a lesson in deportment coming on, but you keep cool. There are predators and prey and witnesses. This room has too many witnesses. "I don't believe in forgiveness," you say finally. "I believe in vengeance."

Hans winces. He can't believe you didn't roll over on your back and beg for a belly scratch as soon as he dropped his greeting card wisdom on you.

"Jesus," Tim says. "You know that never works out."

"Works about as well as blaming yourself for being human. When they freed the slaves from those cotton plantations, the slave owners couldn't believe their victims didn't want to keep working because they'd been 'treated well.' We are those slaves. The people who sent us to the wrong country thank us for our service and patriotism but they don't know what patriotism means."

"Forgiveness is the answer," Hans says. "Don't wait for others to be perfect, perfect yourself."

"I'm not doing anything with feel-good slogans you pulled from Pinterest, dude. You want me to forgive so I can move on? Gimme my slice first. Even in the Bible, to forgive somebody, they gotta line up an apology, repentance and restitution. Dick Cheney and Rumsfeld and all those cats restituted fucking nothing."

"Lefty in the house!" some GI Joebot in the circle pipes up. A few others giggle and mutter.

"It's not about left or right. It's about what's *correct*. If I forgive everything, that means it's okay."

"I disagree, Jesus," Smug Tim says. "Forgiving doesn't make it okay, but it might make *you* okay."

"Forgiveness is divine, huh? To forgive what we've lost takes godlike power. Anybody here a god?"

"I've forgiven everyone." Tim taps his artificial leg with his cane and sits back, as if he can beat you with his disability. That prosthesis is the source of his power. He's one of those asshole cripples who believes a one-legged man can never lose an argument because he's always carrying phantom pain as his trump card.

"Tim, if you've really forgiven everyone, maybe you're a living saint."

He smiles his aw-shucks smile.

You struggle to sit still in your seat. "Or maybe you're an idiot coward who gets a lot of approval for announcing he forgives everybody. If you forgive, you're sure everyone will applaud and say, 'There goes Tim, lost a leg and still a good sport.'"

You're making entirely too much eye contact, but you barrel on. "I see that and say, 'There limps Tim. He's the guy with the little problem with Percocets who's still addicted to the idea of being a good soldier. Yeah, Tim can't stand the idea that not everyone likes him. He's *so* impressive, thinking he's like God, but really, he's just desperate for approval. It's pathetic."

The air is hot. Your mouth tastes like bad coffee. You stare him down and he sees what Hans sensed in you.

"Yours is an interesting perspective," Tim says finally.

The circle ripples as the others shift in their seats. They look at the floor. You called him out and all he's got is "interesting perspective"? Maybe he is a good guy full of forgiveness, but he sure sounds like a wimp backing down.

You turn your lasers on Hans, your voice low, slow and reasonable. "Dude, I don't know what your issue is with me, but Crystal was fucking talking and you want to hear somebody who agrees with you, so let her talk. She's in pain because you're asking her to do the impossible. She blames herself instead of giving a guy like me the names of her superior officers — excuse me, *rapists* — so I can make sure they never have the equipment to do that again to somebody else."

"I don't want that," Crystal says, wiping a tear.

You don't believe her. Her voice lacks conviction. You could convince her you should go castrate her attackers in less than the time it takes a hot coffee to cool. All she'd have to do is give you names and a slight nod and you'd do that for her for free. Or just strangle them the same delicious way you strangled Tia Marta. Serve up forgiveness all day and you're still hungry. Righteous vengeance is more filling.

Everyone else is quiet and sitting far back in their chairs, looking at you in a new way. This is the most you've spoken in Group. That was a mistake.

"Check him!" Hans shouts. "He has a weapon on him! I'm sure! Check him! He carries!" He springs from his chair, but Crystal's hand snakes out and catches Hans' wrist before he can come at you. Tim sticks his cane between you and Hans. It's purely a symbolic boundary, but everybody's ex-military in here, all about defending boundaries: the symbolic, the imaginary and the useless.

It's probably Crystal's pleading eyes that break the spell, because as soon as Hans looks in her face, he softens and steps back.

You raise your hands in a gesture to show they are empty. Your hands tremble. Your body shakes from the inside out, but your voice is steady when you say, "The sign on the front door says no weapons beyond this point, Hans. I am not carrying."

"That's right!" Tim says. "This is a *safe* space. We do *not* bring weapons in here."

That idea must be comforting to Smug Tim.

"And we do not interrupt another member's time," he adds. "Sit down, Hans."

Hans throws a defiant glance your way but sits. He apologizes to Shattered Crystal.

You get up to leave and the group choruses with calls for you to stay. "I'm done for this evening," you say. "Got a headache coming on."

"You going to take anything for that headache, Jesus?" Hans asks. You give him a tight grin.

"Your Indian name is Sees Things That Aren't There. I won't forget your name anymore."

Hans smiles, like he's won something. Or maybe you really have given too much away. "You *are* packing, aren't you?" he says.

You open your trench coat and spin slowly. At the conclusion of your 360-degree turn, you come back to Hans's eyes. "The force is not strong in this one."

Crystal bursts out in a giggle so Group is not entirely unrewarding tonight. "I'm out."

"You don't have to go," Smug Tim calls after you.

"Got a job. Stuff to do," you say. "I'll be back." Then you say "I'll be back," again doing your Arnold Schwarzenegger impression so they don't know if you're serious about returning. That's fine. You don't know, either.

The automatic door squeaks as it slides aside and you gulp in cold breaths to try to settle your heartbeat. The shakes are still there, a tell of your weakness. Hans is probably just crazy, but why did he zero in on you? What bothers you more is what it means. Despite going up against the Lone Wolf and Mr. Bad Birthmark, you're still a bad guy.

This life isn't what you nearly died for: not in the water off Surfside Beach; not in the Miami basement; not in the desert; not in New York. Smug Tim tries to make you run through the past. Like Shattered Crystal, he wants you to tell it, cry over it, make sense of it and maybe even get bored of it. But what's the difference between that and wallowing?

"You won't be back," you tell yourself aloud. "If things are going to change, you have to get things right for you and Willow. It's time to start looking forward, not back," you announce to the whizzing traffic.

Fuck Smug Tim and forget him. He might be mocking you with every optimistic word about life goals, to-do lists and positive reframing.

You hate Shattered Crystal because she's you. Go away, Crystal.

You hate Hans because he was so close to right about you packing heat. What if he's right about evil behind your eyes?

You shut that thought down as best you can. Doubt is for guys with regular jobs.

You hate Group and their politics, their cliques and their phony, self-congratulatory backslapping. Their earnest esprit de coeur exhausts you. You have no mercy for them. That shelf is empty. All you've got for them is distance and indifference.

Heh. Distance and indifference. That makes you sound pretty godlike, after all.

You turn your mind to how lovely Willow is. You think about what a great mother she will make as you step into McDonald's to retrieve your gun. You hid it above a ceiling tile in the men's john.

DOUBLE JEOPARDY

The Super, Miss Iris, acts like a sweet, old woman as long as you're up to date on the rent, which you are not. You slow down as you walk past her door and tread lightly up the metal steps so your footsteps don't echo up and down the stairwell. You need the three s's: shit, shower, and shave. If the military had added another s for sleep, it wouldn't have been so bad.

When you walk into your apartment, there's a fat man in the corner fiddling with an iPhone. You've seen him once before. You can reach for your SIG, but a very tall bald guy puts the muzzle of a sawn off to your head. The only sleep you're in danger of getting any time soon is the long dirt nap.

The bald guy with the shotgun frowns, puts one finger to his lips — his middle finger — to let you know that now is not the time to scream for help, the police, or to engage in witty repartee. Now, you conclude, is an excellent time to shut the fuck up and listen. When you nod your understanding of this unspoken signal, the bald guy smiles and nods back. One canine and a top front tooth are missing from his smile and the rest of his teeth look like caramel corn. The effect is grisly.

"Jesus! How about that? Here you are. C'mon in," the fat man says. "Jesus Salvador! Jesus Salvador Umberto! Jesus Salvador Umberto Luis! Jesus Salvador Umberto Luis Diaz! The burning man! That is *quite* a handle you got there. What was the deal? Insecure? First name, middle and last not good enough for your mother, was it? Or is all that extra nonsense because you come from a huge Roman Catholic family with a lot of old uncles to honor?"

You stare and wait. The fat man doesn't look impatient. He blinks, amiable and avuncular.

"Or maybe it's because you're an only child and your dad had plans for a huge family but your mom said she was going to have one and done? Your dad had big plans and then he had to use up all the boys' names in his head since your mother decided to kill all his progeny while they were still seeds?"

You think of your dead brother Rodolpho. No, you weren't an only child, but you were alone in the world too soon. Rodolpho died in a swirl of red water. Your mother disappeared. Sharks ate your father. You have a long story to tell about how your family suffered so you could live in America. Since their sacrifice landed you in a lousy room with these two, you decide it's best not to get into it. You just shrug.

"You're an eloquent guy, Diaz."

You shrug again.

"Don't overdo it." He gestures toward the only other seat in the room, a wooden chair by the table. Before you can sit down, the fat man holds up a finger to stop you. "One thing. My friend behind you is Lurch. My advice to you is, please, do not piss off Lurch."

You turn to give Lurch the slow scan up and down and he puffs out his chest and smiles again.

"Don't worry," you say. "I'll let the Wookie win."

Lurch stays puffed up but at least that closes his rotting maw. He keeps the sawn off levelled at your gut as he pulls out the chair and turns it backward. He tilts his head and you straddle it, your arms cross the top of the chair.

The fat man sweats even though your room is cold. "I thought you'd be taller."

"I get that a lot. I'm not that short. I just didn't grow up next to a nuclear plant to be a freak like poor Lurch."

Whoever cut the stock on the sawn off did a lousy job of it. When Lurch hits you in the right kidney, there's an extra sharp edge to the blow. The pain makes you forget your headache.

The effect, as Tia Marta taught you, is called the Gate Theory of Pain. Got pain? A fresh new pain from somewhere else can block the original pain signal. Lurch's savage blow eclipses the sun. You swallow your cry. The fat man is patient while you get your breath back.

Tia Marta was a master of pain, but Lurch could give her a few tips. The right kidney is a little lower than the left to make room for the liver. Lurch located your right kidney with such great accuracy, it's clear this isn't his first rodeo. When you wipe away tears to clear your vision, and glance back, his ugly teeth are back on display. Unlike the Lone Wolf, he isn't jittery, either. Violent people who look placid are scarier than using a rattlesnake for a condom.

The fat man leans forward so you're eye to eye. Under your jacket, at your side, you still have the SIG in your waistband. It would be satisfying to shoot Lurch in the kidneys so he gets a feel for what the pain is like, but only a desperate fool would try it. You are enough of a fool to give it a try, yes, but you aren't quite that desperate yet.

"Your landlady, Miss Iris? I had a good conversation with her."

"I bet."

"Don't be angry with her. After I paid your rent, she let us in and was very cooperative ."

"Thanks."

"You're welcome. Miss Iris told me lots of things. You were behind on your rent quite a bit. I paid up till the end of the month. I expect that after our business is concluded, you'll want to move on."

"What business do you and I have? I hear the real money is in coming up with new iPhone apps."

The fat man smiles. "Miss Iris said you were a smartass. How long have you known our friend, Samuel Clemont?"

"Not long."

"How did he get hold of you? Does Old Sam have connections to the New York mob scene? Or do you two have military friends in common? Or is the big black fella a friend of yours?"

They seem to already know everything.

"Chill's a friend."

"Uh-huh. And Samuel's girl?"

"Who?" It would be bad form to give them Willow to use against you.

"Willow Clemont. The tall blonde girl you walked home. Don't tell me *she* slipped your mind. Nobody forgets a girl who looks like that. I've got pictures."

The future Mrs. Diaz is already in the crosshairs. "She needed walking home, that's all."

"Uh-huh." For the first time, the fat man glances at Lurch. "How about that?"

"I didn't catch your name," you say.

The fat man smiles. "I didn't tell you. A guy like you with too many names and a guy like me with none. I like that balance, the yin and the yang of it."

Time to pretend you aren't just a pawn. "So you're from the Recipients and you want the guns."

You see something in his face that passes quickly. What was that? Confusion?

"You're a little brownish man playing in a game where you don't even know the stakes," he says. "You have no idea the trajectory you're on. I see the big picture. That's the hand God dealt you in the big poker game. That's not my fault or my problem. Even better, you're going to help me because I'm appealing to your basic instincts. You want to live, I'll bet."

"That would be good."

"I'll let you live as long as you do as I say."

"What's the magic word?"

Lurch hits you in the right kidney again in exactly the same spot. This time, you fall to the floor gasping as the pain jangles up and down your back. Your jaw drops wide. All you can do is writhe, succumb to your screaming nerves and wait.

"There are people coming, Jesus. A little bunch. They're very important. You're on the floor gasping for air, looking like a landed carp and I'm up here, working on a whole other level."

You manage a nod. It would be churlish not to agree.

"When more of my people arrive, they're going to want everything that

Samuel Clemont has. We know there's a local street gang who wants the Russian shipment. Old Sam's partner, Harry, shouldn't have looked for more buyers after he spoke to us. That was rude."

He waits until you can speak again, studying you as you moan. He looks like a nerdy kid examining an unfamiliar insect whose wings he's just yanked off.

When you can speak, you're feeling cooperative. "I don't know where the shipment is. He's afraid the locals will try to get it before he can sell it to you."

"Good. So we're really on the same team. Simple solution: show those gang members we're serious people and do it right away. We are still prepared to pay what we offered. If Clemont deals with these other people for fear they'll kill him and his daughter, we'll kill him and his daughter. You and the black fella, too, of course. *Heh.* Your death. A mere afterthought. How does that feel?"

"Like any average Tuesday evening." The pain is so bad, you wonder if you'll piss blood, if you dare to try to pee again. Ever. "Clemont already hired me to deal with The Victorious."

"Samuel can only give you a carrot. Now that you know we're very firm about getting the shipment, you have the extra motivation of the stick. A young criminal such as yourself often loses track of key priorities."

You croak out a couple of lines from *The Untouchables*: "That's the Chicago way. Here endeth the lesson." If you were in better form, your Sean Connery impression would come out better. The key to the impression is to pretend you have loose dentures, but your breath is too shallow as yet for the forceful delivery required.

The fat man laughs politely. "We'll call Samuel soon. We'll expect his immediate cooperation. We expect that you'll convince him of all that's at stake. You do understand, right? I don't want Lurch to break a sweat making you understand."

"I get it."

"Clear as glass?"

"Like glass dropped on concrete."

"Excellent. Hey, where'd you learn to speak English?"

"Florida."

"Huh. Of course. Well, my compliments. Even when you cry, you don't sound Hispanic."

The fat man hauls himself out of the chair with a soft grunt and crouches beside you to examine your face as you work through the pain.

The knife in your sock is handy. You could stick that in his eye, taking time to dig for the brain, but Lurch has that sawn off pointed at your groin.

You close your eyes to the agony. The SIG springs into your hand by magic and you double tap Lurch in the face twice before he can cut you in two…You open your eyes. Nah. That doesn't happen, but magic would be useful.

The fat man straightens with another grunt and steps over you on the way out the door. "We'll call soon. Leave him his gun, Lurch. He'll need it to deal with the Wolf."

Lurch keeps his shotgun trained on you as he bends and tucks the PS3 console under his arm. He backs out of the room and, peeking around the corner, stage whispers, *"Bang!"* and disappears.

Their footsteps echo off the metal treads of the staircase as you try to get up. Pain is such a small, inadequate word for all the work it does. They took too much stuffing out of you to risk it. All you can do is crawl to the window and peer out, your breath pulled and pushed through gritted teeth, hissing.

On the street below, the fat man waddles out to a black Ford F150 where he waits for Lurch to open the passenger door for him. The F150 is indistinguishable from every other truck of its kind. It's too far to see the license plate even if the high angle allowed you to spot it. The vehicle sports an extra antenna from its roof with a foxtail tied to the end.

You hold the bruised spot over your right kidney and watch Lurch and the fat man pull away from the curb.

Once they're gone, you roll over and bang the back of your head against the radiator. You experiment with banging it a little harder, but the Gate Theory of Pain doesn't seem to be working in your favor today. The fat man has you in his fist and Lurch has your PS3 and *Lego Batman 2*.

You let the Wookie win.

OUR MAN IN HAVANA

A lot can happen in six minutes. Only six minutes ago Willow packed a bag while Chill tore off in his SUV to lure away anyone following her. A black muscle car peeled off after him, so you felt pretty confident Chill's decoy manoeuvre worked. You took Willow's keys and headed for her yellow hatchback in the parking garage behind her apartment.

Confidence. Silly mistake. Six minutes can feel like just a few seconds.

Six minutes from now, Willow will run to your side, screaming for you not to shove your attacker's own blade up into his throat. You're so angry by then, you want to kill your attacker as if he's a zombie: push the blade through the floor of his mouth, through his tongue, into the roof of his mouth and past the palate's bony resistance up into his brain pan. The long blonde will have her way. The mystery of why you will spare him will interest you almost as much as the fight did. But that's six minutes from now, proving that six minutes can also feel like an ugly hour.

*   *   *   *   *   *

He comes at you from behind, out of the shadows, just as you turn Willow's key and pop the car's hatch. Your attacker could have killed you easily if he had kept the job simple and walked up and shot you in the back of the head. However, a flash of dirty white bandages and a splotch of a birthmark tells you it's the guy you scarred forever with a scalding pot of coffee. You thought of him as the skinny guy. Then he was Mr. Bad Birthmark. Now he's Scarface. If he hadn't taken his burns so personally and came at you with a knife — you figure out the blade is actually a bayonet in the next few seconds — Scarface could have killed you and then probably killed Willow. Or kidnapped her and demanded her father give up the arms shipment before killing her horribly.

Instead, you hear your assailant step in a puddle three steps away and that's just enough warning for you to slip sideways. Instead of puncturing a lung and taking you to the ground to gut you like a pig, Scarface slices the air.

And you're living in the now.

This guy is tall but skinny in the lumpy way skinny guys go once they get too old to eat anything they want. Once he loses the element of surprise, you surprise him by grabbing his wrist and following his momentum. You smash his wrist on the lip of the hatch again and again. The bayonet goes into the trunk. You drive a knee into his side.

He grunts and twists away with strength that rises from fear and desperation. He tags you with a glancing punch to the jaw, but you're already turning away from the blow and, when you spin around, you whip the back of your hand into his nose. It doesn't crack but it stuns him enough for a follow-up left hook to his neck. You throw your hip into it for oomph. The work that goes into putting heft into that punch shoots searing pain from the spot over your kidney where Lurch dinged you less than an hour ago. So far, that's the worst pain Scarface has inflicted.

You're not sure what startles Scarface more. Maybe it's because he had the advantage and suddenly things are going so badly, so quickly. Fights are like that. Maybe it's the agonizing pain in his larynx that paralyzes his speech and muffles all his other senses. Scarface is stunned and breathing heavily, with eyes like shiny pie plates. Maybe he looks so scared because you're laughing.

As he falls backward, he drags you down by your coat, his dirty hands clawing at your lapels. As you go down you lead with your knees and come down on his balls squarely. His eyes bug out and you see the whites all around the perimeter of his irises. You'd think that would end it, but a fight like this doesn't end with a somebody ringing a bell three times and saying, "Okay, you got him."

Scarface shrieks and the fight goes on, though it's pretty much just wrestling after that and you're on top pinning him. When this fight is over, he knows he'll be over. The pull of his hopes and dreams are still, surprisingly, bigger than his pain. Even with his last conscious moments a misery, he fights to keep the pain going as long as possible. A smarter guy would have given up earlier.

You'd forgotten the animal joy of knowing you're going to win. You don't feel that often nor enough. You could have kept that winning feeling if you had just killed him then.

Guys never get knocked cold as easily as they do on TV unless they're hit with a ball peen hammer. You saw that once, back in Havana on the Hudson. You'll never forget the wet crunch and the way the guy crashed stiff, like a tree felled by one swing of a god's ax. It made you sick, but that's the sort of thing that, even as you watch mesmerized, you know you're going to wish you hadn't seen it. Before the struggle with Scarface is over, you wish you had that ball peen hammer.

It ends in an awkward scramble on the ground with short, little punches. Scarface tries to poke your eyes out. He manages to scratch your cheeks a bit, but he's fumbling and weak. You grab a handful of hair and lift his head into an elbow smash. When his eyes roll up, he really does look like a grasping, barely sentient, flailing zombie. You don't feel the pain over your kidney anymore. That will come later. Victory's euphoria eclipses pain better than the Gate

Theory of Pain ever could.

You could finish him with the SIG, but he made it personal and so, stupidly, you do the same. You could cut his throat with the switch in your sock, but instead, as he gasps for breath, you drive the heel of your palm into the sweet spot, just in front of the ear where his jawbone meets his skull. His head is turned and flat against the concrete. There's no give in a concrete floor to lessen the blow.

Scarface sleeps. His bandages are torn away and you can see the mess you made of his face. He'll die ugly, but he'll go to hell in his sleep. When you stop hitting him, all you hear is your heavy breathing and the distant squeal of brakes and a car door. You listen longer, waiting for static from a police radio and urgent voices summoning backup. However, you hear no sirens and see no red, white and blue lights strobing doom.

You stand and retrieve the bayonet from the hatchback. The back door to the apartment building bangs behind you. That's got to be Willow. Best to have this done before she arrives. Before you can turn with the bayonet in your hand, you hear someone moving fast in the shadows and grit under fast footfalls.

You're still breathing hard and waiting for your heart to come down from its full tilt gallop. "Willow?"

The silhouette of a large man appears from out of the shadows. "Shit!"

You recognize that voice. He's twenty paces away, but you can feel where he's aiming, a spot over your heart. It's the Lone Wolf, his right arm in a sling. His trigger and middle fingers are buddy taped and straight out in a splint. In his outstretched left hand, a little .32 catches the light, shining silver.

"I told Skeet not to take you on alone! That idiot! When he wakes up, I'm going to tell him 'I told you so,' every day for the rest of his stupid life."

You both slide a glance to the guy at your feet. All Skeet's resources are focused on breathing. Nothing else works. A quickly spreading stain darkens the unconscious man's pants at the crotch.

"That's supposed to be you on the ground."

"Didn't work out."

"Yeah."

"I guess Chill lost you."

"Hard to crank the wheel fast enough one-handed. He lost me going around too many corners. I can still shoot, though."

You gesture at the .32. "Are you good with that? I mean, even with your left hand?"

"Sure." He points it at your head.

"Are you sure? It's important. You're a little far away. If you're going to shoot me with a peashooter, I'd rather you not take all night killing me. I got places to be."

He lowers the gun again. Either the guy has Attention Deficit Disorder or he's toying with you. That's okay. You're playing for time while Willow sneaks up in the shadows. She's silent, so either she's wearing high heels with felt on the soles or she took off those come-pump-me pumps.

"His name is *Skeet?* I've never known anyone named Skeet."

"There's that actor guy. No relation," the big man offers.

"I figured. I've been calling him Scarface, you know, like they called Al Capone."

"Dude! We are in Chi-fucking-cago! You don't think I know who Al fucking Capone was? I've seen the movies, man. I *live* here. Shee-it!"

"There's an interesting story about Capone you won't find in Wikipedia."

"What do I care?" He raises the gun.

"Quick story. Do you know why they called Capone Scarface?"

"Because he had a scar on his face, you *fucking* moron." He's about to pull the trigger.

"He got the scar in a fight over a girl. I think he was pretty young, still a bouncer at the time. He said he got the scar in the Lost Battalion in France during World War I, but he never served."

"Uh-huh." His first shot misses, but you feel the bullet's breath.

You were just stalling, but it is true he's a bit far away. Not so far away you can reasonably expect to reach behind your back and nail him between the eyes by whipping out the SIG. Most gunfights go down within six feet, up close and personal, not twenty paces. Old-fashioned duels settled disputes at ten paces, though duelling pistols sucked then and it was a one-shot deal. You could dive for it, but still, your best hope is Willow. This isn't some John Woo Hong Kong action flick where the hit man moves in precise slow motion choreographed dance sequences while everyone else has the reaction time of a three-toed sloth trying to figure out the safety on a machine gun.

Yellow phosphorescence catches Willow's blonde hair as she crouches low, still moving, still silent. *That's my girl.*

"Told you, you'd miss at that range." *Please come out into the light and keep your focus on me.*

As if moving by your unspoken command, the big man does step out of the shadows and takes just two steps closer. Pride came before a fall for Scarface Skeet. You? Odds are excellent you're still screwed.

"The interesting story a lot of people don't know about Capone was what happened to him in San Francisco."

The big guy spreads his feet wider, aiming carefully. He won't miss this time. *Hurry, Willow!*

"The guards at Alcatraz said they treated Capone just like any other prisoner. They got him for tax evasion, of course, but did you know about the couple of guys he killed with a baseball bat? Those same guys had served Capone as assassins during the St. Valentine's Day Massacre and he wound up beating them to death at a cocktail party with a Louisville slugger. Imagine being that second guy, waiting for your head to be caved in, watching the other guy getting his head beaten in first."

"Probably felt a little like what you're feeling now."

"Heh. Good point!"

"Still boring, though," the Lone Wolf says. He pulls the trigger again, misses and you hear the ricochet behind you. "Talk faster." He is toying with you.

C'mon, Willow!

"Though the guards treated him the same, to the other inmates, Scarface Al was a celebrity. So you know what some of them wanted to do?"

"Take him down. Make their bones like I'm about to do with you?"

"One of the other inmates came at Al with scissors. Al was still tough, though, even without a bat. He was still street. Al put up his hands, blocked the attack and the scissors went into his hand, between his fingers."

"I should go dump Skeet at an emergency room, so hurry up and finish the story. Places to be." You can feel the spot he's aiming at, like he's pushing a finger into your forehead.

"The funny thing is, Scarface Al? He took his time and beat the shit out of that inmate."

"So? Not much of a story."

"Well, I thought the funny part was that the guards watched the beating go on. They let Al Capone off the leash. They watched, laughed and applauded as it happened, so anybody else who got the idea to go after Capone and make trouble, they'd get the message. Al beat that guy like a rented dick at a porno convention."

The guy chuckles.

She's only one car-length away. She's stealthy, but stealthy is too slow and what you need is firepower.

"Do you know the moral of the story? The moral of the story," — talk slow, give her just a little more time — "is I'm going to beat you down. I'm going to beat you down so hard, you won't feel safe when you crawl up your own ass to try to get away from me."

"You talk pretty."

"Thanks."

His next shot pops as you drop to your belly, using Scarface Skeet's body for cover since he's the only cover you've got. The Lone Wolf lines up the shot that will kill you when he detects movement behind him. Willow tries to hit the big guy in the face with a bright red fire extinguisher but he's a half-step too quick and shoves her back into the side of a car. The car alarm blares immediately, jolting you as you pull your SIG and snap off two rounds. Your first shot goes wide. The second catches him in the meat above the knee. Wouldn't it be sweet if you got him in the femoral artery so he'll bleed out beside Scarface Skeet? He shrieks like a girl with her nipples caught in mousetraps.

The Lone Wolf goes down on one knee and fires at you but you can't throw shots back his way. Instead of doing the sane thing and running, Willow comes at him again. You fire two more rounds, deliberately wide, just to keep him interested and distracted. All the power of the SIG Sauer P220 is reduced to that of a New Year's noisemaker because you're terrified you'll shoot your future wife.

She swings the fire extinguisher again. The big guy is still firing your way instinctively, but his aim sucks worse than ever since his cheekbone is caved in with her first strike. From where you lay prone, the big guy looks quizzical as he turns to look up at Willow. She bashes his handsome face again.

When he's laid out, Willow stands on his forearm and wrist with both bare feet to pull the .32 from his hand.

She looks your way, half her face hidden behind a curtain of mussed hair. If Wonder Woman were blonde, and did her fighting in a tight cream jacket and skirt, she'd look like that.

Scarface Skeet lets out a long groan as you lean on his stomach to get to your feet. "Took you long enough." You try to look casual and cool, but your heart is hammering against your ribs, trying to get out and run away. You're shaking. It seems no matter how many times people shoot at you, you don't get used to it.

"I had to be quiet and the bastard *still* heard me at the last second!" She turns on the Wolf's unconscious form and spits. "That's what you get for taking *me* hostage, fuckface."

"Thanks. Um…if there's a next time, and we should make sure there never is…all I'm saying is, next time, move a little faster."

"I wanted to hear the end of the story, too. Any of that true?"

"Sure. It's all true. I like to travel."

"You went on vacation in San Francisco?"

"Sure. Took the tour at Alcatraz. I'll take you sometime. You've got to have a crab sandwich with sourdough bread at Fisherman's Wharf, though. That was the best part of the tour."

She blows her hair out of her face, a beautiful woman with a shiny .32 in one hand and a fire extinguisher in the other. "Can't wait for the sourdough bread," she says. "I, uh, have a hard time picturing you on vacation taking a tour of Alcatraz."

You tell a lot of lies for a living. It's galling when someone suspects you're full of shit when you tell the truth. Still, her skepticism shows how smart she is. She *should* think you're full of shit all the time because you usually are. Maybe you can change that. "You got me. I was in San Fran to drown a guy in a bathtub."

She laughs and snorts, not taking you seriously.

The car alarm blares on. It's an old alarm that runs up and down annoying scales. Of course, no one's coming, but you shouldn't hang around, either.

Your hands are still shaking when you grab the bayonet. You should shove the bayonet through Scarface Skeet's brain. For some reason you can't explain — a distant memory of something terrible on a Cuban beach — you stop to grab Scarface by the jacket and drag his limp body to prop him into a sitting position against a concrete pillar. Somehow, it doesn't seem right, murdering the guy while he's having a therapeutic nap.

You place the tip of the bayonet under his chin. It's sharp. A trickle of blood slips down the blade as you brace yourself and take a deep breath for one brutal and efficient zombie-killing shove.

"Don't!" Willow screams, her voice cracking.

"He came to me." You promised you'd beat them all down so far they'd never get up. Bloody and piss-stained, Scarface Skeet is a rabid dog. Even with Willow as a witness, you've got to put these thugs down.

A worn memory fires up. You'd rather leave that memory alone.

Willows closes her warm hands around your trembling, cold mitts.

"Don't," she says again, softer. If she'd screamed it again, or tried to order you, you would have done it. Instead, she's asking.

"He came to me," you say again, your voice far away now, weaker, emptier and scared.

Gently, she takes the bayonet from your hands. "He's helpless. We won. Don't be that guy. Stay with self-defence. Be the bodyguard. Don't be the killer."

You stand and step back and Willow smiles. She cups your face with her warm hands and you close your eyes.

You're not living in the now anymore. You're a kid on a Cuban beach. The way the sun is slanted, you're sure it's early in the morning, just past dawn. You shake as terror washes over you. You taste cold saltwater.

You open your eyes and she's staring back, still gentle and forgiving. With Willow, you're the hero. Without her, you are six minutes to Cuba. Without Willow, you are your father.

ARMOR OF GOD

When you close your eyes, your father, Marco Diaz, is not dead. He stands barefoot in cool sand yelling to you as you swim. He tells you to keep your fingers together as you practice your front crawl. You want to quit, but he yells, "Just a few more minutes!" He said that at least thirty minutes ago, too.

You swim, fighting the waves, and, when your father goes quiet, you pause to make sure you haven't swum too far. You pop your head up and scan the beach.

Marco Diaz is no longer watching you. His hands are planted on his hips. A hunched, older man wearing a white shirt and long pants pulled high on his belly stalks toward your father. He yells something. You don't know the words but recognize English and anger. The man has something in his hand. It flashes in the strengthening sunlight.

*　　*　　*　　*　　*　　*

You blink. You're back in a parking garage in Chicago. Willow cups your face gently.

"Will he live?"

"Huh?"

"Scarface. Will he live?"

"Yeah, though he might not want to for a little while."

"I hated him before," Willow says. "I feel sorry for him now."

"I doubt he'll take his beating as a life lesson, turn things around and get right to work on curing cancer."

"You never know," Willow says. "People can change. And if you're not good at something, you probably shouldn't do it. He's not good at whatever it is he did before you, uh…?"

"Racked him up?"

"Yes."

"His name is Skeet."

"Really? He didn't have much of a chance then, did he? The Lone Wolf is bashed up, but he's breathing fine. We should go before he wakes up. He might be, you know, annoyed." She pulls at your elbow.

"You sure? If we wait around for them to wake up, they'll be a lot easier to beat up the second time around."

She doesn't laugh. As you climb into the car stiffly — your hurt kidney reasserts itself for attention — you decide Willow must be one of those beautiful optimists you hear about. She seems so hopeful. How did she get that way? She's the opposite of her father. If that pattern holds true and your kids turn out so different from you, maybe you should find hope, too. From her heights, if she knew your depths, you'd never have a chance with her.

But how different are you from your father? Not different enough, obviously.

Willow wants to talk. "What are you thinking?"

"I was getting kind of emo over Skeet and the Wolf. Don't worry. I think it's passing." You drive, your mind in a fog, criss-crossing the city to make sure no one follows you. The safe house sits on a quiet, well-to-do suburban street, so it's hard to pick out which two-story family home is a family with kids, which is the marijuana grow-op and which is the meth lab. In this economy and with the huge mortgages in an area like this, might there be a few that are all of the above?

When you open the hatchback to grab Willow's bags, you are astonished to see you took Skeet's bayonet. You leave it in the trunk and the garage closes automatically behind you.

Chill opens the back door and gestures you in. Instead of the .357 Magnum, he's got a shiny Ruger Super Redhawk Alaskan in his fist. The .357 must be reserved for impromptu Bible readings. He reads Willow's face. "Any trouble?"

"Trouble doesn't bother me," you say. "I bother it." It sounds like someone else saying it, a tin line from an old film noir. Fine. That's the best you can manage for now. You're afraid that when you close your eyes, you'll be back in the surf, seeing the hunched man stalk toward your father, something flashing in his hands as it catches fresh sunbeams.

"The skinny guy and the Lone Wolf came after Jesus," Willow says.

"Was it bad?"

"They wanted to know if I'd heard the good news about Scientology, so yeah."

Chill looks at the scratches on your face and nods. "When you were done, did they need to be taken away in a coroner's truck or an ambulance?"

"Tupperware."

When Chill frowns, babies cry and strong men grow weak, but Willow ruins your tough guy act. "Jesus let them live."

"Really?" Chill brightens. "Respect!"

You're worried that, just when you had decided you liked Chill, he might try to high five you, as if you'd shown good sportsmanship in an especially brutal little league game. To your relief, he tells you he's going to go check on Willow's dad.

"You stay here and recuperate tonight. I'll check out of my hotel and bring my stuff over in the morning."

"I thought you were staying here," you say. "Who's place is this?"

"My uncle's house," Willow says. "He's out of town."

Once she disappears into the bathroom, Chill eyes you, looking pensive. "Samuel told me to murder the Wolf and Skeet."

"You had the good sense to say no, Chill, so I have to deal with it."

"Mr. Clemont will want to know why the Victorious wannabes aren't dead, Jesus."

You simplify, since you don't quite understand why you held back, either. "I couldn't make his daughter and my future wife an accessory. He'll understand. Tell Samuel I held back for the same reason he didn't shoot them when he had the chance."

"That would make for tension in the family."

"Damn right. What did Clemont tell you about the Recipients?"

"He claimed they were a harmless cult. I told him that was an oxymoron and if I killed any reps from The Victorious, that'd make me an omnimoron."

"Like me?"

"Yeah."

"The Recipients know who we all are, Chill. If I don't take out the wannabes, they'll kill us all before Clemont can pay me enough to skip town with Willow."

"That's inconvenient. What do you want me to tell Samuel? As you'll recall, my policy is I don't know and I don't want to know."

"Tell him I'm working the problem, but he needs to get the shipment out of storage and get the deal with the Recipients done. I need them off my back."

"I'll pass it along. I'm sure Mr. Clemont will be suitably reassured."

Willow walks into the kitchen and pulls a glass from a cupboard. "So guys…how big is Dad's arms deal that we're in this shit this deep? Is it World War III? Should I go hide in the attic?"

You and Chill turn to her together and chuckle nervously, morons in stereo. "I'm supposed to keep you out of that," Chill says. "I don't know —"

"And he doesn't want to know," you finish.

"And your father doesn't want you to know anything about this, either," Chill says sternly.

"It's an accessory after the fact sort of deal," you add.

"Nobody knows where you are and unless the neighbors turn you in, Anne Frank, you're safe," Chill adds. "We just have to stay here and don't so much as look out the curtain."

"Safe. Huh. Great! I'll just go hide in the attic and start working on my journal."

In a sweet gesture only gay guys and Europeans can pull off without feeling and looking like idiots, Chill leans in and kisses Willow on both cheeks. "You're safe, girl. Guaranteed. Just stay off the phone, stay inside and keep the curtains closed."

You're suddenly aware again that you're in a small room with giants. You step back and lean on the counter, trying to look taller, more casual and less battle fatigued.

When Chill's gone, Willow checks the cupboards and finds tea bags and a tea kettle and a couple of chipped teacups. When Willow offers you tea, you accept. You were taught never to turn down tea from a lady. Old habits, even when ingrained under duress, still hold.

"It's just you and me until I can get my iPod recharged," Willow says as you join her in the living room.

"You talk," you suggest. "I'm an excellent listener." More old habits.

"I have another idea."

You smile. Maybe you won't have to wait long to feel those long legs wrap around you. She forgot her iPod charger, but did she remember to throw in a pack of condoms?

Instead, Willow Clemont wants conversation. She wants you to talk. You can tell by the way she sits up straight with her teacup in her lap that this is the job interview part of the introductory dating period.

"I could talk all night about how much I love your eyes. You have kind eyes, Willow. I like that in the future Mrs. Diaz."

"You don't have kind eyes, Jesus. That's why I need to know more. For starters, I'm guessing your parents were Catholic."

"The raving kind. Lots of guilt."

"And did you inherit their sense of guilt?"

"Pass. Next question?"

Willow bestows a patient grin, but the tolerant yet strained kind of smile is loaded in the next chamber. "Where did you learn to fight? In the military?"

You didn't mean to let out that long sigh. Her eyes are still kind, but the rest of her face isn't so sure about you.

"I knew this guy, back in New York. Used to tell this story about how to handle a cop if he stops you. Long story, short, dude's stopped by a cop in Texas. He's got a chopped up body, a shovel and a couple of hundred pounds of marijuana in the trunk."

"True story?"

"Guys bullshit. Who knows? All stories are true mixed with horse shit until neither is both."

"If I give myself a headache, I bet I'd understand what you just said."

"Well, you know. Good stories are all Irish fact. Even if it's not true, it ought to be."

She nods for you to continue.

"So dude's stopped by a cop and the dude has incriminating things in the car. But he's also got a skunk in the back seat."

"Why would he have a skunk in the back seat?"

"I forget what he tells the cop. I just remember that the dude has like, squeezed the skunk juice all over the car and, the stench is so bad, there's no way the cop is going to stick around to ask questions. He talked about how it was just another day at the office to escape heinous criminal prosecution with just a skunk and a smile. No interrogation, no arrest." You give her your best smile.

Her eyes narrow. "Are you saying you wish you had a skunk right now so you wouldn't have to tell me anything about you?"

You smile wider. It doesn't work. She doesn't laugh or snort.

Instead, Willow stands and removes her jacket. She's wearing a matching cream blouse and skirt with no slip. She unbuttons two buttons from the top of the blouse, pauses for drama and sits down. "You were my knight in sh…tarnished armor tonight, Jesus."

"Technically, you saved me," you point out.

"Still, I appreciate you helping me and my dad out. I'd like to show some appreciation."

"I'm down," you say, too quickly.

"But," she sits and crosses her legs, "I don't go to bed with strangers."

You take her in, slow. She's taken the time to apply fresh lipstick that paints her lips cherry red. Through the thin fabric of her blouse, you can make out the dark circles of her erect nipples. She crosses her legs again and you picture her in nothing but the high heels.

You spill your guts.

CONFESSIONS OF A DANGEROUS MIND

"Marco, my father, was the one who first taught me how to fight," you begin. "He was a boxer when he was young. They taught me stuff in the military later, but…Dad was more serious about it."

"More serious than the army? My God, what did he do to you?"

"It wasn't like that."

"How was it?"

"In Cuba, there was a man who came after my father. It was the only time I saw my father in a real fight. He taught me things until we left Cuba. After that…he didn't make it all the way here."

"I'm sorry."

"Don't be. If he'd lived, I probably wouldn't have loved him so much as I do now."

"Dads aren't so bad. You've probably noticed my dad is a little crusty, but I love him."

"Crazy."

"Maybe. What about the man who attacked your father? What was that about?"

You ignore the question. "It's been a while since I was in a fight like that. Scarface Skeet almost got me. If he hadn't made a little mistake at the very first…well, if you make a mistake at the beginning of the fight, it's like buttoning up your shirt wrong." You glance meaningfully at Willow's cleavage. "You start off wrong, you may as well unbutton the whole thing and start again. Scarface should have made a run for it. I probably wouldn't have chased him. I just wanted to get you someplace safe. That's my first priority."

"What did your Dad teach you?"

"The military's policy on hand-to-hand combat makes a lot of sense. Only do it as a last resort, as in just long enough to get to your gun and reload. If I'd gone with that tonight, I not only wouldn't have scratches on my face, I wouldn't have broken a sweat. Also, they say if a fight is going too well, it's an ambush. If I'd just shot Skeet immediately, I would have been out of there before the Lone Wolf doubled back."

Willow gives you a look that might be disappointment so you barrel on, "If the fight is fair, you haven't planned properly. Standard Army manual cliches, all true as far as I know."

"With the gun and without the sweat and scratches? That wouldn't have been so brave or noble."

"I didn't want to be brave. I wanted to win. And you stopped me, so you made me noble, Willow."

"That's kind of sexy."

"I wanted to cut Scarface open just to see the gears inside."

"Not so sexy," she says. "Tell me about your Dad and Cuba and the man who came after him."

You imagine helping her out of that shirt and slipping that tight skirt down her legs slowly, worshipping her with your eyes and lips and tongue.

"Dad taught me the basics. Jabs. Uppercuts. How to throw a hook without wrecking your shoulder."

"How do you do that?"

"The trick to a good hook is not to miss what you're trying to punch. Hitting the target is important. If you pretend the target is a couple of inches behind your opponent's nose, for instance, you hit harder. Keeping distance just right is good. A lot of guys can wail on somebody, but it takes skill to make the other guy miss and waste energy."

"You saw your father fight?"

"Just the once, on the beach. He won, but it wasn't really an even match."

"What happened?"

You clear your throat and have a sip of tea. It felt great when you were sure you were going to beat Scarface Skeet. Maybe that's how Marco Diaz felt, too.

"I learned the most important stuff from those few minutes on the beach. An older man — a guest at the hotel where my father worked — went at my father with a steak knife from the restaurant."

"My god!"

"I was out in the water and by the time I got to shore, it was almost over. The most important stuff is that the guy who hits first almost always wins. Also, you have to deal with the weapon before you take down the man. My dad took the knife away from that tourist like it was nothing. The guy was a bit older, though. Maybe he thought he was going to scare my father, make him run away. Now that I say that, the fight was over so quick, that's probably what was on his mind. He didn't really come to kill. You pull a knife or a gun, you better mean to use it. That was the other man's mistake."

The silence stretches out and when you don't fill it, Willow asks, "What are you not telling me, Jesus?"

You ignore her question again. "The real fancy stuff is what Dad taught me later. It was about fire and water. If you fight like water, you flow around the opponent's attack and go for a body blow or tune up his face. If you take the fire strategy, whatever your opponent throws at you, you burn him. So, like, he tries to kick you? Don't just block it. Break his fuckin' ankle…excuse me."

"I grew up with a Marine for a father. He invented swearing. I don't mind. In fact, tell me more about your family and later I'll tell you how much I like to talk dirty in bed."

"Show, don't tell."

She stares into your eyes and smirks as she opens another button on her blouse. "What happened to the man?"

"I was coming in from swimming. It was very early in the morning and there was no one else around. Only I saw the fight."

"From what you say, it was a short fight."

"Yes. My father took away the steak knife. Then he held it in his fist as he boxed. The jabs were a…. death by a thousand cuts sort of deal."

"Your father knifed a man to death in front of you?"

"Not exactly. As I came out of the water, I was screaming and crying. I ran up to my father as he held the man by the neck. My father slapped me to shut me up."

You touch your cheek, surprised. "I'd forgotten that. I remember him slapping Rodolpho once, too, but that was it. Before the beach, I didn't really think of my father as a dangerous man. He'd taught me boxing, but fighting and being the kind of guy who can…well, which was the real him? The father I knew was a pretty placid, often funny guy, but inside, there was something else waiting to come out."

"What happened to the tourist?"

"He bled, but he was still alive. His white shirt looked like it had big, red flowers. Years later, I was somewhere traveling and saw this ugly shirt with poinsettias on it and this familiar feeling came back. I felt…I thought I might throw up. My father wore a white shirt that day, as well, but his shirt looked more like some art an old girlfriend of mine used to like. The artist had a funny name. Klimt, maybe?"

"So you're saying you were a little kid when you watched your father stab someone to death?"

"No. I'm saying he stabbed him enough to make the old man want to die. Then my father dragged him out into the water and drowned him. I guess he was a mess and wanted the outgoing tide to take his sin out to sea."

Her jaw goes slack.

You shrug. You try to make your shrug look casual, as if you've told this story a hundred times. As if you're bored of it. As if the mind fuckery wasn't such a big deal. "But that wasn't the real fucked up part," you add.

For the first time, Willow cuts her eyes at you and looks skeptical. "Jesus. How could that possibly be the *un*fucked up part?"

* * * * * *

You close your eyes. You can still see Marco Diaz wade back to the beach shirtless. He looks back toward the floating body as if he expects the old man will come back to life and come after him again.

You run at him and throw yourself into your father's arms, crying. Without hesitation, he pushes you back a step and slaps you again. "*Silencio!*" The shock of the wet slap makes you hold your breath.

His face softens a little and he gives you a begrudging, grim smile. "*Mijo,*" he says. "Dry your tears." He cups your face in his big hands. "It's okay."

"What was the man screaming?"

"It's nothing."

"He tried to kill you for *nothing?*"

Marco Diaz makes a disgusted sound in the back of his throat. "Something about me and the man's wife. He was confused and crazy. A misunderstanding. He didn't want to talk. I bet he stayed up all night rehearsing his speech to me, like I was a child. The man was a fool."

"Why? Why did he do that?"

"*Sh. Sh.* It's nothing. The man was very bad. He came after me with a knife. I had no choice. *He* came to *me.* I had to defend myself. I didn't want to die. I don't want to lose you and Rodolpho and your mama."

"B-but, what he said — "

"Quiet, now." Marco Diaz, your beloved father, stares you in the eyes and tells you to keep his secret. "If you don't keep this a secret, I'll have to go away and I'm not willing to do that, *mijo.* I'll do anything to keep me and my family together. You see that corpse floating out there, Jesus? Would you rather it was me?"

"No, papa!"

"Would you rather it was *you?*"

Your eyes go wider but you don't speak, can't speak. You don't know your father at all. He is transformed into someone, some *thing* else.

"Then be quiet now. Don't tell anything about this to anyone. We will never speak of this. It was self-defence and that's all it was. *He came to me.* Don't ever forget that much. Whatever his reasons, *he* came to *me.*"

*   *   *   *   *   *

Tonight, with all that blood…it triggered something you thought was dormant.

Smug Tim says that by using a technique called Flooding — reviewing the worst things we experience over and over — we can get bored of the bad memories. Instead, you suspect the memory of the Cuban beach is *more* entrenched in your memory now because you've reawakened some cruel brain cells that make the scene fresh. They've been waiting to be rediscovered.

"Your father slept with some tourist's wife while they were on vacation?"

"My father was a handsome man. My mother, Maritza…I think she must have suspected him, not of killing that guy, of course, but sleeping around.

When he died…her reaction made more sense to me later. Anyway, just before we left Cuba, my father sold America to her on the basis of the usual stuff…opportunity, promises of riches, awful, overpriced hot dogs and beer in a baseball stadium. The clincher was that he came home one day from his job at the hotel all puffed up with some stupid story about how we should move to America because he had pride and wanted to be treated better."

"Doesn't that make sense?"

"There was some nonsense about buying my brother Rodolpho and me baseball caps. The Cuban police would have picked him up in a minute if the man's wife had told them she'd slept with the help. I guess she kept her mouth shut and got sympathy and all the inheritance."

Willow stares at you differently now. Her eyes are wet.

"Is all this conversation still sexy?"

"No. It's just sad. I wish I had a cigarette."

"I don't want the future mother of my children smoking. Could it be sexy in a sad way?"

"Or a Thai stick. Thai sticks are — you ever tried them? It's a citrusy taste and makes me feel light and breezy. Thai sticks are a sweet high."

You let that go. Instead you say, "I left a couple things out."

"What else could there be?"

"Walking back along the beach, my father held my hand. He never held my hand, not since I was very little. He didn't think it looked right. Wasn't manly enough. That morning he held my hand tight and I looked back toward the corpse. He yanked me to him and told me not to look back. Then he did the weirdest, creepiest thing. He sang. My father had a lovely singing voice, but this he sang just loud enough for only me to hear. He sang, 'That could be *you*. That could be *you*!' Like some kind of sick show tune. I know guys have weird battlefield reactions and euphoria and whatnot, but he sang that to me as we walked away."

Willow shakes her head, disgusted now. Not what you were going for. "That better be the most fucked up part because this is awful and — "

"Exhausting, yeah."

"No," she says. "I'm still with you."

"Would it be sexy again if I told you I kept my father's secret until now?"

Willow's eyes narrow. "Is that a fact or an Irish fact?"

You stand and cross to her. You kneel at her feet and take her hand and kiss her palm. You hold it to your cheek.

Willow stands and drops her teacup and what remains of her tea to the thick, white rug. She pulls you to your feet to lead you upstairs.

At the doorway to the master bedroom, you hesitate. She doesn't know all your quirks yet and the time is inopportune. "I am pretty banged up. I won't be able to get my shirt off without screaming, so I'll have to leave it on, okay?"

"Whatever you need, Jesus. I'll do the work tonight. I'll make you scream, but you'll forget the pain."

"That's called the Gate Theory of Pain."

"What?" She opens her blouse.

"Never mind." You slide the fabric of her shirt across her skin, down and away. "When I first saw you. Oh, man, I can't tell you."

"When I first saw you, I had no idea," she says. "I didn't know at all. And now, after all that's happened, you're my Lion's Mane Jellyfish."

You slip behind her and feel the weight of her breasts in your hands. It feels odd and...unfamiliar...to reach *up* to cup her breasts. Then, "Um, what?"

"Lion's Mane Jellyfish. They are massive, freaky jellyfish that have been swimming or floating or whatever...don't stop that with your hands.... That's nice. I like it slow and gentle...at first." She sinks back and leans against you, lets her head sink back, gives you her throat.

"Lion's Mane Jellyfish have been around the Arctic Ocean since before dinosaurs. I saw a picture of one on Facebook. They have all these tendrils and they grab passing fish and pull them in. The fish never see it coming. They're swimming...yeah...they're swimming and — more! *Rougher now*, Jesus...mmm...oh, god, I can't wait! Um...the prey never see the jellyfish coming. They get stung. They're pulled in. They get eaten. By the way, I *really* enjoy getting eaten, Jesus."

"I'm starving, Willow. Feed me."

She straightens and turns and bends to kiss you, her tongue finding yours. She squeezes you tight. Your body aches, but that's going away as your blood heads south. Willow pulls her head back, but grinds against you as she reaches for the small of your back and pulls your SIG from its home in your belt holster.

Willow holds up the pistol for a moment, studying it. "Boys and their toys. I don't need one of these to blow your brains out." She smiles, winks and slowly, tortuously, runs her long pink tongue across her upper lip. Her lips are full and moist and painted red. She tosses the SIG on the chair and turns her attention to your tie, unknotting it.

You stop her hands at the second button of your Oxford shirt and shake your head.

"I can feel muscles under that shirt," she says as she unbuckles your belt and tosses it aside. "That'll do for now."

You kiss the fingertips of her left hand while she slowly rubs your hard on with the heel of her right. You move to her nipples, kissing them each delicately. She presses against your mouth, urging you to suck harder. Flicking your tongue across her aureolas wins low, approving moans. Except for the high heels, she stands naked.

Her skin is hot against your face and her heavy-lidded gaze is only for you as you slip your hand down her belly and between her legs, teasing and stirring. Wet and panting, she leans against you, her knees buckling, spreading her legs

— an insistent invitation. You kneel to serve.

For the second time tonight, you watch with pleasure as you make someone's eyes roll up to the whites. The future Mrs. Diaz's eyes roll back like a slot machine as she gasps and writhes under your tongue. You want to do that to her every night and every day for the rest of your lives and you tell her so.

"That sounds delightful and impractical. Ooh…" she wriggles. "We'll get dehydrated."

She pulls you up, then pushes you down on the bed and you let her take your pants off. "Mm," she says as she whips off your boxer briefs, eyes widening. "I have plans for that!"

When Willow pulls at your tie — forgotten and hanging around your neck — but you stop her as she reaches for the buttons of your shirt again.

"Please?" She wraps your silk tie around her hands and wrists. She raises her arms behind her head as she sinks into the bed, stretching back, her legs spread wide. "I promise I won't hurt you. And I'll never bite unless you beg me to."

You kiss her and tease her clit until she stiffens. You stop just before she's about to go over the threshold.

"Cruel!"

Willow grasps your cock and slowly licks her lips again, studying your reaction. She doesn't move her fist. She smiles and watches your face as she flicks the tip of her tongue up and down the shaft. She treats you like a lollipop with long slow licks, her gaze locked with yours. Finally, you have memories you want to keep. She makes you slick until you shake with lust and potential, but just as you think she'll give you relief and envelop you in her hot mouth, she pulls back and smiles wider.

"See? I can be mean, too!"

You chuckle and rise to unwind the tie from her fists.

"Still no shirt off?" she pouts. "Doesn't seem fair. Here I am, your buffet."

You raise the tie in two hands, a question. She nods her understanding and leans forward. You gently place the tie across her eyes and knot it firmly behind her head. Willow straddles you and, blindfolded, she unbuttons your shirt with nimble fingers.

When you flip her over onto her hands and knees, she stretches back like a cat, her heart-shaped ass in the air. You tease her and, when she pleads for more, you give Willow the only mercy you ever want to give anyone.

Soon, she's on her back again, her legs straight, her toes pointed. One side of her face is hidden under a fall of long blonde hair again, just like it was after she bashed the Wolf's chiseled cheekbone flat. Your dream comes true when she wraps her long legs around you and pulls you tighter to her.

You are desperate. You are fire. Willow is oxygen.

She urges you in and urges you on. She moans louder, meeting each hard thrust as the pace quickens. Willow is the most beautiful woman in the world and, for a change and for tonight, you are the luckiest man.

In the end, you both are savage addicts. Vicodin highs, feral sex and serrated violence: These are the only ways you know to live in the now and make the world go away.

"I want you to only wear heels and never anything else," you whisper in her ear.

"I can't wear the high heels *all* the time, Jesus!"

"I'll carry you." You turn out the light by the bed, before she can think to remove her makeshift blindfold.

"You can't," she says beside you in the darkness.

"I'll carry you like a secret."

A KISS BEFORE DYING

Chill has a coffee ready for you when you come downstairs at 11:30 a.m. Grocery bags are spread out over the kitchen table, as if he's preparing for a siege, which you guess he is. He hands you a travel coffee mug and the keys to his SUV. "The boss wants to see you. I'll protect Willow until you've sorted out this mess."

"He's putting a lot on one guy, don't you think?"

"Yeah. Long as I'm not the guy, I'm good with it. She sleeping?"

"Yeah. She'll be sleeping in." You can't resist a wolfish grin and strutting a bit on your way out the back door.

Chill raises his coffee mug in a mock toast and rolls his eyes. "Get your ass over to the diner."

"I'm going along with my ass if that's okay," you say. "It's all attached."

"Long as you don't get it shot off, yeah. You've had the gratuitous sex and violence. Be careful. I expect it's mostly violence from here on out."

* * * * * *

Samuel Clemont sits in his wheelchair with the M4 Carbine across his lap. He knows that you and Willow stayed in the safe house last night, so he's probably guessed the rest. Better he think about you and Willow in bed than you and his only daughter fighting the forces of evil in a grimy parking garage. He locks the door behind you and rolls on your heels to the kitchen.

"Chill told me you ran into trouble."

"Let's not live in the past. That was the Wolf. I'm more worried about the meeting I had with the fat guy who paid my rent."

You sit across from him at the kitchen's small table. He offers you nothing so you hold the travel mug in your hands and concentrate on the heat seeping through to your palms as you watch him eat. He's cooked a thin steak for himself, so rare it's bloody, and slapped it on a thick slab of Texas toast made gray with juice from the meat. The grease of the shiny hash browns unsettles your stomach.

"What's in the shipment besides Scorpions?"

He stops chewing and swallows hard.

"Your daughter's in serious danger and the Recipients know who we all are, so let's not dance anymore and get down to it. An anonymous fat man, who keeps a monster named Lurch as a pet, came to see me yesterday. You said they were like the Amish. My right kidney is so bruised, it disagrees. Vehemently."

"Never mind them. I expect you'll take care of The Victorious for me fast so I can do the deal with The Recipients and reopen the diner."

"Well, smell you! Ha! Look, these guys have scoped you out thoroughly and they don't screw around. The Recipients threatened all of us. These are not people you should be doing business with."

"Too late for that. Willow won't move outside for sunshine and fresh air until this is over, so, yeah, we'd all like to get this sorted out before she gets scurvy. I'm holed up here protecting my business. Chill's watching Willow. You are in charge of solving the Wolf problem. If you'd killed him and his pal last night, you'd have made some real progress and the fat man would have no reason to give you more motivation."

"I don't need more motivation. You've held out on me. This can't be just about Scorpions."

"Why are you making this complicated, Jesus?"

"The anonymous fat man I mentioned? He's secretive, but his face did some interesting things when I mentioned the Russian guns. What else do you have to tell me?"

Clemont puts his fork down and sighs. "There's a bit more to the story."

"Better give it all to me this time so we can both make sure Willow stays safe."

"I told you I had a business partner."

"Harry."

"Yeah. Harry got the shipment and I paid him off. It should have been that simple."

"Wait. *You* paid him off?"

"Yeah."

"Up front, in advance, the whole deal, paid 360 degrees? You said before that you 'put money toward it'."

"Yeah. So?"

"See, that kind of pisses me off, Sam. I thought I was just dealing with a guy who owned a diner who was willing to store some guns for the hardcore dealer. The way you described it before, you were just the storage guy, the tube."

He shrugs and points at the grill. "Gotta justify at least some of my income to the IRS."

"I must have been blinded by your daughter's beauty."

"Could be you're just not as smart as you think you are. Nobody's as smart as they think they are."

You take a long, deep cleansing breath. That was the first thing Smug Tim taught you. You squeeze your shoulders to your ears and wait for the muscles to relax. It still doesn't help. "How long have you been an arms dealer, Sam?"

"Since I got blown up and my country failed to pay to get me back to a normal life. Technically, I've been an arms dealer since I was busted down a rank for bringing a pistol back from Iraq after my second tour. They took the pistol, but when I went back I got more and started selling them at gun shows to make up for the loss in pay." For the first time, you see sadness creep in, prying off his mask of anger. "It wasn't for spite. I had bills. Then just before the end of my third tour, I got blown up. Then I had more bills."

When you start to feel sorry for him, you remind yourself he hasn't been straight with you.

He lights up a menthol cigarette and blows smoke at the ceiling. "I had no problems moving rifles and small arms. Ever since Obama was elected, the gun biz got crazy good. The NRA keeps saying the president is going to take away all their guns so the country's gone nuts. Obama hasn't looked sideways at gun laws. Mitt Romney passed more gun control laws than Obama. Romney passed an assault weapons ban, but that doesn't matter to the gun nuts. Since Obama came into office, the diner's done worse but the gun business is better than ever. Remember that shooting in Colorado? The one at the midnight showing of the Batman movie? Applications for gun permits went up fifty percent right after."

"Keep going."

"Anyway, crazy as shithouse rats, some people. They buy more than they can afford and then bury them somewhere, ready for the race war that never comes. If they're so sure of the fall of civilization, they should buy more seeds and learn to become farmers, not fighters. And The Victorious? If they get hold of the shipment, cops and civvies alike are going to be running and screaming everywhere. Chicago will be Tombstone, if the Earps had six shooters and the outlaw cowboys had machine pistols."

He looks away for the first time and studies the floor, his lips a thin line. "Partners in crime. I thought Harry and I were solid. Like brothers, you could say. He was a funny guy. Could tell a great story. You remind me of Harry, actually."

If Samuel Clemont had given you a wink just then, you would have really liked him. Instead, you search and find the hint of a smile at the corner of his mouth. That's the closest you'll come to being friends with the man who would have been your father-in-law. But he only has a few minutes left to live, so what does it matter? Of course, you don't know that yet.

Clemont shrugs with one shoulder, looks at his cold steak and grimaces. "The only way Willow and I can get away from the diner life is a big score and this is big. I tried to play it down before, so you wouldn't be too greedy, but, after last night's incident in the parking garage— "

"You're killing me, man. Spill!"

"The fat man called. He wants to meet at an abandoned warehouse tomorrow night. His people are coming from Florida and he's not going to be put off anymore. A firestorm's coming."

"Just do the deal with the Recipients and I'll figure something out to keep the gang off your back."

"It's already negotiated. When you failed to kill the Wolf and his sidekick last night, he decided you're too soft. A liability. The fat man says I can split up the shipment so The Victorious will get their Scorpions after all."

"But, what are The Recipients getting if The Victorious are getting the Scorpions?"

He sighs. "Mines."

In the sand wars, you thought it was a terrible thing to be ignorant of what you were fighting and dying for. That's one of the reasons you were so anxious to leave the military and get out of the desert. Now you wish you didn't know what you were fighting for. What might The Recipients do with ordnance that heavy? Stage another Waco, Texas where the FBI kills another bunch of women and children in a cult siege? This problem just graduated from worries about the Chicago police, ATF and FBI to an anxiety attack with Homeland Security. This is the kind of homegrown, terrorist-level douchebaggery that could get you stuck back in Cuba, jailed forever in Guantanamo Bay with no salsa music.

Returning to Cuba in chains would be so ironic on a cosmic scale it feels like it's *bound* to happen. The man who would be your father-in-law is right. You aren't as smart as you thought you were.

When the lock turns and clunks in the front door, that thought is confirmed. It's the Lone Wolf, limping but purposeful, coming through the front door. You whip out your SIG as you slip to the kitchen's doorway, already lining up your shot on the big guy.

You shout to Clemont to hunt cover, but when you glance his way, his rifle is pointed at your head.

"It's about time you showed up, Wolf! You're late! I've been stalling this little Cuban asshole for what feels like days! I'm tired of telling him what he wants to hear!"

Of course. The Victorious will get the Scorpions. Your reward for trying to keep Willow pure is delighted vengeance for the wannabes. The Recipients get the mines and the Wolf gets you.

You aren't *nearly* as smart as you thought you were.

IN THE LINE OF FIRE

What's coming isn't impossible, but the scene is so unlikely you have to question if you're really seeing what you're seeing. The left side of his face is bandaged where Willow smashed in his cheekbone last night. He looks like the guy from *Phantom of the Opera*, if the Phantom ran around carrying makeshift explosives. The Lone Wolf stops in the middle of the diner carrying two wine bottles and a longneck: Three molotov cocktails in the hollow of his shoulder sling.

"Hey, baby, I'm home! Did you miss me?" The Lone Wolf looks like a zombie who rose from a hospital bed and stumbled here to eat your brains.

"The Wolf wants *you*," Clemont says. "If he gets you and the Scorpions, all my problems go away. Thanks for pissing off the Wolf so bad you changed his priorities. He wanted the whole thing, too — mines and all — until I offered *you* up. Now everybody can be happy with what they get and Willow and I will still get that big score. I'll tell Willow you said goodbye."

You watch as the Wolf flicks a silver lighter under a rag fuse.

"I don't think so," you say. "I think he means to make sure nobody gets the shipment."

Willow's father laughs derisively, but from his wheelchair in the kitchen, he can't see what you do. The Lone Wolf lights the first fuse, smiling wide. The first bottle arcs over the counter, shatters and bursts in the middle of the kitchen. Clemont stops laughing and starts screaming. One of his shirtsleeves is on fire, which explains why he misses you with his first shot. Frantic, he wheels back from the flame, heading for the doorway to take a shot at the Lone Wolf.

The Wolf throws the next bomb straight to the rear of the diner and you throw yourself backward to dodge the next torrent of flame. Willow's father rolls in your way. You tumble over him and you're both knocked to the floor. The wheelchair clatters and you and Clemont land awkwardly on the hard linoleum. Your SIG skitters out of your grip and away. Crimson, yellow, orange and blue vines of flame race up the walls, chewing through the building's guts. Old construction materials and years of cooking grease strengthen the fire to a roar.

"You will not be selling anything to those Nazis!" the Lone Wolf bellows, coming closer. "Harry wanted to keep the bombs away from them! I'm going to make sure they never get them!"

Nazis?

A smoke detector beeps its jangling alarm from the ceiling.

"You hear?" Wolf screams above the alarm. "*Nothing* to white supremacists!"

"We had a deal!" Clemont looks shaken and confused.

"Harry told us the plan, cracker!"

You struggle to rise and get your pistol, but Clemont manages to hold on to his rifle. The muzzle hovers an inch from your face. Clemont holds the weapon awkwardly, one-handed with his burned arm, his free hand cupping the wound. He grits his teeth against the pain. Despite his screaming nerves, he's still got you locked.

"I'm going to burn alive in here, Jesus, but," he aims between your eyes. "I'll save you that, you sonofabitch."

"The fat man will be on the war path if they don't get those mines. I can still protect Willow. Chill can't do it all alone. Not now. Your daughter needs another bodyguard. Me."

Clemont hesitates a second and sometimes a second is all it takes to change everything. His eyes flick to the Lone Wolf, whose rictus grin is visible in the pass-through. With his good arm, the Wolf raises the last bottle bomb above his head, ready to give you a foretaste of hell.

The M4 booms. The wine bottle shatters and the Lone Wolf screams as the liquid flame rushes over him.

You rip the carbine from Clemont's hands, denying him a second shot. You rise, pointing the rifle at Clemont's head as he pulls himself away from the reaching flames.

It would be best if The Lone Wolf teleported into Lake Michigan and then directly to a hospital burn unit. Since he doesn't have that technology, the next best option, would be to stop, drop and roll. Instead, he runs back and forth in a panic, feeding oxygen to the flames. Not all mercies are tender. You raise the rifle, squeeze the trigger and drop the Lone Wolf with one shot, cutting short his agonized wail.

Clemont's pant cuffs are alight at his knees, but maybe he can't feel anything below the waist because he's focused on tearing off his smoking shirt. Tattoos wind around his body. The dragon wrapped around a burning cross is ironic because in another minute the dragon will look like it's spewing real fire. The letters WC on his upper arm must stand for Willow Clemont. The spiderweb tattoo at his elbow is a lesser known indication that he's killed a black man and he's proud of that fact. The swastika across his belly is also a strong sign that you've made a terrible mistake. The quicker you shoot him, the faster you move on to living in the now, that happy time when you aren't supplying explosives to white supremacists.

Clemont screams for your help and beats at the flames, swearing at his useless stumps. Sweat pops out on your forehead. The tiny kitchen is an oven and the hot air is a giant hand, pushing you backward.

"Where are the mines?"

"Fuck you!"

"Tell me where the goddamn shipment is or I'll leave you!"

"It's in a truck parked at East Wesley and North Main! In a parking lot! Get me out of here!"

The flames climb higher. "Where exactly?"

Instead of answering you, Clemont pulls a set of keys out of his pocket and throws them at you. "You've got it! It's a white panel van at East Wesley and North Main! It's a regular child molester wagon! You can't miss it! Okay? Now get me out of here!"

You have just enough time to grab Willow's father and drag him to the rear of the kitchen. You don't.

Instead you use that precious time to give him the middle finger and back away. "You pointed a gun at me! You were going to give me up to the Wolf! You were going to kill me! I save you, you'll do it again and we both know it. I don't forgive, Sam! *I do not fucking forgive!*"

He curses you. If the venom of spewed hate alone could kill, you'd be in flames along with Samuel Clemont. He shrieks in pain. His hair is on fire. Samuel speaks in tongues. He's still screaming gibberish as you retrieve your SIG from the floor. By the time you give him the double-tap, his death is a microscopic mercy.

We're on the same team, the fat man had said.

How can you ever be pure for Willow now? Samuel Clemont has stained your soul. You'll have to keep this secret from Willow, too. People in love aren't supposed to have secrets, but killing your future father-in-law makes the short list of crimes you have to keep to yourself. Willow's father has cursed you forever. You'll never be the good guy. Your best hope is to find a way back from evil to less bad.

Eyes watering and coughing, you crouch low to get under the smoke filling the diner and rush for the back door. You still have hope right up until you smack into it. The exit door is locked.

No, *not locked!*

Through the tiny wire window, you see a big Chevy parked with its front bumper kissing the door. The door is worse than locked. It's blocked by a couple of tons of metal.

Worse still, Skeet, half his face bandaged, lies slumped on the hood with a shotgun across his legs. With visible effort, he raises his head and his hazy gaze finds you not more than a few feet away on the wrong side of the door. He grins. Hatred shimmers in its purity and righteousness through Skeet's broken face.

The ceiling caves in behind you as a black cloud reaches for you like a choking claw.

You're living in the now, but probably only for another few minutes.

GET SHORTY

"Hi, Skeet!" you shout through the door. "I feel a curious burning sensation! You should tell your mother 'cuz she'll want to see her doctor about it!"

Scarface Skeet smiles back placidly and flips you off. You can't goad him into coming in after you. You're not even sure you deserve mercy so there's no sense wasting the rapidly burning oxygen on him.

The diner's walk-in freezer might buy you a little time. You whirl and burst through the freezer door and slam it behind you. The light is still on and it's chilly in here. It's about the size of a large walk-in closet.

When you were a Military Policeman, you envied firefighters. They dealt with fewer drunks and getting girls was easy. You called them basement savers and bucket heads then. You could sure use them now.

In the movies, a firefighter in full gear would arrive. You'd thank him, raise your pistol and ask politely for him to give you all his gear so you could make a clean escape. That would work if you were Tom Cruise. The script would allow for the rest of the firefighting crew to be incredibly stupid and blind once you got to the safety of the sidewalk.

You need cavalry. Chill's too far away. Willow's with Chill. God never answers your prayers. You only have one ally left in the city and you hope he's not too drunk to answer your call.

The phone rings and rings. You imagine Sgt. Billy's old, arthritic fingers scrabbling for the phone, searching through filthy pockets filled with moldy sandwiches.

"Yeah?" Salvation. Maybe.

"I'm trapped in the back of the diner. God Eats is on fire!"

"Yeah?"

"The only way out is through the back door and a guy has blocked it with a car! He's sitting on the hood with a shotgun!"

"Yeah?"

"Can you help me?"

"Who is this?"

"Sgt. Billy — !"

"Relax, son. Grow a sense of humor. I'm on my way. A couple of minutes." He still has the cell you gave him to his ear as he runs. His breath is short and fast already. Is "a couple of minutes" really two minutes? Or is that the generic two minutes, meaning five or maybe ten?" No smoke is coming in around the cold locker's door, but you resist touching it. If it's hot, you're already fucked and if you're dead by fire, you don't want to know that. Smoke inhalation would have been kinder. You loosen your tie and try to slow your rapid breath.

You look around the locker. Boxes of beef burgers, fruit, vegetables and milk sit in an array on the shelf. Unfortunately, there's not one asbestos suit or oxygen tank to be had. You've got nothing else to do so you hang up on Billy and call 911.

"911. What is the nature of the emergency?"

"Imminent fiery death." You give her the nearest cross street since you have no idea what the address might be.

The operator tells you someone else has called in the fire but asks you your name. "Salvador," you say. "Salvador Dali."

"Is there anyone still in building, Mr. Dali?"

"Yes. One person in the back of the diner in the cold locker...soon to be the hot locker."

"Who is this person?" the operator asks.

The light over your head fries out.

"He didn't live long enough to figure that out." You hang up.

You call Sgt. Billy back. *Ring. Ring. Ring.* Nothing.

You call him again. There's no voicemail on a throwaway phone. You wish you'd sprung for a full cellular plan. You could be leaving a message, telling Willow how sorry you are that you failed her. You'd tell her Sam is dead and promise to say hello to him if you saw him on the other side. Instead, you go to the locker door and listen for a scream or a shout. You need to hear something soon. The words of some forgotten army trainer come back to you again. "Every minute, a fire doubles in size." The diner isn't that big.

You pace. It's four strides, back and forth.

Some things would be better not to know, but it's too late for that. You wish you hadn't seen those tattoos. Did Willow's father go full Nazi after his desert war, or was that from before? He couldn't have gotten into the military with those tatts, could he? Maybe. Samuel Clemont had been a lifer, but maybe he could let it out and be himself later in life.

From experience, you've seen officers look the other way on lots of heinous acts. Plus, after 9/11, some behavioural restrictions were lifted because the brass was desperate for bodies to fill uniforms and body bags. You knew a couple of white supremacists in your unit in Iraq, but by the time they got to Afghanistan they seemed to be cured of their hatred for blacks and reserved all their bigotry for Muslims. It's hard to stay a racist when you serve alongside the same people you were taught to hate. Some guys managed to stay true to dumb and hateful but most of the rest conceded that people of the cool and colorful persuasion serving their country and saving their lives were at least "some of the good ones."

You try the cell again. Again, no answer.

Where is Willow now? You could call her and say goodbye, but you don't want to hear her answer when you tell her Samuel is dead. Besides, she must have known her father was a hateful racist. People don't get tattoos to hide them. She knew he was an arms dealer. Did she…could she know he was selling arms — no, *explosives* — to Neo-Nazis? You're all for capitalism, but there's a common code, even in a world where "Never again," clearly means nothing. If you don't have a code, you're the bad guy. You've already been the bad guy. You're supposed to be beyond that by now. So much for therapy. Fuck you, Smug Tim!

You're still a guy who carries around a SIG Sauer P220 and a switchblade in your sock. You want a bottle of Vicodin more than ever. You could chug that back, be set alight and not really mind. You'd just lay on the floor sleepy and quietly burn to death watching all the pretty colors. Or you could crack open the locker door and let the smoke take you.

There's a crash from the front of the diner. It's really only been a few minutes, but old buildings like this? The insulation is probably old newspapers and ancient Sears catalogues. You put your palm to the wall of the locker. Beyond that wall, you're sure, is another wall of flame. The locker wall is so hot to the touch, it's uncomfortable to hold your bare palm against it for more than a few seconds. The air feels thin as you push it in and out, beginning to gasp. Is the oxygen burning away, or is this panic? If this is just overwhelming panic, it seems like a reasonable time for it to kick in. It feels like you're drowning again.

The weight of the SIG in your palm is reassuring. That's a better option. Take fate in your own hands, close your eyes, put the muzzle in your mouth, pull the trigger and see what comes next. You were always so sure someone else would kill you. Big Denny De Molina or one of his crew would step out of the shadows, put a muzzle to your head and say, "Big Denny says hello."

That would be better than this. *Nazis! Nazis with a plan,* the Lone Wolf had said. Nazis with *mines.* Lurch and the fat man are going to blow something up and that no doubt means the deaths of innocent civilians are on you because you couldn't stop The Recipients.

Something else falls and crashes beyond the freezer's walls.

Too late for hope now. People have told you you're a funny guy all your life, but you'll never be a stand-up comedian like Louis CK, Joe Rogan or Joey CoCo Diaz (no relation). You'll never get the chance to make the world a better place, with laughing crowds applauding and loving you. You'll never see France, or Spain or the Vatican. You really wanted to check out those cool castles in Scotland, hang out in pubs in Ireland and wander around London, too. You'll never see Hollywood. You wanted so much more for yourself. You wanted to be an optimist like Willow. You wanted to be hopeful for the human race, despite the daily news that smacked the shit out of that idea every fucking day. Like the old dude in *The Matrix* said, "Hope is humanity's greatest asset and its greatest weakness." Something like that.

If you shoot yourself right away, you don't have to torture yourself with all the things you never became. You always felt you were meant for bigger things and the profession of hit man was just something that happened to you, not something you chose. If you got another chance, you tell yourself you'd make better choices. Then the quieter voice in your head that you don't listen to enough speaks up. "I'm about to die and I'm still bullshitting myself. Lots of people start out bad but make it to good."

You cross to the locker door and touch it with your bare palm. Hopeful. It is too hot. Sgt. Billy is too late. Death by fire. You sure didn't see that coming. You could douse yourself in cold milk when it gets really hot in here, or will the fire eat up all the oxygen and leave you gasping on the floor until flaming beams crush you from above?

The SIG feels heavy: like a secret kept; like a love denied; like the memory of a disappointed friend you are forced to carry to the end. Good news: the end is here. What's the real rule on suicide? Is that something that really pisses off God? If so, He doesn't understand your problems. Screw Him.

Something shifts and falls against the wall behind you. That must be the bathroom ceiling caving in. Where are the firefighters? Even if they save you, how much better off would you be? With a couple of bodies out front and your record, you may as well burn. You can't talk your way out of the murder investigation back in New York, anyway. Either way, you're dead and Willow's far away. Sometimes clever just isn't enough.

You can't even say you had a good run. You raise the SIG to your mouth and scrape the muzzle across your teeth painfully, chipping a canine, as Sgt. Billy drives the hulking Chevy through the back wall of the diner. He takes out the back wall and the door to the freezer, missing you by inches.

Sometimes clever isn't enough, but brute force often does the job. It's still too late to make it to good. Now is the time to be badass.

THE FUGITIVE

When the Chevy bursts through the freezer wall to the inferno that was the diner, heat and billowing smoke pours over you. Sgt. Billy throws the Chevy into reverse and squeals back out of the fire, nearly running you over twice. The late December air feels like a welcome dip in a cold pool during a heatwave. Fresh oxygen feeds the fire and stokes it to a raging blast furnace that pushes you out of the hole in the rear wall in a swirl of smoke.

Sirens run through discordant scales out front and a crowd has gathered in the back alley to watch the flames stretch up. They are a motley crew of a few teens with scraggly beards and a dumpy woman pushing a stroller. The crowd stands still, wide-eyed and slack-jawed, all eyes on you.

A small child in the stroller sits forward to get a better look at you. Dressed in a pink snowsuit, the little girl peers at you with huge blue eyes.

You stagger out of the flaming building toward them and lean heavily against the old Chevrolet's fender, sucking the crisp air into your lungs between raspy coughing jags. The air is so cold, it cuts. When you're sure you can speak without throwing up, you shout to the alley's assembly, "*Ta da!*"

Only the little girl claps. Tough crowd.

"Again! Again!" she squeals and only then do a few of the teens have the grace to chuckle at your peculiar spectacle. Following the little kid's lead, you get sporadic, confused applause from the slack-jawed onlookers.

Sgt. Billy leans over, pops the passenger door and beckons you in as he guns the engine. "You comin', Chief?"

You tighten and straighten your tie, bow to the crowd and jump in the car. You're still coughing and choking on smoke. Sgt. Billy rounds the corner and slides away just as a cop car turns and powers down the alley, lights blazing and sirens stuttering a staccato warning. If the cop thinks to pursue the Chevy, he won't have any time because, as you glance back, a ladder truck turns after him to attack the fire from the rear of the building. The alley is blocked.

A shotgun sits on the floor of the back seat. "Where's Skeet?"

Sgt. Billy pulls over and turns off the engine. "What is a Skeet?"

"The skinny black guy with the shotgun! What'd you do with him?"

"That fella is in the trunk. Sorry I took so long. It was a real oven in there, huh?" Excited and pale, his breathing is very shallow.

"How'd Skeet end up in the trunk?"

"How do you think? I put him in there. I walked up, grabbed the shotgun and smacked him in the forehead a few times with the stock. It's enough to discourage anyone. He didn't have any fight in him."

"Good thinking. Between his beatings, he's not going to be able to work a cash register for a long time. Hey...he was armed. Respect! You are still a soldier, man!"

"It wasn't like that, dumbass." His eyes narrow. He looks pained and even more pale.

"How was it?"

"I'm an ancient homeless guy. What, you think I tried some bullshit Rambo stuff? I stumbled up and told him I was having a heart attack."

"Wow. That's more good thinking."

He winces. "I wasn't faking, you asshole. I'm an old alcoholic. You think I run every day to stay in shape?" Sgt. Billy takes his pulse, pressing two fingers into his neck and gives you a worried smile. "It was only a couple blocks, but I'm not up to this shit. The job was supposed to be recon only, you dickless fuck!"

You jump out, run around to his side and rip his door open. In a couple of minutes you have him lying across the back seat. Then you're behind the wheel and headed for Mercy Hospital. You push the accelerator as hard as you dare, slaloming through openings in traffic.

"What's this all about, Chief? You said you were doing this to protect your lady."

"I am."

"My left arm hurts bad. I'd like to know what I'm dying for."

"Hold on. We'll be at the hospital soon. I'll get you to Emerge. We're going to take some corners pretty fast in a second, so let me know if you hear any screaming from the trunk."

"And if you don't?"

"Then I'll take those corners a little faster. I'd love to have a chat with Skeet instead of dealing with all this macho bullshit. It would be great to get some answers."

His breathing comes faster now, but Sgt. Billy still manages to ask you the dreaded question. "You one of the good guys, Jesus?"

You hear something dark in Sgt. Billy's tone and you risk turning the rearview mirror down so you can glimpse him. He holds the shotgun. It's pointed at your head. You take his questions more seriously. "I got into this to save a young woman named Willow, the tall blonde I told you to look out for. Her father hired me to kill the man who was dealing her drugs to help her stay clean and sober."

Sgt. Billy emits a tight chuckle. "Only one drug dealer in all of Chicago, is there?"

"I followed her to a couple of meetings. I sat in the back and listened to her talk about her struggle to get past the pills. She wants to quit. Her dad wanted me to cut her supply line so I cut it."

A horn blares to your left and behind you as you weave in and cut off a slower car about to cross an intersection. You lose traction on ice, slide and fishtail as you turn a corner and blow through a red light to more blaring horns and narrow misses.

"And?"

"Then the dad had another job for me. He's got some guns and stuff to sell. He told me to somehow keep his gun shipment out of the hands of the local street gang. He told me they killed his partner Harry. Now I think that's not true."

"So you got me to watch the Victorious's headquarters. Nothing came of that."

"The hell it didn't. If you hadn't been so close by, I'd be bacon."

"The Victorious get the guns?"

"No, but I know now where the shipment is." You flash your lights and honk a warning and a pedestrian caught halfway on a crosswalk sees you speeding toward him. He scampers back to the sidewalk and cowers behind a light stand as you flash by. You don't know the city well, but the hospital must be close.

Sgt. Billy wheezes as he speaks. "Why the fire?" You can hear his pain.

"Willow's father's partner Harry warned the Lone Wolf — the guy from the Victorious who set the diner on fire — that there was more than guns to the deal. White supremacists wanted explosives."

There's the hospital. You take the exit going the wrong way and your tires lose traction in the slush for several feet before the brakes bring the Chevy to a shuddering stop. You jump out. "Somebody get a doctor!" A nurse smoking near the entrance drops her cigarette and runs inside, you presume for a gurney. You pop the back door open, sure that the man who saved you from an awful death is dead.

Sgt. Billy is pale as paper, but he's still got enough strength in his right hand to level the shotgun at your head. "You're telling me you're a hit man who's helping a guy get explosives to Nazis?"

"You put it that way, it sounds bad."

"Make it sound better." He's too weak to hold the shotgun much longer. His aim falls to the center of your chest.

"Sergeant, I'm telling you my father-in-law-to-be played me but I'm going to make everything okay."

"How?"

"Not a clue. I haven't had a lot of time to think about it."

"It's always something with girlfriends and their daddies. Are the doctors coming soon?"

You look back. A security guy is eyeing you, but no help appears to be on the way. "Could we get some help over here? Guy's having a heart attack!" The security guard nods and waves to someone behind him through the glass.

"Willow's father thought he had a deal with the guy from The Victorious to get the guns and kill me, since I pissed 'em off so much, beating the shit out of Skeet and all."

"I get that. I'm kinda pissed at you, too."

"I get that a lot. The Lone Wolf was told about the Nazi side of the equation by Willow's Dad's business partner."

"Harry."

"Right! All I know is the white supremacists have some kind of plot to carry out with the mines that even a badass gang member wouldn't approve of."

"The business partner who warned the gang and soured the deal… Harry. Where is he?"

"I don't know. He flew the coop with a bunch of Willow's Dad's money."

He lowers the muzzle. The shotgun points at your crotch. "If I pulled the trigger right now and made you a eunuch, do you even know why everybody would be better off?"

Pounding feet and a gurney with a screeching wheel come up behind you.

Sgt. Billy points the shotgun at the floor and offers it to you. "Take it. Where I'm going, I won't need it."

You take the shotgun gently and hide it under your trench coat.

"You're not all the way a bad guy, Jesus. I knew that when you bought me a sandwich."

"Thanks."

"You don't operate out of malice. You're just a complete idiot who can't see the forest for the blonde."

"Thanks."

A rough hand pulls you away. Two orderlies, two nurses and a doctor have finally arrived.

"What? Were you guys on a coffee break?"

A black nurse pushes you farther back. "We're swamped in emerge. What happened?"

"He's a homeless guy named Sgt. Billy. He thinks he's having a heart attack."

"What's his last name?"

"As far as I know? Billy."

"Sir! Can you hear me?" one of the orderlies asks.

"Of course, I can hear you! I'm right here! My chest feels tight. Feels like a car is parked on my chest and it hurts like hell. Excuse my language, ladies, but I'm not fucking deaf!"

"Sounds like a heart attack," the doctor says.

"Gee-zuzz fuck, of *course* it sounds like a heart attack! Please excuse my language, ladies. This is my first heart attack."

A nurse titters and tells him to relax as the orderlies yank Sgt. Billy out of the back seat and on to the gurney. "You're feisty. We'll get you inside with some warm blankets, hook you up to a monitor and get you straightened out."

You walk beside him as they roll him toward the entrance to Emerge. "Jesus," Sgt. Billy says, "you aren't seeing the big picture."

"People keep saying that."

"Then *listen!* The father-in-law's business partner who took off with the money?"

"Yeah, yeah. I don't know where he is!"

"Oh, hero. You're too close to see it. You've already met him, you big dope."

"Um…oh." Your scalp heats up. Willow's uncle is out of town and you slept in his bed last night. Harry was Samuel Clemont's business partner, the man he said had been "*like a brother*". Thomas-not-Thomas! The man you left dead in a coffee table was Uncle Harry. You've killed Willow's dad *and* her Uncle Harry. Fortunately, you don't think she has any more family you can fuck up.

Sgt. Billy watches you work it out and whispers, "Moron." He slides a glance at the surrounding crowd and says, "The nurses here are cute."

The nurse who is the least attractive by far titters her approval.

Once inside and down the hall away from the entrance's cold draft, the doctor pulls his stethoscope from his neck and shushes everyone so he can listen to his patient's heart. You take the moment to pull out your half of the ripped $100 bill you owe Sgt. Billy. Before you can put it in his hand, you're denied your grand gesture. The old man stiffens in pain. His eyes go wide as he inhales with a wet, ratcheting sound. You know that sound. You've heard it a few times: The death rattle. He's starting to drown in the mucus stuck in his throat.

The medical team moves with real urgency now and rushes Sgt. Billy into a trauma room and pulls a curtain. You wave goodbye with the ripped bill. "Sorry…. I swear, Billy. I'll look more carefully from now on. All homeless guys look alike, but I'll look more carefully, I promise. I'll see the difference."

"Sir?"

When you turn, a security guard is already taking you by the arm and you have to stiffen and hug the short stock of the shotgun under your armpit so he doesn't see the muzzle at the hem of your trench. He's a large white guy with a kind face who doesn't walk so much as lumbers like a bear. His huge paw is less than an inch from the weapon under your coat. You're not the religious type, but now would be a good time to rediscover a childhood prayer as he escorts you toward the Emerge entrance.

"It was nice of you to pick up a homeless guy, sir. You're a good Samaritan.

A lot of people wouldn't have done that."

"Sure. Had to. He saved my life."

The guard looks at you curiously. "Oh? How's that? You smell of smoke, sir. Was that man in a fire? You pull him out? We'll need to make a full report."

"Long story. To tell you the whole thing would take a book."

"You can't leave your car in front of the ambulance bay. Can you park your car in the parking structure across the street and come back and we'll take your information? You can fill us in."

Once you're outside in the cold air, he lets go and you step back. He's the older sort of rent-a-cop who depends on his size and authority to stop trouble. When trouble does find him, he's the body type to grab hold, wrestle anyone to the ground and sit on them until his buddies arrive with handcuffs. However, looking him up and down, you know this for sure: you can outrun him.

As you and the guard approach the Chevy, a weak but repetitive thumping comes from the trunk. Skeet is awake. "You can have the car, amigo."

"Pardon me? What did you say?"

"The car. It isn't mine. I borrowed it." You open your coat a few inches so he can see the shotgun. "And this." Before he can say anything, you toss him the Chevy's keys. "There's a very unreasonable young black man in the trunk. Could you tell him for me that he should rethink his career choices?"

You back away. The rent-a-cop, wisely, does not move. His gaze isn't on your face, but on the shotgun bulge under your trench. When you get to a corner you yell to him, "He needs medical attention badly! Multiple concussions — and at least one that he deserved. Maybe not. It's still...muddled. His name is *Skeet!* Tell him to change his stupid name, too! And tell him I'm sorry! At least about some of it!"

You turn and hurry on your way. You're even farther away from righteous than you thought.

THE HARDER THEY FALL

It's the logistics that slow any mission. First, you have to get as far away from the hospital as quickly as you can without attracting attention. You want to hold on to the shotgun, so you can't very well grab a cab or a bus or the El. In crowded quarters they'd smell the smoke on your clothes first and spot the bulge under your jacket next. After 9/11, Homeland Security isn't catching many terrorists, but the whole "See something, say something," can really cramp a hit man's style. You search for a good car to steal.

You're pretty desperate to get your style back after old Sgt. Billy spotted the worm in your tequila so easily. You tell yourself you weren't seeing things clearly because you were too close to the action. You wanted to believe Samuel Clemont's cause was just so you could be a hero to Willow. Clemont said you aren't as smart as you think you are. When events happen fast, that can make anyone dumb. At least, that's what you tell yourself.

Heroism is a problem. It's like signing up to kill Osama bin Laden and ending up serving in the wrong country all over again. If Smug Tim were here, you could punch him in his smug face. That would make you feel better, but he would probably give you that same smile, wipe his bloody nose and say something like, "We are doomed to repeat the same painful lessons over and over until we learn the intended lesson." That guy is a longwinded new age Magic Eight Ball.

Waiting for dark to finally creep over Chicago takes a couple hours of zig zagging through the city. You spend that time trying to figure out how to tell Willow that her father is dead. She can never know how he died. You can never tell her how you dispatched her Uncle Harry, the tricky yet noble arms dealer, Thomas-not-Thomas. "Dispatched" is such a good word for what you do. It affirms your image as a modern day Musketeer. It also sounds like you're sending the people you kill somewhere. Most of them end up in Hell probably, but if you make a mistake, maybe they're getting to Heaven faster.

Your Drill Instructor believed in Heaven and Hell (yes, as real places) because he wasn't instructing anyone in the ways of murder. Your DI's motto was, "Kill the enemy and whoever may be standing beside the enemy and let Allah sort them out." Not much of a motto, and too long to put on a bumper sticker or a t-shirt.

And you hate killing civilians. Killing the wrong people makes your stomach ache.

Your cell rings. It's Willow. "Jesus?"

"Hi, baby. I've got some bad news."

"Dad's dead."

"Uh. Yes."

"I know."

"What —?"

"I'm in a car with Lurch and another man who says he has no name."

You grit your teeth. Someone else is listening and you can guess who by his heavy breathing. There's something new in Willow's voice, too. Something thin. That is the sound of creeping terror, like a knife at her throat.

"The fat man is listening then," you say. "Anyone else would say Lurch and the fat man. Go ahead. Tell him he's fat. Friends take friends aside and let them know."

She barrels on. "The man with no name says to find the shipment and call him at dawn. He'll tell you where to come to get me and deliver it."

"Tell the fat man to let you out right now because I don't know where the truck is. Samuel is dead and he's the only one who knew. It could be anywhere in the city."

There's a fumbling sound, a roar and a cry. You recognize the fat man's voice. "If you don't know where the truck is, the girl is useless. If the girl is useless, I'll drop her out of the car right now, but I won't be slowing down to do it. In fact, Lurch! Speed up!"

You made a tactical error there. "I know where the truck is. I've got the keys in my pocket. Don't hurt Willow. You're going to get your way."

"You're sure?"

"I'm sure. And if you hurt her, I'll be coming after you. You know that. Then I'll get my way."

"Less drama, more motion. On your way. We'll be ready for delivery of your shipment by dawn. I'll call you and tell you where to go. I'm sure I don't have to tell you —"

"You have eyes everywhere. No cops, no tricks. We'll meet in some empty lot or something you've already scoped out and we'll do the exchange and I'll be on my merry way with the future Mrs. Diaz."

The fat man clicks off.

Of course, his plan for you and the future Mrs. Diaz isn't quite that neat. He'll shoot you and Willow, perhaps by testing out one of those handy Russian-made Scorpions on your skulls.

*   *   *   *   *   *

You race to the safe house, now known as Uncle Harry's house. It's past eight and the lights are off. The front door is an open mouth. It's knocked out, not in, suggesting Lurch snuck into the house somehow, was in a rush, and made a mess on his exit. You leave the shotgun on the front porch and pull the SIG, checking angles around corners before slipping inside. Your pulse pounds in your ears. You yell Chill's name. The house is still warm. You just missed the excitement.

You run upstairs first. All of Willow's belongings are gone. You doubt Lurch worried she wouldn't have a change of underwear and toiletries. That was the fat man's move to make sure no trail was left for you or the cops. You grab your small pack from the back of the closet and throw it over your shoulder as you rush downstairs.

Chilli Gillie is face up on the kitchen floor, a big knife stuck in his gut. There's so much blood, you have to step carefully, so you don't slip, slide and fall on him.

"They're gone," he says.

"I know. They called me. I thought you'd be dead."

"I'm working on it," Chill tells the ceiling. "No rush."

A cell phone is on the floor, just out of his reach. You're pretty sure it's Willow's. You scoop it up and use it to dial 911. "I'm a huge man and I've been stabbed," you say. "Hurry. I'm bleeding out. Lights and sirens all the way." You give the operator the address and snap the cell shut. You've dealt with enough stupid questions from people in authority today.

You put the pistol away and crouch beside him.

"Don't touch the knife! Don't pull it out. Cuts both ways. Leave it."

"I know. I promise. I won't."

Chill is already putting pressure around the wound with his vest so it looks like he's holding a fake knife. However, all the blood messing up the fancy purple lining is scary and convincing.

"Looks like they got you in the spleen. You can do without that. You'll be okay." *Unless the blade sliced open his colon and shit is spilling around inside, filling his guts with blood and filth.*

Chill looks up at you, but it's as if he's looking through you. "I've been laying here...waiting and thinking."

"Any ideas where they took her, Chill?"

His breath is shallow and rapid, just like Sgt. Billy's was. "Dunno."

"Who was it?"

"Big bald guy with zombie teeth. Could have killed me with his breath. Fat guy was here, too. Laughed at me."

"Say anything useful?"

"Nah. Just...a prick. Asked if I voted Democrat and laughed more."

"The fat man has no name. The muscle was Lurch. I've met them. They're Nazis."

Chill's eyebrows shoot up. "Nazis? Shit. Didn't see that coming when I made breakfast this mornin'. If I'd known, I would have had sausage and eggs instead of oatmeal." He looks down again at the knife. "I've been stabbed by Nazis."

"It's…yeah..."

"Took me by surprise twice then. Don't like him…the Lurch. First clue he was in the house was the knife in my vitals." He sounds so weak and fading.

Sirens call from the distance that they're coming fast. People still always have too much time to think about what waits for them and, no matter how fast the paramedics speed, all ambulances are way too slow.

"How can I find Willow?"

"No idea, man."

"How did Willow know her dad was dead?"

"The cops called. They didn't want to tell her over the phone, but I took the phone and talked to a detective. Got it out of him. The cop didn't want to say on the phone, but he said two bodies were in the diner." Chill takes a few breaths before he can try another long sentence. "They weren't absolutely sure, but a burnt corpse by what was left of a wheelchair…." He winces at the pain, but continues. "Until you walked in, I assumed the other corpse was you." His eyes shift to the cell in your hand. "Told the cops we were in Cleveland and we'd come as soon as we could. Was going to stay here and hole up until I figured out who to go hunting to avenge you."

"Thanks for the thought. How did Lurch find you?"

"As soon as Willow hung up with the cops, she called for drugs. I told her not to, but she was crying about Samuel and she said she needed a fix. Half an hour later…" Chill's eyes shift to the knife protruding from his gut. "I didn't know what to say to her. When she found out about her dad…said she'd be alright as soon as she got her high and jumped to her happy place."

The sirens are getting very close.

"*Run*, man. Po-po's coming. Jesus be nimble, 'cuz they'll be quick. It's a nice neighborhood. They'll assume I'm white…so they're coming as fast as they can." He gives you a half-smile, grimaces and closes his eyes.

"Chill, what do I *do*? Is there someone you want me to call?"

"Wish I could talk to Harry. Don't know where he ran off to. Told him I'd take care of his niece. Messed that up, I guess."

Uncle Harry is a John Doe at the morgue. Then it hits you. "Wait. *Harry's* the guy you were doing the favor for?"

He gives a slight nod. "He told me Samuel was in some deep shit. I told him to skip town and not come back until the drama had blown over. Said he and Clemont had a falling out. He couldn't even talk to his brother anymore. He was a mess on the phone, broken up about her and Clemont. He was drinking more and losing it. Harry wasn't sure, but he thought someone might be following him, too. But the main thing was I keep Willow safe. Damn it! This screws up my perfect record, too."

Harry was right. You followed him quite a bit actually.

"Harry said he had some money hidden for me, too, money he took from Clemont. Figured he'd stop his operation by taking out operating money…and if I'd just do this one sketchy job, we'd be square. I told him I guard celebrities, not waitresses on the edge of an arms trade. He said I owed him one, which I did."

He gasps and, by his face, you guess there's a stab of regret mixed with the stabbing pain. "Man, I *told* him I was out of the deep shit. I should be back home, making sure Sandra Bullock gets from her limo into a restaurant safely. Shit!"

Thomas-not-Thomas was Chill's friend. Now you've got *another* secret to carry to the grave. The way things are going, you won't have to haul that weight long.

"What do I do, Chill?"

Before he passes out, he manages three more words. "Get the girl."

As Chicago's finest come in the front door, you disappear out the back and over the fence. You forgot the shotgun by the front door. You left Chill to die among strangers.

Inventory: you've got Willow's cell phone, a stolen car parked around the block, the keys to a truck parked across town that's loaded with Scorpions and Russian mines, and a burning love for the future Mrs. Diaz that's only a little bit brighter than your glowing hatred for Lurch and the fat man. You've got the SIG and a switchblade and no idea how to get the girl.

THE HUNGER GAMES

The first time you saw Willow Clemont in person, she strode up the sidewalk toward Thomas-not-Thomas's front. There was plenty you didn't know then, like the fact that it was a front. That was crucial information. You didn't know Thomas-not-Thomas was Willow's Uncle Harry or that he was Samuel Clemont's business partner or Chilli Gillie's friend. You didn't know anything about arms deals and Neo-Nazis or the softness of Willow's lips. Maybe you would have found out more, except, after spotting Willow, in particular her legs, you began following her around Chicago instead of the target.

Paulie had sent you the address of the target, a man the client had identified as Willow's drug dealer. Paulie sent you a picture on your phone, one for the target and one for Willow. Paulie didn't tell you her name. He'd labeled the jpeg file only "Total glamazon." The rule was that you could take out the target at that address. "Sooner is better," Paulie said. Cash and drugs awaited. "Exterminate the roach, but make sure the glamazon isn't anywhere near when you do the job. That's solid."

During the week before Christmas, you did follow the man around sporadically in a rental car. You broke into his car when he was at the movies. His registration papers listed him as Thomas LeClerc. He was almost as cagey as the anonymous fat man. In Thomas-not-Thomas's business, dealing with The Victorious and getting bids on mines from white supremacists, he had plenty of people to fear. No wonder he used a front in a scummy neighborhood and commuted back to his life as Uncle Harry in Evanston.

You checked under Thomas-not-Thomas's seats, the glove box and the trunk. Finding no drugs in the car (which was terribly disappointing) you had nothing else to do but to see the movie, too. He saw *The Avengers*. The previews weren't over before you sat directly behind Thomas-not-Thomas. You could have just slit his throat then and be done with the job, but the movie was really too good for that. Harry laughed and rocked in his seat, just like you, when The Hulk slammed Thor. It made you want to leave the target alone and tell Paulie to find another assassin. But there was the promise of money and drugs. Your meagre funds wouldn't last forever. Just driving around in a rental was costing you more for each day you didn't walk up and put a bullet in the target.

After New York, you wondered if you were getting rusty or soft. The hunger for an escape into a sweet high ate at you, though. Mostly the target stayed home. Except for Willow, Harry had no visitors at the scummy address, which, for a drug dealer, didn't make a lot of sense. Harry had been a cautious target dealing with dangerous people. You watched him meet the fat man — no Lurch then — in a tea room in The Loop. They looked like they argued, but that only made sense later.

After your high-profile mess in New York, you wanted to pull off an elegant hit. You considered following Thomas-not-Thomas around in a stolen car and running the target off the road. However, unless there's willful vehicular manslaughter or a bridge involved, a death within city limits on residential streets wouldn't pass a coroner's cursory glance. Also, you might get hurt.

When the target ventured out, usually he drove to the bar where you finally shook his hand on Christmas morning. Harry had a pattern and loved that bar too much. Patterns reveal weaknesses. That's what gave you the idea to make it look like an accident. The drunk driving angle was so obvious, you thought that was the only way to get him. You considered breaking his head with a baseball bat and then somehow driving him into a light pole, but that was way too complicated, with doomed shades of *The Postman Always Rings Twice*. If it didn't work for Jack Nicholson, it wouldn't work for you.

Then one night after Harry left the bar, you struck up a conversation with Chinese Rick about alcoholism. You told him you had a handle on sobriety but you missed hanging out in bars. You told him the model plane hobby didn't get you out of the house and away from your bitch of a wife. You asked him to keep the Cuba Libres coming — you'd pay — but not to put any alcohol in them. Chinese Rick thought you were crazy, but kept his judgments to himself after you tipped him harder. Chinese Rick didn't blink when you sat down and got social with one of his regulars, Thomas-not-Thomas.

If you hadn't hesitated and gotten so fancy about the mission, you wouldn't be in this deep now. Maybe you would have figured out more in advance if you hadn't switched your recon to the glamazon. You had to know her name. It was her long legs that made you want to follow her at first. Her shape was pleasing, of course, and her long blonde hair made her look innocent and wholesome. Her look was too girl-next-door for you to believe she could be a serious druggie.

When you followed her from the target's house to a meeting, you slipped in at the back. The air turned blue with cigarette smoke, surely a rebellion against city ordinances, but such rules are unreasonable to expect from a bunch of addicts. The usual cast of people who had gone through addiction's gauntlet came forward and shared their stories.

They were the same stories that are repeated across America several times a day: the cop who hit his wife when he drank so he turned to pills; the son who stole Dilaudid from his aging father (making the old man suffer more back pain so he'd have his fix); the mom who didn't think she had a serious problem because they were all prescription pills; the young mother who wanted to quit because another baby was on the way; the young father who tried to commit suicide after his toddler got into his stash and almost died.

And then there was Willow. That's how you first heard her name. "Hello. My name is Willow and I'm an addict."

"Hi, Willow!" everyone replied. There are armies of people in church basements and rec centers and library multipurpose rooms across the country, doing this ritual, making time sacred, fighting the hunger.

"The first time I took drugs was in high school," Willow said. "My father was away and my Mom was sick with cancer and I started by taking some of her drugs. The first ones made me sick, because I didn't know what I was doing. I thought I'd get high and instead I threw up. I think it was something to help my mother with hormone levels or something. I threw up all over my bed. Got it out of my system before I grew a dick, though."

Everyone burst out laughing, you included. You peered at her from between the heads of people in front of you, yearning to get a closer look.

"Then I got hold of some of her pain meds and my pain went away. It was great at first. People call it a crutch, but everybody's got a crutch and I needed a powerful one to lean on. People who would call us weak? They've got cigarettes and fried food and coffee and chocolate croissants and Honey Boo Boo and true crime and unanswered prayers and football."

The room got unnaturally quiet then. Willow did not waver. "The people who judge us? When they win they call it smarts, but lots of it was luck. They were lucky to be born into the right family. It wasn't their intelligence or hard work that saved them from breast cancer. My mother had breast cancer and she was the hardest working, smartest woman I ever knew."

She spoke as if lit by a spotlight, her eyes just above the crowd. You had the eerie feeling she wasn't really talking to the crowd at all. She spoke as if to the ghost of her dead mother, floating above her fellow addicts.

"The people who judge us, the ones who don't want a methadone clinic in their neighborhood or who scream at you at a family get-together…they don't know our struggle. They don't know our hunger. They don't sympathize with our sadness because the taste for pills just happened to miss them. The straight edges? I think they're like those screaming personal trainers you see on TV angry at fat people. They were born skinny and think they've earned something. They've got their addictions. Lots of people call this a journey to sobriety, but since I quit pills, I'm more aware of all the addictions around me. Love, hate, judgment, self-righteousness…those are addictions, too."

She gets a smattering of applause from the uncertain. Some around the room nod. A few more look worried about where Willow's speech is going. This isn't the usual rote "sharing time" about condemning her former lifestyle and wondering what she was thinking. This is *Look into the Existential Abyss. We May as Well Party*. But then Willow takes her defiance out of its dive.

"Nothing is as good as that first hit," she said. "After that? I'm tired of all addictions. They aren't healthy. Getting high feels more and more like another job. When I talk to people at these meetings, there's something I notice. We talk about our addictions and how good it felt early on. Later, getting to feel good gets to be more of a chore. It's a shit job on top of your regular shit job that costs you too much money. For me…well, you can get high, but you can't get to happy. It's like I can eat but never feel full. Does anybody know an addict who uses daily and looks happy? I don't."

The room resonated with the group's murmured agreement.

"I try every day not to use," Willow said. "I've already got a shit job. I don't need another one."

"One day at a time!" a woman called out.

"I know that's true," Willow said. "But some days, I look at my phone and I want to make that call and go get some candy, you know?"

"We know!" the same woman called. "Don't do it!"

"I know. I'm trying. The thing about candy is, you can't have just one. So I'm trying not to make that call. If I start, I know I'll take more and things will get out of control again. After my mom died, I was dog shit for a long time. Mom wouldn't have wanted that for me. I have to go without the candy. Vicodin. Percocet. Poppers. I have to stop but I'm tempted every day. Kind people and my family are trying to help me. I just know that I can't stop at one pill, so I have to make sure I don't start at one pill. I'm working on that. Soon, I think I can be confident in my new life. The really key thing for me is, if you love yourself enough and if you love other people enough, no matter what the cost, you'll ask for help. I'm asking for help."

It was like she was speaking directly to you, telling you to make her life easier by killing her dealer. She said she wanted to quit. You heard, "I can't quit cold turkey, please help me."

The group applauded her all the way back to her seat. You slipped out at the next break, but for a moment before you left, Willow's gaze met yours, through the crowd and across the room. In that second, you felt a new yearning and you wanted to sate that new hunger. You desperately wanted to substitute your old needs for Willow. You wanted to be pure for her. You wanted to kill the man who gave her all that dangerous candy. If not for Willow, you never would have returned to Group at the VA and sat still to listen to Smug Tim's dull cliches about getting past the past and forgiving the unforgivable.

The Vikes you found behind Thomas-not-Thomas's toilet tank were Willow's stash. He hid it from her, trying to help his niece quit.

Harry Clemont gave you a nostalgic story about journalism school. That was probably all lies, a well-rehearsed cover story. Or maybe that part was true and he was lonely, getting drunk in a shitty bar on Christmas, and trying to connect with a dangerous stranger. Maybe he thought he was making you feel better about being there with him, a fellow drunk who'd been kicked out by his ex.

Thomas-not-Thomas stole money from his brother Samuel Clemont to get away from a deal with white supremacists he wanted nothing to do with. He called in Chill to protect Willow. If you'd gotten to know Harry, you're pretty sure you would have liked him. He told convincing lies. He may not have been a civilian — as a gun runner, he was in your war zone — but Thomas-not-Thomas was a gun runner with a conscience.

He was a better man than you, but you didn't know that yet.

* * * * * *

The bag of Vicodin is still in your flop, hidden in the bottom of the chair in the corner. If you can find Willow, you can both keep each other clean and out of trouble. You're almost sure. If you can't find Willow, you want to eat every pill and then go find more.

Where to begin to look?

Your superior officer when you were an MP, Lt. Mathers, was a real bloodhound. To find a missing person or an AWOL soldier, he would run down family first. That doesn't help you much. You've shot and killed Willow's known relatives.

That leaves known associates. Chill said that when Willow found out Samuel was dead, her hunger overcame her quest to be clean. She called someone, but it must have been on the landline back at her uncle's house because when you check her cell's most recently used numbers list, all you find is calls back and forth to the diner.

Several contact numbers are listed on Willow's cell: her hair salon, some names you don't know with area codes that aren't local and Connie's Pizza.

The light cast up from the cell lights your face as snowflakes kiss the screen. Then, a spark of hope. You find a telephone number that reads: Candy.

SOME LIKE IT HOT

Your superior officer in the Military Police was a tricky guy. On your first meeting, Lt. Chuck Mathers slid it in sideways that he was Eminem's long lost uncle. The last time you saw him, he confessed that was bullshit, but he said that little detail got him laid and made young idiots like you listen more carefully.

"The little details are a rabbit's warren and you have to keep an eye on them if you're to find your way and get rabbit stew." Mathers was a smart MP, an antidote to the gorilla-busting-heads-in-a-bar cliche. When a grunt was in trouble after beating up his girlfriend, Mathers always knew when to go soft and when to go hard with the questions. Mostly he let bad soldiers talk, playing down the cause and consequence of their crimes. He gave bad soldiers rope until they hanged themselves.

"Getting information and confessions? It goes easier if they like you. They won't like us when we're done. In fact, they'll hate us later, but so what?" he said. "Weeds hate the hoe."

Going into a strip club to break up a fight, Mathers went straight to the biggest man first to let the others know the chaos they revelled in was over for the night. Mathers could be up on adrenaline from the bar fight arrests one minute and in the next switch gears to talk a sad guy who was AWOL into coming back to base. He'd go gentle, avoid unnecessary drama, and cut the dude the needed slack to get him in off the ledge. He began every shift with the reminder, "Have a plan A and a plan Z. Strong peters out by 30. Clever lasts."

Mathers's lessons come to mind as soon as you see Willow's candy girl, Liberty Montano, walk into the coffee shop. Dressed like a starlet out of the '40s in a floaty, feathery white jacket, she wears a black beret and teardrop-shaped sunglasses that make her look vaguely like a cute, huge-eyed alien. She spots you immediately from your description on the phone and plops into the booth seat across from you.

You're drinking a regular decaf to keep your nerves from jangling too hard at the thought of Willow at the fat man's mercy. The double espresso Liberty told you to order for her is still hot and ready.

She isn't what you expect from a drug dealer. She looks like a college girl and you tell her so.

"I *am* in college, moron. It's the only way to afford the tuition. I'm working on an MBA, though I've probably learned more in my off hours." She slides her sunglasses down delicately. She sports two black eyes. Your best friend did that to you not long ago in New York. You wince in sympathy.

"Lurch's work?"

"Swift." She rolls her eyes as she slides her glasses up.

"Have you known Willow long?"

"A while. We've partied a few times. Interesting girl. When she comes into money, I see more of her. She jumps on and off the wagon, weeks at a time."

"Do you like her?"

"Sure. As much as I like anybody. She's a client. Most of the job is schmoozing, so you know…." She sips the espresso, frowns and reaches across the tabletop to the sugar. She dumps a steady stream into the small cup and stirs the thick mixture into a brown sludge.

"Help me out here," you begin. "Lurch gave you a couple of black eyes to get you to give up Willow?"

She gives you a curled lip. "He punched me in the face before any questions, just to get my attention. He got it. The wide guy asked all the questions. Lurch has got the Bond villain thing going on. It was brutal. In the exquisite. They convinced me pretty quick that when Willow called, I was to tell her I was on my way with her medicine. They went instead. Took the pills, too."

"What number did the fat man give you to call?"

"He didn't. They waited with me."

"Shit. How long was that?"

"Most of today. Like, from around noon."

"What was that like?"

"Excruciating. First Lurch smacked me around. Then the fat one gave me a lecture about the history of the Civil War. Then they noticed I had Netflix and they forced me to watch *Toddlers and Tiaras* with them. Made me wish they'd get back to the beating."

"But they knew she'd call you?" You wonder how long Lurch and the fat man followed Willow to figure out Liberty was her supplier?

"I told them Willow hadn't called me in a couple weeks or more, but they were sure she'd call and she did. They knew all about her. The wide one said her dad just died in a fire. Poor kid. Sounded like the dad was an asshole a lot of the time, but still…. Easy trigger for candy lovers."

"I know a bit about that subject."

"Then you know that whether it's peanut butter cheesecake or Vikes, anything that happens that's good or bad means you deserve a reward, so people call me for pills. There's a reason it's a booming business. There's no bad time to get high and, when your dad dies in a fire, that's a really good time to get about as high — "

"As satellites, yeah. But how'd they know about the fire so quick?"

"Back when I was sampling the product, I'd occasionally watch stars go nova on the other side of the galaxy and talk with shamans in a jungle made entirely of mushrooms and patrolled by giant jaguars. However, despite these amazing experiences, I don't have any answers for you, Jesus. You want wisdom? I say, keep calm, bang a gong and call the cops." Montano shrugs and drinks her sweet caffeine sludge.

Plan A is a straight plea for mercy for Willow and vengeance for herself. "I need to find the fat man and Lurch. They've got Willow. I'm worried they'll do worse than a couple of black eyes."

"Yeah, and when you find them, I'm sure you'll give them each a stern talking to."

"I might even get very cross with them, yes."

"I don't know where they are, Jesus. They didn't leave a forwarding address. Like I said, call a cop if you're so worried. Just leave me out of that noise."

"Cops aren't an option. Willow's my mission."

"I'm not a helpful option, either. I'm thinking of taking some time off to travel. California's warmer and, after meeting Lurch, I'm not scared of mud slides, earthquakes and radiation from Japan anymore. Hollywood might be a good move. It's Vicodin Heaven, especially for all those poor rich stars who aren't allowed to eat food. It's all pills and booze for fame whores. They live on wine spritzers, adoration and Roxy, knocking back 30 mg at a time to hasten the cozy slide to has-beens on *Where Are They Now?*"

"How did Lurch and the fat man track you down?"

She shrugs again, hiding behind those cartoonish sunglasses, as readable as Sanskrit.

"Who were Willow's friends? The ones she partied with? Did she have a best friend or"— this kills you a little — "anyone special recently?"

"So I should give you client names? I don't think so. Besides, the only guy I ever met through Willow was her uncle."

"Uncle...?"

"Harry."

Damn. He used his real name around his niece's drug dealer. If he'd used his real name with you, maybe he'd still be alive. Mm, no, you still would have shot him. The hit was address-specific, not name-specific. If you'd done more of your own recon, instead of relying on the lie Samuel told Paulie, you'd have figured out Liberty Montano was Willow's dealer. You'd have killed this annoying girl instead.

"Harry is such a jerk. A real bloviator. He broke Willow's cell once, as if she wouldn't know my number by heart. You don't touch a girl's cell. He was always trying to keep me away from Willow. He even came to me in person once. Relatives don't get it. I don't have to call anybody. People come to me.

"Last I saw Willow, I sold her a big bag of Vicodin. Ever since she came into money, she's quite the hoarder. Her drunk asshole uncle — who was *driving* her, by the way — comes up and takes that big bag of Vikes right out of her hands. He told her he'd hold them and if she really wants them, he'll give her a little at a time because he's worried her kidneys will shut down because she's such a greedy gobbler. Some people don't get irony. The *drunk* kept trying to get his druggie niece to go to a meeting! Naturally, from my perspective, he's spreading out the time between my sales. Right in front of me. Galling."

"So…you didn't think Willow was going to quit?"

"Oh, sure. It's just a question of time. Girls Willow's age either don't do pills or try it once and throw up. The ones that stick, girls like Willow? They quit when they turn thirty, get married, have kids…whatever gives them that life-change mojo. Willow will take door number three. She's just a smart girl going through a tough time that makes her dumb. She won't be a customer forever. If it weren't for her mom…you know about her mom, right?"

"The cancer, yeah."

"Terrible thing. Without that and her dad ending up in a wheelchair, she'd never be calling me for medicinal stress relief."

"But," you persist, "you sound sure about Willow being able to kick?"

"Some go for the full Marilyn Monroe, too, I suppose, though there's compelling evidence that Marilyn Monroe's death wasn't suicide. It was murder. Did you know that?"

You shake your head. "I'm more of a JFK assassination buff."

"*Hmph. That* one? No way Oswald acted alone."

"Okay, but about Willow — "

"Seen it a hundred times. Willow will be okay if she can just stay away from trauma and drama. I'm going to miss her. And, not for nothing, by your questions, I obviously know her better than you do."

"You're making me sad."

"People make themselves sad. There's only one way I make people happy. You want to buy some happy? If not, I'm making travel plans. I was hoping for some more money for the road west."

You're missing something, but what? You better be missing something, or you and Willow are dead at dawn. To live to see past sunrise, you have to choose the battleground and that's going to be whatever hole the fat man and Lurch have crawled into with the future Mrs. Diaz. But the fat man was so cagey, he wouldn't even give Liberty Montano a cell number. He was so smart, he found Willow's drug dealer and waited for the call from Willow he was sure would come.

You prepared several stories to tell Willow's candy dispenser. You'd prepared lies to convince her to help find Willow before dawn. But Plan B, C, D, and E won't help because Liberty Montano *has* no information.

How could the fat man be that all-seeing? How did he know about the fire so quickly that he could instantly jump on the opportunity to grab Liberty?

How long had he been following Samuel and Willow around, gathering data? He must have done more recon than you did with Uncle Harry/Thomas-not-Thomas.

You watched the target, not just to find your opening for the hit, but to make sure Paulie's mission for you wasn't just a trap to get you arrested by the FBI or murdered by your former associates from New York. It took you a week to convince yourself that Paulie was legit and not setting you up so Big Denny De Molina could walk up and decapitate you with a shotgun blast. The last time you saw Big Denny, you both stood in a burning house and you never want to see him again.

Wait. When you met the fat man in your apartment, he called you "the burning man." *And there it is.* When we're rushed, we're dumb.

The fat man knew you threw the coffee pot in the diner to scald Skeet. The fat man knows so much, you have a clue how you can find Willow. He must have eyes on the street, just like you did when you hired Sgt. Billy for the job that killed him. The homeless blend in with the streetscape so well, they may as well wear concrete camouflage. The fat man hired an invisible man.

The candy dispenser must be a whiz at reading faces. "You've got an idea."

"Yeah. I do."

"That's impressive because I'm useless."

"Yes. No. Uh…you gave me an idea."

"By being useless?"

"Yeah."

"Okay."

"There is something you can do for me," you add as you stand to leave.

"What? For free? The coffee isn't that good."

"You'll want to do this." You point under the table at a canvas shopping bag. "I swung by my apartment on the way here. It's that big bag you were talking about. If pleading, negotiation and torture wasn't going to work, my last resort was to buy the information from you with all those delicious Vikes. There's a bit less in there, but still a lot. Take it. Willow and I are going on the wagon. We won't wait until we're thirty. We're quitting cold turkey. We'll do it together. Weaning is not an option."

She gives you a pitying smile. "I've heard that before. I doubt it'll work. You can't make that decision for somebody else, and you did say letting go of the happy pills was your *last* resort. It is your girlfriend's life on the line, right?"

In that moment, you aren't sorry Lurch punched her in the face a few times. "It's for real this time, Liberty. No more pills."

"What makes you think it's real? People stop, sure, but nobody kicks in one shot."

"It's not one shot. We've been playing around growing up for a while. Besides, in the next few hours, Willow and I will probably have several near-death experiences. I hear they're life-changing. That should give us that mojo you mentioned."

"Good luck," she says. "But, dude? You wanted my opinion about Willow. I got one for you, too. I look at you and I see a guy who doesn't quit cold turkey. You've got the stink all over you. Whatever your drug of choice is, you're not the type to ever stop chasing that high."

"Sounds less like a prediction and more like a curse."

Liberty Montano sips her espresso sugar sludge and stares in your eyes. Her smile is not kind. "You? You're a Marilyn. Maybe they'll make it look like suicide, but you are definitely *so* Marilyn."

FROM DUSK TILL DAWN

As you head down the street from the cafe, you pause to check over your shoulder. It would have been helpful if you looked in a window and caught Lurch's uniquely Frankensteinian silhouette in the reflection. Instead, you stay watchful and find, to your disappointment, that no one follows you. Dawn is hours away, but you still have to get to the truck filled with Russian mines and Scorpions.

With no one to catch in the shadows, you wonder, what would Lt. Mathers do? The lieutenant was not universally loved, but he taught you to think clearly in difficult circumstances. You want to rush to the truck to make sure it's waiting where Samuel Clemont told you to find it, but finding Willow is your highest priority. The Nazis have her and could be killing her, or worse, right now. You want to run in circles with your arms over your head as you scream long vowel sounds. Instead, you prioritize your emotions and make a mental note to lose your fucking mind later.

There's no time to wait for your tail to show up. You've got to go to them. You have a hunch you spotted the person who followed you between the diner and Willow's place. You grab a cab and head that way.

God Eats is an empty hulk. The front of the restaurant's shell is still intact, but beyond the yellow police tape, lies a ruin. You tell the driver to drop you off down the block and walk up the opposite side of the street. You hike the collar on your trench coat against the settling cold. A police cruiser is parked in the mouth of an alley nearby. A van marked *Fire Investigation Unit* stands next to where the diner's front doors once stood. A klieg light casts a bright white shine down the ashen throat of the dead building and you glimpse two flashlights bobbing at the rear. The dead neon sign that had flashed "God Eats." is not lit. *Hm. God Eats. If He's Hephaestus, the God of Fire, He sure does.* (Tia Marta skipped a lot of important subjects, but the classics interested her.)

A few blocks on, you expect a darting shadow to slip in from behind, slitting your throat and stealing the keys to Samuel's panel van. Instead, in a narrow alley across the street from Willow's apartment, the man who followed you sits on a mattress of cardboard, his back resting against a garbage can. He rubs his gloveless hands together as he watches her building. Ezekiel, or at least the homeless man with Ezekiel 25:17 emblazoned in white across his black hoodie, doesn't see you coming until it's too late to run.

You promised Sgt. Billy you wouldn't think of all homeless people as a wandering mass of lookalikes. You'd take them as individuals, not clones hiding behind similar beards and identical masks of bewildered distraction. How often had you passed Ezekiel in the street, never suspecting that he was looking back with more than a casual interest? When you saw him in the street after kissing Willow the first time, the bastard even asked you if you knew someone was watching over you!

He's no poser. You can't fake that homeless look without layers of Hollywood makeup, daily humiliation, persistent lice and dejection. They hired him just like you hired Sgt. Billy. Both sides needed invisible observers.

"The fat man sent me," you say. "You can stop watching the apartment."

Ezekiel looks up at you warily, his eyes wide. You give him a reassuring smile and offer him a hand up.

Instead of taking it, he squints and says, "What's the code?"

"Morse?"

"That ain't it."

"Damn, the fat man is a smartie, isn't he?"

"Smarter than most."

"Got a name?"

"Daniel. Just Daniel."

"So, you know you're an accessory to kidnapping, Daniel Just Daniel?"

"One, you ain't a cop. Two, do I look that ambitious to you?"

"Do you know who I am?"

"Jesus Diaz. I'm supposed to keep an eye out for you."

"What did the fat man tell you about me?"

"I don't ask what I don't need to know. Keeps me from accessorizing kidnapping." He smiles. "I was outside the diner watching when you nailed that dude with the pot of hot coffee. I don't know much about your particular *who*, but, the way you did it, I can guess *what* you are."

"You caught the show, huh?"

"Hells, yeah. That shithead almost knocked me over when he come screaming out of the place. Threw himself into a snowbank."

"The fat man has the girl."

"Mm. Willow Clemont. The fat man told me. She's a tall girl. A looker. Saw you smoochin' the other night. If it were me getting kissed like that, I wouldn't have been in such a hurry to leave. What's wrong with you?"

"That question has baffled experts."

"I see it. It's in your aura. You got a lot of yellow in your aura. That's fear. Not judging. I can see you're worried about the tall girl. And red. You got a lot of red. At the right time, that's passion. This is the wrong time, so I see it's a lot of mad. You're a real angry man. You need more purple, guy. Violet is royal and divine. Clears out all that bad shit."

"Thanks."

"You say that, but I see more red lighting up your chakras. Dangerous for your karma."

"What's the fat man's name?"

"Dunno. Didn't say."

"Where is he?"

"Didn't tell me that, either."

"I need to know where Willow Clemont is before they hurt her."

The man shrugs and looks away. There is no defiance in that look. "Sorry, Jesus. I can't help you, but I would if I could."

"How come you can't?"

"You've met Lurch, right?"

You nod. Daniel is a pawn, not a douchebag white supremacist. He's more afraid of Lurch than he is of you. Plan A: Keep it nice, but make sure he knows you aren't going to stop asking until he tells you something useful.

"True story," you say. "Tony Jacob was a kid I knew in Union City. He would go into the city to snatch purses. His theory was that the farther away from home he was, less likely he'd get caught. Like married people? They figure if they go to another country, they're temporarily single and adultery doesn't count."

The man bobs his head.

"Despite Tony's awesome theory, he did get caught one day. He grabbed a purse off a lady in Hell's Kitchen and ran. An off-duty cop — big, brawny ox — was out jogging, spotted my man Tony and chased him down an alley. He dropped the purse, but this cop kept coming after him. He was a young cop from the neighborhood, cocky and badge-heavy."

"I know the type."

"I bet you do. So, this cop runs down Tony, tackles him and gets him into a double arm bar, his foot planted between Tony's shoulder blades."

"So?"

"So the cop's in a back alley and he doesn't have a cell phone. He's got no back up and no friends. Tony struggles hard and he can't drag him out to the street. The cop can't let him go, either. The cop holds him, just barely, but can't do much more. Tony's on his belly, but it's a standoff."

"What did the cop do?"

"He calls up the alley. He shouts for help. He asks passersby to call the police. They're New Yorkers. They pretend they don't hear him. They gawk a little and they keep walking. The useless wrestling continues, but the cop still can't get anybody to help haul Tony off to jail. Time goes on and the cop sees his only option is to beat the shit out of Tony until he cooperates. He beats on my buddy until he begs for his life. Just then, a few of the local toughs look down the alley and see this cop kicking the poor innocent citizen's ribs in. He's the local badge-heavy cop, remember, so naturally, they recognize the prick. Next thing you know, it's the cop on his belly in a double arm bar and Tony is wheezing down the alley while the cop begs for his life."

"So your buddy got away to steal again another day? Nice story."

"Well, not quite. Up the alley, Tony spots the lady's purse beside the dumpster where he threw it. He bends over and somebody said later that, when he bent over? There was a series of crunches and clicks. One of the gang beating the shit out of the cop said he heard it from more than a dozen feet away. Like a sack of wet bones shifting and clicking. Next thing you know, Tony's on the ground sucking wind again. A bunch of his ribs cracked and his lungs got punctured when he bent over. Tony was dead before the ambulance arrived."

"Hard way to go. Why'd you tell me that, Jesus? Are you the cop in this story?"

"My point is, you should tell me what I need to know because I'm more trouble than I'm worth. All red through my chakras and all. I am Captain Relentless. I won't stop, so help me."

He looks at you, but shrugs. "I can see you're serious, but I got nothing for you."

You're going to have to reach deeper into the alphabet. Plan B: The Not-so-veiled Threat.

You crouch on one knee, so you're eye to eye with Daniel. "Another guy from the old neighborhood. Gayle Ott. Funny name for a guy. *Gayle* Ott."

"You're named after a God."

"*Heh*. That's been mentioned to me once or twice. Anyway, we called him Otter."

"You called a guy named Ott, Otter? Y'all got imagination."

You sigh, trying to picture violet swirls of divinity cleaning away your reds and yellows. Holly Go-lightly from *Breakfast at Tiffany's* had mean reds, but her mean reds and your mean reds are different. Yours end with somebody getting shot in the face.

"Otter worked in a drug supply chain, delivering things. It was a non-prescription sort of deal, operating somewhere between a meth maker and the meth dealers. Otter shorted the count. He kept a little back and sold the extra little bit on his own. He said he only did it once, but thieves are like pedophiles. When they're finally caught, they all say that the time they were caught was the first time they stepped over the line. It never is. The boss wanted Otter punished, of course, but he also wanted to know who Otter sold the stuff to. His customer needed a mild tuning up, maybe a couple of black eyes, for instance, so they'd remember who it was proper to do business with."

"So what'd you do?"

"I threatened to cut off his toes, one by one. Pulling off a sock and a shoe was almost all that was necessary to convince him I was serious. He told me what I needed to know without the need for too much violence. Two toes later, problem solved. You take the little toe, nobody misses it much. Take the big toes and your balance is all messed up for life and you walk funny. Most guys start with the little toes, but that's just sadistic, dragging it out like that."

He gazes back. "I could scream rape. People are around. I'm not worried about a guy in a suit who talks to me in a public place. I'm worried about waking up to a monster with breath like death. Worse than all the guys I know from the shelters. Lurch is…I've never met anybody like Lurch. He doesn't talk. He's the kind who just breaks things. No offense, but he's like…movie monster scary."

Daniel Just Daniel is smart and isn't scared of you. Maybe he even figured out that you've never cut off anyone's toes. Big Denny De Molina told you Otter's story, but apparently the magic of persuasion doesn't translate when you tell it.

Plan C: Get biblical.

"Ezekiel 25:17," you say. You grab Daniel by his jacket and pull him up as you stand and slam him against the wall. You pull the SIG out and dig it into his crotch. "The path of the righteous man is beset on all sides by the inequities of the selfish and the tyranny of evil men. Blessed is he," you say, your voice rising with the rhythm and flow of the words, "who in the name of charity and good will, shepherds the weak through the Valley of Darkness, for he is truly his brother's keeper and the finder of lost children."

Daniel struggles and makes a half turn as if to run. You catch him by the shoulder and spin him back. You place the muzzle of the roscoe at the tip of his nose and the man goes cross-eyed. You whisper, "And I will strike down upon thee with a great vengeance and *furious* anger those who would attempt to poison and destroy my brothers! And you will know my name is the Lord when I lay vengeance upon thee."

"I got the fat man's cell phone number. That's all I got."

"That'll do."

Daniel gives you the cell number and you make the SIG disappear under your trench coat again.

"You sure know your Bible," Daniel says. "Should have expected as much from a guy with a name like Jesus."

"The Bible I don't remember much at all, but I love Jules."

"Who?"

"I know movie dialogue, especially everything Quentin Tarantino ever bestowed upon us. Blessed be the Tarantino. May peace forever fall upon Saint Tarantino. It's one of the best scenes in *Pulp Fiction*."

"Fuck," Daniel says.

"Blasphemer."

"The fat man is going to send Lurch after me. Lurch will kill me twice."

"Not if I get him first."

"How are you going to get a thing like Lurch? His name is *Lurch*, for Christ's sake!"

"No problem. If all goes according to plan, in a couple of hours, you're going to make a phone call for me, Daniel. You'll never have to worry about Lurch again. Willow will be safe and no one will get Medieval on your ass as long as you do exactly as I say."

"And what if I don't?"

"If Willow's hurt or dead and you could have helped me save her and you didn't? That would make you a true bad guy. After I get Lurch and the fat man, then it'd be suitable for me to hunt you down. If you don't help me and I find them anyway, maybe I'll fail. With my last breath, I'll make sure they know you helped me."

You give him a moment to work it through.

"Okay," he says. "A phone call."

"I'll throw in $100 for your happy help and genial cooperation." Evil is a mystery, but capitalism he understands. You give Daniel Just Daniel the other half of Sgt. Billy's torn hundred-dollar bill.

THE NIGHT OF THE HUNTER

Daniel does as he's told and joins you for a cab ride to the truck. Maybe it's the torn bill. Maybe he's still thinking of what the cold muzzle of a heater feels like at the end of his nose.

The cab smells like burnt cabbages and sweaty feet. You give the cabbie an address that's a couple of blocks from your actual destination. His dirty ID card on the dash has an unpronounceable name you can only guess is Egyptian. For a cabbie on the graveyard shift, he's mercifully uninterested in chatting. Instead, the guy plugs his white earphones back in. He points at his head and almost yells, "I'm listening to computer radio! Mike Schmidt! Comedy! *The 40-year-old Boy*! Podcast! Hilarious!"

When he catches your thousand-yard stare, he turns to his work and slams the old cab into drive. Daniel doesn't talk too much, either, still uncertain whether he's a paid informant or if you'll shoot him in the face.

Lt. Mathers had a knack for finding AWOL soldiers and getting them to come back to base without excess drama. With Willow in the hands of a couple of white supremacists, and more crazies on the way, a pant load of drama is guaranteed. However, you have the fat man's cell number and Lt. Mathers taught you an elegant solution for finding people who don't want to be found.

"Whatcha gonna do?" Daniel asks.

"Find the fat man. The best defense…"

"How are you going to do that?" Maybe Daniel is still worried about Lurch, crazed and tearing out a jugular with his dental nightmare of ruined fangs. To be fair to Daniel, Lurch does have zombie-worthy teeth.

"Are you going to track his phone?" Daniel asks. "Triangulate coordinates? I heard there was this guy in Colorado. Guy got lost in the woods and a mountain lion attacked. He managed to blind the cat with a pen and it ran off, but not before the animal ripped up his legs real bad. He thought he was going to die, but the cops tracked him down with the cell phone in his pocket!"

Closed Chicago storefronts flash past and each streetlight is a slow strobe that illuminates the anxiety in the creases and contours of Daniel's weatherbeaten face. He could be thirty or fifty. He's not meant for this. As soon as you don't need him anymore, you'll cut him loose and get him out of harm's way.

You sigh. "I figured I'd put a call out to my crack team of ninja monkey clone assassins. Then I'll just call for a helicopter with infrared cameras to zero in on the fat man. After that, I'll go all Klingon Christopher Plummer on his ass and 'Cry havoc! And let slip the dogs of war!'"

"I think that's Shakespeare," Daniel mumbles. "And I've heard the government can listen in if you just have a cell phone with you. You don't even have to be using it. As long as the battery is in, they've got you."

"Do I look like I'm the guy with the office under an active volcano, a monocle and a white Persian cat? I'm not exactly overloaded with resources, or cavalry for back up and a trunk full of cash, Daniel. I have an idea, that's all. The pizza trick works eight times out of ten." You try to sound confident, but you've had enough plans suddenly tip upside down that your voice comes out jittery. He gets your vibe and shuts up.

You pay the cabbie and urge Daniel to keep up with you. You're almost surprised when you turn a corner to find the white panel van — "a regular child molester wagon" Samuel had said just before he burned to death. It's parked exactly where Samuel said it would be: East Wesley and North Main.

You make the first phone call and Mathers' old hound dog trick doesn't work. You dial again and strike out again. Then you try a smaller pizza chain: Meanie Giodinni's. It's a go.

"I have a pizza order."

"Your telephone number, sir?" comes the bored voice from some wage ape praying for death.

You give the pizza place the fat man's cell number.

The order taker confirms the number is in their system. "So you want this order delivered to 19 Victor Young Street?"

"Sure, oh, uh…change of plan. Cancel that order and I'll call back. Thanks!" To Daniel, you grin. "Bingo. I know where the fat man is. "

"Slick. It's actually a little scary how easy that was."

"Now I need to make a car bomb to deal with Lurch." You've got a panel truck full of mines, but you're in a hurry so, to rig this device in a jiffy, you'll need to find an all-night convenience store.

The van's engine sputters to life. A few blocks away, Daniel points out a mom-and-pop with a dimly lit yellow sign that looks like a mallard in flight. The sign reads: 24-hour Convenience! Duck in! You do duck in, but you take the fat man's cell, the keys to the van and Daniel's request for a Slushie.

A few minutes later you return with a plastic bag that contains two long canisters of room freshener, a cheap little clock sporting a "Chicago Bears" logo, a ball of twine, a roll of duct tape and a tube of super glue. "No Slushie machine," you tell Daniel. "I got you a Coke and a Baby Ruth."

It takes all your self-control not to break the speed limit on the way to the address where the fat man and Lurch are holding Willow. However, a traffic stop would make you more queasy than you already feel.

In this area, the streets are dotted with for sale signs. You miss the address and have to double back. Why doesn't anybody have their address displayed plainly? Very few houses seem to have numbers in this neighborhood, and many of those that do are either spelled out in an illegible script or the numbers are half-hidden behind bushes or posts. "I hope these people need an ambulance in a hurry some day. Serve 'em right!"

You had expected an abandoned warehouse or a broken down shack on the edge of the city. Instead, you spot the black Ford F150 with the foxtail tied to the roof antenna parked in front a two-story white house with fresh paint. The sign on the front lawn advertises that the house is for sale. Another piece of wood tacked to the bottom of the sign reads like a depressing capitulation: Reduced!

"Clever. So many underwater mortgages, there are plenty of empty houses to hole up in. I could have saved a lot of rent if I'd thought of that. I should have known the fat man would be squatting somewhere out of the way where he wouldn't have to use a name. He's so cagey he's almost invisible, except for visits from the pizza delivery guy."

"Think how I feel, looking at all these empty houses."

"Sorry, Daniel." For a minute there, you'd forgotten you sat next to a homeless guy.

You pull the van around the next corner. It's a decent observation post. You can see the front door clearly and the houses are spread out enough that you'd spot someone trying to sneak up on you through a side yard. You tell Daniel to stay frosty while you hurriedly construct the device that will help you kill Lurch.

You wind the duct tape around both air freshener canisters and yank the short red and black wires from the little clock's battery compartment. You attach the leads from the clock to the ends of the cylinders and apply even more tape. You wrap the twine around the whole contraption until you're satisfied it will hold together solidly.

"That's going to kill Lurch?" Daniel asks, frowning.

You pop the top on the tube of super glue and cut off the tip of the applicator with your knife. "You know, Daniel, for a guy with a Bible verse painted on his clothing with —what is that? White out? You don't seem to have much faith. Trust me. I'm Jesus."

HIT MAN

The trick will be to get the device in a spot Lurch will have to reach for it. Willow's on your mind and the thought of her at Lurch's mercy makes you want to run, but Lt. Mathers taught you well. "Run and people act like rabbits. Wander up casually and we won't get into a footrace with a guy fresh out of bootcamp," he said. "Those clowns are in the best shape of their lives."

You can't manage to go so slow it's a sidle, but you keep your speed to a solid amble as you approach the Ford F150. You stick to the sidewalk at first. No lights are visible in the house, so Lurch could be at the window, watching you come at him. If he runs at you out of the house, you'll lose both the element of surprise and the chance to outflank the enemy. Willow will be in even more danger. You don't know how long you have until dawn, but there's a better than even chance everyone left in this post-mortgage crisis/pre-apocalyptic neighborhood is still asleep. That just leaves meth head vampires on their way to bed and the bakers and morning shock jocks on their way to work to get in the way.

You pass the truck to get a glimpse in the back. Nothing there. Daniel's watching from the van. If Lurch popped out of the Ford's bed to slit your throat, you might die of embarrassment before all the blood loss took you away. A streetlight casts enough shine to see inside the cab. At a glance, you guess that antenna is for a CB radio. Very retro. Or for coordination of an attack.

You step into the street and look over your shoulder before you duck down behind the truck. This plan might work better in summer. You get your back and pants wet squirrelling under the truck to place the device. If Lurch spotted you already, you're in a vulnerable position. Your ears strain for the bang of a door or the crunch of a footstep in the snow.

You apply the super glue in several spots along the top of your device and press it into the truck's undercarriage with the clock face pointed at you. It's got to be attached solidly or you're screwed. The instructions told you to count to ten seconds for the adhesive to stick properly, but you've got to be *sure* it won't fall off. You force yourself to count slowly — one hippopotamus, two hippopotamus, three hippopotamus...— all the way to twenty. When that's done, you give the device a yank and it holds fast.

You scramble up and stalk away, trying to look purposeful, like you have urgent business elsewhere and can't seem to remember where you left your car. Cold and wet have soaked through your clothes and by the time you make it back to the van, the shivers have taken over your body and your teeth are chattering. If you live through this, you promise yourself you will start to dress more appropriately for these jobs. A black knit cap, a pea coat and a black turtleneck are a hit man's cliche, but they'd make more sense for Chicago in winter. On the job, you're always dressed like you're going to church or a funeral, which makes sense in its own way.

"What now, Jesus?" Daniel asks.

"Now you make a phone call for me. Here. Use the phone the fat man gave you."

Daniel takes the phone like it might be contaminated. "What should I say?"

"Warn him there's a bomb under his truck, of course."

"You want him to *know*?"

"Yep."

"What if he doesn't believe me?"

You point over your shoulder at the five wooden crates crammed into the back of the van. "He already knows I've got a van full of Russian mines. He'll believe it."

"But how would *I* know you put a bomb under his truck?" Daniel whines.

Your knuckles go white on the steering wheel and you count ten hippos before you answer. "*Relax*, Daniel. Do you remember the anthrax scare, not long after 9/11?"

"No."

"Doesn't matter. Listen. The FBI chased ghosts trying to figure out who was sending anthrax through the mail. Some people died. It was quite a panic. There was even worry that there would be copycats who'd send baby powder packages and shut down the mail service everywhere."

"Uh-huh. How does that help me?"

"The powers that be had to warn everybody that if you get an envelope with powder in it, *don't sniff it!* Think about that for a second. The World Trade Center had just come tumbling down and we thought terrorists were behind every rock and tree and people still had the survival instincts of deer in headlights. They'd get a letter full of powder and their first reaction is to take a deep snootful to see if it smelled like baby powder or anthrax, as if they'd know what anthrax smelled like."

"What if the fat man answers? He's not stupid."

"Everybody's stupid if you don't give them time to think. Tell them there's a bomb under their truck and it will go off at dawn."

"What do I say when he asks how I know that?"

"You don't wait for them to ask questions, Daniel. You hang up. I thought

I'd made myself clear, but perhaps I didn't explain in enough detail." You whip out your SIG Sauer and let the cold muzzle graze Daniel's temple.

Daniel begins to hyperventilate. Hands shaking, he makes the call. "Th-there's a b-b-bomb!" He hangs up.

Since it's not helping, you pocket the SIG and sigh. "It would have been better if you'd been more specific, Daniel."

"I'm nervous! I get that way when anybody points a gun at me! Don't point a gun at me!"

"It's okay. It's okay. They'll call you back in a second. Just…just remember to tell them it's under their Ford F150 and it will go off soon. Say dawn."

The cell rings. Despite the fact that it's a cheap throwaway phone, you guess that it was the fat man who downloaded the ringtone. To your surprise, it's *"I Get By"* by Everlast, proving that even evil assholes can have taste.

"Should I answer it now?"

"Yeah. Presuming Willow is still alive, I'm in kind of a rush."

"It's Daniel."

You urge him to get to it, circling an index finger.

"There's a bomb under your car! Uh, under your truck! Under your Ford F1…"

You take the phone from Daniel and yell, "It'll blow at dawn!" and close the cell with a snap. It rings again, almost immediately. You roll down your window and toss it into a snowbank.

"What now?"

"Wait."

"It didn't work! Let's go! Call the cops and let them handle it! SWAT will clear this up and give your lady the best chance!"

"Wait."

"I screwed it up! I'm sorry! We've got to get out of here! When that bomb goes off and, you know, what with the gas tank — ! Oh, my god! If you hadn't pointed that g— "

"That's not a bomb, Daniel. The worst you can do with a couple of cans of air freshener is make somebody's asthma worse or maybe give them cancer over the long haul."

You pull the SIG out so fast this time, you accidentally bang him in the temple a bit with the butt.

At that moment, you spot Lurch burst out of the front of the house. The door bangs and echoes through the pre-dawn stillness. Daniel scrabbles for his passenger door, yanking at the handle but forgetting to unlock it. Before he starts clawing at the upholstery or trying to climb out of the window, you reach across Daniel, pull the lock and shove him out.

You twist the key in the ignition and the engine sputters to life as Lurch frantically circles his F150, searching. In a moment, standing in the street, he's spotted the device and doesn't hesitate to throw himself underneath to try to yank it clear. You pull out, but not so fast you risk attracting Lurch's attention. You need to act like normal traffic, not an avenging angel bearing down on your enemy, engine screaming.

You speed up as much as you dare and you see Lurch's long legs pointed out into the street. He got under the truck quick, but by the way his legs are jumping and wriggling, he's got two hands on the dummy bomb and he's struggling with all his might to overcome super glue. He may as well try to pry up a boulder with his dick.

At the last second, Lurch hears your van's engine and pulls his knees up, but you drive the van so close to the Ford that its rear fender takes out your driver's side mirror and it's not just a scratch you leave down the sides of both vehicles, but a layer of paint. The van lurches over each of Lurch's legs, bouncing over him in a sickening double bump.

His scream is…what's the word Liberty Montano used to describe the pain he inflicted? *Exquisite.*

You lock up the brakes and open your door and turn in your seat to peer back at him. Lurch is a real trooper. He's already flipped over on his stomach. He pulls himself out from under the truck by his elbows.

They made you do that in bootcamp, crawling for hours through deep mud that felt like it would suck you down to Hell and you'd be grateful for the rest despite the pitchforks and flames.

Sgt. Devin, AKA The Devil, would cackle, "You girls aren't dirty enough yet! Your legs and dicks are blown off! Pull yourself to cover by your elbows before Haji fires another RPG! Faster!" It was like Sgt. Devin was doing his best Samuel L. Jackson impression, if Samuel L. Jackson was having a bad day.

"Get your faces in that mud and *pull*, goddammit! Be my dirty girls! Nothing to it but to do it!" the Devil would say. In retrospect, by the way he enjoyed his job, The Devil was probably into some pretty sick German torture porn.

Lurch is in agony. You can't leave him like this. You did Samuel Clemont the favor of shooting him after he'd burned a while. You can do no less for Lurch on the off chance that it was he who likes Everlast's music and therefore may find forgiveness in the afterlife. He'll get no forgiveness from you, of course, but after he's dead, grace is somebody else's business.

"Hey! Speedbump! Justice is served, Nazi boy!"

Lurch raises his head to snarl at you, baring those ugly teeth one last time. Lurch is a big guy. The elevation of his forehead is just about even with the height of your back bumper when you slam the van into reverse and floor it. The sound surprises you. You thought it would be more of a crunch, but instead, when Lurch's head snaps back, it's a wet slap. He's under your left rear wheel and when you put the van in drive, the tires lose traction and spin red, white and brown gore. Lurch is a meat skid mark.

You shouldn't smile, but there's a little bit of a smirk on your face as you park. You jump out of the van and raise the SIG. *Nothing to it but to do it!* But

Lurch is beyond need of earthly mercies.

A familiar feeling, like the ghost of a memory of a spider, crawls on the back of your neck. A pistol's hammer cocks behind you. You raise both hands slowly and turn, expecting that Daniel has turned on you.

Instead, it's the fat man pointing a nickel plated .38, so shiny it gleams in the streetlight's yellow glow.

"Shit." You drop the SIG in the snow gently.

"No swearing." He gestures with his weapon, once for you to put your hands down and twice for you to walk across the street.

You look right and left, confused. The Ford F150 was parked in front of the address the pizza place gave you. Lurch ran to his truck from that house. However, the fat man is so canny, he broke into the house for sale across the street, too. When the fat man gestures for you to climb into the trunk of a car in the garage, resistance is futile.

You've been had. Bad. Again.

THE USUAL SUSPECTS

"What, do you suppose, is the most painful way to die, Mr. Diaz?" Burning to death is pretty fresh in your mind, but you don't mention that in case the fat man takes your whimsy as a suggestion. You're in a large cool room with a pillowcase over your head. At any moment you expect the fat man to do something terrible. He's taken your pistol and duct taped your hands in front of you and your legs are taped to the chair just below your knees. You still have the switchblade in your sock — the fat man was too uncomfortable in a crouch to reach that far — but you know from experience how useless it is to take a knife to a gunfight.

When you don't answer he continues. "Well, let's not talk about dying yet, Mr. Diaz. It happens I need your peculiar expertise, so let's talk about what's most painful that doesn't kill you."

"Old age is the worst. Let's try that."

"I recall the IRA's favorite trick with informants was to kneecap them. A shot in the patella is very persuasive."

"I'm allergic."

"One in each leg and you beg for death, I bet. What do you think?"

"I only bet on pool and when the Queen of England will die."

"Another thought occurs. When Reagan was shot, one of the Secret Service agents did what he was trained to do and took a bullet in the gut. I *loved* that assassination attempt. You're too young to remember, but they showed it on television, over and over in slow motion. Very instructive. Did you know one of the people who helped foil that one was a hero construction worker who jumped on John Warnock Hinckley Jr.? They say it's easy to kill a head of state, but it's harder than it looks. Anyway, the Secret Service agent must have been wearing body armor under that suit, but the way he rolled around? It looked like agony. Don't worry. I could probably get all the information I need out of you before you die."

"Too risky for you. If you clip the inferior vena cava with that gut shot, I could bleed out before you could start regretting your terrible sin."

You listen carefully as the fat man moves around you, his breathing and footsteps heavy. "How is it that a guy like you knows words like 'inferior vena cava?'"

"A guy I knew died that way. I thought he was going to make it until his gut filled up like a balloon."

"I see."

"Well, let's just keep in mind that I have a lot of options. Whoever had this house before just walked away from it. The mortgage crisis in this country…terrible what criminals are allowed to get away with as long as they wear suits and work on Wall Street."

"I love wearing good suits," you say, "but I'm beginning to regret my vocational choices."

"My point, Mr. Diaz, was that upstairs in the kitchen, there's probably a carrot scraper. Keep that in mind when you don't feel like cooperating. I have lots of choices as to how I deal with you."

"Cool! I'm a big fan of free will. You might even decide to let me go."

"Oh, Lurch's widow would be very upset with me if I allowed that."

"His widow? Really? I thought you and Lurch made a lovely couple."

"This does not end well for you."

"I've heard that before. Let's not get ahead of ourselves. What do you want to know? I'm in a giving mood."

"I have a mine from your van. Soon I will go get all the mines. One at a time, I will soak them in hot water in the bathtub," the fat man says. "You're going to walk me through the bomb construction."

"Your informant got away," you say. "He was pretty freaked out and running for his life last time I saw him."

"Daniel," the fat man says. "I thought of him as Ezekiel. I like Ezekiel. Interesting fellow. He was a priest — the one in the Bible, I mean. I have no idea what Daniel's profession might have been before living on the streets, but Ezekiel? He had an amazing vision. He reported that he saw a wheel in the sky. Some crazies think he was talking about a UFO, but my favorite thing about the biblical Ezekiel was his prediction of the End Times. 'Wail…for the day of the Lord is near. A day of clouds' — nuclear, I suppose — '…a time of doom for nations.'"

"That's what I love about the Bible. All the emo Goth poetry."

The fat man moves closer. If you've offended his Christian values, he's probably about to make you bleed. You jump when he whispers in your ear, "How about Ezekiel's warning that no foreigner should be allowed in the temple? I wonder if that is God's little joke on us? A foreigner in the temple could mean a Kenyan in the Whitehouse, couldn't it?"

You sigh. Political talk makes you tired. However, one thing the military taught you was, if captured, keep the assholes talking, smoke their smokes and prolong the non-torture part of the adventure in the dim hope that you will get a chance to kill them. "Kenyan, secret Muslim…the dude was elected fair and square. By the way, even if he was Muslim, this is America. That's not supposed to matter. I get the feeling if he was a white guy — a secret Belgian, let's say — birthers wouldn't be so excited about his birth certificate."

"I believe in Manifest Destiny, Mr. Diaz. That doesn't simply imply we'll take over Canada one day, though we will. It means that, as a caucasian American, I'm one of the owners of this country. As an original master, I don't care to listen to lectures by a man who's not only Latino, but wasn't even born in my country."

"If you have to swim and fight for it, you appreciate citizenship more," you say.

"You imagine I'm the bad guy."

"I was thinking 'evil' with a capital E, but *po-tay-to, po-taw-to*."

"No. Not Evil." He sounds hurt. "When voters want to get something done and it doesn't get done, we're told to be patient. The politicians say we shouldn't make the Perfect the enemy of the Good. I'm not the enemy of the Good. I'm trying something new and different. New, unfamiliar things always look evil at first, but what all the sheeple don't understand is, what's coming? It's not simply about Good versus Evil. I serve the *greater* Good."

"Said every evil dude in history."

"And every patriot who wasn't too queasy about the relationship between ends and means."

"I wonder when Daniel will be back with the cops? I wish he'd hurry up. Shouldn't be long now."

He pulls the pillowcase off your head. You blink at the bright light. Daniel sits on the floor across the room. No, propped up in a corner and drenched in blood. His eyes are marbles, drained of life, accusatory.

"I caught up with him in your van not more than a couple of blocks from here. Sorry about the upholstery." The fat man points the SIG at your face. "I'm going to have a seat over there. You will help me do my job." He points at a long table eight feet away. "If you think you can tear out of that chair before I empty your pistol into you, feel free to try it."

"I won't." You mean it.

THE HURT LOCKER

A couple of beer bottles stand within easy reach of the fat man's seat behind the long table. Tools are strewn before him, including a roll of duct tape, brown butcher paper, three kettles, a row of screwdrivers, an adjustable wrench, and a large, flat plastic container usually used to store clothing under a bed. It is filled with water and through the plastic you glimpse a mine. You recognize it. It's a Russian TM40.

So far, your captor has demonstrated his confidence in what he knows. You have to drag him deeper into your world, where doubt can seep into his skin. "Did the clean up outside go okay? Are you sure nobody else called the police? SWAT's probably already circling the house."

"Actually, I didn't even drag Lurch's body into the garage," he replies breezily. "Before I drove over and picked up our homeless friend, I grabbed a snow shovel and covered Lurch up. All that blood, too. You sure made a mess, but the van is safely backed up in the driveway. No police. Thank you for your concern, but thanks to all those underwater mortgages, this street is the most deserted residential area in all of Chicago. I checked."

The fat man is going to kill you without a care in the world because some fat cat on Wall Street robbed people with bad deals and predatory mortgages years ago. It's all the little things that add up to the big picture, and that always seems to lead to blood and guts. Every misstep at the wrong moment, every turn left instead of right and a gift for bad timing: once again, loving the wrong woman has got you tied to a chair. If you believed God was interested in your tiny life, you'd be sure He has it in for you.

"You're going to help me, Mr. Diaz. Explosives aren't exactly my area of expertise. That was Lurch's thing. He loved to 'blow shit up' as he would say. I have four young men coming up here from Florida tomorrow at noon and I have to have the bombs ready. I need car bombs that will detonate on impact. I have to rig it so, in case the driver loses his nerve, I can be behind him, detonating it remotely."

"Just like they do with those suicide bombers in the Middle East," you say, hoping to provoke your captor and getting him off-balance. You won't be able to convince him you find the tenets of The Recipients' cause delightful —

you're the wrong color for that — but nervous, angry people make mistakes. It'll take a huge mistake on his part to get you out of this chair.

"One for the Lincoln in the garage, one for the Ford F150, one for your van and I'll have to have one ready to install for the car the boys are bringing. We're on a tight schedule. You have no idea how hard it is to sucker four twits into becoming suicide bombers."

"Just like they do with suicide bombers in the Middle East," you offer again.

Instead of irritating him, the fat man smiles with pride. "Not at all like that. They've got bombs going off on the other side of the world every day. I really had to work hard to scare up four true believers. Between you and me, Osama Bin Laden had that part right. He tricked most of the terrorist teams on 9/11 into their suicide mission. That's what it takes. Discontent, malcontents and idiot true believers. Don't get me wrong. There are plenty who believe in the cause and the inner circle of The Recipients are some deep people. For the dabblers…let's just say it's difficult to convince a young fella to kill himself if he's got Internet access."

"Too much access to the 21st century?"

"Can't tear them away from the porn. In fairness, if we could get al-Qaeda more porn, we wouldn't have half the problems we do."

"I get it. You found some self-righteous, self-hating loser assholes."

"Oh, I wouldn't judge. From what I gather, a bunch of people might take you for a tool and an asshole, too. I looked into your background, so I know you have some history with technical problems like this. That car bomb you rigged back in New York? Did it take out the whole house?"

"Mostly just the front. But it was a *stone* house."

"I see. Well, you see the position I'm in. I wish Lurch were here. If he were, I'd put a bullet in your head and tell Lurch to get to work. I could be upstairs making bacon and eggs. Instead…well, here we are."

You hold up your bound hands, duct taped palm to palm in prayer position. "I don't miss Lurch. He didn't appreciate me as a person. I was thinking about that when the back tires were spinning and turning him into paste."

The fat man plops himself into his chair. He puts your SIG down delicately on the tabletop, picks up a beer bottle and takes a swig. It's infuriating. If he were a little closer and if your hands were free and if a freak asteroid strike obliterated him in a cloud of dust, you might have a chance at getting out of this basement alive.

"Where's Willow?"

"Upstairs. She's safe as long as you answer my questions and talk me through my technical problem."

You don't believe him but you let that go. Anything you could say about that now wouldn't help Willow and you're not going to go out a petulant whiner.

"I must say, munitions are fascinating," he says. "I was more interested in politics and history in school. Right now, I wish I'd studied more chemistry. When they talked about IEDs on the news, I never pictured mines. They used to call them boobytraps. Do you know why they changed that?"

The fat man is back in lecture mode. No wonder he doesn't know anything. He answers his own questions. "Fog of war. IED means Improvised Explosive Device, I know, but, to most people like me? Not so long ago, IEDs connoted explosives that the terrorists somehow cobbled together out of kitchen supplies and a visit to a desert hardware store. I never thought about Russian mines. Funny that. I mean, I was a member of Mensa in college. I possess a superior intellect. And yet, it never occurred to me, it's the Middle East. There are mines everywhere. We sold a lot of them and they all can be used against us...or for us, as the case may be."

He sets his beer on the table, all business. "This mine has been soaking in warm water for forty minutes. Is that enough time?"

You actually have no idea about that, but you nod earnestly.

"What do you know about these old mines?"

"The Hummers we had weren't armored, especially early in the war."

"Yes, I remember Rumsfeld telling the troops that you go to war with the army you have, not the one you wish you had."

"Yeah. The prick!"

"Proceed."

"We armored up vehicles as best we could and we packed sandbags on the floorboards of everything we drove. That saved some lives. Then a couple of my buddies got blown up about two-hundred yards from my checkpoint. The tangos got clever again and stacked the mines so the IED wasn't one explosive. It was three."

"Uh-huh. But do you know how to extract the explosive from this mine?"

"They taught us stuff. What I pick up, I remember."

"A good student, hm?" He looks dubious. Given where you sit, you can't blame him.

"You'll have to unscrew the top detonator. It's that cap in the center. Unscrew it."

"If I blow up, it won't just be you and me who will die. Your girlfriend is just upstairs."

"Then don't pull that pin as you unscrew the fuse housing."

"Good. Just so we understand each other." Nervous, his hands shake. "VBIEDs! Vehicle-borne IEDs! Military jargon. They do love the alphabet, don't they? I think it should stand for Very Best Idea Ever, Dummies! Samuel Clemont assured me there'd be enough explosive to destroy the target. It's very important we use it all. I have people to answer to, for one thing," he says fussily — almost to himself. "We have to use it all because the target will be in a vehicle and other vehicles will be around the target. They drive in defensive patterns."

Uh-oh. You have more than an inkling what this is about, and now this asshole just *has* to die.

He tries to unscrew the cap and fails.

"The stuff that makes this an explosive was injected at the factory," you say. "Try the wrench and don't be a wimp about it. It's not going to go off that easily."

His hands shake more and his face gets red as he tries to twist off the cap and fails again. You watch him strain and puff as more minutes tick by.

"I can't get the cap to turn!" he says and gives up.

"Hey. Mensa. Righty, tighty. Lefty loosey."

"Oh." A lot of guys would have shot you in the knee then, just because. The fat man is too embarrassed. "I couldn't figure out how to turn the hot water on in a hotel shower once. Same sort of thing," he says. These mines must have been sitting in a warehouse beside the crate of Scorpions for a long time. There's no rust and, when the fat man finally turns the cap the right way, it comes off.

"Lift off the top plate so you can access the inside." You lean back in your chair and wait while he pulls the metal casing up and away. He acts like it could blow up in his face any moment, but you're sure now that's not how he's going to die. It's all you can do not to smile.

"See that stuff inside? Does it look like it's in good shape?"

"How would I know that?"

"Does it look like green plasticine?"

He nods.

"Now smell it."

"What?"

"It's been in a warehouse for decades. Who knows if it's still good? Stick your face down in there and take a long drag. What does it smell like? Grandma's feet? Roses? What?"

The fat man picks up your SIG and points it at your crotch. "Respect, boy."

"Respect, man."

"Are you toying with me? Maybe I seem out of my element here, but I'm a fixer, Mr. Diaz. I problem-solve. Mess with me, and it won't just be you who suffers horribly."

"It should smell like almonds."

He puts his nose next to the casing and inhales deeply, coughs, and inhales again. "It does, in fact, smell like almonds, Mr. Diaz." He puts your pistol back on the table beside him and has another swallow of beer. "Now what?"

"If the water is warm enough, it should make the explosive material easier to scrape out."

He takes up a tablespoon and pulls out a few flakes of the green stuff.

"It'll be colder in the middle. Get in there and scrape it out from the sides."

"Ah. Yes." He's breathing heavier already and empties the bottle of beer before he continues.

You watch him work as the little pile of explosive clay becomes a bigger pile on a torn square of brown butcher paper. Toward the end, it's like he's trying to scrape very cold ice cream out of the bottom of a pail. He's red and sweating before he's done.

"What will we do after this, Mr. Diaz?"

"One step at a time. The longer it takes, the longer I live. It sucks a lot of the time, but I still enjoy breathing. Weird, huh?"

"You're thinking short-term. You should be more expansive. Help me here and you die quickly. I'm not a sadist. I'm not like Lurch. He was…like you. Animals. You two had a lot in common, I imagine."

"Maybe the same taste in music."

He coughs again and rubs an eye with the back of his hand. "I told you, I'm playing a much larger game than you can imagine. I see all the chess pieces. If it makes you feel any better, you're a small but critical part in something huge. I am not constructing bombs. I'm building history."

If this were an old Arnold Schwarzenegger movie, you could say, "You *are* history." However, you're still a long way from being able to stand without getting shot in the crotch. You lean back and try to breathe shallowly out of the corner of your mouth, unsure your distance will protect you.

"What now?"

"Pretend you're in elementary school. Remember making snakes out of Play-Doh? Roll the green plasticine between your palms."

"What does that do?" he asks, finally more suspicious, his breath coming shorter.

"The snakes make up the packing material for your bomb. Everybody thinks of car bombs as dynamite sitting under the hood. You can pack the stuff in the hub caps or the trunk, too. The wheel wells are a good place. You're fitting the bomb to the space so you can fit in more."

"I hadn't thought of that." He begins making snakes out of the explosive material. His cheeks are like stop signs. Sweat soaks his shirt.

"Is this on the test to get into Mensa? Maybe I qualify."

He laughs for the first time, though it turns into a ragged cough at the end. Then it hits him and he grabs his head and moans. The spoon clatters. He grabs for the SIG as he tips to the side, but he tips the wrong way and crashes to the floor.

You bend and get your knife. It takes a few minutes to cut through the tape and extricate yourself from the chair, but you have time. The fat man holds his head and writhes in helpless agony.

"Hey, Mensa. I've got some bad news." You remove your jacket and fashion a mask over your face with your shirt to avoid inhaling particles from the explosive. When you come around the table, the fat man's eyes roll your way and he goggles at your bare torso. Not many people have seen the grid of savage scars that criss cross your chest and abdomen.

You tuck the pistol in your waistband and bend to cut his sweaty shirt open. You knew it had to be there and it is: a large blue swastika tattooed over his heart. You use the arms of the sign of hatred as a guide for your cuts. When he tries to stop you, you cut his palms and fingers, too. He howls. The fat man's bloodshot eyes bulge wide.

He thinks his pain is bad. No. Not yet.

You lift the butcher paper — heavy with what looks like green plasticine — and, careful not to touch the explosive material, press it to the fat man's chest. His pain eclipses his ideas about how vast agony can be. His pain stretches out past Jupiter.

You step away and watch.

Nitroglycerine in a cut may be the worst pain on earth. Think wasps full of battery acid and then multiply that by fire and repeated kicks in the nuts followed by salt in the wound. Inhaling the mine's chemicals causes severe headaches and blurred vision. Handling explosives without gloves? He must have been lying about being a member of Mensa. When he clutches his chest with his cut hands, the nitro sears through his nerve endings and he flops around.

You watch the pain shudder up and down, like an earthquake has chosen only him to torment. You watch his torture the way straight men watch pornography together: transfixed, yet uncomfortable at having company. You won't have company long. His darkness closes around him. He's a traitor to his country, but the only kind of arrest he'll have is cardiac.

The fat man's rigid body starts to loosen. The would-be history maker stares up at you. Maybe, blurry vision and all, he finally sees the real you. You wonder which you he sees? The demon or the angel? You talk to yourself all the time, trying to separate your warring halves.

Or maybe you aren't at war with yourself. Everyone in group, in movies, in the world...they all talk about the war between good and evil. Maybe God needs you to be his avenging angel. With all you've done, you can never be the good guy, but perhaps God places you in these situations because he needs you to be the bad guy. Good guys finish last, but against evil? A bad guy has a chance.

As his heart pumps itself dead, your heart soars. You feel like you might be lifted off the floor and hover with sheer power and elation.

"I'm smiling," you tell him, "but it's not that I'm a sadist. I'm God's bad guy. I just realized — and I don't think it's just the aerosolized nitro talking — I get high on vengeance. Give me that, and I can feel good. I can even forgive you now."

His jaw finally drops, face muscles slack. The fat man dies surprised.

JESUS SAVES

Beyond the bedroom door, you hear a television or a radio playing. You pause. If it's locked, Willow is a captive and you're here to save her. If it's unlocked, Willow is probably dead. The permutations and combinations start piling up: raped and murdered, dead of an overdose, or perhaps just so high she's lying on the bed staring at…is that a *SpongeBob Squarepants* cartoon?

Another terrible possibility looms. What if Willow played you all along and she's a Neo-Nazi, too? Samuel Clemont was a racist asshole, but he was still her father. It's a gamble. Either the senseless hate took hold and she was just using you to get rid of the Lone Wolf and Skeet, or she's rebelled against her father like every other kid in America.

You bet on America and try the knob. It's locked, but the door is light and hollow. You break it down with one kick.

Willow is curled in the fetal position on an unmade bed. She looks up at you slowly, lids heavy, pupils spun wide, her mind in a half-world made of cozy dreams, thick quilts and heavy gravity. It is as if she sees through you. She turns back to watching television.

You recognize the *SpongeBob* episode. It's Pat Morita's last job before he died. The actor who played Mr. Miyagi in the original *The Karate Kid* does some voice-over work. In the movies, the damsel in distress rushes into the hero's arms, the music swells and all problems are erased. Instead, there's a couple of dead guys in the basement, a monster buried in a snowbank, four white supremacists on the way and you and Willow are watching a *SpongeBob Squarepants* cartoon.

But you aren't the movie hero, you remind yourself. You shot Chilli Gillie's friend and Willow's uncle, Thomas-not-Thomas. You let Willow's father burn a while before you shot him. That's a lot of secrets to keep before you even get to say, "I do."

"Willow?"

"Hm?"

"We can go."

"Go where?"

"I don't know."

"Okay."

She turns back to watch SpongeBob get rescued by a squirrel from Texas who is a superb martial artist.

A bottle of Vicodin sits on the night table. There are still lots of pills for both of you. You walk to the bathroom and flush them. When that's done, you're astonished you didn't even hesitate.

You guide Willow to the car in the garage. The Lincoln is more comfortable in the driver's seat than the trunk.

"Will. I want to be with you, You know that, right?"

"Mm-hm."

"But it won't work out."

"Um. Mm-hm."

"I'm sorry about your dad."

Now she looks at you, returning from the half-world. "My father's dead."

"Yes. I'm sorry."

"People always say they're sorry when someone dies. I don't know why. Sorry for what? It's not like they killed him."

"Uh…yeah."

Willow falls asleep against the passenger door. You drive in circles with no particular destination for a couple of hours. When you have a plan, you take her back to her apartment and tuck her into her own bed like a little girl. Maybe she'll wake up tomorrow and decide to change and live a life without drama and danger.

Willow's done it before. She could do it again, but not if you're around. Drama and trauma follow you around like hungry puppies. She can't have that in her life. The addiction counsellors were right. Relationships that start too fast, end too fast. You can't have girlfriends and instant future-wives, anymore…or at least not for a while. An evil guy might keep Willow by lying about who killed her father and uncle and never care that each happy day was a casual betrayal. You're just God's bad guy, so you have to go away and carry the weight of your sins with you.

But it's not as easy to walk away as you imagined. You watch the Queen of the Giants sleep, yearning to touch her blonde hair, fearing that she'll wake and you'll lose yourself to her eyes. Maybe you could lie every day. If you could make Willow happy, maybe redemption and forgiveness is possible for you.

Willow slowly opens her eyes. You don't know how long she pretended to sleep, but her tears reveal her deception. "Jesus," she says.

"Yes, my queen?"

"You think you love me, right?"

"I don't think. I know."

"Then what did you do with my Vicodin?"

"Flushed it."

She sits up. You were mistaken. Her eyes are not blue pools of gratitude. "If you love me so much, how come you didn't call the fucking cops, you moron? If you gave a shit about me, it would have been SWAT saving me, not you! Get out! Get away from me, you stupid asshole! And how could you throw away my Vikes? You fucking *dwarf!* "

You hesitate and look back but she just shakes her head and points you to her bedroom door.

"Little person. Dwarf is politically incorrect," you whisper and head out the door.

"Jesus!"

You turn around, hopeful.

"Of all the diners, in all the towns, in all the world, you walk into mine!" She rips the drawer from her night table and hurls it. The drawer cracks on the doorframe by your head and its contents spill across the floor. You lean in and close the door behind you to muffle her crying.

Since there is none for you, you now know the value of forgiveness. You should have fled to Nevada. What happens in Vegas, stays in Vegas. What happens in Chicago, stays with you.

JESUS DELIVERS

You glance at your watch. It will have happened by now. You don't mean to, but you speed up a little. The front wheels eat pavement. The back wheels push the miles behind you. In a couple of days, you'll be in LA. You need a lot of miles between you and Chicago.

Los Angeles is about as far as you can get without boarding a plane and you hate boats. With all the security cameras fitted with facial recognition technology and scanners that even detect your gait, airports aren't a safe place for you.

Chill rides stiff in the passenger seat, complaining about the potholes. He's out of the hospital, officially AMA, Against Medical Advice. "I'm stitched. I'll rest all the way to LA. Hospitals are full of sick people. The best place for me is in my own bed, healing in my own home." The big man sits slumped against the passenger-side door of his SUV as you play pilot on the Eisenhower Expressway past the Columbus Park Golf Course. You let your eyes linger there, wondering how many times Willow will pass this spot, seeing what you see, being where you are.

Willow will probably grow old in Chicago, but like Paulie said, she's a glamazon. She won't be alone for long. Liberty Montano is right. Willow's too smart not to kick the Vikes. Kids who should have been your kids are waiting, ahead in her time stream. Some summer day, she might even go golfing over there in some far off future with a husband who is…let's say an orthodontist.

In Group, Smug Tim said, "The two most powerful words in the English language, when slammed together, are 'Begin again'." You hope he's not wrong about everything. No matter how much you want to kick somebody in the teeth, the chances they're wrong about *everything* are pretty small, right?

Chill frowns at you. "Jesus. What are those two crates in the back of my truck?"

"Used to be more. It'll be fine as long as we don't get stopped by the cops."

"Oh, well, that's just peachy then. A brown man driving my car and me sitting in the passenger seat and he says, 'As long as we don't get stopped by the cops.' You better be avoiding Arizona altogether! You cross into Arizona even for a minute, they're going to be pulling over your brown ass and my black ass with it."

Sgt. Billy rises from the back seat. "Heart patient, here! Trying to sleep!"

"Sorry," you and Chill chorus.

"I can drive if you want. They'd leave an old white guy alone. I don't have a driver's license, but it's just a little dog's leg through Arizona if we cross into Nevada at Mesquite. And, hey! There's no White Castle in California! We need to stop at White Castle. In fact, we need to stop at White Castle every time we stop for as long as we can. I'm looking forward to seeing the Pacific Ocean before I die, but no White Castle is a heavy trade-off."

"Said the heart patient," Chill says.

"I won't be coming back this way."

"Fine. We'll go around Arizona. We'll hit a White Castle and you, old man, are not driving my SUV." Chill turns back to you. "And don't think I didn't notice you didn't answer my question, Jesus."

You glance at your watch again. 4 pm. You switch on the radio to catch the news update. In a moment, it's revealed why numerous alphabet agencies will want to talk to the Cuban assassin who's already linked to murder and a car bombing in New York.

"On the brink of President Obama's New Year's Day visit and speech tonight in the city where he began his political ascendance, and just weeks before his inauguration in Washington for his second term as president, the FBI reports that they have foiled a group of terrorists."

You can feel Chill's eyes on you.

The news announcer continues, "The investigation is ongoing and details are classified, but around noon today, a powerful explosive device, or several bombs, rocked a quiet Chicago neighborhood. An anonymous tipster called the FBI and several media outlets to say the terrorists were homegrown and members of the neo-Nazi affiliated Recip — "

You stab the button to shut it off and keep your eyes on the road, your teeth grinding. "Damn! It's New Year's Day! I totally missed out on making my resolutions last night and I was supposed to start work at a gym this week!"

Chill's laugh rumbles up to a high pitch. "You can make a new resolution any day, man. Like staying out of trouble from now on."

"I'm not in trouble. As long as they don't set up roadblocks or something, but…you know…"

"The FBI reports *they* foiled something, huh? How'd that happen, do you suppose?"

"Hypothetically? I'm guessing someone with excellent penmanship left a note on the front door telling Nazis to come on in and go down to the basement to see the fat man."

"What else would such a note say? Hypothetically."

"That's not the important bit. It's what the note didn't say, like maybe there were four charges rigged to the door in the basement. That might have made the house explode and slaughtered some assholes."

"That's a pretty specific guess," Chill says.

"I'm out of my mind with grief over a very recent failed relationship. Pay me no attention."

"So you avenged me and slopped extra vengeance on top, too?"

"Chill, in my defence, point one: You're a big, gay black guy. None of those assholes were going to make your Christmas card list. Second, it wasn't all about you. I was working out some rage issues at the time I rigged the detonators. Three, they were white supremacist suicide bombers. That shouldn't even count against me. They suicided earlier than they planned, that's all. And four, it would have been faster and easier to litter a bunch of mines all around the front yard, under the snow. I held back on that plan. I think I showed a lot of responsibility and restraint, don't you?"

"What held you back? You find God?"

You shake your head. "I remembered the Devil. But I knew I wouldn't be there to watch, so there didn't seem to be any point in going overboard."

"You blew up a neighborhood!"

"That's a gross exaggeration."

"Well, you blew up a house."

"It was foreclosed. Might have hurt the bank. Count that as a win for the little guy."

You spare Chill a glance, but he's not amused. He's wearing his serious face. "Jesus, what's in the crates?"

"It's an investment fund for a coffee shop. I'm going to sell it on the Silk Road and get Willow back on her feet. I think the woman who was going to be the future Mrs. Diaz should work in a nicer part of town. I'm going to set her up. One day, once I'm sure she's clean and sober and on track, she's going to get a beautiful anonymous surprise in her mailbox."

"Explosives?" Sgt. Billy asks.

"Money," Chill answers for you.

"Slow down," Sgt. Billy says. "You said Silk Road. What are you, trading with the Chinese?"

"The Silk Road is the Internet beneath the Internet. It's a place to buy and sell contraband. If that doesn't fly, there are always other ways. I'm thinking the best way to go is a bidding war among collectors for the Scorpions. That usually works out."

"Nah, man. Nah!" Chill says, waving his hands. "I owe you a favor. Here's what it's going to be. You come work for me."

"What's it pay?"

"It pays in not being in jail. It's a new year, man. Make a new resolution. It's pay enough that you don't have to sell a crate full of arms! You have to start planning for the long-term."

"I've never had much shot at a long-term, Chill."

"From now on, you're my Vice President in Charge of Special Projects."

"That sounds good. What's that like? Bodyguarding Beyonce?"

"Guarding Beyonce's chihuahuas, maybe. I just don't want you selling a bunch of weapons to assholes." He looks back at the crates again. It's wedged in, covered with a couple of bags of clothing Chill brought. Sgt. Billy has nothing but the clothes on his back and all you have is a backpack and the PS3 game station with *Lego Batman 2* you stole from Willow's uncle. Lurch hadn't even set it up for himself. He just took it from you for spite.

"Jesus, that *is* just the Scorpions, right? You didn't put any old Russian mines in my truck, did you?"

You smile and shake your head, your gaze riveted to the highway west. "That would be...bad. Right?"

"Oh, god. Watch for potholes."

"If you love her that much, how could you leave her?" Sgt. Billy asks.

You wait a long time for the answer to come. "I do love her, but," you admit, "too much to stay." You tell them how you found Willow on the bed watching *SpongeBob Squarepants*, high as angel pussy. "Someday, maybe soon, she'll climb down off that ride," you say. "When she does, she deserves better. We'd have made beautiful children together, and they'd have to love me. No matter what, you love your mother and father."

"But —?" Chill prompts.

"But there'd always be a but."

You drive automatically, switching lanes and keeping up with traffic, picturing what your children with Willow might have looked like. Chill talks about the bombing, but it's all a background buzz. You finally glance his way when, in some pain, Chill reaches out and gently covers your hand on the steering wheel. "Thank you, Jesus. He will never know of your secret service. But I know."

"Chill, I think this is the beginning of a beautiful friendship, but I do wonder when I'll ever get used to your *lithp*. Calling me *Hay-thuth, Hay-thuth, Hay-thuth*? Will I ever get used to that?"

"*Athhole*." Chill puts his head against the glass and closes his eyes to sleep.

You watch the road, eager to get out of the ice and into the sun that's always shining on California's picturesque mud slides, forest fires and earthquakes.

No, not evil, the fat man had said. He was so *sure*.

That's the hell of it, because you're pretty sure your story is classic bad versus evil, too. You could only forgive the fat man after you'd extracted the ultimate vengeance.

"You're named after someone who forgave, Jesus," Smug Tim once said. "Christ is for giving and forgiving. It's a good example, don't you think?"

"Asking me to forgive is like asking you not to run funny." Looking in Smug Tim's eyes, you wanted to rip off his prosthesis and beat him to death with his steel leg. Maybe then you could forgive him.

You're more the Old Testament kind of kick-ass. As long as you're confronting evil, you're sort of okay with that. Maybe more righteous kills will balance out the sins and close up some wounds.

Nothing to it but to do it! the Devil would say.

You can begin again, yes, but you're still the child watching your brother die in red water. You're always the kid in the Miami basement praying to God for help and hearing no divine reply. You're still the young teenager begging your captors to kill you. Tia Marta and the Bug Man were so beyond evil, they wouldn't allow such an easy escape.

In the rearview mirror, you catch Sgt. Billy shaking his head. He looks thinner than before. The lines on his face make a roadmap to a few laughs and many more tears. He lies down again in the backseat. His frail, papery voice reaches up to you like a ghost's whisper, "Remember? I ran away from the perfect girl once. I warned you. You find a woman like that, you stay and *change for her.*"

Does anyone really change, or are they actors, pretending they are the characters they play? Given time, you might have conned Willow, charmed her, helped her grieve and eventually won her back. You could even con yourself and kept the secrets of her father's and uncle's deaths forever. Killing off her family sure would make for an awkward wedding, though. Nobody on the bride's side of the church and all you've got on the groom's side are ghosts, the FBI and assassins.

The snow that had whispered down so gently now thickens, coming at you with purpose. You listen to the rhythm of the windshield wipers, smile and daydream of what might wait beyond Chicago's storm. With what you've got packed in those crates, any evil assholes on the West Coast better buckle up and brace themselves.

You don't need love and Vikes anymore. Justice is your addiction and there's no rehab for righteous violence. Vengeance is your drug now and nobody gets higher than Jesus.

HOLLYWOOD JESUS

Robert Chazz Chute

BRING GROOVY BACK.

When numerous alphabet agencies hunt you, it is best to keep a low profile.

Rule #1: Avoid the limelight's burn.

Rules #2 and #3 are to eschew drama's sting and to duck trauma's pain. You didn't do that and now, here you are. The FBI agent on the floor is face-down dead and the bad guy, Detective Hank Reles, has a gun — *your* SIG Sauer P220 — aimed at your forehead. Worse? This is not at all how you'd planned to tear up Hollywood. It's apparent you have failed, again, to observe the rules of *The Divine Assassin's Playbook*. You made up those rules. You'll surely die for it.

"Take out your phone, Mr. Diaz," Reles says.

With shaking hands, you do as you're told.

"Call her," he says.

"I wouldn't. It won't do you any good."

"Call her or I'll kneecap you and then you'll call her anyway, but crying hard." He takes a step closer. He gestures with the pistol, urging you to hurry.

If you call and she answers, you're pretty sure he'll empty his magazine into you without a blink.

What will your obituary read? Possibly: "Originally from Cuba and a former Military Policeman, Jesus Salvador Umberto Luis Diaz was largely misunderstood and he didn't mean to get into the assassination and vengeance-for-hire business. He killed a lot of bad people but left no legacy besides death. In his heart, he was always pure. Sometimes he actually thought he served Justice. But hey, shit happens."

"Now!" the big man roars.

You take a deep breath, squeeze your eyes tight and three…two…one….you hit *Send*.

Is this all there is? Time to find out. You open your mouth, but not to speak. This is how it ends.

* * * * * *

Your story starts, if any story can be said to have one beginning, with a call from your boss, friend and Ving Rhames lookalike, Chillie Gillie.

"Who's the client?"

Chill won't say, so you know the client is a friend — an even better friend than you. When pressed, Chill admits the client is "tight like family, so I need you for an extra-special, special project."

Chill's lisp makes it, "extra-spethial, spethial."

"Okay, shoot."

"I need you to find something on a guy named Oswald. But no shooting."

"What'd Oswald do besides take the fall for assassinating Kennedy?"

Chill tells you what address to go to and leaves it at that, maybe thinking you won't notice your question went unanswered.

"That's in Montecito. That's not the book depository in Dallas. What did Oswald do?"

"Maybe nothing, but that's not the way to bet. All we know for sure is he's an asshole. This is a search for evidence, off-the-books deal. Go in, but he's a raccoon, not a cockroach, you hear? Don't be a hard rock."

This is Dirty Tricks Department shorthand: raccoons you trap. Cockroaches require extermination.

Knowing your history, Chill feels he needs to drive the point home. "This is *not* a search and destroy mission. Recon, only, you dig?"

"Recon the raccoon. I dig, Shaft."

"Shut your mouth."

"What? Just haven't heard anybody say 'dig' in a long time."

"I'm bringing it back. I'm also thinking of bringing back the word 'groovy'."

"Groovy. I can dig it."

"There you go. But, seriously, you don't have to pull your pistol out every time, man. Use a little finesse."

You end the connection and leave your regular phone with Sgt. Billy. If you're caught, nothing ties you to Chill. That's standard Dirty Tricks Department policy. The entire department is you, but you stick by your rules. Chill gave you a job when no one else would. You owe, therefore you pay.

Sgt. Billy pours black coffee into a thermos. The coffee is sour and stiff, perfect for a long drive and a long wait. Black bag jobs are mostly boring recon followed by a few frantic minutes of anxiety or even terror.

"Big job?" Sgt. Billy asks.

"Maybe, Chill was light in detail so either he doesn't know enough or he knows it could turn into a shit storm. He says I can keep my bullet in my chest pocket so all's quiet on the Western front tonight."

"I'm old enough to get the Barney Fife in Mayberry reference, Jesus, but the Western Front thing — "

"War movie."

"Oh."

The old man will watch pretty much any show with you. You've got a voracious appetite for anything on the old movie channel. However, Sgt. Billy doesn't watch war movies. *Platoon* gave him flashbacks.

Billy hands you the burrito he's cooked on the hotplate, shovelled into a roll of newspaper. "Don't be out too late. I worry." He smiles. "Now gimme a dollar."

You give him a man-hug — one arm clasped low to avoid any chance of accidental pelvic grind, the other goes high to clap him on the back. "Thanks, Mom."

He pushes you away. "Just stay out of trouble, you little monster."

"Staying out of trouble is not the business we're in." You had practiced that in the mirror a few times. You looked good saying it, but Hollywood never calls for you to star in a movie. Hollywood only needs you for raccoons in the garbage and cockroaches under the bed.

You're Jesus Diaz, once a hit man and now in charge of black bag gigs for Chill's security outfit. You keep the stalkers away. You tell yourself your assassin-for-hire days are over. You haven't completely ruled out knocking off anybody who deserves a long dirt nap, though. This is Hollywood.

It's a beautiful place where aspiring gods and goddesses can live, however briefly, in the sun. But raccoons and cockroaches and agents are everywhere.

IF THE TREES ARE DYING, IT'S A METH LAB.

From your black Ford Fairlane, you watch Oswald's house, a big Spanish villa constructed of pink stucco and bad taste. He doesn't appear to have any domestic servants around the place. You would have watched longer, but it's a nice neighborhood. Hesitate too long and a police cruiser might roll up on you, patroling the nice white neighborhood for unfamiliar brown people. You've got fake ID, of course, but you're too well-dressed to claim you're the gardener waiting for Oswald's return.

Stage One: Look for something incriminating outside the house. The nearby trees aren't dying so the villa is not a meth lab. The windows aren't all blacked out and the curtains aren't all pulled shut so it's not a marijuana grow op. So far, the place looks like all the other big houses down the block except no basketball nets and bicycles litter the driveway. This could be a neighborhood filled with orthodontists and their families.

A few minutes later, you get the text from Chill on your throwaway phone. To dodge tracking, he sends it through an anonymous remailer account. Chill says the client is anxious and in a hurry and you need to do this recon "with alacrity".

"Alacrity?" you text back.

"Hurry da fuck up, in & out, report."

Like all orders, that demand proves inconvenient. You're elbow deep in Oswald's garbage at the back of the house trying to find something useful. So far, his worst crime is that he does not recycle. The state of California doesn't execute non-recyclers unless they are serial offenders. Time to casually fracture a few laws. You begin Stage Two of the recon.

On TV, the hero slips a credit card into the edge of a door to pick a lock. That destroys the credit card — who needs that hassle unless it isn't your card? Also, that isn't nearly as easy as it looks except with old doors at cheap motels. The next option is to pull out a lock pick set and get to work, hoping a nosy neighbor doesn't spot you while you struggle to overcome the lock.

That's not just picky work. It's nit-picky and plenty of locks are different so you have to take the time to learn each lock. More hassle. If television episodes went down in real time, they'd be longer and even more boring.

You've used the hockey stick and bicycle chain trick to rip off doorknobs, but since you'd look suspicious walking around with that sort of bulge under your sports jacket, you've left that tool at home. That's your only complaint about West Coast weather: The sun always shines in California. No stylish trench coat concealing bulky tools of the trade for you.

Nineteen Eighty-four has come to the Golden State and Big Brother is watching. Between the LAPD and wandering bands of TSA VIPR teams — Visible Intermodal Prevention & Response — a brownish fellow like you wearing a heavy trench in the sunshine would be marked for interrogation and a search. It would be grossly unjust, but Homeland Security would send you back to Cuba forever if they had the chance. If they found out your real identity, you'd end up on the Gitmo/water-boarding end of the island, not the cheap tourist destination side.

Why, you wonder again, would Bush call it Homeland Security? The term reeks of Nazis, fascists, *"unt zee Fazaland."* The chief tormentor of your childhood, Tia Marta, had a thick German accent. Plus, you had your fill of real Nazis back in Chicago. Maybe you're a little sensitive on that subject.

Focus. What are you going to do about Oswald's back door?

Keeping a low profile and being a smart ninja requires finesse. If you were a brainless thug, the quickest way into Oswald's house would be to make sure your heel connects full force by the lock and kick it in. That's almost always effective. Paranoid homeowners may spend a grand on a security door, but everybody spends the least they can on the installer so the frame is $25 worth of wood and the screws that hold it in place are usually way too short. One or two kicks would get you in quicker than fumbling with a key.

An amateurish B&E makes plenty of noise, though. That choice could end badly: Nosy neighbor appears, garden trowel still in hand. You've got a rule about keeping civilians safe from the secret war so you'd smile and try to bluff your way past him.

Suppose the old man repays your consideration by sticking the blade of his garden trowel in your throat. Or, you tie up the nosy old man from next-door with the electrical cord from his hedge trimmer. Suppose you ask him politely to shut up while you go about your mission. One heart attack later, that's another murder charge against you. Who needs it?

The key to a happy life is less stress, so you do the brainy thug thing: you look. The key isn't under the mat or on top of the doorframe. It's under the second flower pot you check. The homeowner would have had half a chance of keeping you out a little longer if he'd thought to stick the spare key in the pot's dirt. That would have stymied you easily, but since no one wants dirty fingernails, a moment later you're standing in Oswald's house.

BIG IN JAPAN: AWESOME SONG BY ALPHAVILLE

As you step into the living room, a motion detector shines red and a shrill alarm goes off, jangling your nerves. However, alarms are even easier to deal with than people who leave their house keys in predictable places. It's the sort of alarm system where a little box makes a big whoop. Then an agent from the alarm company calls to warn you that police are on the way so you better identify yourself or they'll be really mad.

The police, of course, are not on their way. That's a stupid bluff. Homeowners get charged for false alarms so alarm companies don't call 911 unless they're sure somebody's in the house who shouldn't be. Besides, though the LAPD claims a response time of 5.7 minutes, you'd have to be skinning a live puppy while tossing grenades at a nunnery to get attention that fast. For burglaries, the cops might take an hour or not show up at all. Lucky you.

You pull the switchblade from your sock and cut the wires to the little box. The alarm company's agent will still get through to the phone, but all they can do is leave a concerned message on voicemail. With no connection through the alarm box, they'll assume the alarm is bogus since there's no burglar to scold. The LAPD charges $115 for each false alarm, so the alarm company's default is caution. The security system company doesn't want to lose a subscriber, never mind that a charge of $115 for a false alarm is couch change to a guy who owns a house worth many millions. Oswald must be rolling in long paper.

Alarms easily defeated with a knife? You don't worry about those too much. Dogs, you worry about. However, Oswald doesn't have a dog. He has fish, mostly angels and yellow tangs, hanging in place or swimming in slow circles amid coral.

You've heard fish have such short memories, a fish tank may as well be the ocean. To the fish, the ocean floor is littered every few feet with armies of scuba divers standing beside pirate chests spewing oxygen bubbles. Civilians are like that, you suppose. Every day looks the same — their routines, their beliefs, their lives of habit and the expectation they'll get to do it all again tomorrow. Most people seem to forget why they're here, hanging in place and swimming in slow circles.

Each day is different for you, but maybe it would be nice to forget the past, to believe in permanence. It would be good to have something nine to five and reliable to depend upon. Instead, you wander through the rooms of a stranger's house, counting four huge aquaria and wondering what you're supposed to find.

The first to-do on your list is to make sure you have an alternate exit. That's the smart ninja strategy. However, you pause to take in the rich decor: leather furniture, a long marble countertop in the huge kitchen, marble everything in the bathrooms. It's irritating when assholes have such nice things. Your third-floor flop is an old industrial warehouse, empty except for you, Sgt. Billy and the run down Japanese restaurant on the first floor.

The restaurant is called Big in Japan, but that's a lie. It was never big in Japan. The waiter tells you the name is stolen from a fancy restaurant in Montreal. The owner tells you he got it from a song released in 1984 by a forgotten German band called Alphaville. You believe the owner because, though the old cook is a little bent and slow now, when he talks about dancing in hot clubs in Holland over thirty years ago, he gets a wistful look in his eyes.

You run across a table piled with mail. It's a federal offence to read someone else's mail, so you're really in trouble now, mister.

Ross Oswald III is an accountant for a firm that serves some of Hollywood's biggest stars or, as everyone from waiters and car wash slaves to top Scientologists say here, Oswald is "in the Industry." You suspected this already because Oswald's mailbox reads: Ross Oswald III, *Esquire*. There you have it: plenty of independent corroboration he's a douchebag.

Usually, that alone wouldn't be enough to require your skill set. You've often considered going on a rampage — especially when LA traffic pokes at whatever gland in your brain is responsible for road rage. Who in L.A. hasn't had those dark thoughts on the 405?

Realistically, taking down or knocking off every jerk in Hollywood would be a round the clock job for an army. Besides, it would also eliminate a good chunk of on-screen talent, some of the directors and all of the agents. The continued functioning of the world's entertainment machine depends on your restraint. If you destroy Hollywood, that leaves Bollywood to take over the world, and no one wants that. Too much weird, happy dancing.

In an amateur B&E, the desperate crackhead runs straight for the master bedroom, rips out the sock drawer and fills it with valuables and is out and running down the street in two minutes. You're a pro, so you take it slow and check the office off the foyer. The computer is, of course, left on all day so you plug in a jump drive and check his internet history. You don't have to be a hotshot hacker to get into anyone's computer. You just have to walk into their home and be nosy.

No real surprises, but Oswald's got enough kinky porn on his hard drive to tire out a teenaged boy whose parents are away for the weekend. It's the mean bondage stuff that makes you uncomfortable, like your soul wears tight shoes on the wrong feet. You got introduced to BDSM as a kid and seeing it again puts you back in that basement in Miami, sweating.

On your first day in America, you watched your family drown. After the Bug Man kidnapped you off Surfside Beach, you survived slavery for three years. Bludgeoning Tia Marta with a heavy silver tray was step one in your emancipation. You strangled her with the necklace that held the key to your escape. The Bug Man disappeared forever.

You left Miami with a duffel full of clothes, a SIG Sauer P220, a switchblade and Tia Marta's newest pet, little Denny De Molina. You still carry the pistol, the switchblade and a taste for vengeance.

Oswald's porn sites turn your stomach — what happened to porn where no one gets slapped, gagged or strangled? Regular sex on camera is soft core nostalgia from a more innocent time when both partners looked like they were having a good time. The nasty stuff reminds you too much of Tia Marta hurting you. For her, pain was sex.

Clicking through numerous directories, it's not like Oswald has a file folder on his desktop that reads: "Stuff that will put me away for life" or "Lord Vader's Nefarious Plans for the Death Star." The jump drive copies spreadsheet files. Follow the money, like Deep Throat said in *All The President's Men*.

You click on a folder labeled "Vacation pics" to see how much better a rich accountant lives. It's more porn, but by the lighting, it's amateurish and homemade. A picture on the wall shows the guy who must be the accountant shaking hands with an old lady and smiling as he holds a shiny gold plaque.

You glance back at the grainy video. That's Oswald tying up a crying blonde who looks awfully young. Hard to tell for sure and you can't bring yourself to keep watching. Oswald holds a leather cat-o-nine tails in one hand and his dick in the other. That little old lady with the plaque had no idea she was shaking the dick hand of a sadist. Shuddering, you click through his email, looking for clues and copying everything you can.

Check your watch. Move on.

THE DIVINE ASSASSIN PREFERS ARMANI.

The place is spotless and smells like lemons, like the house is ready for one of those *Better Homes and Gardens* specials that makes a house look like an abandoned shrine. It's an atmosphere you associate with vacant people whose empty consumerism makes them obsessed with appearances. Obsessive cleanliness also makes you think of soulless serial killers trying to erase any trace of blood.

When you were a cop in the military walking into a case of a missing wife, the smell of bleach was a sure sign the grieving husband was actually "a person of interest." Technically speaking, you suppose you're a serial killer, too, but that doesn't count as long as you stay on the side of the angels. Mostly.

You explore the house, starting with the basement. If someone shows up looking for an intruder, you don't want to be the dumbass ninja stuck in the basement without multiple exits. There's a small storage area filled with old furniture. Most of the basement's square footage is a fancy games room with a sunken floor: full bar, huge sectional couches, a hot tub that's empty and dry, big flat screen and a pool table that makes you drool a little. It's a giant man cave.

Oswald is an asshole, but he still seems to have had more friends than you. However, this is the one place in the house with a coat of dust, so thick you might be the first person down here in months. Maybe Oswald was a big wheel, screwed up somehow and now Chill's client wants something on him for vengeance?

Hollywood is full of deals gone bad. Rifts, feuds and grudges aplenty result. You're going to have to find out. You don't like jobs where you don't know all there is to know about the client. Not knowing has gone badly in the past, but for a simple recon, you didn't want to press Chill. You trust him even if that means he doesn't trust you to spill everything up front. You can be patient.

There are three bedrooms, but two are empty to the bare walls. Oswald looks a youngish thirty, handsome and about your size, playing the field in kink. Those stark rooms tell a story: He's got no family who will ever visit. If he had a family, he's not tight with them now. Maybe his dad was eaten by sharks, too.

In the master bedroom, the bed is a king but Oswald sleeps alone. There are two nightstands, but the far one is empty. In the nightstand closest to the door, you discover a shiny .32 revolver in the drawer. You let him keep it, but in case Chill wants you to come back later, you empty the pistol and take all of Oswald's ammo.

You put the weapon back the way you found it and poke through more drawers. A wad of cash is rolled up in black socks so it stands to reason the house has no safe. You stuff the wad in your pocket and keep looking. Tie pins, a dead watch, mismatched socks waiting for a lost mate. Nothing useful.

The walk-in closet is magnificent. It's more like another room than a closet. He's got rows and rows of shoes, each pair on a bamboo rack. Sadly, none of them are your size.

When you open the cedar cabinet to your left, you savor the smell of the wood. A line of linen dress shirts hangs ready and pressed, each in a plastic sheath from the dry cleaner. Each shirt is hung precisely two inches apart. The motorized tie rack proves he must be color blind, but the six sets of cufflinks are nice. The tie pins are gold and silver. You pocket the platinum cufflinks.

To your right, you find Oswald shares your taste in suits: all hail Armani. He's got suits like Batman has backup capes and cowls. You hope Chill will send you back here. You're going to want to steal more than you can carry. You sift through the suits. They're all black, except for a few pinstripes. You check the tags. They look a little long in the sleeve for you, but you can get that altered. It's Christmas in July.

A metallic scrape reaches your ear.

You pull the SIG as you spin, but you're alone. You wait. Hold that breath. Strain to the full range of your hearing.

Another, subtle scrape?

Yes. You're sure of the direction, but not of the source. You step toward the rack of suits, divide them, push them back. It's got to be a panic room. If Oswald is in there with a cell, you're already screwed. You can't let the cops take you alive. That leaves putting the muzzle under your chin and finding out what's next.

But it's not a panic room. There's a small lock at the rear of the closet, just under the shelf. A gold key sits in the lock. Panic rooms, even disguised ones, lock from the inside. You turn the lock and, despite your effort to be quiet, the long dead bolt slides with a clunk. Expecting a shotgun blast to cut you in half, you spring back.

The desperate sob reaches out before the stench hits you. You know those smells: Meat gone bad and feces mix to make degradation. It's dark in there. "Hello?"

It's rough echolocation, but from the sound your voice makes, the room is bigger than you expected. You fish a small flashlight out of your pocket and peer in. You turn back to flick the switch in the walk-in closet and the fluorescents buzz and snap on with a low insectile hum.

You are unprepared for the utter horror that meets your eyes. The light spilling in through the secret door falls on a girl, tied to a wooden chair. Naked. Slumped. Dead. Half her head is shaved. The other half is a fall of red hair reaching past her broken shoulders. The hair runs to blood at the tips — her blood — like a paintbrush dipped in red. Her skin is a wretched map of criss-crossed welts and blossoms of old bruises.

The sob comes again. Your flashlight beam finds the beautiful Asian woman in the cage. Her red dress is ripped. One side of her face is a little swollen but otherwise? It's clear that Oswald hadn't started in on her yet.

You've known a lot of killers, but whoever did this? Worse. Monsters. Monsters erase humanity before they take the last breath and heartbeat.

This room is a torture chamber like the one that trapped you in a Miami basement for three years. You want to throw up, but this is a crime scene so you hold your burrito and sour coffee down.

You know better, but for some reason that denies reality, you try for a pulse at the woman's neck. You don't have to search for a pulse to confirm what you already know. The girl's skin is cold. You crouch at her feet. Her eyes stare back, the whites visible around the pupils.

Your stomach cramps and you curl up, fall to your knees and bow at her feet, as if in worship. The smell hits you harder and you can't keep your gorge down. You throw up the burrito and black coffee. You spew DNA all over the crime scene.

Soon, that won't matter. You aren't here to trap and relocate raccoons.

You just graduated to the role of exterminator. Again.

HAVE A FRIEND ON CALL WITH A LOAD OF GAS CANS.

When your stomach is empty, you straighten up and wipe your mouth on your sleeve. It's then that you realize the captive woman is staring and you're still holding your SIG in your hand, a little tighter than usual.

"I won't hurt you," you say, soft as you can. You drop the gun to your side and move a step toward her, but the light from the open door dims. The room is even darker and it takes you a second to work through what's going on.

"Jesus Diaz?" a gravelly voice asks.

You haven't heard that name, your real name, in months. *Uh-oh.*

He's large enough to almost fill the doorway. He has a barrel chest and a misshapen head too small for his body. Even in this light, pitted acne scars throw shadows across his face. He looks like a heavy sent over from Central Casting. Judging by the pictures in the living room and the video you saw, that's not Oswald. That's good news. The bad news is he knows your real name and you're sure the dark shape in his mitt is a pistol aimed your way.

"*Sí?*"

"*Senor Diaz, quiero hablar con usted en privado.*"

You're nine feet apart in a very dark room. If you step closer to the light thrown through the secret door, you'll be going toward the light in the cosmic sense. You throw yourself behind the corpse in the chair and his gun barks twice. The woman in the cage screams.

You'd scream in terror, too, but you're busy. Flat on your belly behind the chair, the poor girl's body rocks above you. If you had stuffed your SIG back in its holster, the heavy would rush in and shoot you in the face at point blank range. You'd be shaking and fumbling for your weapon and dead. Instead, you're lining up your shot.

Your first two shots rip into his legs. You hoped for his knees, but a couple of chunks of meat and bone are sufficient.

He goes down on his back in the doorway with a grunt, half in the torture chamber and half out. "Esteban! Esteban!" He gets off another wild shot, but you can't miss your target now. You let the air out of that barrel chest and make his head more misshapen. When you click empty, you roll up and change mags.

The woman is still screaming. That's good because Esteban is coming and you need him distracted.

When you were a little boy in Cuba, you were in charge of babysitting your little brother, Rodolpho. You kicked a soccer ball back and forth, wandered the beach and begged for money from tourists. You were cute and Rodolpho was a painfully thin and sickly child so begging was the best use of your time.

Occasionally, you would entertain yourselves by spying on your father as he cleaned the hotel pool. The game was to see how long you both could stalk him before he spotted you. When he was really little, Rodolpho proved to be too much of a giggler to be effective for long, but he got better at it under your stern tutelage.

Once, you told Rodolpho to sneak around to the stairs on the other side of the pool to spy on Marco Diaz. Meanwhile, you snuck up on your father, less than six feet away. Just as you were about to close the distance and lay a hand on your father's shoulder to surprise him, little Rodolpho pounded down the stairs on the other side of the pool. He might have weighed fifty pounds, but it was all in his heels. He slowed down the last few feet to go on tip-toe and peered around a potted palm. You and your father burst out laughing at your little brother's poor ninja skills.

You're reminded of your dead brother now as the heavy's ally, Esteban, pounds up the stairs in a blind rush screaming "Sergio! Sergio!" That is a tactical error.

You slip to the side of the door, your back flat against the wall. The dead guy stares up at you, blood still pumping from his wounds. With his hard looks, it's impossible to imagine he could ever have been anything else but the thug he was. With a face like that, you don't get to be a florist.

"Sergio!" Esteban arrives, breathing heavy. His gun hand pokes in the doorway first, arm straight.

"Don't! Don't!" The woman in the cage screams louder though you're sure she's huddled in a ball on the floor of her cage.

You hear the gunman's sharp intake of breath. That's surprise. He didn't expect to see the dead girl in the chair and he pauses to curse, "*Me cago en todo lo que se menea!*"

Before you learned English swear words, you translated the Spanish curses you knew from your father directly into English. When you tried to defy your captors, the worst thing you could think to say to them in broken English was, "I shit on everything that moves!" Hearing that expression again from the thug now makes you understand why the Bug Man and Tia Marta giggled a little before they reached for the hot iron to burn the defiance out of you.

"Diaz? A donde estas?" Esteban takes a half a step across the threshold. *"Te voy a matar!"* I will kill you!

That, you've heard many times.

On TV, the hero cracks the gunman's wrist with the butt of his pistol and easily disarms him. That would be good. You have a lot of questions that need answers. However, this ain't TV. Nothing goes that smooth and there are no second takes. The muzzle of the SIG grazes Esteban's left earlobe.

A single gunshot in a closed room sounds so loud, echoes of angry sound waves shimmer off the walls.

Esteban collapses atop Sergio. In the dim light, it looks like love.

JEUS PREFERS THE TERM
TROUBLESHOOTER.

You don't want to leave the woman in the cage, but smart ninjas aren't soft ninjas. You step over the would-be assassins and quickly peek around the door, checking your angles. No one. Now that the gunfire is over, the house seems more still, as if everything, including the fish downstairs, are pausing to listen, too.

If Esteban had crept up the stairs and waited patiently for you to come out of the chamber of horrors, he could have easily shot you dead in the closet/shrine to Armani.

A window in the upstairs hallway to the street shows your car is where you left it, but a maroon Ford Shelby Mustang GT 500 sits behind it. The driver must have heard the shots and spotted you in the window. The engine roars to life and he peels out. You can't see the driver, but you're sure you'll meet soon. Next time, if he's smart, the guy in the Shelby will bring assassins who know better than to stand like silhouette targets in backlit doorways.

You didn't win today because you were especially smart. You're just smarter than the average hit man. That's usually enough. Hit man is a profession no different from plumbers and doctors and mechanics: there are few geniuses.

Before you turn on the torture chamber's light switch, you ask Oswald's prisoner, softly, not to scream. She does, anyway.

"*Sh. Sh.* You're out of danger."

She shakes her head and hugs herself. "No, I'm not."

She looks a little younger than you with skin that appears poreless. Her complexion is dark cream. She could be a model, which you suppose is why Oswald decided to trap her in his nightmare. You glance at your watch. When will Oswald return from work? You need back-up. Whatever schedule Chill had in his head, events have changed them.

There's a padlock on the woman's cage. Fortunately, the keys are on the floor a few feet away. That's a relief because shooting off the lock is another common trick in movies that requires special ammo. Try it in real life and the ricochet could kill you or her.

Before you open the lock, you look in her eyes. "Who's the girl in the chair?"

"Ginger Snap."

"So, a call girl?"

She nods. "Me, too."

"What's her real name?"

"Tabby Bernstein. She's from Indiana."

"Of course, she is. Where's your muscle?" Girls who look this good always have a driver who minds the girls when they go out on a job.

She shakes her head. "Ross said we'd make twice the money if we came to work on our day off, off the books, you know? He told us he could get us into movies. They all say that, but you keep hoping for a way out, you know?"

"I know." You ask her name.

"Sugar Cane."

"What's your real name?"

"Sugar Cane."

"C'mon."

"My parents hung out at Esalen a lot. That's what they named me. My sister's name is Candy."

"That's a great stripper name."

"My sister is a dental hygienist in Des Moines."

That tells you all you need to know about Sugar for now. "Excuse me, Sugar. I have a headache coming on."

Chill answers on the first ring. "Find anything?"

"Trouble."

"The cops show up?"

"Something about as bad. Emissaries from an ex best friend."

"What do you need?"

"Send Skunk to evac a vic to a hospital." You glance her way and she eyes you suspiciously. "Not the nearest hospital. I need time and I need Berb over here with gas cans. As many as he can get. Full."

"On the way." He clicks off.

"I'm not a 'vic'," Sugar says.

"You're crying. It's an easy mistake to make."

"I'm not a victim! I'm a casualty. Wrong place, wrong time. But her?" She nods to the dead naked woman. "He made me watch."

"Guy named Oswald, right?"

"Yes."

She knows his name, so he didn't plan for any prisoner in this room to survive captivity.

"Every terrible, filthy, disgusting thing he did to her, he made me watch. He told me I was next if I didn't cooperate. For, like, the second half of it? She didn't even make a sound. Cried from pain sometimes, but she didn't beg or plead. It was the bravest thing."

Before you can stop yourself, you say, "It wasn't bravery. It was surrender."

She's shocked for a moment and angry at you. "How would you know?"

You holster the SIG and pull up your shirt so she can see the crosses of scars across your belly. You've never willingly shown any woman your scars from Miami, but you need her to trust you. She needs to know you understand.

"I've been the person tied to the chair," you say. "Many times."

"You aren't a policeman," she says.

"I'm…something else."

"Don't call the police."

You glance at the bodies in the doorway. "Good advice."

"Not because of them."

"Oh?"

"The police are part of it. Prostitution, slavery, snuff films. There are police, high up. Oswald was saving me for the highest bidder."

This day was much better when you thought you were going to get some free suits out of an easy recon job.

"They're evil," Sugar says.

"How many in the ring?"

"Four that I've seen."

"It'll be okay," you say, feigning a self-assurance you don't feel. "I can fix this. Evil's my specialty." You pause. "Troubleshooting evil, I mean."

BETTER ASSASSINS ARE NOT TRACEABLE.

Chill hadn't told you the boys were on standby. They must have been because Skunk's red Crown Victoria rocks to a halt out front in a few minutes.

The crew calls him Skunk because he has a thick stripe of white through his black hair that reaches to the back of his head. Tall, 50ish, fit, ex-navy and the most experienced security guy in the company. He's reliable, but his moral inflexibility makes him the choice to spirit the girl to safety. He's not up for Dirty Tricks Department shenanigans.

After she steps over the dead men, Sugar looks back at you. "What will you do?"

"Something...fitting. Go with the nice man, now. He'll get you to an ER, okay?"

"Will I see you again?"

"Probably not."

"These men...they don't know mercy."

"I know the type. Thanks, Sugar. I'll take it from here. Why don't you disappear for a few days, in case I don't find them all right away."

You shoo her out and Skunk hustles her away. It's a relief to see her go. You let her see your scars. Before you spoke English well, you called them your "scares." You weren't wrong, either.

While you wait for Berb to bring the gas cans, you search pockets. Esteban carried an ugly Smith & Wesson and a pack of Nicorette gum.

"Good news!" you announce to the half of Esteban's head that's still together. "You've quit smoking, scumbag. Lung cancer is a tough way to die. You're welcome. *Hombres necios...*"

Sergio had a Springfield Armory XD-S.45, good for concealment but comically small in his huge ham of a fist. Sergio carried enough extra mags to suggest he was either a terrible shot, a hoarder or he was expecting a shoot out with dozens of gunmen.

Neither would-be assassin carries a wallet, ID or even keys. Even the tags are ripped out of their sports jackets. They got everything right except the "deadly" part of ninja assassin.

All you really know is they spoke Spanish and they wanted to get information out of you before killing you. Most important, they knew your real name. In California, you're Dr. J.D. Fix. No one besides ex-girlfriends, New York's Spanish Mob, the FBI, Homeland Security, Chill, Sgt. Billy — and now Sugar — know your real name. The first four might shoot you on sight. The last three, you have to trust.

You've never met these guys, of course. They're undoubtedly locals working for The Machine. New York's Spanish Mob knows your name and they have not forgotten what you did to them.

You glance at your watch. There's no point calling Berb. He's coming as fast as he can and the timing will be tight. You need the gas cans before Oswald comes home. Berb doesn't want to take part in what you're about to do any more than Skunk, but he'll show with the accelerant.

In the torture chamber, you notice something disturbing and possibly useful. In the corner sits a tripod. There's no camera, but someone recorded what went on in this room. You hope you never have to see that recording.

Deep breath.

You step to the girl in the chair. She stares at you. That's another thing TV and movies get wrong. You can try to close the eyes of the dead, but it doesn't work. They keep staring back, asking why. Or maybe, "Is that all there is?"

A large mattress with no box spring or bed frame sits on the floor. There's a single soiled sheet that will have to serve as the girl's shroud. You cut her bonds with your switchblade and catch her before she slips from the chair. Despite the blood, shit and piss, you cradle her to your chest, carry her, and lower her to the mattress gently. You wrap her in the sheet slowly, with reverence.

"I'm so sorry this happened to you. Don't be embarrassed," you say. "You did nothing wrong. I promise they won't do it again. I'll make sure they never hurt anyone again. I'll make sure they're sorry they did this."

The girl couldn't have been older than eighteen.

You whisper the only prayer you really believe: "They don't have it in them to feel for other people. There's something wrong with their brains. Don't worry, though. I'll make sure they feel regret. They have no empathy, but they've got nerves for pain, just like everybody else. I'll make them find regret, somewhere deep down in the bone. I promise, over your dead body. Amen."

You finish crying before Berb arrives.

HIT MEN KNOW WHAT EXOCULATE MEANS.

When Ross Oswald III pulls up to his house in his BMW, you wonder what he's thinking about. Do monsters so compartmentalize their lives that they're pretty much like everyone else when at work? Does he really focus on his spreadsheets, or is the background music playing in his mind a constant pounding drum: rape, murder, destroy, rape, murder, destroy?

You could ask him, but you have more pressing issues on your mind. You have to take him down before the smell of gas everywhere tips him that something is amiss. You're also concerned how many times you can use the stun gun without killing him. You don't want to be premature on that, but you'll just have to experiment.

When he opens the front door, briefcase in hand, you greet him with a cheery, "Science can be fun!" Two barbed darts deliver lightning to his face.

You zap him five times before he rolls around enough to tangle himself in the wires. Tetany through his muscles makes his hands into claws. His throat and face strain and his eyes goggle up at you, bewildered. Through the miracle of electricity, he looks more like the monster he really is beneath the nice suits.

"Good evening, Oswald. I notice in all your correspondence, nobody seems to call you Oz. Oswald sucks but Oz is a cool name. How come no one calls you Oz?"

After a while, through tears and gasping for breath he manages, "What?"

"We're all here to learn, pal." You zap him again. "Try to focus, Oz. I was talking about your name and waiting for you to give me the slightest reason to pull this trigger again. Unfair of me, I know, but we both know you don't have a right to ask for what's fair. If I run out of juice in this stun gun — I think the limit on this battery charge is twenty-five electrocutions — I'll have to switch to low-tech tactics. Did you know that there's a two percent chance with every zap that you could experience the agony of testicular torsion? Usually when I want testicular torsion, I have to go old school and do it manually, but through the miracle of technology — "

Zaaaaaap!

Crying. Drooling. It looks like a seizure, but he's fully awake, conscious of every amp and volt shooting through his body, racking him with spasms. When you took your training as a Military Policeman, they called the stun guns "conducted energy weapons." That sounded pretty fancy and futuristic for what they are.

Your instructor, Sgt. "The Devil" Devin, would call the agony Oswald is now suffering "temporary neuromuscular disruption." When you pull the trigger and let the current ride, he is your puppet. The girl in the chair was no doubt his puppet, too. You wonder if she's watching. You'd like to think so.

"Come to think of it, given what you are, maybe I should have shot you in the nuts instead of the face. Or I could use your own cattle prod on you. I found it up in that secret room. That would be justice, wouldn't it, Oz?"

His eyes are huge with fear and his pupils are pinpricks. He nods minutely.

"That's the right answer."

He nods harder, eager to please.

You zap him again, the electric gun ticking as it delivers the volts. "Nobody likes a suck up, Oz."

FOR INTERROGATION, PREPARE THE DONNY OSMOND PATTER.

You give Oswald some time to recover and let his fear grow. "You a Donny and Marie fan, Oz? Don't answer that. *Everybody's* an Osmond fan, though I'm a little higher on Donny than Marie. She's sweet, but he did that really funny video with Weird Al called *White & Nerdy* a few years ago. You see it? Hilarious. I'd tell you to YouTube that shit, but you don't have that kind of time."

He studies you, looking for an angle. If he knew about your childhood in Miami, he'd rediscover a childhood prayer instead of trying for a way out.

"If they're old enough, everyone thinks of Donny in his early purple socks and *Puppy Love* days. They forget about his stab at a comeback. He made a really good song and kind of a sexy video. That was toward the end of music videos being relevant. Do you remember that? He sang a song called *Soldier of Love*. Pretty catchy. I liked it so I ended up getting hooked on the stuff from when he was young. Movies and happy music…such beautiful escapes. If you had it here, I'd play *Soldier of Love* for you. When I go, I'd be okay with that as the soundtrack for my death scene. How about you? What music would you like to play you off the stage?"

"I can give you money."

"I've been upstairs, Oz. You don't have that level of moolah."

"I could! I could get it to you! Lots of money!"

He shuts up when you raise the stun gun. "After what I saw, you'd need more money than the Sultan of Brunei for me to pause just for two seconds. You'd need more money than God, Oz. You'd need Pope-level money for me to give you another night on earth. Read me?"

When he nods you lower the stun gun, sit down and get comfortable. "Where was I before you interrupted?"

"You…you…were talking about Donny Osmond."

"Right! Great performer. Caught him and Marie in Vegas on my trip out here. Good show, but weird show. She makes surprisingly bawdy jokes. She's still cute. And you know what, thinking about you and Donny…it got me thinking about redemption. I was thinking about how we're all looking for redemption. We all want to stay on top or make a comeback. We all want to be right and we all want to be loved. Sometimes we have to change our names and, what would an uber-corporate wage ape like you call it? Rebranding!"

He's nodding, which makes you want to zap him again, but if he has a stroke, he'll be much less coherent.

"Anyway, years back, when *Soldier of Love* came out, some VJ suggested that Donny reinvent himself. She said he should change his name to Oz or maybe it was *The* Oz. Or maybe The Great and Powerful Oz. He hasn't aged a bit, you know. He's one of those guys like Rob Lowe. Makes you wonder if they have a deal with the devil. Have you got a deal with the devil, Oz? You seem pretty well set up here, rich…lots of pricey fish…secret torture chamber and all. I'm wondering who the devil is? Can you tell me? Who is the devil behind you?"

"What do you want to know?"

"Names."

"Which ones?"

"All of them."

"You don't know these people."

"You don't understand me yet, Oz. Think of me as your opposite number. I'm a lot like you. You're bent wrong. I'm bent right. Like Jimmy Cagney said in *The Strawberry Blonde*, 'That's the kind of hairpin I am.' You know that movie? 1941. Kinda sappy, but it's still Cagney."

"They'll kill me."

"You *know* you're dead already."

"Then what's in it for me if I cooperate?"

You eye the stun gun and set it down on the floor as you pull out the switchblade. His gaze is fixed on the knife. Strangely, from your experience with situations like this, a blade scares guys much more than a handgun, at least until they get shot. It's time to pull back and use a little finesse.

"I knew somebody like you when I was a kid, Oswald. She taught me how to speak English like an American, among other things. She thought having a large vocabulary was important. For instance," you show him your shiny blade, "do you know what 'exoculate' means? I'll give you a clue. It has to do with your eyes."

Oswald begins to weep. "C'mon, man! Give me *something* here!"

"I'll give you a choice of how you die. I promise you that. You *will* have a choice."

"That's not much of a deal."

"This isn't a negotiation. With those darts in your face, I might make you dance all night. Or I could use this knife and make you my puppet the old-fashioned way and shove it up your ass. Take the deal and spill everything, or I promise you, we'll go through my full vocabulary, E - Z. We'll start with 'exoculate.'"

JESUS & ANDREW DICE CLAY DRIVE A FORD FAIRLANE

His face is bloody from where you ripped out the darts. Oswald's still begging you to shoot him as he climbs on the chair.

You aim the SIG at his crotch. "If I shoot you, it'll be in the left testicle. It'll hurt, but you'll still end up in that tank." You raise the Zippo. "Get in there."

Oswald tumbles into the big aquarium, frightening clouds of yellow tangs. Displaced water gushes over the floor. His head pops up and he sputters. "Call the cops! I'll confess everything! I'll go to prison!"

"And let you get repeatedly beaten, tortured and raped? That would be wrong, Oz. I don't want to sink to your level. That would be evil and I'm just bad. In fact, I'll prove to you I'm not the monster you are."

You raise the stereo remote and click play. Oswald's Bose sound system blasts out *Hard Knock Life* by Jay-Z. It's not *Soldier of Love*, but it's not bad at all. The song is far too fine for the thing in the aquarium that's been impersonating a human being.

You step to the front door and toss the Zippo behind you. The flame's blossom is a beautiful rush, taking over the room, climbing walls and circling the fish tank.

"Shoot me! Shoot me, you son of a bitch! You said I had a choice! Shoot me! You said I had a choice!"

Over the roar of the inferno chewing through the house, a rhyme occurs to you. "Maybe you'll boil! Maybe you'll fry! Drown or broil, prepare to die!"

Oswald looks back at you uncomprehending. *"What?"*

Some people just don't appreciate rap.

"I never said I'd shoot you, Oz! Your choice is drown or burn! It's up to you!"

"You're so sure what's wrong with me!" he sputters. "What's wrong with *you?*"

"Gandhi said, 'Be the change you want to see in the world!' That's what I'm doing!" You turn from the wall of heat, leaving him to hell.

But you are more than a little haunted by his question. What is wrong with you? The real answers? Trauma, drama and a tragic lack of choices, you suppose. But who cares? Everybody has an opinion on how people should be, but you are what you are. You tell the night, "I am a special snowflake. I love me."

You walk back to the Fairlane and climb in, watching the orange light spread from window to window. Smoke pours out the front door. You left a trail of gasoline to a couple of gas cans in the torture room. It doesn't take long for the spreading flames to find that fuse and race into the torture chamber.

When the explosion hits, the concussion is bigger than expected. Oswald's next-door neighbors' car alarms begin to blare and people come out of their homes, all reaching for their cell phones at once, pointing and yelling to each other. Despite all the noise, Oswald's screams penetrate the din.

You thought it was possible the fire could suck up all his oxygen. Maybe he'd drown or maybe, since he was all wet anyway, he'd try to make a run for it through the field of flame. In the end, it's the roof collapsing that cuts his last scream short.

Satisfactory.

You've destroyed *two* very nice houses and one crappy one in your career as the divine assassin. Some people might begin to think something is seriously wrong with you. However, you tell yourself nothing is a habit until you do it consistently for much longer. Three weeks straight, the productivity experts say. Yes, burning down a house each day for three straight weeks? *That* would be excessive. You do feel bad about the fish. There wasn't time to save them.

Strangely, there's still power in the flaming ruins. The roof collapse didn't get the stereo yet. You can still just catch the little kids singing the chorus to *Hard Knock Life*.

The Fairlane's engine cranks to a soothing rumble that drowns out the music. The shouts of excited neighbors are all that's left now. You pull away as sparks fly and embers drift into an orange sky toward the white gaze of a ripe moon.

You gave up on God when Tia Marta beat that hope out of you, but, figuring it can't hurt, you offer a prayer for the girl's eternal rest as she cremates.

Sirens reach through the night to announce that the firefighters are on their way. You have some names and more fires to put out. You slowly motor away from what was supposed to be a simple recon mission.

The two would-be assassins don't get any prayers from you. However, you do thank Ross Oswald III for all the fine Armani suits and silk shirts stuffed in the trunk.

CALIFORNIA WOMEN ARE WORTH THE
EARTHQUAKES.

Whenever you get to a new town, you act like a tourist. You take the bus tours, fitting in easily with all the slack-jawed rubes. Some tours are better than others but they hit most of the same hot spots: the Chinese Theater, Hollywood Boulevard, The Hollywood Bowl, Universal CityWalk and the Hollywood Sign. The best tour went through the Hills, pointing out various celebrity homes.

You took a double decker bus with the same tour guide twice because he was so entertaining and appeared so knowledgeable. "That one belongs to director Kevin Smith! This beautiful house belongs to comedian Joe Rogan! That one belongs to Molly Ringwald from *The Breakfast Club* and various John Hughes' movies!"

On the second tour, the guide didn't assign the same mansion to the same star twice. Kevin Smith's house was now Ben Stiller's place. Rogan's compound became Bill Maher's. That's so Hollywood. You laughed until you could hardly breathe. Even hairpins like you who have already been duped plenty. You've played deception games of your own, too, but anyone can be conned. It's often surprisingly easy.

In the neighborhoods reserved for celebrities and the idle rich, you don't actually see the really fabulous houses. The really nice mansions, like Johnny Depp's place — or at least the place you *think* belongs to Johnny Depp — is far behind high hedges concealing razor wire. Bus tours allow the rubes to admire the smaller mansions you can see from the road. These are probably the houses that belong to the armies of lawyers and accountants who work for celebrities and the idle rich. "Accountants of the Idle Rich." That would be a great name for a band.

You drive aimlessly, using the time to think. You got Sgt. Billy to buy you the Ford Fairlane at a police auction. The engine needs tuning, but as you drive with the windows rolled down and the wind in your hair, the uneven rumble under the drum of the hood is soothing.

You rarely drove in New York. California is for driving. You've been up and down the coast many times to visit Hearst Castle, The Mystery House and to ride the streetcars in San Francisco. The best driving is out of the city. L.A.'s traffic is so congested and slow, it actually makes the city feel much bigger than it already is. Just a few miles as the crow flies can take at least an hour, picking your way through the city's sprawl and bumper-to-bumper traffic. Miles are not covered well within the city. Time is wasted.

One weekend, with no work from Chill to hold you, you drove to San Jose and sang along with Dionne Warwick as the CD played *Do You Know the Way to San Jose?* You sang it over and over until Sgt. Billy reached up from the back seat, ejected the CD and threw it out of the car window. He called you a little kid that day. He hasn't stopped. That makes you happy, like you've got a father again (but new and improved from the murderous Marco).

You should be dead, or at least pacing in a tiny concrete cell, so you relish everything California has to offer: a better father, a boss who's a friend and scenery accented with palm trees and beautiful women. Tens are everywhere (and even the fives dress like tens).

Beautiful women are to California what windmills are to Holland: they define the landscape. The women move alone and in groups, heads up and always going somewhere with a confident stride. Women in New York have a similar stride, but always look harried, hurrying on like they're perpetually late for an appointment.

California women move with equal purposefulness, but they seem assured that even if they're late, they're worth the wait. They are powered by the sun and always sure the future is bright. California during the day is all smiles and summer dresses. The view is worth the earthquakes.

By the time you find yourself in Pompano Beach, you're ready to work out your next move. Around Progresso Village, you park when you find a Wifi connection that's not locked up. On any street, there are still people who do not password protect their modems, much to the delight of sex offenders looking for untraceable downloads. And avengers like you.

You text Chill and he texts back right away. "Smooth?"

"Shiny."

"News?"

"Oswald did *not* act alone."

You touch the icon for Evernote and send him the names. Four targets. Then you tell Chill you really need to know who the client is and chat with him.

It's not a him. It's a her and it's a name everyone knows: Legs Gabrielle.

He sends you a photo. You've seen the starlet nearly naked in Esquire in the "Women We Love" photo shoot. Another pic of Legs isn't necessary, though you do appreciate it.

Chill sends another pic. However, this one is not Legs Gabrielle. It's a thick-necked bruiser, all steroid jaw and dead eyes under a blonde brush cut. The insolent slash of his mouth makes his look more Aryan Nations than ex-military.

You go cold when you see Chill's next text. It reads: *Detective* Hank Reles. LAPD. 6'4, and trouble. Claims to be Ex Spec Ops for the navy. He's the client's stalker."

Shit. He's one of the names you squeezed out of Oswald.

Chill tells you where to find her. He's on his way soon.

It seems your night is far from over. You smell like gasoline, so you change in a gas station, wash up as best you can and ditch your ruined clothes in a dumpster eight blocks away before turning around.

Time to catch a rising star, but how are you going to kill the devil without drawing all of hell's heat?

DO THE TIME? YOU GET TO DO THE CRIME.

Sal's Comedy Hole on Melrose. You find a place to park a couple of blocks away and head in. You've been here before. It's a fun, funky place with no drink minimum and a different atmosphere than most comedy clubs. There are couches, for one thing. It reminds you of a couple of cozy clubs back in New York.

When you walk in, you don't have to scan the crowd for Legs. She's already onstage doing a set. A movie star doesn't have to do stand-up anymore. However, you've seen Conan and Kimmel interview her. It doesn't matter how beautiful she is or how many movies she's in. Legs Gabrielle was funny first and loves the work.

The crowd laughs in all the right places. The way she paces the stage, a panther in a cage, reminds you of Chris Rock's early days. Most female comics stand still and are conversational. Legs is balls out aggressive, daring the audience not to laugh.

You scan the crowd for Reles. Given his size, he'll be hard to miss. You slip to the side so you can watch Legs, the crowd, the front door and the exits.

"Where my stoners at?" Legs Gabrielle scans the crowd. "It's okay! You can tell me! It's just between us!"

One guy half-way back raises a hand.

"What's your name, sweetie?"

"Paul."

"That's nice. What's your last name?"

"Um…Burnell."

She pounces. "Awesome. Paul Burnell! Now where are my law enforcement officers? Gotta be at least one in the crowd! You better have your card for that weed, Paul, or you're headed to jail!"

No one raises a hand, but she slips into her saver for the joke. "That's cool. That's cool. The cops are undercover tonight. There's an easy way to spot 'em, though. Narcs can't help themselves. Any hecklers show up? We'll know, *that's* a narc. Humor narc, weed narc. Same thing. They see somebody else having fun and they gotta smack that right down! That or the narc will show himself by giving my new friend Paul here a cavity search out front of the club later!"

The laughter barely dies down when she hits again. "Don't be confused. If Paul is getting a cavity search in the men's room between sets, that's not necessarily a narc. That could just be a friend of Paul's, so don't be hatin'!"

The crowd is really going with it, but she manages to top herself. "I was just up in Canada and the cops up there are cool about weed. Besides, if the guy's got a gun, you *want* him to chillax and chillaze with some weed. Up there? They give you a stern talking to, steal your weed and go smoke it right in front of you on their horse. Maybe even give the horse a puff just to piss you off. That's not bad. Bad is, in most states? They take away your house, your car, your job, your life, your kids and toss your ass in prison for years for the victimless crime of talking stupid while you look up at the stars!"

You're scanning the room for a monster, but she's got you chuckling a little bit.

"Which would you rather? Have a trip to the principal's office or have everything taken away? Stern talking to or have sex in a very small room next to a toilet with a guy named Mary, like our poor stoner friend, Paul Burnell, here? I'll take that trip to the principal's office. Go ahead, Mr. Mountie! Get your horse high and taunt me with my own stash! I'll take it! It's better than having prison sex with Paul!"

The room erupts and Burnell stands, puts both hands in the air and bows to Legs like he's worshipping her.

"…just kidding, Paul! Give me a call when you get some good weed, baby! I prefer the AK Kush or BC Bud, cool?"

Her voice is still sweet, but her pace is machine gun fast and she has the crowd in her fist. "Of course, weed is a luxury. It's not weed we really want. You know what women want, fellas? I'm sorry to tell you, size does matter. When we pull you into bed, we want a big…strong…meaty…*jaw!* No! You don't get to breathe until I say you can breathe. You get to breathe, maybe, when I'm done! Now get in there and enjoy dessert first if you even *hope* you're going to have a shot at the main course!"

The audience roars, even the few who look disapproving and embarrassed. Legs calls out a woman who's frowning and shaking her head but laughing despite herself.

"Oh, no, bitch, you can't have it both ways. You don't get to laugh first and then call my act dirty! You laughed. We saw you. You can't take it back. And later tonight, when you take your man home, you'll be *telling* him that joke over and over. Hell, you'll be acting it out. It's just a joke, baby! Don't smother him!"

You don't know how long she's been up there, but she only waits a moment before the next line of attack.

"And fellas, if you're going to watch that nasty porn, take it as an instructional video. You will be graded on this oral exam if you ever expect to test me on the supplementary anal."

The room goes nuts again and when that wave of laughter subsides, Legs goes into crowd work, setting up the next punch. "What about it, ladies? When you catch your man watching porn, is that cheating?"

A couple of women near the front answer yes. Legs zeroes in on the closest couple. "Do you know this man?"

"That's my husband."

"I was hoping since you have your hand in his crotch," — the woman jumps in her seat, raises both hands and laughs — "but I didn't want to assume. I thought maybe you're just friendly. What's your name, sweetie?"

"Challa," the woman answers, loud and proud.

"And your man's name?"

"Dave!" Dave, a wimpy-looking dude in a yellow sweater vest, looks like he might crawl under his chair to escape. His cheeks flush crimson.

"Dave, have you been on those websites? Did you forget to clear out your browser's history, you poor dumb bastard?"

To his credit, the guy smiles, nodding. The crowd cheers his embarrassment and he tries to wave Legs Gabrielle off, begging for mercy. He might as well have been waving a slab of red meat at a tiger.

"Dave, Challa is very angry with you. I can tell. She's calling you out in front of all these people, man! She's telling you very clearly that pornography is cheating!"

A basso rumble of discontent reaches her from the back of the crowd and Legs wheels on them. "Some of your boys are thinking they should come to your defense, Dave, but those guys are either single or they're sitting beside their date right now and pretending they don't even know what porn is! They make it all in Pasadena, fellas! You trying to tell me you've never heard of youporn? Or xhamster.com? Dave knows those sites and," she points to another victim, "and this guy here is taking notes so he won't forget the name of that website when he gets home! You can tell he's alone. He's one of those small-jawed guys!"

Legs points at another man standing off to the side at the front and you're surprised to find it's Berb, her bodyguard for the evening. As soon as he left you, he must have reported for his babysitting shift.

"See the jaw on this guy?" Legs says. "Dude's got a jaw like a steam shovel." She mimes holding a phone, winks and smiles and mouths, "Call me."

People are rocking in their seats with laughter. It's not just laughter, though. It's energy that bounces off the walls and moves through the crowd, amping everyone up.

"So guys, here's the real deal. Dave, Challa feels that porn is cheating so you have to stop that shit. I'm not saying I agree. I'm saying that's your lady's policy so now it's your policy. Pornography is cheating! So, Dave. You know what you gotta do now, right? You gotta delete those nasty websites, tune up your jaw muscles — chew a lot of gum — and head on over to some nasty *dating* websites. Hook me up *now* dammit! dot com…Just blow me quick cuz I don't want to do any of the work...dot org...I need a guy with a steam shovel jaw...dot net. Get out and find yourself a *real* woman, Dave! You know why? Because Challa *already* thinks you're a cheater! If you're going to do the time, Dave, you get to do the *crime*!"

Women scream and men howl with laughter and before that can die down, Legs leaves the stage on a high note, pausing to give a dainty curtsy, blowing kisses as she exits.

BODYGUARD? NAH, YOU'RE AN ATTACK DOG.

Berb spots you and waves you over. He only knows you by one name. "Fix! Chill told me you're getting called in on this one."

He doesn't ask about the gas cans. Berb is a professional so he's got instant amnesia. If you brought up the evening's earlier adventures, he'd look at you like a bulldog looks at a ceiling fan, bewildered maybe, but not curious.

Not curious is good. He's a bodyguard. You're something else Hollywood security firms never speak of. He plays defense. You play offense. Sometimes you wish you had his job.

You tell Berb you're here to keep an eye out for the same threat he is: Reles.

"You met Legs, yet?"

"Uh-uh. How long you been babysitting?"

"For a month at least. Me, Skunk and the new Samoan. It's been one on one until a couple of days ago. Then Chill put us all on her. Threat's up, but I don't know the details why."

"I think I know why. What's she like?"

"She's nice," Berb says. "Unlike some people in her profession, she's not always on, so she's almost like a regular human when she isn't in front of a crowd."

"Almost?"

"Well, look at her. Gorgeous, funny, smart, rich and getting richer. The whole package."

"I'll be glad to see the client and congratulate her on a great set. She destroyed."

"No time. We're on the move in a second. You'll have lots of chances to talk, though," Berb adds. "We're headed back to Legs' place right away. I already put the call in to Chill — he's still on his way — but we need you, too. We're calling in reinforcements."

"What's up?"

Berb can't be older than twenty-five, but his face is heavy and as serious as an old man. "A security nightmare. I like Miss Gabrielle a lot, but she's throwing an impromptu party. She must think she's out of danger because she's not listening to me at all, man."

"Cabin fever?"

He nods. "They all get it eventually. Chill called her and she was suddenly acting like a princess sick of being locked in the tower. I get it. Everybody gets tired of being surrounded by babysitters."

Chill must have told her he had his special ops guy (i.e. you) on the case. "Her relaxation of vigilance and celebration is premature."

"That's okay. We'll stay frosty. Skunk's already got the egress covered and the Samoan's by the car watching for stage door Johnnies. Next stop: Legs Gabrielle's house." He flashes you the address from his phone.

It will be nice to hang out in a mansion with no hidden horrors in secret bloody rooms. Not blowing up a mansion will also be a positive change of pace.

Berb tells you what he knows. Chill proposed that the easiest way to deal with Detective Reles was to get Legs out of town. However, she's got auditions to attend and stand-up gigs to do. All her work is in Los Angeles so she can't give her stalker a cooling off period.

She wants to live her life, do her work and live her dream unharassed. That's reasonable. You understand. However, once Reles finds out one of his torture ring buddies is dead, things could get hot. In your mind, it's a torture ring. You refuse to think of what happened to that poor girl as sex.

You're on your way out when you spot Reles near the door. He's on his way out, too. He must have been pressed against the back wall in the shadows behind a pillar. He's cagey. You need to know more but you can't come straight at the guy. You know Reles is dangerous because you had to zap Oswald until the stun gun's battery drained. Then you had to use old school, manual techniques to get the predator's name. Oswald gave up Reles last.

Reles is the scariest kind of crazy. He's got a badge.

Your power and authority comes from the weight of Ginger's dead gaze. Her name in the real world was Tabby. Tabitha. It was a beautiful name for a girl who didn't get a chance to pull herself out of Hollywood's underground.

Tonight, it's time for another recon mission. In the best case scenario, Reles and his circle of monsters disappear. Then you'll disappear, too, preferably to another country, at least for a while.

How you're going to manage all that? You have no idea.

You think of Ginger's dead gaze again. All you do know is, tonight? Vengeance wears Armani.

WHEN CONFRONTING EVIL, LOOK FRIENDLY AT FIRST

You don't have to follow him far. Reles crosses the street to a coffee shop, orders a drink and sits on the tiny outdoor patio. When you cross the street, he appears to stare at you. Then you realize he looks at everyone that way, mad at the world. He looks like a cannibal who hasn't eaten in days and has a new bottle of barbecue sauce at the ready.

Reles is one of those big, sandy-haired California dudes who looks like he spends all his spare time pumping iron and trying to make his neck bigger. His shoulders are so yoked, he looks out of place in the cafe's patio lawn chair, like an adult in a child's plastic chair.

Slap on your happiest smile. As Jack Lemmon used to say before the camera rolled, "It's magic time!" You throw Reles a flirty wink as you pass him. His jaw tightens and he looks away.

The woman in front of you in line has a complex order and a problem with her credit card. You take the opportunity to call Chill on your throwaway and tell him where you are.

"What's your plan?"

"I have no idea, so…improv. I'll take his temperature."

"Don't use the rectal thermometer until you've got a solid plan, Jesus."

"Roger that."

"Go full drama," Chill suggests. "From what Legs tells me, he thinks of himself as a tough guy."

"He has the look that tells me that's real."

"Then shake him up with your musical theater schtick."

"It's not a schtick. It's a character."

"Sure, sure, Pacino. Just get him off balance and come up with a plan. The fact that he's a cop…it's complicated."

"Yes, mother."

The clog in the artery to the barista is finally clear. Everyone has a story, so for practice you take what you think is a pretty good guess about the young woman behind the counter. The barista speaks to the customers in a monotone that suggests she's on some kind of downer but she enunciates each word, so maybe she has a mild case of Aspergers. She's about twenty-three and thin with that sinewy, unhealthy look Yoga vegans get when they do too many of the wrong drugs. She has a hard look around her mouth and her eyes are squinty, as if she's perpetually looking at the world through smoke.

Slathered in tattoos of mythical animals and awash in retail boredom, you spot what you think is phoenix doing battle with a gryphon. The blue tattoos — not yet completed so she's probably saving up for color — spread up from her push-up bra cleavage to her throat.

She wears a name tag that reads: Raven. Her grandparents probably went to Berkeley and her parents are stoners but she's working a Starbucks because she's living with some dude studying neo-fascism AKA law school at UCLA.

"Darling!" you burst. "I am *so* in need of a decaf venti latte with a dusting of cinnamon, I can't tell you!" You might have overshot the runway. Your first attempt sounds more like Truman Capote on helium, so you try to dial it back when you say, "Thanks, sweetie. Love the dragon eating the gryphon. Very neo-D&D revivification."

Raven gives you a plastic smile that tells you to drop dead. Despite the traffic, Reles must have heard you out on the patio so there's no way he'll think you're any danger to him. Macho guys like Reles always assume gay guys are no threat, even though that's obviously stupid. Chill is gay and he could pound just about anybody to dust. You happen to know he has on several occasions.

You get your drink, swish out to the patio and slide into a seat at the little table next to Reles. The key to meeting people is not to wait and let the tension build where it's obvious you're speaking out of loneliness as a last resort. To make this play work, you have to channel crazy Aunt Sadie. Everybody knows a crazy Aunt Sadie who can't shut up for a minute as long as she's conscious.

"Hello! Do you know who I just saw in that club across the street?"

Reles turns his head slowly and looks you up and down, assessing. When you wink and smile again, taking his threat assessment as a sexy invitation, his upper lip curls. Misinterpreting a threat as a come-on is the easiest way to throw off a threat assessment.

"Not interested."

"Oh, really? Do you know who Legs Gabrielle is?"

His head snaps around again. "What about her?"

"She's a dolly. Just a dolly."

"Yeah, she is." At the corner of his mouth, he allows a hint of a grudging smile.

"I talked to her and you know what? She talked to me! It was like the television just came alive!"

"What name do you go by, muchacho?"

Like dialogue from an old Western, you think. "Delgado, but you can call me Armando. Everybody does. And what's your name, kind sir?"

"Hank," he says, taking another sip of his coffee. "What did Legs say?"

"Oh, my God, yes. I have a friend who works backstage. I spoke to Legs Gabrielle. And you know what's better? She couldn't have been sweeter."

"What'd she say?" He's intrigued and impatient.

"I asked her what her perfume was because it was beautiful. It smelled like roses."

"Armando," Reles says. "I didn't ask what you said. I asked what she said."

Typical cop mentality: entitled. You probably sounded the same when you first became a Military Policeman. A lot of guys get badge-heavy and stay badge-heavy. Give anybody a special hat and power over others and they will abuse that power. Studies prove it. Given how you held Oswald's life in your hand tonight and squeezed, you don't need to google a scientific study. You know it personally. Subtract the sex crimes and maybe you aren't so different from Reles.

When you pick up your drink for another sip, your hand shakes. You were supposed to rattle him. Instead, he's shaking you.

CHILDREN ARE HOLY TO THE DIVINE ASSASSIN

"Hello?"

There's something familiar about Reles. Something about him makes you want to wipe the smug off his face with a power sander.

You take another swig of coffee to give yourself time and think about what to say next. Just because you're playing a gay guy doesn't mean you have to play the role without dignity. "Bitch, please, I'm getting to that. I asked her about her perfume and she said she only wears lavender."

An ex of yours wore that scent. The lovely Lily. To this day, the scent of lavender still stirs happy memories, way back last summer, before the New York mob wanted you punished, then dead. Somewhere out there, another guy much like you is no doubt hunting you. It's like it's always rabbit season and your only hope is to lose yourself in the city's warren of dives. You're always hiding in a hole and, behind the scenes of every day life, there are so many hunters.

"Miss Gabrielle said she got the perfume on her last trip to Canada," you add. "They were shooting her latest film. Something awful. Another horror movie."

"I love her horror movies."

"That's not my cup of pee, Hank, but to each his own. I prefer her stand-up. I saw a clip of her work…the Montreal Comedy Festival, I think it was. Very funny. Very racy, as I recall."

"Yeah. I've heard all her stuff." His gaze never leaves the entrance to the comedy club. "She's a dirty bitch. I'd love to see her on her knees with clothespins on her nipples."

You drop out of character for a second and just say, "Shit, man."

"She's a buffet." Reles looks at you for the first time in several minutes and you see something in his eyes you recognize. "With lots of cinnamon! I can't tell you!" he adds, mocking you.

You know that face. His is the confidence of a wolf among sheep. The woman and man who kidnapped you, Tia Marta and the Bug Man, had the same dead eyes.

LAPD's psychologist must have been asleep the day they let this guy in the door. A lot of candidates fail those tests simply because they answer the crucial question wrong. When asked why they want to be cops, the correct answer is, "To serve and protect." Blather a few banalities about respect, love of order and being a peace officer and you're in.

Most monsters are so dumb, they think the correct answer is, "To enforce the law and finally get the respect I deserve." Then they're out the door and wondering why they can't ever be police officers. Then they go into low level security jobs or they become deputies in remote Texas towns shaking down brown people and tourists. Or the rejects get elected governor of Texas. They go anywhere they can wield power unchecked. Detective Hank Reles has the look of a guy who should definitely *not* be in authority.

That look in his eyes…you've caught that look in mirrors sometimes. You tell yourself again that you're nothing like this asshole. You're just a guy who finds himself in bad circumstances, repeatedly. When you were a soldier, they told you killing people was heroic. When you were an enforcer, the mob said you did your duty when you squeezed a lowlife for money owed. As a hit man, the people you were sent to kill were killers themselves. You don't kill civilians and kids are considered holy and off limits.

You've killed for money, in self-defense and as a preemptive strike. The pleasure you take in your work comes from winning and knowing you're taking out someone who deserves it. Now you only answer to Chill, yourself and God (in no particular order) and you're okay with it.

An ex-girlfriend once asked what made you okay with your job. You told her that no one you killed was destined to cure cancer. Regular people look down on guys like you, but you're making the world a more beautiful place. You are the garbage man.

Reles is about power and you're about justice. You'll cling to that distinction to your dying breath to stay righteous, just in case anybody really is up in the sky, counting your sins in a big ledger. You hope they count the sorrows you corrected, too.

"What else did Legs tell you?" Reles asks.

"She said she's going away for a long vacation. Greece, maybe."

He grimaces. "When?"

"I don't know. She has these big, burly men with her. Nice looking fellows. I'd love to be part of her entourage. Imagine getting to be with Legs Gabrielle all the time. A woman like her could turn a guy like me *straight*, honey!"

"Yeah."

He tips his hand. "How many big, burly guys was she with, Armando?"

You tell Reles you saw six men with her.

"Six?"

You went overboard trying to discourage him from bothering the client. "It was a tight squeeze back there, but that's how I got such a good whiff of that lovely perfume."

"Lavender, huh? I'll have to get some of that for my lady."

Reles gets up. "Bye, Mr. — "

"Armando, please!"

"Sure. *Armando*. Heh. When you prance back to Mr. Chillie Gillie, tell him Detective Hank Reles says hello."

ONE MISSTEP AND YOU'RE SHIT ON TOAST

"What gave me away?" you ask.

"Three things: First, when I was rude to you, you should have bitched me out more and left in a huff. Instead, you stayed. Why? Because you're here for something else. Me. Second, *six* guys? I've followed her around. I know how many guys are on her security detail."

A power sander won't do the job. You want to wipe the smug off his face with the rear tires of your car. You did that once to a guy in Chicago and it proved very satisfying. "What was the third thing?"

"You asked me what gave you away. That's when I knew for sure you've got to be a snitch for Gillie Security Associates."

"Shit." Your head heats up. You've used that same trick. Now you know how he got over on the qualifying interviews for the LAPD. Most monsters are stupid. He's not. He knows the right thing to say to get what he wants and no one understands how dangerous he is until he peels back the mask. Reles frightens you in a way few men do. He might be as good at his job as you are at yours. He might be better.

"Tell Legs I look forward to meeting her again. Tell her to drive carefully. I'm always watching…out for her." He stands over you, smiling. "Oh, and, Armando? Did you know that…I think, last time I checked, sixty-two people have died from pepper spray? Sixty-two! Probably more. I wonder how many pepper spray cans it would take to kill you? You'd be begging for death a long time before it would actually happen."

"Hypothetically?"

He shrugs. "Sure. Hypothetically, I could use MK-9. That might speed up the experiment. Heh. That's military grade pepper spray. I'd start with your eyes, of course. They say you throw up for hours with MK-9. After the first bit, there's nothing to throw up anymore and all you know is pain. It's like your eyes and nose and mouth and stomach are on fire but it doesn't stop. Hell must be filled with MK-9 and napalm. That's the fire that burns and burns but never consumes so the pain just goes on and on and it feels like an eternity until your heart gives out."

"Yeah, yeah. Mr. Policeman is our friend, but to me and Legs, you're just another pest going through the garbage who needs to be put down."

His laugh is that of a very convincing robot. "If I ever see you again, I am going to do things. You can't even imagine how bad."

"I've got a pretty good imagination."

"Good. Stay out of my way."

"You know that's not going to happen."

"Then I'll catch you later…*Armando*."

He's out of earshot by the time you think to reply, "I look forward to when next we meet, Professor Moriarty."

That would have been a pretty cool retort if it had come to you fast enough, but you were busy sweating. You make a mental note to pick up bottles of Pepto Bismol, just to have on hand in case you have to pour it into your eyes and mouth to neutralize a pepper spray attack. Milk or Coke will do in pinch, but the pink stuff is best. Now that you've met Reles face-to-face, you're sure you have to make more elaborate and desperate plans of attack.

It's not just that he's a very bad dude threatening a nice lady that spurs your fear for her. Despite all you've done, the fact that this asshole is supposed to serve and protect pisses you off. You used to serve. Sure, you're a hit man, but that doesn't make you a dick. Reles is a disgrace to every other decent guy in uniform.

Gay improv didn't work so when next you meet Hank Reles, you won't be Armando Delgado, non-threatening snitch. Next time you'll be the divine assassin.

SOME NIGHTMARES NEVER GO AWAY

Legs Gabrielle's house isn't the monster mansion you expected. A very successful cardio-thoracic surgeon could live here, but it's far from Johnny Depp-level housing. It's not exactly small, but it's not hidden and anonymous behind tall, impenetrable hedges and razor wire, either. The house has four bedrooms and the piano-shaped pool out back stands drained and dry.

You look for Chill in the gathering crowd but he's not here yet. Glasses clink and drinks flow and someone fires up *Play that Funky Music (White Boy)* by Wild Cherry. Under different circumstances, you'd love to dance. Instead, you plug in your earpiece with the coiled wire and find out who else from Gillie Security Associates has arrived to deal with the influx of strangers parking in the circular driveway.

The driveway is full and people park up and down the road, wander in out of the dark and come through the open front gate. You had to park up the road too far and no one's checking IDs, so the situation is already out of control.

"This is Fix on the perimeter," you say. "Check in."

"Two. Check. In the foyer." That's Berb.

"Three! Check. In the kitchen." That's Jeremy, the big Samoan bodyguard (and too loud in your ear.) He has the look needed for intimidation gigs. Babysitting celebrities is often about having the steroid freak or the fattest and tallest out front. A show of potential force eliminates the need for violence in most cases.

Jeremy is green. Last month, he was a repo man in Pasadena. He's shaped like a barrel and he either wants to stake out the kitchen or be where the ladies are. He's one of those guys who aspires to be a rapper and he seems to think he could do a better job guarding beautiful women by sitting beside them in hot tubs.

Chill caught him flirting with a client too hard last week. The Samoan was then tasked with walking yappy little dogs that fit in Louis Vuitton purses. Chill handed Jeremy a wad of plastic bags and told him to make sure he didn't forget to stoop and scoop. Jeremy snarled, "Yes, Mr. Miyagi. I'll paint your damn fence."

Everybody laughed, even Chill. Then Jeremy got more errands and yappy little dogs to stoop and scoop after.

You told Jeremy he didn't have to stoop and scoop.

"Really?" he asked, his pumpkin head split into a Jack-o'-lantern grin.

"The yard, yes. You have to clean that up, sure. But if the Reality TV star of the moment has a happy, snappy little Brussels Griffon that shits in her purse, that's not your responsibility. Don't go sniffing women's purses, kid."

Jeremy stared blankly. The kid doesn't get your sense of humor yet.

"Four," Skunk whispers, "In the front main room."

It seems like a long time has passed since you handed Sugar, wrapped in one of Oswald's blankets, over to the oldest of the crew. Skunk will be hanging back, trying to blend in with the curtains, watching eyes and hands and memorizing faces.

No word from One. That's Chill. In his absence, you give the orders you're sure he would issue.

"Three, head upstairs and keep people out of the bedrooms. We don't want any plants in there. As soon as the party's over, somebody has to stay up and go through the whole house to scan for bugs and cameras. You guys draw straws to see who stays up all night and tomorrow."

There's no hesitation. Berb congratulates Jeremy. "I've just drawn straws and it's low man on the totem pole again."

"Aw!" Jeremy's mouth seems to be full of potato chips.

"Clear the channel. One will be listening," you say. "All hail One."

"Hail," each guard says in sequence.

If Chill has arrived and is parking his car, he's not laughing.

You don't recognize any of the actors — this must be the wannabes and B actor brigade — but you recognize a comedian named Redban coming up the driveway. He's sharing a joint with a young woman who, by her look and dress, is a porn star before the anger and sadness has kicked in. Between her giggles, you catch the first half of a joke he tells onstage about dating Asian girls.

You envy his confidence. Tia Marta beat your confidence out of you and, given what happened with your last two girlfriends, you're in no hurry to hook up with the next one.

You circle the perimeter, but with no walls and no cameras, there's nothing to even slow any intruder who wants to slip in with the party goers. Legs seems destined to be a big star, but since she hasn't gone full legend yet, she's actually harder to protect. Most big stars have compounds and a full-time security staff that lives on the premises. The smart celebs who are running really hot don't go out in public much.

Chill sometimes gives fatherly lectures to some of his youngest clients. When they tire of being surrounded by security, they need to know that one day they'll be able to go to the grocery store without being mobbed. He tells them to send a maid for errands and enjoy the easy money while it lasts. When the fame goes away, and it almost always does, it's cold outside of the limelight.

Old bodyguards don't retire. They just hope to get shot. Chill gives work to some old buddies in the business sometimes. He assigns them to be paid friends to former celebrities who don't really need protection anymore. When celebs are young they don't really want to bother with security. After the trends cast them aside, those same celebs sometimes miss the image that having bodyguards projects.

Legs is on the upswing now and, seeing her onstage tonight, it's impossible to imagine she'll ever lack attention (the good type of attention that pays and the stalking kind that pains).

Chill's team is inside the house watching Legs so you play wallflower and hang around outside. Since the party has just started, everyone's inside raiding the bar. The pool is drained of water so the patio isn't very attractive and there are only a couple of people out here.

How will Reles come at Legs? You suspect you've made a tactical error. The easiest thing in the world is to walk up behind someone and pull a trigger. However, Reles doesn't want to kill Legs. He wants to possess her. He's the kind of cat who only kills the mouse after he's done tormenting it.

Chill has been holding you back since the events in Chicago, insisting you can find more peaceful ways to deal with assholes. Until today, you've managed pretty well, coloring within the lines. But remembering the look in Reles's eyes, you feel like an eager dog on a choke chain. When you see a guy like Reles wreaking havoc and terrifying a woman whose only crime is trying to entertain people, you want to use the Russian mines on him. Erasing the asshole would be easy, but dealing with more attention from the FBI would not. The Russian mines are leftover prizes from your Chicago adventures, stored away in a relatively safe place. One of those Russian beauties might be an easy way to blow up Reles in his car...or on his toilet. That would be good. Everybody poops.

You wonder about the girl in the chair. Is her body fully incinerated yet? Her horror gives you a familiar bout of nausea. That room reminded you too much of Miami. Rats crawled over your naked body in the dark, waking you with a start from fitful sleep and tortured dreams. The nightmares kept coming long after you got out of that basement.

You wish the recon in Montecito could have gone differently, but leaving a crime scene intact would be a gift to CSI nerds. There should be evidence of what those men did, but what could trip them up could also lead the police your way.

Justice for Reles and his friends is up to you. You had better go inside and talk to the client to find out what she knew that led you to the crime scene that will haunt your dreams.

JESUS AGREES! NO CAPES!
#THEINCREDIBLES

When you spot Legs by the bar, she has changed into a long white sheath slit up one side to display one of her famous gams. She's surrounded by a clutch of friends and admirers, but her eyes get big when she spots you. Chill must have described you to her. You give her a wink and a nod. With numerous apologies, she extracts herself from the center of the group quickly. In a moment, she joins you on the terrace overlooking the backyard.

"Great set tonight."

"Thanks!" Her eyes are bright. "Mostly, when guys say 'great set,' they're staring at my tits."

"I'll do that, too, but I'll be sneaky about it."

She nods. "Comedy is the best high there is and I've tried a bunch." She holds up her champagne flute in a little toast and smirks, "Better than this stuff. I got this bubbly for thirty bucks and it tastes like five. Somebody stomped the grapes with dirty feet. The toe jam makes it too sweet."

"Nice."

"So you've got to be Dr. Fix."

"Right now? I'm just the babysitter. J.D. to my friends. You can call me J.D."

"Chill calls you his Agent in Charge of Special Projects."

"Sounds better than Thug in Charge of Dirty Tricks, doesn't it? I've asked Chill if I could go by Emissary of Righteous Vengeance."

"He wouldn't go for it?"

"He wouldn't buy me a cape, either. Chill said capes are gaudy, though making him say 'emithary' ith fabulouth!"

"Don't be mean. I love his lisp…*hith lithp!* It softens him a little. Besides," she adds, "You're a couple of centuries too late to rock a cape. That look rarely works in modern life."

"So, I guess this is a bad time to ask if you're a Marvel or DC fan."

"Batman and Superman have it wrong — "

"Sacrilege!"

She shrugs. "Like in *The Incredibles*, you'd strangle yourself to death in a revolving door or something."

You take in her high cheekbones and full lips.

"You're staring," she says.

"Sorry. Women who are fans of *The Incredibles* are sexy. Just putting that out there." Jeremy the Samoan can't get away with flirting with clients, but you figure you're mildly cuter. You've always been shy around women, but gorgeous women do make you aspire to extroversion. Given that she already has a stalker who packs heat, you pause to consider that your timing is lousy.

Legs Gabrielle's smile is tolerant but she lets the moment pass so you move on briskly. "Really funny stuff tonight. There aren't many comediennes, but you sure stand out." Your mistake.

"Cut that shit," she says. "Women in comedy don't like that. We're just comedians or comics. Comedienne sounds like something Elayne Boosler had to put up with when she was breaking ground. That ground's broke." Seeing you look stricken at offending her, she softens. "Besides, I prefer the term 'Professional Goofist'."

"And do you prefer actor or actress?"

"So far, I'm mostly a screamer in a tank top in B horror movies. Most critics would say the label of actor or actress applied to me is an insult to real thespians."

"You know what they say about thespians, Miss Gabrielle? A lot of girls just experiment with thespianism for a semester or two in college."

With that stupid joke you make a movie star laugh. Most comedians have to feel like they're the only ones in any room who can get a laugh, so you decide not to put it off: you like Legs a lot.

"I thought you'd be taller," she says.

Okay, you like her a little less. "I get that a lot."

"People dare to call you short a lot?"

"Oh…gee whiz. Up until now, I thought they were just quoting the line from *Roadhouse*. Everybody tells Patrick Swayze's character — "

"Dalton!"

"Yeah! Everybody tells him they thought he'd be taller."

She touches your arm and you feel better about the world. "*Roadhouse!* Man, I love that movie!"

Legs is a funny movie star who loves *Roadhouse*. You promised yourself you wouldn't fall in love so easily again, but your shields are down. "Everybody loves that movie," you say, "but no one is supposed to. It's not allowed. I love it non-ironically, though."

"I know what you mean. I hate it when people call my work 'a guilty pleasure.' They bought the ticket and they laughed their asses off or at least they had a good time. I can't stand critics who think they could do better or worry that they shouldn't have enjoyed themselves. The pricks."

She looks up and her cheeks redden. "Sorry, J.D. I know nobody gives a shit about lucky white girl problems. I had a weak moment of honesty there. When I win the Oscar someday, I'll try to remember people are starving in Africa."

"Heavy is the head that wears the diamond tiara," you say.

She smiles and you want to see more of that so you risk going back to the well and add, "Golly, though! I'm short? This is terrible news! I thought I was tall since my legs reach all the way to the ground."

She cracks up a little, but it could be the cheap champagne.

"My God! Apparently I'm a little person and I didn't notice until now!" To your immense relief, Legs cracks up again. Her easy laughter encourages you.

"But me and Patrick Swayze? We're *strong* dwarves." You strike a pose and flex a bicep.

It wasn't that funny, so she's probably nervous around you. You try to set her at ease with a nod to her world. "I might have an okay bit if poor Patrick Swayze wasn't dead. I guess I'll have to hold off a bit longer on my dreams of doing stand-up, at least until I update my material."

"A guy like you…sorry, you're not what I expected. You're so thin."

"I prefer 'wiry.' Most guys who work security details just slap a mean look on their faces, like they just ate barbecued baby and are hungry for a juicy toddler." You shrug. "Cliches are so…"

"Cliche?"

"Right."

She toasts you and takes a gulp of the bubbly. Her gaze moves to the gate, wary again and searching. Reles might be out in the dark, watching her from the deep shadows under the trees.

Legs has not asked about Oswald. Chill probably told her she doesn't need or want to know the details of what you do. She's an actress, so you can't be sure, but she must not know about the fire you set today. Not yet.

All you want to do is talk to her about comedy and superhero comics and *Roadhouse*. Instead, it's time to move past the introductory pleasantries. She sent you to a monster's house and four people are dead, three by your hand. What's her connection to the dead girl in the chair?

WHEN QUOTING HIGHLANDER, I SOUND
LIKE PETER LORRE

"I went to Chill about Reles. I've had plenty of stalkers, but he's the only one who scared me. I wanted him out of my life, but I couldn't figure out how. He said he had a guy for that."

"That's me. Raccoons and roaches are my business."

"Huh?"

"Raccoons, I discourage from coming around and I keep them out of your attic. We started calling stalkers 'raccoons' because they're always going through celeb garbage looking for toenail clippings and whatnot."

Legs asks you for details about your job.

Working security assignments in Hollywood is much safer compared to the dangers of your last gig. That included running guns and trading in Russian mines with evil people, plus explosions and nearly burning to death.

Blending in with a crowd of anxious, autograph-seeking fans standing behind a velvet rope? Until today, most of your work in Hollywood has been easy. You skip the details that include blood and bone and give her a summary of the light lifting you do.

"I discourage stalkers, often using their own douchebag tactics. They go through celeb garbage so I go through theirs, for instance. I'm the garbageman. Somebody cyber stalks you, I cyber stalk them right back, but harder."

Using some of the less subtle intimidation techniques you learned back East? That's called 'going Jersey' and it's better than working a retail job and trying to sell khaki pants to hipsters for a few bucks an hour at The Gap.

You leave 'going Jersey' out of your story, too. "Chill sometimes slips me anti-stalker assignments. Occasionally, I do some undercover bodyguard work."

"What's an undercover bodyguard?"

"That usually involves hanging out in malls, protecting the teenage children of celebs. They aren't aware they've got a bodyguard unless there's trouble. Kids like the idea of bodyguards. They even brag about needing us. That's the first week. Then they want to go to the movies with their friends and not worry we'll tell their parents they're having sex or smoking pot. The parents still worry about kidnapping, so I sit in the dark and watch kids watch movies."

"And do you watch them have sex and smoke pot?"

"I'm discreet," you say. "Speaking of discreet, you shred anything that has phone numbers, bank records…anything personal that could be used against you, right?"

"Dude! I've met enough creeps and paparazzi, I run my tampons through the shredder before I throw them out."

"Tampons. Yeah. When fans turn to fanatics, things can get really weird."

As a former mob enforcer, you're still having a hard time adjusting to your new lifestyle. You have a little money set aside now, thanks to Chill, but you can't go out and spend it on much that's fun. Movies are okay because you can slip into a darkened theater and maintain your low profile. Walking up and down Rodeo Drive in Armani and Ray-bans, you manage to fit in. However, you are still a fugitive and that means living off the grid.

You don't have to turn caveman to elude the Feds, but you have to be so ridiculously careful that sometimes you think life would be much easier if you went full Harrison Ford in *Witness* and hid out among the Amish. Building barns wouldn't be so bad if you could fall in love with a hot chick in a bonnet.

"You said roaches and raccoons. What do you mean when you say 'roaches'?"

That's your segue. "Reles is a roach. He needs to be stepped on. How'd you meet Hank Reles, Miss Gabrielle?"

"He came to one of my parties. He tagged along with Ross Oswald. He's my agent's accountant. Mort's my agent."

"Mort Sheldrake?"

"You know him?"

"I know the name."

She spoke of Oswald almost as an afterthought. She doesn't have to know the slime is now burning in the land of the past tense. That knowledge will have to wait. You'll let Chill break it to her that you had to go into extermination mode. When this is over, you'll have to disappear for a while. Maybe you'll drive up the coast to Seattle and let things cool down. You could drink coffee and…what else do people do in Seattle?

"You're very worried about Reles," you say. "What did he say to you?"

"He told me he likes the way I scream in the movies," Legs says. "He said he'd like to make me scream like that. I'm tortured and die in the movie he loves most."

"*The Tar Pit Killings?*"

"You've seen it?"

"Piece of shit," you say and the muscles around her mouth go slack. "Uh, sorry. Horror movies with torture aren't my sort of thing. I'm not saying everybody has to hate it, but I've got a sore spot." For instance, you've still got a sore spot over your right kidney where a bad guy thumped you with the butt of his sawn off shotgun.

What you don't say is that you've endured too much real torture to ever get some kind of vicarious thrill through a cheap horror movie. "But I heard you were great in it," you hasten to add.

Legs breaks into a laugh. For such a delicate looking woman, her laugh is full-throated and raucous. "You're from back East, aren't you?"

"Yeah."

"Where?"

You do your best Christopher Lambert impression from *Highlander* and say, "Lots of places." It comes out more like Peter Lorre and she's confused.

"I'm sorry, Miss Gabrielle. I forgot my manners. I was supposed to give you the Hollyweird answer and say you were, 'Simply fabulous!'"

You love her easy smile. If you hadn't sworn off falling in love recently, Legs Gabrielle could definitely be The Future Mrs. Diaz. If she could read your thoughts, she'd call you a crazy stalker, too. You'd have to shoot yourself in the face.

"I so rarely hear honesty," Legs replies, "that whenever I hear it around here, it's like the person speaking has lapsed into another language."

"No offense taken?"

"No, no. Thanks for the slap of cold water. I'm from Maine. I'm used to cold water. *Tar Pit* did suck. I told them so at the time."

"Obsequious hipster suck ups are supposed to say you were fabulous. Failing that, how about I give you a line? I look forward to you starring in movies that are worthy of your talent."

"Hipster douchebags don't know what 'obsequious' means," she says, "but people toss so much bullshit my way, especially men, they must think I'm a mushroom and they're trying to make me grow."

That seems to remind her of something and her smile fades again. "I deal with flirts and fans all the time, J.D. I never have a problem because I usually stick them with a joke or, if they get too mouthy, I treat them like a heckler in the club. That won't work with this guy. Hank Reles is something else. Something…"

"Less than human."

"I was about to say that."

"It's all in the eyes," you say. You've seen Reles's marble gaze. You recognize the fear in Legs Gabrielle.

Her instincts are correct.

A LABRADOODLE IS BETTER THAN A LIFE OF PROSTITUTION

A couple of peroxide blondes holding champagne flutes approach, their eyes on Legs. Their eyes have that star struck look that says, *I'd go lesbo for one night for bragging rights.* A couple of guys trail them, their gaze fixed on the girls' asses. They look like eager frat boys who've stumbled into the Playboy Mansion.

You do a half-turn and give the group your mean look and a dismissive wave of your hand. They get the message and veer off.

"Why did you ask Chill to get me to check Oswald's house if it's Reles you're worried about?"

"There was this girl. I was worried about her. Oswald didn't treat her well. Neither did Reles. I tried to be tolerant for a while because they were Mort's friends, but…people make choices. They've got their lives, but that doesn't mean I have to see it."

"Be specific."

"The girl was one of those high-priced escorts, the classy kind you spot with old rich guys with faces like raisins. Watch any Academy Awards and you can play spot the john. Something Mort said about Oswald and this girl he brought to the parties…it set me off."

"What did Mort say?"

"I forget the exact wording, but it set off alarm bells. Something about treating a whore like a whore and that's what they're paid to do. Then Reles said her work was no different from any actress but the hours were shorter."

"Is Mort tight with Reles?"

"He said Reles was his bodyguard."

"Agents only need guarding from their clients."

"I think Mort likes a posse. It's about getting girls for each other."

"Nothing shadier than that? Anything worse than hiring hookers, for instance?"

She looks confused. She has no idea how ugly and deep this goes. She still thinks this is about Reles and his obsession with her. It's about Ginger and who knows how many more young women tied to chairs in the dark.

Someone's got to the stereo. The music is *Celebration* by Kool & the Gang. It doesn't fit the mood on the terrace.

"Mort called this morning to tell me he had a big gig for me, but if I wanted it, I'd have to go to a private party at Oswald's house. I declined. Then Oswald called me up. Mort must have given him the number or it's in my tax paperwork. Anyway, Oswald said, 'Be an actress for us.' I got his meaning."

"And you knew that meant sex."

She nods. "At least sex. I'd talked to the escort a lot. She was actually a nice girl. She came to L.A. looking for work in the movies like all of us do. I could have been her. Lots of girls could have been her. Everybody's gotta pay the rent. Last I saw the girl, she said she was thinking of getting out of the business. It was getting too rough, is what she said."

"What did you tell Mort?"

"We'd already fought about Mort's friends — Reles and Oswald. I didn't want them to come around to my parties anymore. I'm so pissed at Mort, I'm looking for new representation. That's why I got back onstage tonight. Mort didn't want me to play around onstage. Said stand-up was hurting my brand. He said directors were looking for a more demure me."

"What was the name of the girl who worked as an escort?"

"Called herself Ginger. Nice young woman. Sugar introduced me to her. Sugar hung out with Oswald, too. She was a working girl, but I thought she had designs on graduating to trophy wife. Don't get me wrong. She's nice, but she acted like she enjoyed Oswald's company more than Ginger did."

Maybe Legs is right about Sugar's demeanor. Or maybe call girls have more in common with actresses than Legs knows. The lovely, terrified Asian woman didn't look like she had any love for Oswald when you found her locked in his cage.

"Were there other girls?"

"There was a string of them with Oswald. Sugar must have been a favorite since she lasted the longest."

"What can you tell me about Ginger?"

"Not much. She liked dogs. She wanted to buy a labradoodle puppy. She told me she was thinking about moving back East somewhere. Home, I guess. Haven't seen her in weeks. I hope she did move back home. I don't think she was cut out for the life she was trapped in. I offered her money to go back home. She said she had money and she'd save up. Just a couple more months she said, and she'd leave."

The dead girl in the chair. Half her head was shaved. The other half was long red hair. And the somewhere she never made it back to was Indiana. The dead girl in the chair was Tabitha Bernstein, dog lover. She'd been a person with dreams and a life and a name before Oswald and Reles got to her and erased everything. There are several names on the list Oswald gave you, and that trash has to be taken out, Garbageman.

You close your eyes. You see the dead girl in the chair again. She raises her head and blinks at you. She says in a whisper, "Makes you want to paint the town red with blood, doesn't it, Jesus?"

HINCKLEY FOCUSED ON STEPHEN KING FIRST

Legs filed a complaint against Reles. The policeman she spoke to doubted her and didn't even want to file a report on the detective. "The detective told me that, even if what I say is true, the best course of action is to ignore Reles and hope he goes away."

"Chill finds that can be a point of contention with cops. It's true that many stalkers move on if ignored and you shouldn't engage them. Remember John Hinckley Jr.?"

"The nut who tried to impress Jodie by killing Reagan? Of course. I'm slightly older than I look but I'm also much smarter than I look. Besides, I know Jodie."

Sometimes you forget that many of Chill's clients don't think of movie stars as movie stars. They're the people they hang out with on golf courses or know personally from the set. They watch each other's kids from the sidelines at little league.

To you, every big star's name is a unit: first name, last name. Jodie Foster is Jodie Foster. Miss Foster, maybe, but just Jodie? Never.

"Uh, Jodie Foster, yes…" you say finally. "What a lot of people don't know is, Hinckley was focused on Stephen King and some other celebrities first. Stalker psychology is variable. It can take them a while to decide on their target. Sometimes attention from law enforcement, restraining orders or a simple reply to a fan letter actually encourages them. Still…"

"Still, what?"

You take a deep breath and lay it out for her. "The official line is not to pay too much attention to stalkers or they suck you into their psychodrama. They become sure they've got a relationship with you. They go to great lengths to rationalize their actions, even if it means breaking into your home. Some stalkers focus on their idols for years."

She studies the carpet, losing hope again. "The same psycho was focused on Dave for a long time and kept breaking in," she says.

"Dave?"

"Letterman," she answers. "I tried to be nice to Reles, but I was firm when

I turned him down."

"It's not your fault, Miss Gabrielle. He's bent. You could have spit in his face and he would have taken that as a come on. It sounds like he did get your message. You aren't interested, so then he decided to come at you sideways. From the information I gathered today, it looks like these men have a…well, I don't know how else to say it. They treat all women like whores."

"And actresses…" she says. "I should have seen the signs earlier. Since that first party Reles acted like a creep. I would have kicked him out earlier, but he was part of Mort's entourage. Everywhere I went after the first night I met him — over two months ago — it feels like someone's watching me. Just when I think I'm not being followed, I turn around and there he is again, watching and smiling. He's been following me around, off and on, for weeks. I wonder sometimes if he's just sitting out there in his car jerking off or if he's getting up the nerve to come and shoot me in the face or…or…make me scream for him like I did in that movie. I should have seen it coming earlier."

"The first thing to keep in mind at all times is that the stalker is the psycho, not you. You aren't crazy and you did nothing to invite this."

She looks unconvinced and distracted, her eyes searching the dark uselessly again.

"A few years ago, there was a story out of Jersey," you offer. "A supermarket chain cranked up a new policy to try to make their stores friendlier. They told the staff on the cash registers to smile more, call customers by the name on their frequent shopper card. It was supposed to be innocuous, public relations stuff to get people to shop at their stores more."

"Did the customers go into shock? You said this happened in Jersey? Polite cashiers must have freaked some of them out."

"Maybe, but the big issue that emerged were a lot more problems with male customers. Some of the old ladies didn't like it because getting called by name in a line up at the supermarket felt too personal, like the lower classes were taking liberties with them. But the men? A bunch of them looked at these young female cashiers suddenly smiling at them and they thought the checkout girls were trying to pick them up, even hideous old guys."

"It's not my fault. Thanks. I get it. But it is my problem. What else can you tell me about stalkers?"

You shrug. "It's often a no-win situation. If you aren't responsive, you're a bitch. Some think they're helping you. Or their career will be boosted up. Or they think you'll rescue them from their messed up lives. They want money and love. They're narcissists starved for attention."

"The detective I talked to…he said I could try to take out a restraining order but he said some things — "

"Restraining orders are made of paper, not Kevlar, so their resilience under the strain of bullets is a shade low. Also, most cops would acknowledge that stalkers have a worrying tendency toward threat escalation. Today's Peeping

Tom is tomorrow's panty sniffer and, if they don't get derailed, eventually they can become rapists or worse. They start out small, building up their nerve. If the stalker breaks into your house, of course, the police can haul him away, but mostly, police are for after — "

You shut off that sentence before you get to the end of it and clear your throat. Honesty is fine, but she's already plenty scared. "Trouble is, there's a double standard. Even with high profile clients, the cops figure you've got your own security, a ton of fans or fanatics and most stalkers go away or lose interest if *you* go away. Careers are often short in Hollywierd and maybe the cops are trying to manage their caseload by attrition."

Her eyes are focused on you again. Despite the topic, it gives you a warm feeling. "What's the double standard?"

"If you were the President of the United States, the Secret Service doesn't wait around to see if the threat is viable. They go interview suspects and get in their face with a threat assessment and stern words." You smile. "Maybe more than stern words."

"Okay, but I don't want extra security around me all the time and forever. Your guys aren't bad. This isn't about them. It's just that extra security makes everything a hassle. If I want to go out, I have to plan ahead. I can't just jump in the car and go. I'm never alone and I feel like I'm under house arrest. This stalker is different. From this guy, I can never feel safe and just…I want to be left *alone*! The rest of my crazy life is already enough of a strain. This guy has already been in my house a few times with Mort and Oswald. It feels like a much more personal violation than a creepy fan letter from some guy writing all the way from Topeka."

A lot of people would exchange places with her without hesitation. Most wouldn't pause to say goodbye to their children if they could be her. You run your eyes over her body and reconsider. Most probably couldn't handle the ongoing borderline anorexia, heavy workouts and pressure it takes to be an up-and-coming starlet. It's not so rosy at the top and you know what it's like to have friends betray you. You want to give her a hug, tell her the truth and let her know that one of the monsters is already dead and gone. The rest are on your list and you're good at this sort of thing.

Of course, you can't do any of those things. Down here at the bottom sucks, too.

"The cop I talked to? It was more than just a case of one cop protecting another. He suggested that a restraining order might not fly. He said a judge probably wouldn't believe a rich bitch slut like me."

Your jaw goes slack. "You didn't go to the station, right? You called the police and I'm guessing a guy named Mueller showed up at your door, probably without a partner, am I right?"

"Yeah. How'd you know?"

"Because the cop at your door wasn't representing the best and brightest and finest of the LAPD. He was repping for Reles."

"Shit."

"That's the name of the cop you spoke to, right?"

"Detective Mueller, yeah."

You don't have to add another target to your list of names. His name is already there. He doesn't know it yet, but he's a bowling pin. You're the ball.

Her eyes are wet. "I'm totally screwed, aren't I?"

"Not yet."

"This is a nightmare."

"Ever hear of a guy named Bekhti? Odd name. Stands out."

"No."

"We'll save him for last since we know the others. He'll turn up. Break a hornet's nest, they all come out to swarm."

"What are you going to do? There's a bunch of them."

"A handful. Slightly fewer than a bunch."

"We've got to call the FBI, right? This is going to tear up my life. I'll never be safe. What if Reles and Mueller have more friends?"

"That's the hell of it, Legs. Most cops take serve and protect very seriously. Some cops think that motto is all about them and their own. If you bring in the FBI, there's no way to tell which way the investigation will break. They might even try to bring you down, smearing you to silence you."

"What do I do?"

"Leave it to me."

"What can you do?"

She looks so scared, you want her to feel a little safer. You break a rule from your playbook and hope Legs can handle it. "I said I had names. There are fewer names now. Used to be a bunch."

THIS IS NOT A MOVIE. BAD THINGS HAPPEN TO HEROES.

You give Legs Gabrielle your best encouraging look. She's strong, but she's been pretending to be strong for a long time, like a rope pulled at either end by powerful, relentless machinery until it snaps. When Chill put you on the case, she thought J.D. Fix meant an easy fix. Finding out there's more than one cop involved? Twice as bad.

"Can you really stop these guys?" Miss Gabrielle asks.

"If I fail, I'll fail in such a way that they still won't bother you or anyone else again."

"What does that mean?"

"If things go bad...it beats dying old of tumors spreading out from the prostate." When they write your obituary, the headline will read: *He never worried about dying old.*

"Careful," she says. "Reles is a lot bigger than you. Mueller, too."

"No worries. I'll be a smart ninja. Every guy has to have a thing. That's my thing."

Brave, goofy words. Even as you utter them, your throat goes dry. You swallow with a hollow click. Words are as useless as an empty gun. What you haven't learned yet is that you aren't as brave as you think you are — certainly not as brave as you sound. The whole prostate cancer dare was bravado to impress a beautiful woman. However, you are just stupid enough to still believe macho bullshit. Deep down, you think the law of cause and effect won't apply to you. Laws are for suckers. You're the hero of your own movie so naturally you believe nothing really bad can happen to you. You share the same delusion as everyone else and so, when the surprises come, your suffering shall be all the more egregious.

When you begin to turn away, she catches you by the shoulder. "Chill said I shouldn't ask, but, did you find something we can use against Reles and his buddies? Is Mort involved?"

"I've got nothing on your agent besides the fact he sounds like a sewer rat. For the rest, when Chill says you shouldn't ask, don't. I've already told you too much. In fact, I was never here."

"But at least tell me you found Sugar. Is she safe?"

You allow a slight nod.

She sighs heavily. "Thank you. Did Ginger go back home?"

"Could be. Um…so, look, this thing has barely begun. We'll keep you safe, but all these people wandering in doesn't make it easy. We usually have to prepare for events like this."

"Sorry, but I feel safe in a crowd and another moment given up to fear makes me feel like Reles has already won. I can't stand anyone winning but me."

"What did Chill tell you, Miss Gabrielle? About me, I mean?"

"You say 'what'. You really mean 'how much.' From what Chill says, keeping me safe isn't your department. That's up to those other three. Mr. Berbniak didn't want me to have the party tonight, either —"

"How many people are coming tonight?"

"I think at some point I told you to call me Legs or…wait. You're about to tell me something unpleasant, aren't you?"

"Would you cancel tonight's party?"

"It's not a party, J.D. It's a get-together."

"Do get-togethers have guest lists?"

"No, that's a party thing. Parties have themes and caterers. At get-togethers, it's much less formal so somebody gets naked and drunk and ends up on TMZ."

"How do people know to come?"

"In my world, I tell one person and the cell phone tree takes over. We had a similar thing back in Maine when some idiot gets lost in the woods. The whole town comes out for a search and rescue. I prefer get-togethers, actually. With formal invitations, someone always gets left out and they get pissy and you have to take them to lunch so they still feel the love."

She drains the champagne from her glass and, as she tips her head back, you take that moment to admire her cleavage.

"In Maine, people are nosy and you hate them for it. Out here? People tell you everything. Why people need psychoanalysts anywhere on the West Coast is a mystery. They sure aren't holding anything back."

How you envy these people. You've got an ugly history to "get over," whatever that means. You'll never live long enough to forgive the past.

THE DESERT IS HARD IN NEVADA. USE PICKS, NOT SHOVELS.

"Can I tell you something else before I go?"

"Not if it's going to ruin my evening," she says. "I've had enough of that."

"Sorry. It's just that staying low profile is safer. Are you sure you can't get out of town?"

"And there goes the evening. I have security here: you're here and all my friends are here."

"Are they all your friends?"

Legs looks around and shakes her head. "There are people here I don't know. That's how get-togethers work. But aren't I safer surrounded by a crowd in my own house?"

"You'd think so, but no."

"This is ridiculous. I'm sorry, but I've given up enough time and headspace to Reles and his friends."

You catch her arm and give her your best smile. "Legs, I need to let you in on something. I really am trying to help you here."

She gestures with her empty glass to give you the floor.

"If I were a psycho cop who wanted to kidnap a star such as yourself — "

"Starlet, I think."

You give her a heavy sigh and she pays attention. "A couple of hours from now, when the party — the get-together, is really rocking, I'd phone in an anonymous noise complaint. I'd arrive, maybe with another cop who's a tight friend and maybe not. Maybe I'd have another accomplice in the crowd. That wouldn't be hard. Anyway, if I were him and I wanted to take you off in my cruiser, the accomplice would drop a baggie of cocaine on the coffee table in plain sight as I arrived to deal with the noise complaint."

"Is this how your mind works all the time, or are we just talking about Reles?"

"I'm picturing a scenario where you could easily end up locked in the back of a cruiser."

"I have lawyers."

"You're still thinking like a human, Legs. He could take you back to his precinct and have you all to himself for a while, far too long before your lawyers could spring you. But if I were him, I'd pull the same trick the NYPD pulled with Occupy Wall Street protesters. I'd take you to some far flung precinct so it would take longer to find you. All the while you're in processing, you're in handcuffs and maybe you're in a private interrogation room with the cameras turned off."

"Oh, God."

"They can do anything and get away with it. Whatever happens to you, they'd call it the consequences of resisting arrest. Or maybe Reles is really unhinged and he might not take you to a police station at all. He might take you for a ride all the way to Nevada and lose you in the desert. Or he might take you down the coast and dump you off a cliff into the Pacific once he's done with you. Guys like Reles are unstable, so it's difficult for me to predict how he'll react. The next move is his."

"You're scaring me."

"Only to protect you. I was thinking of holding back, but now I think you should know the real deal."

"How do you get to be the guy who thinks like this?"

"Would you believe I'm a genius security strategist?"

"Maybe, but it would be simpler to assume you're another psycho who just happens to be on my side. Psychos are everywhere. Last month I auditioned for a part and the director couldn't stop staring at my feet. Breasts, I get all the time, but this dude was obsessed."

"Was it Tarantino? I understand he's into feet. I bet a film student somewhere must be writing his graduate thesis on the number of shots there are of Uma Thurman's feet in *Kill Bill*."

"No, it wasn't Quentin and that was mildly amusing, but," — a hard tone enters her voice — "I haven't forgotten that when you talk about Reles, you sound like you share his brain."

You try to look innocent, but does innocence look like a shy smile or should you appear hurt by her accusation? "According to Occam's Razor, the simplest solution is probably the right answer, but quoting Occam's Razor is something a brilliant strategist would say, so I can't help you there. How I can help you is, please, call off the party and let's batten down the hatches until I'm sure I've discouraged Detective Reles. I haven't stuck a sword in the bull yet. I've just waved a red cape at him."

"Just do your job, J.D. If the cops show up, we'll deal with them and I've got my lawyers on speed dial."

You reply, "Your lawyers are irrelevant to a guy like Reles unless they're well-armed." But you say it to her back.

She's already returning to her friends, back to that make-believe dimension where everything works out just fine, according to the script. However, before she's back inside she turns her head and freezes. She almost walks into the door.

You slide up beside her and follow her gaze. A man and a woman stand by the empty pool.

"Mort is here. I fired that son of a bitch this morning and he dares to show up at my own house with one of his girls!"

"Does Mort carry a weapon?"

"No. He's a shark. Isn't that enough? Watch out for his teeth."

"Keep calm. Stay inside. I'll speak with him."

"He's trespassing and he's an agent, not a cop. I can call the cops to get rid of him."

"No. Reles and Mueller might be waiting for that call so they can roll up and take you away."

"What will you say to him?"

"When I said I'd 'speak' with him, I didn't really mean I'd speak with him."

"This is my house. Don't hurt him. Not here."

"I promise. I won't hurt him."

You'll never be back here, so you take a chance. You put your arms around Legs Gabrielle and kiss her softly on the mouth. Surprised, she stiffens and then surrenders to you, kissing back. It's an act to savor. A decade of her full lips on yours would be a good beginning.

Before you step off the terrace, you whisper in her ear, "You will never see me again, so remember this: you didn't set any of this in motion. You asked for help because *they* started this. I have the names. If you are ever tempted to feel sorry for any of these men, know that if you hadn't brought us in, you'd be their next victim. Whatever happens to them, it's for you and all the victims they've already made and all the victims they were going to make. Whatever happens is righteous and it's on me."

Her breath smells of champagne but her lips taste of strawberries. She puts her hands on your chest and gently, slowly pushes herself away.

Before you turn to deal with Mort Sheldrake you add, "And don't forget that kiss. I won't."

IN THE MOVIE, JOHN LEGUIZAMO COULD DO THE JOB.

Girls begin to dance with each other on the terrace, casting long, reaching shadows that play over Mort Sheldrake's face. He's kind of handsome. He might still be handsome, past the plugs that look like doll hair and the waxy look people get after too many facelifts. Not even Hollywood money can hold back time. He's a fit 55, looking like 45, but reaching for 35 using the questionable miracles of cosmetic surgery.

Sheldrake talks in low tones to a woman in a red dress. He speaks with an intense, staccato rhythm so you can hear the k's and t's.

You wander closer but at a tangent, just another party guest inspecting the empty pool. The pool is shaped like a piano. Berb told you some one-hit wonder owned this place before Legs and thought he was on the way up until the music industry collapsed and he had to sell the place to pay the IRS.

Sheldrake rings alarm bells but it's the woman who pulls your gaze. Her backless dress displays smooth skin, naked but for a tattoo of a jaguar prowling down the right side of her spine. She shifts from side to side but not in time to the music. She's either nervous or impatient. Her long black hair reaches down her back so the jaguar appears and disappears, appears and disappears.

The woman in the red dress shakes her head. "Don't!"

Sheldrake's face twists into an ugly snarl. He balls his fist and swings at her face. Just before his punch makes contact, he stops and steps close to give her a hug. She flinches in a way you recognize. That's someone who is used to being hit. You used to be like that. Learned helplessness is tough to break.

Then he does it again. His fist comes closer this time. When he steps into another hug, she turns so you catch half of her face in the light. That half is terrified and desperate so you take a wild guess and extrapolate the rest.

You clear your throat.

The guy looks over at you and smiles. "Don't need a drink right now, Jose."

"Ginger sent me."

That startles him. He pushes the girl back, focuses on you.

"Ginger? Ginger who?"

"That was weak. Try again."

"Who are you?"

"I'm Dr. Fix. I fix things. Ginger says you need to get fixed. I'm a vet. I can do that."

"When did she tell you this?"

"I met her late this afternoon."

"I don't think that's the same Ginger I know."

"Did you shave half her head? Or did you just help hold her down while Mueller or Reles — "

He shakes. Not just his head. His hands shake. His body trembles. It's fear, not rage, you see in his eyes. He's not an alpha dog in the rape and murder ring. He doesn't have the stones to be a leader. An innocent man wouldn't wear the face Sheldrake wears now.

"Did Reles tell you to do those things? Is that what helps you sleep at night? You were only following orders?"

"I don't know what you're —"

"You're a murderer, Sheldrake. A john, a pimp, and even, I'm told, a big time agent. What makes a thing like you? Are you a new thing? There are more serial killers than there used to be. Is it the Internet? Is that how sickos find each other?"

Sheldrake turns to the girl with the Jaguar tattoo. She's already slipped away. She runs down the driveway holding her six-inch stilettos high. Makes you smile. Another life saved.

"These things you think you know…"

"Oswald's dead. He died horribly."

"How do you know? When?"

"Earlier this evening. I know because I killed him."

His face does some interesting, subtle things, like it's fighting the paralyzing effects of all that Botox. Mostly his lips push in and out, trying to think fast in panic mode. No one thinks fast, or well, in panic mode.

"Is it money you want?"

"Rich people always think that."

"So…we can negotiate."

"You would think that, wouldn't you? However, you aren't Miss Gabrielle's agent anymore. I'm her agent."

"What?"

"I'm her Agent of Delicious Violence, Divine Vengeance Division."

The guy moves in to push you back. The main mistake rich, white Hollywood douchebags make in these situations is that they don't really want to fight. Whatever confrontations they've been in always crank up slow. It starts with dirty looks and idle threats and slowly escalates to shouting about lawsuits. Even if the guy amps himself up enough to actually fight, he has to warm up to it and get talky. A gawking crowd must gather and his pride must be hurt before he risks his perfect teeth and bloodies his knuckles.

With sex, you start slow, slowly get faster and make it last as long as possible. Strategy in a fight is the opposite of sex: start strong, finish fast. No foreplay. Even in a boxing match, you start out with a couple of jabs and feel out the opponent. That's not the way to go here.

"Don't you know who I — ?"

You knock him sideways with your strongest punch, a right hook to his perfect jaw throwing your hip forward so all the weight of the punch is where it needs to be. His mandible goes sideways. He hasn't even put up his hands yet. With your left hand, you grab the knot of his tie and twist, turning off his air. You use the tie to pull him into the next two punches. His perfect Roman nose pushes off to one side. He still hasn't put up his hands but you give him one more hook to be sure those hands stay down.

Your father, Marco Diaz taught you about the button. A couple of inches in front of the ear is the temporomandibular joint. To allow for chewing, the jaw has to move. The same joint, the button, that allows humans to eat? That's a design flaw in combat. Marco called a vicious hook to that spot, "ringing the bell."

Buttons or bells, you swing on Sheldrake and put your hip behind it again. If he didn't know it before, he gets it now. All his life, Morton Sheldrake has been a fake tough guy.

You were going to finish him with an uppercut. Civilians might think that's overkill, but every fight must be won decisively. If a guy's jaw clicks every time he tries to chew steak, he'll cross continents to avoid meeting you again. However, you don't finish him with an uppercut because Legs holds your arm. She doesn't try to restrain you. Her touch is gentle. She's asking with soft fingers on your shoulder, *don't kill him.*

You open your fist and, placing your hand in the center of his chest, gently push him backward into the pool. He twirls in midair. He's so far gone, he does a Superman and doesn't have it in him to protect himself as his face meets the concrete. It's the deep end, about ten feet down.

"Without water, should we still call it a pool?" you ask. "It should really be called a hole until there's water in it."

"Oh, my God!" she says. "You said you wouldn't…you *killed* him!"

"Maybe he's not dead, but I hope he is because, if not, I'll have to climb down there, drag him up and toss him in again head first."

She winds up and slaps you as hard as she can, which is pretty hard. Sheldrake lets out a ghostly moan of agony.

"It's okay. See? He's okay. Hey! Sheldrake! If you live, tell 'em John Leguizamo did this to you!"

"Chill said you could deal with problems quietly! Chill said you're supposed to be some kind of ninja!"

You look up and the girls on the terrace have stopped dancing. They're staring at you, memorizing your description for when the cops show up, no doubt.

Legs heads for the house. You're about to leave when you see Detective Hank Reles step out of the dark. He's already spotted you and he's marching for you, his gun already out and pointed your way.

His first shots go wide, but not by much. You feel the breath of the slug as it passes your left ear, whispering death. You have practiced many clever replies and movie catchphrases in the mirror. All words abandon you now.

MICRO UZI. 28 ROUNDS PER SECOND. THAT WOULD DO.

There's screaming and chaos in the house. Berb will be on top of Legs Gabrielle. Lucky guy. Skunk will be on his way and maybe Jeremy the Samoan will extricate himself from the refrigerator long enough to come to your rescue, but that's iffy. You might have to save yourself.

Before Reles can shoot again at close range, you throw yourself to the only cover there is: the pool. Mort is struggling to his knees when you land on his back. Some bones crack and give, but it's him, not you. He has cushioned your fall. Sheldrake doesn't even yell. The air goes out of him. He collapses into the concrete, silent. You roll to your back and pull him on top of you.

Reles appears at the edge, peering down at you, pointing his revolver. Mort makes for a pretty flimsy human shield. You key your mic.

"I told you if I ever saw you again, Armando, I'd fuck you up!"

"You don't want to do that!"

He shoots out a chunk of concrete by your head. "Yeah, I really do."

"*Witnesses*, genius! The cavalry is on the way! Security to the pool! Scramble!" You keep the mic open, but you're talking to Reles now. "Detective Hank Reles has just beaten the green shit out of a guest and he's got a gun!"

You dare to show him the mic at your wrist and the coil of wire to your earphone so he knows you aren't bluffing. "It's attempted murder right now. It'll be murder in a second."

You read somewhere that what makes a person smart is that they go through much the same thinking process as the average dummy, but faster. Reles works through the equation fast. He takes one last hurried shot at you and runs.

The bullet misses you, but takes Mort through that precious face he's been getting a Beverley Hills surgeon to tighten up all these years.

You roll Mort off and sprint to the shallow end of the piano, up the steps, and pull your SIG.

Berb shows up at your side, pistol drawn. Skunk appears on the terrace. He's pulled out his Micro Uzi, but looks disappointed he has no target to perforate at twenty-eight rounds per second.

"Client secure?"

"With Jeremy," Skunk barks. "Where'd he go?"

"I'd guess the road and to his car but back up Jeremy in case he doubles back."

As if in answer, a woman's high, anguished scream goes up from the house. That's soon joined by another woman's voice cutting through the night. The natural thing to do would be to run to the screams, but that's no way to proactively deploy forces. Skunk runs to check the commotion. You run for the gate. Keying your mic as you go, you order Berb to keep everyone inside and down. "If I see Reles, he'll be returning fire in this direction."

When you get to the road, it's lined with cars. The only sound is noise from the house you can't make out. It's all just inarticulate shouting. The quiet road is lined by trees. Cold steals over you and, standing out on the dark highway alone, you feel stupid and exposed. You're trying to keep your head, but you just ran out into the road without pause. You slip behind a black Yukon and crane your neck, afraid Reles is behind you and lining up his shot.

"Berb! Report! Did I bet wrong?"

"Reles is not here, Fix."

Speaking must have helped Reles zero in. You hear a guttural report followed by *spang!* Reles puts a hole in the truck's side.

You're relatively safe behind the engine block, but all he has to do is move to get a better angle. A hundred people with cell phones must be, at this moment, calling the cops. You're a fugitive in a gun fight with a cop. That scenario can't end well.

You move around the back of the Yukon until the macadam is under you and you can peer up the road. There's nothing to see but the outlines of cars so you fire a shot to let him know where you are and twist away. Two more shots smack the pavement behind you. You're moving up the side of the road, staying low and sprinting from car to car, hoping he'll get stupid and show himself.

That realization stops you cold. You're hoping a smart guy, trained with weapons, will do something stupid in order for you to succeed. You wait, try to get your breathing under control, and listen. You need back-up to outflank Reles. Chill should have been here by now. With any luck, he's almost here, ready to put holes in Reles's back with his big Redhawk.

Eyes darting, you pull out your phone and call Chill for help.

Chill's ringtone reaches your ears: *It's Raining Men* by the Weather Girls. You make out the outline of Chill's midnight blue Escalade two cars up. Chill didn't report in when he arrived. You already know you're going to get bad news when you open the door to Chill's ride. The question is, how bad will the news be?

FLOATING BOX OF SURVEILLANCE VEHICLES, NOT DUKES OF HAZZARD

A black pickup pulls out fast, fishtailing. You run to Chill's Escalade and haul the door open. The dome light pops on and, out of habit, you glance in the back seat before you jump behind the wheel. Chill's beside you, his bald head bloody and his eyelids swollen closed. He's not up to a conversation.

You check the pulse at his neck. His chest rises and falls regularly. His pulse is strong but he's been beaten badly and blood's everywhere.

"Chill? I need you to wake up, man!" With two knuckles, you dig into his sternum, rubbing up and down hard. Chill stirs from the pain, but he doesn't come around, either.

You bark quick orders into your mic. "Berb, secure the client. Skunk, 10-2 out by the gate."

"10-4," Skunk replies.

"What's going on?" Jeremy asks.

Before you can reply, Skunk chews out the junior bodyguard for you. "Watch the crowd from the stairs and don't let anyone up. Keep the channel clear unless you spot something suspicious."

You fish Chill's keys out of his jacket and leave the door open so he'll be easier for Skunk to find in the dark. You run for the gate.

Skunk is in your ear. "Who needs EMS?"

"Number One. He's in the back of his ride, just west of the gate. Door's open, no bad guys in sight."

"Roger that."

Skunk's still in your ear and you almost run into each other by the gate. You order Skunk to give you his keys. He doesn't hesitate and he points at his red Crown Vic a few cars down the road, parked so it's pointed back to the city. Good man.

Berb chimes in, but only to report, "Client's secure." His tone is flat and angry. There's something else in his voice, but you can only process so much at one time.

At Skunk's Crown Vic, you pause and use the pen light from your shirt pocket to check it before you jump in. No one's in the back seat waiting to brain you with a lead pipe. There's no time for this. The bad guy is getting away. You hop behind the wheel and gun the engine.

"Fix?" Skunk's breathing hard.

"How bad is he?"

"He's out. He's lost a lot of blood."

The road winds through the Hills. If you had time to check out your phone's GPS you'd have a better sense of where you are. You've rarely ventured into this part of Los Angeles and nothing looks familiar. Big, well-lit homes far from the road flash by here and there. To your right are sheer drops. To your left are tight corners you take at ill-advised speeds. There's a wonderful view of city lights from up here, but a moment's distraction will kill you. You were too far away to catch the license plate on the pickup so you have to catch up to Reles.

Horns blare as you pass slower vehicles and a couple of times you're forced to cut in quick to avoid a head-on collision. You hate this. Some guys love to race cars and learn to do donuts in high school parking lots. You never went to high school and the first thing you drove was an Army Jeep. The only vehicle you ever really enjoyed was a Humvee in the desert, government issue and armored up. There was a lot more room for error then, even when jumping a sand dune.

If you overtake Reles up in the Hills, you have a chance at getting him. Once he hits the rabbit's warren of city streets, he'll lose you easily. You press the accelerator harder.

This is no way to chase anyone. To do this properly, you should have five cars keeping him in a floating box of surveillance vehicles. Chasing people in a car is stupid. Better to pick them up when they aren't looking for you in the rearview mirror. With a car set up so the brake lights don't light up, you can even follow any bad guy surreptitiously from in front. Since he already knows you're after him and you don't have access to a helicopter, you're going at this all wrong, as if this is some kind of car chase from bad TV.

An ambulance roars past, lights and sirens all the way, climbing to rescue Chill. You click your body rig radio to let them know the paramedics are just minutes away, but all you get is static. You're beyond the broadcast range of Chill's crew. If you catch up to Reles, you forgot to pack another handy human shield. Your cell rings and you almost wreck as you dig it out of your suit jacket.

"Fix?"

"Kinda busy right now, Berb." You don't bother to explain. The squeal of your tires in that last turn should do that. "The client's secure, right?" Your pulse was already racing. Now it's a very fast drumbeat.

"She's not feeling very secure. In her bedroom, there's blood all over the walls."

"Shit."

"Some of that, too," Berb says. "How'd he get past us?"

"He must have already been in the house before the party started. I guarantee he was in the closet in the master bedroom, probably taking pictures of Legs as she changed into that fabulous dress." You catch an anguished cry in the background.

"Uh, got you on speakerphone, dude. Miss Gabrielle is right here."

The Crown Vic slides sideways too much on the shoulder and you almost tip. You wrestle the wheel, ease up on the gas and get the car back under control.

"Take me off goddamn speakerphone, Berb!"

"Done."

"Convey my apologies and assure Miss Gabrielle that when I catch Reles, I'll bring back his phone. I'll also present her with any pictures that are on said phone and whichever hand he jerks off with. Relay that just as I said it. She'll feel better."

"What's your location? Can you see the guy's vehicle? I'll call it in to the cops."

"Negative, boy scout. Call the cops to the house. I've got the takedown."

"Gotta be honest, it's pretty freaky here."

"Whose blood is on the walls? Have you found a body yet?"

"It's bad, but it's roadkill. He left a message in blood."

You hit a straight shot at the bottom of a hill and catch a glimpse of the black pickup ahead, turning left through a red light at the next intersection. You're out of the Hills and exactly where you don't want to be, careening though the city. "Don't keep me guessing. I hate a mystery. What's the message?"

"It says, 'Catch you later.'"

Those were Reles last words to you back at the cafe. He's playing, as if Legs's life is just a game and no one else matters. Is that a message to Legs alone, or is he putting you on notice, too?

"How do you know the blood's from roadkill?"

"It's still here. There's a dead raccoon in her bed."

"Uncool, dude. That'll spoil the mood."

STARCHASE IS REAL. DRIVERS, SLOW DOWN.

You're almost on top of Reles when the lights and sirens fire up behind you. You turn on Skunk's police scanner and, naturally, they're talking about you.

"You got him?"

"Got him," the CHP cop behind you answers. "Now that I'm on him, pull over and see if he stops."

Under different circumstances, you would stop and hash this out. Those "different circumstances" include not being wanted by the FBI. If an officer of the law is going to decide about a difference of opinion between Detective Reles and a brownish Hispanic man such as yourself? You're going to get beaten senseless before you're murdered.

In the best case scenario, this chase ends with you shot or beaten. If you don't end up dead, they'll put you in a federal prison or in Gitmo wishing you were dead. The things you did right won't matter. They don't even have to charge you to keep you in a cage forever anymore if it doesn't suit them. Better write a new best case scenario fast.

Reles slows and pulls over like a law-abiding citizen. You give him the finger as you shoot past him. More sirens fire up and the police scanner chatters at you as more of the LAPD joins the chase.

You weave in and out of slower traffic — all traffic is slower than you tonight — but you've got no plan that could possibly end well. Not yet. Just as you're thinking you've got to lose them before they bring a helicopter into the pursuit, you hear the whir of rotor blades overhead.

The cop behind you speeds up close and tells you through his speaker to pull over. As if you didn't understand the premise of Cops and Robbers.

This couldn't get worse. At least you thought so until you hear a light thunk behind you. The cop on the scanner can't contain his enthusiasm when he says, "Got him! Starchase deployed."

Things just got worse.

A supervisor somewhere back there tells the officer in closest pursuit to back off. They've tagged the Crown Vic with a GPS stuck to the back with an epoxy compound. It sounds like something out of a sci-fi movie, but the LAPD have been using these little tattle tale devices since 2006.

You wrench the wheel right and head west. As long as you keep your speed high, they won't try to box you in. You weave right and left every few intersections so they won't anticipate where you're headed and set up a spike belt. They think they already have you, which is the only hope you have.

When you're speeding through city streets, it's difficult to wipe away your fingerprints. By the time you get to Santa Monica Pier, the cops have lost patience and the helicopter's bright white searchlight beams down on you like the eye of God. The cruisers in pursuit hang back so maybe they're hoping you'll come to your senses and slow down, or at least run out of gas. If there were a busy mall, you could try to lose yourself there, but nothing nearby is that busy this time of night.

The police have got the copter and the tracker on you so they're trying to avoid pushing you to speed faster in the city. Prudent. You're driving crazy so you're very close to killing someone besides yourself. If you slow down, they might try a pit maneuver and bump you, forcing you to fishtail and spin out. If this chase goes on much longer, they'll try ramming you repeatedly.

You pull out your phone and dial Sgt. Billy. He doesn't answer. You call back, cursing him. You end up driving in circles and then figure eights, keeping your pattern unpredictable. Your pursuers will be smiling. In every other car chase they've ever been in, the perp was trying to get home. When they're in trouble, everyone heads home. You aren't an ordinary perp. You're a force for divine justice whose sidekick won't answer the fucking phone.

"Yeah?"

"Billy!"

"Yeah?"

"Why didn't you answer the phone?"

"I got a life. Havin' a bath."

"Me, too, in a minute. Get yourself to that place you like, not far from Santa Monica pier. As soon as you can."

"Why?"

"They've got good food."

"Anything else?"

"Bring donuts! Copy?"

"Yeah, yeah. Fine."

"I love you, Sergeant!"

"Oh, shit! It's serious!"

You hang up on him, grip the wheel and press the accelerator so Skunk's old Crown Vic roars as the new Interceptor engine broils under the hood. The floorboards are cut so the accelerator pedal can go a little deeper and open the monster's throat a little wider, delivering a little more punch. Skunk is going to be pissed about what you're going to do to his refurbished car.

BUTTON MAN IS A TOUGH JOB. BECOME A DENTIST INSTEAD, KIDS!

It's so late, it's almost early, which is good because only a few young couples and late-night tourists wander the pier this time of night.

You lay on the horn and keep it pressed. You floor it again, heading straight out for the water. The Bubba Gump Shrimp company flashes by on your left. You've never eaten there and now you probably never will. There's a Ferris wheel back there. The last time you were on a Ferris wheel was Coney Island with your first real love and your best friend. If there was one good, uncomplicated day, it would be that one. You'll try to think of that in your last moments as you drown.

You arrested a Navy Seal for making trouble in a bar in Germany once. He told you that when he was trained, the other candidates drowned him. Every Seal got drowned and then resuscitated by the other trainees. As you put him in the drunk tank, he told you, "You get high from the lack of oxygen to your brain and feel euphoria when you stop struggling against the water." You hope he was telling the truth and that's not just macho bullshit.

You will not allow yourself to be taken alive. Whatever happens, you aren't going to prison and there's no macho bullshit about that vow. You spent years as a prisoner to two sadists as a kid. Prison or that terrible basement in Miami: it's all the same to you and you won't go through that horror again.

Maybe this end is as it should be. You should be dead several times over: Miami, New Jersey, New York, Chicago. You could have died many times. You should have treated this trip to California as something extra. Instead, you soaked up the sun's heat and told yourself you wanted to live forever. You got greedy for more life and now God's going to show you how wrong that bit of whimsy was.

You destroy a sign that reads: Closed to traffic. Now that you're on the pier, the boards under the Crown Vic sound like a hundred thundering hoofbeats.

Maybe the seatbelt will save you or maybe you'll be trapped in the car all the way to the bottom. A crazy thought crosses your mind: *My father will be waiting for me there.* But, of course, whatever might be left of Marco Diaz is amongst the deep coral off Florida's coast, somewhere around Surfside Beach if the currents didn't carry his remains farther out after the sharks were done.

The steel fence along the dock looks strong. At this speed, you figure it will part for you like balsa wood. Instead, the crash into the fence slows you and the car hits the edge of the dock like a pole vault. The nose goes down and the airbags deploy and you're cartwheeling. When you're airborne, your foot's still pressing the accelerator through the floor and the engine revs up, as if exhilarated at the sudden lack of friction.

Then things…slow…down. It's as if you're already underwater and trying to make sense of the world with eyes that perceive with hyperacuity. A spring in your brain is sprung and the works are turning at a quarter speed.

It feels like the roller coaster at Coney Island, the way your butt is lifted out of the seat a little, but this time you're upside down.

Now you're not.

Now you're upside down and now you aren't sure as you squeeze your eyes tight and throw up across the dashboard.

Ah, you were right side up, judging by the arc of the vomit. If not for the seatbelt, you'd break your neck when your head hit the roof.

Should you brace for impact with the water and risk breaking a leg? Or try to relax and imagine you are boneless and let the seatbelt do the work? The airbags are already deflating.

Before you can work out the right answer, the Crown Vic hits the water harder than you expect (and you expected the impact to feel like you were running into a brick wall).

Time and your brain slowed together when you were flying through the air. Now time speeds up, going way too fast to keep up. You aren't thinking anymore. You are not the smart ninja assassin you thought you'd finally become.

Dr. Fix is fucked and not in a good way.

READ THE PLAYBOOK FOR DATING TIPS A LA
ALBERT CAMUS

Your mother drowned. Your brother was chopped up by boat propellers and drowned. Your father drowned. That was a tough day off Surfside Beach.

You only lived because a murderous monster you called the Bug Man saved you for his torture chamber in a basement. Since you escaped the Bug Man and his evil mistress, Tia Marta, you've always suspected you were cursed. Despite all the bullets that habitually fly in your direction, you expected to die drowning at the bottom of the ocean.

Vicodin got you away from those dark thoughts for a while. Then you found vengeance was a higher high. As the car hits the water, you realize you probably should have stuck with Vicodin. As you begin to sink, you remember Dallas and Albert Camus.

You met Dallas in a military jail in Germany. You'd just punched a superior officer. Dallas was charged with stealing stuff from the PX to sell on the black market. You'd killed a couple of people by then, but you didn't consider yourself a criminal. Not yet.

What impressed you most about Dallas was his overwhelming confidence. Prison didn't bother him. When he said, "Yes, sir," his emphasis was always on the *yes*. He dipped the *sir* so low, it's amazing he didn't get regular shit duty for insolence.

Dallas was a Private, six feet high and four feet wide. He got into the Army after 9/11 like you did, but he got in after the powers that be were desperate and loosened the physical fitness restrictions. He hadn't done a pushup since boot. Despite his lowly status, Dallas was supremely confident with women. He was everything you were not.

"I got into the Army for the uniform, man," he said. "Ladies dig the uniform. I'da gone with fireman, but they wouldn't take me."

As you waited for your court martial, Dallas schooled you on his pickup artistry. "Uniform's the first thing. After I get out of here, I'll still wear it. What's the Army gonna do? Keep me from buying stuff at military surplus stores? Shit, I shoulda thought of that before. I'da had me a chest full of fruit salad. The ladies love medals and ribbons. I could go to any house party and tell 'em how I won the war."

"We didn't win," you told him.

"Maybe so, but we'll never say so, am I right?"

"You're right."

"I'll tell you something else, man…I run the ladies several at a time. I never get caught."

You looked at him wearily and asked how he got caught stealing from the PX.

He shrugged and smiled and refused to say. He'd seen you around the base with MP on your shoulder just days before so he wasn't going to talk about his case. You suspected he was stealing so he could finance all the dating he did with the local German women.

"I don't understand a word they say, but I sure like the way they say it," Dallas said. "They say what they want to say and I imagine the translation is all, 'Dallas, you're the best! Dallas don't leave me! Dallas, no man has ever made me feel this way!'"

"Maybe they're saying, 'Dallas, you sweat too much!'"

"Oh, man! Why'd you have to go and say that? I was about to give you the key to dating several women at a time with no problems. You're cut off. Suffer in silence, man."

Jail is boring. You said nothing for twenty minutes. It was Dallas who caved first. He laid out his dating strategy.

"Flirt with your eyes, man. That's the first thing."

"I thought the uniform was the first thing."

"*Sh.* I'm giving you the keys to the palace here. Next…where was I?"

"Flirting with your eyes. Even the lazy one?"

"My mother says that gives me character."

"Well, she would say that, right? What next?"

"Smile wide. That's the second thing. Chicks love a man who isn't the strong, silent type. That gets boring quick. I learned watching my older brothers. The shy ones don't date. Next is, be deep. You gotta keep it light and flirt, but you gotta throw some intelligence around. Talk about Albert Camus."

"Who?"

"That's it, right there. That's why you're in here for violence and I'm in here for spreading the love, man. You don't know Camus, you don't get laid. You got to know Camus. You don't get laid, some of that fluid pressure builds up and the next thing you know, you're taking a swing at your C.O. or something. You wanna be a swinger, you gotta be one with the Camus!"

"I'm listening."

"You gotta be sly. You slide it in that you're reading this book by Albert Camus. Suppose you're at a party and you give a lady the eye and she gives you a second glance. She don't know it, but you're already halfway to third base.

You're looking sharp in your uniform."

"And if you aren't in uniform?"

"At least wear nice shoes. Sneakers are for dudes who hang out with other dudes in the gym. Don't be that guy. You dress nice, ladies notice."

"Okay. So she's given me a second look. Then what?"

"Lots of guys got lines and they're all bad. Don't put a line on a girl. You walk right up, eye contact, big smile and you introduce yourself. You get her name and you use it right away so you don't forget it."

"Is this a party girl you're talking to or are you trying to pass around business cards at a Toastmaster's meeting?"

Dallas laughed. "That's the pickup artist's problem. He's always looking for the shortcut. He don't know Camus. Besides, you wanna see somebody naked, she's gotta know you see her as a person. You wanna get to first base, you gotta let her know your mama churched you and raised you right."

"My mom's dead. We didn't do church."

"Hold off on the dead mom, man. If you aren't getting anywhere by the third date, you could try going dark. I don't recommend it. Dark ain't deep. It's just depressing. I'm talking about first date action."

"Okay."

"So…where was I?"

"You were about to sell her aluminum siding and take her to church."

"Right. Handshake. Smile. You tell her, 'Hi, I'm Jesus Diaz. It's spelled like the Son of God but pronounced Hay-soose.'"

"Yeah, I'm kind of tired of that."

"Never mind. Tell her your Jose Conseco. Whatever. I'm getting to the good stuff."

"Sorry."

"You tell that party girl who's been hit on all night, 'What books are you reading?' And make sure you say books, not book. You're subtly communicating to her fine ass that you're intelligent but you also think she's intelligent. No pickup line does that."

"I do have a thing for women who wear glasses," you admit.

"All right, all right, roger-dodger. Now you have to let her know your lights are on. This is where you slide in the Camus."

"Is that a dick joke?"

"No. No, man. It's not."

"Oh."

"Can I continue?"

"Sure."

"You tell her you're blown away by this Algerian philosopher you been reading. You say, 'People think he was an existentialist, but he was actually an absurdist.'" Dallas clapped his hands and showed his palms like he'd just performed a startling magic trick.

You stared at him for a moment. "I'm going to have a nap now."

"You're *missing* it, man! Camus wrote these cool ass stories about how he's gotta go to his mother's funeral and he kills a dude."

"Sounds depressing. I thought down wasn't the same as deep?"

"Context for your play, Jesus. It's all about context. She's thinking you're a deep, sensitive kind of guy and then you add the magic spell. You tell her how fascinating Camus was because he was all for personal and *sexual* freedom. You drop that on her and then you can get with the flirty and the double innuendos."

"Double entendres?"

"Yeah. Whatever. French shit's good, too."

"This works? It can't. You don't even understand any German!" You laid back on your bunk and closed your eyes.

"No, man. This is for running your game when we get out of here and head back home."

"So, here, you're just going to German prostitutes."

"Man, I'm trying to pass the time and giving you gold and here you come, all about judgment and shit."

"Fine. You done?"

"You're being rude, but I'm going to give you the secret formula that lets you run several ladies at a time without one of them waking you up one morning by cutting your dick off."

You sat up and nodded. "I do want to know how to avoid that."

"When you're all flirty and she's all flirty and you both know it's going somewhere? You tell her, 'It is a fucking tragedy I have a girlfriend.'"

"*What?*"

"Yeah. I know, right?"

"You're insane."

"No, no, man. Now she knows you got value. If you're single, there's something wrong. You're communicating to her that she's a fantasy and you're already proven and tested your own self."

"I'm going to sleep. Some girl is going to kill you."

"Lemme finish. I haven't laid the magic words on her yet. You make like you're about to go. You begin with a goodbye handshake, but then you kiss the back of her hand, like you can't help yourself. Then you say, 'You are such a beautiful person…such a *sexy* woman…my God, what fun we could have had if you only could keep a secret…*Ta-da!*'"

"Ta-da? What then?"

"Then you walk away."

"I walk away?"

"You walk away." Dallas smiles. "She'll follow you out to your car. Don't chase women, man. Let them chase you. You find one you like, you let 'em catch you."

"This is your dating strategy?"

"Absolutely. Do that five times a night and you never go home alone. One of five girls will follow you out to your car. You're letting her take the responsibility of being the predator for a change. You're just a little rabbit who can't help himself in the face of her stunning beauty."

"What about the other four girls who laugh in your face?"

"They aren't smart enough for you. Any girl gets with me, she's gotta be down with the Camus and personal and sexual freedom. You want a big life after we get out of here? Read some Camus."

"I still think somebody's going to cut your dick off."

"Not before I make full use of it," Dallas said. His belly convulsed in ripples as he giggled.

As you sink into the Pacific, that memory of Dallas sitting in the corner of a cell, shirtless, his torso convulsing with each high giggle, comes back to you.

Why now? Because you're about to drown. Your life is about to be cut short and you have not made full use of it.

HOW NOT TO ESCAPE DROWNING IN A CAR

Exhibit 1 in your diary of a death by drowning in a car: The seatbelt is way too hard to figure out.

Your hands shake and your feet are cold. You try to slow your breathing because smart ninjas don't die by drowning. Your body doesn't want to cooperate with your orders. Though the autopsy report will say death by drowning, it should read: Death by the intersection of Panic and Stupid.

Exhibit 2: Your feet are already wet and you still aren't out of that seatbelt. Is the buckle jammed or are your fingers just numb, cold and dumb as all the blood rushes to your core? You glance in the rearview mirror. The face you barely recognize looks frantic, wild-eyed and white with shock.

Exhibit 3: You should have tried to open the door immediately, while there were only a few inches at the bottom of the door. Did you float for long while you sat in the driver's seat, dazed, confused and staring ahead at the Pacific's expanse stretching to Japan? You'll never see Japan, now, bonehead.

Exhibit 4: You finally figure out the deep intricacies of the seatbelt buckle and free yourself. You push at the door, but the water's already up to the window. You should be saving your strength for the nosedive to the bottom. You're plunging into darkness. How far a drop is it to the bottom? Maybe you should have kept that seatbelt on. Damn.

Exhibit 5: When the Pacific closes over the car, instinctively, you duck. Clearly, your instincts suck. Plus, that happened a minute ago but you're only remembering it now. Nothing makes sense. Time is messed up.

Exhibit 6: You're scrambling to get the seatbelt back on when the front bumper hits the bottom with a muted crash, and the car goes over unevenly, like it's hit sand and rock and silt. You had pictured a soft landing on all four tires. Instead, the bang rattles your teeth and you're plunged into the darkness of a dust cloud that blots out the headlights. Cold water climbs to your neck, shaking you further and jangling every nerve.

Exhibit 7: The water inside and outside should equalize the pressure on the door. You push hard. The door doesn't budge. The impact with the fence or with the Pacific's bottom must have jammed the doors shut. When you dig out your pen light, you discover your door is locked. The lock on a new Crown Vic should pop even if it is locked. This is an old Crown Vic. You should have listened when Skunk carried on about his alterations to his precious ride. Instead, you nodded politely and tuned out. You're losing time.

Exhibit 8: The lights are out, but for some reason you can't fathom, you're wasting more time trying the electric windows. You want to take a deep breath to calm down, but the cabin is quickly filling with water. The cold slap in your face says you don't have the luxury of the time it takes to be Zen about your looming demise.

Exhibit 9: You close your eyes and Lily pops up. You thought you were going to marry her. You've thought you were going to marry several women, but you walked away from them. Lily's the one who walked away from you. Lily's saying something. She looks angry. Lily often looked angry but no less beautiful. Then you get it. She's screaming, "You don't have time for this! Wake up, Jesus. *Resurrect, bitch!*"

It's time to be Batman, if Batman packed a SIG Sauer P220. You take a last breath, pull your pistol and fire out the window. The driver's side window splinters and the rest of the Pacific runs in to the roof.

The rear tires aren't down, either because you're tipped on the ocean floor or because there's an air bubble back there. There's supposed to be. You've got an SAS manual and they always sound sure about these things. However, the SAS manual is about escaping a submerged vehicle. They didn't have a chapter devoted to escaping the police after escaping a submerged vehicle.

Your father taught you how to swim in Cuba, but you haven't been in the ocean, or even a pool with water in it, since you were a kid. Nearly drowning and the subsequent kidnapping in Florida messed up your plans for more beach-going fun. You swore you'd never get in the water again. You pull yourself through the window and head back toward the pier, into the teeth of your pursuers. That still feels cozier than the trap of an underwater metal tomb.

You break the surface and cling to the bottom of the pier, gasping. You're cold, but the air tastes sweet. A police helicopter comes into view and you dive again, heading around the pier. It's a long swim back to the pilings underneath the amusement park.

Somewhere in the long swim underwater, you lose your Tanini Crisci shoes. You're exhausted, but memories drive you on. The image of your drowning father chases you to shore.

Losing $1,200 shoes puts things in perspective. Some guys would get spiritual about escaping near-death. A lot of men would take this perilous misadventure as a sign to disappear to Mexico and start a quiet life of charity, peace and contemplation. But you aren't going to start chewing granola, go barefoot and become a vegan now.

The attack on Chill makes you want to kill Hank Reles very much, of course. Losing those expensive shoes makes you want to kill him, but to do the job slower.

And what those men did to Ginger in Oswald's secret slave room? That makes you think an Apocalypse would be a peachy idea right about now. If that's what the world is underneath, why live?

HOW TO EQUIP A SURVEILLANCE VAN

When you reach the shore and hide under the pier, there's still a better than even chance that the police chopper will spot you. However, they're focusing on where you went, not where you are. The helicopter hovers a few feet above the water drilling deep with their searchlight. Reles pulls to the edge of the pier first and stands there, staring at the water, hands in his pockets, probably smirking.

The CHP cruiser screeches to a stop behind him. That hero doesn't hesitate to pull off his shoes, holster, belt and radio gear. The cop slams his stuff on the hood of his car and jumps into the Pacific, intent on saving you.

You forgot. They aren't all bad. You were one of them once. Okay...so don't blow up the world. A few are worth saving.

You creep away before the forces for earthly justice expand their search and set up a perimeter.

You walk away, then you run, then you walk, alternating between inconspicuous and terrified. Finally, you rest and shiver under a table at the International Chess Park. It's not really a park. There isn't any grass. It's just a place people come to play chess with strangers.

The irony isn't lost on you. You've had three run-ins with Detective Hank Reles. At the coffee shop he saw through your play too easily. In Legs Gabrielle's dry pool, you played him to a draw. As car chases go, he beat you bad. You're alive and not in custody, but that was mostly dumb luck.

Before dawn, you pull yourself up and make your way toward the rendezvous point. It's two miles. The police could pick you up at any time. You hope Sgt. Billy remembered to bring the surveillance van. You won't relax until you're safely hidden behind those tinted windows and blackout curtains. If you'd had time to plan ahead, you would have asked for a towel, a change of clothes and shoes. A different face, a fresh name and a new life would be good, too. Something safe, possibly in advertising.

Chill keeps a white panel surveillance van in a garage not far from his office. Behind its tinted windows are three pieces of gear: low-light, very low light and zoom cameras. Chill paid close to $10,000 just for the cameras. There's also a periscope, a computer, remote joysticks to control the cameras from a custom console and audio and video recording equipment. It looks like any other commercial van on the street except for the dual antennae, but that's only a tip off to people who look closely.

Unlike a typical surveillance van, Chill also invested in commercial camouflage. Several different magnetic signs can plaster the sides of the vehicle. Chill's crew calls it the bakery wagon because, most of the time, the sign across the hood and rear reads: *Grace's Baking.*

Grace's Baking is a tribute to Chill's mother, Grace Gillie. Down the side, the slogan reads in bright yellow letters: *Try our donuts! The burnt ones are free!* Chill says the company name is a subtle nod to Grace's marijuana habit. The slogan acknowledges that his mom's cooking sucked.

The Rose Cafe and Market opens at 7 a.m. You arrive there by 7:15. Sgt. Billy is waiting for you in the van, chewing Eggs Scandia. That's poached eggs on a croissant with lox. He's got one for you, too. You're grateful and starving.

Sgt. Billy waits until you're seated, hands you the food and a little plastic fork. The coffee is still hot. You take a deep breath and get comfortable in your chair. It's a race to see if you can finish breakfast before you fall asleep. But you can't eat or sleep. You can only cry because Billy tells you Chill, your boss and friend, is dead.

HOW NOT TO MEET A CELEBRITY

Sgt. Billy delivers you safely home, such as it is. The ceiling leaks when it rains and the wood is rotting around you. When your business is done in L.A., you'll have to move on. Hollywood will never be the same without Chill. Without Chill, who will save you from yourself?

From the moment you met Chillie Gillie in Chicago, he showed you a way out of the thug life. Like you, he'd done things of which he was not proud. He'd put the bad stuff behind him and gave you a job and a future. Chill took you in and encouraged you to use your talents more cleverly.

Sgt. Billy hands you a cappuccino. The espresso machine, the laptops and the weaponry are the only fancy bits of tech in this dump. You've got a hotplate for a stove and a tiny fridge for the cream. Your bed is a futon thrown on the floor.

Sgt. Billy used to live on the streets of Chicago so this is a step up for him. For you? The hope Chill offered was what kept you here. The California sunshine elevated your mood. Now? You might need to hit the anti-depressants again. And by "anti-depressants" you mean seek an even more terrible vengeance against Reles and his crew.

"How you doin', Chief?"

"Okay. Did you call Skunk?"

"Yeah. He reported his car stolen. The cops haven't called him yet, but he knows the deal." The old man sighs. "I never thought Chill would go before me. My heart works at forty percent and I'm so creaky in the morning. Have to get up six times in the night to piss. Prostate's prolly the size of a softball. And Chill was such a tough son of a bitch."

He was. After he was stabbed in Chicago, he pulled himself out of a hospital bed early so he could get back to his life in Hollywood.

"You're awfully quiet, Ace. Longest time I've heard you go without crackin' off a joke. I don't get your jokes all the time, but — "

"I'm thinking of something Chill said to me, Billy. He said I don't have to pull my pistol out every time. He asked me to use a little finesse and stay righteous."

"Chill was smarter than you."

"Yeah."

"We're in a crazy business, Jesus. We see pretty people up on a screen forty feet high, the nuts get jealous or they think they know 'em or own 'em. It's just a matter of time before somebody kills or captures the idols they worship."

A few people do get insane about celebs, but they aren't all as crazy as Detective Hank Reles is about Legs Gabrielle. You've definitely felt star struck, too. You met Joe Rogan in a Whole Foods parking lot once and you still curse yourself and burn with embarrassment at the memory.

You couldn't seem to stop yourself from quizzing Rogan about his old sitcom, *News Radio*. The episode in which the cast bid a fond farewell to comedian Phil Hartman was the only episode of a television show that made you cry. Funny and loveable, Hartman was murdered in his sleep.

Murdered while helpless. That's your second biggest fear, next to drowning.

"Chill was proud of you most when you held back a little, Jesus. His favorite was the game show case." Sgt. Billy's cackle ends in a cough and a wheeze.

Despite everything, you allow a small smile. In the case of the Tank versus the game show host, Chill approved your play. A powerlifter named Chris Gardenia ran a gym in Pasadena. He shot steroids into his ass so heavily, he was known to police as a habitual 'roid rager and road rager. ("Known to police" is a cop euphemism for "an asshole we can't seem to keep in jail for long.")

His fellow gym rats called him Tank because of his penchant for getting into fights with bouncers. His move was to run at club security from behind and slam them into walls. Then the floor. The guy had an unhealthy obsession with moving heavy shit up and down in the form of barbells. He was such a hard juicer that the steroids had swollen his jaw east and west, much like Reles. Tank also had an obsession with a top game show host.

Think of the top game show hosts. The one that first comes to mind was Tank's intended victim. Tank Gardenia — all muscle, obsessive personality and zero charm — was determined to become best friends with said game show host, even if it meant doing something stupid. Doing something stupid is usually what's required for an ordinary mortal/stalker to meet a celeb. However, few stalkers of your experience are smart enough to get on a game show (even the most moronic game shows.)

Tank's solution was to follow the talk show host from a taping at the studio. When the host backed out of a Trader Joe's parking space, the stalker saw his chance. Tank shot forward in his Camaro — yes, of course, it was a fucking Camaro — and made sure the celebrity backed into him. One dented fender later, Tank had the game show host's insurance information, including the celeb's address and phone number.

This minor accident did not blossom into the game show guy and Captain Road Rage becoming besties forever. The friendly phone calls imploring the celeb to train with Tank began. Those phone calls soon got less friendly. Next, Tank demanded the host take him to dinner at Melisse.

"If you don't want to meet with me for dinner, take me to lunch and hang out, instead," Tank said. "I'll show you what you should be eating."

The host politely declined.

"I understand. But you'll understand if I do something crazy with your address. I could put it up on the net, for instance. So if I were you, I'd get with my program and forget about calling the police or getting a restraining order. You do that, maybe I'll bang your girlfriend or shoot your dog. I'm trying to be nice, here, but you don't seem to want to listen to reason. I'm not like your regular fans, bro. I'm your super fan. I'm looking out for you!"

The host gave Tank the name and number of his lawyer for any further inquiries about fixing his car. Game show guy hung up and changed his number and tried to forget the crazed muscle man.

Then a shitty old Camaro with a dent in its front fender started sliding by his front gate each night. Game show guy spent more money on his security system and put another lock on his bedroom door. The Camaro came back, three or four nights a week at odd times, driving slow as the driver laid on the horn.

When Tank appeared at the dog park and held the host's little pug in his massive hands, smiling and petting the animal, the game show host finally got really scared.

Sitting safe in Chill's office, game show guy shook as he told about the look on the steroid freak's face.

"Tank said, 'I own you. You think you're so high and mighty and rich and famous, but backing into my car is all it takes for me to be your lord and master. It's so easy. I know where you live. I know who your friends are. I know where your mom lives. What are you going to do? Nothing. Nothing but what I tell you.'"

Game show guy promised to take Tank to lunch. Then he hurried away with his little dog and ran to Chill. Tank's target didn't need a restraining order or more police patrols in his neighborhood. He called the professionals because he needed a smart ninja on his side.

HOW NOT TO KILL A STALKER

"Don't kill the Tank," Chill said.

"He needs it," you said.

"Find another way."

"What if we don't call it a shooting? How about…lead poisoning at 1,150 feet per second?"

"How about no?"

"But one trigger pull is so easy."

"Think about it longer. Be imaginative," Chill said.

You didn't have to destroy Tank's computer and set fire to his house. He'd left his computer on and his browser open when he went off to work. It would have been fun to get into Tank's bank account and make some bank transfers to charity. However, you didn't have those passwords.

Fortunately, Tank left the file on the computer's desktop with all the information he'd gathered on Chill's client. It wasn't just the game show host that Tank obsessed over. Tank had a list of targets. As you scanned the names, you realized he had a stalker file on the entire cast of *Family Ties*. You tossed that in the computer's trash can, too, and erased it.

To take out Tank, you needed something strong. You searched his apartment. The rich have safes for money, jewels and guns. The poor keep their cash, porn and guns under the mattress. The middle class always keep their valuables in the sock drawer. Tank had a spare credit card hidden in his sock drawer in the bedroom. You spent half an hour downloading child porn to Tank's computer using his credit card.

There are, of course, too many sex offenders in the world for the police to get to in a timely manner. It was necessary to get the cops' attention. You printed some labels.

You checked in with Sgt. Billy. Your elderly sidekick was in the donut van, inches from Tank's back bumper in a traffic jam on the Glendale Freeway. Plenty of time.

You emailed Tank's boss and, pretending to be Tank, announced that you were quitting immediately because you were "sick of dealing with his shit."

You wrote that Tank had taken a copy of all the gym's account information.

You wrote that data would be useful for when he opened his own gym. You railed on quite a bit — spewing hatred, curses and racial epithets on Tank's behalf.

You implied that if you didn't cool off over the weekend, you might return to work and "shoot the whole gym in the goddamn face."

Workplace shootings almost always involve a disgruntled employee facing Monday morning. You added a link to an old video of the Boomtown Rats singing about a school shooting. *I don't like Mondays.* Good song, and sure to earn Tank a no-knock entry from SWAT.

You set the email so it wouldn't send until Tank was home so he'd have no deniability. As strained as police forces are — and strained they must be since they haven't caught you, yet — two more stops were in order.

At a sleazy corner store where most of the security cameras were obvious fakes, you loaded up on the most explicit and imaginative porn you can find in paper: Gay, straight and fetish. You had no idea there were still so many varieties of these kinds of magazines. Really poor perves can't afford computers, so there must still be a market for the paper variety of porn.

The magazines are strangely specific: whole magazines devoted to one subject, like footjob cuckolding. This is the sort of lunacy the Internet was built for. Who still buys this stuff unless they're on a mission to get rid of a stalker?

To whit, your next stop is the nearest library. In the car, you stick the labels on each of the magazines. Each label reads the same:

This generous donation of literature made possible by Chris Gardenia. Train with me at my gym so you look this good naked, too!

As you browse the library shelves, you slip the magazines at random intervals among the books in the Religion section.

The police will get several irate calls from elderly library patrons and, of course, Tank's boss, in short order. The boss will want to retrieve the information on Tank's computer, which, of course, isn't there. Though that beef is a civil matter, the added boost of an anonymous tip from an anguished librarian should get a warrant to cart off his computer.

In your call to the tip line, you will complain that a man matching Tank's unique description wanted to take naked pictures of your son. You followed him from the elementary school down the street to Tank's address. That will surely light a fire under the asses of local law enforcement. Tank's tiny mind will be fully occupied with other pursuits besides threatening famous game show hosts. There will be no more midnight runs past his favorite game show host's house.

You also added Tank's home address to the labels, in case some devout NRA-loving churchgoer wants to have a productive chat with Tank about putting all-anal porn in amongst the old issues of *Guns & Ammo.*

Sgt. Billy rouses you from your warm reverie. "Do you think you may have overdone it on that job, Jesus? Even though you didn't shoot anybody?"

"The cops are overworked and there are too many bad guys to catch. They need all our support and encouragement."

"When will Tank get out of jail, anyway?"

"He'll be away so long, when he comes out he'll no longer be 'known to police.'"

"So…what's next for us? Now that the boss has passed on?"

"Chill didn't pass on, Billy. He died of a brain hemorrhage after Reles fractured his skull."

Sgt. Billy stares at you for a moment more. "You want to use your imagination again, don't you?"

You shrug. "Mostly I just want to shoot Hank Reles and Detective Mueller in the face. But maybe I can come up with something more imaginative. With Chill's death, I feel the need to make a statement. Execution is too easy."

"Reles and Mueller…they're still *cops*, Jesus. Killing's easy. Walking away…well, running away, is hard."

"Chill's not here. No holding back now."

"They'll kill you. If not them, their buddies. These are sick in the head bastards."

You lie back on your futon and stare up at the water stained boards in the rotting ceiling. "That's okay. I gotta be me."

When you open your eyes, Sgt. Billy is shaking you awake. Skunk stands in the doorway. Legs Gabrielle and Sugar Cane stand with him. Legs can't stop crying.

SIDEKICKS NEED EMERGENCY CODE WORDS SO THEY KNOW WHEN TO PANIC.

You pull yourself to your feet stiffly. You put a hand out to Skunk. "Sorry about your car, man."

Skunk startles you by pulling you into a hug. His eyes are wet. "I'm just so sorry about Chill. That's all I can think about. Insurance will take care of the car. Money can't bring back a downed soldier. Chill was the best of us. They must have bushwhacked him, Fix."

Your gaze slides to the ladies. Legs has been crying. Sugar looks scared, but the woman you rescued from Oswald's cage looks better than when you saw her last. Evidently, Sugar kept your true identity to herself, but her presence still screws up operational security. "Sergeant, could you go down to the bodega and get us some more cream for coffee? Soy, this time, please? That'd be good for us."

Sgt. Billy nods and dips his head to the women on his way out. He knows that if you ask for soy, he's on recon duty.

Skunk whispers in your ear. "Sorry to take them to your lair, man. Miss Gabrielle insisted. She and Chill go way back. Berb and the Samoan weren't available and I couldn't leave them both alone."

"It's…not optimum, but it's fine." You live in a hovel with a futon on a bare wood floor. It's not the image your Armani suits project when you're out in the world. Your poverty is embarrassing. Worse, you're embarrassed that they know you're embarrassed. Letting people see you as you are gives up too much power.

You take a deep breath and focus on Skunk. "I didn't expect to see Sugar again."

"I dropped her off at the hospital as ordered."

"Sugar came to me," Legs says. "I heard what happened to Oswald. Sugar told me enough about her kidnapping…about Ginger. We all know he deserved what he got."

"Legs took me in," Sugar says. "I didn't know where else to go. I can identify these men. What if they come after me?"

You nod. "My fault. I should have told you how to disappear. Too pressed for time to think straight, I guess."

Skunk pipes up. "Sugar said you told her to keep me out of this. I appreciate it, Fix, but this is Chill we're talking about now. You need me for anything? I'm down, dog."

You can't help but smile. Skunk's a solid dude, but somebody should stay pure. "The first night I met Chill," you reply, "we came to an agreement. I'd take care of the dirty tricks and morally ambiguous stuff. He'd take care of things on his end. 'I don't know and I don't want to know,' was Chill's official policy."

"I can work unofficially on this one," Skunk says.

You shake your head. "Eventually, Chill and I worked it out so I kept him informed on cases on a need-to-know basis. Let's keep that approach with you, man. Take care of the funeral and deal with questions from 5-0. I'll get my hands dirty. Chill would want to keep you clean. Somebody's got to be the face of the company now. That's you."

You nod to Legs. "Exactly how far do you go back with Chill?"

"I gave him his first bodyguard job when he quit trying to be an actor. Way back."

"Like family," you say.

She nods. Her jaw is tight. She's not just sad. She's furious.

"Skunk, what are you driving now?" you ask.

"Caddy. Rental."

"Could you go check out the seats? Make sure they're comfortable. The ladies and I need to have a quick chat upstairs."

You need to make sure neither of them will lose their nerve and call in the police or the FBI. You hate depending on strangers, but for you to do your job, you have to make sure they can keep their mouths shut. If Legs and Sugar come to their senses and fall back into acting like ordinary, good citizens, you're dead before you can even begin your campaign of vengeance.

SERIOUSLY CONSIDER RUNNING AWAY. LIVE LONGER.

You show Sugar and Legs the stairs to the roof. The view from your dreary little piece of Los Angeles shows busy streets and wandering homeless people. The sun shines as if it doesn't care that Charles "Chill" Gillie is dead. People go about their business as if his murder doesn't matter. If the universe had a face, you'd punch it.

"You okay?" Legs asks.

"Pretty broken up, but I'm finding my rage."

"Why did Reles kill Chill?"

"Because he would have stood in the way of getting to you." The look on her face tells you that wasn't diplomatic enough. Dealing with clients and being charming is Chill's job...*was* Chill's job.

"Why don't you just leave town?" The way Sugar says it, it's more of a statement than a question. "You can't win against Reles and Mueller. Just run. We should all get away."

"Let me worry about that. I still don't know anything about Bekhti. What can you tell me about him?"

"I heard Mueller call him Gaston. He likes to watch. He finds the girls, too. He watched Ginger die. Reles did it. Mueller recorded it. He joked about how he had often photographed crime scenes, but never before the fact."

"Where did Bekhti find you?"

"Craigslist."

"And?"

"He was a generous older man."

"What was the ad?"

"Searching for submissives into BDSM."

"If you're so submissive, how come I had to drag the information out of you?"

"Hey!" Legs says sharply.

Sugar avoids your gaze, her eyes fixed on the big, dead rooftop air conditioning unit that sits over your flop. "I'm not proud," she says. "Ginger was a friend. I brought her in. We both needed the money."

"Don't we all?" As soon as you say it, you realize you're standing next to someone for whom money is not a problem. "You should get out of town, Legs. I know it's not convenient, but — "

"You're not going anywhere, right?"

"Nope."

"You're going to do something. For Chill?"

"In his memory, yes. I feel like I have to."

"Sugar's right. We should run."

"He won't," Sugar says. "I've seen his scars." She begins to cry. She runs at you. Her embrace begins as a hug. Then she's pulling your shirt off.

You stand in the presence of two women in broad daylight. They stare at your torso. Legs's mouth drops open. Your chest and stomach are a road map of scars. Crosses.

Sugar stands close, your shirt forgotten in her hand. "Who did this to you?"

"People. Two of them. I was a kid."

"That's why you won't run," Sugar says. She reaches out tentatively and caresses your chest where the worst scar lies.

It's in the shape of a cross, too, but thicker than the others. When you insisted on using your name, Tia Marta tried to make you forget your name is Jesus. She heated a crucifix in fire and hung it around your neck. Tia Marta branded you. She thought that was an ironic joke.Sugar's voice is barely above a whisper. "You won't try to get away from Reles or Mueller or Bekhti. You'll come right at them because, like me, you are a glutton for punishment."

You grab Sugar's hand and push it away, burning in embarrassment at being exposed like this. You've spent most of your adult life having sex with your clothes on, trying to avoid conversations like this. "I am not a glutton for punishment."

Sugar shrugs. "Sure looks like it."

"Every time I talked back, they'd punish me. I thought they would kill me dozens of times over. I kept talking back until I couldn't talk anymore. Then it got worse."

You turn your naked back to the women. They gasp in unison. "If I tried to escape, they'd burn me with the edge of an iron."

"It…it looks like…wings!" Sugar says.

"Yes. Another of Tia Marta's little jokes. She said if I kept trying to defy them, she would give me wings before she killed me."

"It's beautiful," Sugar said. "So…symmetrical."

"No!" You and Legs say it at the same time.

You twist and grab the shirt from Sugar's hand. "It's not beautiful, Sugar. My point is, I'm not a glutton for punishment. Like you and Ginger, I was a victim. Now I'm a glutton for justice."

You walk to the edge of the roof and pull your shirt on, covering up quickly and buttoning up slow so you give yourself time to calm down.

"I'm sorry for what happened to you," Legs says. "I understand...I'm glad you aren't walking away from this."

You hang your head. "I'll finish it."

Below you is a dark blue van parked on the far side of the street. It looks like any other commercial van, except for the dual antennae. You squint and look closer. It has a periscope. Its telescopic microphone is pointed at you.

It's not LAPD. If it were, they'd be coming through the door and shooting you already.

It's not the Spanish mob. They'd wait for you to go down to the bodega, pull you into a van and shoot you in the back of the head. It's not your one-time friend, Big Denny De Molina. If he knew where you were, he'd come straight from LAX to shoot you in the face.

It's probably the FBI, but your imagination runs wild. It could even be the CIA for all you know. The Company would prioritize gathering information above busting you. First they gather data. Then they use you. When they're done with guys like you, you don't see the inside of a court. They might put a hood over your head and you'd wake up at a black site naked and primed for torture. Best case scenario, they simply kill you.

Chill warned you that you couldn't walk away with a shipment of Russian TM40 mines and expect no one to come looking of them. They won't have to look far to find the explosives.

Whatever spy agency it is, you're in Big Brother's sights and in the open. Time to knot your tie nonchalantly, casually step out of sight and run and run and run.

CLEAN GETAWAYS GET DIRTY EASILY.

You meet Billy on the stairs and you both whisper "Feds!" at the same moment.

"Take the ladies out the back, through the restaurant. If it looks clear, get them in the van. Take off the bakery signs, change the plates and get out the magnetic signs for the plumbing business." (*Gill's Plumbing. We lay pipe and open your drain!*)

"How will I know if it looks clear?"

"You'll only know for sure when you get away. They've got nothing on you anyway, so don't sweat it."

"What about you?"

You give the old man a hug. "I'll be okay, Mother."

"But what about your cache — "

"Go. We're walking away from it. When I have an assignment for you, I'll call. You know where I'll be until then."

He was a soldier. Heart attacks and age don't change a thing. Sgt. Billy still follows orders. He knows better than to tell you to stay safe. Instead, when he tosses you a glance over his shoulder, he says, "Jesus? Win."

You can't recall ever achieving an unqualified victory. Winning is a tall order.

Legs wishes you good luck and hurries after Billy. Sugar pauses at the door and blows you a kiss. "Bye, sweetie!"

"Bye."

She disappears down the stairs.

Well...that's a lonely feeling. You used to crave being alone. All you wanted was for the world to leave you alone. Too bad you still don't feel that way because, if this play goes wrong, at best you're going to spend a lot of time in a SHU. Though "Segregated Housing Unit" sounds awfully fancy for getting thrown in Solitary when the your cell will be nothing more than a small, dark hole.

You click your comm rig twice and Skunk rolls up to your door a moment later. As you exit the door, you're carrying as many Armani suits as you can, high and on their hangers, still in their plastic sheaths from the dry cleaners.

You've already changed into a dark blue suit, almost identical to that of Skunk. Your hands shook as you hurried to change, wondering if the Alphabet Agency would burst through the door at any moment.

You give Skunk the nod to pop the trunk but you open the Caddy's back door and slip in the back seat. The surveillance van is down the block a bit on the other side of the street. You wait for a truck to rumble by. Skunk goes back to close the trunk and you slip back out of the Caddy, head down until you're back in Big in Japan.

Skunk stands in the street at the driver's door and appears to be having an animated conversation. Talking to an empty back seat full of your suits would be funny if your freedom wasn't on the line. He makes a gesture of exasperation, really selling it, and jumps in the Caddy. Then he peels out.

The surveillance van does not move. However, two identical cars pull out to follow him. As they pass your window, you think, "Goodbye, Powers Without Judgment."

You turn to find Agent John Smith from Elizabeth, New Jersey staring at you from his seat, a half-eaten bento box of unagi in front of him. Nobody who wants to eat that much eel can be a good guy. You haven't seen Smith since New York. He's sweating through a blue Oxford shirt. His 9 mm is pointed at your chest.

You smile. "Hello, Power Without Judgment."

"Jesus Diaz AKA Dr. JD Fix."

"Yup. So, that was an FBI van watching me. I hope you got my good side. I've got a great ass. You should see me twerk on Instagram."

"I told them you'd come downstairs for some sushi eventually. Keep your hands where I can see them, don't move and sit down."

"Okay. Shall I not move first? Or should I sit and then not move?"

He directs you to your seat with the gun. The restaurant is empty except for the cook and one waiter and he's fled to the kitchen.

"Can I have some of your sushi? I'm not sure what the food is like at Gitmo. I understand it's often what they can blend up and force feed you."

"Shut up."

"Okay."

"I have two messages for you. The first is from Big Denny."

"How is he?"

"He's feeling better. Losing weight. Barbara's getting him to eat organic and they're into green juicing."

"Nice. They married yet?"

"Barbara wants to wait a while longer before walking down the aisle again. Since you killed Jimmy…guess she doesn't wanna look like the merry widow."

He's not calling you in. He doesn't even have his earbud in. John Smith is a pretty good sport considering that the last time you saw him you made fun of his name and screwed up his assignment. You took over his observation post in a post office so your ex-girlfriend could get away with a lot of money.

Every good deed, mistake and misstep ties itself to the next until you've got enough trouble to hang yourself.

MAKE WEAK ENEMIES. YOUR BATTLES WILL GO EASIER.

"**D**id you get in trouble?" you ask. "After New York? Demoted? Did they make fun of you, I mean besides for your stupid white guy name? When I took your gun and radio, did the other agents razz you a bit? Make you leave meetings for sandwiches and coffee? I guess every office is like that. I dunno. I never really worked in an office."

He doesn't look eager to exchange pleasantries. "My career advancement options would have been limited, but since I'm the only FBI agent who can positively ID you in person, I got assigned to track down my favorite domestic terrorist."

"Dude! Please! Not everybody who blows shit up is a terrorist. Is that your disdain face? That looks like it must be your disdain face."

"Mr. Diaz, we live in a country with Ag Gag laws. If a hippie who tries to take pictures at a slaughterhouse can be classified as a terrorist, you certainly are a terrorist."

"Denny must be paying you so goddamn much money, it hurts! What's the plan? If Denny's paying you to take me somewhere for a long, drawn out torture session, pull the trigger now. I've been tortured enough in my life. Actually, if you plan to arrest me, I'll reach for my SIG right now and we can finish — "

"Shut up."

You sigh. "Okay."

"Big Denny says hello and he says keep doing what you're doing. You're on the right track."

"What?"

"You have a common enemy, apparently. Big Denny wants you to do what you do."

You take a deeper breath. Your heart rate begins to slow. Agent Smith is not going to shoot you. However, you've been set up for the long con. "How did you pick up my trail again, exactly?"

He smirks. "Denny's a big wheel now. He's got reach."

"Denny's got money mojo now, sure, but enough to get you to turn a blind eye?"

"I'm not turning a blind eye for long, Mr. Diaz. Nobody's got that much money. You threatened my family."

"I didn't mean it, John."

"Felt like it."

"Sorry, but believing that I would kill your family was kind of key to the bit, right? How would it have gone down if you hadn't taken me seriously?"

"You aren't getting away again, Jesus. We've got you dialed in. You aren't leaving LA. Satellites. Surveillance. Pictures. Meta-data. Data. Shoe size. We know all your associates. I even have a photo of you kissing Legs Gabrielle. That won't bode well for her career, palling around with known terrorists."

"One, leave her out of it. Two, you're quoting Sarah Palin and 'palling around with terrorists' didn't stop Obama's election. Besides which, if the President knew what I did for him in Chicago, I'd get a pardon."

"Chicago. Thanks for the confirmation. Do you have to leave a trail of blown up houses *everywhere* you go?"

"It's a bad habit. I'm trying to quit."

"You aren't hearing me, Jesus. I *own* you."

"That's what all stalkers say. So I go ahead with my mission — "

"Whatever you have planned, I don't want to know."

"I get that a lot. What happens when I'm done?"

Smith smiles ear to ear. "Well, then I get to shoot you, of course. Denny's not paying me to be a traitor, you piece of shit. He's paying me to wait a few days before I'm declared a hero."

He's startled when you push your chair back and stand. "Well, you know what they say. When you work by the hour, slow the fuck down. Let's revisit this when I'm done, okay? Did Denny mention which common enemy I'm taking out for him?"

"You were both enforcers for The Machine, right? Betcha you guys made lots of enemies together."

"I think Big Denny might have pointed an old enemy my way hoping I'd kill or be killed, am I right?"

"Jesus?" Smith raises his pistol, points it at your crotch and yells, "Bang!"

You jump back and come very close to shitting your pants and peeing at the same time. "That's just mean, man."

"That was the second message. From me to you, bitch."

You won't give him the satisfaction of watching you run away so you walk fast and fight to keep the pace below a scurry. Your heart doesn't stop hammering in your chest until you're two blocks away. Yes, that was definitely Smith's disdain face. He intends to shoot you, but only if you give him one chance.

Mental note: Don't do that.

WHEN POSSIBLE, DRESS LIKE BRUCE LEE.

Your backup hideout is a storage facility in West Carson. It's not much more comfortable than the dump over Big in Japan. There's no working air conditioner in either location. You're back to sleeping on the floor so it feels pretty much the same.

You need to find the mystery man, Gaston Bekhti. If you had more manpower, you'd take them all down at once. Maybe there's a way to do that by going after the trio's weakest point.

Since the cops did not find your body off the end of the Santa Monica pier, Reles is bunking at LAPD's Thai Town precinct. Sgt. Billy put a tracker on his pickup and the Samoan is watching the precinct's comings and goings from a restaurant across the street.

Reles must have a comfortable cot in there because Jeremy hasn't spotted him yet. Despite your best research and recon efforts, it's as if Hank Reles doesn't have a home. Whatever rock he lives under, he's good at keeping the address a secret. Once again, Reles proves better than you at your own game.

Finding him in a vulnerable place is up to Sgt. Billy's tracker and Jeremy. The restaurant owner doesn't mind if Jeremy keeps the table by the window as long as the big Samoan keeps eating. He complains he's eating so much he's going to develop a peanut allergy. You tell him to pay the restaurant owner more for the table rental and to pace himself eating his way through the menu.

Detective Mueller ran interference for Reles. He's not as good at keeping his home a secret. Sgt. Billy followed him home. Mueller can't hide because he's got a family and his wife spends her days taking the kids to school and to soccer. Then she documents their lives on Facebook. Detective Mueller wasn't hard to find. He's the soft target in the open, so Mueller will feel your wrath first.

When Sgt. Billy reports in, you give him his orders. He has a lot of stuff to shop for at Home Depot. A minute later, you call him back. "On second thought, Billy, go to several Home Depots. Load up. Don't attract attention. Make sure you aren't followed."

There's no getting at Reles, but if all goes well tonight, he'll be exactly where you need him to be.

At the appointed time, you spot Berb sprinting along the line of storage units. He's dressed for battle, just in case: yellow jumpsuit and all a la Bruce Lee in *Game of Death*. Uma Thurman looked great in the same outfit in *Kill Bill*. Chill gave Berb that outfit as a joke Christmas gift, but Berb loves it. He even started dieting and running more so he could fit into it.

You wish you were guarding Uma Thurman's body right about now. Or Legs. Life would be so much simpler if you could be the guy who sweeps Legs Gabrielle off her feet. Kevin Costner had his chance with Whitney Houston in *The Bodyguard*, but he walked away from her. That was the most unbelievable moment in a movie full of unbelievable moments. If all goes well with Mueller, you'll be able to walk away from this mess instead of being wheeled away.

Berbniak doesn't stop to chat and, judging by the amount of sweat he's pumping out, he's been running through the city for a while. A fast runner zig-zagging through back alleys is difficult for the FBI to follow surreptitiously. As he runs by, he doesn't even look your way. He drops the item you asked for. You wait a few minutes to see if the Feds show up. Just because Smith won't shoot you doesn't mean the rest of the FBI is so patient.

The Feds do not appear so you go out and retrieve the IronKey flash drive. Finally, it's statement making time. This one, everyone will remember.

STAY RIGHTEOUS

The smart ninja's friend is super glue. You've used it before to great effect. When Sgt. Billy returns, he confirms he's got everything on your shopping list. He's noted the make and model of the car Mueller drives, a 2014 Hyundai Sonata. Most important, that model has a sunroof and Mueller's house has a two-car garage.

The complication is the detective has a wife and two young girls who live with him. From the cell phone picture Sgt. Billy took, Mueller's wife is about thirty-five and blonde. The kids can't be more than five or six. Mueller's double life is going to be tough on them.

As night falls, you take off the Armani suit, slip into a black t-shirt, black jeans and black Nikes. Inspecting yourself in the shard of mirror taped to the steel wall, you look like any other hipster who should be shopping for a black beret on the way to a weeknight poetry slam at UCLA.

Clearly, something iconic is needed for the drama to come. A Scream Halloween mask might seem too funny. A Billy puppet mask from the Saw movies would be appropriate. You looked into a Pinhead mask, but it cost too much. Instead, you top off your outfit with a *luchadore* mask. The Mexican wrestling mask is black with a skeleton's bone-white face and red flames around the eye slits. You hope the kids stay in bed and the wife is a deep sleeper.

It would be better if you stole a truck but Chill's van is already packed with your supplies. You look in the mirror again. Is this what a grown ass man should be doing?

Would Chill approve? *Thtay righteouth, Hey-thuth.*

You tell yourself you're doing this for Chill and for all the Gingers in the world. You probably should have given therapy more of a shot because you're also working through your own issues.

You reach under your shirt and trace the map of scars. The very first time Tia Marta cut you, she used the edge of an envelope. She laughed at you. You were so unused to pain then. Then she squeezed lemon juice into the paper cut. Soon she graduated to knives and salt. Then, the hot iron.

Looking back, you sure were a slow learner. But your whole life is a pile of shit, isn't it? Gotta start shoveling somewhere.

Tonight, ladies and gentlemen, the character of the clever hit man will be played by Jesus Diaz. The actor's motivation will be supplied by his lost childhood and tortured fool's soul.

Take a deep breath. Step closer to the mirror. Look into your eyes and try to find the man behind the scary mask. What happens tonight shouldn't be narrated by Morgan Freeman. Tough guy voice-over work for tonight's movie should be supplied by the cowboy in the *Big Lebowksi*, Sam Elliot. Or maybe Dennis Leary could put a funny, edgy spin on what's about to unfold, like he does for those truck commercials.

Somebody really badass should play you. If John Leguizamo isn't available, could Jason Statham play a short Cuban?

SOLID ADVICE: DON'T STEP IN THE BUTTER.

Magic tricks are fascinating. It's always disappointing to discover how they are achieved. For instance, when Detective Mueller pulls his Sonata into his garage and steps out of his car, you step out from behind his wife's car. Mueller is startled to see you come out of the shadows. All he sees is the bone white of the skull at first. What happens next only *looks* like magic.

By the time he processes that you're wearing a *luchadore* mask, he's focused on the muzzle of the pistol pointed at his head. The automatic garage door isn't quite down yet so he tries to make a run for it as he fumbles for his gun. Mueller is startled to see his feet in the air in front of him. He crashes to his back.

That's a cool magic trick.

The thin film of liquid butter on the floor converts the smooth soles of his dress shoes into surprise ice skates. See? Disappointing.

You land on his right arm first so he can't reach for the pistol in his shoulder harness under his left armpit. If he were a lefty, you might have had a problem, but since most people are right-handed, that's the way to bet. You go to work, pistol-whipping Mueller to soften him up. When he's tenderized, you reach for his weapon — a standard LAPD-issue revolver. Toss it aside.

It's late and the kids are in bed asleep. Mrs. Mueller is watching Jimmy Fallon in her bedroom on the second floor. You pause to listen for the pitter patter of little feet and complications. All you hear is Mueller's labored breathing. He's okay. It's labored because all your weight sits on his chest. One knee to the balls curls him up and in a moment you're rolling him face down.

When he tries to speak, you put the SIG's muzzle against his ear and whisper. "Sh. I've been in your house. Just on the first floor. If you make too much noise, I'll have to go read your kids a bedtime story. I found *Goodnight Moon* on the living room floor. Do you want me to read *Goodnight Moon* to your kids?"

He shakes his head.

"Good. Be quiet until I tell you to speak. I have questions. You will not speak until I'm ready. Otherwise it's *Goodnight Moon.*"

He's freaking out and bug-eyed but he stays quiet. You'd feel sorry for him, but you're bad and he's evil.

This is where Sam Elliot or Dennis Leary would say, *Try to remember that when you see what Jesus Diaz does next.*

When you look at Mueller, you don't see a cop who's a normal family man. You see a monster. You see a dead red-haired girl tied to a chair with half her head shaved. Her eyes stare, still wide and frightened, even into death. But now that you've kneed Mueller in the balls, Ginger's dead staring face sports a wide Joker grin.

This guy has daughters and he did that to somebody else's daughter? Unfathomable. Some things, no one should understand. Given the nature of Mueller's crimes, it's fitting you use a ball gag on him. Soaking the ball gag in vinegar and menthol is just an added touch to keep him distracted and his eyes watering while you manhandled him into position.

Use the extra-long zip ties to pin his wrists to each thigh, just above the knee. When he tries to get up, the buttered floor slams him back down into the concrete before you have a chance to do the same. Next, zip tie the ankles.

Next? This is complicated. Follow the checklist.

Don't step in the butter.

Make sure all the windows are rolled up (but leave a couple of inches down on the driver's side window.

Open the sunroof.

Pop the Sonata's hood.

Before you apply super glue to the car's steering wheel, it is critically important to disable the horn. In a moment, when Mueller discovers he can't take his hands off the wheel, he does the expected and slams his head into the center of the wheel. No car horn sounds because you ripped the wires. Now Mueller has a headache, though, so that was fun.

You cuff his ear with the SIG once, just because, and then blindfold him. You remove his tie and wrap it around his throat. Knot it behind the head rest to hold him still.

You've used piano wire and heavy fishing line in the past, but it's likely to cut your hands. Despite what every caper movie you've ever seen suggests, it's really hard to wear gloves and do delicate work like tying knots, especially when the adrenaline is pumping, your hands are shaking and time is a factor.

With the super glue applied to the wheel, you take out your carpet knife. The short, sharp, hooked blade fits precisely around any Adam's apple. It's also best for slipping under tight zip ties. Mueller resists putting his hand on the steering wheel, but he's got no leverage and a quick bash with your elbow into his solar plexus makes him cooperative. You take his handcuffs. They're good for smashing him in the face and opening up some deep cuts, too, but the fight is out of him so there's no need to be sadistic.

You want to be sadistic, but you don't need to be. That's the slim difference between you and your prey at this moment. You have prey. He has victims.

He doesn't give you a hard time placing his other hand on the steering wheel because, this time, after you cut the zip tie, you put the tip of the cold blade at his throat. Live and learn.

You pause to reflect on your work to make sure your tasks match your checklist. You made the mistake of putting super glue on a bad guy's palm once. Before you could glue him to the wall, he made a grab for your face and his hand came away furry. That was a painful lesson and you never could grow a beard again after that mishap.

You take off the *luchadore* mask. It's hot and sweaty. It's not half as hot and sweaty as Mueller is about to be.

Here's where Sam Elliot or Dennis Leary intone, *Don't try this at home, kids!*

HIT MEN: YOU'RE GOING TO NEED A COOL CODE NAME.

Double-check the door to the house. You've already cut the land line, super glued the back and front doors and you've taken the cell phone that was charging in the kitchen.

Creeping around the house barefoot and trying not to wake the kids or alert the wife was strangely more nerve wracking than beating up Mueller. You can't hit a kid or a woman. If one of the girls starts to cry, that would send you running. With the monster in the man suit, though? The easy answer is hit him harder.

You picked up the little rubber wedge for 99 cents from Dollarmania. It's still jammed safely under the door between the garage and the house so you won't be interrupted now. The most dangerous, and loudest part, is over. It's time for construction work to begin.

You bring out the cartons of foam insulation tubes. Each tube's application tip is already cut open and ready to go. It's the kind of insulation that expands to fill big spaces behind walls as soon as it emerges from the tube. The instructions say it's good for "irregular spaces." Perfect. You begin with spraying the well at Mueller's feet. It comes out as a sticky beige cloud that quickly fills the space beneath the brake and accelerator.

He doesn't know what's going on and he's nervous. "Relax, Mr. Mueller. I won't set you on fire. I did that to Oswald and I hate to repeat myself. We don't want to suck the drama and tension from the moment, right?"

"Hmph?" he says through his gag.

It takes fewer tubes than you expected to get the car's cabin filled to his neck with foam insulation.

You slide the length of PVC pipe through the sunroof and line it up with his mouth. The super glue coats the edge of the circle of pipe. You remove the ball gag and jam the pipe over his mouth. You count to sixty to make sure it's secure. You repeat the procedure with a short length of pipe attached to his left ear.

You have extra tubes of insulation left over. You fill the rest of the Sonata's passenger compartment. It gives Mueller time to think and sweat. It gives the insulation time to harden.

By the time you're packed up and ready to whisper your questions down the tube and into his ear, Mueller is eager to answer. To be sure, you play tough guy a little harder.

"I already know the answers to several of my questions," you say. "You'll never know which ones so don't try to be cute. If I detect any deception on your part…I notice you like Coke, Mr. Mueller. You have a case in the corner of your garage. You're hot and itchy and terrified right now. Imagine how awful it will be when I start pouring Coke down that pipe until you drown. Now, if I say please, are you ready to answer my questions?"

His disembodied voice croaks up the PVC pipe. "Yes."

You have no doubt this is the most polite he's been to anyone. He gives you passwords. He tells you exactly what you need to know to bring down Detective Hank Reles. He knows nothing about Gaston Bekhti except he's from out East and he's rich. He doesn't know anything about the Spanish mob, either. He's never heard of Big Denny De Molina. That's okay. You have a feeling that, after tonight, the monsters will get flushed out of hiding.

Before you leave him to cook a while, you give him a small sip of Coke, but not enough to drown him. He'll live, if the cops come fast enough.

Your plan is not to call 911. That would lack imagination. Instead, you take the wedge out of the bottom of the door to the house and head for his computer. The files you need are in a deep sub-directory under old taxes labeled Gun Warranties. These files are not Gun Warranties. They are snuff films.

You don't have time to search through them all. Somewhere in there, video awaits of Ginger in the chair. Maybe Sugar's in the background in the cage screaming, "Don't!" You wish you hadn't come to the rescue too late.

You don't look at the videos. You don't want to watch Ginger die. Instead, you begin the email campaign.

You take out the IronKey flash drive and load the email addresses. Every network including the Fishing Channel gets a copy. Every journalist from CNN to the podcast networks gets a copy. Every address you have for the FBI and Homeland Security gets a copy. Everyone from Chill's list and from Detective Albrecht Mueller's address book gets the video files. That's just about everyone in the Los Angeles Police Department.

Al's Mom will get the bad news, too.

The subject line reads: *Warning. Snuff films are in the attachments.*

You type a brief message:

Protect the identities of the victims. Stop these monsters: Gaston Bekhti, Detective Hank Reles and Detective Albrecht Mueller of the LAPD. This is what they do to women.

Detective Mueller is anxiously awaiting arrest in his home. He'll live, if you hurry. It's up to you if you decide to hurry.

Sincerely,

The Divine Assassin

You really like the sound of "The Divine Assassin." If you get out of this clean, that's what you'll call yourself all the time. Sure, it'll sound obnoxious after a while, but when it comes down to it, we are all defined by what we do.

The moment you click send is perfect except that *The Tonight Show* is long over. Mueller's wife stands in the doorway with a shiny .38 pointed at your head.

If she doesn't shoot you to death, you promise yourself you'll flee to Canada. In Canada, not every goddamn house is an arsenal.

HAVE SOME STYLE. DON'T BE AVERAGE JOE GUNSLINGER.

She stands in the doorway, taking you in. You're wearing the *luchadore* mask again. It's a good bet she didn't see that coming when she pulled on her jeans this morning. You aren't terribly worried, though her hand is shaking and that's the hand that's holding the gun.

"Good evening, Mrs. Mueller. May I call you Marsha?"

Her eyes widen. "How do you know my name?"

"*Sh.* The girls are sleeping and we don't want to disturb them."

"I'm calling the police."

"I already did, after a fashion. They'll be here soon."

"Good, then. We'll wait."

You decide to like her then. She's scared out of her mind but she's standing her ground. It would have been smarter to hide in her kids' room and cower, pointing her gun at the door. Still, Marsha Mueller is spunky.

"Did you call on your cell phone, mister? The phone doesn't work. If you lie to me, I'll shoot you right here."

The threat sounds so close to what you told her husband, you have to nod your appreciation. It's a good threat and you have no intention of lying to this woman. You take off the mask and give her a small smile. "Marsha? Why don't you hold that pistol in both hands and relax your elbows a bit. You're so stiff and nervous, you're shaking. If you could point it a little off target, just enough to avoid an unhappy accident, that would be great. Please."

"I'll shoot you if you try anything!"

"I don't doubt it. I'm not going to move from this chair. I just need to show you something and then we can talk some more or wait for the cops. Whatever you want to do, okay? You've got the gun. I'm sitting down. You can see my hands. You're in control, okay? Can I show you something now?"

You don't wait for her answer. Instead, you spin the laptop around and press enter. Her ice-blue eyes widen so much you see the whites all the way around her irises.

"This isn't the decoy laptop you use for Facebook and Pinterest, Marsha. I found this one in the back of the closet, just where Al said I'd find it, hidden between two boxes of old LPs in a shopping bag. That's your husband doing that, Marsha."

Her lip curls. Her lips tremble. She wants to look away and she can't.

"That's an innocent girl he's doing that to. There's nothing consensual happening there, is there? Al and Hank are having fun. See their smug smiles, so secure in the knowledge they will never be caught? You probably know Hank, I'm guessing. Does he come over on the fourth of July? Join the barbeque, maybe? Does he play with your kids? I've come to stop Hank and your husband from doing these — "

The gun drops to the floor with a heavy *thunk*. She throws up.

"…atrocities."

This is the first time you've disarmed anyone by making them vomit.

You pull her up from her knees and rub her back. "Easy. You'll be okay. He's not hurting anyone anymore. I saw to that."

She heaves again and coughs and sputters. The floor of the Mueller family's den tells you she had Kung Pao chicken for dinner.

When Marsha's finished, she straightens and wipes drool from her chin. "Is Al dead?"

You look at your watch. "No. Not yet, barring unforeseen circumstances."

"Where is he?"

"In the car. In the garage."

Marsha Mueller scoops up the pistol and races out of the room. You grab the IronKey drive from the laptop's USB port and your mask from the desk. You leave to follow her. Then you double back and close the laptop in case the kids get up.

When you enter the garage, Marsha is yelling at Al. Judging by the weak voice of hot misery creeping out of the black PVC pipe sticking out of the Sonata's sunroof, Al Mueller is still alive and probably wishing he wasn't.

"Gee-zuzz! Why didn't you just kill him?" Marsha asks.

You blink. You're not sure. The quick and easy answer is, Chill's wishes were that you be more imaginative. He always thought you could be better than the average Joe Gunslinger. Or maybe you worried that if you tortured and shot Mueller, you'd like it too much and you'd become him. You got what you needed and no more.

Oddly, you don't regret letting him live. That's new. A cop in a deviant sex ring who is also murderer of young women? Prison will be hard. Death would let him off too easy.

Marsha's staring at you, still waiting for an answer. Why did you let him live?

You clear your throat. "Um. Because…reasons."

Thtay righteouth, Hey-thuth.

LEARN THE BASKET HOLD.

She raises the gun, pointing it at the Sonata's windshield. You sweep one arm up under her arm. One shot is fired into the ceiling and now she's fighting you. Marsha Mueller tries to push you back, punches your chest and slaps your face. You step behind her as you twist the gun from her hand. You toss the gun behind you and grab her wrists in a basket hold, pinning her crossed arms.

"Sh. Marsha. You've got kids. I've seen their pictures. They're still little. You pull that trigger and you won't see them except at Thanksgiving and Christmas and your birthday. Read me?"

"Did he? Did he touch my girls?" She's weeping.

"I don't know, Marsha. But whatever happened or didn't, they'll get help. You'll get help. It's going to be okay, but you've got to do as I tell you now. Don't kill him. Your daughters are going to need you."

The fight drains from her. Her knees are weak. You let her slide to the floor. Mueller is trying to scream.

The cops will be here soon. "Marsha, do you know a man named Gaston? Gaston Bekhti?"

She stares at the car blankly and shakes her head.

"Are you sure? It's important. He's described to me as an older man, silver hair. Maybe an old guy you know by another name with an accent?"

"No."

She's staring at the car and listening to her husband beg to be let out of the oven created by his body heat. She's staring at the checklist you slapped on the hood. You left it as a present for the FBI.

At the bottom of the checklist you used to spring Detective Mueller's trap, you added a note. It reads:

Special thanks to Agent John Smith of the FBI for making this possible. Also, kudos to Big Denny De Molina for paying John not to arrest me.

You wanted to be a hero, John. You put off murdering me and I appreciate it. Now you are a hero.

You're welcome,
The Divine Assassin

You stiffen when you hear a tiny voice behind you, coming from the kitchen. Marsha is deep in shock and she doesn't hear it. You slip back into the house.

A little blonde girl, about five, looks up at you, bewildered and trying to rub sleep out of her eyes. Kids shouldn't be awakened by gunshots. Kids should have a childhood. You didn't, but maybe the girl and her sister will have a chance at one now.

"Where's Mommy?"

"She's with Daddy. They're having a grown-up talk."

"Who are you?"

"Right now?" You smile wide. "Right now I'm the babysitter."

"*Not* a baby."

You crouch. "You're right. You aren't a baby. Or you're very tall for a baby. I don't know about that. Maybe you're the world's tallest baby."

She smiles.

"It's way past your bedtime, isn't it? What's your name?"

"Cindy."

"Cindy. Of course! You're Cindy Lou Who. And you're out of bed. You better go back to bed, okay?"

The kid doesn't move.

"Go back to bed…please."

She holds out her hand. "You're the babysitter? Really?"

"Yep. Professionally."

"We never had a *boy* babysitter."

"Well. That doesn't seem fair, does it?"

"I want a bedtime story."

"I bet you and your sister already had a bedtime story tonight."

"Want another one," she whines.

Her hand is so small and delicate in your palm.

When the first uniforms arrive, they'll find Marsha in the garage standing next to the car. The Sonata will be filled with beige clouds of quick-set foam insulation and muted screams.

You've made a statement. You've announced to the world you aren't a terrorist. You're no Iron Man or Thor, but you're an avenger.

Maybe you aren't so far gone that you can at least aspire to a Robert Downey Jr.-level of awesome.

FIREFIGHTERS DON'T LIKE BEING CALLED BUCKETHEADS AND BASEMENT SAVERS.

You imagine Marsha telling Al Mueller how much she hates him through the PVC tube glued to his ear, dripping well-deserved hate into his fetid brain. The first uniforms on the scene will call the fire department to cut Mueller out. The cops will find both girls asleep in their beds, tucked in tight and safe.

The LAPD claims a response time of 5.7 minutes. Despite your massive email campaign, they take ten minutes to get to Al's house. According to your scanner, they waited for a supervisor so they take fifteen minutes to set up a perimeter to secure the scene.

You keep one eye on the clock as you drive away in Chill's surveillance van. You listen to the chatter on the police scanner as red, white and blue strobes flash by. You have to grin about the hyper-response. The scene is just so weird, are they really calling for backup? Or are they calling their buddies to have a look before the bucketheads and basement savers cut Mueller out with the jaws of life?

They don't need backup now. They need an ambulance, Child Protective Services and CSI. The Golden State's teams that deal with trouble will pick up the pieces and put the puzzle together. Somebody will help those kids. The girls have a chance at a life now, but you had to break the lie they had first.

Marsha Mueller will change her name and she'll never really trust anyone again. She won't want to talk about the betrayal and how deeply she was deceived. She'll blame herself. Someone will tell her she should forgive him. Someone well-meaning will say poor Al was mentally ill. Marsha will hate those people almost as much as she hates her soon-to-be ex. Her rage will always be close at hand, ready to fire.

At least, that's how you handled it.

But sometimes, in moments like these, you can pause to relax. After all that relentless action, you take just a moment for a deep breath to reflect on an elaborate job well done. The escape was the smoothest part of the mission.

It took you a couple of minutes to slip out of a second-floor window and drop to the ground. Jumping the neighbor's fence took a few more seconds.

You didn't get away by much. Little Cindy drove a hard bargain. To avoid waking her sister sleeping in the next bed, you read her a bedtime story. She insisted you read it twice. Fortunately, *Goodnight Moon* is a short book.

You enjoyed reading to the girl more than you enjoyed stewing her father in a car made into a crock pot. Chill would have been proud of you.

Maybe you *aren't* still you. Not quite.

You allow yourself to feel good about that for another whole minute. You feel…what is that unfamiliar feeling? *Pure*. You feel pure.

The Divine Assassin bit started as a cutesy joke. However, heading to Legs Gabrielle's house to debrief and smoke a joint with Sgt. Billy, you feel high in a way that feels like falling in love.

No.

You feel like you *deserve* somebody's love and not just anybody's love. Maybe Legs will swoon at your exploits. You could spin what started as a wicked torture story into a clever caper. Maybe you will escape to Canada. Maybe Legs can shoot more movies in Vancouver or Toronto. Maybe this is the start of a beautiful friendship (with benefits).

Chill's voice pops into your head with a cheery, *Groovy, baby! I can dig it!*

Your smile fades when the scanner chatter heats up from Thai Town. While you were congratulating yourself, Detective Hank Reles shot and killed two uniformed cops as they tried to arrest him.

Shut your mouth.

It's not over.

47,000 PEOPLE ON THE NO-FLY LIST. SOON?
JUST A FLY LIST.

Y ou won't be slipping away and across the Canadian border anytime soon. Like you, Reles is now a desperate fugitive. You're pretty sure he won't flee to Canada, either. Not yet.

Last you checked, the powers that be had 47,000 people on the No-fly list. Of the 680,000 stuck on the KST list — "known or suspected terrorists" — almost half have no known affiliation with a terrorist group. That's many more than the number of those on the watch list for Al Qaeda, Hamas and Hezbollah combined. The government keeps adding to the pile at a rate of 900 new names a day. No wonder they can't keep track of you.

Reles knows what you know. The powers that be won't catch him, either. They're too busy adding to the pile of names they can't manage. Maybe they'll realize their mistake when everybody's on the watch list.

Domestically, the spy agencies concentrate their watch list efforts on New York. Since 9/11, that makes sense. But the city they watch most, after New York, is Dearborn, Michigan. With only 96,000 people, it has a high percentage of Arab-American names in the phone book. The counterterrorism agencies keep staring at groups as perpetual suspects instead of focusing on deserving individuals. Despite all their tech, the alphabet agencies have buried themselves in data so deep, you have to wonder if they're out to stop real terror threats. Or is Homeland Security just another employment program for the otherwise unemployable, like massive infantry hires in the time of drones?

China builds one out of every four cars in the world. Japan is second. Germany comes in third, then South Korea and India. Finally, your beloved USA comes in sixth. America used to build cars. Now they manufacture law enforcement, prison guard jobs and paranoia.

You heard these factoids on NPR because sometimes you joined Chill on protection details. Chill was always good company and a good conversationalist (as long as you shut up while he listened to *Wait, Wait, Don't Tell Me*).

You wish you'd spent more time sitting in cars with Chill and just talking. He had the body and presence to be an intimidating bodyguard, but it seemed he got into the business because he really loved celebrity gossip. You wish Chill was here now.

Big Brother's ability to peer through every web cam, ATM camera, and stoplight cam won't help. They can sift through every bank record and credit card transaction, but the feds still couldn't stop a couple of kids from bombing the Boston Marathon. How are they going to stop a cop if the cop is smart?

From what you've seen, Reles is smart and Sugar says Bekhti has money. They've got the resources to escape. If they hole up until the heat dies down, they could be at large and destroying lives for a long time to come. Theoretically, Reles and Bekhti could be on a boat and in the wind already.

But no, Reles is not going anywhere yet. He'll want to end his time in Los Angeles on a win. When you push a monster, no matter how smart they are, they push back. That's what monsters do. He's going to want the human prize with whom he has been so obsessed. He'll want to make a statement.

You call Sgt. Billy.

"Hey, Chief."

"On my way. Circle the wagons."

"They're already circled, Ace. Legs and Sugar are locked up tight and I'm on the castle wall ready with burning oil in case there's a siege."

"Double the guard on the Princess's chamber. Everyone in to protect the castle?"

"Skunk and Berb are here with me, armed and ready."

"What about the kid?"

That's how you find out Jeremy the Samoan isn't answering his phone.

You call and call again. When Jeremy doesn't pick up, cold spider feet run down your spine and hot sweat trickles down your face. He was supposed to be watching for Reles. Reles must have been watching for the Samoan.

You tell yourself the battery on Jeremy's cell could be dead. You try to come up with more scenaria where Jeremy doesn't try to play the hero against a cop who has just killed two cops. You worry that you and the crew ribbed the newbie too much and now maybe Jeremy's done something stupid to try to prove himself. Or maybe the kid is a goof who is stuck on the toilet because he's stuffed himself with too much pad thai.

But in your heart you already know. America manufactures paranoia now, but in your experience, paranoia is rarely wrong.

Your cell lights, vibrates and plays the chorus to ZZ Top's *Sharp Dressed Man*.

It's Jeremy's cell number showing in the caller ID.

Of course, it's not Jeremy.

WHAT WOULD JESUS DO?

"**H**ello, Jesus."

You expected Reles to call you Armando. This is bad. How does he know your name? "Let me talk to Jeremy. I need proof of life."

"No can do."

"Then we don't have anything to talk about."

You hang up. Too bad you can't hang up on anyone dramatically anymore. That used to be a thing you could do with a phone, hang up with a clatter and a bang and a loud, indignant click. Somebody should write an app to replicate the experience.

The cell lights up again.

You answer, "Sex line. Ramone the Sexy Vampire speaking."

"Jesus! If you hang up on me ag — "

You hang up.

Reles must be seething. A monster like him, treating people the way he does, is all about control. Deny him anything and his rage is dangerous. You might have just sealed the Samoan's fate. Or he was dead already. It's so easy to make a tactical error when you're pressed for time and dealing with lunatics. You prefer the organization a checklist provides.

Maybe Alaska is your answer. Anywhere the population is spread thin is the place for you. More people close together? More friction. Friction means heat and heat leads to burns. Unfortunately, you don't imagine there are many hermits with a penchant for Armani suits and Tanino Crisci shoes. It's hard to get a good latte, go to the movies and enjoy a quiet afternoon in a bookstore when you're hiding out from humanity high above the Arctic Circle.

You drive. You sweat. You count slowly to one hundred. You tell yourself you'll call back when you reach one hundred, but you force yourself to take a deep breath with each number. You're afraid the next time you answer the phone it will be Jeremy screaming. Instead, it's Jeremy.

"He's got a gun to my head, Jesus."

"Hang in there, kid." (That's about the stupidest thing a man has ever said to anyone, but what else is there?)

Reles comes back on the line. "Proof of life."

"Good for you. You've just bought yourself one of your testicles back."

"What?"

"You've let Jeremy live. I'm going to let you keep a testicle for that demonstration of good judgment."

"You don't seem to understand. I've got your little buddy hostage."

"Barely know him. Don't care. What do you want?"

"I need you to pick up some stuff for me. Do that and your Gilligan lives."

"My Gilligan? Haven't heard that one in a long time."

"I like old television. I used to watch a lot of old TV."

"Me, too. I prefer old movies…and candlelight dinners and long walks on the beach. What do you want me to pick up at your house?"

"You're swift."

"If you could do it yourself, you would. Thanks to a bunch of videos just released everywhere, you can't leave whatever rock you're hiding under, can you? What's the matter? Gaston wouldn't do it for you?"

"Gaston isn't answering my calls. Guess he ran away."

He gives you the address. You plug it into the van's GPS. Then he tells you what he wants. There's a go-bag in the back of his bedroom closet.

"There will probably be cops there already, Reles."

"That's your problem."

"Okay."

"Call me back in two hours and I'll tell you where to drop the go-bag. I get the bag, you get your Gilligan."

"I'll call you back in two hours and we'll meet at my place. Top floor of the building — "

"Your dump over Big In Japan?"

"Er…yeah." He's showing off, telling you he's still way ahead of you and even had time to map the territory.

"Yeah, well, we'll just have to negotiate about negotiating after you've got my bag," he says. There's laughter behind his tone. "Back of the upstairs closet. Get it. Get it?"

"Peachy. Anything else?"

"Just one thing. They're plastering my name and picture over every channel!"

"Gee, I wonder why?"

"My picture's on TMZ right now! It's behind George Clooney!"

"Yeah?"

"How did you get George Clooney's email address?"

"The man whose skull you fractured? Chill Gillie? He had a lot of cool friends and they all want you dead."

"Okay…but George fucking *Clooney*? He's holding a press conference about me? My name is trending as a hashtag on Twitter! That and #YesAllWomen.

It's crazy."

"Congrats, Reles. You're a celebrity. I've been meaning to get on Twitter myself, actually. Catch the news, follow some of the people I've been watching out for…maybe tweet some inspirational quotes or something."

"Sure, that's nice for you. George Clooney is mad at me! Tell me, what's he really like?"

"Maybe he'll do lunch with you if you turn yourself in, Reles. How bad do you want to get to know the real George?"

You hang up and try to figure out how you can get the go-bag and save Jeremy. He only gave you two hours so there's no time for stealth. The crime scene in Mueller's house is fresh so you're hoping the LAPD isn't too organized yet. However, it's probably too much to hope that the city's police force will have a slower response time than TMZ and Clooney's publicist.

If there are only a few uniforms in the house, you'll have to try a hit and run. How are you going to do that without hurting somebody who is just doing their job? You feel good and pure, but it's going to be difficult maintaining your good-guy mojo as The Divine Assassin. As you speed on to your destination in Pacific Heights, it seems kind of fitting that the word *assassin* has two asses in it.

You tell yourself you'll improvise once you get there, but going in? You have no idea how to execute the mission without trading shots and maybe executing a few cops.

What would Jesus do?

DON'T BE A HIT MAN UNLESS THE HIT IS A SONG AND YOU'RE JAY-Z.

If Jeremy knew the closest you can park to the address Reles gave you is two blocks, he'd pray harder. The street is blocked with fire engines. There's no fire, but they're ready for one.

You'd hoped the cops would still be reeling and acting dumb. Instead, with two cops dead by Reles's hand, they're working faster, sticking to that 5.7 minute average response time. LAPD has swooped in with all their forces. Judging by their numbers, the police are well aware of Reles's military background and they're worried about IEDs. You don't see one way to complete your mission to get the bag and save the Samoan.

The crowd stares down the street with a mixture of anxiety and anticipation. People say they go to the Indianapolis 500 race to watch cars turn left at high speeds. Everyone knows the real entertainment is in watching beer cans rattle from the deafening noise and wondering when somebody's going to die ugly. Pacific Heights feels like the Indy 500 tonight.

You ask the nearest guy in a bathrobe what's going on. He tells you to shut up and get yourself a TV. Then he turns back to staring down the street. You want to smack him, but his casual rudeness also makes you homesick for New York. You let it pass.

An elderly woman touches your elbow. "I'm Eleanor," she says. She smiles and gives you a flirty wink. "Don't mind him. He's grouchy. The police told us to evacuate. There's a fugitive in the neighborhood."

The nearest fugitive is you. You return the woman's smile.

She looks in your eyes and touches her hair. She straightens to push out her chest. She's pretty old, but the breast implants are probably no more than half her age. Breast implants have been around since the sixties. You suspect Eleanor was one of the brave, early pioneers. Her thick collagen lips are new, too.

You don't know for sure what's going on in her head. However, you're pleased to get a few seconds' relaxation from being on a suicide mission for a maniac. You sigh. It's flattering that you can still inspire an eighty-year-old to flirt.

The numerous beatings and breaks you've received over time have made your nose a little thicker and angle a little to the right. You used to be pretty. Now you've got what Big Denny called, "tough-guy good looks." That means you've got a bad case of thug mug. Your features are coarsening. At least you never got cauliflower ears.

If you thought your chances of living another night were better, you'd worry about the trend your face is following. You're suddenly past thirty and there is no little house with a picket fence, or a wife and a couple of kids in your future. You should have been a lawyer. When divorce attorney's think like merciless assassins, they make long paper.

You thought you'd improvise, but you still have no ideas. The big Samoan is still screwed to the wall. There's just no way to ninja your way in. Too many cops and too many bright lights. Reles's house doesn't just have a few policemen surrounding it. The bomb squad is here. Once they give the all clear, a small crowd of investigators will crawl through the house in booties, masks and white overalls.

If there were fewer cops to blow past — and if you had a fake badge — you might have considered bluffing your way in. You'd still have a hard time walking out of the scene with a bag over your shoulder. Everything has to be bagged and tagged. If Hank Reles still has a teddy bear from childhood in there, it's considered evidence.

If you had a few days, you might have been able to set up diversions all over town, use some magic misdirection and maybe set up a few harmless explosions on office tower rooftops. There's no way you can get in and out.

"They sure moved fast to block off the street, huh?" you say.

The old man in the bathrobe looks your way again. "That's my next-door neighbor's house. Hank Reles. Borrows my lawn mower twice a month and hasn't refilled the damn gas tank once."

"Well…you should have guessed he was criminally insane, then, huh?"

BLACK BAG OPS ARE ALWAYS MORE DANGEROUS THAN YOU THINK.

"This is my husband, Uri," the old woman says.

"Pleased to meet you both." You shake her hand. "I'm J.D."

Uri ignores you and stands on his tiptoes to try to get a better look through the crowd. He doesn't notice when she holds your hand and won't let go.

"Do you think they'll let us get back to our bed soon, J.D.? I really need to get back to my nice warm bed right now. Don't you?"

"Um…dunno."

"How long do you think this will take?" she asks.

You shrug. "Did the police give you any hint?"

"They said they'd give us an estimate when they knew. That was twenty minutes ago."

"I saw a bomb squad truck," Uri says. "Hank's Special Forces or something. I thought that was hooey, but I guess they're taking him seriously."

"They have to, dear," Eleanor says. "It's all over the news. Horrible sex crimes that man was involved in. Murder is so unnecessary."

The old lady looks at you in a way you recognize and you shift your weight from foot to foot uncomfortably.

"Hank is a good-looking young man," she says. "It's terrible, treating women like that. Doesn't he know there's plenty of opportunities on the Internet? Latex and leather and whips and chains and whatnot? Just about everything a body needs." She looks you up and down and licks her lips slowly. "It can be so good. It doesn't have to be mean. Do you know what I mean, J.D.? I bet you do."

When you tear your gaze off Eleanor, Uri's staring at you and his wife. "This isn't the time, Eleanor! For God's sake, girls are dead, woman!"

She straightens and seems like a prim grandmother for a moment. "Yes, Uri. I know. It's sick. It's a terrible thing to do to a person, especially to young girls. It's such a waste! When will pigs like Hank understand that no means no? All this sex and violence comes out of repression, I think. The most conservative places in the world always download the freakiest porn, don't you know?"

You realize she's still holding your hand when she gives a little squeeze with bony, Crypt Keeper fingers and adds, "No means no and yes means yes."

"Um." You pull your hand away gently.

She leans closer. "Uri's right. Now is not the time. But..." Eleanor whispers, "when it is the time, Uri and I swing."

"Eleanor! Have you got an off button?"

"Shut up, you old bastard! You couldn't find *my* on button with a map and a gynecologist to guide you!"

People turn to stare and giggle. You take a step to the left, slowly melting back from the crowd. This, you suspect, is the quintessential Hollywood moment. Old people who were young when they came west lived life a little crazy and never really backed away from the edge. But maybe old people have sex lives in Utah, too.

You check your watch. Ten minutes before time's up.

The answer comes to you. Call Reles and tell him you have the go-bag. He said it was a black bag. Jeremy's only chance is for you to go buy one on the way to the rendezvous. You have to take the chance the bags will look alike, at least long enough for you to put a bullet in the monster's head. It's dark. Maybe you can sell it.

Uri and Eleanor yell louder and you step back, out of the press of bodies. Everyone is watching the elderly couple yell angrily at each other.

Everyone but John Smith of the FBI, of course. The one agent who can most easily pick you out of a crowd does so. You turn to find his pistol pointed at your nose.

"Hi," you say.

"Hi."

Two beefy guys clamp their hands on you and force you to the ground. All three yell at you to comply or they'll shoot you in the head. One screamer slinging one set of orders would have been sufficient.

Smith takes your SIG, the knife in your sock and your phone. Strong hands cuff your wrists behind your back. When they pull you up, Smith smiles wide. "Jesus Salvador Umberto Luis Diaz AKA Dr. J.D. Fix! You are under arrest for multiple counts of murder and domestic terrorism. Who are the fossils you were talking to?"

"Reles's neighbors. Don't really know them. They seem...nice."

Smith glances at one of his fellow agents and tells him to question the old couple. "Be sure to get their names and addresses. I'll send them a fruit basket. If not for them, I would never have spotted Mr. Diaz in the crowd. Anything to say now, smart ass?"

"Shit."

FREE WILL OFTEN COSTS QUITE A BIT.

Smith gets excited when you tell him about the go-bag. He seems less concerned about rescuing Jeremy. He's sure whatever's in the bag must be valuable evidence. He marches you past the yellow crime scene tape and up the block to Reles's house.

It's just another two-story house indistinguishable from all the others. You aren't sure what you expected. It's not like the mailbox is made of human skulls. It's just another house where, until very recently, a monster lived. How many other houses hold monsters? Or maybe you're still a little freaked out by Eleanor and Uri. Is anybody really normal or is that just one of those things everyone pretends to believe? Maybe normal is like Bigfoot. Everybody says it's out there somewhere but proof is thin on the ground.

Agent Smith gets into a huddle with his team out of your earshot. You can't hear the words but you recognize the tone. Urgent orders are being slung and men with guns are running somewhere, bent on a task that could get them killed.

"I didn't much like that note you left at Mueller's house," Smith says. "However, given who you are and who I am, you're not doing me any damage."

"Nobody listens to Jesus."

"Goddamn right." Smith sits you in the back of a cruiser in the street in front of the house. They bag your weapons and put them in the trunk. You're beside the bomb squad truck but if you lean, you can see the house well enough.

Smith keeps the cruiser's back door open and sweeps his arm toward the house in a magnanimous gesture. "After what you did for us with Detective Mueller," he says, "you deserve a front row seat to the show. That was a hell of a thing. I've never seen anyone work that hard to fuck somebody up."

"I've lived through worse for much longer. Does all this newfound gratitude mean you aren't going to shoot me?"

He chuckles. "Oh, I have a strong feeling I'm still going to shoot you. But every Christmas Eve, I'll toast you with some eggnog and, for a second or two? I'll have a doubt about whether I made the right decision."

"Sounds reasonable." You try to look cool, but you don't really know if he's just busting balls or not. Back in New York, you did imply you were willing to kill his family to get what you wanted. Technically. Smith seems the type to hold a grudge.

The FBI agent directs the bomb squad tech searching the house to the upstairs bedroom to search the closet.

"Did you check the basement first?"

Smith looks annoyed but nods. "Yeah. We thought we'd find bones or a dozen bodies chained to the walls. Instead, I'm told Reles has a really kickass man cave. Sectional couch with a beer fridge and a huge HD TV. My bet was there'd be at least a couple of girls from the Dominican or Guatemala down there. Those are the hot countries for human trafficking right now."

"His video collection will be hideous," you say.

"Yeah, we know our jobs, Jesus."

"Sure."

"You used to be an MP, huh?"

"You've read my file a hundred times, I'm sure."

"What makes a guy like you, anyway?"

"Violent video games and too much corn syrup in the after school snacks?"

He cuffs your ear. It hurts but you try not to let that show. "Sorry. I didn't think it was a serious question. I didn't realize you were trying to have a moment with me."

Smith cuffs you again in the same spot. Your eyes bug and your left ear rings.

"So," Smith asks, "what makes a guy like you, anyway?"

"Lack of choices."

"Everybody's got a choice."

"Then why aren't you a hit man, Agent Smith?"

"Because that's a stupid choice."

"When did you decide that?"

Smith smiles. "You're asking me if I sat down with my high school guidance counselor and went over my options? Law enforcement or killing people for money?"

"So, no. You didn't make the choice, one way or the other. How do you know you really had any choice at all, then? You say you know your job. Okay. Maybe you became what you are because that's what you're good at. That's your design. That's not a choice. You were a calf in high school who thinks he made a choice to be a cow for the rest of his life."

The FBI Agent looks at you for a moment before telling you to shut the fuck up.

"I don't just kill for money, by the way. Sometimes it's just called being righteous."

Smith hits you again, harder. You decide this is an excellent time to choose to shut up. Free will and all that.

WITH BOMBS, ALWAYS ASSUME THERE'S MORE THAN ONE DEVICE.

Smith asks an LAPD lieutenant if the bomb tech has found the bag in the upstairs closet yet.

"We don't want to rush it, sir. LAPD says we take it slow to ensure there are no booby traps."

"This guy wasn't about those kinds of boobies. He's a pathetic perve, pure and simple."

You aren't usually the type to blurt things, but to everything there is a season. "No! Take it slow! He was Spec Ops before he was LAPD!"

Agent Smith whirls on you. "But he was *always* a perve. Kind of like you, huh? A torturer, right? You and Reles share lots in common, I bet." He punches you in the gut and you fold up.

When you can get your breath, you say through clenched teeth, "Owie! That's a nasty menstrual cramp I've got going on."

A couple of cops standing nearby burst out laughing. They turn their attention back to Reles's house when Smith gives them a dirty look.

The radio chatter goes back and forth. The bomb tech has found an impressive weapons cache. With these guys, there's always a huge weapons cache, isn't there?

You wonder what Cuba will be like. It's been a long time since you were in Cuba, but you were on the other side of the island. Guantanamo Bay won't be quite as nice. There's a bunch of innocent guys there who will never get out. There's a few real assholes who will also never get out. They'll ask you to commit to their hunger strike but the tubes they use for force feeding are an absolute misery. You don't have the stomach for it. Once again, you don't have that many choices in life. Suicide by cop is still an option.

Then you have a chilling thought. The government has Rendition and Detention sites all over the world. What if they send you to a secret prison in the Middle East? The food there would (almost) make you wish you were detained in Gitmo.

On the other hand, Agent Smith has promised to shoot you. He probably hasn't forgotten that.

The bomb squad's radio receiver in the nearby truck is turned up. "I found a bag in the upstairs closet. It's a black bag."

"Smith! Let me call Reles."

"We've already got the number off your phone, dumbass. We don't need you to call him. SWAT's already got a team coming down on him as we speak. They're zeroing in. We don't need you to do our jobs."

"Let me call Reles, anyway. I'll tell him I've got what he wants. At least if he thinks I'm coming with his stuff, maybe he won't do damage to his hostage. I can talk to him, distract him while your guys get into position."

"They're almost there, Diaz. I don't need you talking to Reles and spooking him. If there is a hostage, we have pros to deal with that. You're a murdering, torturing scumbag. You are in my custody. You will not be in contact with our target. Understand?"

"The guy he's got. He's just a kid, Smith. He's been a bodyguard for a few weeks."

"I'm not responsible for his poor vocational choices. Or maybe your theory is right and he was *designed* to be a sacrificial cow."

"Smith, you must have been designed to be a prick."

The bomb squad's radio clicks on again. "It's a device."

The cops and firefighters go quiet.

Shit. Reles didn't want anything except to blow you up. That seems oddly personal for a guy you met only once. Most bad guys meet you a few times before they feel that strong an urge to burn you in hell.

Smith turns to you with the kind of toothy grin that makes you want to knock each tooth down his throat one by one with a small piano-tuning hammer.

"No problem," the bomb tech says. "It's crude. And…disarmed."

Everybody relaxes and Smith's laughing at you as his cell rings. The FBI agent who's liaising with LAPD SWAT reports they've found Reles' hideout. It's a warehouse in West Hollywood.

Smith puts the caller on speaker and stares into your eyes as the happy report comes in.

"They have eyes on the hostage. Alive."

Jeremy is alive!

"Looks like he's alone, tied to a chair."

Wait. The phone is there, but Reles isn't?

Time for more blurting. "No!" you shout. "*T-t-trap!* Reles is — "

The explosion in West Hollywood cuts off your warning and finishes your argument for you.

It takes a moment before the FBI agent comes back on the line. "Smith! We've got men down! The whole *building* came down!"

Sorry, Jeremy.

Smith curses. The radio cross-chatter sounds like a fight. Amid all the angry and urgent conversations, only you seem to hear the bomb tech in Reles's house. Over the open channel, he says, "Uh-oh."

You lie down on the cruiser's back seat and then roll to the floor.

Take a breath. Screw eyes tight.

HOW TO STINK UP THE PLACE

The explosion doesn't bring down Reles's entire house, but the concussive wave feels like a padded hammer in the chest.

You bring your knees up and pull the handcuffs under your heels. It's a tight squeeze but if Javier Bardem can do it in *No Country for Old Men*, a ninja like you should be able to do it. It looked easier in the movie but you manage to get your hands in front of you without dislocating a shoulder.

When you pop your head up for a quick peek, people in the street are picking themselves up off the ground. You crane your neck but you don't see much smoke or dust. This moment of confusion would have been a good time to run, but Agent Smith is at the door with his gun out and pointed at your chest shaking his head. He looks judgmental and jittery.

A bomb specialist in full gear stumbles out of the front door and a cloud of thin, white smoke pours out after him. He's waving his arms wildly. Everyone stops and stares for a couple of seconds, more than a little amazed as the tech falls off the front steps. A group of cops and firefighters rush forward to help the man, but several slow and then drop back.

A senior firefighter waves the group back. The cops stumble toward the street, coughing and heaving. Two firefighters pull their oxygen masks up from their Scott Air Packs and rush forward. They grip the bomb tech under his armpits to yank him away from the advancing cloud. With his heavy gear, it's a hard slog but they pull him across the grass. The senior firefighter is screaming, but his mask makes him incomprehensible until he's halfway to the street.

"Carbide! *Carbide bomb! Carbide gas!*"

Calcium carbide, when exposed to air or water, makes a big boom. It also produces a cloud of noxious gas. Reles must have used a lot of carbide for the secondary device. A little carbide can kill gophers. A lot sends humans screaming and gasping.

Everyone's forced back to the street, but it seems the carbide bomb hasn't killed anyone. If Reles wanted mass casualties...this doesn't make much sense. What purpose would a carbide bomb serve?

Agent Smith notices your hands are no longer behind your back and he leans into the car. He smacks the back of your head and pushes you down to the floor by the back of your neck. "I won't have to shoot you, Jesus. Maybe I'll just leave you in the car and let the gas — "

You figure out Reles's play when the chatter of gunfire from an AK starts up from behind you. M43 rounds put holes in the car's windshield, making deadly little stars in the glass with each shot. The next rounds shatter the side and rear windows.

For a moment, you're sure you are shot. It's hard to breathe.

Agent Smith's hand is no longer on your neck. He slumps forward, draped across your back. His pistol thunks to the floor. There's a sound that hot, fast metal makes when it hits a body. You feel the vibration as each round tunnels through him. Smith doesn't scream as he goes. Just a soft grunt and his last hot breath escapes his slack jaws into your ear. It's as if Agent Smith softens and melts away into death.

Smith was human a moment ago. Now he's a sack of meat in what was once a decent suit.

Death is always a surprise, even when it's expected. It's awful when it's slow, but sometimes it's so lightning quick there's no transition time for the victim. A person is there and suddenly they are not. There's no time for Smith to process what's happening to him, no moment of clarity and noble last words. When death happens this quick, it makes you worry there's no meaning at all. Smith's erasure seems to carry no more significance to the universe than the death of a rabbit in the jaws of a coyote. Maybe less so. At least the rabbit sees the predator coming and has a chance to run.

You're under heavy, dead weight as the metal rain continues in short bursts. The shooter has moved on to other targets. By the screams, you can tell he's aiming to wound. You don't have to risk poking your head up. You know what he's doing. Reles must be in a high window in a house directly across the street from his own house. He's spreading the misery around, creating chaos.

Kill a man and he's down. Wound a man and two others may risk their lives to save the fallen. The short bursts continue. The screams go on and on.

TO HUNT A MONSTER, YOU MUST BE ONE.
TAKE THAT, NIETZSCHE.

In your mind's eye, you picture knees exploding, feet turned to red mash and fingers lost. The regular cops will be pinned down. Pistols are useless against rifles at this range. Whoever's left of SWAT will be organizing, looking for a safe route from cover so they can outflank him. They'll be crouching behind engine blocks and calling for more backup, an LAPD helicopter and God.

They'll need the Medcat, an armored vehicle with four litters, to pull out the casualties. A Ballistic Engineered Armored Response Counter Attack Truck AKA a BearCat is also on the menu so SWAT can safely approach Reles's position.

You can't hear Reles laugh, but you'd bet anything he is laughing. He might even have an erection. Guys like him, whatever he does is about power. He works out hard to intimidate. He trains hard to make himself scarier. He victimizes girls and women. Behind the monster's mask, to feel such a need to be what he is, how incredibly weak Reles must be. Under his suit of muscle, Reles is terrified all the time.

"Fear leads to anger. Anger leads to hate. Hate leads to suffering." Yoda was goddamned right. Beneath the anger is always fear.

The street will be filled with men and women in uniform trying to save themselves and each other under fire. Helping people is so hard. Hurting them is too easy.

If you were Reles, you'd have two Remington ACRs up in that high window. As soon as both mags on the Adaptive Combat Rifles clicked empty, you'd throw smoke and run, leaving the weapons behind, probably rigged with an IED if you had enough time to plan ahead. Maybe Reles will toss a grenade or two, as well. He doesn't seem to have any respect for his brothers and sisters in arms, but then, he was never really one of them. He's a maniac and a criminal who somehow managed to slip through the screening process.

You didn't really become a criminal until you were out of the military and the legit world had no more use for you. You remind yourself that you're very different from Reles. That's a good thing to try to remember because you know what happens next. When the police mount a counterattack, Reles will be long gone, but he'll leave behind plenty of toys to slow the cops down.

How many IEDs did Reles leave behind him to cover his retreat? How many feet of detcord trail through that house? How many decoy devices and spoilsport time bombs await anyone who tries to get to his position? He might even have a claymore waiting for his pursuers.

You would.

As soon as the shooting stops from the neighbor's house, you push Agent Smith off you and out through the open door. He lands in the street with a wet smack. His left eye stares at the sky. His right eye points at you.

"Sorry, man." Staying low, you slip through the passenger side door. The keys to the handcuffs hang from Smith's belt. Your hands shake as you crawl into the driver's seat. The car keys are in the ignition.

Before the police can recover from the attack, you roar away as the first smoke bombs hit the pavement. Between the gas cloud behind them and the billowing smoke screen in front of them, both you and Reles have plenty of cover for your escape.

No police stand at the cordon. The civilians have run for their lives or they're cowering in clutches behind sparse cover. You hit the lights and sirens. It's a long time since you drove a cruiser under lights and sirens, except back then it was a Jeep. It feels good. With all the broken windows, the experience is weirdly familiar.

As you speed past, one of the strobes freezes Eleanor and Uri in light. In their terror, the old couple clutch each other.

The tires squeal as you tear around the back of the block, hoping to catch Reles on the run. You've got Agent John Smith's blood all over you and his 9 mm at the ready. Your weapons are in the trunk. You're on a righteous mission.

However, the universe doesn't care about what feels right. Indifferent to your need for vengeance, it's about the distance between stars and people. Nature is hot chemistry and cold physics. You are alone and Reles gets away.

You get away, too, because you think like him. You're the star of your movie. You're the hero. You tell yourself that you are not like Hank Reles. But somewhere, from far away — in the chasm between the fearful boy you were and the man you've become — there is an echo of doubt from a basement in Miami.

You slip out of character. Just for a moment, you let the mask fall. You aren't *you*, anymore.

I am. I am like Hank Reles.

Before you begin to weep, you reach for your rage. That's never far away. All you have to do is to think of Tia Marta with her hot iron. You summon the memory of the Bug Man of Surfside Beach. That memory is as ready as ever. You see him standing over you with his big mirrored aviator sunglasses. He asks, "Paper or plastic?" before slipping a bag over your head.

The sunglasses made him *look* like a bug, but he had an uncaring, insectile heart, too. As the bag slipped over your head — before the hot plastic clung to your face to take your air and thoughts away — you glimpsed your face in the mirrors concealing the Bug Man's eyes.

Yours is a little boy's face confronted with the truth of the universe too soon. That is the face of fear and helplessness and utter incomprehension.

The hate roars back.

You're powerful and righteous again. Your hate will lead to Reles's suffering. Knowing this, the little boy in the basement slips back into the dark, out of sight, back to Miami, swept away into history.

You are very much like Hank Reles. That's why you're the one to kill him.

HOW TO GET THE BLOOD OFF

At the home of Legs Gabrielle, Sgt. Billy opens the back door. His eyes are wide as he takes you in.

"I know. It's a lot of blood but none of it's mine. The van is parked down the hill."

You remove your shoes so you don't track blood through the house. Sgt. Billy promises to run them under a hose out back and points you upstairs to a bedroom suite with a shower.

Big Denny told you once that, when covered with someone else's blood, it's best to shower with cold water first. "You want to keep the pores closed. People are filthy. Who knows what they've got or where they've been?"

You're not sure the cold water trick really works, but you scrub and shiver as long as you can stand it under a cold blast. You get all of Smith's blood off before you chance spinning the shower dial to hot. Soon the bathroom is steamed to a fog. You're still scrubbing when you hear the door open and there's a human figure beyond the fogged glass.

For a second, you're sure it must be Reles, as relentless as the devil. When you realize you aren't dead at the bottom of the shower yet, you hope it's Legs.

It's Sugar.

"Brought a towel for you."

"Thanks."

"You okay?"

"I will be."

"How do you know?"

"Experience. At least, that's how it's worked out so far. I expect that will continue until it doesn't."

"Did you see Detective Reles?"

"No. But it was him."

"How do you know?"

"Because of what he planned and how he slings bullets."

"It's all over the news. They're looking for you, too. Wolf Blitzer is on CNN calling Pacific Heights a war zone."

"War zones are everywhere, but usually they're confined to bedrooms and living rooms and kitchen tables. How many cops are dead?"

"Two. Plenty more injured. They aren't saying for sure yet."

"Thanks for the update. Will you excuse me while I clean up?"

"Sure. Go ahead." Sugar doesn't leave.

"I need some time here."

"Take your time."

"What do you want?"

"Tell me…about what you do…what's the worst thing you ever did?"

"Why do you want to know, Sugar?"

"Maybe so I can feel better about the things I've had to do."

You let the hot water wash over you for a minute before answering.

There's a lot of competition for the worst thing you've ever done. You pick the first thing that comes to mind. You tell Sugar about the time you killed the Ghost.

SMART HIT MEN WORK ON AN EMPTY STOMACH.

The Ghost moved like an old man but he was really only fifty or so. This was the first job you pulled for The Machine. Big Denny said you had to make your bones so the boss, Vincent Lima, would know you were solid.

When you came back from Iraq via Germany, you'd scrounged for jobs but no one would hire you. Meanwhile, Big Denny had a car and wasn't worrying about how to pay for his next meal. He said the hours were easy and it was better than living on the street. You'd done plenty of that already and didn't want to go back.

Big Denny drove you out to a shack in the middle of nowhere. Wantage, New Jersey. He parked by the side of the road and you both watched the place for a while. Plastic flamingos crammed the front yard. The maple tree out front was all wind chimes. Concentric metal and plastic rings twisted hypnotically in the breeze. The mailbox was topped with a wooden sculpture of two men on either end of a little saw that moved back and forth when the wind was just right. A pink, hand-painted sign read: Yard Art 4 SALE.

"It's a guy selling a bunch of crap. What business does the Spanish mob have way out here?"

"Their business."

"C'mon, man. I can't kill some guy without knowing why."

Big Denny shook his head. "That's not how this works. You only get to know what you need to know. It's just like the Army, Jesus. Did they let you do a lot of thinking for yourself?"

"No. They didn't, but if I'm going to do this, I need to know he's a bad guy who deserves it."

Big Denny put a paw on your shoulder and stared into your eyes. "The Ghost is a bad guy who deserves it."

"You know this for sure?"

"Valid. I know it."

"Fine. Gimme the throwaway gun."

"The boss says no."

"What?"

"Sorry, buddy. The assignment comes straight from Vincent but Jimmy added a twist."

"Who the hell is Jimmy?"

"That would be the boss's son."

"Of course."

"You gotta go in without a gun or a knife to do it."

"Jimmy doesn't want to hire me at all, does he?"

"I vouched for you, but Jimmy's got a hard on for Cubans. He says if you do the job as ordered, you're in and they'll start you off with nice bank and a no-show job in construction. If I have to do the job, you're out. You can't no-show on the hit, man."

You stared at your oldest friend for a long minute. "You mean if I don't do the job, you're supposed to kill me, too, right?"

"Jesus!" Big Denny put on his hurt feelings look with puppy dog eyes. He looked like a scolded pug. "After all we've been through together, you can ask that?"

"Denny. Dude."

"Yeah, okay, I'm supposed to do you if you don't do him, but you know I wouldn't. You'd have to disappear, though. It would be a whole…thing, you know. Let's not make this a big thing. No complications, no danger. You Scooby Doo the Ghost, we go get pancakes. There's a great pancake place in West Orange on the way back."

"I don't want to go get pancakes after ending somebody!"

"Well, Christ! Then you box up yours for later, drama king. I come all the way out here? I want pancakes. Now get out of the car and do him. Remember, I vouched for you. Maybe nothing good happens to me if you don't pan out. You ever think of that?"

You got out of the car and looked around. The metal circles within circles twisted faster as a cold breeze wafted over you. You shivered, but you were sweating, too.

Big Denny rolled down his window. "He lives alone. I'll honk if somebody shows up but nobody's going to show up. One other thing. You're supposed to make it look like an accident. But you're supposed to make a statement."

"What does that mean?"

"A statement."

"Yeah?"

"You know…like…drama…like…I don't fuckin' know. Do what you can. It's from Jimmy. He's a little off."

Before you could argue further, Big Denny De Molina rolled up the window, locked the door and waved you on.

You walked to the front door and knocked. You jumped when a cat in the front window leapt away. You hadn't realized it was there until you caught the movement in the corner of your eye.

The Ghost came to the door. You had assumed he got the name from being some kind of spy worthy of the moniker. The guy who answered the door wasn't the sort who looked like he could pass through borders and assume multiple identities. He stood at the door in his pyjamas, bent at the waist and neck and leaning on an IV pole.

"Hey," you said.

A moment passed. "Well?"

"I wanna buy all your flamingos. My boss is having a birthday. I need forty-seven. He's forty-seven."

"That right?" The Ghost peered around you to look at Big Denny in the car. He frowned. "You drove all the way out from New York for my flamingos?"

"Yes. Yes, I did."

He looked you up and down. "Bullshit. You've come to kill me."

"I — "

"Come on in. Let's get it over with."

WHERE TO HIDE THE GUN

The Ghost sat in a plaid chair the cat had scratched to shreds. The television was a huge old set with rabbit ears pulling in a ragged signal from FOX News.

"Well?"

You stood in the Ghost's house and looked around. No pictures of his loved ones. No hint of what he did for the mob that got him in trouble. You don't know what you expected, but never this.

"This is a test, isn't it?" you asked.

"More for me than you, I hope. What's a matter? First time?"

You didn't answer and his face fell. "Oh, shit. They sent me a rookie. That's less respect than I was hoping for."

"I've killed people," you said.

The Ghost looked you up and down and smirked. "Self-defense, though, right? Not like this? Not a sick guy in a chair." He nodded at his IV pole and the tube snaking into the back of his wrist. He tapped the pole with a finger. "Kidneys. Never had a family or enough friends to scrounge up a spare kidney for a transplant."

"That sucks."

"Yup. But now it's harder for you like this, isn't it? You're wondering why they don't just let me die in peace."

"Why aren't they?"

"Whaddayou? The Ghost of Christmas Past? I'm the Ghost of Your Future, you little shit. I ben a *bastid*, okay?"

"Oh."

"Yeah. Oh. And now I've got a wet behind the ears wannabe assassin. You'll probably fuck it up. You look like a fuck up."

"And this is why you have no friends."

He smiled. "A good, quick death would be better than fading away. I'm sick of sittin' there in the clinic, going for dialysis. I'm not much of a reader. Other people read while they get the dialysis. I sit there watchin' the pretty nurses and wish I was twenty years younger." He sighed and stared at you. "So on a cold autumn day in Wantage, New Jersey, you show up at my door on the last day of my life to do me the favor of a quick death. Feels like I'm doin' *you* the favor, fuck up."

"I'm starting to think I should turn around and let you die slow, Ghost. You're too rude to die quick."

He laughed at the joke. Then he laughed at you. Then he farted loudly and got up abruptly. "Outta my way! I haven't had a decent shit in days and if you aren't going to do it, let me poop out a present for you to take with you, back to New York."

He disappeared into the bathroom but left the door ajar.

The cat looked at you as if to say, "Well?"

You spotted the Metamucil on the kitchen counter.

You kicked the door open and he sat on the toilet with a revolver pointed at your gut. You grabbed for it. The Ghost failed to get off a shot. The cylinder couldn't turn in your grip. You twisted it away from him. "Dude!"

"Always keep a back-up gun behind the toilet tank, kid. If you're going to last in this business, learn your craft, for Christ sake! Be observant. Be a smart ninja."

"Any last words?"

"Don't give assholes the chance to say any last words. They'll pop you if you play by the rules."

"Okay. That it?"

"Why are you doing this, kid? I don't think your heart's in it."

You looked around his bathroom. The tub had never been scrubbed. The paint flaked off the walls. Whatever he'd done, it sure didn't look like it paid. "Why did you do whatever you did for the mob, Ghost?"

He smiled. "Wantage. I live in Wantage. I'm filled with wantage."

You unscrewed the cap off the Metamucil canister and told him to tip his head back and open wide. He cooperated. You poured the orange powder in and he started to cough immediately.

His saliva turned the powder to sludge too slowly so you poured in a little water from the sink. Not so much for him to swallow. Just enough that the sludge expands in his throat and cuts off his airway. He died thrashing, bare assed on the toilet.

You thought you killed him. You sort of did, though, a week later, the newspaper reported that he'd died of a heart attack. His real name was Leonard Meinhof. The coroner's report didn't mention more details, but the home care nurse who found Ghost told the newspaper that she'd found the man's face eaten by his cat.

You told yourself you'd done the dying man a favor. Back in Denny's car, you realized the wheel gun from behind the toilet tank was empty. Ghost had done you the favor. It still wasn't self-defense, but you'd thought yourself a smart ninja for using a common household medication for constipation to your advantage. The Ghost had made it easier for you.

"Congratulations," Denny said. "Cherry's broken. You're in and the pancakes are on me."

"Waffles."

"Whatever."

"Denny?"

"Yeah?"

"I'm in, right?"

"Balls deep."

"What did he do?"

"What? The Ghost?"

"What did he *do*, Den? Between us. He's a bad guy. You said it. I Scooby Doo'd the Ghost, just like you said. I'm in. So? What's his deal?"

Big Denny laughed. "No fuckin' clue. Welcome to The Machine, Jesus."

"You said he deserved it! You sonofabitch!"

Denny just shrugs and laughs and you promise you'll get back at him.

"Yeah, sure," he says. "Someday. Everybody swears they'll get even someday. Nobody gets even a little bit of justice."

The waffles in West Orange did taste good, but by the time Denny got you as far as East Orange he pulled over so you could puke in a ditch. You were still so mad at him you refused to get out. Big Denny was still trying to push you out of his car when you yelled, "A little bit of justice, bitch!" and threw up all over him.

CONFESSION IS GOOD FOR THE
PROSECUTING ATTORNEY.

You've never confessed all the details to anyone but Big Denny. Sugar was the wrong person to open up to. She stands outside the shower, laughing. It's not a funny story. At least, it isn't a funny story to you.

Legs pokes her head in. "Now's not the time for fun and games, kiddies. Everyone out of the pool. You'll get your fingers all pruney."

You poke your head out of the shower stall and you and Sugar say together, "We didn't do anything."

Legs rolls her eyes.

Sugar gives you a hard look. This morning, Sugar does not look sweet but you figure PTSD takes many forms. For a girl you found kidnapped, beaten and threatened in a cage, she's actually doing remarkably well.

Legs grabs the towel, throws it at you and pulls Sugar out the door. After you dry yourself off, you discover Sgt. Billy has retrieved clothes for you from the van.

You're still getting your shirt on when Legs pounds on the door. "We need to talk, Jesus!"

You tell her to come in and, as she rushes in with Sugar behind her, you turn away to finish buttoning your shirt, hiding your scars again.

"I'm sorry," Legs says. "I didn't mean to embarrass you."

"It's okay." Your tone tells her it's not okay.

Sugar puts a soft hand on your shoulder. "It is okay, though. Scars mean life. Everybody's got them, seen and unseen." She buttons your top two buttons for you, smiles and knots your tie. An Oxford knot. She's done this before. She pats your cheek and sits on the bed. "Who taught you to be ashamed of your scars? The person who gave them to you?"

"No. Tia Marta liked scars too much. She enjoyed giving them. Skin without a scratch was an invitation to her."

"So? Who made you feel bad?"

You smile. "The truth is, it was a girl from Princeton. In the Army, scars were a macho bullshit sort of badge of honor. But once I was out...I don't go swimming in public pools. Let's leave it at that."

"No," Sugar says. "Tell us about the girl from Princeton."

Legs moves to stand by the bed. "I need to talk about Reles."

"Wait," Sugar says. "Let him tell it. He tells good stories."

You sigh. "Not much to tell. I was self-conscious, especially about the burns. When I was dating, I tried to stay clothed. Even making love in the dark…well…a woman putting her hands on my bare back…you know. You can feel thick scars and next thing, they want to turn on the light."

"Is that what the girl did?"

"Something like that. We were alone in her dorm and we'd already been making out pretty heavy. She…well, you know…she got to feeling pretty good."

"You got her off, you mean?" Sugar asks.

"Ehm. Yeah. I turn off the light and now that she's achieved some satisfaction, we're basically two strangers in the dark. I thought I knew where this was going, but now that she's had her…er…climax, she doesn't seem too concerned about mine."

"Women can be such bitches sometimes," Sugar says.

You clear your throat. "Um…anyway, things slow down and she's smoking beside me in the dark and she's gotten quiet. I've made my move and I thought we were already on a trajectory, you know? A glide path where we land at a happy airport. Instead, she's put us in a holding pattern."

"What'd you do?" Sugar asks.

"I start talking to her about her life at Princeton. She's already tired of college guys and she's thinking about maybe becoming a professor or traveling more, but she doesn't know what she really wants. Eventually, she finishes her smoke and it looks pretty bleak."

"And you've got blue balls," Sugar says. She smiles and licks her lips in a way that makes you need to look away.

The licking thing reminds you of the old lady, Eleanor. Also, the fact that Sugar is a submissive prostitute makes you squeamish about her advances. Legs is smart and funny. Smart, powerful women are more to your taste. You wish it was Legs looking at you and licking her lips that way.

"Anyway," you say. "The girl gets off the bed and tells me to take off my shirt and pants. I start to get nervous, but she keeps the room dark. She opens up a tiny fridge and in a moment she's back with whipped cream in a can."

"Oh, yeah!" Sugar says.

"For me, it's more like 'Oh, no!' She unbuttoned my shirt and put cold whipped cream on my nipples. I should be thinking about the sex, but I'm just hoping she doesn't touch the crucifixion scar on my chest. She'll either think I'm part of some Catholic cult or — "

"She'll think it's ugly," Sugar says.

"Hey!" Legs says sharply.

"Yeah. No. She's right," you admit. "So I'm feeling nervous and I start trying to get the attention back on her. I start talking…well…heh. I start rambling, really. An Army buddy had this patter he used on girls. He started talking philosophy with them, about sexual freedom and being your own autonomous person and whatnot. I was nervous. I don't know what the hell I was doing. When she stops licking my nipples, I know I've fucked up."

"She felt the scar, huh?" Legs asks.

"No. I was talking about the short life and deep thoughts of Albert Camus. I'd read all about him. I was trying to pick up girls at Princeton, for God's sake! I wanted to impress them. Some of them liked the uniform well enough, but when I talked, I felt too stupid to share their air. A guy named Dallas suggested the way to a smart girl's heart was to talk about Albert Camus. I'd read his stories. The novels were short and better than his philosophy, really. But I'd never stepped into a classroom. I'd never heard his name…well, I'd never heard his name spoken by someone who knew how to pronounce it. Dallas steered me wrong. I pronounced it like '*Kay-muss.*' It's pronounced '*Ka-moo!*'"

"So?" Sugar wouldn't have cared. That fact makes you like her a little more.

"What happened?" Legs asks.

"She thought my mistake was hilarious. She started giggling. Then she sat up quick and turned on the light. And there I am, naked with nothing but three columns of whipped cream to hide me."

"*Three?* Oh. Not three nipples." Sugar has a wicked smile.

"It's another of those stories that should be funny, I guess. Except that's when she started screaming. You two ladies are the first to see my scars since then."

Legs smiles, too, but not unkindly. Still, she's a comic. If Reles doesn't kidnap and kill her first, this story is going to be retold onstage in a club in Denver to a roaring drunk audience someday. You're guessing that Legs will assume the role of the hapless naked goof in the bed and the embarrassment will be over an appendix scar. It won't be as good, but she'll find a way to amp it up and sell it for laughs.

"Sorry that happened to you," Legs says. "But we need to talk about how you're going to track down Reles."

You were about to explain how you need to use her as bait. Instead, Sugar's cell rings. She hands you the phone. It's Hank Reles.

He tells you to meet him at your abandoned apartment over Big in Japan.

"The FBI are sitting on that place. That's why I'm not there."

"I've taken care of the FBI. That's why I'm here."

"What does that mean?"

"You can imagine."

"What if I don't come?" you say. "It would be easier to just call the cops on your ass."

"You won't. What if I get away again? I could just disappear. Got that all planned out. Then one day I could resurface. You'll know when that day happens because Legs Gabrielle, my fair lady, will have disappeared off the face of the Earth. Don't worry, though. I'll keep that bitch in a little dog cage, alive for a while, anyway. She doesn't know how to behave yet, but I can crate her, train her, bring her to heel and rub her nose in it."

"I see your point."

"Don't get cute, Jesus. If the cops get to me before you do, you'll never find out what happened to your mother."

"I don't — "

"*After* Surfside Beach."

"She's — "

"Maritza Diaz. You remember Surfside Beach, don't you? I'll bet you do."

"When do we meet?"

"As soon as you get here."

"On my way."

THE FBI HAS OVER 85,000 ACTIVE MISSING PERSONS CASES.

In the United States, about 1,800 people disappear every day. You've seen stats as high as 2,300 a day. Where all the people go is a mystery. Where are all the people kicked out of their homes in Detroit, for instance? Where could they all go?

Dallas, the fat pickup artist and Albert Camus fan, told you the missing persons phenomenon comprised crazy people, teenage runaways and black ops renditions, but the renditions were really a cover up for alien abduction. On further consideration, you shouldn't have been taking any dating advice from Dallas.

Many of the missing are found or wander back home on their own, but the FBI has 85,000 active missing persons cases. Maritza Diaz, your mother, is one of them. You looked for her yourself, of course. Later, you accepted that she drowned that day at Surfside Beach and never got a proper burial.

Now the hope that you aren't alone in the world is back. Hope burns bright, even in dark places. That's what speeds you back to the little parking lot behind Big in Japan and up the back stairs. Your hope dims quickly.

You find the first FBI agent at the bottom of the stairs. He's nailed to the wall: pinned, dead and staring, arms outstretched. Hank Reles counts a nail gun among his toys. There's a big knife still sticking out of his gut. It's a crude crucifixion and a message to you. The agent didn't take two or three days to die, though. The blood streaming down his face isn't from a crown of thorns. He was beaten about the skull, just like Chill.

You point your SIG up the stairs. "Reles? You up there?"

"Yeah, we're here."

"Who is we?"

"We is me and my new buddy, Agent Caruthers. C'mon up. Don't worry. He's disarmed and having a nap."

"How do I know you won't shoot? You've already tried to kill me."

"Took out your guard and covered your escape from the Federal Bureau of Injustice, didn't I?" He laughs. "Would you feel better if you knew I was only following orders?"

"Did the order come from Big Denny?"

"Shit, no. Gaston wants you dead. Wouldn't really surprise me if a bunch of other people want you on the dirt side of the grass, too."

"Common problem. We share that."

"Funny you're so hard to kill. Guess you got toughened up young, huh?"

"Why do you want to talk now?"

"C'mon, Jesus! You killed Tia Marta for me, so I owe you for that much."

"What?"

"What I said."

"I'm intrigued. I am not reassured. Go on. Why the big light show for the cops?"

"No, stupid. For Gaston. If I follow orders, he gives me a free ride out of here on a yacht. It's always good to do what Gaston tells you to do. He's a rich guy."

"What do you want to know, Reles? You didn't call me here for gits and shiggles."

"Heh. I've got everybody looking for me thanks to you. Maybe I wanna see the man who screwed up my shit, eye to eye. You want to know what I want? How about this? How long did you have to beat on Mueller before he gave me up?"

"Oh, that. All I had to do was say please."

"Heh. He was a bitch. You want to know where Maritza is now? Let's talk like men. I want something from you. You got a gun. I got a gun. But what I have to say will need a face to face."

You take out your phone and select the camera. You crawl on your belly down the narrow hallway until you can reach the bottom corner of the door. You snap a quick picture and pull back.

The tactic is half recon but mostly it's a test. The picture shows Reles standing behind a guy in a suit. The guy in the suit is slumped in a chair. The hostage does not fit Gaston Bekhti's description. The hostage who isn't really a hostage trick had to be ruled out first.

As to the test, it's important to note that Reles didn't try to shoot you through the wall when you took the picture. He's just standing there, his gun at his side. Also of note, Detective Reles is shirtless. This is a significant detail. He's not just showing off the rock hard abs and slabs of muscle. He's letting you see his scars.

As you enlarge the photo on your screen, you gasp. Your scars are like wings across your back. The raised crescents of iron burns spread across Reles's chest. You've seen that burn pattern once before, across a boy's chest.

What name do you go by, muchacho? Like dialogue from an old Western.

He'd asked you that. Back in the cafe across from the comedy club, he didn't simply ask your name. He was asking what your alias was. You should have asked him the same question.

"*Darren?*"

"Darren Hill from Sarasota. You didn't recognize me before, but I guess we didn't know each other very long. You were my replacement."

"I thought you were dead. And you weren't built like the Hulk then. And mostly we were in the dark."

"Last time I talked to you," Reles says, "you didn't speak English."

You step into the doorway, pistol ready. He sinks, his gun is against the unconscious man's head. The FBI agent is a human shield. Kind of ironic since Agent Smith was your shield.

"Hi, Jesus. Funny that we were kids together and now here we are again. Reunion time." He points his pistol at you. You might be able to clip him, but if he fires, he'll definitely hollow you out.

You drop the SIG.

As soon as your weapon thunks to the floor, Reles pushes the chair over and the FBI agent falls flat. His neck shouldn't move that way, or that far to the side. It's loose, like the bones have melted. You watch the agent's chest, but of course it doesn't move.

You fell for the false hostage trick, after all.

A GOOD CHOKEHOLD TAKES YOU OUT FAST.
THINK BLOOD, NOT AIR.

Reles orders you to take out your cell phone.

With shaking hands, you do as you're told. You went with the Android because you can take the battery out of an Android. iPhones are easier to trace. You wish you had an iPhone with you now. The cops could be surrounding the place, rescuing you. Ha! No. SWAT would shoot you both.

"Call Legs," he says.

"It won't do you any good."

"Call her or I'll kneecap you and then you'll call her anyway, but crying hard."

You have to agree with his logic so you dial the number that might just save your life. That's extremely unlikely, of course, but when you're dealing with a crazed stalker who also happens to be a cop killer, it's important to make them feel loved.

He takes a step closer, menacing and meaning business but not so close you can make a desperate lunge and play hero. He picks up your gun and gestures with the SIG to make you hurry up so he can speak with Legs Gabrielle. Maybe he'll lure her out of hiding. Maybe he'll shoot you between the eyes and taunt her.

You thought the movie reel of your life would flash by in your last moments. You didn't want to endure that because, frankly, your childhood was brutal and filled with death. However, your brain doesn't rehash all that. Instead, you get one of those short, independent films that plays in art cinemas that nobody sees. You get the most recent replay of the brutality, death and stupid mistakes that landed you at this place and time. Like the rest of your life, if not for the funny bits, the replay would be too much for your heart to take. It's hard to say which part of your life weighs heaviest on you. Too late to make corrections now.

The childhood stuff happened to you and none of that was your fault. The little film that runs through your head now? This is your fault. It's a clever and funny story, but mostly desperate. Call it *The Dumb Assassin's Playbook* by Jesus Diaz, the bullshit artist who died because he believed his own hype. You thought you were so smart, which — more irony and embarrassment — is a key component of winding up with a target on your forehead.

"Now!" the big man roars.

Push that button. But don't expect escape. No one escapes the past. You hope to die and be reborn for another shot at a long boring life among kind people.

You take a deep breath, squeeze your eyes tight and three...two...one...you hit *Send. Is this all there is?* Time to find out. You open your mouth, but not to speak.

The mines you hid in the dead air conditioning unit explode and the cave-in takes the roof. The ceiling collapses under the weight of three tons of steel. Detective Hank Reles isn't just killed. He is erased. The air conditioner squashes him flat and keeps going through the second floor. It crashes through, all the way to the ground floor and the basement.

Monsters shouldn't die so quickly, but you went with the only play you had left.

The concussive wave slams you back, but fortunately, your mouth was open and you remembered not to hold your breath. Anticipating an explosion, that's anyone's natural instinct, but that's not the smart ninja's play. If you had held your breath that close to the explosion, your lungs would have popped like balloons and your first and last clue you were dead would have been the taste of blood. An open mouth lessens the effect of the wall of air that just got displaced, too, but the headache is still epic. It feels like your head is trapped in a vice and your brain is a throbbing, aching thing slamming around the inside of your skull trying to get out of the dark.

But you don't die. Instead, you're trapped in the present tense, living and dying in the awful now. You claw at the door frame at the edge of the apartment so you won't get sucked down the hole. The choking dust and debris hangs in the air. What's left of your futon is on fire as it slides into the expanding hole in the middle of the floor. Your ears ring with a whine that goes on and on. You stumble to the stairs and lean on the railing, feeling your way through a cloud of brown dust.

When you emerge from the building at the bottom of the rear stairs, you can't stop coughing. The dizziness consumes. It feels like your brain has slipped a gear. The mines you got from the Chicago gig were your trump card. You thought you'd use the explosives if Big Denny De Molina's enforcers ever found you. Sometimes it pays to have lots of enemies.

Sugar pulls up in Legs Gabrielle's car. She steps out and beams a smile at you. She's wearing a splashy red party dress. You're still coughing and dizzy, but seeing her makes you smile. You wave to let her know you're okay. She waves back. You feel like you've saved your little sister from the wolf. Another monster's dead. One more monster to find.

"Paper or plastic?" A voice speaks from behind you. A plastic bag slips over your head. Somehow, the Bug Man of Surfside Beach has found you again. A sinewy forearm wraps around your windpipe as you gasp for breath.

Nightmares live.

The building is on fire. Smoke and sirens fill the air. Your air won't last long enough for any help to arrive.

"You could have been a king," the Bug Man says. "In another life, you could have come with us, been one of us. You could have been drinking beer on a yacht and heading to South America. We could have lived like gods in Uruguay. We could have lived on sangria on ice and women on tap and Viagra and poppers forever. But you killed Marta and Hank! You took my best from me, you thieving, filthy little pig."

Ah. Right. You stole the Bug Man's Armani suits when you fled North, too. But the Bug Man took your mother and brother. Tia Marta took your childhood. Worse than all that, the Bug Man is directly behind you, killing you as he promised. Hank Reles took your pistol. Your hope for vengeance is dying as fast as you are.

Seconds left.

REVENGE IS BEST SERVED WHILE YOU'RE STILL YOUNG ENOUGH TO ENJOY IT.

You screwed up the future, but the future is a tiny thing now. Soon, you will no longer exist.

Desperate to play for time and break his grip, you slump to the ground, letting your dead weight pull him down. He doesn't break the chokehold. Instead, he follows you down like a pro. Your head slams into the pavement.

Stars. You see stars, darting back and forth and getting brighter as your vision becomes a dark tunnel. The tunnel gets longer. Through the plastic, at the end of the tunnel, you see a figure in red. Sugar is coming. The only light at the end of your tunnel is the color of blood.

"Your mother made it to shore, you know, Jesus." The Bug Man grunts from the effort. He's older now, of course, but still plenty strong enough. He's sure he's won. You can feel his breath coming hard and fast, crinkling the plastic at your ear. Your dying flame of rage leaps higher when the Bug Man says, "I made Maritza one of my girls. She didn't last long. She didn't give up like you. Some women have too much spirit."

You flail weakly, one hand trying to pry his fist open. If you could get just one finger in your palm, you could peel him off you. But the Bug Man knows how to choke a man out. He's no doubt had lots of practice on boys and girls.

You can't do it.

You can't get away.

You can't.

Your other hand closes on the hilt of the switchblade in your sock. The Bug Man screams as you plunge the blade into his crotch.

His arm isn't wrapped around your throat anymore. You twist away and pull the hot plastic off your face and gasp. That first full breath is like a tall glass of ice water in the desert. When you turn to look the Bug Man in the eyes and slash his throat open, that's even better than that first full breath.

It is no surprise at all that the Bug Man of Surfside Beach must be the elusive Gaston Bekhti. As soon as you knew that Detective Hank Reles was really Darren Hill from Sarasota, you guessed the rest. Sex slavery, snuff films and all manner of depravity require networks and infrastructure and providers. Monsters, in other words.

Blood pumps from the Bug Man's throat in spurts. Each geyser of blood is a little lower with each beat of his stone heart. His eyes are still furious.

Beat.

Beat.

Beat…beat…

His eyes are glass.

You're covered in blood. You can't help but smile. The Bug Man was once your god. He made you what you are. It was he and Tia Marta who decided if and when you would eat, when and how much you would suffer. They threatened death each day you were trapped in the basement. Rather than graduate from the basement to become one of his soldiers, you slew your god and his kingdom has fallen.

No one really escapes their past but maybe you can change your future.

You roll to your back, breathing hard, waiting for your head to clear. Sugar is crying. Her thick mascara drains down her face in black trails.

"It's okay." You hold out your hand for Sugar to help you to your feet. If she gets you to the car, in a few minutes, all this will be a dot in the rearview mirror.

Sugar holds out her hand but she's not reaching for you. There's a Ruger LCP 380 in her fist. The pistol's frame is hot pink. Sugar Cane does not cry for you. You twist away as she fires twice. Two rounds rip through your side. Getting shot hurts, like you're on fire.

Reles knew so much about you and now you know why. Sugar must have heard you prowling around Oswald's house. She locked herself in the cage and tore her dress and smacked her face against the cage bars.

You fell for the false hostage trick, after all. Twice. Sugar Cane is another Tia Marta.

You want to talk to her. You want to air accusations and hear explanations. You never will. Sugar Cane's dress blossoms a deeper red. Her jaw drops. Her bright eyes dull. Her pink pistol drops from her slack hand. She drops to the hot pavement.

WHEN YOUR HIT MAN HAS WARM FEELINGS, HE'S EITHER HIGH OR ON FIRE.

You lie between two corpses and you're about to bleed out, the third sack of meat. You will no longer exist. Surprise. You aren't surprised. You should have become a bus driver or a professional salsa dancer or…well….just about anything else besides a guy who lives by the gun.

Big Denny De Molina looms above you, shaking his head. "What happened to you, man? You forgot where we came from."

Close your eyes. Let it all go away. Hope for the best. Expect oblivion. If not oblivion, maybe you'll see Chill in heaven. That would be far out and groovy. You can dig it. More likely, you'll wake up in hell, burning with all your deserving victims.

You feel numb. Death can't be far from here.

Open your eyes. Big Denny points his pistol your way. You somehow manage to lift the knife, which now seems to weigh about seventy pounds. Denny smirks and kicks it away. The knife spins away in slow motion. Denny steps closer. Then he steps on your forearm and pins you. You can't move and you've got no fight left.

Fight? Fight is a cold thing far away. Fight is a distant star. It will take eons for the light from Fight to reach Earth. By then you'll be skeleton dust and worm shit.

You look up at Denny and your eyes are so wet, it's as if you're looking up at him through water. This isn't the death scene you were hoping for. You aren't Jimmy Cagney in *White Heat* screaming, "Top of the world, ma!" in defiance. You wanted to be a hero. You hoped you'd have time to balance out the pain and find redemption. Instead, you're drowning in self-pity. You're helpless.

Big Denny fires and fires and fires until the gun clicks empty. With every shot, Gaston Bekhti's body shakes and shudders beside you.

You close your eyes. Strong arms pick you up. Gently, you are carried away.

An old memory surfaces, perhaps your earliest memory. You are on a burning beach in Cuba. Your legs are very tired and your bare feet are too hot in the sand. You dance to ease the heat. You hold your arms up, waiting, hoping. You are tiny. The sunlight dazzles.

Someone picks you up and carries you away. You close your eyes, relieved to be held and cared for. A wisp of long hair caresses your cheek. It must have been your mother. Goodbye, Maritza.

You hear voices but it's as if the words echo down a long tube. You don't understand what they are saying, but the tones are soothing. You think of the good people in your life and you wish them well. You hope Skunk stays righteous and carries on Chill's legacy of protecting people. You wish Berb all the best and you're so sorry you couldn't save Jeremy. You hope Sgt. Billy understands you love him. He was one of the few constants in your life, at least for a while.

You want them all to understand that with every action, you were doing the best you could at the time. First you were just trying to survive. Later, you tried to redeem yourself. You tell yourself you had a rough start, but you ended where you did for reasons that were your own. You forgave yourself for failing too easily.

You hope Legs Gabrielle gets every award and reward she so rightly deserves in Hollywood. It's a town famous for building up stars for everyone to worship. This place is also infamous for wishing upon falling stars, delighting in their crash to Earth.

When all these feelings flood in, you know you must be high. When you were addicted to Vicodin, you were full of benevolent feelings like this. Whatever is pumping through your blood and brain, the drug has emptied the word *hate* of all meaning.

You struggle to open your eyes. Tile ceiling. A monitor beeps along, steady and regular as your heart.

I am not dead.

You are back.

Jesus is resurrected.

LIFE IS A TRAIN THAT HITS THE END OF THE LINE WITHOUT BRAKES.

Big Denny De Molina sits in the chair beside the hospital bed, his chin on his chest and fast asleep.

Surprise! You are not dead or in federal custody. It hurts to laugh.

Big Denny startles, raises his huge head, and looks your way. A slow smile spreads across his face.

"The enemy of my enemy is my friend, huh?" Your throat is dry. Your voice comes in a rasp. "But our common enemy is dead now. Why didn't you let me bleed out? I'm getting too old for repeated beatings, if that's what you saved me for."

Denny shrugs. "You saved me from the basement, Jesus, from Tia Marta and the Bug Man. I forgive you for the misunderstanding in New York."

"What? You found Jesus?" This time, you don't pronounce it like your name. You say, "Gee-zuzz."

"I finally found you. I found Bekhti's boat first. I was stakin' that out. Figured if I'd followed him around long enough, you'd show up and we could kill him together, just like old times."

"How many houses do I have to blow up to give you the idea I want out? Did I forget to leave a memo? What? Does The Machine require two weeks' notice?"

He laughs. "Look at you. Makes me sick, seeing you go all Hollywood like this, all shot up and still trying to take on the world alone. What you get for hanging out with the swells without me, all fancy and shit. You was never meant for that world, man. People change, but nobody changes so much as you'd need to change to hang out with a chick like Legs Gabrielle. Who do you think you are?"

"I dunno, man. That's the problem."

Legs Gabrielle…you'll never see her again. Once again you've met the perfect woman and, again, the perfect woman is not for you. How many times must the same lesson be repeated until it is learned?

Denny leans in, watching your eyes get wet. "You okay, buddy? You need more painkillers? Bedpan? Hankie? Sponge bath?"

There aren't enough painkillers in the world. Shake it off, genius. "How is it you showed up at my back door, Denny? You follow Bekhti?"

"I wish. Didn't work out that way. Smith told me the FBI staked out that dump you were living in, but Smith didn't think you'd be stupid enough to go back there for any reason."

"But you thought I'd be stupid enough."

"Yeah. I had one of my guys keep an eye on the place." When he catches your look, he shrugs. "Dude! Smith was dirty. Everything is available for a price. Anyway, when my guy spotted Reles going in, they called me. I knew you'd show up. I left a comfortable seat watching Bekhti's boat just in time to save your life. And you're welcome, by the way."

"Uh…*gracias.*"

He makes the sign of the cross your way. "And now you're free of the Bug Man. Go in peace, bro."

But nothing is ever that easy. You've lived too long in this world to expect an easy ending. Forgiveness isn't enough. "What else, Denny?"

"What else, what else?"

"For starters, where am I and what's this gonna cost me?"

"You're in a private clinic."

"Private. Sounds pricey. Where?"

"Rosarito."

"Where?"

"Mexico."

"How?"

"Gaston has a very nice yacht. We borrowed the boat and his crew. Sorry you slept through the trip. Heavy sedation will do that. I got you fixed up in LA. Then I got you out."

"And me without my passport and no travel insurance. Gee. I could get in trouble, couldn't I?"

"You'll have a new passport soon. New identity. Jesus Diaz and Dr. J.D. Fix are dead."

"Deep down, I knew those guys couldn't last."

"Well, we're almost even, but you owe me for the two guys you killed at Oswald's. They were freelancers, but still, it's the principle of the thing. They worked for me and now I gotta pay off a couple of widows and make things smooth."

"Knew this was gonna cost me big. Those guys were careless and impolite, Denny. Now what do you want from me?"

He shrugs. "Tit for tat. Quid for quo. I scratch your back, you shave mine. You know…capitalism. That's life. You owe me. That's America."

"We're in Mexico."

"That's the bonus of being an American, Jesus. No matter where we go, we act like we're home. I always carry a little bit of Jersey with me." He pats his jacket over the left armpit where his shoulder holster bulges.

"Yeah. I know the rule. You owe, you pay. But those freelancers came at me heavy, Denny."

"Yeah, well, they weren't my best operators. But you'll do, if you're smart enough to take the job I'm offering you."

"Look at you, all grown up and talking like a boss."

"You haven't been keeping track of what's going on in New York, have you?"

"You're the boss?"

"Nah. Not quite. A boss. Not the boss. I still have people to answer to, just like always. Besides, nobody calls nobody 'boss', anymore. Get some class."

"Yeah? What do they call you now?"

"Sir."

"Oh. No shit?"

"Yeah."

"What do you want for the guys who came after me and were rude about it?"

"Lily."

"What?"

"You heard me."

"I haven't seen Lily since — "

"Since you helped her walk away with my money."

"It wasn't yours at the time."

"It is now."

"I thought she was going to Spain to check out some paintings."

"She was in Spain, then Prague. I don't know where Prague is. Then she was in London. Now she's in New Orleans."

"Doing what?"

"You'll find out."

"Yeah? I'm shot and we're quits. She's my ex, man. I have no special powers when it comes to Lily. Not anymore. I don't think I ever had special influence over her, really."

"We need the skim back, Jesus. If you go after her, maybe she'll live. If I have to send somebody from my crew, my higher ups will notice. I'll have to report to them. They'll require things to be done that neither of us want to happen. Not to Lily. I need somebody I can trust, off the chain, but not so off the chain that they'll come at Lily heavy. Take care of this and we're cool."

"Why so generous, Denny?"

"You're like a brother and Lily was like a sister-in-law. I don't want her dead. I just need the money back. Whatever's left of it. I hear she's frugal."

"I don't remember her that way."

"I need what she has. It'll be a lot. As soon as you're up and around, I need you to go get it."

You watch Denny's eyes. Each blink takes a fraction of a second too long. He's lying about something.

"You need the money for something big. You owe a lot of money or you're going to use it for something off The Machine's books. You lose big betting on the ponies?"

He stares at you for what seems like a full minute and hardly blinks at all. "You in or out?"

Maybe he'll kill you, after all.

No.

No, he won't. Not after going to all this effort to save you. Not yet. Big Denny needs you to be his outside talent.

You give him a warm smile. A real smile. In the end, you tell yourself, no one's smarter than Jesus. But if you heal, save Lily and somehow manage to bring him the money? You're still you and Denny is still Denny. You can get a new switchblade and a new SIG Sauer, but you're stuck with your luck.

Go ahead. Follow orders again. Save Lily. You can even throw Denny a "sir" or two to make him feel good. You tell yourself all the time you're the smart ninja, but you know if your life was really a movie, you wouldn't live past the first reel. No matter what you do, no one will really see you as the good guy. You tell yourself you're bigger than The Beatles. You kid yourself that no one is harder than Jesus. Like the Olympic motto, you're faster, higher, stronger. The lies make you brave, but you know that you're on a one way trip that doesn't end with a little house surrounded by a white picket fence.

God put a gun in your hand and he won't let you put it down. No choices. There is no free will. Every time you try to use your will, the bill is too high and you pay in blood. In the end, no one will be deader than Jesus.

It's time for a new identity. It's time to grow up and try to stop talking to yourself. It's especially time to stop telling yourself lies to get through each day. But if you can't be you, anymore, who will you be?

"It's always out of the frying pan, into the napalm with you, Jesus. In or out, man? I need to know now, 'cuz if you're out, you know you gotta be all the way out."

"Just like the first time, doing that guy in Wanton, New Jersey."

"Huh? Who?"

"I haven't forgotten…sir." You smile wider at Denny. "The Divine Assassin is in. Goodbye, Hollywood Jesus."

THANK YOU!

Thanks for reading the first three books in the *Hit Man Series*!

Books and writers live and die by reviews. If you dig these stories (or any of my work), please leave a happy review wherever you purchase your inky entertainment.

Turn the page for a sneak peak at the next book in this series, *Resurrection, A Hit Man Thriller*.

Links to all my books follow at the end of this book. Whether it's killer thrillers, time travel, or apocalyptic epics you crave, I have something for you to love.

Cheers!

~ Robert

SNEAK PEAK OF
RESURRECTION
A HIT MAN THRILLER

CHAPTER 1

We become the stories we tell about ourselves.

Like you, I want a lot of things. I want rich, dark coffee every morning, two cream, one sweetener. I don't want to have to be anywhere in particular by nine o'clock. I would prefer warm breezes and a fine house on a tropical beach. Some think I want too much. On the night in question, my chief desire was to avoid getting shot.

While normal folks hustled to their jobs, appointments and errands, I used to do touristy things in London. I lingered in cafes and read novels without paying attention to the time, no schedule or routine. I had a cozy out-of-the-way flat and I'd built a gaming computer. My only furniture was a bed, a gaming chair, a desk for the computer's two screens and an easel in the corner by the window.

Games on Steam and Twitch would have to wait. Trouble had found me. In my case, Trouble was the corpse slumped in my gaming chair and, to stay alive, I had to make more people into corpses.

I'd been avoiding trouble quite well by staying on the move for the last couple of years. Sun-drenched Spain was warmth and happiness. Smiles and laughter seemed to come to the Spanish more easily. Though I have Spanish blood, New York beat that capacity for easy smiles out of me. I kept going, losing myself *in* crowds but never managing to lose myself *to* crowds.

I thought Italy would be my home for a while. Rome is a castle that contains all the history and art we want to remember.

Though I loved the city, my mother didn't feel I was safe there. "At the Vatican, you are too close to God and He is always watching," she told me. "People like us are meant for the Colosseum, maybe, but not for churches full of old men praying hard because they're too scared of dying."

So I kept moving.

Echoes of ancient Rome haunt London's architecture. I enjoyed the friendly energy in the pubs as I sipped dark beer. I drank in arch British accents spoken in hushed tones in old bookstores. I liked to people-watch while I traveled on the Tube. The smooth tone of the recorded voice that warned me to "mind the gap" cheered me. I loved London's sights, especially the Sherlock Holmes statue at Baker Street Station and Madame Tussauds wax museum.

The freaky torture chamber in the wax museum was good mental preparation for the horrors ahead. I didn't know it then but my history had set me on one path to the future. No more detours or carefree afternoons in cafés.

Losing oneself had been such comfort but Camberley is a small city of about 38,000. I stepped off the train in Camberley and paused to get my bearings. I envied the other passengers returning home late from work. Their day was at an end. The night shift was just beginning for me.

I was only a couple of hours from my home in London but I felt exposed. This was the kind of place that was small enough for people to make eye contact. A small population invites familiarity, observation and casual conversation. Those are dangerous behaviors for someone like me. I was born for the underworld.

The sky brightened at random intervals as sporadic fireworks burst over Camberley. *Guy Fawkes Day*. "Gunpowder, treason and plot," I said aloud to no one. My life in New York used to be about those three things. Despite my best efforts, I was about to return to that life. I should have gotten back on the train. I should have taken those fireworks as an omen and run.

The Guy Fawkes celebration was not that big a deal in Camberley. I regretted missing the light show over Parliament. However, history is indelible. It asserts itself in a way that the unknown future cannot. Ghosts from my old life had traveled all the way from New York to haunt me. I didn't use my New York name anymore but somehow they tracked me down.

When I crossed the ocean to escape New York, I left dead men in my wake. It was fight or flight. To escape, I had to do a little of both. NYC had come to Camberley and it would be — *had to be*— bloody. There was no other way. I wished I was walking with Jesus. Jesus Diaz would understand my plight.

The wind picked up as I wandered away from the train station, wary of CCTV. That was London's one negative for people like me: too many surveillance cameras.

The first cabbie I found had a Cockney accent so thick I could barely understand him. He spoke loudly, shout-talking as if the back seat of the cab was the back of a theater. He turned in his seat to talk to me often, his gaze felt like mice crawling over my chest.

"Take me here," I said, and held out a scrap of paper. The address was a scrawl that was not my own. I scratched out some numbers and added a few to put some distance between me and the target. I would be close but the cab wouldn't drop me off in front of a future crime scene, either.

The cabbie turned on the dome light to peer at the address again as if he was deciphering a complex code. Before he was done, he turned to take another long look at me.

I'm used to creepy stares from ogling men. I try to take lust as a compliment if guys aren't too piggy about it. As long as their rudeness doesn't get in my way or hold me back, I ignore them. However, that night I was in a hurry. "Hey! Can you get me there or not? If not, let me know now and I'll grab another cab. I'm not here so you could gawk at my tits."

He shrugged, turned off the dome light and went about his business, embarrassed. I'd come off too strong, not because I called him out but because I didn't want to be memorable. When I lived in New York, I had to be aggressive all the time. It's how you make your way through the city. Push, or you're a pushover.

The cab rolled to a stop in front of an old, narrow house. No light shone from the building's windows. I grabbed my duffel bag and climbed out. I tossed the cabbie his fare with a couple of pounds for a tip.

He waited to watch me go into the house. Maybe he was thinking of my safety or perhaps he was staring at my ass in his headlights. I headed toward a small shop, the only source of light on the street. By the time I came back out with a pack of cigarettes and a Coke, the cab had disappeared.

Up the hill, the silhouettes of iron gates stood tall against the city shine. I walked that way and, on the stone wall by the gate, spotted the numbers I was looking for.

I wanted to go back to my flat in Muswell Hill. After a calming hour or two of playing *GTA 5* or *Fortnite* or *Black Ops 4*, I might relax. But there was still the problem of the dead woman in my gaming chair. I didn't know how I was going to get rid of the body yet.

To calm myself, I could have tried my hand at copying Salvador Dali's style of painting. Getting the colors right is relatively easy, but to imitate the master's brush strokes is like forging another person's handwriting. Dali's work was chock-full of surreal images. I love surreality because, too often, reality sucks.

But I had to face reality. My father was Pete Vasquez, a captain for New York's Spanish mob. Dad started out as an enforcer and graduated to bookie, sometimes a shylock. I knew he was a made guy early on but he admitted nothing about his membership in the Machine for a very long time.

It was my mother who trained me to run *at* problems, not *from* them. Like the Devil, I have used many aliases. My real name is Lily Olivia Vasquez. I am a target but I will not be a victim anymore.

CHAPTER 2

The buzzer at the front gate had no cameras that I could see. I tossed the duffel over the fence and climbed the stone wall. I do a lot of Pilates. I'm up to it. I managed to avoid rolling my ankle when I dropped to the other side. The easy part was over.

The ground was soft from the day's rain so I left a footprint behind me with every step. Since I'm not a ninja, I didn't know what I could do about that. My policy is I don't dwell on things I can't control.

I'd come for men trying to track, control and kill me. I had heavy experience dealing with men who tried to tell me what to do, to dominate and own me. They were all history. If they were not forgotten, they soon would be.

I stuck to the tree line and ducked behind a hedge where the trees thinned. A light popped on. Two men were speaking in weirdly aggressive tones. They spoke in that tone men use when the subject is sports and each is loyal to rival sports teams. Breakin' balls, in other words.

As I crept closer I discovered their accents were American. Specifically, this pair was brought up in Brooklyn. They were so careless and loud, they couldn't have suspected they were being observed. Unless I'd stumbled upon a mansion that's a halfway house for hearing-impaired bad guys, these big dopes must have been at least a little drunk.

The light went out again as I heard a door close. The two men remained, smoking and relaxed, far too lackadaisical have been on guard duty. They weren't expecting trouble. They probably assumed I was dead. That was good. My death was an integral part of my plan.

Both men — one tall and skinny, the other short and round — looked startled as I stepped out from behind the hedge not ten feet away. They turned and stared. Maybe it was the booze or perhaps they'd always had brains that worked arduously, as if they were mired in deep mud.

"Hey, Red!" the tall one called out.

I tossed my hair and beamed a smile. The red locks were new. I'd bought the wig in Kensington. People would remember the bright red hair. They were less likely to remember my face. One defining feature blurred the other details. After that night, I couldn't pretend to be a redhead again, not on this continent, anyway.

The tall one smiled at me with a mouthful of teeth that seem to wander across his wide mouth aimlessly. "Ooh, what's your name?"

"Cherry's the name, boys." My English accent wasn't bad. My voice was steady as I tested it on them. If I failed the accent test, the evening would end prematurely and badly. I liked my new black leather jacket. I didn't want to see it turned into a sieve with my blood leaking through.

Both men looked me over. It was an appraising look, different from those of flirts and oglers. They knew the name Cherry. They were deciding how nervous they should be around me.

Pulling off a scam requires confidence. I'd always had my share of that. My mother taught me how to swagger the same week I got my first period. "Walk like you're somebody who is going to own the world," she told me, "because you are."

She had me walk back and forth across the room. "No, not like a dude with your shoulders up. Move like a panther. A woman who owns herself moves like a panther."

I'd seen one panther asleep at the Bronx Zoo. Still, I knew what she meant. I tried my stride again and Mama gave me a slight nod that I took for grudging approval. I almost had it, but obviously, I didn't have it quite right.

"How will I know for sure when I've got it?" I asked.

"You'll know when you walk like me," Mama said.

The short one wasn't as friendly as his fellow guard. "You lost? You might be lost, pretty lady."

"She said she was Cherry," the tall one said.

"I heard what she said," the short one replied, "but we have to be sure. You're on private property, Miss … uh — "

"Cherry. I was on a job for your boss and — "

"What kind of job?"

The short one thought he was a big guy but he was just a fat guy. As he slipped from curiosity to a lascivious stare, I decided to kill him first.

"Take it easy, Short Round," I said. "It was a collection job." I slipped the duffel from my shoulder, pulled it open and flashed the cash, lots of it. Money was the calling card that opened doors everywhere.

Short Round peered in. "Now, how'd you get all that?"

"Sold a lot of Girl Scout cookies. What do you think?"

"Have you still got your Girl Scout uniform?" the tall one asked.

I liked him even less then. "I retrieved the money and killed the bitch. Your boss will want the dough, am I right?" My New York accent slipped in a little just then but the guards' gaze was fixed on the duffel.

"Arms up. We'll have to frisk you." The tall one said it but they both stepped closer.

"Both of you?"

"Thoroughly."

I decided I didn't like the tall one any better than the short one.

"Where you from, girl?" Short Round asked.

When I'm in situations like this, I always ask myself the same question: What would Jesus do? Jesus Diaz was good at talking himself out of tight spots. I should do that. However, when Short Round came at me with his big hands, palms out and aiming for a free grope, I decided to be myself instead. I dropped my attempt at an English accent. "I'm the woman you meet at the place where your dreams and nightmares meet."

Short Round looked at me like a terrier confused by an escalator. I pulled my handgun out of the bag and shot him in the face. Predictably, one shot did the job. Short Round crumpled to the ground.

I lined up my next shot. The tall one was pulling a pistol from his belt when I nailed him, two in the chest, one in the head. That appeared very pro but I meant to group three in the chest. I only got the headshot because he was falling backward.

A ruckus rose from inside the house: running feet and shouting. No time to run. I wouldn't survive a shootout with a bunch of bad guys at once. I'd been impatient, like always.

I dropped to my knees to cradle the corpse with three new holes in it. Double-plus-dead and laid out flat on the gravel, the tall one was now the long one. I didn't know his name so I decided his post-mortem monicker should be Longfellow.

Three guys rushed out of the front door, guns drawn and eager to kill somebody. They were impatient people, too. Our business was full of them. If we weren't this way, we'd have 401Ks, drive the speed limit and maybe work at a bank.

"They went that way!" I gestured dramatically and begin to cry. "Toward the front gate!" The trick to selling a good cry is to add a wet snort. They'd never think anyone would do that on purpose.

"Who did? Who went where?" the third man bringing up the rear asked in a Cockney accent.

"The killers! Two of them! Guys in black t-shirts and jeans! They're headed for the gate! Quick! They'll get away!"

The dumbest of the trio sprinted in the direction I had pointed. The one that was a little less dumb ran to the Land Rover parked in front of the garage. Gravel flew as his tires spun and he took off in hot pursuit.

Wild goose chase: Engaged. They were gone without giving me another thought.

Bad Guy #3 stopped and stared at me. It dawned on him that he'd never seen me in his life. He was the smartest of the three stooges. I guessed that made him the stooge with the bowl cut. *Moe.* The smartest stooge was named Moe. My dad used to laugh at that silly shit. I didn't get it.

"Where'd you come from?" Moe was armed, but his pistol hung in his hand at his thigh.

Smarter but not smart enough.

My hand was slick with blood when I pulled my pistol out from under the corpse. I pointed it at Moe's head. "*Sh.*"

Moe dropped his weapon in the gravel and backed up. I scooped up the handgun. It was a CZ 75 that fit in my hand nicely. My dad always bought American and disliked guns from the Czech Republic. However, Moe's choice of weapon held sixteen rounds. I didn't know if I would need all that ammo before I was done but the weapon's sleek lethality was a comfort.

I waved Moe toward the front door. He interlaced his fingers behind his head without me having to ask. He didn't say a word and nodded when I told him what to do.

Him, I liked.

CHAPTER 3

I remembered the man I was looking for. I'd met him many times in New York when he was just another thug in the Machine's crew. "Take me to Lonnie."

"Lonnie's not here," Moe said.

"That's a shame. I'm going to have to splatter your brains and slip out the back."

"I could be wrong," he replied. "In fact, I think you'll find him in the panic room."

"Any cameras in there?"

"Um...."

"Answer quick. A man who answers too slow is lying."

"There's a camera outside the panic room, yeah."

"But none out in the yard or in the house?"

"No."

Idiots. Good.

I imagined Lonnie cowering in his panic room. Any minute, he'd call to find out what all the shots were about. As if on cue, Moe's phone rang. He handed it over with no bullshit.

Good boy!

"Lonnie?"

"Who's this?" The guy on the other end of the line was breathing heavily. He sounded big and sweaty.

"Cherry. I've brought the long paper Big Denny De Molina is looking for."

"What's with the gunfire?"

"I had a misunderstanding with your boys. There wasn't a man among them."

"Where's Church? Gimme Church!"

I looked at my captive. "Your name Church?"

He nodded miserably.

"He's right here, Lonnie. Can't come to the phone right now. He's been kneecapped."

"What? How?"

"I showed up with the cash and your guys wanted to take it. That wouldn't be good for me. Big Denny wouldn't like it. Wouldn't be much good for you, either. You should hire a better class of assistants next time."

I gave Lonnie time to get all that nasty cursing out of his system. It took a while. The fact that he was upset only proved me right. His crew was low grade. He wouldn't have believed me so easily otherwise.

Denny sent Lonnie to get his money back but this guy was no boss. He was just another also-ran from New York. Without inspiring respect, any boss could lose control of his crew. Lonnie expected less from his men. Real leaders didn't do that. They expected more. If Big Denny really wanted his money back, he shouldn't have sent the B-team.

"We need a face-to-face," I told Lonnie. "You'll want to get hold of Denny and tell him he's got a lot of his money back, not all of it, but a lot. I'll need you to count out my finder's fee — "

"How do I know you haven't taken out your finder's fee already?"

"Because nobody crosses Big Denny and lives. He's the boss of the Machine and he's much more savage than Vincent Lima ever was. It's been, what? Two years? Still, Denny sent me after that girl. If you owe Denny, he'll find you. It's worse if you make him chase you. Earth's not big enough to play hide-and-seek with Big Denny. He's the elephant who doesn't forget. You should have seen what I did to that bitch. Denny said send a message. There's blood on the floor and hair on the walls."

Lonnie was more scared of Denny than he was of me so he didn't waste time thinking. "C'mon up to the second-floor office, Cherry."

A minute later, I stood upstairs in an office with a desk and a poker table. From the look of things, I'd interrupted a card game. I kept my captive ahead of me as a human shield.

The panic room door opened. Before he emerged, Lonnie called out, "Did you skin that thieving bitch with a carrot peeler like I told you?" He came to a stop when he saw my hostage. The rusty gears in Lonnie's brain began to crank again. "Church? I thought you got kneecapped. What — "

"Oh, right." I shot Church in the right knee. He went down screaming. I pointed the CZ 75 at Lonnie's crotch. "Sorry. That was on my to-do list."

Lonnie stared and his mouth hung open. His mind's gears started to turn faster but they were still pretty creaky. I gave him a minute to catch up. Finally, he said, "You ain't Cherry."

"Good guess. Do you remember me, Lonnie?"

"Lily. I remember. Everybody who's left in the Machine remembers you."

"Good for you," I said. "For a minute there, I thought I was going to have to draw diagrams and explain it with puppets."

"Where's Cherry?"

"Well, I didn't skin her alive with a carrot peeler like she was going to do to me."

"Shit."

"Don't feel too bad for her. She gave you up quick and told me how to find you. She also blabbed that you had only spoken with her on the phone."

"Aw, shit."

"And now here I am, talking to the man who sent that crazy bitch to torture and kill me."

"Aw, shit."

"You're an eloquent guy, Lonnie."

Dad was wrong about always buying American. I loved the feel of the Czech pistol in my hand. Not too much kick in the recoil, either.

CHAPTER 4

Forearm skin does not peel the same way a carrot does. Cherry the Ginger Assassin had managed to take some skin off my forearm before I got back in control of the situation. The key to taking down any enemy was to find their weakness.

We all have a fatal flaw. For instance, when I was eight, a girl named Mandy beat me up after school. I don't think it was personal. She was a big girl and had a rep around the school for beating up a lot of kids.

When I came home with a black eye, I complained to my mother. She handed me a bag of ice and told me to learn from the experience.

Outraged at her hands-off parenting style, I demanded, "Learn what?"

"Learn how not to have the experience again."

"How?"

"Find her weakness."

"I was hoping her weakness would be for you to tell her mom and her mom would beat her up."

"If it has to come to that, I'll have to go over to her house and beat her ass and her mother's ass."

"Good."

"No, Lily. No good. You got a problem to solve. How are you going to handle it?"

"Bring a gun to school?"

"That is not a proportionate response. That's a weak-ass way to go. You can do better."

"A stick? A brick?"

"Better than that."

"I don't know, Mom — "

"You're a Vasquez. Do we run from our problems?"

"No."

"What do we do?"

"We run *at* them. But what can I do? She's bigger than me."

"But is she more savage?"

When I didn't answer, Mom told me, "She better not be more savage than you. It's a bad world. If you can't handle a schoolgirl, how are you gonna deal with a real life problem? The world is all business and self-preservation. How you gonna deal with it? You gonna let somebody take your life and your dignity? Life's too important and precious to live like that, baby girl."

I took roundabout ways to get home. My elaborate detours saved me a beating for three days. On the fourth day, my bully caught me again. She threw me to the ground and sat on my head, laughing and demanding money. I discovered, quite by accident, that the insides of the bully's thighs were ticklish. That's how I got out from under my tormentor. Mandy was still on her knees and giggling when I got to my feet. Then I started punching. I had my opening. Between punches, I started screaming, "You think you're bad? You got no idea!"

Some boys from the neighborhood formed a circle around us and laughed as I stopped that girl cold. I kept screaming. My punches were wild and out of control but I kept going, sure that if I let her get to her feet, she'd kill me.

"You're never going to bother me again! Don't even look me in the eyes! Never look me in the eyes! Never!"

Before long, the boys stopped laughing and their concern turned to fear. Some pulled me off her and tried to calm me down. Others ran away and didn't look back.

Mandy lived but she came to school the next day with two black eyes, a swollen purple jaw and a chipped front tooth. She did not look my way. She didn't pick on anybody else, either.

When I came home with bloody knuckles, Mom had the ice pack ready again. She didn't ask what happened to the bully. All she said was, "Next time you punch somebody, put a roll of quarters in your fist."

The Ginger Assassin's fatal flaw was that she enjoyed her job too much. Sadists are careless. They lose sight of the mission with their gory distractions. As she attempted to peel my forearm with a rusty carrot peeler, she stared too long at my blood. It was as if she was thirsty. I guess *bloodthirsty* is a real thing.

When Cherry caught me, I asked myself what Jesus would do. The answer: I begged for my life but I spoke softly, just a whisper. I told her that if she let me go, I'd tell her where all of Big Denny's money was hidden. The window of opportunity was small and I only had one chance. As my captor bent closer, I headbutted the brains out of that psycho bitch.

Cherry held on to the carrot peeler but dropped her gun into my lap. After that, I was the one asking the questions. Never bring a carrot peeler to a gunfight.

Lonnie had his own exploitable flaws. Aside from being a weak leader, he was easily distracted watching Church roll around on the floor.

"Goodnight, Moe." I shot the henchman a couple of times in the chest and he stopped his annoying moaning.

Lonnie paled as he stared at the face of his dying man. I snugged the muzzle of the Czech pistol into Lonnie's crotch. That seemed to cure his ADHD.

I had questions. I got answers. Then I spent more bullets.

Lonnie's burner phone had Big Denny's number on it. Men tasked with killing me and retrieving the skim were dead. Big Denny had waited years to get this close. He was going to be so pissed that he missed this chance.

But trouble doesn't stop coming. The wild goose chasers returned. I heard the Land Rover skid to a stop out front and in a moment both of them pounded around downstairs shouting Lonnie's name and cursing. They checked the house as if they were cops, shouting, "Clear!" for each room they searched. These goons were not smart ninjas.

I tiptoed into a bedroom and took off my shoes. The pair I decided to call Larry and Curly ran upstairs, a couple of freaked-out amateurs. I guess their mothers never taught them how to take care of themselves.

They found the man I'd dubbed Moe and they shouted at each other even more. Then they spotted Lonnie. As blood spread across their boss' crotch and wet brains slid down the wall behind his desk, Larry and Curly's shouts went up an octave. There's something about seeing a man shot in the crotch that bothers men much more than seeing splattered brains. I guess they don't value things they don't use.

Transfixed, the bad guys stood with their backs to me gibbering with adrenalin, not a single cogent thought in their heads. These poor morons were local recruits, definitely new to this sort of thing. I have seen it all before so, soundless in bare feet, I stepped out of the bedroom. They might have been chattering about the price of parrots if Godzilla destroys Tokyo again. Cockney really is impenetrable to me when it's cranking out of an idiot's mouth at full tilt. Creeping closer, I got the gist: Larry and Curly were arguing about who was more to blame for failing to guard Lonnie.

I gripped Lonnie's heavy .38 in my left hand and the CZ 75 in my right. I decided I could solve their argument for them. Both thugs stopped talking when they felt the muzzles on their necks. The CZ 75 pistol was warm. Lonnie's weapon was cold. Both of them went stiff.

"Don't blame yourselves, boys," I said, flat and calm. "You think you're bad? You got no idea."

I dropped them both. Lonnie's gun was too loud in the small space and my ears rang.

CHAPTER 5

I was prepared to deal with the aftermath. I really was a Girl Scout, briefly. I liked the little sash but otherwise, the organization's fashion sense did not appeal to me. I stayed with the Scouts long enough to learn to be prepared. I took the weapons and every cell phone.

Mom taught me the utility of savagery.. From Jesus, I learned to improvise on the fly. I found a big gas can in the Land Rover. The corpses in the front yard were too heavy to pull up the stairs so I poured gasoline on Short Round and Longfellow where they fell. Pardon me, I should have said *petrol*.

Ever wondered what it sounds like to torch a mansion? As soon as I dropped the match, the flame was like a rushing wind. The trail of liquid fire raced up the stairs. The fire looked eager. When the flame reached the gas can I had propped on Lonnie's chest, I heard a tinny bang, the shattering of glass and another whoosh as flames burst from the windows.

As the fire spread, the mansion's empty windows glowed like angry orange eyes. It happened faster than I expected. I didn't stay to watch. I did what Jesus would do. I left ashes for the cops to investigate and took off in the Land Rover.

I had to transfer Lonnie's data to my cell and dump the rest of the phones. I couldn't keep the getaway vehicle for long but I put some distance between me and the mansion. Surely someone would soon noticed a funeral pyre the size of a huge house. As I pulled onto the street, I counted the cost: Longfellow, Short Round, Church AKA Moe, Larry, Curly and Lonnie.

I'd become the assassin who'd tried to torture and murder me for one night. Only when I was safely on the road and away did my hands begin to shake. I can't say it was all terrible. Playing the Ginger Assassin was empowering. I'm not crazy, though (or at least I'm still sane enough to know I shouldn't feel good about it). My breath came in little gasps.

I'd taken the money to escape New York and make a better life. In the scheme of sins, theft was a smaller sin than murder. You could even call it self-defense and, unless you're Amish or something, pretty much everybody's for self-defense. This was business and self-preservation.

Those were seven killers who would have killed me if I'd given them a chance. I would not weep for them but my hands continued to shake as I drove away from my sins. I yanked the red wig off and swore I'd never be a ginger again.

Many blocks away, I was still thinking about the surprised look on Lonnie's face when I pulled the trigger. As adrenaline burned off, my exhaustion began to set in. I couldn't wait to escape into sleep. I ditched the car and cleaned myself up. I had rags and alcohol in the duffel. Like a good Girl Scout, I came prepared. A long walk and two cabs later, I got back to my flat.

In the dim light coming in from the streetlight, I spotted two things wrong with my small living room. There were two bodies. When I left, there had been only one.

Cherry's corpse lay on the floor. I was more worried about the silhouette of the man slumped in my gaming chair. I pulled out Lonnie's piece and aimed it at him. "Who's been sleeping in my — " I didn't finish my Goldilocks joke.

The man awoke and looked up. The light struck his face as he smiled down the barrel of the .38. It was as if he looked Death in the face every day. His sharp eyes fixed on mine and he smiled wider. "Hi, Lily."

"*Jesus*, Jesus!" The first Jesus was the popular hippie deity. The second Jesus was pronounced, "Hay-soose."

Jesus Diaz rose from the chair. I lowered the weapon.

THINK YOU KNOW JESUS?

You ain't seen nothin' yet!

Thus ends the sneak peak for *Resurrection, A Hit Man Thriller.* To pick up where you left off and find out what mayhem Lily and Jesus Diaz get up to, please follow the book link at AllThatChazz.com or search for it on your Amazon store.

Enjoy!

(*Psst!* More book links ahead, too!)

ABOUT THE AUTHOR

Robert Chazz Chute is a former crime journalist, speech writer, book doctor and an award-winning writer living in Other London. He writes killer thrillers, suspense and apocalyptic science fiction. To find out more about his books, please visit his author page at AllThatChazz.com and sign up for updates and deals.

*If you love Robert Chazz Chute's work and want even more interaction, join us on the Facebook fan page here for daily updates and fun chat.

ALSO BY ROBERT CHAZZ CHUTE

All book links are available at AllThatChazz.com.

~ CRIME THRILLERS ~

Bigger Than Jesus, Book 1 of The Hit Man Series
Higher Than Jesus, Book 2 of the Hit Man Series
Hollywood Jesus, Book 3 of the Hit Man Series
The Divine Assassin's Playbook
(Omnibus Edition of the first three Hit Man books)
Resurrection, A Hit Man Novel Book 4 of the Hit Man Series
Brooklyn in the Mean Time
The Night Man
Sometime Soon, Somewhere Close
(anthology)

~ DYSTOPIAN & APOCALYPTIC FICTION ~

Amid Mortal Words

* * * * * *

This Plague of Days, Season 1
This Plague of Days, Season 2
This Plague of Days, Season 3
This Plague of Days, Omnibus Edition

* * * * * *

AFTER Life INFERNO
AFTER Life PURGATORY
AFTER Life PARADISE
AFTER Life (Box set)

* * * * * *

Robot Planet, The Complete Series

*   *   *   *   *   *

Haunting Lessons, Book 1 of The Dimension War
Death Lessons, Book 2 of The Dimension War
Fierce Lessons, Book 3 of The Dimension War
Dream's Dark Flight, Book 4 of The Dimension War

~ TIME TRAVEL ~
Wallflower

~ COLLECTIONS ~
Murders Among Dead Trees
Self-help for Stoners
All Empires Fall

~ NON-FICTION ~
Do the Thing: The Last Stress-busting Book You'll Ever Need

www.ingramcontent.com/pod-product-compliance
Lightning Source LLC
Chambersburg PA
CBHW031025030726
47497CB00004B/1004